The Third
Inspector Morse
Omnibus

The Third Inspector Morse Omnibus

Last Bus to Woodstock
The Wench is Dead
The Jewel That Was Ours

Colin Dexter

MACMILLAN
LONDON

Last Bus to Woodstock first published 1975 by Macmillan London Limited
The Wench is Dead first published 1989 by Macmillan London Limited
The Jewel That Was Ours first published 1991 by Macmillan London Limited
This omnibus edition published with corrections 1993 by
Macmillan London Limited

a division of Pan Macmillan Publishers Limited
Cavaye Place London sw10 9pg
and Basingstoke

Associated companies throughout the world

ISBN 0-333-59691-9

3 5 7 9 8 6 4 2

A CIP catalogue record for this book is available from
the British Library

Typeset by Cambridge Composing (UK) Limited, Cambridge
Printed by Mackays of Chatham PLC, Kent

Contents

Last Bus
to
Woodstock

PRELUDE

'Let's wait just a *bit* longer, please,' said the girl in dark-blue trousers and the light summer coat. 'I'm sure there's one due pretty soon.'

She wasn't quite sure though, and for the third time she turned to study the timetable affixed in its rectangular frame to Fare Stage 5. But her mind had never journeyed with any confidence in the world of columns and figures, and the finger tracing its tentatively horizontal course from the left of the frame had little chance of meeting, at the correct coordinate, the finger descending in a vaguely vertical line from the top. The girl standing beside her transferred her weight impatiently from one foot to the other and said, 'I don' know abou' you.'

'Just a minute. *Just a minute.*' She focused yet again on the relevant columns: 4, 4A (not after 18.00 hours), 4E, 4X (Saturdays only). Today was Wednesday. That meant . . . If 2 o'clock was 14.00 hours, that meant . . .

'Look, sweethear', you please yourself bu' I'm going to hitch i'.' Sylvia's habit of omitting all final 't's seemed irritatingly slack. 'It' in Sylvia's diction was little more than the most indeterminate of vowel sounds, articulated without the slightest hint of a consonantal finale. If they ever became better friends, it was something that ought to be mentioned.

What time was it now? 6.45 p.m. That would be 18.45. Yes. She was getting somewhere at last.

'Come on. We'll get a lif' in no time, you see. Tha's wha' half these fellas are looking for – a bi' of skir'.'

And, in truth, there appeared no reason whatsoever to question Sylvia's brisk optimism. No accommodating motorist could fail to be impressed by her minimal skirting and the lovely invitation of the legs below.

For a brief while the two girls stood silently, in uneasy, static truce.

A middle-aged woman was strolling towards them, occasionally stopping and turning her head to gaze down the darkening length of the road that led to the heart of Oxford. She came to a halt a few yards away from the girls and put down her shopping bag.

'Excuse me,' said the first girl. 'Do you know when the next bus is?'

'There should be one in a few minutes, love.' She peered again into the grey distance.

'Does it go to Woodstock?'

'No, I don't think so – it's just for Yarnton. It goes to the village, and then turns round and comes back.'

'Oh.' She stepped out towards the middle of the road, craned her neck, and stepped back as a little convoy of cars approached. Already, as the evening shaded into dusk, a few drivers had switched on their sidelights. No bus was in sight, and she felt anxious.

'We'll be all *righ*',' said Sylvia, a note of impatience in her voice. 'You see. We'll be 'avin' a giggle abou' i' in the morning.'

Another car. And another. Then again the stillness of the warm autumn evening.

'Well, you can stay if you like – I'm off.' Her companion watched as Sylvia made her way towards the Woodstock round-about, some two hundred yards up the road. It wasn't a bad spot for the hitchhiker, for there the cars slowed down before negotiating the busy ring-road junction.

And then she decided. 'Sylvia, wait!'; and holding one gloved hand to the collar of her lightweight summer coat, she ran with awkward, splay-footed gait in pursuit.

The middle-aged woman kept her watch at Fare Stage 5. She thought how many things had changed since she was young.

But Mrs Mabel Jarman was not to wait for long. Vaguely her mind toyed with a few idle, random thoughts – nothing of any moment. Soon she would be home. As she was to remember later on, she could describe Sylvia fairly well: her long, blonde hair, her careless and provocative sensuality. Of the other girl she could recall little: a light coat, dark slacks – what colour, though? Hair – lightish brown? 'Please try as hard as you can, Mrs Jarman. It's absolutely vital for us that you remember as much as you can . . .' She noticed a few cars, and a heavy, bouncing articulated lorry, burdened with an improbably large number of wheel-less car-bodies. Men? Men with no other passengers? She would try so hard to recall. Yes, there had been men, she was sure of that. Several had passed her by.

At ten minutes to seven an oblong pinkish blur gradually assumed its firmer delineation. She picked up her bag as the red Corporation bus slowly threaded its way along the stops in the grey mid-distance. Soon she could almost read the bold white lettering above the driver's cab. What was it? She squinted to see it more clearly: WOODSTOCK. Oh dear! She had been wrong then, when that nicely spoken young girl had asked about the next bus. Still, never mind! They hadn't gone far. They would either get a lift or see the bus and manage to get to the next stop, or even the stop after that. 'How long had they been gone, Mrs Jarman?'

She stood back a little from the bus stop, and the Woodstock driver gratefully passed her by. Almost as soon as the bus was out of sight, she saw another, only a few hundred yards behind. This must be hers. The double-decker drew into the stop as Mrs Jarman rasied her hand. At two minutes past seven she was home.

Though a widow now, with her two children grown up and married, her pride-and-poverty semi-detached was still her real home, and her loneliness was not without its compensations. She cooked herself a generous supper, washed up, and turned on the television. She could never understand why there was so much criticism of the programmes. She herself enjoyed virtually everything and often wished she could view two channels simultaneously. At 10 o'clock she watched the main items on the News, switched off, and went to bed. At 10.30 she was sound asleep.

It was at 10.30 p.m., too, that a young girl was found lying in a Woodstock courtyard. She had been brutally murdered.

PART ONE
Search for a girl

CHAPTER ONE
Wednesday, 29 September

From St Giles' in the centre of Oxford two parallel roads run due north, like the prongs of a tuning fork. On the northern perimeter of Oxford, each must first cross the busy northern ring-road, along which streams of frenetic motorists speed by, gladly avoiding the delights of the old university city. The eastern branch eventually leads to the town of Banbury, and thence continues its rather unremarkable course towards the heart of the industrial midlands; the western branch soon brings the motorist to the small town of Woodstock, some eight miles north of Oxford, and thence to Stratford-upon-Avon.

The journey from Oxford to Woodstock is quietly attractive. Broad grass verges afford a pleasing sense of spaciousness, and at the village of Yarnton, after only a couple of miles, a dual carriageway, with a tree-lined central reservation, finally sweeps the accelerating traffic past the airport and away from its earlier paralysis. For half a mile immediately before Woodstock, on the left-hand side, a grey stone wall marks the eastern boundary of the extensive and beautiful grounds of Blenheim Palace, the mighty mansion built by good Queen Anne for her brilliant general, John Churchill, 1st Duke of Marlborough. High and imposing wrought-iron gates mark the main entrance to the Palace drive, and hither flock the tourists in the summer season to walk amidst the dignified splendour of the great rooms, to stand before the vast Flemish tapestries of Malplaquet and Oudenarde, and to see the room in which was born that later scion of the Churchill line, the great Sir Winston himself, now lying in the once-peaceful churchyard of nearby Bladon village.

Today Blenheim dominates the old town. Yet it was not always so. The strong grey houses which line the main street have witnessed older times and could tell their older tales, though now the majority are sprucely converted into gift, antique, and souvenir shops – and inns. There was always, it appears, a goodly choice of hostelries, and several of the hotels and inns now clustered snugly along the streets can boast not only an ancient lineage but also a cluster of black AA stars on their bright yellow signs.

The Black Prince is situated half-way down a broad side-street to the left as one is journeying north. Amidst the Woodstock peerage it can claim no ancient pedigree, and it seems highly improbable, alas, that the warrior son of King Edward III had ever laughed or cried or tippled or wenched in any of its precincts. Truth to tell, a director of the London company which bought the old house, stable-yards and all, some ten years since, had noticed in some dubiously authenticated guidebook that somewhere there-abouts the Prince was born. The director had been warmly congratulated by his Board for this felicitous piece of research, and not less for his subsequent discovery that the noble Prince did not as yet figure in the Woodstock telephone directory. The Black Prince it was then. The gifted daughter of the first manager had copied out from a children's encyclopaedia, in suitably antique script, a brief, if somewhat romantic, biography of the warrior Prince, and put the finished opus into her mother's oven for half an hour at 450°. The resultant manuscript, reverently brown with age, was neatly, if cheaply, framed and now occupied a suitable position of honour on the wall of the cocktail lounge. Together with the shields of the Oxford colleges nailed neatly along the low stained beams, it added tone and class.

For the last two and a half years Gaye had been the resident 'hostess' of the Black Prince – 'barmaid', thought the manager, was a trifle *infra dignitatem*. And he had a point. 'A pint of your best bitter, luv,' was a request Gaye seldom had to meet and she now associated it with the proletariat; here it was more often vodka and lime for the bright young things, Manhattan cocktails for the American tourists, and gin and French – with a splash of Italian – for the Oxford dons. Such admixtures she dispensed with practised confidence from the silvery glitter and sparkle of bottles ranged invitingly behind the bar.

The lounge itself, deeply carpeted, with chairs and wallseats covered in a pleasing orange shade, was gently bathed in half light, giving a chiaroscuro effect reminiscent, it was hoped, of a Rembrandt nativity scene. Gaye herself was an attractive, auburn-haired girl and tonight, Wednesday, she was immaculately dressed in a black trouser-suit and white-frilled blouse. A flash of gems on the second and third fingers of her left hand, betokened gentle warning to the mawkish amateur playboy, and perhaps –

as some maintained – a calculated invitation to the wealthy professional philanderer. She was, in fact, married and divorced, and now lived with one younger son and a mother who was not unduly chagrined at the mildly promiscuous habits of a precious daughter who had been unfortunate enough to marry such 'a lousy swine'. Gaye enjoyed her divorced status as much as she enjoyed her job, and she meant to keep them both.

Wednesday, as usual, had been a fairly busy evening, and it was with some relief when, at 10.25 p.m., she politely, but firmly, called for last drinks. A young man, seated on a high stool at the inner corner of the bar, pushed his whisky glass forward.

'Same again.'

Gaye glanced quizzically into unsteady eyes, but said nothing. She pushed her customer's glass under a priority whisky bottle and placed it on the counter, holding out her right hand and mechanically registering the tariff with her left. The young man was obviously drunk. He fumbled slowly and ineffectually through his pockets before finding the correct money, and after one mouthful of his drink he eased himself gingerly off his seat, measured the door with an uncertain eye, and made a line as decently straight as could in the circumstances be expected.

The old courtyard where once the horses had clattered over the cobbled stones had access from the street through a narrow archway, and had proved an invaluable asset to the Black Prince. A rash of fines for trespassing on the single and double yellow lines which bordered even the most inhospitable and inaccessible stretches of road was breeding a reluctant respect for the law; and any establishment offering 'PATRONS ONLY, cars left at owners' risk' was quite definitely in business. Tonight, as usual, the courtyard was tightly packed with the inevitable Volvos and Rovers. A light over the archway threw a patch of inadequate illumination over the entrance to the yard; the rest lay in dark shadow. It was to the far corner of this courtyard that the young man stumbled his way; and almost there he dimly saw something behind the further car. He looked and groped silently. Then horror crept up to the nape of his neck and against a padlocked stable door he was suddenly and violently sick.

CHAPTER TWO

Wednesday, 29 September

The manager of the Black Prince, Mr Stephen Westbrook, contacted the police immediately after the body was found, and his call was acted upon with commendable promptitude. Sergeant Lewis of the Thames Valley Police gave him quick and clear instructions. A police car would be at the Black Prince within ten minutes; Westbrook was to ensure that no one left the premises and that no one entered the courtyard; if anyone insisted on leaving, he was to take the full name and address of the person concerned; he should be honest if asked what all the trouble was about.

The evening's merriness wilted like a sad balloon and voices gradually hushed as the whispered rumour spread: there had been a murder. None seemed anxious to leave; two or three asked if they could phone. All felt suddenly sober, including a pale-faced young man who stood in the manager's office and whose scarcely touched whisky still stood on the counter of the cocktail lounge.

With the arrival of Sergeant Lewis and two uniformed constables, a small knot of people gathered curiously on the pavement opposite. It did not escape their notice that the police car had parked immediately across the access to the courtyard, effectively sealing the exit. Five minutes later a second police car arrived, and eyes turned to the lightly built, dark-haired man who alighted. He conversed briefly with the constable who stood guard outside, nodded his head approvingly several times and walked into the Black Prince.

He knew Sergeant Lewis only slightly, but soon found himself pleasurably impressed by the man's level-headed competence. The two men conferred in brisk tones and very quickly a preliminary procedure was agreed. Lewis, with the help of the second constable, was to list the names, home addresses, and car registrations of all persons on the premises, and to take brief statements of their evening's whereabouts, and immediate destinations. There were over fifty people to see, and Morse realized that it would take some time.

'Shall I try to get you some more help, Sergeant?'

'I think the two of us can manage, sir.'

'Good. Let's get started.'

A door, forming the side entrance to the Black Prince, led out into the courtyard and from here Morse stepped gingerly out and looked around. He counted thirteen cars jammed tight into the limited space, but he could have missed one or two, for the cars furthest away were little more than dark hulks against the high back wall, and he wondered by what feats of advanced-motoring skill and precision their inebriated owners could ever negotiate the vehicles unscathed through the narrow exit from the yard. Carefully he shone his torch around and slowly perambulated the yard. The driver of the last car parked on the left-hand side of the yard had presciently backed into the narrow lot and left himself a yard or so of room between his nearside and the wall; and stretched along this space was the sprawling figure of a young girl. She lay on her right side, her head almost up against the corner of the walls, her long blonde hair now cruelly streaked with blood. It was immediately clear that she had been killed by a heavy blow across the back of the skull, and behind the body lay a flat heavy tyre-spanner, about one and a half inches across and some eighteen inches in length – the type of spanner with its undulating ends so common in the days before the inauguration of instant tyre repairs. Morse stood for a few minutes, gazing down at the ugly scene at his feet. The murdered girl wore a minimum of clothing – a pair of wedge-heeled shoes, a very brief dark-blue mini-skirt and a white blouse. Nothing else. Morse shone his torch on the upper part of the body. The left-hand side of the blouse was ripped across; the top two buttons were unfastened and the third had been wrenched away, leaving the full breasts almost totally exposed. Morse flashed his torch around and immediately spotted the missing button – a small, white, mother-of-pearl disc winking up at him from the cobbled ground. How he hated sex murders! He shouted to the constable standing at the entrance to the yard.

'Yes, sir?'

'We need some arc-lamps.'

'It would help, I suppose, sir.'

'Get some.'

'Me, sir?'

'Yes, you!'

'Where shall I get . . . ?'

'How the hell do I know,' bellowed Morse.

By a quarter to midnight Lewis had finished his task and he reported to Morse, who was sitting with *The Times* in the manager's office, drinking what looked very much like whisky.

'Ah, Lewis.' He thrust the paper across. 'Have a look at 14 down. Appropriate eh?' Lewis looked at 14 down: *Take in bachelor?*

It could do (3). He saw what Morse had written into the completed diagram: BRA. What was he supposed to say? He had never worked with Morse before.

'Good clue, don't you think?'

Lewis, who had occasionally managed the *Daily Mirror* coffee-time crossword was out of his depth, and felt much puzzled.

'I'm afraid I'm not very hot on crosswords, sir.'

' "Bachelor" – that's BA and "take" is the letter "r"; *recipe* in Latin. Did you never do any Latin?'

'No, sir.'

'Do you think I'm wasting your time, Lewis?'

Lewis was nobody's fool and was a man of some honesty and integrity. 'Yes, sir.'

An engaging smile crept across Morse's mouth. He thought they would get on well together.

'Lewis, I want you to work with me on this case.' The sergeant looked straight at Morse and into the hard, blue eyes. He heard himself say he would be delighted.

'This calls for a celebration,' said Morse. 'Landlord!' Westbrook had been hovering outside and came in smartly. 'A double whisky.' Morse pushed his glass forward.

'Would *you* like a drink, sir?' The manager turned hesitantly to Lewis.

'Sergeant Lewis is on duty, Mr Westbrook.'

When the manager returned, Morse asked him to assemble everyone on the premises, including staff, in the largest room available, and drinking his whisky in complete silence, skimmed through the remaining pages of the newspaper.

'Do you read *The Times*, Lewis?'

'No, sir; we take the *Mirror*.' It seemed a rather sad admission.

'So do I sometimes,' said Morse.

At a quarter past midnight Morse came into the restaurant-room where everyone was now gathered. Gaye's eyes met and held his briefly as he entered, and she felt a strong compulsion about the man. It was not so much that he seemed mentally to be undressing her, as most of the men she knew, but as if he had already done so. She listened to him with interest as he spoke.

He thanked them all for their patience and co-operation. It was getting very late and he didn't intend to keep them there any longer. They would now know why the police were there. There had been a murder in the courtyard – a young girl with blonde hair. They would appreciate that all the cars in the courtyard must stay where they were until the morning. He knew this meant that some of them would have difficulty getting home, but taxis had been ordered. If anyone wished to report to him or to Sergeant Lewis anything at all which might be of interest or value to the inquiry, however unimportant it might seem, would such a person please stay behind. The rest could go.

To Gaye it seemed an uninspired performance. Happening to be on the scene of a murder ought surely to be a bit more exciting than this? She would go home now, where her mother and her young son would be fast asleep. And even if they weren't, she couldn't tell them much, could she? Already the police had been there over an hour and a half. It wasn't exactly what she'd come to expect from her reading of Holmes or Poirot, who by this time would doubtless have interviewed the chief suspects, and made some startling deductions from the most trivial phenomena.

The murmuring which followed the end of Morse's brief address died away as most of the customers collected their coats and moved off. Gaye rose, too. Had she seen anything of interest or value? She thought back on the evening. There was, of course, the young man who had found the girl . . . She had seen him before, but she couldn't quite remember who it was he'd been with, or when. And then she had it – blonde hair! She'd been in the lounge with him only last week. But a lot of girls these days peroxided their hair. Perhaps it was worth mentioning? She decided it was and walked up to Morse.

'You said the girl who has been murdered had blonde hair.' Morse looked at her and slowly nodded. 'I think she was here last week – she was with the man who found her body tonight. I saw them here. I work in the lounge.'

'That's very interesting, Miss – er?'

'Mrs. Mrs McFee.'

'Please forgive me, Mrs McFee. I thought you might have been wearing all those rings to frighten off the boys who come to drool at you over the counter.'

Gaye felt very angry. He was a hateful man. 'Look, Inspector whatever your name is, I came to tell you something I thought might be helpful. If you're going . . .'

'Mrs McFee,' broke in Morse gently, looking at her with an open nakedness in his eyes, 'if I lived anywhere near, I'd come in myself and drool over you every night of the week.'

At just after 1.00 a.m. a primitive, if reasonably effective, relay of arc-lamps was fixed around the courtyard. Morse had instructed

Lewis to detain the young man who had found the murdered girl until they had taken the opportunity of investigating the courtyard more closely. The two men now surveyed the scene before them. There was a great deal of blood, and as Sergeant Lewis looked down on her, he felt a deep revulsion against the violence and senselessness of murder. Morse appeared more interested in the starry heavens above.

'Do you study the stars, Lewis?'

'I read the horoscopes sometimes, sir.'

Morse appeared not to hear. 'I once heard of a group of schoolchildren, Lewis, who tried to collect a million matchsticks. After they'd filled the whole of the school premises, they decided they'd have to pack it up.' Lewis thought it his duty to say something, but all appropriate comment eluded him.

After a while, Morse reverted his attention to more terrestrial things, and the two of them looked down again at the murdered girl. The spanner and the solitary white button lay where Morse had seen them earlier. There was nothing much else to see but for the trail of dried blood that led almost from one end of the back wall to the other.

The young man sat in the manager's office. His mother, though expecting him to be late, would be getting worried; and so was he. Morse finally came in at 1.30 a.m. whilst the police surgeon, the photographers, and the fingerprint men busied themselves about the courtyard.

'Name?' he asked.

'Sanders, John Sanders.'

'You found the body?'

'Yes, sir.'

'Tell me about it.'

'There's not much to tell really.'

Morse smiled. 'Then we needn't keep you long, need we, Mr Sanders?'

The young man fidgeted. Morse sat opposite him, looked him hard in the eye and waited.

'Well, I just walked into the courtyard and there she was. I didn't touch her, but I knew she was dead. I came straight back in to tell the manager.'

Morse nodded. 'Anything else?'

'Don't think so.'

'When were you sick, Mr Sanders?'

'Oh yes. I was sick.'

'Was it after or before you saw the girl?'

'After. It must have upset me seeing her there – sort of shock, I suppose.'

'Why don't you tell me the truth?'

'What do you mean?'

Morse sighed. 'You haven't got your car here have you?'

'I haven't got a car.'

'Do you usually have a stroll round the courtyard before you go home?' Sanders said nothing. 'How much drink did you have tonight?'

'A few whiskies – I wasn't drunk.'

'Mr Sanders, do you want me to find out from someone else?' It was clear from Sanders's manner that he hardly welcomed an enquiry along such lines. 'What time did you come here?' continued Morse.

'About half-past seven.'

'And you got drunk and went out to be sick.' Reluctantly Sanders agreed. 'Do you usually drink on your own?'

'Not usually.'

'Who were you waiting for?' Sanders did not reply. 'She didn't show up?'

'No,' he said flatly.

'But she did come, didn't she?'

'No, I told you. I was on my own all the time.'

'But she did come, didn't she?' repeated Morse quietly. Sanders looked beaten. 'She came,' continued Morse in the same quiet voice. 'She came and you saw her. You saw her in the courtyard, and she was dead.'

The young man nodded.

'We'd better have a little chat, you and me,' said Morse ungrammatically.

CHAPTER THREE
Thursday, 30 September

As he stood alone in the bedroom of Sylvia Kaye, Morse felt measurably relieved. The grim duties of the night were over, and he switched on the natural defence mechanism of his weary mind. He wished to forget the awakening of Mrs Dorothy Kaye, and the summoning of her husband from his night-shift in the welding division of the Cowley car plant; the fatuous, coarse recriminations and the overwhelming hurt of their bitter, empty misery. Sylvia's mother was now under sedation, postponing the day and the reckoning; whilst Sergeant Lewis sat at headquarters learning what he could from Sylvia's father. He took many pages of careful notes but doubted if it all amounted to much. He was to join Morse in half an hour.

The bedroom was small, one of three in a neat semi-detached house in Jackdaw Court, a quiet crescent with rotting wooden fences, a few minutes' walk off the Woodstock Road. Morse sat down on the narrow bed and looked around him. He wondered if the neatness of the bed was Mum's doing, for the remainder of the room betrayed the slack and untidy living of the murdered girl. A vast coloured portrait of a pop artist was pinned rather precariously above the gas fire in the chimney breast, and Morse reminded himself that he might understand young people rather better if he had a teenage family of his own; as it was, the identity of the handsome youth was cloaked in anonymity and whatever pretensions he may have had would for Morse be for ever unknown. Several items of underwear draped the table and chair which, with a whitewood wardrobe, substantively comprised the only other furniture. Morse gingerly picked up a flimsy black bra lying on the chair. His mind flashed back to that first glimpse of Sylvia Kaye, rested there a few seconds and slowly returned through the tortuous byways of the last unpleasant hours. A pile of women's magazines was awkwardly stacked on the window-sill, and Morse cursorily flicked his way through make-up hints, personal problems, and horoscopes. Not even a paragraph of pornography. He opened the wardrobe door and with perceptibly deeper interest examined the array of skirts, blouses, slacks, and dresses. Clean and untidy. Mounds of shoes, ultra-modern, wedged, ugly: she wasn't short of money. On the table Morse saw a travel brochure for package trips to Greece, Yugoslavia, and Cyprus, white hotels, azure seas, and small print about insurance liability and smallpox regulations; a letter from Sylvia's employer explaining the complexities of VAT, and a diary, the latter revealing nothing but a single entry for 2 January: 'Cold. Went to see *Ryan's Daughter.'*

Lewis tapped on the bedroom door and entered. 'Find anything, sir?' Morse looked at his cheerful sergeant distastefully, and said nothing. 'Can I?' asked Lewis his hand hovering above the diary.

'Go ahead,' said Morse.

Lewis examined the diary, turning carefully through the days of September. Finding nothing, he worked meticulously through every page. 'Only one day filled in, sir.'

'I don't even get that far,' said Morse.

'Do you think "cold" means it was a cold day or she had a cold?'

'How do I know,' snapped Morse, 'and what the hell does it matter?'

'We could find out where *Ryan's Daughter* was on in the first week of January,' suggested Lewis.

'Yes, we could. And how much the diary cost and who gave it to her and where she buys her Biros from. Sergeant! We're running a murder inquiry not a stationery shop!'

'Sorry.'

'You may be right though,' added Morse.

'I'm afraid Mr Kaye hadn't got much to tell me, either, sir. Did you want to see him?'

'No. Leave the poor fellow alone.'

'We're not making very rapid progress then.'

'Oh, I don't know,' said Morse. 'Miss Kaye was wearing a white blouse, wasn't she?'

'Yes.'

'What colour bra would your wife wear under a white blouse?'

'A lightish-coloured one, I suppose.'

'She wouldn't wear a black one?'

'It would show through.'

'Mm. By the way, Lewis, do you know when lighting-up time was yesterday evening?'

'Afraid I don't, off hand,' replied Lewis, 'but I can soon find out for you.'

'No need for that,' said Morse. 'According to the diary you just inspected, yesterday, 29 September, was St Michael and All Angels' day and lighting-up time was 6.40 p.m.'

Lewis followed his superior officer down the narrow stairs, and wondered what was coming next. Before they reached the front door, Morse half turned his head: 'What do you think of Women's Lib, Lewis?'

At 11.00 a.m. Sergeant Lewis interviewed the manager of the Town and Gown Assurance Company, situated on the second and third storeys above a flourishing tobacconist's shop in the High.

Sylvia had worked there – her first job – for just over a year. She was a copy-typist, having failed to satisfy the secretarial college at which she had studied for two years after leaving school that the ungainly and frequently undecipherable scrawls in her shorthand notebook bore sufficient relationship to the missives originally dictated. But her typing was reasonably accurate and clean, and the company, the manager assured Lewis, had no complaints about its late employee. She had been punctual and unobtrusive.

'Attractive?'

'Well – er, yes. I suppose she was,' replied the manager. Lewis made a note and wished Morse were there; but the Inspector said he felt thirsty and had gone into the Minster across the way.

'She worked, you say, with two other girls,' said Lewis. 'I think I'd better have a word with them if I can.'

'Certainly, officer.' The manager, Mr Palmer, seemed a fraction relieved.

Lewis questioned the two young ladies at considerable length. Neither was 'a particular friend' of Sylvia. She had, as far as they knew, no regular beau. Yes, she had boasted occasionally of her sexual exploits – but so did most of the girls. She was friendly enough, but not really 'one of the girls'.

Lewis looked through her desk. The usual bric-à-brac. A bit of a broken mirror, a comb with a few blonde hairs in it, yesterday's *Sun*, pencils galore, rubbers, typewriter ribbons, carbons. On the wall behind Sylvia's desk was pinned a photograph of Omar Sharif, flanked by a typewritten holiday rota. Lewis saw that Sylvia had been on a fortnight's holiday in the latter half of July, and he asked the two girls where she'd been to.

'Stayed at home, I think,' replied the elder of the two girls, a quiet, serious-looking girl in her early twenties.

Lewis sighed. 'You don't seem to know much about her, do you?' The girls said nothing. Lewis tried his best to elicit a little more co-operation, but met with little success. He left the office just before midday, and strolled over to the Minster.

'Poor Sylvia,' said the younger girl after he had gone.

'Yes, poor Sylvia,' replied Jennifer Coleby.

Lewis eventually, and somewhat to his surprise, discovered Morse in the 'gentlemen only' bar at the back of the Minster.

'Ah, Lewis.' He rose and placed his empty glass on the bar, 'What's it to be?' Lewis asked for a pint of bitter. 'Two pints of your best bitter,' said Morse cheerfully to the man behind the bar, 'and have one yourself.'

It became clear to Lewis that the topic of conversation before his arrival had been horse racing. Morse picked up a copy of *Sporting Life* and walked over to the corner with his assistant.

'You a betting man, Lewis?'

'I sometimes put a few bob on the Derby and the National, sir, but I'm not a regular gambler.'

'You keep it that way,' said Morse, with a note of seriousness in his voice. 'But look here, what do you think of that?' He unfolded the racing paper and pointed to one of the runners in the 3.15 at Chepstow: the Black Prince. 'Worth a quid, would you say, Sergeant?'

'Certainly an odd coincidence.'

'10 to 1,' said Morse, drinking deeply on his beer.

'Are you going to back it, sir?'

'I already have,' said Morse, glancing up at the old barman.

'Isn't that illegal, sir?'

'I never studied that side of the law.' Doesn't he want to solve this murder, thought Lewis, and as if Morse read his unspoken words he was promptly asked for a report on the deceased's position with Town and Gown. Lewis did his best, and Morse did not interrupt. He seemed rather more interested in his pint of beer. When he finished, Morse told him to get back to headquarters, type his reports, then get home and have some sleep. Lewis didn't argue. He felt dog-tired, and sleep was fast becoming a barely remembered luxury.

'Nothing else, sir?'

'Not until tomorrow when you'll report to me at 7.30 a.m. sharp – unless you want to put a few bob on the Black Prince.' Lewis felt in his pocket and pulled out 50p.

'Each way, do you think?'

'You'll kick yourself if it wins,' said Morse.

'All right. 50p to win.'

Morse took the 50p and as Lewis left he saw the barman pocket the coin, and pull a further pint for the enigmatic Chief Inspector.

CHAPTER FOUR

Friday, 1 October

Prompt at 7.30 next morning, Lewis tapped on the inspector's door. Receiving no answer, he cautiously tried the knob and peered round the door. No sign of life. He walked back to the front vestibule and asked the desk-clerk if Inspector Morse was in yet.

'Not seen 'im.'

'He said he'd be here at half-seven.'

'Well, you know the Inspector.'

I wish I did, thought Lewis. He walked along to pick up the reports he had wearily typed out the previous afternoon, and read them through carefully. He'd done his best, but there was little to go on. He walked on to the canteen and ordered a cup of coffee. Constable Dickson, an officer whom Lewis knew fairly well, was enthusiastically assaulting a plate of bacon and tomatoes.

'How's the murder job going, Sarge?'

'Early days yet.'

'Old Morse in charge, eh?'

'Yep.'

'Funny bugger, isn't he?' Lewis didn't disagree. 'I know one thing,' said Dickson. 'He was here till way gone midnight. Got virtually everyone in the building jumping about for him. I reckon every phone on the premises was red hot. God, he can work, that chap, when he wants to.'

Lewis felt a little shame-faced. He himself had slept sweetly and soundly from six the previous evening until six that morning. He reckoned that Morse deserved his sleep, and sat down to drink a cup of coffee.

Ten minutes later a freshly shaven Morse walked brightly into the canteen. 'Ah, there you are, Lewis. Sorry to be late.' He ordered a coffee and sat opposite. 'Bad news for you, I'm afraid.' Lewis looked up sharply. 'You lost your money. The constipated camel came in second.'

Lewis smiled. 'Never mind, sir. I just hope you didn't lose too much yourself.'

Morse shook his head. 'Oh no, I didn't lose anything; in fact I made a few quid. I backed it each way.'

'But . . .' began Lewis.

'C'mon,' said Morse. 'Drink up. We've got work to do.'

For the next four hours the two of them were busy sorting the

reports flowing in from the wide-flung enquiries Morse had initiated the previous day. At twelve noon, Lewis felt he knew more
about Sylvia Kaye than he did about his wife. He read each report
with great care – Morse's orders – and felt that many of the facts
were beginning to fix themselves firmly in his mind. Morse, he
noticed, devoured the reports with an amazing rapidity, reminiscent of someone skipping through a tedious novel; yet occasionally
he would re-read the odd report with a fascinated concentration.

'Well?' said Morse finally.

'I think I've got most things pretty straight, sir.'

'Good.'

'You seemed to find one or two of the reports very interesting,
sir.'

'Did I?' Morse sounded surprised.

'You spent about ten minutes on that one from the secretarial
college, and it's only half a page.'

'You're very observant, Lewis, but I'm sorry to disappoint you.
It was the most ill-written report I've seen in years, with twelve –
no less – grammatical monstrosities in ten lines! What's the force
coming to?'

Lewis didn't know what the force was coming to and hadn't
the courage to enquire into the Inspector's statistical findings on
his own erratic style. He asked instead, 'Do you think we're
getting anywhere, sir?'

'Doubt it,' replied Morse.

Lewis wasn't so sure. Sylvia's movements on the previous
Wednesday seemed established. She had left the office in the High
at 5.00 p.m., and almost certainly walked the hundred yards or so
to the No 2 bus stop outside University College. She had arrived
home at 5.35 p.m. and had a good meal. She told her mother she
might be late home, left the house at roughly 6.30 p.m. wearing –
as far as could be established – the clothes in which she was
found. Somehow she had got to Woodstock. It all seemed to Lewis
a promising enough starting-point for a few preliminary enquiries.

'Would you like me to get on to the bus company, sir, and see
the drivers on the Woodstock run?'

'Done it,' said Morse.

'No good?' Disappointment showed in the Sergeant's voice.

'I don't think she went by bus.'

'Taxi, sir?'

'Improbable, wouldn't you think?'

'I don't know, sir. It might not be all that expensive.'

'Perhaps not, but it seems most improbable to me. If she'd

wanted a taxi, she'd have rung up from home – there's a phone there.'

'She may have done just that, sir.'

'She didn't. No phone call was made by any member of the Kaye household yesterday.'

Lewis was experiencing a dangerous failure of confidence. 'I don't seem to be much help,' he said. But Morse ignored the comment.

'Lewis, how would you go from Oxford to Woodstock?'

'By car, sir.'

'She hadn't got a car.'

'Get a lift with one of her friends?'

'You wrote the report. She doesn't seem to have had many girl friends.'

'A boy friend, you think, sir?'

'Do you?'

Lewis thought a minute. 'Bit odd if she was going with a boy friend. Why didn't he pick her up at her house?'

'Why not, indeed?'

'She wasn't picked up at home?'

'No. Her mother saw her walking away.'

'You've interviewed her mother then, sir.'

'Yes. I spoke to her last night.'

'Is she very upset?'

'She's got broad shoulders, Lewis, and I rather like her. Of course she's terribly upset and shocked. But not quite so heart-broken as I thought she'd be. In fact I got the idea her beautiful daughter was something of a trial to her.'

Morse walked over to a large mirror, took out a comb and began to groom his thinning hair. He carefully drew a few strands across a broad area of nakedness at the back of his skull, returned the comb to his pocket and asked a perplexed Sergeant Lewis what he thought of the effect.

'You see, Lewis, if Sylvia didn't go by bus, taxi or boy friend, how on earth did she ever get to Woodstock? And remember that get to Woodstock somehow she assuredly did.'

'She must have hitched it, sir.'

Morse was still surveying himself in the mirror. 'Yes, Lewis, I think she did. And that is why,' he took out the comb again and made some further passes at his straggling hair, 'that is why I think I must put in a little TV appearance tonight.' He picked up the phone and put through a call to the Chief Superintendent. 'Go and get some lunch, Lewis. I'll see you later.'

'Can I order anything for you, sir?'

'No. I've got to watch my figure,' said Morse.

The death of Sylvia Kaye had figured dramatically in Thursday afternoon's edition of the *Oxford Mail*, and prominently in the national press on Friday morning. On Friday evening the news bulletins on both BBC and ITV carried an interview with Chief Inspector Morse, who appealed for help from anyone who had been on the Woodstock Road between 6.40 p.m. and 7.15 p.m. on the evening of Wednesday, 29 September. Morse informed the nation that the police were looking for a very dangerous man who might attack again at any time; for the killer of Sylvia Kaye, when brought to justice, would face not only the charge of wilful murder, but also the charge of sexual assault and rape.

Lewis had stood in the background as Morse faced the camera crews and joined him after his performance was over.

'That damned wind!' said Morse, his hair blown into a tufted wilderness.

'Do you really think he might kill someone else, sir?'

'Doubt it very much,' said Morse.

CHAPTER FIVE

Friday, 1 October

Each evening of the week, with rare exceptions, Mr Bernard Crowther left his small detached house in Southdown Road, North Oxford, at approximately 9.40 p.m. Each evening his route was identical. Methodically closing behind him the white gate which enclosed a small, patchy strip of lawn, he would turn right, walk to the end of the road, turn right again, and make his way, with perceptible purposefulness in his stride, towards the lounge bar of the Fletcher's Arms. Though an articulate man, indeed an English don at Lonsdale College, he found it difficult to explain either to his disapproving wife or indeed to himself exactly what it was that attracted him to this unexceptional pub, with its ill-assorted, yet regular and amiable clientele.

On the night of Friday, 1 October, however, Crowther would have been observed to remain quite still for several seconds after closing the garden gate behind him, his eyes downcast and disturbed as if he were pondering deep and troublous thoughts; and then to turn, against his habit and his inclination, to his left. He walked slowly to the end of the road, where, on the left beside a row of dilapidated garages, stood a public telephone-box. Impatient at the best of times, and this was not the best of times, he waited restlessly and awkwardly, pacing to and fro, consulting his watch and throwing wicked glances at the portly woman inside the kiosk who appeared ill-equipped to face the triangular threat of the gadgeted apparatus before her, an uncooperative telephone exchange and her own one-handed negotiations with the assorted coinage in her purse. But she was fighting on and Crowther, in a generous manner, wondered if one of her children had been taken suddenly and seriously ill with Dad on the night-shift and no one else to help. But he doubted whether her call was as important as the one he was about to make. News bulletins had always gripped his attention, however trivial the items reported; and the item he had watched on the BBC news at 9.00 p.m. had been far from trivial. He could remember verbatim the words the police inspector had used: 'We shall be very glad if any motorist . . .' Yes, he could tell them something, for he had played his part in the terrifying and tragic train of events. But what was he going to say? He couldn't tell them the truth. Nor even half the truth. His fragile resolution began to crumble. He'd give that wretched woman another minute – one minute and no longer.

At 9.50 p.m. that same evening an excited Sergeant Lewis put through a call to Chief Inspector Morse. 'A break, sir. I think we've got a break.'

'Oh?'

'Yes. A witness, sir. A Mrs Mabel Jarman. She saw the murdered girl . . .'

'You mean,' interrupted Morse, 'she saw the girl who was later murdered, I suppose.'

'That's it. We can get a full statement as soon as we like.'

'You mean you haven't got one yet?'

'She only rang five minutes ago, sir. I'm going over straight away. She's local. I wondered if you wanted to come.'

'No,' said Morse.

'All right, sir. I'll have the whole thing typed up and ready for you in the morning.'

'Good.'

'Bit of luck, though, isn't it? We'll soon get on to this other girl.'

'What other girl?' said Morse quietly.

'Well, you see, sir . . .'

'What's Mrs Jarman's address?' Morse reluctantly took off his bedroom slippers, and reached for his shoes.

'Bit late on parade tonight, Bernard. What's it to be?'

Bernard was well liked at the Fletcher's Arms, always ready to fork out for his round – and more. All the regulars knew him for a man of some academic distinction; but he was a good listener, laughed as heartily as the next at the latest jokes, and himself occasionally waxed eloquent on the stupidity of the government and the incompetence of Oxford United. But tonight he spoke of neither. By 10.25 p.m. he had drunk three pints of best bitter with his usual practised fluency and got up to go.

'Another one before you go, Bernard?'

'Thanks, no. I've had just about enough of that horse piss for one night.'

'You in the dog house again?'

'I'm always in the bloody dog house.'

He walked back slowly. He knew that if the bedroom light was on, his wife, Margaret, would be reading in bed, waiting only for her errant husband to return. If there was no light, she would probably be watching TV. He came to a decision as foolish as the ones he had made as a boy when he would race a car to the nearest lamppost. If she was in bed, he would go straight in; if she was still up, he would ring the police. He turned into the road, and saw immediately that the bedroom light was on.

Mrs Jarman gave her testimony in a brisk, if excited, fashion. Her memory proved surprisingly clear, and Sergeant Lewis's notes grew fat with factual data. Morse left things to him. He wondered if Lewis had been right in thinking this was the big break, and considered, on reflection, that he was. He himself felt impatient and bored with the trained and thorough pedanticism with which his sergeant probed and queried the chronology of the bus stop encounter. But he knew it had to be done and he knew that Lewis was doing it well. For three-quarters of an hour he left them to it.

'Well, I want to thank you very much, Mrs Jarman.' Lewis closed his notebook and looked, in a mildly satisfied manner, towards his chief.

'Perhaps,' said Morse, 'I could ask you to come to see us in the morning? Sergeant Lewis will have your statement typed out, and we'd like you to have a look through it to see that he's got it all right – just a formality, you know.'

Lewis stood up to go, but Morse's veiled glance told him to sit down again.

'I wonder, Mrs Jarman,' he said, 'if you could do us one last favour. I'd just love a cup of tea. I know it's late but . . .'

'Why, of course, Inspector. I wish you'd said so before.' She hurried off and the policemen heard a spurt of water and a clatter of cups.

'Well, Sergeant, you've done a good job.'

'Thank you, sir.'

'Now listen. That bus. Get on to it as soon as you can.'

'But you said you'd checked the buses, sir.'

'Well check 'em again.'

'All right.'

'And,' said Morse, 'there's that articulated lorry. With a bit of luck we can trace that.'

'You think we can?'

'You've got a definite time – what else do you want, man?'

'Anything else, sir?' said Lewis in a subdued voice.

'Yes. Stay and make a few more notes. I won't be long.'

The kitchen door opened and Mrs Jarman reappeared. 'I was just wondering whether you gentlemen would like a little drop of whisky, instead of tea. I've had a bottle since Christmas – I don't usually drink myself.'

'Now, now,' said Morse, 'you are a very resourceful woman, Mrs Jarman.' Lewis smiled wanly. He knew what was coming. *Déjà vu.*

'I think a little drop of Scotch would do me the power of good. Perhaps you'll have a drop youself?'

'Oh no, sir, I'll have a cuppa, if you don't mind.' She opened a drawer in the cupboard and brought out two glass tumblers.

'Just the one glass then, Mrs Jarman,' said Morse. 'It's a pity, I know, but Sergeant Lewis here is on duty and you will appreciate that a policeman is not allowed to consume any alcoholic drink whilst on duty. You wouldn't want him to break the law, would you?'

Lewis muttered to himself.

Morse smiled into his liberal dose of whisky whilst his assistant soberly stirred a diminutive cup of wickedly dark brown tea.

'Mrs Jarman, I just want to ask you one or two more questions about what you've said to Sergeant Lewis. I hope you don't feel too tired?'

'Oh no.'

'Do you remember how this "other girl" seemed? Was she a bit cross? A bit nervous?'

'I don't think she was – well, I don't know. Perhaps she was a bit nervous.'

'A bit frightened?'

'Oh no. Not that. A bit sort of, er, excited. Yes, that's it, a bit excited.'

'Excited and impatient?'

'I think so.'

'Now, I want you to think back. Just close your eyes if you like, and picture yourself at the bus stop again. Can you recall anything, anything at all, that she said. She asked you if the next bus went to Woodstock. You've told us that. Anything else?'

'I can't remember. I just can't seem to remember.'

'Now, Mrs Jarman, don't rush yourself. Just relax and picture it all again. Take your time.'

Mrs Jarman closed her eyes and Morse watched her with keen anticipation. She said nothing. Morse at last broke the embarrassing silence. 'What about the girl who was murdered? Did she say anything else? She wanted to hitchhike, you said.'

'Yes, she kept saying something like "Come on".'

' "It'll be all right"?' added Morse.

'Yes. "It'll be all right. We'll have a giggle about it in the morning." '

Morse's blood froze. He remained utterly motionless. But Mrs Jarman's memory had dredged its last.

Morse relaxed. 'We've kept you up late, but you've been wonderful. And this must be a real priority brand of Scotch?'

'Oh, would you like a little drop more, sir?'

'Well, I think I wouldn't perhaps say no, Mrs Jarman. Yes, a drop of the finest Scotch I've tasted in years.'

As Mrs Jarman turned her back to refill his glass, Morse sternly motioned Lewis to stay where he was, and for the next half hour he tried with every subtlety he knew to jog the good lady's recollection of her chance encounter with the murdered girl and her companion. But to no avail.

'Just one more thing, Mrs Jarman. When you come to see us in the morning, we shall be holding an identity parade. It won't take more than a minute or two.'

'You mean you want me to . . . Oh dear!'

At 11.45 p.m. Morse and Lewis took their leave of Mrs Jarman. They were standing by their cars when the door of the house suddenly opened again and Mrs Jarman came hurriedly towards Morse.

'There's just one more thing, sir. I've just remembered. When you said close your eyes and just picture things. I've thought of something. That other girl, sir. When she ran, she ran with a sort of splay-footed run – do you know what I mean, sir?'

'Yes I do,' said Morse.

The two men returned to HQ. After enquiring whether any further calls had come through and learning there were none, Morse called Lewis to his office.

'Well, my friend?' Morse looked pleased with himself.

'You told her we're going to have an identity parade?' asked a puzzled Lewis.

'We are. Now tell me this. What would you say was the most vital fact we learned from Mrs Jarman?'

'We learned quite a few pieces of valuable information.'

'Yes, we did. But only one fact that really made your hair stand on end, eh?' Lewis tried to look intelligent. 'We learned, did we not,' said Morse, 'that the girls would have a bit of a giggle about it all in the morning?'

'Oh, I see,' said Lewis, not seeing.

'You see what it means? They would be meeting in the morning – Thursday morning, and we know that Sylvia Kaye was in employment and we know where, do we not?'

'So the other girl works there, too.'

'The evidence would seem to point very much that way, Lewis.'

'But I was there, sir, and none of them said a word.'

'Don't you find that very interesting?'

'I don't seem to have done a very good job, do I?' Lewis looked disconsolately down at the Chief Inspector's carpet.

'But don't you see,' continued Morse, 'we now know that one of the girls – how many were there?'

'Fourteen.'

'That one of the girls is at the very least withholding vital evidence and at the best telling us a heap of lies.'

'I didn't talk to them all, sir.'

'Good God, man! They knew what you were there for, didn't they? One of their colleagues is murdered. A sergeant of the murder squad comes to their office. What the hell did they think you'd gone for? Service the bloody typewriters? No, you did well,

Lewis. You didn't force our little girl to weave her tangled web for us. She thinks she's OK and that's how I want it.' Morse got up. 'I want you to get some sleep, Lewis. You've got work to do in the morning. But just before you go, find me the private address of Mr Palmer. I think a little visit is called for.'

'You're not thinking of knocking him up now, are you, sir?'

'Not only am I going to knock him up as you put it, Lewis, I am going to ask him, very nicely of course, to open up his offices for me and I am going to look through the private drawers of fourteen young ladies. It should be an exciting business.'

'Won't you need a search warrant, sir?'

'I never did understand the legal situation over search warrants,' complained Morse.

'I think you ought to have one, sir.'

'And perhaps you'll let me know where the hell I find anyone to sign a warrant at this time of the night – or morning, whatever it is.'

'But if Mr Palmer insists on his legal rights . . .' began Lewis.

'I shall tell him we're trying to find out who raped and murdered one of his girls,' snapped Morse, 'not looking for dirty postcards from Pwllheli!'

'Wouldn't you like me to come with you, sir?'

'No. Do as I say and go to bed.'

'Well, good luck, sir.'

'I shan't need it,' said Morse. 'I know you'd never believe it, but I can be an officious bastard when I want to be. Mr Palmer will be out of bed as if he'd got a flea in his pyjama bottoms.'

But the manager of the Town and Gown Assurance Co., though condescending to get out of bed, flatly refused to get out of his pyjamas – top or bottom. He asked Morse for his authority to search his offices, and once having established that Morse had none, he proved adamant to all the cajolings and threats that Morse could muster. The Inspector reflected that he had badly underestimated the little manager. After prolonged negotiation, however, a policy was finally agreed. All the staff of the Town and Gown would be assembled in the manager's office at 8.45 a.m. the following morning, where they would all be asked if they had any objection to the police opening any incoming private correspondence. If there were no objection (Palmer assured Morse), the Inspector could open all correspondence, and, if need be, make confidential copies of any letter which might be of value. Furthermore

all the female employees would be asked to attend an identity
parade at the Thames Valley HQ some time later the same
morning. Palmer would need some time to arrange a skeleton
servicing of the telephone exchange and other vital matters. It was
a good job it was Saturday; the office closed at midday.

Perhaps, thought Morse in retrospect, things hadn't worked
out too badly. He wearily drove to HQ and wondered why, with
all his experience, he had rushed so wildly into such an ill-
considered and probably futile scheme as he had contemplated.
Yet, for all that, he thought that he had in some strange way been
right. He felt in his bones that there was an urgency about this
stage of investigation. He felt he was poised for a big break-
through, though he did not at this stage realize how many breaks-
through would be required before the case was solved. Nor did he
realize that in an oddly perverse way Palmer's refusal to allow him
unauthorized entry to his premises had presented him with one
gigantic piece of luck. For a letter, addressed to one of the young
ladies in Palmer's employ, was already on its way, and no power
on earth, except the inefficiency of some unsuspecting sorting-
clerk, could – or indeed did – prevent its prompt delivery.

Morse returned to HQ and spent the next hour at his desk. He
finished at 4.15 a.m. and sat back in his black leather chair. Little
point in going home now. He pondered the case, at first with a
slow, methodical analysis of the facts known hitherto and then
with what, if he had been wider awake, he would wish to have
called a series of swift, intuitive leaps, all of which landed him in
areas of twilight and darkness. But he knew that whatever had
taken place on Wednesday evening had its causation in the
actvities of certain persons, and that these persons had been
motivated by the ordinary passions of love and hate and greed
and jealousy. That wasn't the puzzle at all. It was the interlocking
of the jigsaw pieces, those pieces that would now be coming into
his hands. He dozed off. He fitfully dreamed of an attractive red-
headed barmaid and a blonde beauty with blood all over her hair.
He always seemed to dream of women. He sometimes wondered
what he would dream about if he got himself married. Women
probably, he thought.

CHAPTER SIX

Saturday, 2 October, a.m.

'What *next*?' said Judith, Mr Palmer's confidential secretary. 'Opening our letters, he said!'

'You could have said no,' replied Sandra, an amiable, feckless girl, who had, on merit, made no advance either in status or in salary since joining the office three years ago.

'I almost did,' chimed in Ruth, a flutter-lashed girl with the brains of a butterfly. 'If Bob sent me one of his real passionate ones, coo!' She giggled nervously.

Most of the girls were young and unmarried and lived with their parents, and because of late morning postal deliveries and a fear that parents might pry into matters not concerning them, several of them had invited their correspondents to address mail to the office. Indeed, so many incoming letters were marked 'Private and Confidential', 'Personal' and the like, that an unsuspecting observer might have surmised that the Town and Gown was the headquarters of a classified intelligence department. But Palmer countenanced such mild abuse of his establishment with philosophic quietude, whilst at the same time keeping a hawk-like eye on the office telephone accounts. It seemed to him a fair arrangement.

Each girl in her own way had been a little overawed by Morse, and his quietly spoken requests were conceded with no audible murmur of dissent. Of course they all wanted to help. In any case he was only going to get copies of the mail and everything would be treated with the utmost confidentiality. Nevertheless Ruth had given an audible sigh of relief on discovering that this was a morning when Bob had temporarily exhausted his supply of lecherous suggestions. However broadminded they were, well . . .

'I think we all ought to help them find out about poor old Sylvia,' said Sandra. For all her low-geared intellect she was a girl of ready sensitivity and had been deeply saddened, and a little frightened, by Sylvia's death. She wished in her own innocent way that she could contribute something to the inquiry, and she sensed disappointment, though little surprise, that no one had written to her.

There were seven personal letters and two postcards for Morse to study, and as he cursorily cast his eye over each before placing it in the copying machine, he felt it was all rather foolish. Still, there was the identity parade, of which he had high hopes, although here again in the sobering light of morning the expectancy index had already fallen several points.

'Have you been on an identity parade before?' said Sandra.

'Of course not,' replied Judith. 'People don't get involved in murders every week, do they?'

'Just wondered.'

'What do we *do*?' asked Ruth.

'We do what we're told.' Judith believed passionately in the virtues of authority, and she sometimes wished that Mr Palmer, though he was very nice of course, would be just a little firmer and not quite so friendly with one or two of his employees.

'I saw one once at the pictures,' said Sandra.

'I saw one on the telly,' said Ruth. 'Will it be like that?'

Afterwards they decided it was like that. Disappointing really. A nondescript woman walked along and looked at each of them as they spoke the words, 'Do you know when the next bus is?' You couldn't really be frightened of her. Wouldn't it have been awful, though, if she'd put her hand on your shoulder? But she didn't. She'd walked past all the girls and then walked back and then walked off. That Inspector – he'd been hoping, hadn't he? And that was a bit funny at the end, wasn't it? Running to the door at the far end of the yard. What was that all about?

'They got the crook in the picture,' said Sandra.

'And on the telly,' said Ruth.

'You shouldn't believe all you see,' said Judith.

Morse was sitting in his office at midday, when Lewis came in. 'Well, sir? Any good?'

Morse shook his head.

'No good at all?'

'She thought two or three of them might be her.'

'Well, that narrows it down a bit, sir.'

'Not really. I've heard defending counsels make powdered mincemeat out of witnesses who swore on their grandfathers' graves that they were absolutely *positive* about an identification. No, Lewis. It doesn't help us much, I'm afraid.'

'What about your other idea, sir? You know, the girl had a funny splayed sort of run.'

'Oh, we got them to run all right.'

Lewis sensed he had landed on a sore point. 'No good, sir.' It was a statement, not a question.

'That's right, Lewis. No good. And it might have occurred, it might just have occurred, Lewis, to members of the crime squad, to me, Lewis, and to you, that all girls run in the *same ham-footed bloody way*.' He blasted the last few words at his sergeant, who waited for the hurricane to subside.

'You could do with a pint of beer, sir.'

Morse looked a little happier. 'You may be right.'

'I've got a bit of news, sir.'

'Let's have it.'

'Well, the bus – that's out. I got the driver and conductor of the 6.30 p.m. 4E from Carfax. There were only a dozen or so on the bus anyway, most of them regulars. Our two girls pretty certainly didn't get to Woodstock by bus.'

'We don't know for certain that both of them got to Woodstock anyway,' said Morse.

'But Sylvia got there, didn't she, sir, and the other girl asked for the bus there?'

'I'm beginning to wonder if Mrs Jarman is such a helpful witness, after all.'

'I think she is, because that's only the bad news.'

'You've got some *good* news?' Morse tried to sound a bit more cheerful.

'Well, it's that lorry the old girl told us about. Quite easy really to trace it. You see at Cowley there's this system with car-bodies. When they . . .'

'Yes, I know. You did a sharp job, Lewis. But cut the trimmings.'

'He remembers them. A Mr George Baker – lives in Oxford. And listen to this, sir. He saw the two girls getting into a car. A *red* car – he was sure of that. Chap driving – not a woman. He remembered because he often picks up hitchers, especially if they're girls; and he saw these two just beyond the roundabout – about fifty yards ahead. He would have given them a lift, he said, but this other car pulls up, and he has to pull out to get past. He saw the blonde all right.'

'We're a despicable lot, aren't we?' said Morse. 'Would you have picked them up?'

'I don't usually, sir. Only if they're in uniform. I was glad of a few lifts myself when I was in the Forces.'

Morse reflected carefully on the new evidence. Things were certainly moving.

'What did you say about a pint?'

They sat silently in the White Horse at Kidlington and Morse

decided that the beer was drinkable. Finally he broke the silence.
'A red car, eh?'

'Yes, sir.'

'Interesting piece of research for you. How many men in Oxford
own red cars?'

'Quite a few, sir.'

'You mean a few thousand.'

'I suppose so.'

'But we could find out?'

'I suppose so.'

'Such a problem would not be beyond the wit of our efficient
force?'

'I suppose not, sir.'

'But what if he doesn't live in Oxford?'

'Well, yes. There is that.'

'Lewis, I think the beer is dulling your brain.'

But if alcohol was dimming Lewis's intellectual acumen, it had the
opposite effect on Morse. His mind began to function with an easy
clarity. He ordered Lewis to take the weekend off, to get some
sleep, to forget Sylvia Kaye, and to take his wife shopping; and
Lewis was happy to do so.

Morse, not an addictive smoker, bought twenty king-sized
cigarettes and smoked and drank continuously until 2.00 p.m.
What had really happened last Wednesday evening? He was
tormented by the thought that a sequence of events, not in
themselves extraordinary, had taken place; that each event was
the logical successor of the one before it; that he knew what one
or two of these events had been; that if only his mind could project
itself into a series of naturally causal relationships, he would have
it all. It needed no startling, visionary leap from ignorance to
enlightenment. Just a series of logical progressions. But each
progression landed him at a dead end, like the drawings in
children's annuals where one thread leads to the treasure and all
the others lead to the edge of the page. Start again.

'I'm afraid I shall have to ask you to drink up,' said the landlord.

CHAPTER SEVEN

Saturday, 2 October, p.m.

Morse spent the afternoon of Saturday, 2 October, sitting mildly drunk in his office. He had smoked his packet of cigarettes by 4.30 p.m. and rang for more. His mind grew clearer and clearer. He thought he saw the vaguest pattern in the events of the evening of Wednesday, 29 September. No names – no idea of names, yet – but a pattern.

He looked through the letters he had copied from the Town and Gown: they seemed a sorry little package. Some he dismissed immediately: not even a deranged psychiatrist could have built the flimsiest hypotheses on five of the nine pieces of evidence. One of the postcards read: 'Dear Ruth, Weather good, went swimming twice yesterday. Saw a dead jellyfish on the beach. Love, T.' How very sad to be a jellyfish, thought Morse. Only three of the communications held Morse's attention; then two; then one. It was a typewritten note addressed to Miss Jennifer Coleby and it read:

Dear Madam,
    After asessing the mny applications we have received, we must regretfully inform you that our application has been unsuccessful. At the begining of November however, further posts will become available, and I should, in all honesty, be sorry to loose the opportunity of reconsidering your position then.
    We have now alloted the September quota of posts in the Psycology Department; yet it is probable that a reliably qualified assistant may be required to deal with the routnie duties for the Principal's office.
Yours faithfully,

It was subscribed by someone who did not appear particularly anxious that his name be shouted from the house-tops. An initial 'G' was clear enough, but the surname to which it was floridly appended would have remained an enigma to the great Champollion himself.

So Miss Jennifer Coleby is after a new job, said Morse to himself. So what? Hundreds of people applied for new jobs every day. He sometimes thought of doing so himself. He wondered why he'd thought the letter worth a second thought. Typically badly written – unforgivable misprints. And misspellings. No one in the schools cared much these days about the bread-and-butter

mechanisms of English usage. He'd been brought up in the hard
school: errors of spelling, punctuation, and construction of sentences had been savagely penalized by outraged pedagogues, and
this had made its mark on him. He had become pedantic and
fussy and thought back on the ill-written travesty of a report he
had read from one of his own staff only two days before, when he
had mentally totted up the mistakes like an examiner assessing a
candidate's work. 'Assessing.' Yes, that was wrong in this letter –
among other things. The country was becoming increasingly
illiterate – for all the fancy notions of the progressive educational-
ists. But if his own secretary had produced such rubbish, she
would be out on her neck – today! But she was exceptional. Julie's
initials at the bottom of any letter were the sure imprimatur of a
clean and flawless sheet of typing. Just a minute though . . .
Morse looked again at the letter before him. No reference at all.
Had G. Thingamajig typed it himself? If he had – what was he? A
senior administrator of some university department? If he had . . .
Morse grew more and more puzzled. Why was there no letter
heading? Was he worrying his head over nothing?

Well, there was one way of deciding the issue. He looked at his
watch. Already 5.30 p.m. Miss Coleby would probably be at home
now, he thought. Where did she live? He looked at Lewis's careful
details of the address in North Oxford. An interesting thought?
Morse began to realize how many avenues he had not even started
to explore. He put on his greatcoat and went out to his car. As he
drove the two miles down into Oxford, he resolved that he would
rid himself as far as he could of all prejudice against Miss Jennifer
Coleby. But it was not an easy thing to do; for, if Mrs Jarman's
memory could be trusted, the ambitious Miss Coleby was one of
the three girls who may have made the journey to Woodstock that
night with the late Miss Sylvia Kaye.

Jennifer Coleby rented, with two other working girls, a semi-
detached property in Charlton Road where each paid a weekly
rent of £8.25, inclusive of electricity and gas. It meant a fat rake-
off of almost £25 a week for the provident landlord who had
snapped up two such properties for what now seemed a meagre
£6,500 some six years since. But it was also a blessing for three
enterprising girls who, for such a manageable outlay, were reasonably happy to share the narrow bathroom and the even narrower
lavatory. Each girl had a bedroom (one downstairs), the kitchen
was adequate for their evening meals, and all of them used the

lounge in which to sit around, to chat and watch TV when they were in. These arrangements, apart from the bathroom, worked surprisingly well. Seldom were the girls in together during the day, and so far they had avoided any major confrontation. The landlord had forbidden men-friends in the bedrooms and the girls had accepted his diktat without contention. There had, of course, been a few infractions of the ban, but the household had never degenerated into overt promiscuity. One rule the girls imposed upon themselves – no record players; and for this, at least, their elderly neighbours were profoundly grateful. The house was kept tidy and clean, as Morse immediately saw as the door was opened by a sad girl eating a tomato sandwich.

'I've called to see Miss Coleby, if I may. Is she in?'

Dark, languorous eyes looked at him carefully, and Morse found himself tempted to wink at her.

'Just a minute.' She walked leisurely away, but suddenly turned her head to ask, 'Who shall I say?'

'Er, Morse. Chief Inspector Morse.'

'Oh.'

A cool, clean-looking Jennifer, dressed in blouse and jeans, came out to greet Morse, without apparent enthusiasm.

'Can I help you, Inspector?'

'I wonder if we could have a few words together? Is it convenient?'

'It will have to be, I suppose. You'd better come in.'

Morse was shown into a lounge, where Miss Dark-eyes sat pretending to be deeply engrossed in a report on the Arsenal v. Tottenham match.

'Sue, this is Inspector Morse. Do you mind if we speak here?'

Sue stood up, and a little too theatrically, thought Morse, switched off the set. He observed her slow, graceful movements and smiled to himself, approvingly. 'I'll be upstairs, Jen.' She glanced at Morse before she left, saw the incipient smile at the corners of his mouth and afterwards swore to Jennifer that he had winked at her.

Jennifer motioned Morse to sit on the settee, and sat opposite him in an armchair.

'How can I help, Inspector?'

Morse noticed a copy of Charlotte Brontë's *Villette* balancing like a circumflex accent over the arm of her chair.

'I'm having – purely routine, of course – to check the movements of all the er . . . persons . . .'

'Suspects?'

'No, no. Those who worked with Sylvia. You understand that this sort of thing has to be done.'

'Of course. I'm surprised you haven't done it before.' Morse was a little taken aback. Indeed, why *hadn't* he done it before? Jennifer continued. 'Last Wednesday evening, I got home a bit later than usual – I went round Blackwells to spend a book token. It was my birthday last week. I got home about six, I should think. You know what the traffic's like in the rush hour.' Morse nodded. 'Well, I had a bite to eat – the other girls were here – and went out about, let's see, about half-past six I should think. I got back about eight – perhaps a bit later.'

'Can you tell me where you went?'

'I went to the Summertown library.'

'What time does the library close?'

'Seven thirty.'

'You spent about an hour there.'

'That seems to be a reasonable conclusion, Inspector.'

'It seems a long time. I usually spend about two minutes.'

'Perhaps you're not very fussy what you read.'

That's a point, thought Morse. Jennifer spoke with an easy, clear diction. A good education, he thought. But there was more than that. There was a disciplined independence about the girl, and he wondered how she got on with men. He thought it would be difficult to make much headway with this young lady – unless, of course, *she* wanted to. She could, he suspected, be very nice indeed.

'Are you reading that?'

She laid a delicately manicured hand lightly upon *Villette*. 'Yes. Have you read it?'

'Afraid not,' confessed Morse.

'You should do.'

'I'll try to remember,' muttered Morse. Who was supposed to be conducting this interview? 'Er, you stayed an hour?'

'I've told you that.'

'Did anyone see you there?'

'They'd have a job not to, wouldn't they?'

'Yes, I suppose they would.' Morse felt he was losing his way. 'Did you get anything else out?' He suddenly felt a bit better.

'You'll be interested to know that I got that as well.' She pointed to a large volume, also lying open, on the carpet in front of the TV set. 'Mary's started to read it.' Morse picked it up and looked at the title: *Who was Jack the Ripper?*

'Mm.'

'I'm sure you've read that.'

Morse's morale began to sag again. 'I don't think I've read that particular account, no.'

Jennifer suddenly smiled. 'I'm sorry, Inspector. I'm very much of a bookworm myself, and I have far more spare time than you, I'm sure.'

'Coming back to Wednesday a minute, Miss Coleby. You say you were back about eight.'

'Yes, about then. It could have been quarter-past, even half-past, I suppose.'

'Was anyone in when you got back?'

'Yes. Sue was in. But Mary had gone off to the pictures. *Day of the Jackal* I think it was; she didn't get back until eleven.'

'I see.'

'Shall I ask Sue to come down?'

'No. No need to bother.' Morse realized he was probably wasting his time, but he stuck it out. 'How long does it take to walk to the library?'

'About ten minutes.'

'But it took you almost an hour, perhaps, if you didn't get back until eight-thirty?'

Again the pleasant smile, the regular white teeth, a hint of gentle mockery around the lips. 'Inspector, I think we'd better ask Sue if she remembers the time, don't you?'

'Perhaps we should,' said Morse.

When Jennifer left the room Morse was looking around with sombre, weary eyes, when suddenly a thought flashed through his mind. He was deadly quick as he picked up *Villette*, turned to the inside of the cover and deftly replaced it over the arm of the chair. Sue came in, and quickly confirmed that as far as she could remember Jennifer had been back in the house at some time after eight. She couldn't be more precise. Morse got up to take his leave. He hadn't mentioned the very thing he had come to discuss, and he wasn't going to. That could come later.

He sat for a few minutes in the driving seat of his car and his blood ran hot and cold. He had not quite been able to believe his eyes. But he'd seen it in black and white, or rather dark blue on white.

Morse knew the Oxford library routine only too well, for he rarely returned his own irregular borrowings without having to pay a late fine. The library worked in weeks, not days, for books borrowed, and the day that every 'week' began was Wednesday. If a book was borrowed on a Wednesday, the date for return was exactly 14 days later – that Wednesday fortnight. If a book was borrowed on Thursday, the date for return was a fortnight after the following Wednesday, 20 days later. The date-stamp was changed each Thursday morning. This working from Wednesday to Wednesday simplified matters considerably for the library assistants and was warmly welcomed by those borrowers who found seven or eight hundred pages an excessive assignment inside just fourteen days. Morse would have to check, of course, but he felt certain that only those who borrowed books on Wednesday had to return books within the strict 14-day limit. Anyone taking out a book *on any other day* would have a few extra days' grace. If Jennifer Coleby had taken *Villette* from the library on Wednesday last, the date-stamp for return would have read Wednesday, 13 October. But it didn't. *It read Wednesday, 20 October.* Morse knew beyond any reasonable doubt that Jennifer had lied to him about her movements on the night of the murder. And why? To that vital question there seemed one very simple answer.

Morse sat still in his car outside the house. From the corner of his eye he saw the lounge curtain twitch slightly, but he could see no one. Whoever it was, he decided to let things stew a while longer. He could do with a breath of fresh air, anyway. He locked the car doors and sauntered gently down the road, turned left into the Banbury Road, and walked more briskly now towards the library. He timed himself carefully: nine and a half minutes. Interesting. He walked up to the library door marked PUSH. But it didn't push. The library had closed its doors two hours ago.

CHAPTER EIGHT
Saturday, 2 October

Bernard Crowther's wife, Margaret, disliked the weekends, and effected her household management in such a way that neither her husband nor her twelve-year-old daughter nor her ten-year-old son enjoyed them very much either. Margaret had a part-time job in the School of Oriental Studies, and suspected that throughout the week she put in more hours of solid work than her gentle, bookish husband and her idle, selfish offspring put together. The weekend, *they* all assumed, was a time of well-earned relaxation; but they didn't think of her. 'What's for breakfast, Mum?' 'Isn't

dinner ready yet?' Besides which, she did her week's wash on
Saturday afternoons and tried her best to clean the house on
Sundays. She sometimes thought that she was going mad.

At 5.30 on the afternoon of Saturday, 2 October, she stood at
the sink with bitter thoughts. She had cooked poached eggs for
tea ('What, again?') and was now washing up the sticky yellow
plates. The children were glued to the television and wouldn't be
bored again for an hour or so yet. Bernard (she ought to be
thankful for small mercies) was cutting the privet hedge at the
back of the house. She knew how he hated gardening, but that
was one thing she was *not* going to do. She wished he would get
a move on. The meticulous care he devoted to each square foot of
the wretched hedge exasperated her. He'd be in soon to say his
arms were aching. She looked at him. He was balding now and
getting stout, but he was still, she supposed, an attractive man to
some women. Until recently she had never regretted that she had
married him fifteen years ago. Did she regret the children? She
wasn't sure. From the time they were in arms she had been
worried by her inability to gossip in easy, cosy terms with other
mums about the precious little darlings. She had read a book on
Mothercraft and came to the worrying conclusion that much of
motherhood was distasteful to her – even nauseating. Her matern-
al instincts, she decided, were sadly underdeveloped. As the
children grew into toddlers, she had enjoyed them more, and on
occasion she had only little difficulty in convincing herself that she
loved them both dearly. But now they seemed to be getting older
and worse. Thoughtless, selfish, and cheeky. Perhaps it was all
her fault – or Bernard's. She looked out again as she stacked the
last of the plates upright on the draining rack.

It was already getting dusk after another glorious day. She
wondered, like the bees, if these warm days would never
cease . . . Bernard had managed to advance the neatly clipped
and rounded hedge by half a foot in the last five minutes. She
wondered what he was thinking about, but she knew that she
couldn't ask him.

The truth was, and Margaret had descried it dimly for several
years now, that they were drifting apart. Was that her fault, too?
Did Bernard realize it? She thought he did. She wished she could
leave him, leave everything and go off somewhere and start a new
life. But of course she couldn't. She would have to stick it out.
Unless something tragic happened – or was it *until* something
tragic happened? And then she knew she would stand by him –
in spite of everything.

Margaret wiped the formica tops around the sink, lit a cigarette, and went to sit in the dining-room. She just could not face the petty arguments and the noise in the lounge. She picked up the book Bernard had been reading that afternoon, *The Collected Works of Ernest Dowson*. The name was vaguely familiar to her from her school-certificate days and she turned slowly through the poems until she found the lines her class had been made to learn. She was surprised how well she could recall them:

> I cried for madder music and for stronger wine,
> But when the feast is finish'd and the lamps expire,
> Then falls thy shadow, Cynara! the night is thine;
> And I am desolate and sick of an old passion,
>   Yea, hungry for the lips of my desire:
> I have been faithful to thee, Cynara! in my fashion.

She read them again and for the first time seemed to catch the rhythm of their magical sound. But what did they *mean*? Forbidden fruits, a sort of languorous, illicit, painful delight. Of course, Bernard could tell her all about it. He spent his life exploring and expounding the beautiful world of poetry. But he wouldn't tell her because she couldn't ask.

It must have been an awful strain for Bernard meeting another woman once a week. How long had she known? Well, for certain, no more than a month or so. But in a strangely intuitive way, much longer than that. Six months? A year? Perhaps more. Not with that particular girl, but there may have been others. Her head was aching. But she'd taken so many codeine recently. Oh, let it ache! What a mess! Her mind was going round and round. Privet hedge, poached eggs, Ernest Dowson, Bernard, the tension and deceit of the past four days. My God! What was she going to do? It couldn't go on like this.

Bernard came in. 'My poor arms don't half ache!'

'Finished the hedge?'

'I'll finish it off in the morning. It's those abhorrèd shears. I shouldn't think they've been sharpened since we moved here.'

'You could always take them in.'

'And get 'em back in about six months.'

'You exaggerate.'

'I'll get it finished in the morning.'

'It'll probably be raining.'

'Well, we could do with a drop of rain. Have you seen the lawn? It's like the plains of Abyssinia.'

'You've never been to Abyssinia.'

The conversation dropped. Bernard went to his desk and took out some papers. 'I thought you'd be watching the telly.'

'I can't stick being with the children.'

Bernard looked at her sharply. She was near to tears. 'No,' he said. 'I know what you mean.' He looked soberly and almost tenderly at Margaret. Margaret, his wife! Sometimes he treated her so thoughtlessly, so very thoughtlessly. He walked across and laid a hand on her shoulder.

'They're pretty insufferable, aren't they? But don't worry about it. All kids are the same. I'll tell you what . . .'

'Oh, don't bother! You've made all those promises before. I don't care. I don't care, I tell you. As far as I'm concerned they can go to hell – and you with them!'

She began to sob convulsively and ran from the room. He heard her go into their bedroom above, and listened as the sobs continued. He put his head in his hands. He would have to do something, and he would have to do it very soon. He was in real danger now of losing everything. He might even have lost it already . . . Could he tell Margaret everything? She would never, never forgive him. What about the police? He'd almost told them, or, at least, he'd almost told them part of it. He looked down at Dowson's works and saw where the page was open. He knew that Margaret had been reading it and his eyes fell upon the same poem:

> *Surely the kisses of her bought red mouth were sweet;*
> *But I was desolate and sick of an old passion,*
> *When I awoke and found the dawn was gray:*
> *I have been faithful to thee, Cynara, in my fashion.*

Yes, it had been sweet enough, it would be dishonest to pretend otherwise; but how sour it tasted now. It would have been a huge relief to have ended it all long ago, above all to have broken free from the web of lies and deceit he had spun around himself. Yet how beguiling had been the prospect of those extra-marital delights. Conscience. Damned conscience. Nurtured in a sensitive school. Fatal.

Though not a believer himself, Bernard conceded the empirical truth of the Pauline assertion that the wages of sin is death. He wanted desperately to be rid of the guilt and the remorse, and remembered vaguely from his school days in the Bible-class how lustily they had all given voice to many a chorus on sin:

> *Though your sins be as scarlet, scarlet, scarlet,*
> *They shall be whiter, yea whiter than snow.*

But he couldn't pray these days – his spirit was parched and desolate. His primitive, eager religiosity was dulled now and overlaid with a deep and hard veneer of learning, culture, and cynicism. He was well rehearsed in all the theological paradoxes, and the fizz of academic controversy was no longer a delight. Whiter than snow, indeed! More like the driven slush.

He walked over to the window which looked out on to the quiet road. Lights shone in most of the windows. A few people walked past; a neighbour was taking his dog to foul some other pavement. An L-driver was struggling to turn her car around, and was painfully succeeding, though the line of symmetry through MAC's Self-drive Zodiac rarely progressed more than seven or eight degrees at any one manoeuvre. More like a thirty-three point turn, he thought. The instructor must be a patient chap. He had tried to teach Margaret to drive once . . . Still, he had made up for that. She had her own Mini now. He watched for several minutes. A man walked by, but though he thought he seemed familiar, Bernard didn't recognize him. He wondered who he was and where he was going, and kept him in sight until he turned right into Charlton Road.

As Morse had walked past, he too was wondering what to do. Best have it out with Jennifer now? He didn't know, but he thought on the whole it was. Conscious that he had not covered himself with glory at the earlier interview, he decided mentally to rehearse his new approach.

'You want to ask me some more questions?'
'Yes.' Tight-lipped and masterly.
'Won't you come in?'
'Yes.'
'Well?'
'Thus far you've told me nothing but a pack of lies. I suggest we start again.'
'I don't know what you're talking about . . .' Slowly and pointedly he would get up from the chair and walk towards the door. He would utter not one further word. But as he opened the door, Jennifer would say, 'All right, Inspector.' And he would listen. He thought he had a good idea of what she would tell him.

That he would have been wrong, he was not to learn for some time yet; for he discovered that Jennifer had gone out. The languid Sue, her long legs bronzed and bare, had no idea where she had gone. 'Won't you come in and wait, Inspector?' The full lips parted and quivered slightly. Morse both looked and felt alarmingly vulnerable. He consulted his wrist-watch for moral support. 'You're very kind but . . . perhaps I'd better not.'

CHAPTER NINE
Sunday, 3 October

Morse slept soundly for almost twelve hours, and awoke at 8.30 a.m. He had returned home immediately after his second call to Charlton Road with a splitting headache and a harassed mind. Now, as he blinked awake, he could scarcely believe how fresh he felt.

The last book Morse himself had taken from the library and which now lay, three weeks overdue, on his writing desk, was Edward de Bono's *A Five-Day Course in Lateral Thinking*. He had followed the course conscientiously, refused to look at any of the answers in advance, and reluctantly concluded that even the most sympathetic assessment of his lateral potential was gamma minus minus. But he had enjoyed it. Moreover he had learned that a logical, progressive, 'vertical' assault upon a sticky problem might not always be the best. He had not really understood some of the jargon too well, but he had grasped the substantial points. 'How can one drive a car up a dark alley if the headlights are not working?' It didn't matter what the answer was. The thing to do was to suggest *anything* a driver might conceivably do: blow the horn, take the roof rack off, lift the bonnet up. It didn't matter. The mere contemplation of futile solutions was itself a potent force in reaching the right conclusion; for sooner or later one would turn on a blinker and, hey presto!, the light would dawn. In an amateurish way Morse had tried out this technique and had surprised himself. If a name was on the tip of his tongue, he stopped thinking directly about it, and merely repeated anything he knew – the state capitals of the USA – anything; and it seemed to work.

As he lay awake he decided temporarily to shelve the murder of Sylvia Kaye. He was making progress – he knew that. But his mind lacked incision; it was going a bit stale. With a rest today (and he'd deserved one) he'd be back on mental tip-toe in the morning.

He got up, dressed and shaved, cooked himself a succulent

looking mixture of bacon, tomatoes, and mushrooms, and felt good. He ran a leisurely eye through the Sunday papers, checked his pools, wondered if he was the only man in England who had picked in his 'any eight from sixteen' permutation not a single score-draw, and lit a cigarette. He would sit and idle the time away until noon, have a couple of pints and get lunch out somewhere. It seemed a civilized prospect. But he was never happy without something to do, and before long was mentally debating whether to put some Wagner on the record player or do a crossword. Crosswords were a passion with Morse, although since the death of the great Ximenes he had found few composers to please his taste. On the whole he enjoyed the *Listener* puzzles as much as any, and for this purpose took the periodical each week. On the other hand he delighted in Wagnerian opera and had the complete cycle of *The Ring*. He decided to do both, and to the opening bars of the richly scored Prelude to *Das Rheingold*, he sat back and turned to the penultimate page of the *Listener*. This was the life. The Rhine-maidens swam gracefully to and fro and it was a few minutes before Morse felt willing to let the music drift away to the periphery of his attention. He read the preamble to the crossword:

'Each of the across clues contains, in the definition, a deliberate misprint. Each of the down clues is normal, although the words to be entered in the diagram will contain a misprint of a single letter. Working from 1 across to 28 down the misprinted letters form a well-known quotation which solvers . . .'

Morse read no more. He leapt to his feet. A solo horn expired with a dying groan as he switched off the record player and snatched his car keys from the mantelpiece.

His in-tray was high with reports, but he ignored them. He unlocked his cabinet, took out the file on the Sylvia Kaye murder, and extracted the letter addressed to Jennifer Coleby. He knew there had been something wrong with the whole thing. His mouth was dry and his hand trembled slightly, like a schoolboy opening his O-level results:

Dear Madam,

  After asessing the mny applications we have received, we must regretfully inform you that our application has been unsuccessful. At the begining of November however, further posts will become available, and I should, in all honesty, be sorry to loose the opportunity of reconsidering your position then.

We have now alloted the September quota of posts in the Psycology Department; yet it is probable that a reliably qualified assistant may be required to deal with the routnie duties for the Principal's office.

Yours faithfully,

How wrong-headed he had been! Instead of thinking, as he had done, with such supercilious arrogance, of the illiteracy and incompetence of some poor blockhead of a typist, *he should have been thinking exactly the opposite*. He'd been a fool. The clues were there. The whole thing was phoney – why hadn't he spotted that before? When you boiled it down it was a nonsense letter. He had first made the mistake of concentrating upon individual mistakes and not even bothering to see the letter as a synoptic whole. But not only that. He had compounded his mistake. For if he had read the letter as a letter, he might have considered the mistakes as mistakes – *deliberate mistakes*. He took a sheet of paper and started: 'asessing' – 's' omitted; 'mny' – 'a' omitted; 'begining' – 'n' omitted; 'loose' – 'o' inserted; 'Psycology' – 'h' omitted. SANOH – whatever that signified. Look again. 'our' – shouldn't it be 'your'? 'y' omitted; 'routnie' – 'n' and 'i' transposed. What did that give him? SAYNOHIN. Hardly promising. Try once more, 'alloted' – surely two 't's? 't' omitted. And there it was staring him in the face. The 'G' of course from the signature, the only recognizable letter therein: SAY NOTHING. Someone had been desperately anxious for Jennifer not to say a word – and Jennifer, it seemed, had got the message.

It had taken Morse two minutes, and he was glad that Jennifer had been out the previous evening. He felt sure that faced with her lies about the visit to the library, she would have said how sorry she was and that she must have got it wrong. It must have been Thursday, she supposed; it was so difficult to think back to events of even the day before, wasn't it? She honestly couldn't remember; but she would try very hard to. Perhaps she had gone for a walk – on her own, of course.

But she would find things more awkward now. Strangely Morse felt little sense of elation. He had experienced an odd liking for Jennifer when they had met, and in retrospect he understood how difficult it must have been for her. But he must look the fact squarely in the face. She was lying. She was shielding someone – that someone who in all probability had raped and murdered Sylvia. It was not a pretty thought. Every piece of evidence now pointed unequivocally to the fact that it was Jennifer Coleby who had stood at Fare Stage 5 with Sylvia on the night of the 29th; that it was she who had been given a lift by a person or persons unknown (pretty certainly the former) as far as Woodstock; that there she had witnessed something about which she had been warned to keep her silence. In short that Jennifer Coleby *knew the identity of the man who had murdered Sylvia Kaye*. Morse suddenly wondered if she was in danger, and it was this fear which prompted his immediate decision to have Jennifer held on suspicion of being an accessory to the crime of murder. He would need Lewis in.

He reached for his outside phone and rang his sergeant's home number.

'Lewis?'

'Speaking.'

'Morse here. I'm sorry to ruin your weekend, but I want you here.'

'Straightaway, sir?'

'If you can.'

'I'm on my way.'

Morse looked through his in-tray. Reports, reports, reports. He crossed through his own initials immediately, barely glancing at such uncongenial titles as *The Drug Problem in Britain*, *The Police and the Public*, and *The Statistics for Crimes of Violence in Oxfordshire* (second quarter). At the minute he was interested only in one statistic which would doubtless, in time, appear in the statistics of violent crime in Oxfordshire (third quarter). He'd no time for reports. He suspected that about 95% of the written word was never read by anyone anyway. But there were two items which held his attention. A report from the forensic lab on the murder weapon, and a supplementary report from the pathology department on Sylvia Kaye. Neither did more than confirm what he already knew or at any rate suspected. The tyre-lever proved to be a singularly unromantic specimen. Morse read all about its shape, size, weight . . . But why bother? There was no mystery about the lever at all. The landlord of the Black Prince had spent the afternoons of Tuesday, 28th and Wednesday, 29th tinkering with an ancient Sunbeam, and had unwittingly left his tool kit outside the garage on the right at the back of the courtyard where he kept the car. There were no recognizable prints – just the ugly evidence, at one of the lever's curving ends, that it had crashed with considerable force into the bone of a human skull. There followed a gory analysis, which Morse was glad to skip.

It was only a few minutes before Lewis knocked and entered.

'Ah, Lewis. The gods, methinks, have smiled weakly on our enquiries.' He outlined the developments in the case. 'I want Miss Jennifer Coleby brought in for questioning. Be careful. Take Policewoman Fuller with you if you like. Just held for questioning, you understand? There's no question at all of any formal arrest. If she prefers to ring up her legal advisers, tell her it's Sunday and they're all playing golf. But I don't think you'll have much trouble.' On the latter point, at least, Morse guessed correctly.

Jennifer was sitting in interrogation room 3 by 3.45 p.m. On Morse's instructions, Lewis spent an hour with her, making no mention whatever of the information he had been given earlier in the afternoon. Lewis mentioned quietly that, in spite of all their enquiries, they had not been able to trace the young lady, seen by two independent witnesses, who had been with Sylvia Kaye an hour or so before she was murdered.

'You must be patient, Sergeant.'

Lewis smiled weakly, like the gods. 'Oh, we're patient enough, miss, and I think with a little co-operation we shall get there.'

'Aren't you getting any co-operation?'

'Would you like a cup of tea, miss?'

'I'd prefer coffee.'

Policewoman Fuller hurried off; Jennifer moistened her lips and swallowed; Lewis brooded quietly. In the tug-of-war silence which ensued it was Lewis who finally won.

'You think I'm not co-operating, Sergeant?'

'Are you?'

'Look, I've told the Inspector what I know. Didn't he believe me?'

'Just what did you tell the Inspector, miss?'

'You want me to go over all that again?' Jennifer's face showed all the impatience of a schoolgirl asked to rewrite a tedious exercise.

'We shall have to have a signed statement in any case.'

Jennifer sighed. 'All right. You want me to account for my movements – I think that's the phrase, isn't it – on Wednesday night.'

'That's right, Miss.'

'On Wednesday night . . .' Laboriously Lewis began to write.

'Shall I write it out for you?' asked Jennifer.

'I think I ought to get it down myself, miss, if you don't mind. I haven't got a degree in English, but I'll do my best.' A quick flash of caution gleamed in Jennifer's eyes. It was gone immediately, but it had been there and Lewis had seen it.

Half an hour later, Jennifer's statement was ready. She read it, asked if she could make one or two amendments – 'only spelling, Sergeant' – and agreed that she could sign it.

'I'll just get it typed out, miss.'

'How long will that take?'

'Oh, only ten minutes.'

'Would you like me to do it? It'll only take me about two.'

'I think we ought to do it ourselves, miss, if you don't mind. We have our regulations, you know.'

'Just thought I might be able to help.' Jennifer felt more relaxed.

'Shall I get you another cup of coffee, miss?'

'That would be nice.' Lewis got up and left.

Policewoman Fuller seemed singularly uncommunicative, and for more than ten minutes Jennifer sat in silence. When the door finally opened it was Morse who entered carrying a neatly typed sheet of foolscap.

'Good afternoon, Miss Coleby.'

'Good afternoon.'

'We've met before.' The tide of relaxation which had reached high-water mark with Lewis's departure quickly ebbed and exposed the grating shingle of her nerves. 'I walked down to the library after I left you yesterday,' continued Morse.

'You must enjoy walking.'

'They tell me walking is the secret of perpetual middle age.'

With an effort, Jennifer smiled. 'It's a pleasant walk, isn't it?'

'It depends which way you go,' said Morse.

Jennifer looked sharply at him and Morse, as Lewis earlier, noted the unexpected reaction. 'Well, I would like to stay and talk to you, but I hope you will let me sign that statement and get back home. There are several things I have to do before tomorrow.'

'I hope Sergeant Lewis mentioned that we have no authority to keep you against your will?'

'Oh yes. The Sergeant told me.'

'But I shall be very grateful if you can agree to stay a little longer.'

The back of Jennifer's throat was dry. 'What for?' Her voice was suddenly a little harsher.

'Because,' said Morse quietly, 'I hope you will not be foolish enough to sign a statement which you know to be false' – Morse raised his voice – 'and which I know to be false.' He gave her no chance to reply. 'This afternoon I gave instructions for you to be held for questioning since I suspected, and still suspect, that you

are withholding information which may be of very great value in
discovering the identity of Miss Kaye's murderer. That is a most
serious offence, as you know. It now seems that you are foolish
enough to compound such stupidity with the equally criminal and
serious offence of supplying the police with information which is
not only inaccurate but demonstrably false.' Morse's voice had
risen in crescendo and he ended with a mighty thump with his fist
upon the table between them.

Jennifer, however, did not appear quite so abashed as he had
expected.

'You don't believe what I told you?'

'No.'

'Am I allowed to ask why not?'

Morse was more than a little surprised. It was clear to him that
the girl had recovered whatever nerve she may have lost. He clearly
and patiently told her that she could not possibly have taken out
her library books on Wednesday evening, and that this could be
proved without any reasonable doubt. 'I see.' Morse waited for
her to speak again. If he had been mildly surprised at her previous
question, he was flabbergasted by her next. 'What were *you* doing
at the time of the murder last Wednesday evening, Inspector?'

What was he doing? He wasn't quite sure, but any such
admission would hardly advance his present cause. He lied. 'I was
listening to some Wagner.'

'Which Wagner?'

'*Das Rheingold.*'

'Is there anyone who could back up your story? Did anyone see
you?'

Morse surrendered. 'No.' In spite of himself, he had to admire
the girl. 'No,' he repeated, 'I live on my own. I seldom have the
pleasure of visitors – of either sex.'

'How very sad.'

Morse nodded. 'Yes. But you see, Miss Coleby, I am not as yet
suspected of dressing up in women's clothes and standing at the
top of Woodstock Road hitching a lift with Sylvia Kaye.'

'And *I* am?'

'And you are.'

'But presumably I'm not suspected of raping and murdering
Sylvia?'

'I hope you will allow me a modicum of intelligence.'

'You don't understand.'

'What's that supposed to mean?'

'Hasn't it occurred to you that Sylvia probably enjoyed being raped?' There was bitterness in her tone, and her cheeks were flushed.

'That seems to assume that she was raped *before* she died, doesn't it?' said Morse quietly.

'I'm sorry – that was a horrid thing to say.'

Morse followed up his advantage. 'My job is to discover what happened from the moment Sylvia and her friend – *and I believe that was you* – got into a red car on the other side of the Woodstock roundabout. For some reason this other girl has not come forward, and I don't think the reason's very hard to find. *She knew the driver of the car,* and she's protecting him. She's probably frightened stiff. But so was Sylvia Kaye frightened stiff, Miss Coleby. More than that. She was so savagely struck on the back of the head that her skull was broken in several places and lumps of bone were found in her brain. Do you like the sound of that? It's an ugly, horrible sight is murder and the trouble with murder is that it usually tends to wipe out the only good witness of the crime – the victim. That means we've got to rely on other witnesses, normal ordinary people most of them, who accidentally get caught up at some point in the wretched business. They get scared: OK. They'd rather not get mixed up in it: OK. They think it's none of their business: OK – but we've got to rely on some of them having enough guts and decency to come forward and tell us what they know. And that's why you're here, Miss Coleby. I've got to know the truth.'

He took the statement that Jennifer had made and tore it into pieces. But he could not read her mind. As he had been speaking she had been gazing through the window of the little office into the outside yard, where the day before she had stood with her office colleagues.

'Well?'

'I'm sorry, Inspector. I must have caused you a lot of trouble. It was on Thursday that I went to the library.'

'And on Wednesday?'

'I did go out. And I did go on the road to Woodstock – but I didn't get as far as Woodstock. I stopped at the Golden Rose at Begbroke – that's what, about two miles this side of Woodstock. I went into the lounge and bought a drink – a lager and lime. I drank it out in the garden and then went home.'

Morse looked at her impatiently. 'In the dark, I suppose.'

'Yes. About half-past seven.'

'Well – go on.'

'What do you mean – "go on"? That was all.'

'Do you want me to . . .' began Morse, his voice fuming. 'Fetch Lewis!' he barked. Policewoman Fuller read the gale warning and hurried out.

Jennifer appeared untroubled, and Morse's anger subsided.

It was Jennifer who broke the silence. 'You mustn't be too angry with me, Inspector.' Her voice had become little more than a whisper. Her hand went to her forehead and for a while she closed her eyes. Morse looked at her closely for the first time. He had not noticed before how attractive she could be. She wore a light-blue summer coat over a black jumper, with gloves in matching black. Her cheek bones were high and there was animation in her face, her mouth, slightly open, revealing the clean lines of her white teeth. Morse wondered if he could ever fall for her, and decided, as usual, that he could.

'I've been so flustered, and so frightened.'

He had to lean forward slightly to catch her words. He noticed that Lewis had come in and motioned him silently to a chair.

'Everything will be all right, you see.' Morse looked at Lewis and nodded as the sergeant prepared to take down the second draft of the evidence of Miss Jennifer Coleby.

'Why were you frightened?' asked Morse gently.

'Well, it's all been so strange – I don't seem to be able to wake up properly since . . . I don't seem to know what's real and what's not. So many funny things seem to be happening.' She was still sitting with her head in her hand, looking blankly at the top of the table. Morse glanced at Lewis. Things were almost ready.

'What do you mean – "funny things"?'

'Just everything really. I'm beginning to wonder if I know what I *am* doing. What am I doing *here*? I thought I'd told you the truth about Wednesday – and now I realize I didn't. And there was another funny thing.' Morse watched her keenly. 'I had a letter on Saturday morning telling me I'd not been chosen for a job – *and I don't even remember applying for it*. Do you think I'm going mad?'

So that was going to be her story! Morse experienced the agony of a bridge player whose ace has just been covered by the deuce of trumps. The two policemen looked at each other, and both were conscious that Jennifer's eyes were on them.

'Well, now.' Morse hid his disappointment and disbelief as well as he was able. 'Let's just get back to Wednesday night, shall we? Can you repeat what you just told me? I want Sergeant Lewis to get it down.' His voice sounded exasperated.

Jennifer repeated her brief statement and Lewis, like the Inspector before him, looked temporarily bewildered.

'You mean,' said Morse, 'that Miss Kaye went on to Woodstock, but that you only went as far as Begbroke?'

'Yes, that's exactly what I mean.'

'You asked this man to drop you at Begbroke?'

'What man are you talking about?'

'The man who gave you a lift.'

'But I didn't get a lift to Begbroke.'

'You *what?*' shrieked Morse.

'I said I didn't get a lift. I would never hitchhike anyway. I think you ought to know something, Inspector. *I've got a car.*'

While Lewis was getting the second statement typed, Morse retreated to his office. Had he been wrong all along? If what Jennifer now claimed was true, it would certainly account for several things. On the same road, on the same night and one of her own office friends murdered? Of course she would feel frightened. But was that enough to account for her repeated evasions? He reached for the phone and rang the Golden Rose at Begbroke. The jovial-sounding landlord was anxious to help. His wife had been on duty in the lounge on Wednesday. Could she possibly come down to Kidlington Police HQ? Yes. The landlord would drive her himself. Good. Quarter of an hour, then.

'Do you remember a young lady coming in to the lounge last Wednesday night? On her own? About half-past seven time?'

The richly ringed and amply bosomed lady wasn't sure.

'But you don't often get women coming in alone, do you?'

'Not often, no. But it's not all *that* unusual these days, Inspector. You'd be surprised.'

Morse felt that little would surprise him any more. 'Would you recognize someone like that? Someone who just dropped in one night?'

'I think so, yes.'

Morse rang Lewis, who was still waiting with Jennifer in the interview room.

'Take her home, Lewis.'

The landlady of the Golden Rose stood beside Morse at the enquiry desk as Jennifer walked past with Lewis.

'That her?' he asked. It was his penultimate question.

'Yes. I think it is.'

'I'm most grateful to you,' lied Morse.

'I'm glad I could help, Inspector.'

Morse showed her to the door. 'I don't suppose you happen to remember what she ordered, do you?'

'Well, as a matter of fact, I think I do, Inspector. It was lager and lime, I think. Yes, lager and lime.'

It was half an hour before Lewis returned. 'Did you believe her, sir?'

'No,' said Morse. He felt more frustrated than depressed. He realized that he had already landed himself in a good deal of muddle and mess by his own inadequacies. He had refused the offer of the auxiliary personnel available to him, and this meant that few of the many possible leads had yet been checked and documented. Sanders, for example – surely to any trained officer the most obvious target for immediate and thorough investigation – he had thus far almost totally ignored. Indeed, even a superficial scrutiny of his conduct of the case thus far would reveal a haphazardness in his approach almost bordering upon negligence. Only the previous month he had himself given a lecture to fellow detectives on the paramount importance in any criminal investigation of the strictest and most disciplined thoroughness in every respect of the inquiry *from the very beginning*.

And yet, for all this, he sensed in some intuitive way (a procedure not mentioned in his lecture) that he was vaguely on the right track still; that he had been right in allowing Jennifer to go; that although his latest shot had been kicked off the line, sooner or later the goal would come.

For the next hour the two officers exchanged notes on the afternoon's interrogation, with Morse impatiently probing Lewis's reactions to the girl's evasions, glances, and gestures.

'Do you think she's lying, Lewis?'

'I'm not so sure now.'

'Come off it, man. When you're as old as I am you'll recognize a liar a mile off!'

Lewis remained doubtful: he was by several years the older man anyway. Silence fell between them.

'Where do we go from here, then?' said Lewis at last.

'I think we attack down the other flank.'

'We do?'

'Yes. She's shielding a man. Why? Why? That's what we've been asking ourselves so far. And you know where we've got with that line of enquiry? Nowhere. She's lying, I know that; but we haven't broken her – not yet. She's such a good liar she'd get any damned fool to believe her.'

Lewis saw the implication. 'You could be wrong, sir.'

Morse blustered on, wondering if he was. 'No, no, no. We've just been tackling the case from the wrong angle. They tell me, Lewis, that you can climb up the Eiger in your carpet slippers if you go the easy way.'

'You mean we've been trying to solve this the hard way?'

'No. I mean just the opposite. We've been trying to solve it the easy. Now we've got to try the hard way.'

'How do we do that, sir?'

'We've been trying to find out who the other girl was, because we thought she could lead us to the man we want.'

'But according to you we *have* found her.'

'Yes. But she's too clever for us – and too loyal. She's been warned to keep her mouth shut – not that she needed much telling, if I'm any judge. But we're up against a brick wall for the time being, and there's only one alternative. The girl won't lead us to the man? All right. We find the man.'

'How do we start on that?'

'I think we shall need a bit of Aristotelian logic, don't you?'

'If you say so, sir.'

'I'll tell you all about it in the morning,' said Morse.

Lewis paused as he reached the door. 'That identification of Miss Coleby, sir. Did you think it was satisfactory – just to take the landlady's word for it?'

'Why not?'

'Well, it was all a bit casual, wasn't it? I mean, it wasn't exactly going by the book.'

'What book?' said Morse.

Lewis decided that his mind had got itself into a quite sufficient muddle for one day, and he left.

Morse's mind, too, was hardly functioning with crystalline lucidity; yet already emerging from the mazed confusion was the germ of a new idea. He had suspected from the start that Jennifer Coleby was lying; would have staked his professional reputation upon it. But he could have been wrong, at least in one respect. He had tried to break Jennifer's story, but had he been trying to break it *at the wrong point*?

What if all she had told him was perfectly true? . . . The same revolving pros and cons passed up and down before his eyes like undulating hobby-horses at a fairground, until his own mind, too, was in a dizzying whirl and he knew that it was time to give it all a rest.

CHAPTER TEN
Wednesday, 6 October

The cocktail lounge of the Black Prince was seldom busy for the hour after opening time at 11.00 a.m., and the morning of Wednesday, 6 October, was to prove no exception. The shockwave of the murder was now receding and the Black Prince was quickly returning to normality.

It was amazing how quickly things sank into the background, thought Mrs Gaye McFee as she polished another martini glass and stacked it neatly among its fellows. But not really; only that morning an incoming air-liner had crashed at Heathrow with the loss of seventy-nine lives. And every day on the roads . . .

'What'll it be, boys?' The speaker was a distinguished-looking man, about sixty years old, thick set, with silvery-grey hair and a ruddy complexion. Gaye had served him many times before and knew him to be Professor Tompsett (Felix to his friends, who were rumoured not to be legion) – Emeritus Professor of Elizabethan Literature at Oxford University, and the recently retired Vice-Principal of Lonsdale College. His two companions, one a gaunt, bearded man in his late twenties, the other a gentle-looking bespectacled man of about forty-five, each ordered gin and tonic.

'Three gin and tonics.' Tompsett had an incisive, imperative voice, and Gaye wondered if he got his college scout to stir his morning coffee.

'Hope you're going to enjoy life with us, young Melhuish!' Tompsett laid a broad hand on his bearded companion's shoulder, and was soon engrossed in matters which Gaye was no longer able to follow. A group of American servicemen had come in and were losing no time in quizzing her about the brands of lager, the menu, the recent murder, and her home address. But she enjoyed Americans, and was soon laughing good-naturedly with them. As usual, the lager-pump was producing more froth than liquid substance and Gaye noticed, waiting patiently at the

other end of the bar, the bespectacled member of the Oxford
triumvirate.

'Shan't be a second, sir.'

'Don't worry. I'm in no great rush.' He smiled quietly at her,
and she saw the glimmer of a twinkle in his dark eyes, and she
hurriedly squared the acount with the neighbourly Americans.

'Now, sir.'

'We'd all like the same again, please. Three gins and tonics.'
Gaye looked at him with interest. The landlord had once told her
that if anyone ordered 'gins and tonics' instead of the almost
universal 'gin and tonics' – he really *was* a don. She wished he
would speak again, for she liked the sound of his voice with its
sarft Glarcestershire accent. But he didn't. Nevertheless, she stayed
at his end of the bar and lightly repolished the martini glasses.

'Whatawe done to you, honeybunch?' and similar endearing
invitations emanated regularly from her other clients, but Gaye
quietly and tactfully declined their ploys; she watched instead the
man from Gloucestershire. Tompsett was in full flow.

'He didn't even go to my inaugural when he was up. What do
you think of that, Peter, old boy?'

'Don't blame him really,' said Peter. 'We all sit and salivate over
our own prose, Melhuish, and we kid ourselves it's bloody
marvellous.'

The Professor of Elizabethan Literature laughed good-
humouredly and half-drained his glass. 'Been here before,
Melhuish?'

'No, I haven't. Rather nice, isn't it?'

'Bit notorious now, you know. Murder here last week.'

'Yes, I read about it.'

'Young blonde. Raped and murdered, right in the yard out there.
Pretty young thing – if the newspapers are anything to go by.'

Melhuish, newly appointed junior fellow at Lonsdale, very
bright and very anxious, was beginning to feel a little more at
home with his senior colleagues.

'Raped too, was she?'

Tompsett drained his glass. 'So they say. But I've always been
a bit dubious myself about this rape business.'

'Confucius, he say girl with skirt up, she run faster than man
with trousers down, eh?'

The two older men smiled politely at the tired old joke, but
Melhuish wished he hadn't repeated it: off-key, over-familiar.
Gaye heard the clear voice of Tompsett rescuing the conversation.
He was no fool, she thought.

'Yes, I agree with you, Melhuish. We mustn't get too serious about rape. God, no. Happens every day. I remember a couple of years back there was a young gal here – you'd remember her, Peter – quick, clear mind, good worker, marvellous kid. She was taking Finals and had eight three-hour papers. She'd done her seventh paper on the Thursday morning – no it was the Friday, or was it . . . but that's beside the point. She took her last but one paper in the morning with just one more fence to jump in the afternoon. Well, she went off to her digs out at Headington for lunch and – beggar me! – she got raped on her way back. Just think of the shock for the poor lass. You remember, Peter? Anyway, she insisted on taking the last paper and do you know, Melhuish – she did better on the last paper than she'd done on all the others!'

Melhuish laughed heartily and took the empty glasses.

'You make it up as you go along,' muttered Peter.

'Well, it was a good story, wasn't it?' said Tompsett.

Gaye lost the thread of their talk for a few minutes, and when she picked it up again, it was clear that the conversation had taken a slightly more serious turn. They always said that gin was a depressant.

'. . . not necessarily raped *before* being murdered, you know.'

'Oh, shut up, Felix.'

'Bit revolting, I know. But we all read the Christie business, didn't we? Wicked old bugger, he was!'

'Do they think that's what happened here?' asked Melhuish.

'Do you know, I might have been able to tell you that,' said Tompsett. 'Old Morse – good chap! – he's in charge of the case, and we've had him at the college guest-evenings. He was invited tonight, but he had to cry off. Had a minor accident.' Tompsett laughed. 'Fell off a ladder! Christ, who'd ever believe it? Here's a chap in charge of a murder inquiry and he falls off a bloody ladder!' Tompsett was highly amused.

The Americans had abandoned all hope and the bar had emptied now. The three men walked across to the table by the window.

'Well, we'd better see what they can offer us for lunch,' said Peter. 'I'll get the menu.'

Gaye held out a large expensive-looking folder and presented it, already opened, like a neophyte offering the collect for the day to an awesome priest.

Peter looked through quickly, a gentle cynicism showing on his face. He looked up at Gaye and found her watching him. 'Do you recommend "Don's Delight" or "Proctor's Pleasure"?' He asked it in an undertone.

'I shouldn't have the steak if I were you,' her voice as quiet as his.

'Are you free this afternoon?'

She weighed up the situation for several seconds before nodding her head, almost imperceptibly.

'What time shall I pick you up?'

'Three o'clock?'

'Where?'

'I'll be just outside.'

At four o'clock the two lay side by side in the ample double-bed in Peter's rooms in Lonsdale College. His left arm was around her neck, his right hand gently caressing her breasts.

'Do you believe a young girl can get raped?' he asked.

Gaye considered the problem. Contented in mind and in body, she lay for a while contemplating the ornate ceiling. 'It must be jolly difficult for the man.'

'Mm.'

'Have you ever raped a woman?'

'I could rape you, any day of the week.'

'But I wouldn't let you. I wouldn't put up any resistance.'

He kissed her full lips again, she turned eagerly towards him.

'Peter!' she whispered in his ear, 'rape me again!'

The phone blared suddenly, shrill and urgent in the quiet room. Blast!

'Oh, hullo Bernard. What? No. Sitting idling, you know. What? Oh, tonight. Yes. Well, about seven, I think. Why not call in for me? We can have a quick drink together. Yes. Felix? Oh, he's well tanked-up already. Yes. Yes. Well, look forward to it. Yes. Bye.'

'Who's Bernard?'

'Oh, he's an English don here. Good chap. Pretty bad sense of timing, though.'

'Does he have a set of rooms like this?'

'No, no. He's a family man is Bernard. Lives up in North Oxford. Quiet chap.'

'*He* doesn't rape young girls then?'

'What, Bernard? Good lord no. Well, I don't think so . . .'

'You're a quiet man, Peter.'

'Me?' She fondled him lovingly, and abruptly terminated all further discussion of Mr Bernard Crowther, quiet family man of North Oxford.

PART TWO
Search for a man

Beginning its life under a low (Head Room 12 ft) railway bridge, and proceeding its cramped and narrow way for several hundred yards past shabby rows of terraced houses that line the thoroughfare in tight and mean confinement, the Botley Road gradually broadens into a spacious stretch of dual carriageway that carries all west-bound traffic towards Faringdon, Swindon, and the sundry hamlets in between. Here the houses no longer shoulder their neighbours in such grudging proximity, and hither several of the Oxford businessmen have brought their premises.

Chalkley and Sons is a sprawling, two-storeyed building, specializing in household fittings, tiling, wallpaper, paint, and furniture. It is a well-established store, patronized by many of the carpenters (discount), the interior decorators (discount), and almost all the do-it-yourselfers from Oxford. At the furthest end of the ground-floor show rooms there is a notice informing the few customers who have not yet discovered the fact that the Formica Shop is outside, over the yard, second on the left.

In this shop a young man is laying a large sheet of formica upon a wooden table, a table which has a deep, square groove cut longitudinally through its centre. He pulls towards him, along its smoothly running gliders, a small automatic saw, and carefully lines up its wickedly polished teeth against his pencilled mark. Deftly he flicks out a steel ruler and checks his measurement. He appears content with a rapid mental calculation, snaps a switch and, amid a grating whirr, slices through the tough fabric with a clean and deadly swiftness. He enjoys that swiftness! Several times he repeats the process: lengthways, sideways, narrowly, broadly, and stacks the measured strips neatly against the wall. He looks at his watch; it is almost 12.45 p.m. An hour and a quarter. He locks the sliding doors behind him, repairs to the staff wash-room, soaps his hands, combs his hair, and, with little regret, temporarily turns his back upon the premises of Mr Chalkley and his sons. He pats a little package which bulges slightly in the right-hand pocket of his overcoat. Still there.

Although his immediate destination is no more than ten minutes' walk away, he decides to take a bus. He crosses the road and traverses in the process as many lines, continuous, broken, broad, narrow, yellow, white, as one may find in the key to an Ordnance Survey map; for the Oxford City Council has escalated its long war of attrition against the private motorist and has instituted a system of bus lanes along the Botley Road. A bus arrives almost immediately, and the dour Pakistani one-man crew silently discharges his manifold duties. The young man always hopes that the bus is fairly full so that he may sit beside one of the mini-skirted, knee-booted young girls returning to the city; but today it is almost empty. He sits down and looks mechanically around him.

He alights at the stop before the railway bridge (where the bus must make a right-hand detour to avoid a scalping from the iron girders), threads his way to a dingy street behind the shabby rows of houses, and enters a small shop. The legend above the door of Mr Baines' grimy, peeling shop-front reads 'Newsagent and Tobacconist'. But such is the nature of Mr Baines' establishment that he employs no cohorts of cheeky boys and girls to deliver his morning and evening newspapers, nor does his stock of tobacco run to more than half a dozen of the more popular brands of cigarettes. He sells neither birthday cards nor ice-cream nor confectionery. Mr Baines – yes, he is a shrewd man – calculates that he can make as much profit from one swift, uncomplicated transaction as from the proceeds of one day's paper rounds, or from the sale of a thousand cigarettes. For Mr Baines is a dealer in hard pornography.

Several customers are standing along the right-hand side of the narrow shop. They flick their way through a bewildering variety of gaudy, glossy girlie magazines, with names that ring with silken ecstasies: *Skin* and *Skirt* and *Lush* and *Lust* and *Flesh* and *Frills*. Although the figures of the scantily clad models which adorn the covers of these works are fully and lewdly provocative, the browsers appear to riffle the pages with a careless, casual boredom. But this is the appearance only. A notice, in Mr Baines's own hand, warns every potential purveyor of these exotic fruits that 'the books are to be bought'; and Mrs Baines sits on her hard stool behind the counter and keeps her hard eyes upon each of her committed clients. The young man throws no more than a passing glance at the gallery of thrusting nakedness upon his right and walks directly to the counter. He asks, audibly, for a packet of twenty Embassy and slides his package across to Mrs Baines; which lady, in her turn, reaches beneath the counter and passes forward a similar brown-paper parcel to the young man. How Mr Baines himself would approve! It is a single, swift, uncomplicated transaction.

The young man stops at the Bookbinder's Arms across the road and orders bread and cheese and a pint of Guinness. He feels his usual nagging impatience, but gloats inwardly in expectation. Five o'clock will soon be here and the journey to Woodstock is infinitely quicker now, with the opening of the new stretch of the ring-road complex. His mother will have his cooked meal ready, and then he will be alone. In his own perverted way he has grown almost to enjoy the anticipation of it all, for over the last few months it has become a weekly ritual. Expensive, of course, but the arrangement is not unsatisfactory, with half-price back on everything returned. He drains his Guinness.

Sometimes he still feels guilty (a little) – though not so much as he did. He realizes well enough that his dedication to pornography is coarsening whatever sensibilities he may once have possessed; that his craving is settling like some cancerous, malignant growth upon his mind, a mind crying out with ever-increasing desperation for its instant, morbid gratification. But he can do nothing about it.

Prompt at 2.00 p.m. on Wednesday, 6 October, Mr John Sanders is back in the Formica Shop, and once more the gyrating saw, whining in agony, can be heard behind the sliding doors.

On Wednesday evenings during term-time the Crowther household was usually deserted from 7.00 p.m. to 9.00 p.m. Mrs Margaret Crowther joined a small group of earnest middle-aged culture-vultures in a WEA evening class on Classical Civilization; weekly the children, James and Caroline, swelled the over-subscribed membership of the Wednesday disco at the nearby Community Centre; Mr Bernard Crowther disliked both pop and Pericles.

On the night of Wednesday, 6 October, Margaret left the house at her usual time of 6.30 p.m. Her classes were held about three miles away in the Further Education premises on Headington Hill, and she was anxious to secure a safe and central parking-lot for the proudly sparkling Mini 1000 which Bernard had bought for her the previous August. Diffidently she backed out of the garage (Bernard had agreed to leave his own 1100 to face the winter's elements in the drive) and turned into the quiet road. Although still nervous about her skills, especially in the dark, she relished the little drive. There was the freedom and independence of it all – it was her car, she could go wherever she wanted. On the by-pass she took her usual deep breath and concentrated inordinately hard. Car after car swished by her on the outside lane, and she fought back her instinctive reaction to raise her right foot from its gentle pressure on the accelerator and to cover the brake pedal. She was conscious of the headlights of all the oncoming cars, their drivers, she was sure, brashly confident and secure. She fiddled with her safety belt and daringly glanced at the dashboard to ensure that her lights were dipped. Not that she ever had them on full anyway, for fear that in the sudden panic of dipping them she would press the switch the wrong way and turn them off altogether. At the Headington roundabout she negotiated the lanes competently, and uneventfully covered the remainder of her journey.

When she had first considered committing suicide, the car had seemed a very real possibility. But she now knew that she could never do it that way. Driving brought out all her primitive instincts for safety and self-preservation. And anyway, she couldn't smash up her lovely new Mini. There were other ways . . .

She parked carefully, getting in and out of the car several times before she was perfectly happy that it was as safely ensconced and as equidistanced from its neighbours as she could manage, and entered the large, four-storeyed, glass-fronted building that ministered to the needs of the city's maturer students. She saw Mrs Palmer, one of her classmates, starting up the stairs to Room C26.

'Hullo, Mrs Crowther! We all missed you last week. Were you poorly?'

'What's wrong with those two?' asked James.

A quarter of an hour after Margaret's departure, Bernard had caught the bus down to Lonsdale College, where he dined one or two nights a week. The children were alone.

'Not unusual, is it?' said Caroline.

'They hardly talk to one another.'

'I 'spect all married people get like that.'

'Didn't used to be like that.'

'*You* don't help much.'

'Nor do you.'

'Wha' do you mean?'

'Ah – shut up!'

'You misery.'

'F— off!'

These days their conversation seldom lasted longer. With a few minor permutations and, in the presence of Mum and Dad, a few concessions to conventional middle-class morality, their parents had heard it many times. It worried Margaret deeply and infuriated Bernard, and each wondered secretly if all children were as vicious, ill-tempered, and uncooperative as their own. Not that James and Caroline were uppermost in either parent's mind this Wednesday evening.

As one of the senior fellows of his college, Bernard had naturally been invited to the memorial jamboree for the ex-Vice-Principal who had retired the previous summer. The dinner was to begin at 7.30 p.m., and Bernard arrived in Peter's rooms with half an hour to spare. He poured himself a gin and vermouth and sat back in a faded armchair. He thought he liked Felix Tompsett – the old sod! Certainly he ate too much, and drank too much, and, if many-tongued rumour could be believed (why not?), he had done a lot of other things too much. But he was a good 'college man'; it was on his advice that the college had bought up a lot of property in the early sixties and his understanding of interest rates and investment loans was legendary. Odd really, thought Bernard. He finished his gin and shrugged into his gown. Preprandial sherry would be flowing in the Senior Common Room, and the two friends made their way thither.

'Well, Bernard! How are you, old boy?' Felix's smile beamed a genuine welcome to his old colleague.

'Can't grumble,' replied Bernard lamely.

'And how's that lovely wife of yours?'

Bernard grabbed a sherry. 'Oh fine, fine.'

'Lovely woman.' Felix mused on. He had obviously begun to celebrate his own commemoration with pre-meditated gusto, but Bernard couldn't match his *bonhomie*. He thought of Margaret as the conversation burbled around him . . . He tuned in again just in time to laugh convincingly at Felix's discovery of a recent inscription on the wall of the gents in the Minster bar.

'Bloody good, what?' guffawed Felix.

The party moved next door and sat down to the evening's feast.

Bernard always felt that they had far too much to eat, and tonight
they had far, far too much to eat. As he struggled his way through
the grapefruit cocktail, the turtle soup, the smoked salmon, the
tournedos Rossini, the gâteau, the cheese, and the fruit, he
thought of the millions in the world who had not eaten adequately
for weeks or even months, and saw in his mind the harrowing
pictures of the famine victims of Asia and Africa . . .

'You're quiet tonight,' said the chaplain, passing Bernard the
claret.

'Sorry,' said Bernard. 'It must be all this food and drink.'

'You must learn to take the gifts the good Lord showers upon
us, my boy. You know, as I get older I must confess to the greater
appreciation of two things in life – natural beauty and the delights
of the belly.'

He leaned back and poured half a glass of vintage claret towards
his vast stomach. Bernard knew that some men were naturally fat
– all to do with the metabolic rate, or something. But there were
no fat men in Belsen . . .

But whatever other confessions the good chaplain may have
been about to divulge were cut short by the toast to Her Majesty
and the clearing of the Principal's throat as he rose to his feet to
begin his encomium on Felix Tompsett. They had all heard it all
before. A few necessary alterations in the hackneyed, hallowed
phrases – but basically the same old stuff. Felix would be leaving
holes in so many aspects of college life; it would be difficult to fill
the holes . . . Bernard thought of Margaret. Why not leave the
bloody holes unfilled . . . One of the foremost scholars of his
generation . . . Bernard looked at his watch. 9.15 p.m. He couldn't
go yet. Anecdotes and laughter . . . Bernard felt pretty sure they
would all be reminded of that incident when a disgruntled
undergraduate had pissed all over Felix's carpet two years ago . . .
Back to the academic stuff. Top-of-the-head. Phoney . . . His work
on the Elizabethan lyric poets . . . why, the old bastard had spent
most of his time doing first-hand research on the historic inns of
Oxfordshire. Or with the women . . . For the first time Bernard
wondered if Felix had made any overtures to Margaret. He'd better
not . . .

Felix spoke well. Slightly drunk, amiable, civilized – quite
moving really. Come on! 9.45 p.m. The presentation was made
and the company broke up by 10.00 p.m. Bernard rushed out of
college and ran through the Broad to St Giles', where he found a
taxi immediately. But even before the taxi stopped, he saw some

movement outside the darkened house. His heart raced in panic-stricken despair. James and Caroline stood beside the front door.

'You might have . . .' began Caroline.

Bernard hardly heard. 'Where's your mother?' His voice was hard and urgent.

'Don't know. We thought she must have been with you.'

'How long have you been waiting?' He spoke with a clipped authority the children had seldom heard.

'About half an hour. Mum's always been here before . . .'

Bernard opened the front door. 'Ring up the tech. at Heading-ton. Ask if they've finished.'

'You do it, Caroline.'

Bernard brought his right hand with vicious force across James's face. 'Do it!' he hissed.

He went to the gate. No one. He prayed for the sound of a car, any car. Car! A cold sweat formed on his forehead as he darted to the garage. The door was locked. He found the key. His hand shook convulsively. He opened the door.

'What on earth are you doing?'

Bernard started, and in his heart blessed all the gods that were and are and are to be. 'Where the hell have you been?' In a fraction of a second his terrible, agonized fear had flashed to anger – relieved, fierce, beautiful anger.

'As a matter of fact the starter-motor's gone on the Mini. I couldn't get anyone to fix it and in the end I had to catch a bus.'

'You could have let me know.'

'Oh yes, of course. You want me to ring round all the garages, then you, and then presumably the kids.' Margaret herself was becoming very angry. 'What's all the fuss about? Just because *I'm* late for a change!'

'The children have been waiting no end of a time.'

'So what!' Margaret stormed into the house, and Bernard heard the high-pitched voices within. He closed the front gate and then the garage. He locked and bolted the front door. He felt happy, happier than he had felt for many days and many hours.

CHAPTER TWELVE
Wednesday, Thursday; 6, 7 October

Morse did not know what had persuaded him, after seven months of promises and prevarications, to fill in the ragged, gaping hole above the kitchen door where the electrician had led in the wires for a new power-point. Everything had been wrong from the start anyway. The Polyfilla powder, purchased some two years previously, had hardened into a solid block of semi-concrete within its packet; the spatula he used for cracking eggs and filling cracks had mysteriously vanished from the face of the earth; and the primitive household steps never had stood four-square on their rickety legs. Perhaps he had taken inspiration from Mr Edward de Bono and his recipe for lateral thought. But whatever the motive for his sudden urge to see the wretched hole filled in, Morse had taken a vertical plunge, like some free-fall parachutist, from the top of the steps, when the cord restraining the uprights to a functional 30° angle suddenly snapped and the whole apparatus collapsed into a straight line beneath him. Like Hephaestus, thrown o'er the crystal battlements, he landed with an agonizing jolt upon his right foot, lay with a feeling of nausea for two or three minutes, wiping the cold sweat which formed upon his brow, and finally limped his way to the front room and lay breathing heavily on the settee. After a while the foot was a little easier and he felt somewhat reassured; but half an hour later the swelling began and a fitful, sharp pain nagged away at his instep. He wondered if he could drive, but knew it would be foolish to try. It was 8.30 p.m. on Tuesday, 5 October. Only one thing for it. He hobbled and hopped across to the telephone and rang Lewis, and within the half hour he was sitting disconsolately in the accident room of the Radcliffe Infirmary, waiting for the result of the X-ray. A young boy sitting on the bench next to Morse was wringing his left hand in some agony (car door) and two men badly injured in a road accident were wheeled by for priority treatment. He felt a little less depressed.

He was finally seen by an almost unintelligible Chinese doctor who held up his X-ray pictures to the light with the disinterestedness of a bored guest having a casual glance at one of the holiday slides of his host. 'Nobrocken. Creepancrushes.' From the competent nurse into whose hands he was now delivered, Morse gathered that no bones were broken and that the treatment prescribed was crêpe bandages and hospital crutches.

He expressed his thanks to the nurse and doctor as he swung along diffidently towards the waiting Lewis. 'You,' shouted the doctor after him. 'You, Mr Morse. Nowork twodays. You rest, OK?'

'I think I shall be all right, thanks,' said Morse.

'You, Mr Morse. Youwangebetter, eh? Nowork. Twodays. Rest. OK?'

'OK.' Oh God!

Morse hardly slept through Tuesday night; he had a vicious toothache in each of the toes on his foot. He swallowed Disprin after Disprin and finally towards dawn dozed off from sheer exhaustion. Lewis called several times during the prolonged agonies of Wednesday and watched the Inspector fall into a blessedly deep sleep at about 9.00 p.m.

When Lewis greeted him the next morning, Morse felt better; and because he felt better, his mind reverted to the murder of Sylvia Kaye, and because his mind was not now wholly preoccupied with the tribulations of his right foot, he felt a great depression grow upon him. He felt like a quiz contestant who had almost got some of the answers right, had others on the tip of his tongue, but had finished up with nothing. One always longed to start again . . .

He lay with these troubled thoughts on his mind. Lewis was fussing around. Good old Lewis. They'd all be having a good laugh at the station, he thought. Humiliating, falling off a ladder. Well he hadn't fallen *off* a ladder. He'd fallen *through* one.

'Lewis! You told everybody what happened, I suppose?'

'Yes, sir.'

'Well?'

'They think you're making it up. They think you've got gout really. You know – too much port.'

Morse groaned. He could picture himself limping round with every other person stopping him to enquire into the circumstances of the disaster. He'd write it all out, have it photocopied, and distribute the literature around the station.

'Still painful, sir?'

'Of course it bloody well is. You've got millions of nerveendings all over your bloody toes. You know that, don't you?'

'I had an uncle, sir, who had a beer barrel run over his toes.'

'Shut up,' winced Morse. The thought of anything, let alone a beer barrel, being within three feet of his injured foot was quite unbearable. Beer barrel, though. Morse was getting better.

'Are the pubs open yet?'

'Fancy a drink, sir?' Lewis looked pleased with himself.

'Wouldn't mind a jar.'

'As a matter of fact I brought a few cans in last night, sir.'

'Well?'

Lewis found some glasses, and positioning a chair a goodly distance from 'the foot', poured out the beer.

'Nothing new?' asked Morse.

'Not yet.'

'Mm.'

The two men drank in silence. Some of the answers almost right . . . others on the tip of his tongue . . . What, wondered Morse, if he had been right, or almost right? If only he could start again . . . Suddenly he sat up, forgot his incapacity, yelped 'Oh, me foot!' and leaned back again into his nest of pillows. He *could* start again, couldn't he? 'Lewis. I want you to do me one or two favours. Get me some writing paper – it's in the writing-desk downstairs; and what about some fish and chips for lunch?'

Lewis nodded. As he went off for the writing paper, Morse interrupted him.

'Three favours. Open a few of those cans.'

A thought had been floating around in Morse's mind for several days, elusive as a bar of soap in a slippery bath. In the beginning was the thought, and the thought became word, and Morse unwrapped the text carefully and read the message. *Im Anfang war die Hypothese*. In the beginning was the hypothesis. But before formulating any hypothesis, even of the most modest order, Morse decided that he would feel sharper in body, mind, and spirit with a good wash and a shave. Slowly and painfully he got out of bed, tacked crabwise around the walls and ended up by hopping over the last few feet of the bathroom floor. It took him almost an hour to complete his toilet, but he felt a new man. He retraced his irregular progress and gently heaved his right foot into a comfortable niche alongside a spare pillow stuffed down at the bottom of the bed. He felt exhausted but wonderfully refreshed. He closed his eyes and fell fast asleep.

Lewis wondered if he should wake him, but the pungent smell of fried batter and vinegar saved him the trouble.

'What's the time, Lewis? I've been asleep.'

'Quarter-past one, sir. Do you want the fish and chips on a plate? Me and the wife always eats 'em off the paper – seems to taste better somehow.'

'They say it's the newsprint sticking to the chips,' replied Morse, taking the oily package from his sergeant and tucking in with relish. 'You know, Lewis, perhaps we've been going about this case in the wrong way.'

'We have, sir?'

'We've been trying to solve the case in order to find the murderer, right?'

'I suppose that's the general idea, isn't it?'

'Ah, but we might get better results the other way round.'

'You mean . . .' But though Morse waited it was clear that Lewis had no idea whatsoever what he meant.

'I mean we ought to find the murderer in order to solve the case.'

'I see,' said Lewis, unseeing.

'I'm glad you do,' said Morse. 'It's as clear as daylight – and open some of these bloody curtains, will you?'

Lewis complied.

'If,' continued Morse, 'if I told you who the murderer was and where he lived, you could go along and you could arrest him, couldn't you?' Lewis nodded vaguely and wondered if his superior officer had caught his skull on the kitchen sink before landing on his precious right foot. 'You could, couldn't you? You could bring him here to see me, you could keep him at a safe distance from my grievous injury – and he could tell us all about it, eh? He could do all our work for us, couldn't he?'

Morse jabbered on, his mouth stuffed with fish and chips, and with genuine concern Lewis began to doubt the Inspector's sanity. Shock was a funny thing; he'd seen it many times in road accidents. Sometimes two or three days afterwards some of the parties would go completely gaga. They'd recover, of course . . . Or had Morse been drinking? Not the beer. The opened cans were still unpoured. A heavy responsibility suddenly seemed to descend on Lewis's shoulders. He was sweating slightly. The room was hot, the autumn sun bright upon the glass of the bedroom window.

'Can I get you anything, sir?'

'Yep. Flannel and soap and towel. By Jove, your wife's right, Lewis. I'll never eat 'em off a plate again.'

A quarter of an hour later a bewildered sergeant let himself out of the front door of Morse's flat. He felt a little worried and would have felt even more so if he had been back in.the bedroom at that moment to hear Morse talking to himself, and nodding occasionally whenever he particularly approved of what he heard coming from his own lips.

'Now my first hypothesis, ladies and gentlemen, and as I see things the most vital hypothesis of all – I shall make many, oh yes, I shall make many – is this: that the murderer is living in North Oxford. You will say this is a bold hypothesis, and so it is. Why should the murderer not live in Didcot or Sidcup or even Southampton? Why should he live in North Oxford? Why not, coming nearer home, why not just in Oxford? I can only repeat to you that I am formulating a hypothesis, that is, a supposition, a proposition, however wild, assumed for the sake of argument; a theory to be proved (or disproved – yes, we must concede that) by reference to facts, and it is with facts and not with airy-fairy fancies that I shall endeavour to bolster my hypothesis. *Im Anfang war die Hypothese*, as Goethe might have put it. And please let it not be forgotten that I am Morse of the Detective, as Dickens would have said. Oh yes, a detective. A detective has a sensibility towards crime – he feels it; he must feel it before he can detect it. There are indications which point to North Oxford. We need not review them all here, but the *ambience* is right in North Oxford. And if I am wrong, why, no harm is done to our investigation. We are propounding a hypothesis, that is, a supposition, a proposition, however wild . . . I've said all that before, though. Where was I, now? Oh yes. I wish you to accept, provisionally, dubiously, hopelessly if needs be, my premier hypothesis. The murderer is a resident of North Oxford. Now I mentioned facts, and I shall not disappoint you. Aristotle classified the animals, I believe, by subdividing them, and subdivision will be our method of procedure. Aristotle, that great man, divided and subdivided – species, subspecies, genera (Morse was getting lost) genera, species, subspecies and so on until he reached – what did he reach? – *the individual specimen of the species*.' (That sounded better.) 'I, too, will divide. In North Oxford there are, let us say, "*x*" number of people. Now we further hypothesize that our murderer is a male. Why can we be confident of this fact? Because, ladies and gentlemen, the murdered girl was *raped*. This is a *fact*, and we shall bring forward at the trial the evidence of eminent medical personnel to . . .' Morse was tiring a little, and fortified himself with another can of beer. 'As I was saying, our murderer is male. We can therefore divide our number *x* by, let us say, er, four – leaving the women and children out of our reckoning. Now can we subdivide again, you will ask? Indeed, we can. Let us guess at the age of our murderer. I put him – I am diffident, and you will accuse me of formulating sub-hypotheses – between 35 and 50. Yes, there are reasons . . .' But Morse decided to skip them. They weren't all that convincing, perhaps, but he had reasons, and he wished to sustain the impetus of his hypothesis. 'We may then further subdivide our number *x* by two. That seems most reasonable, does it not? Let us continue. What else can we reasonably hypothesize? I believe – for reasons which I realize may not be fully acceptable to you all – that our suspect is a married man.' Morse was feeling his way with an increasing lack of confidence. But the road ahead was already clearing; the fog was lifting and dissipating in the sun, and he resumed with his earlier briskness. 'Now this means yet a further diminution in the power of *x*. Our *x* is becoming a manageable unit, is it not? But not yet is the focus of our *camera hypothetica* fixed with any clear delineation upon our unsuspecting quarry. But wait! Our man is a regular drinker, is he not? It is surely one of our more reasonable claims, and gives to our procedure not only the merits of hypothetical plausibility, but also of extreme probability. Our case is centred upon the Black Prince, and one does not visit the Black Prince in order to consult the tax inspector.' Morse was wilting again. His foot was throbbing again with rhythmic pain, and his mind wandered off for a few minutes. Must be those Disprin. He closed his eyes and continued his forensic monologue within his brain.

He must, too, surely he must, figure in at least the top 5% of the IQ range? Jennifer wouldn't fall for an ignorant buffoon, would she? That letter. Clever chap, well schooled. *If* he wrote it. If, if, if. Carry on. Where's our *x* now? Go on. He must be attractive to women. Yet who can say what attracts those lovely creatures? But yes. Say yes. Subdivide. Cars! God, he'd forgotten cars. Not everyone has a car. About what proportion? Never mind, subdivide. Just a minute . . . *red* car. He felt slightly delirious. Just a fraction longer . . . That really would be a significant subdivision. The *x* was floating slowly away, and now was gone. The pain was less vicious. Comfortable . . . almost . . . comfortable . . .

He was woken at 4.00 p.m. by Lewis's inability to manage the front door without a disturbing clatter. And when Lewis anxiously put his head round the bedroom door, he saw Morse scribbling as furiously as Coleridge must have scribbled when he woke up to find, full grown within his mind, the whole of *Kubla Khan*.

'Sit down, Lewis. Glad to see you.' He continued to write with furious rapidity for two or three minutes. Finally he looked up.

'Lewis, I'm going to ask you some questions. Think carefully –
don't rush! – and give me some intelligent answers. You'll have to
guess, I know, but do your best.'

Oh hell, thought Lewis.

'How many people live in North Oxford?'

'What do you call "North Oxford", sir?'

'I'm asking the questions, you're answering 'em. Just think
generally what *you* think North Oxford is; let's say Summertown
and above. Now come on!'

'I could find out, sir.'

'Have a bloody guess, man, can't you?'

Lewis felt uncomfortable. At least he could see that only three
of the beer cans were empty. He decided to plunge in. 'Ten
thousand.' He said it with the assurance and unequivocal finality
of a man asked to find the sum of two and two.

Morse took another sheet of paper and wrote down the number
10,000. 'What proportion of them are men?'

Lewis leaned back and eyed the ceiling with the confidence of a
statistical consultant. 'About a quarter.'

Morse wrote down his second entry neatly and carefully
beneath the first: 2,500. 'How many of those men are between 35
and 50?'

Quite a lot of retired people in North Oxford, thought Lewis,
and quite a lot of young men on the estates. 'About half, no more.'

The third figure was entered: 1,250. 'How many of them are
married, would you say?'

Lewis considered. Most of them, surely? 'Four out of five, sir.'

Morse formed the figures of his latest calculation with great
precision: 1,000.

'How many of them regularly go out for a drink – you know
what I mean – pubs, clubs, that sort of thing?'

Lewis thought of his own street. Not so many as some people
thought. The neighbours on either side of him didn't – mean lot!
He thought of the street as a whole. Tricky this one. 'About half.'

Morse revised his figure and went on to his next question. 'You
remember the letter we had, Lewis. The letter Jennifer Coleby said
she knew nothing about?' Lewis nodded. 'If we were right in
thinking what we did, or what I did, would you say we were
dealing with a man of high intelligence?'

'That's a big if, isn't it, sir?'

'Look, Lewis. That letter was written by our man – just get that
into your head. It was the big mistake he made. It's the best clue
we've got. What the hell do they pay us for? We've got to follow

the clues, haven't we?' Morse didn't sound very convinced, but Lewis assured him that they had to follow the clues. 'Well?'

'Well what, sir?'

'Was he an intelligent man?'

'Very much so, I should think.'

'Would you think of writing a letter like that?'

'Me? No, sir.'

'And you're pretty bright, aren't you, Sergeant?'

Lewis squared his shoulders, took a deep breath and decided not to minimize his intellectual capacity. 'I'd say I was in the top fifteen per cent, sir.'

'Good for you! And our unknown friend? You remember he not only knows how to spell all the tricky words, he knows how to misspell them, too!'

'Top five per cent, sir.'

Morse wrote down the calculation.

'What proportion of middle-aged men are attractive to women?' Silly question! Morse noticed the derision in Lewis's face. 'You know what I mean. Some men are positively repulsive to women.' Lewis seemed unconvinced. 'I know all about these middle-aged Romeos. We're all middle-aged Romeos. But some men are more attractive to women than others, aren't they?'

'I don't get many falling for me, sir.'

'That's not what I'm asking you. Say something, for God's sake!'

Lewis plunged again. 'Half? No, more than that. Three out of five.'

'You're sure you mean that?'

Of course he wasn't sure. 'Yes.'

Another figure. 'How many men of this age group have cars?'

'Two out of three.' What the hell did it matter?

Morse wrote down his penultimate figure. 'One more question. How many people own red cars?'

Lewis went to the window and watched the traffic going by. He counted. Two black, one beige, one dark blue, two white, one green, one yellow, one black. 'One in ten, sir.'

Morse had shown a growing excitement in his manner for the last few minutes. 'Phew! Who'd have believed it? Lewis, you're a genius!'

Lewis thanked him for the compliment and asked wherein his genius lay. 'I think, Lewis, that we're looking for a male person, resident in North Oxford, married – probably a family, too; he goes out for a drink fairly regularly, sometimes to Woodstock; he's a well-educated man, may even be a university man; he's about 35 to 45, as I see him, with a certain amount of charm – certainly, I think a man some of the young ladies could fall for; finally he drives a car – to be precise a red car.'

'He'd be as good as anyone, I suppose.'

'Well, even if we're a bit out here and there, I'd bet my bottom dollar he's pretty likely to fit into most of those categories. And, do you know, Lewis, *I don't think there are many who fall into that category*. Look here.' He passed over to Lewis the sheet of paper containing the figures.

North Oxford?	10,000
Men?	2,500
35–50?	1,250
Married?	1,000
Drinker?	500
Top 5%?	25
Charm?	15
Car?	10
Red Car?	1

Lewis felt a guilty sense of responsibility for the remarkable out-come of these computations. He stood by the window in the fading light of afternoon, and saw two red cars go by one after the other. How many people *did* live in North Oxford? Was he really in the top 15%? 25% more likely. 'I'm sure, sir, that we could check a lot of these figures.' Lewis felt constrained to voice his suspicions. 'I don't think you can just fiddle about with figures like that, anyway. You'd need to . . .' He had a dim recollection of the need for some statistical laws operating on data; the categories had to be ordered and reduced in logical sequence; he couldn't quite remember. But it was all little more than an elaborate game to amuse a fevered brain. Morse would be up in a day or so. Better look after him and humour him as best he could. But was there any logic in it? Was it all *that* stupid? He looked again at the paper of figures and another red car went by. There were nine 'ifs'. He stared gloomily out of the window and mechanically counted the next ten cars. Only one red one! North Oxford was, of course, the biggest gamble. But the fellow had to live somewhere, didn't he? Perhaps the old boy was not so cuckoo as he'd thought. He looked at the sheet yet again . . . The other big thing was that letter. *If* the murderer had written it.

'What do you think then, Lewis?'

'Might be worth a go.'

'How many men do you want?'

'We'd need to do a bit of thinking first, wouldn't we?'

'What do you mean?'

'The local authorities could help a good deal. First we'd need some up-to-date lists of residents.'

'Yes. You're right. We need to think it through before we do anything.'

'That's what I thought, sir.'

'Well?'

'We could get straight on to it in the morning, sir, if you felt up to it.'

'Or we could get straight on to it now if *you* felt up to it?'

'I suppose we could.'

Lewis rang his long-suffering spouse, and conferred with Morse for the next two hours. After he had left, Morse reached for a bedside phone and was lucky to find the Chief Superintendent still in his office. And half an hour later Morse was still talking, and ruefully cursing himself for having forgotten to reverse the charges.

CHAPTER THIRTEEN

Saturday, 9 October

On the morning of Saturday, 9 October Bernard Crowther sat at his desk in his front room reading Milton, but not with his usual thrilled enjoyment. He was lecturing on *Paradise Lost* this term and in spite of his thorough and scholarly mastery of the work he felt he should do a little more homework. Margaret had caught the bus to Summertown to do her shopping and his car was ready outside to pick her up at midday. The children were out. Goodness knew where.

He was surprised to hear the front door bell ring, for they had few callers. Butcher perhaps. He opened the door.

'Why, Peter! What a surprise! Come in, come in.' Peter Newlove and Bernard had been firm friends for years. They had arrived at Lonsdale College the same term and since then had enjoyed a warm and genuine relationship. 'What brings you here? Not very often we have the pleasure of seeing you in North Oxford. I thought you played golf on Saturday mornings, anyway.'

'I couldn't face it this morning. Bit chilly round the fairways, you know.' The weather had turned much colder the last two days, and the autumn had suddenly grown old. The day seemed bleak and sour. Peter sat down. 'Working on Saturday morning, Bernard?'

'Just getting ready for next week.'

Peter looked across at the desk. 'Ah. *Paradise Lost*, Book I. I remember that. We did it for Higher Certificate.'

'You've read it since, of course.'

'*From morn to noon he fell, from noon to dewy eve, a summer's day.* What about that?'

'Very fine.' Bernard looked out of the window and saw the white hoar-frost still unmelted on his narrow lawn.

'Is everything all right, Bernard?' The man from Gloucestershire spoke with an abrupt kindliness.

'Course everything's all right. Why did you say that?' It was clear to Peter that everything was far from right.

'Oh, I don't know. You just seemed a bit on edge on Wednesday night. Scuttled away like a startled hare after the dinner.'

'I'd forgotten that Margaret would be late, and I knew the kids would be waiting outside.'

'I see.'

'Was it that obvious?'

'No, not really. I was watching you, that's all. You didn't seem your old self when we had a drink together, and I thought you might be a bit under the weather.' Bernard said nothing. 'Everything OK with you and er Margaret?'

'Oh, yes. Fine. I've got to collect her, by the way, at twelve. What's the time now?'

'Half-past eleven.' Peter rose to his feet.

'No, don't go! We've got time for a quick drink. What'll you have?'

'Are you going to have one?'

'Of course I am. Whisky?'

'Fine.'

Bernard withdrew to the kitchen to get the glasses, and Peter stood in front of the window, looking out into the narrow street. A car, white and pale blue, with a light (not flashing) on the roof and POLICE marked in bold black lettering across its side, was parked across the way, two or three doors to the left. It had not been there when Peter arrived. As he watched, a police constable, with a black and white chequered band around his flat, peaked hat, was coming out of a front gate. A middle-aged woman walked with him and the two were talking freely, pointing between them to every point of the compass. More talk and further pointing arms. Was she pointing here? The constable had a list in his hand and he was clearly checking some names. The woman stood with her apron around her, clutching her arms about her middle to keep warm and chattering interminably on.

Bernard came in, the glasses clattering a little on the tray. 'Say when!'

'I see you've got a few criminals in the road, Bernard.'

'What did you say?' Bernard looked up sharply.

'Is the law always prowling around here like this?' Peter got no further. The door bell rang twice; shrill, peremptory. Bernard opened the door and stood face to face with the young constable.

'Can I help you, officer?'

'Yes, I think so, sir, if you will. Won't take more'n a minute. Is this your car, sir?' He pointed to the red 1100 outside.

'Yes, it is.'

'Just checking, sir. We've had a lot of cars stolen recently. Just checking.' He made a note in his book. 'Can you remember the registration number, sir?'

Mechanically Bernard recited the number.

'That's yours all right then, sir. Have you got your log-book handy, sir?'

'Is it necessary?'

'Well, it is rather important, if you don't mind, sir. We're checking as thoroughly as we can.'

Peter heard the conversation through the open door and felt strangely worried. Bernard came in and poked about haphazardly in his desk. 'Where the hell's Margaret . . . They're checking on stolen cars, Peter. Shan't be a minute.' He looked ashen, and could find nothing. 'I'm sorry, officer,' he called. 'Come in a minute, will you?'

'Thank you, sir. Don't worry if you can't put your hand on the log-book, sir. You can give me the information yourself quite easily.'

'What do you want to know?'

'Full name, sir?'

'Bernard Michael Crowther.'

'Age, sir?'

'Forty-one.'

'Married, sir?'

'Yes.'

'Children?'

'Two.'

'Occupation?'

'University lecturer.'

'That's about all, sir.' He closed his book. 'Oh, just one more thing. Have you left your car unlocked recently? You know what I mean. Is it locked now, for example?'

'No, I don't think so.'

'No, it isn't, sir. I tried all the doors before I called. It's an open invitation to car thieves, you know.'

'Yes, I'm sure you're right. I'll try to remember.'

'Do you use your car much, sir?'

'Not a great deal. Running around a bit in Oxford. Not much really.'

'You don't take it out when you go for a drink, for example?'

Peter thought he saw the daylight. Bernard had been drinking and driving, had he?

'No, not very often,' answered Bernard. 'I usually go round to the Fletcher's. It's not far; I always walk there.'

'Would you take the car if you went drinking outside Oxford, sir?'

'I'm afraid I would,' said Bernard slowly, in a helpless sort of way.

'Well, don't drink too much, sir, if you're driving. But I'm sure you know all about that.' The constable glanced quickly round the room and looked drily at the two large tumblers of whisky; but he said nothing more until he reached the door. 'You don't know anyone else in the road who's got a red car, do you, sir? I've got to make a few more enquiries.'

Bernard thought, but his mind was swimming. He couldn't think of anybody. He closed his eyes and put his left hand on his forehead. Every day in term time he walked to the far end of the road. Red car? Red car? His was the only one, he was pretty sure of that.

'Well don't worry, sir. I'll just make one or two more, er . . . Anyway, thank you for your help, sir.' He was gone. But not, Peter noticed, to make any more enquiries in that particular road. He walked straight to the police car (left unlocked) and immediately accelerated away.

Some ten minutes later as he drove along to Woodstock, Peter Newlove was glad he'd never married. The same woman – thirty, forty, fifty years! Not for him. He couldn't imagine poor old Bernard jumping into bed that afternoon for a riotous half-hour romp with Margaret. Whereas . . . He thought of Gaye undressing, and his right foot pressed hard upon the accelerator.

*

An immensely excited Constable McPherson rushed across the forecourt of the Thames Valley HQ where earlier the same morning he had seen poor old Morse staggering painfully along, his arms encircling the shoulders of two of his burly mates. Wow! McPherson felt like a man with eight draws up on the treble-chance pool. As he had driven the few miles from North Oxford to Kidlington, he sensed a feeling of unprecedented elation. For the last four years his uniformed career had been uniformly undistinguished; he had apprehended no significant villain; he had witnessed no memorable breach of either the civil or the criminal code. But blessed indeed he was today! As he had neared the Banbury Road roundabout he had switched on the wailing siren and the winking blue light, and had delighted in the deference accorded to him by his fellow motorists. He felt mightily important. Why not? He *was* mightily important – for today, at least.

Inside the station, McPherson debated for a second or two. Should he report to Lewis? Or should he report his intelligence direct to the Inspector? The latter course seemed on reflection the more appropriate, and he made his way along the corridors to Morse's door, knocked and just caught the muffled 'come in' from the other side.

'And what can I do for you, Constable?'

McPherson made his report with an accuracy and incisiveness that was impressive, and Morse congratulated him upon the prompt and efficient discharge of his duty. McPherson, though mightily gratified with the compliment, was a little surprised that Morse himself seemed not immediately anxious to summon the cohorts of the law. But he'd done his own job – done it well.

'Excuse me if I don't stand up – gout, you know – but . . .' He shook McPherson's hand warmly. 'It won't go unnoticed, believe me.'

After McPherson's departure, Morse sat silently and thoughtfully for a few minutes. But so he had been sitting when the constable had entered. It would have been so disappointing for McPherson to have known, and anyway McPherson had been the immediate cause. No, he could never have had the heart to confess that Mr Bernard Crowther had telephoned in at 11.45 a.m. wishing, he said, to make a statement.

Crowther had insisted that he should present himself, that on no account were the police to collect him, that he expected the authorities at least to allow to a witness, coming forward

voluntarily with what might be valuable information, the normal
courtesy of not being picked up like a common felon. Morse had
agreed, and Bernard promised to be with him at 2.30 p.m.

Morse found himself apologizing for his immobility and his first
impression of Crowther was surprisingly agreeable. The man was
nervous – that was plain for all to see; but there was an odd charm
and dignity about the fellow; that sort of middle-aged schoolmas-
ter-type that some of the girls might have a crush on.

'Look, Inspector – you are a Chief Inspector, I think – I have
never in my life been inside a police station until this moment. I
am not conversant with normal police practice and procedure. So
I have taken the precaution of writing out, very rushed, I'm afraid,
the statement I wish to make.'

CHAPTER FOURTEEN
Saturday, 9 October

On the evening of Wednesday, September 29th, I left my house in
Southdown Road at 6.45 p.m. I drove my car to the roundabout at
the north end of the Banbury Road, where I turned left and travelled
the four hundred yards or so along Sutherland Avenue to the
roundabout at the northern end of the Woodstock Road. I turned
off the A40 and took the road north to Woodstock. Night was
already drawing in and I switched the sidelights on, in common, I
noticed, with the majority of the other motorists. Yet although it
was that awkward half light in which it is most difficult to drive, it
was not dark enough for full headlights; it was certainly not dark
enough for me to miss two young girls standing a little way beyond
the roundabout on the grass verge alongside the self-service filling-
station. The girl nearer to the road I saw clearly. She was an
attractive girl with long fair hair, white blouse, short skirt and a coat
over her arm. The other girl had walked on a few yards and had her
back towards me; she seemed to be quite happy to leave the
business of getting a lift to her companion. But she had darkish
hair, I think, and if I remember correctly was a few inches taller
than her friend.

I must now try to be completely honest with you. I have often
been guilty of romantic day-dreams, even vaguely erotic day-

dreams, about picking up some wildly attractive woman and finding her a rare and disturbing combination of brains and beauty. In my silly imaginings the preliminary and diffident skirmishing would lead gradually but inevitably to the most wanton delights. But this, remember, has always been a day-dream and I mention it simply to excuse myself for having stopped at all. I shouldn't feel guilty and apologetic about such things; yet in all honesty I do feel so, and have always felt so.

But that is by the way. I leaned over and opened the nearside front door and said that I was going to Woodstock, if that would help. The blonde girl said something like 'Oh, super'. She turned round to her companion and said (I think), 'What did I tell you?' and got into the front seat beside me. The other girl opened the rear door and got in also. What conversation there was was desultory and disappointing. The girl beside me reiterated at intervals that this was 'a real bi' of luck' (she had a typical Oxford manner of speech) because she had missed the bus; I think the girl sitting in the back spoke only once and that was to ask the time. I mentioned as we passed the gates of Blenheim Palace that this was about it, and I understood that it would do them fine. I dropped them as soon as we reached the main street, but I didn't notice where they went. It was natural for me to believe, as I did, that they were going to meet their boy friends.

There is little more to say. What I have written above is a true record of the events which, as I now realize, later in the evening led up to the murder of one of the girls I had driven.

I have just re-read what I have written and am conscious that it perhaps says little which can help your investigation. I am also aware that my statement will give rise to two questions: first, why was I myself going to Woodstock on the night of 29 September, and second, why did I not come forward earlier with my evidence? The two questions are really one, and I shall feel a great weight off my shoulders to be able to answer it; nevertheless, it is my earnest hope that what I have to say can be treated by the police with the strictest confidentiality, since other people, themselves completely inno-cent, would be hurt beyond telling if it were to become generally known.

For the last six months or so I have been having an affair with another woman. We have been able to meet regularly once a week, almost always on Wednesday evenings, when my wife and children are away from home and when no awkward questions are likely to arise. On Wednesday, 29th, I was on my way to meet this woman by the side gates of Blenheim Palace at 7.15 p.m. I parked my car outside the Bear Hotel and walked there. She was waiting. We walked into Blenheim gardens, beside the lake, and through the trees – it is a most beautiful spot. It was, of course, dangerous for us, since so many people from Oxford go out for a meal in Woodstock. But we were always careful, and the element of risk was itself perhaps part of the excitement.

I need say no more. I read the account of the murder and later watched Detective Chief Inspector Morse make his appeal on television. I wish you to know that I almost telephoned there and then; in fact I waited outside a telephone box in Southdown Road for several minutes that same evening with a firm resolve to come forward immediately. But this is making excuses, and I have none to offer. I fully understand, as you will, that I have not, even at this late stage, come forward of my own volition. When a police constable called at my home this morning, I realized that you were on to me, and thought it best to offer this statement straight away. I perpetuated to my wife the rigmarole which the constable had given me about stolen cars, and I told her that I would be coming here. I would do anything in the world to avoid hurting her (yet, it is probable, I know, that I have hurt her already), and I should be most grateful if any part of my statement not relevant to the strict terms of the inquiries you are conducting can be kept secret.

That I am genuinely sorry for the inconvenience and needless extra work which I have caused, will, I trust, be obvious from what I have said here. If it is not, let me hasten to state now my profound apologies for my selfish and cowardly course of action.
I am,
  Your humble servant,
  Bernard Michael Crowther.

Morse read the statement slowly. When he had finished he looked across the table at Crowther, then looked down again at the statement and re-read it with even greater concentration. When he had finished, he leaned back in his black leather chair, carefully picked up his injured right foot, put it across his left knee, and rubbed it lovingly.

'I've hurt my foot, Mr Crowther.'

'Have you? I'm sorry to hear that. My medical friends say that feet and hands are about the worst things to knock about – something to do with the multiplicity of nerve endings.'

He had a pleasant voice and manner. Morse looked him fully in the eyes. For several seconds neither man flinched, and Morse thought he saw a basic honesty in the man. But he could not conceal from himself a draining sense of disappointment and anticlimax; like Constable McPherson he had thought of a big pools win, only to find that instead of 'telegrams required' the forecast was very low. 'Yes.' He picked up the conversation. 'I shan't be walking round Blenheim Park tonight, sir.'

'Nor shall I,' said Bernard.

'Very romantic, I should think, having a bit on the side like that.'

'You make it sound very crude.'

'Wasn't it?'

'Perhaps so.'

'Are you still seeing her?'

'No. My philandering days are over now, I hope.'

'Have you seen her since that night?'

'No. It's all off. It seemed better.'

'Does she know that you picked the two girls up?'

'Yes.'

'Is she upset – that it's all over, I mean?'

'I suppose so, a bit.'

'What about you?'

'To be truthful, it's a great relief. I'm not a very accomplished Casanova and I hated all the lying.'

'You realize, of course, that it would help a great deal if this young lady – is she young, by the way?'

For the first time Bernard hesitated. 'Fairly young.'

'If this young lady,' continued Morse, 'would come forward and corroborate your evidence.'

'Yes. I know it would.'

'But you don't want that.'

'I'd rather you disbelieved my story than dragged her into it.'

'You're not going to tell me who she is? I can promise you that I will handle the business myself.'

Bernard shook his head. 'I'm sorry. I can't do that.'

'I could try to find her, you know,' said Morse.

'I couldn't stop that.'

'No, you couldn't.' Morse moved his foot carefully back to the cushion strategically placed under his desk. 'You could be with-holding vital evidence, Mr Crowther.' Bernard said nothing. 'Is she married?' persisted Morse.

'I'm not going to talk about her,' he said quietly, and Morse sensed a steely resolve in the man.

'Do you think I could find her?' His foot shot with pain, and he picked it up again. Oh, what the hell, he thought; if this bit of stuff likes him to tickle her tits under the trees, what's that got to do with me? Bernard had not answered and Morse changed his tack. 'You realize, I'm sure, that this other girl, the one who sat in the back seat, she's the one who might be able to give us a line?' Crowther nodded. 'Why do you think we haven't heard from her?'

'I don't know.'

'Can't you think of any reason?'

Bernard could, that was clear, but he did not put his thoughts into words.

'You can, can't you, Mr Crowther? Because it could be exactly the same reason which accounted for your reluctance to come forward.' Bernard nodded again. 'She could tell us, perhaps, who Sylvia Kaye's boy friend was, where she was going to meet him, what they were going to do – she might be able to tell us such a lot, don't you think?'

'I didn't get the idea they knew each other very well.'

'Why do you say that?' asked Morse sharply.

'Well, they didn't chatter much together. You know how young girls do: pop music, dances, discos, boy friends – they just didn't talk much – that's all.'

'You didn't catch her name?'

'No.'

'Have you tried to think if Sylvia used her name?'

'I've tried to tell you all I can remember. I can't do any more.'

'Betty, Carole, Diana, Evelyn . . . no?' Bernard remained impassive. 'Gaye, Heather, Iris, Jennifer . . .' Morse could not make out the mildest flicker of response in Bernard's eyes. 'Had she got nice legs?'

'Not so nice as the other's, I don't think.'

'You noticed those?'

'What do you think? She was sitting next to me.'

'Any erotic day-dreams?'

'Yes,' said Crowther, with a fierce burst of honesty.

'It's a good job it's not a criminal offence,' sighed Morse, 'otherwise we'd all be inside.' He noticed a light smile play for a brief second on Crowther's worried face. I can see him being attractive to some women, thought Morse. 'What time did you get home that night?'

'About a quarter to nine.'

'Was that the usual time, you know, because of er your er wife and so on?'

'Yes.'

'An hour a week, was that it?'

'Not much longer.'

'Was it worth it?'

'It seemed so – at the time.'

'You didn't call at the Black Prince that evening?'

'I've never been in the Black Prince.' It sounded very definite. Morse looked down at the statement again and noticed the beautifully formed handwriting; it seemed a pity to type it out. He questioned Crowther for a further half an hour, and gave it up soon after 4.00 p.m.

'We shall have to keep your car here a while, I'm afraid.'

'You will?' Crowther sounded disappointed.

'Yes, we might just find something, you know – hair, that sort of thing. They can do wonderful things these days, our forensic boys.' He got up from his chair and asked Crowther for his crutches. 'I'll promise you one thing,' said Morse. 'We'll keep your wife out of it. I'm sure you can make up something to tell her. After all, you're used to that sort of thing, aren't you, sir?'

Morse limped out behind Crowther and ordered the desk sergeant to get some transport. 'Leave your car keys with me please, sir,' said Morse. 'You should have the car back early next week.' The two men shook hands and Crowther was to wait only a few minutes before he was ushered into a police car. Morse watched him go with mixed feelings. He felt he'd handled things satisfactorily. He needed to think now, not to talk. Funny, though, that about the other girl's legs; Mrs Jarman said she was wearing slacks . . .

He summoned assistance and was helped across to Crowther's car. The doors were open. He struggled his way into the nearside front seat and sat back, manoeuvring his foot as carefully as he could, and stretching his legs as far as possible in front of him. He closed his eyes and pictured the legs of Sylvia Kaye, long, tanned, finely formed, rising up to her brief skirt. He thought she might have leaned back, too. 'Hot pants!' he said, almost to himself.

'Pardon, sir?' said the sergeant who had helped him into the car.

By an odd coincidence (or was it?) Studio 2 in Walton Street was presenting a double sexploitation bill whose titles were calculated to titillate even the most jaded appetite. The first, 2.00–3.05 p.m., was *Danish Blue* (not, judging from the mounds of female flesh that burst their bounds in the stills outside, a film about the

manufacturing of cheese) and from 3.20–5.00 p.m. the main
attraction of the week, entitled *Hot Pants*.

At 5.00 p.m. the earlier addicts were leaving, and a small group
of men stood inside the foyer waiting for admission. One of these
would normally have joined the early brigade, for this was for him
a weekly occurrence. But he had been needed by Messrs Chalkley
and Sons for two hours' overtime in the Formica Shop. He would
not, this week, be able to stay round and see the programme
twice; but the films seldom met his inflated expectations or the
infinite promise of the coming-shortly trailers. On these occasions
he seldom looked about him, and it was just as well in the late
afternoon of Saturday, 9 October, that once again he averted his
eyes from his fellow voyeurs. For standing no more than four feet
away from him, ostensibly checking the times of the next programme, but keeping himself carefully and unobtrusively out of
the limelight, was the sergeant seconded to Detective Chief
Inspector Morse for the inquiry into the murder of Sylvia Kaye.
Lewis thought that this was one of Morse's more rewarding
assignments, and he suspected that, but for his accident, his chief
might well have undertaken it himself.

CHAPTER FIFTEEN
Monday, 11 October

The weekend drifted by, and the leaves continued to fall. Morse
was feeling more cheerful; he could now put a good deal of weight
on to his foot, and on Monday morning, deciding that he could
exchange his crutches for a pair of sticks, he arranged for
McPherson to drive him down to the Radcliffe Infirmary Outpatients' (Accident) Department.

He questioned McPherson closely as they drove. What
impression had he formed of Crowther? What had been Crowther's immediate reactions? What was he like at home, did he think?
What had he been doing when McPherson called? Morse found
the young constable surprisingly intelligent and observant, and
told him so. Furthermore he found a good deal in the information
he had been given that interested him and aroused his curiosity.

'What had he been reading – did you manage to see?'

'No, sir. But books on literature, I think. You know, poetry.'
Morse let it pass.

'He had a writing-desk, you say?'

'Yes, sir. You know, papers all over it.'

Morse mentally resolved not to count up the 'you knows' he'd had so far and the 'you knows' he was surely going to get. 'Was there a typewriter there?' He said it casually enough.

'Yes. You know, one of those portable things.'

Morse said no more. Waved through the narrow yards of the Infirmary, that seemed in conspiracy to prevent too many injured citizens from gaining immediate access to the Outpatients' Department, the police car parked itself, with no objections from porters, orderlies, or traffic wardens, on a broad stretch of concrete marked 'Ambulances Only'. A policeman's parking lot was sometimes not an unhappy one. Morse had foreseen the swopping of crutches for sticks as a straightforward transaction; but it was not to be. There appeared to be an unbreached egalitarianism in the world of all injured brothers, and Morse was constrained to take his proper place and wait his proper time whilst the proper formalities were completed. He sat on the same bench, skipped through the same old edition of *Punch*, and felt the same impatience; he heard the same Chinese doctor, his sang-froid seemingly disturbed by the inability of a little boy to sit still: 'Youwannagetbetter, li'l boy, youbetter sidstill.'

Morse stared gloomily at the floor and found himself watching the nurses' legs go by. Not much to make the blood boil really. Except one pair – beautiful! Morse would like to have seen the rest of the delicious damsel, but she had walked swiftly past. Fat, so-so, thin, so-so – and then those legs again and this time they stopped miraculously in front of him.

'I hope you're being looked after all right, Inspector Morse?'

The Inspector was visibly stunned. He looked up slowly, straight and deep into the sad, come-hither face of darling Dark-eyes, co-resident of the cool Miss Jennifer Coleby. 'You remember me?' said Morse; a little illogically, thought the girl standing directly above him.

'Don't you remember *me*?' she asked.

'How could I forget you?' said the Inspector, slipping at last in to a smooth forward gear. How lovely she was! 'You work here?'

'If I may say so, Inspector, you must have asked a great many more intelligent questions in your time.' She wore her uniform becomingly – and Morse always thought a nurse's uniform did more for a girl than all the fine feathers of the fashion houses.

'No, not very bright, was it?' he confessed. She smiled – delightfully.

'Have a seat,' said Morse, 'I'd like to have a chat with you. We didn't say much before, did we?'

'I'm sorry, Inspector. I can't do that. I'm on duty.'

'Oh.' He was disappointed.

'Well . . .'

'Just stay a minute,' said Morse. 'You know, I really would like to see you, some time. Can I see you when you come off duty?'

'I'm on duty until six.'

'Well, I could meet . . .'

'At six I shall go home and have a quick meal, and then at seven . . .'

'You've got a date.'

'Well, let's say I'm busy.'

'Lucky bugger,' mumbled Morse. 'Tomorrow?'

'Not tomorrow.'

'Wednesday?' Morse wondered mournfully if the progression through the remaining days of the week was anything more than a hollow formality; but she surprised him.

'I could see you on Wednesday evening, if you like.'

'Could you?' Morse sounded like an eager schoolboy. They arranged to meet in the 'Bird and Baby' in St Giles' at 7.30 p.m. Morse tried to sound more casual: 'I can take you home, of course, but perhaps it would be better not to pick you up. You can get a bus all right?'

'I'm not a child, Inspector.'

'Good. See you then.' She turned away. 'Oh, just a minute,' called Morse. She walked back to him. 'I don't know your name yet, Miss . . .'

'Miss Widdowson. But you can call me Sue.'

'Is that just for special friends?'

'No,' said Miss Widdowson. 'Everyone calls me Sue.'

For the first week of the case Morse had felt confident in his own abilities, like a schoolboy with a tricky problem in mathematics to work out who had the answer book secretly beside him. From the very beginning of the case he thought he had glimpsed a Grand Design – he would have to juggle about a bit with the pieces of evidence that came to hand, but he knew the pattern of the puzzle. For this reason he had not, he realized, considered the evidence *qua* evidence, but only in relation to his own prejudiced reconstruction of events. And having failed to work out an answer to his problem which bore the faintest similarity to the agreed solution in the answer book, he was now beginning seriously to wonder if, after all, the answer book was wrong. Sometimes on the eve of a big horse-race he had read through the list of runners and riders, closed his eyes and tried to visualize the headlines on the sports page of the following morning's newspaper. He'd had little success with that, either. Yet he still thought he was on the right track. He was, as he saw himself, a perservering man, although he was wide awake to the possibility that to Lewis (sitting across the table now) his perseverance might well be considered stubbornness, and to his superiors sheer pig-headedness.

In fact Lewis was not at that moment considering the stubbornness of his chief at all; he was contemplating with great distaste the orders he had just received.

'But do you think it's proper to do it this way, sir?'

'I doubt it,' said Morse.

'But it's not legal, surely?'

'Probably not.'

'But you want me to do it.' Morse ignored the non-question. 'When?'

'You'd have to make sure he was out first.'

'How do you suggest . . .?'

Morse interrupted him. 'Christ, man, you're not in apron strings. Use your nous!'

Lewis felt angry at he walked across the canteen and ordered a cup of coffee.

'What's the matter, Sarge?' Constable Dickson was eating again.

'That bloody man Morse – that's what's the matter,' muttered Lewis, setting down his cup with such vigour that half the contents slopped messily into the saucer.

'I see you like your coffee half and half, Sarge,' said Dickson. 'Half in the cup and half in the saucer.' He was highly amused.

McPherson walked in and ordered coffee. 'Solved the murder yet, Sergeant?'

'No we bloody haven't,' snapped Lewis. He got up and left the grey-looking apology untouched – half in the cup and half in the saucer.

'What's eating him?' asked McPherson. 'God, he don't know how lucky he is. Damn good chap, Inspector Morse. I tell you, if he don't get to the bottom of that Woodstock business, nobody will.'

*

It was a nice compliment and Morse could have done with it. After Lewis had left, he sat for a long time, his hands together in front of his face, fingertips to fingertips, eyes closed, as if praying to some benign divinity for light along the darkening path. But Morse had long ago, albeit unwillingly, discounted the existence of any supernatural agency. He was fishing patiently in the troubled waters of his mind.

He got his bite about 4.30 p.m., and limped across to the file on the Woodstock murder. Yes, they were both there. He took them out and read them again – for the umpteenth time, it seemed. He must be right. He had to be. But still he wondered if he was.

The first thing (but it was a minnow, not a shark) that arrested his attention was that in both the letter from the (pretty certainly) bogus employer, and in the statement made by Crowther, the writer had used the form 'I should'. Morse, not as conversant as he should have been with some of the niceties of English grammar, more often than not – almost always now he thought of it – used the form 'would'. He could hear himself dictating: 'Dear Sir, I would be very glad to . . .' Ought he to have said 'I should'? He reached for Fowler's *Modern English Usage*. There it was: 'The verbs, *like, prefer, care, be glad, be inclined*, etc., are very common in first-person conditional statements (*I should like to know* etc.). In these *should*, not *would*, is the correct form in the English idiom.' Well, thought Morse, we learn something new every day. But somebody knew all about it already. So he should, though; he was an English don, wasn't he? What about Mr G— undecipherable who had something to do with a mis-spelt Psychology Department? (Blast – he'd not even checked that yet.) But Mr G was a university man, too, wasn't he? said a still small voice at the back of Morse's mind. A very little minnow! Interesting, though.

He read the documents yet again. Just a minute. Hold on. Yes. This wasn't a minnow. Surely not! 'Yet it is not improbable . . .' The phrase appeared in each document. A mannered phrase. 'Yet' standing at the beginning of its clause; not the commonest of syntactical structures. And what about 'not improbable'. That was a figure of speech Morse had learned at school. 'St Paul was a citizen of no mean city.' He consulted Fowler again. That was it. *Litotes*. Parallel expressions raced through his mind. 'Yet it is probable . . .'; 'But it is probable/likely . . .'; 'But it may be . . .'; 'Maybe . . .'; 'I think . . .'; 'But I think . . .' Odd. Very odd. A very mannered phrase.

And there was another coincidence. The phrase 'in all honesty' also appeared in each letter. What would he himself have written?

'Frankly', 'honestly', 'to be frank', 'truthfully'? Come to think of it, it didn't mean very much at all. Three little weasel words. The letter really was most odd. Had his first appraisal of its significance been over-sophisticated, too clever-clever? But people *did* do that sort of thing. Wives and husbands did it in war-time, communicating to each other a wealth of factual data unsuspected by the army censors. 'I'm sorry to hear little Archie's got the croup. Will write again soon,' might well have concealed the military intelligence that Trooper Smith was to be posted from Aldershot to Cairo next Saturday. Fanciful? No! Morse believed that he had been right.

The evening shadows fell across his desk, and he replaced the Woodstock file and locked the cabinet. The answer was slowly coming, and it seemed to be the answer in the answer book.

CHAPTER SIXTEEN
Tuesday, 12 October

On Tuesday morning at 11.00 a.m., half an hour after Crowther had boarded a bus to the city centre, a small business van, bearing the legend 'Kimmons Typewriters' drew up outside the Crowther residence in Southdown Road. A man, wearing a lightweight grey jacket with 'Kimmons' embroidered across the pocket, alighted from the van and walked through the white gate, past the scraggy lawn, and knocked. Margaret Crowther, wiping her hands on her apron, opened the door.

'Yes?'

'Mr Crowther live here, please?'

'Yes.'

'Is he in?'

'No, not at the minute.'

'Oh. You Mrs Crowther?'

'Yes.'

'Your husband rang to ask us to look at his typerwiter. He said the carriage was getting stuck.'

'Oh, I see. Come in, will you?'

The typewriter man rather ostentatiously took from his pocket a small box, containing, one must have supposed, the requisite tools of the trade, stepped with an obvious diffidence into the narrow hallway and was ushered into the room off the right-hand side of the hall where Bernard Crowther spent so much of his time

considering the glories of the English literary heritage. He spotted
the typewriter immediately.

'Do you need me?' Mrs Crowther seemed anxious to resume
her culinary duties.

'No, no. Shan't be more than a few minutes – unless it's really
wonky.' His voice sounded strained.

'Well, call me when you've finished. I'm only in the kitchen.'

He looked carefully around, made a few perfunctory tappings
on the typewriter, slid the carriage tinkling to and fro several
times, and listened carefully. He could hear the clink of plates and
saucers; he felt fairly safe and very nervous. Quickly he slid open
the top drawer on the right of the small desk; paper-clips, Biros,
rubbers, elastic bands – nothing very suspicious. Systematically he
tried the two lower drawers, and then the three on the left. All
pretty much the same. Wadges of notes clipped together, bulky
agendas for college meetings, file-cases, writing paper, more
writing paper and yet more – ruled, plain, headed, foolscap, folio,
quarto. He repeated his pathetic little pantomime and heard, in
welcome counter-point, an answering clatter of crockery. He took
one sheet from each of the piles of writing paper, folded them
carefully and put them into his inside pocket. Finally taking one
sheet of quarto he stood it in the typewriter, twiddled the carriage
and quickly typed two lines of writing:

> After asessing the mny applications we have received,
> we must regretfully inform you that our application

Mrs Crowther showed him to the door. 'Well, that should be all
right now, Mrs Crowther. Dust in the carriage-bearings, that's all.'
Lewis hoped it sounded all right.

'Do you want me to pay you?'

'No. Don't bother about that now.' He was gone.

At twelve noon Lewis knocked on Bernard Crowther's door in the
second quad of Lonsdale College and found him finishing a
tutorial with a young, bespectacled, long-haired undergraduate.

'No rush, sir,' said Lewis. 'I can wait perfectly happily until
you've finished.'

But Crowther had finished. He had met Lewis the previous
Saturday, and was anxious to hear whatever must be heard. The
youth was forthwith dismissed with the formidable injunction to
produce an essay for the following tutorial on 'Symbolism in
Cymbeline', and Crowther shut the door. 'Well, Sergeant Lewis?'

Lewis told him exactly what had occurred that morning; he made no bones about it and confessed that he had not enjoyed the subterfuge. Crowther showed little surprise and seemed anxious only about his wife.

'Now, sir,' said Lewis. 'If you say you expected a man from Kimmons to come and look at your typewriter, no harm's been done. I want to assure you of that.'

'Couldn't you have asked me?'

'Well, yes, sir, we could. But I know that Inspector Morse wanted to make as little fuss as possible.'

'Yes, I'm sure.' Crowther said it with an edge of bitterness in his voice. Lewis got up to go. 'But why? What did you expect to find?'

'We wanted to find out, sir, if we could, on what machine a certain, er, a certain communication was written.'

'And you thought I was involved?'

'We have to make enquiries, sir.'

'Well?'

'Well what, sir?'

'Did you find out what you wanted?'

Lewis looked uneasy. 'Yes, sir.'

'And?'

'Shall we say, sir, that we didn't find anything at all, er – at all incriminating. That's about the position, sir.'

'You mean that you thought I'd written something on the typewriter and now you think I didn't.'

'Er, you'd have to ask Inspector Morse about that, sir.'

'But you just said that the letter wasn't written on—'

'I didn't say it was a letter, sir.'

'But people do write letters on typewriters don't they, Sergeant?'

'They do, sir.'

'You know, Sergeant, you're beginning to make me feel guilty.'

'I'm sorry, sir. I didn't mean to do that. But in a job like ours you've got to suspect everybody really. I've told you all I can, sir. Whatever typewriter we're looking for wasn't the one in your house. But there's more than one typewriter in the world, isn't there, sir?'

Crowther did not contest the truth of the assertion. A large bay window gave a glorious view on to the silky grass of the second quad, smooth and green as a billiard table. Before the window stood a large mahogany desk, littered with papers and letters and essays and books. And in the centre of this literary clutter there sat, four-square upon the desk, a large, ancient, battered typewriter.

On his way back to Kidlington, Lewis drove through the broad tree-lined sweep of St Giles' and took the right fork to follow the Banbury Road up through North Oxford. As he passed the large engineering block on his right, he saw a tallish woman in dark slacks and a long heavy coat walking along, every few steps sticking out a thumb in what seemed a particularly demoralized and pessimistic way. She had long blonde hair, natural by the look of it, reaching half-way down her back. Lewis thought of Sylvia Kaye. Poor kid. He passed the blonde just as she turned her head, and he blinked hard. What a world we live in! For the lovely blonde had a lovely beard and side-whiskers down to his chin. Interesting thought . . .

Morse had been unable to conceal his exasperation when Lewis had reported to him earlier and when, with ridiculously rapid certitude, he had established that the letter on which he had pinned his faith had been written neither on Crowther's personal typewriter nor on any of the brands of writing paper so carefully filched from Crowther's personal store. His one worry then had been to paper over the cracks of irregularity in police procedure, and it was for this reason that he had immediately dispatched Lewis to talk to Crowther. To the report of this inteview he listened with care, if without enthusiasm, when Lewis returned at 1.00 p.m.

'Not the happiest of mornings then, Sergeant.'

'No. I'd rather not do that sort of thing again, sir.'

Morse sympathized. 'I don't think we've done any harm though, have we, Lewis? I'm not worried so much about Crowther – he's hardly been above-board with us, has he? But Mrs Crowther . . . could have been tricky. Thanks, anyway.' He spoke with genuine feeling.

'Never mind, sir. At least we tried.' Lewis felt much better.

'What about a drink?' said Morse. The two men went off in lighter spirits.

It had occurred to neither of the policemen that women of the intelligence and experience of Mrs Margaret Crowther would do anything but automatically and unquestioningly accept the *bona fides* of any Tom, Dick, and Harry of a tradesman. Furthermore, Mrs Crowther had herself been a confidential secretary before she married Bernard; in fact the typewriter was hers and that very morning she herself had typed out two letters on the same machine, one addressed to her husband and one addressed to Inspector Morse, c/o Thames Valley Police HQ, Kidlington. The typewriter was in perfect order, she knew that; and she had seen the nervous man from Kimmons Typewriters as he had slid open the drawers of Bernard's desk. She wondered what he was looking for, but she didn't really care. In a gaunt, weary way she had even smiled as she closed the door behind him. She would fairly soon be ready to post the two letters. But she wanted to be sure.

Morse worked at his desk through most of the afternoon. The report on Crowther's car had come in, but appeared to signify little. One long blonde hair, heavily peroxided, was found on the floor behind the nearside driving seat, but that was about it. No physical traces whatsoever of the second girl. Several other reports, but again nothing that appeared to advance the progress of the investigation. He turned his attention to other matters. He had to appear the next morning in the Magistrates' Court: there were briefs and memorandums to read. His mind was grateful to have, for a change, some tangible data to assimilate and he worked through the material quite oblivious to the passage of time. When he looked at his watch at 5.00 p.m. he was surprised how swiftly the afternoon had gone by. Another day over – almost. New day tomorrow. For some reason he felt contented and he wondered to himself if that reason had anything to do with Wednesday and Sue Widdowson.

He rang Lewis, who was about to go home. Yes, of course he could come along. Perhaps he could just ring his long-suffering wife? She'd probably just got the chips in the pan. 'You say, Lewis, that Crowther has got another typewriter in his rooms in college. I think we ought to check. Well?'

'Anything you say, sir.'

'But you'd like to do it straight this time, wouldn't you?'

'I think that would be best, sir.'

'Anything you say, Lewis.'

Morse knew the Principal of Lonsdale College fairly well and he rang him up there and then. Lewis was a little surprised at Morse's request. The chief was doing it properly this time. He listened to the monologue. 'How many typewriters would there be? Yes. Yes. Including those . . . Yes. As many as that? But it could be done? Well that would be an enormous help, of course . . . You'd rather it that way? No, doesn't matter to me . . . By the end of the week? Good. Most grateful. Now listen carefully . . .'

Morse gave his instructions, iterated his thanks at inordinate length, and beamed at his sergeant when he finally cradled the phone. 'Co-operative chap that, Lewis.'

'Not much option, had he?'

'Perhaps not. But it will save us a lot of time and trouble.'

'You mean save *me* a lot of time and trouble.'

'Lewis, my friend, we're a team you and me, are we not?' Lewis nodded a grudging assent. 'By the end of the week we shall have evidence from every typewriter in Lonsdale College. What about that?'

'Including Crowther's?'

'Of course.'

'Wouldn't it have been a bit easier . . .'

'To fire straight at the bull's-eye? It would. But you said you wanted to do this in accordance with the great unprejudiced principles of English law, did you not? We haven't got a thing on Crowther. He's probably as innocent as my Aunt Freda.'

Since Lewis had never seen or heard of the said Aunt Freda he refrained from direct comment. 'Do you think Crowther's our man, sir?'

Morse stuck his thumb in the corner of his mouth. 'I don't know, Lewis. I just don't know.'

'I had a bit of an idea today, sir,' said Lewis after a pause. 'I saw what I thought was a girl and when I got close and she turned round she wasn't a she, she was a he.'

'You explain yourself very succinctly, Sergeant.'

'But you know what I mean.'

'Yes, I do. When we were boys we tried to look like boys; if you looked like a girl you were a cissy. Nowadays you've got young fellows with eye make-up and handbags. Makes you wonder.'

But Morse hadn't quite seen his point and Lewis filled in the picture. He was no ideas man, he'd always realized that, and felt great diffidence in putting his notion forward. 'You see, sir, I was just thinking. We know Mrs Jarman saw the two girls' (he needn't have gone on, but Morse held his peace) 'at the bus stop. She must have been right. She actually spoke to one of them and the other one was Sylvia Kaye. All right. The next thing is that the lorry driver, Baker, saw the girls being picked up at the other side of the roundabout by a man in a red car. But it was getting dark. He said they were two girls. *But he might have been wrong.* I could have sworn I saw a girl this morning – but I was wrong. Everybody has been dazzled by Sylvia – all the eyes were on her and no wonder. But what if the lorry driver had seen Sylvia with another person, and what if this other person looked like a girl but wasn't. *The other person could have been a man.* Remember, sir, the other girl Mrs Jarman saw was wearing slacks, and the descriptions we had from Baker fitted so well we thought they must be the same two people. But what if the other girl decided in the end not to hitchhike to Woodstock. What if she caught up with Sylvia, told her she wasn't going to bother to go to Woodstock after all, and what if Sylvia met up with some man, probably someone she knew anyway, who'd been waiting for a lift before she got there, and the two of them hitched together. I know you've probably thought of this anyway, sir' (Morse gave no indication either way – he hadn't) 'but I thought I ought to mention it. We've been trying to find the man who did this and I just thought he might have been in the car with Sylvia all along.'

'We've got Crowther's evidence you know, Sergeant,' said Morse slowly.

'I know, sir. I'd like to see that again if I could. As I remember it he didn't have *much* to say about his second passenger, did he?'

'No, that's true,' admitted Morse. 'And I can't help thinking he knows more than he's told us anyway.' He walked over to the filing cabinet, took from his files the statement of Bernard Crowther, read the first sheet, passed it over to Lewis, and read the second. When both men had finished, they looked at each other over the table.

'Well, sir?'

Morse read it out: '"The girl nearer to the road I saw clearly. She was an attractive girl with long fair hair, white blouse, short skirt and a coat over her arm. The other girl had walked on a few yards and had her back towards me; she seemed to be quite happy to leave the business of getting a lift to her companion. But she had darkish hair, I think, and if I remember correctly was a few inches taller than her friend . . ." What do you think?'

'Not very definite is it, sir?'

Morse searched for the other relevant passage: '"I think the girl sitting in the back spoke only once and that was to ask the time . . ." You may have got something, you know,' said Morse.

Lewis warmed to his theory. 'I've often heard, sir, that when a couple are hitching the girl shows a leg, as it were, and the man keeps out of the way. You know, suddenly shows himself when the car stops and it's too late for the driver to say no.'

'That didn't happen here though, Sergeant.'

'No. I know that, sir. But it fits a bit doesn't it: "seemed quite happy to leave the business of getting a lift to her companion".' Lewis felt he should quote his evidence, too.

'Mm. But if you're right, what happened to the other girl?'

'She could have gone home, sir. Could have gone anywhere.'

'But she wanted to go to Woodstock very badly, didn't she, according to Mrs Jarman.'

'She could have got to the bus stop.'

'The conductor doesn't remember her.'

'But when we asked him we were thinking of two girls, not one.'

'Mm. Might be worth checking again.'

'And another thing, sir.' The tide was coming in inexorably and was lapping already at the sand-castles of Morse's Grand Design.

'Yes?'

'I hope you don't mind me mentioning it, sir, but Crowther says that the other girl was a few inches taller than Sylvia.' Morse groaned, but Lewis continued, remorseless as the tide. 'Now Sylvia Kaye was 5' 9", if I remember it right. If the other girl was Jennifer Coleby she must have been wearing stilts, sir. She's only about 5' 6", isn't she – '

'But don't you see, Lewis? That's the sort of thing he *would* lie about. He's trying to put us off. He wants to protect this other girl.'

'I'm only trying to go on the evidence we've got, sir.'

Morse nodded. He thought seriously that he should take up schoolteaching – primary school would be about his level; spelling, he thought, the safest bet. Why hadn't he thought about that height business before? But he knew why. In the Grand Design it was Crowther who had been the guilty man.

And now the waves were curling perilously close to the last of the sand-castles; had already filled the moat and breached the rampart. It was 6.00 p.m., and Lewis's second batch of chips was getting cold.

Morse limped out of the building with Lewis, and the two stood talking by the sergeant's car for several minutes. Lewis felt rather like a pupil in Morse's putative primary school who had caught his master out in the spelling of a simple word, and he hesitated to mention a little thing that had been on his mind for several days. Should he keep it for tomorrow? But he knew that Morse had a busy day in front of him at the courts. He plunged in.

'You know the letter, sir, addressed to Jennifer Coleby?'

Morse knew it by heart. 'What about it?'

'Could there have been some fingerprints on the original copy?'

Morse heard the question and stared blankly into the middle distance. At last he shook his head sadly. 'Too late now.'

The primary school became a distinctly firmer prospect as the minutes ticked by. The sand-castle lurched forward and prepared to topple headlong. It was time someone else took over; he would see the Commissioner.

A police car stopped a few yards from him. 'Want some help, sir?'

'I'm all right, thanks.' Morse shook off his gloom. 'I'll be back in training next week. You'll see me in the first-team squad for the next home game.'

The constable laughed. 'Bit of a nuisance, though. Especially when you can't drive.'

Morse had almost forgotten his car. It had been locked up for over a week now. 'Constable, jump in the front with me, will you? It's high time I had a try.' He climbed into the driving seat, waggled his right foot over the brake and accelerator, pushed the foot with firmness on the brake-pedal, and decided he could cope. He started the engine, drove off round the yard, tested his ability to do the right things, came to a stop, got out and beamed like an orphan handed a teddy bear.

'Not bad, eh?' The constable helped Morse into the building and along to his office.

'You'll be able to use your car again tomorrow, won't you, sir?'

'I think I shall,' said Morse.

He sat down and thought of tomorrow. The Commissioner. In the afternoon would be best, perhaps. He rang the Commissioner's number, but there was no reply. He was seeing someone else, too, in the evening. He was looking forward to seeing Sue Widdowson – it was little use pretending he wasn't. But what a mess he'd made of it. The 'Bird and Baby' indeed! Why on earth hadn't he invited her to the Elizabeth or the Sorbonne or the Sheridan. And why hadn't he arranged to pick her up, like any civilized man would have done? Hang Jennifer Coleby! It wasn't too late, though, was it? She would be home by now. He looked at his watch: 6.30 p.m. The *Oxford Mail* lay on his desk and he scanned the entertainments page. *Hot Pants* and *Danish Blue*, he noticed, had been retained for a second week 'by public demand'. He could have taken her to the pictures, of course. Perhaps not to Studio 2, though. Restaurants. Not much there. Then he spotted it. *'Sheridan Dinner Dance*: double ticket – £6. 7.30–11.30 p.m. Bar. Dress informal.' He rang the Sheridan. Yes, a few double tickets still available, but he would have to collect them tonight. Could he ring back in a quarter of an hour or so? Yes. They would keep a double ticket for him.

Jennifer Coleby's telephone number was somewhere in the file and he soon found it. He thought over what he was to say. 'Miss Widdowson' – that would be best. He hoped that Sue would answer.

Brrr Brrr. He felt excited. Fool.

'Yes?' A young girl's voice, but whose? The line crackled.

'Is that Oxford 54385?'

'Yes, it is. Can I help you?' Morse's heart sank. It was unmistakably the cool, clear voice of Jennifer Coleby. Morse tried in some inchoate way to speak as if he wasn't Morse. 'I want to speak to Miss Widdowson if she's there, please.'

'Yes, she is. Who shall I say is calling?'

'Oh, tell her it's one of her old school friends,' replied the unMorselike voice.

'I'll get her straight away, Inspector Morse.'

'Sue! Su-ue!' he heard her shouting. 'One of your old school friends on the line!'

'Hello. Sue Widdowson here.'

'Hello.' Morse didn't know what to call himself. 'Morse here. I just wondered if you'd like to make it the Sheridan tomorrow night instead of going for a drink. There's a dinner-dance on and I've got tickets. What do you say?'

'That'd be lovely.' Morse thought he liked her voice. 'Absolutely lovely. Several of my friends are going. Should be great fun.'

Oh no! thought Morse. 'Not too many, I hope. I don't want to have to share you with a lot of others, you know.' He said it lightly with a heavy heart.

'Well, quite a few,' admitted Sue.

'Let's make it some other place, shall we? Do you know anywhere?'

'Oh, we can't do that. You've got the tickets anyway. We'll enjoy it – you'll see.'

Morse wondered if he would ever learn to tell the truth. 'All right. Now I can pick you up, if you like. Would that suit you?'

'Oh, yes please. Jenny was going to run me down in her car – but if you . . .'

'All right. I'll pick you up at 7.15.'

'7.15 it is then. Is it long dresses?' Morse didn't know. 'Never mind – I can easily find out.'

From one of your many friends, doubtless, thought Morse. 'Good. Looking forward to it.'

'Me, too.' She put down the receiver and Morse's own endearing adieu was left unspoken. Was he really looking forward to it? They were usually a bit of an anticlimax, these things. Still it would do him good. Or serve him right. He didn't much care. He'd have a decent meal anyway, and it would be good to hold a young girl in his arms again, tripping the light fantastic . . . Oh hell! He'd forgotten all about that. He was going out of his mind, the stupid, senseless fool that he was. He could no more invite the fair Miss Widdowson to share the delights of a dreamy waltz than invite a rabbi to a plate of pork. He hobbled to the enquiry desk. 'Get me a car, Sergeant.'

'There'll be one in a few minutes, sir. We've got to . . .'

'Get me a car now, Sergeant. And I mean *now*.' The last word resounded harshly through the open hall and several heads turned round. The desk sergeant reached for the phone. 'I'll be waiting outside.'

'Want some help, sir?' The desk sergeant was a kindly man, and had known the Inspector for several years. Morse waited by the desk. He was angry with himself and he had many reasons for feeling so. But why he should think he had a right to take things out on one of his old friends he could not imagine. He cursed his own selfishness and discourtesy.

'Yes, Sergeant, I could do with some help.' It had not been Morse's day.

CHAPTER SEVENTEEN
Wednesday, 13 October, a.m.

A freak storm struck the Oxford area in the early hours of Wednesday morning, demolishing chimneys, blowing down television aerials, and lifting roof-tiles in its path. The 7.00 a.m. news reported a trail of devastation in Kidlington, Oxon, where a Mrs Winifred Fisher had a narrow escape when the roof of a garage broke its moorings and crashed through an upstairs window. 'I just can't describe it,' she said. 'Terrifying.' The portable radio stood on the bedside table along with a telephone and an alarm clock which, at 6.50 a.m., had wakened Morse from a long, untroubled sleep.

He got out of bed when the news had finished and peered through the curtains. At least his own garage seemed intact. Funny, though, that the storm had not awakened him. Gradually the memory of yesterday's events filtered through his consciousness and settled like a heavy sediment at the bottom of his mind. Gone were the flights of angels that had guarded him in sleep and he sat on the edge of his bed fingering the rough stubble on his chin and wondering what this day would bring. Increasingly, as the case progressed, the graph of his moods was resembling a jagged mountain range, peaks and valleys, troughs and elations.

At a quarter to eight he was shaved, washed, and dressed, and feeling fresh and confident. He swilled out the dregs from his late-night cup of Horlicks, rinsed his late-night whisky glass, filled the kettle, and turned his attention to a major problem.

For the last few days he had worn, around his wounded foot, an outsize white plimsoll, loosely laced, and slit down the heel. It was time to get back to something normal. He was loth to appear in the court in such eccentric footwear and he could hardly believe that Miss Widdowson would be overjoyed with a semi-plimsolled escort at the dance. He had two pairs of shoes only and a dangerously low supply of suitable socks; and with such limited permutations of possibilities, the prospect of being presentably shod that day was somewhat remote. He slipped his faithful battered plimsoll back on, and decided to buy a large pair of shoes from M and S, his favourite store. It was going to be an expensive day. He drank a cup of tea, and looked out of the window. His dustbin lid was leaning against the front gate, with litter everywhere. He must remember to have a look at the roof-tiles . . .

In retrospect he thought he had got yesterday's events out of all perspective; he had been standing too close to the trees, and now he thought he saw again the same familiar wood, labyrinthine, certainly, as before – but still the same. He was feeling his old resilient self, or almost so. But the drastic course of action he had contemplated – what about that? He would have to consider things again; he had a more immediate problem on his mind. Where were his pen, his comb, and his wallet. Amazingly, and with deep relief, he found them all in the same heap on the bedroom mantelpiece.

The faithful old Jaguar was still there. It had been a good buy. Powerful, reliable, and 300 miles on a full tank. He had often thought of changing it but never had the heart. He eased himself into the narrow gap between the door of the driver's seat and the whitewashed wall of the garage. It was always a tricky manœuvre and he was getting no thinner. But it felt good to sit at the wheel again. He gave the old girl a bit more choke than usual – after all she had been standing idle for a week – and pressed the starter. Chutter . . . chutter . . . chutter . . . chutter. No. Bit more choke? But he mustn't flood her. Again. Chutter . . . chutter . . . chutter . . . chutter . . . chutter . . . Odd. He'd never had much difficulty before. Third time lucky, though. Chutter . . . chutter . . . chutter. Battery must be getting a bit low. Oh dear. Give her a minute or two's rest. Let her get her breath back. This time, then! Chutter . . . chutter . . . Bugger! Once more. Chutt . . . 'Just my bloody luck,' he said to himself. 'How the hell am I supposed to get about without . . .' He stopped and shivered involuntarily. A grey dawn was breaking in his mind and the purple mysteries of the morning were shot with the rays of the rising sun. 'Bliss was it in that dawn to be alive.' Wordsworth, wasn't it? It had been in *The Times* crossword last week. The waves were at last receding from the beach. The white crests of the breakers rolled ceaselessly and tirelessly towards the shore, but their strength was gone. He saw the Grand Design before him and the last little sand-castle had survived the mighty sea.

The manager of Barker's garage in Oxford was so impressed by Inspector Morse's courteous call upon his services that a new battery was on its way in ten minutes, and installed in fifteen. The clouds were high and white and the sun shone brightly. Open weather, as Jane Austen would have called it. Morse retrieved the dustbin lid, and meticulously gathered up all the litter from his garden.

The university city of Oxford was busy this morning, the third full day of the Michaelmas term. First-year undergraduates, with spankingly new college scarves tossed over their shoulders, eagerly explored the bookshops of the Broad, and a trifle self-consciously strode down the High into the crowded Cornmarket, into Woolworths and Marks and Spencer and thence, according to taste, into the nearest pubs and coffee shops. At 1.00 p.m. Morse was sitting on a chair in the self-service men's shoe department in the basement of M and S. He normally took size 8, but was now experimenting with patience and determination. Size 9 seemed of little use, and after considerable trafficking in stockinged feet between the show counter and his chosen chair, he plumped for size-10 black leather slip-ons. They seemed huge and were, of course, potentially useless in the long run. But who cared? He could wear two pairs of socks on his left foot. Which reminded him. He paid for the shoes, adjusted his plimsoll, much to the bewilderment of a large, morose-looking cashier, who looked as if she might wear size 10 herself, and proceeded to the hosiery counter where he purchased half a dozen gaudy pairs of light-weight socks. If he had been able, he would have walked out into Cornmarket with a light step. The car was functioning, the courts were finished, the case was flourishing.

Others, too, were making their purchases. Trade was thriving this morning, and not only in the large stores in the main streets in Oxford city centre. At about the same time that Morse, the megapode, tucked his purchases beneath his arm, one further swift, uncomplicated transaction was being effected in the run-down back street behind the Botley Road, and it could be argued that this time, at least, John Sanders had struck the better bargain.

CHAPTER EIGHTEEN
Wednesday, 13 October, p.m.

At Lonsdale College Wednesday, 13th was the first full guest-night of the Michaelmas term and Bernard Crowther left home a little earlier than usual. At 6.15 p.m. he knocked on Peter New-love's rooms and walked in, not waiting for a reply.

'That you, Bernard?'

'It's me.'

'Pour yourself a drink. Shan't be a minute.'

Bernard had passed the Lodge as he came in and had picked up three letters from his pigeon-hole. Two he opened raggedly and relegated cursorily to his jacket pocket. The third was marked 'Confidential', and contained a card 'From the Principal':

'The police, in the course of their investigations into the recent murder at Woodstock, are anxious to trace the provenance of a typed letter which has come into their possession and which they think may be material evidence in their enquiries. I have been asked by the police to see that every typewriter in the college is checked and I am asking all my colleagues to comply with this request. The Bursar has agreed to undertake this duty and it is my view, and also that of the Vice-Principal, that we must readily accede to this proper request. I have therefore informed Chief Inspector Morse, who is heading the murder enquiries, that we as a collegiate body are most anxious to co-operate in any way possible. The Bursar has an inventory of all college typewriters; but there may be private typewriters in the rooms of several Fellows, and I ask that information concerning them should be given to the Bursar immediately. Thank you for your help.'

'What's up, Bernard? Don't you want a drink?' Peter had come in from the bathroom and stood combing his thinning hair with a thinning comb.

'Have you had one of these?'

'I have indeed received a communication from our revered and reverend Principal, if that's what you mean.'

'What's it all about?'

'Don't know, dear boy. Mysterious though, isn't it?'

'When's the great investigation due?'

'Due? It's done. At least mine is. Little girl came in this afternoon – with the Bursar, of course. Typed out some cryptic message and then she was gone. Pity really. Lovely little thing. I must try to spend a bit more time in the Bursary.'

'I shan't be able to help much myself, I'm afraid. That bloody thing of mine was manufactured in the Middle Ages and hasn't had a ribbon in it for six months. I think it's what they call "seized-up", anyway.'

'Well, that's one suspect less, Bernard. Now are you going to have a drink or not?'

'Don't you think we shall have enough booze tonight?'

'No, dear boy, I don't.' Peter sat down and pulled on an expensive pair of heavy, brown brogues: size 10s, but not purchased from the self-service shoe department at Marks and Spencer.

'We've just got time for a quick one, I think.' It was almost 7.30 p.m. 'What would you like?'

'Dry sherry for me, please. I shan't be a minute. Must powder my nose.' She went off to the cloakroom. There were only a few people in the lounge bar and Morse, served without delay, took the drinks over to the corner of the room and sat down.

The Sheridan was the most fashionable of the Oxford hotels and most visiting stars of stage, screen, sport, and television found themselves booked in at this well-appointed, large, stone building just off the bottom of St Giles'. A striped canopy stretched out over the pavement and a flunkey stood his station beside the gleaming name-plate on the shallow steps leading down to the street from the revolving doors. Morse suspected that the management kept a red carpet rolled up somewhere on the premises. Not that it had been rolled out this evening; in fact he had been unable to find any parking space at all in the hotel's narrow yard and had been forced to park his car along St Giles'. It wasn't perhaps the best of starts, and they had said little to each other.

He watched her as she came back. She had parted with her coat and walked with enviable elegance towards him, her long deep-red velvet dress gently affirming the lines of her graceful body. And suddenly, sweetly his heart beat stronger, and their eyes met and she smiled. She sat beside him and he was aware again, as he had been as she sat beside him in the car, of the strange and subtle promise of her perfume.

'Cheers, Sue.'

'Cheers, Inspector.'

He didn't know what to do about this name trouble. He felt like an ageing schoolmaster meeting one of his old pupils and being rather embarrassed by the 'sirs' in every other sentence, and yet feeling it phoney to have it otherwise. He let the 'Inspectors' pass. Things could change, of course. Morse offered her a cigarette but she declined. As she sipped her sherry Morse noticed the long and delicately manicured fingers: no rings, no nail-polish. He asked her about her day's work and she told him. It was all a little strained. They finished their drinks and walked out of the lounge and up the stairs to the Evans Room, Sue lifting her dress slightly as she negotiated the stairs, and Morse trying to forget the tightness in his right shoe and frenziedly arching the left foot to prevent the shoe from falling off completely.

The room was arranged with subdued and delicate decorum: around a small, well-polished dance-floor tables were set at regular intervals, the silver cutlery gleaming on the white tablecloths and a red candle lit on each table, the blue and yellow flames tapering into a slimness, almost as exquisite, thought Morse, as Sue Widdowson herself. Several couples were already seated and it was sadly clear to Morse that some of her wretched friends were among them. A small band played some languorous melody that lingered in the mind and as they were shown to their table a young couple took the floor, blithely and obliviously, feeding deep upon each other's eyes.

'You've been here before?'

Sue nodded, and Morse followed the young couple with his eyes and decided not to give too free a rein to his imagination. A waiter came to them with the menu, and Morse welcomed the diversion.

'Do they throw in the wine?'

'We get a bottle between us.'

'Is that all?'

'Isn't that enough?'

'Well, it's a special occasion, isn't it?' Sue was noncommittal. 'What about a bottle of champagne?'

'You've got to drive me home, remember?'

'We could get a taxi.'

'What about your car?'

'Perhaps the police will pick it up.' She laughed and Morse saw her white teeth and the fullness of her lips. 'What do you say?'

'I'm in your hands, Inspector.' Would you were, he thought.

Several other couples were now dancing and Sue was watching them. 'You enjoy dancing?' Sue kept her eyes on the dancers and nodded. A young Adonis waved a hand in their direction.

'Hello Sue. All right?' Sue raised a hand in greeting.

'Who's that?' asked Morse aggressively.

'Doctor Eyres. He's one of the housemen at the Radcliffe.' She seemed almost hypnotized by the scene. But she turned back into Morse's orbit with the arrival of the champagne, and after a while the conversation took a freer course. Morse chattered as amiably and interestingly as he could and Sue seemed pleasantly relaxed. They ordered their meal, and Morse poured another glass of champagne. The band stopped; the couples on the floor clapped half-heartedly for a few seconds and retired to the perimeter tables. Dr Eyres and his heavily mascaraed young brunette made their way towards Morse's table, and Sue seemed glad to see them.

'Doctor Eyres, this is Inspector Morse.' The two men shook hands. 'And this is Sandra. Sandra, this is Inspector Morse.' The leaden-eyed Sandra, it transpired, was also a nurse and worked with Sue at the Radcliffe Infirmary. The band resumed its plangent strains.

'Mind if I had this dance with Sue, Inspector?'

'Of course not,' smiled Morse. You lousy, lecherous medico. Sandra sat down and looked at Morse with obvious interest in her eyes.

'I'm awfully sorry not to be able to ask you to dance,' he said, 'but I've had an accident with my foot. Nearly better, though.'

Sandra was sympathy itself. 'Oh dear. How did that happen?'

For the fiftieth time in the last seven days Morse repeated the attendant circumstances of his escapade. But his mind was all on Sue. As she escorted the houseman to the floor he thought of Coleridge:

> *The bride hath paced into the hall,*
> *Red as a rose is she.*

He watched them dance; he saw Sue's arms closely round her partner's neck, her body close to his; and then his cheek was brushing her hair, her head happily resting on his shoulder. Morse felt sick of a jealous dread. He turned his eyes away from the smooching couples. 'Do you know, I reckon I could just about cope with this dance myself,' he said. 'May I?' He took her hand, led her to the floor and, firmly placing his right arm round her waist, drew her towards him. Rapidly, however, he realized the extent of his own stupidity. His injured foot was working like a dream, but lacking the confidence to lift his other foot more than a centimetre off the dance-floor he was soon kicking his partner's toes with monotonous and ill-received regularity. Mercifully the dance was quickly over, and mumbling profuse apologies about his ill-educated feet Morse slopped his way back to the haven of his table. Sue was still talking in an animated way to Doctor Eyres, and after Sandra had rejoined them, the trio erupted into peals of laughter.

Ten minutes earlier Morse had anticipated that even the most succulent steak would taste tonight as dry as the Dead Sea apples, but he tucked into his meal with a will. At least he could eat. Even if he couldn't dance, even if he'd forgotten how middle-aged he'd now become, even if Sue was yearning for someone else, he could still eat. And jolly good it was. They said little and when something was said, as they drank their coffees, it came as a big surprise.

'Why did you ask me out, Inspector?'

Morse looked at her, the hair light-brown and lifted softly from her face, her face itself all freshness and delight, the cheeks now

faintly flushed with wine; and above all the magic of those wide
and doleful eyes. Had he asked her with any firm purpose? He
wasn't sure. He put his elbows on the table, rested his chin on his
clasped hands. 'Because I find you so very beautiful and I wanted
to be with you.'

Sue looked at him for several seconds, her eyes unblinking and
gentle. 'Do you mean that?' she asked quietly.

'I don't know if I meant it when I asked you. But I mean it now
– I think you know I do.' He spoke simply and calmly and he held
her eyes with his own as he spoke. He saw two splendid tears
forming on her lower lids and she reached across and laid her
hand upon his arm.

'Come and dance with me,' she whispered.

The floor was crowded and they did little more than sway
slowly to the sweet, low rhythm of the band. Sue leaned her head
lightly against his cheek and Morse felt with a wonderful joy the
moisture of her eyes. He wished the world would stop and that
this heavenly moment could be launched on the eternal seas. He
kissed her ear and said some awkward, loving things, and Sue
nuzzled deeper and deeper into his arms and pulled him even
more closely to her. They stood together as the music ended, and
Sue looked up at him. 'Can we go now, please. Somewhere on
our own.'

Morse remembered little of the next few minutes. He had
waited in a dream-like state beside the revolving doors and arm-
in-arm the two had slowly walked along St Giles' towards the car.

'I want to talk to you,' said Sue when they were sitting in the
car.

'I'm listening.'

'You know when you said that you might not have meant . . .
might not have meant what you said. Oh, I'm getting all muddled.
What I mean is – you did want to ask me something, didn't you?'

'Did I?' asked Morse.

'You know you did. About Jennifer. That's where we both came
in, wasn't it? You thought she'd got something to do with the
Woodstock murder . . .' Morse nodded. 'And you wanted to ask
me about her boy friends and that sort of thing.'

Morse sat silently in the darkness of his car. 'I'm not going to
ask you now, Sue. Don't worry.' He put his arm around her and
drew her towards him and tenderly kissed the softest, heavenliest
lips that ever the Almighty made. 'When can we meet again, Sue?'
As soon as he had spoken he knew that something was wrong.

He felt her body tauten; she moved away from him, felt for her handkerchief and blew her nose. She was on the verge of tears. 'No,' she said, 'we can't.'

Morse felt a hurt that he had never known before, and his voice was strained and unbelieving. 'But why? Why? Of course we can meet again, Sue.'

'We can't.' Her voice for the moment seemed matter-of-fact and final. 'We can't meet again, Inspector, because . . . because I'm engaged to be married.' She just managed to blurt out the last word before burying her head on Morse's shoulder and bursting into anguished tears. Morse kept his arm tightly around her and listened with unfathomable sadness to her convulsive sobs. The front window had steamed over with their breath and Morse perfunctorily wiped away the moisture with the back of his right hand. Outside he saw the massive outer wall of St John's College. It was only 10.00 p.m. and a group of undergraduates were laughing gaily outside the Porter's Lodge. Morse knew it well. He'd been an undergraduate there himself; but that was twenty years ago and life since then had somehow passed him by.

They drove in silence up to North Oxford and Morse pulled up the Jaguar directly in front of Sue's front door. As he did so the door opened and Jennifer Coleby came out with her car-keys in her hand, and walked towards them.

'Hello, Sue. You're home early, aren't you?'

Sue wound the window down. 'We didn't want to get stopped for drinking and driving.'

'Are you coming in for a coffee?' asked Jennifer. The question was directed obliquely through the car window to Morse.

'No. I think I'd better get home.'

'See you in a minute then,' said Jennifer to Sue. 'Just going to put the car away.' She climbed into a smart little Fiat and drove smoothly off to her rented garage in the next street.

'Good little cars, Fiats,' said Morse.

'No better than English cars, are they?' asked Sue. She was bravely trying not to make a fool of herself again.

'Very reliable, I'm told. And even if something does go wrong, there's a good agent pretty near, isn't there?' Morse hoped he sounded casual enough, but he didn't really care.

'Yes, right on the doorstep, really.'

'I've always found Barkers pretty good myself.'

'She does, too,' said Sue.

'Well, I suppose I'd better go.'

'Are you sure you won't come in for some coffee?'

'Yes. I'm quite sure.'

Sue took his hand and held it lightly in her own. 'You know I shall cry myself to sleep, don't you?'

'Don't say that.' He didn't want to be hurt any more.

'I wish you were going to sleep with me,' she whispered.

'I wish you were going to sleep with me for ever, Sue.'

They said no more. Sue got out of the car, waved as the Jaguar slowly moved off, and turned towards the front door, her face blinded with tears.

Morse drove to Kidlington with a heavy heart. He thought of the first time he had seen Miss Dark-eyes and now he thought of the last. Would things had been otherwise! He thought of the saddest line of poetry he had ever read:

Not a line of her writing have I, not a thread of her hair

and felt no better for the thought. He didn't want to go home; he had never realized before how lonely he had become. He stopped at the White Horse, ordered a double whisky, and sat down in an empty corner. She hadn't even asked his name . . . He thought of Doctor Eyres and his dark-eyed Sandra and supposed, without a hint of envy, that they were probably getting into bed by now. He thought of Bernard Crowther and doubted if his illicit liaisons with his girl in Blenheim Park were tinged with half the sadness that he himself now felt. He thought of Sue and her fiancé and hoped he was a good fellow. He bought another double whisky and, maudlin and fuddled, left soon after the landlord shouted time.

He put away the car with exaggerated care and heard the phone ringing before he could open the door. His heart raced. He rushed into the hall just as the phone stopped. Was it her? Was it Sue? He could always ring back. What was the number? He didn't know. It was in his files at Police HQ. He could ring there. He picked up the phone – and put it down. She'd probably been ringing all the time he'd been sitting in the White Horse. Blast it. Ring again, Sue. Just to let me hear you speak. Ring again, Sue. But the telephone rang no more that night.

CHAPTER NINETEEN

Thursday, 14 October

Bernard Crowther had a hangover on Thursday morning. He would be lecturing in the Schools at 11.00 a.m. and he contemplated his notes on 'Influences on Milton's Poetical Style' with a growing sense of apprehension. Margaret had brought him a cup of hot black coffee at a quarter to nine; she always knew – and usually said so. She had been up since half-past six, cooked the children's breakfast, washed some shirts and blouses, made the beds, hoovered the bedrooms, and she was now putting on her coat in the hall. She put her head round the door. 'You all right?' How Bernard hated the reminder!

'Fine.'

'Do you want anything from town – Milk of Magnesia tablets?' They seemed perpetually in a state of eruptive belligerence, staring at each other over a long-disputed frontier. Margaret! Margaret! He wished he could talk to her.

'No. No thanks. Look, Margaret, I've got to go down myself pretty soon. Can you wait a few minutes?'

'No. Must be off. You home for lunch?'

What was the point? 'No. I'll have a bite to eat in college.' He heard the front door bang and watched her as she walked quickly to the end of the road and round the corner and out of sight. He went to the kitchen, filled a glass with cold water, and dropped in two tablets of soluble Disprin.

Morse and Lewis conferred from nine to ten that morning. There were several loose ends to tie up and several interesting trails to follow. At least, that's how Morse explained things to Lewis. After Lewis had left him, he had a call from a young reporter on the *Oxford Mail*, as a result of which a brief paragraph would appear in the evening edition. Routine answers. He couldn't tell anyone much, but he tried to sound as confident as he could. It was good for morale.

He got the Kaye file and spent the next hour reading the documents in the case. At 11.00 a.m. he put the file away, reached for the Oxford and District telephone directory, looked under the Cs for the number he wanted, and rang the manager of Chalkley and Sons, Botley Road. He was unlucky. John Sanders had not come in that morning; his mother had phoned – bad cold or something.

'What's your opinion of him?' asked Morse.

'He's all right. Quiet, little bit surly, perhaps. But most of them are these days. Works well enough, I think.'

'Well, I'm sorry to have bothered you. I wanted a quick word with him, that's all.'

'About this murder at Woodstock?'

'Yes. He found the girl, you know.'

'Yes. I read about it and of course everyone tried to talk to him about it.'

'Did he have much to say?'

'Not really. Didn't seem to want to talk. Understandable, I suppose.'

'Yes. Well, thanks once again.'

'You're very welcome. Do you want his home address?'

'No thanks. I've got it here.'

Lewis was rather more fortunate. Mrs Jarman was at home, dusting the stairs.

'But I don't understand, Sergeant. I'm *sure* they were both girls.'

Lewis nodded. 'Just checking up on one or two things.'

'But I spoke to one of them, as you know, and the other poor girl – well, you know . . . And I thought they were *about* the same height; but it's ever so difficult to remember you know . . .' Yes, Lewis knew. He left her to dust the stairs.

He found the bus conductor drinking coffee in the canteen at Gloucester Green.

'*One* girl getting on the bus? But you said *two* before.'

'Yes, I know. But we've got an idea that perhaps only one got on.'

'Sorry. I can't remember. I am sorry, honest – but it's a long time ago now.'

'Yes. Don't worry. As I said – just an idea. If you do happen to think of anything . . .'

'Of course.'

George Baker was digging his garden. 'Hullo mate. I seen you before.'

'Sergeant Lewis – Thames Valley Police.'

'Ah. Course. Wha' can a do forya?'

Lewis explained his visit but George's answer was only marginally less discouraging than those of the others.

'We-ell, I s'pose it *could* a been a fella, bu' swipe me mate, I could a swore as both of 'em was women.'

Memories were fading and the case was growing stale. Lewis went home for lunch.

At 2.00 p.m. he was ushered into the office of the car service manager of Barkers Garage on the Banbury Road, where he spent more than an hour working his way methodically through hundreds of carbon copies of work-sheets, customers' invoices, booking-ledgers, and other sundry records of car repairs for the weeks beginning September 20 and 27. He found nothing. He spent a further hour going back to the beginning of September, increasingly conscious that his task was futile. Miss Jennifer Coleby, although she had an account with Barkers, had not brought in her car for any repairs or service since July. She had bought the car new from the garage over three years ago; HP nearly finished; no trouble with payments; no serious mechanical faults. 6,000 service on 14 July, with a few oddments put right. £13.55. Bill paid July 30.

Lewis was disappointed if not surprised. Morse seemed to have a bee in his bonnet about this Coleby woman. Perhaps this would put him off for good? But he doubted it. He walked over the road to the newsagents and bought the evening newspaper. A caption near the bottom right-hand corner of the front page caught his eye:

WOODSTOCK KILLING
BREAKTHROUGH NEAR

Following intensive activity, police are quietly confident that the killer of Sylvia Kaye, found raped and murdered at the Black Prince, Woodstock, on the night of 29 September will soon be found. Chief Inspector Morse of the Thames Valley HQ, who is heading the murder inquiry, said today that several key witnesses had already come forward and he considered that it would only be a matter of time before the guilty party was brought to justice.

Lewis thought it must be a hoax.

The confident head of the murder inquiry, if ever invited to take his eight discs to a desert island, would have answered 'Committees' to the inevitable question about what he would be most glad to have got away from. The meeting called for this Thursday afternoon to consider pensions, promotions, and appointments stretched on and on like an arid desert. His only contribution throughout was a word of commendation for Constable McPherson. It seemed a justifiable excuse for contravening his customary and caustic taciturnity. The meeting finally broke up at five minutes past five, when he yawned his way back to his office and found Lewis reading the prospects for Oxford United's visit to Blackpool the following Saturday.

'Seen this, sir?' Lewis handed him the newspaper and pointed to the caption portending judgement day for the Woodstock killer.

Morse read the item with weary composure. 'They do twist things a bit, these reporters, don't they?'

Sue Widdowson's day, too, dragged drearily by. She'd wanted desperately to talk to Morse again last night. Who knows what she might have said? Was his phone out of order? But in the cold light of morning she had realized how foolish it would have been. David was coming on Saturday for the weekend, and she would be meeting him at the station at the usual time. Dear David. She had received another letter that morning. He was so nice and she liked him so very much. But . . . No! She had just *got* to stop thinking of Morse. It had been almost impossible. Sandra had been full of questions and Doctor Eyres had patted her bottom far too intimately, and she was lousily, hopelessly miserable.

Mrs Amy Sanders was worried about her son. He had seemed listless and off-colour for a week or so now. In the past he had taken the odd day or two off work, and more than once she had had to lay it on a bit thick in describing to Messrs Chalkley the symptoms of some fictitious malady which had temporarily stricken her dear boy. But today she was genuinely concerned. John had been sick twice during the night and was lying shivering and sweating when she had called him at 7.00 a.m. He had eaten nothing all day and, against her son's wishes, she had rung the doctor's surgery at 5.00 p.m. No, she had not thought it urgent, but would be most grateful if the doctor could call some time.

The bell rang at 7.30 p.m. and Mrs Sanders opened the front door to find a man she had never seen before. Still, the doctors these days were always changing around.

'Does Mr John Sanders live here?'

'Yes. Come in, Doctor. I'm ever so glad you could call.'

'I'm not a doctor, I'm afraid. I'm a Police Inspector.'

*

The landlord of the Bell at Chipping Norton took the booking himself at 8.30 p.m. He consulted the register and picked up the phone again.

'For tomorrow night and Saturday night, you said?'

'Yes.'

'I think we can do that all right, sir. Double room. Do you want a private bathroom?'

'That would be nice. And a double bed if you've got one. We never seem to sleep well in these twin beds.'

'Yes. We can do that.'

'I'm afraid I shan't have time to confirm it in writing.'

'Oh don't worry about that, sir. If you could just let me have your name and address.'

'Mr and Mrs John Brown, Hill Top, Eaglesfield (all one word), Bristol.'

'I've got that.'

'Good. My wife and I look forward to seeing you. We should be there about five.'

'We hope you'll enjoy your stay, sir.'

The landlord put down the phone and wrote the names of Mr and Mrs J. Brown in the booking register. His wife had once added up the number of John Browns booked into the Bell: in one month alone there were seven. But it wasn't his job to worry too much about that. Anyway, the man had sounded most polite and well educated. Nice voice, too: West Countryish – rather like his own. And there must be one or two quite genuine John Browns somewhere.

CHAPTER TWENTY
Friday, 15 October, a.m.

Morse woke up late on Friday morning. *The Times* was already on the floor in the hall and one letter was protruding precariously through the letter box. It was a bill from Barkers – £9.25. He stuck it, with several of its fellows, behind the clock on the mantelpiece.

The car purred into life at the first gentle touch. He had the sticks in the back of the car and decided to run down to the Radcliffe Infirmary before going to the office. As he joined the patiently crawling, never-ending line of traffic in the Woodstock Road, he debated his course of action. He could see her quite by chance, of course – as he had last time; or he could ask for her. But would she want that? He longed just to *see* her again and, dammit!, she would be there. What could be more natural? He had dreamed about Sue the previous night, but in a vague, elusive sort of way which had left her standing in the forecourt of his mind. *Had* it been her on the phone on Wednesday night?

He turned off, across the traffic, into the yard of the Radcliffe, stopped on double yellow lines, collared the nearest porter, gave him the sticks and the promissory note of the bearer to return the same, and told him to see to it. Police!

The road was clear as he left Oxford and he cursed himself savagely every other minute. He should have gone in – stupid fool. He knew deep down he wasn't a stupid fool, but it didn't help much.

Lewis was waiting for him. 'Well, what's the programme, sir?'

'I thought we'd take a gentle bus ride a little later, Lewis.' Ah well. His not to reason why. 'Yes. I thought we'd go to Woodstock on the bus together. What about that?'

'Has the car conked out again?'

'No. Going like a dream. So it should. Had a bill for the bloody battery this morning. Guess how much?'

'Six, seven pounds.'

'Nine pounds twenty-five!'

Lewis screwed up his nose. 'Cheaper if you'd gone to the tyre and battery people up in Headington. They don't charge for any labour. I've always found them very good.'

'You sound as if you're always having car trouble.'

'Not really. Had a few punctures lately, though.'

'Can't you change a tyre yourself?'

'Well yes. Course I can. I'm not an old woman you know, but you've got to have a spare.'

Morse wasn't listening. He felt the familiar tingle of the blood freezing in his arms. 'You're a genius, Sergeant. Pass me the telephone directory. Consult the Yellow Pages. Here we are – only two numbers. Which shall we try first?'

'What about the first one, sir?'

A few seconds later Morse was speaking to Cowley Tyre and Battery Services. 'I want to speak to the boss of the place. It's urgent. Police here.' He winked at Lewis. 'Ah, hullo. Chief Inspector Morse here. Thames Valley . . . No, no. Nothing like that . . . Now, I want you to look up your records for the week beginning 27 September . . . Yes. I want to know if you supplied a battery or mended a puncture for a Miss Jennifer Coleby.

C-O-L-E-B-Y. Yes. It might have been any day – probably Tuesday or Wednesday. You'll ring me back? Get on with it straight away, please. It's most urgent. Good. You've got my number? Good. Cheers.' He rang the second number and repeated the patter. Lewis was turning over the Sylvia Kaye file that lay open on Morse's desk. He studied the photographs – large, glossy, black and white photographs with amazingly clear delineation. He looked again at the shots of Sylvia Kaye as she lay that night in the yard of the Black Prince. She'd been really something, he thought. The white blouse had been torn sharply on the left-hand side, and only the bottom of the four buttons remained fastened. The left breast was fully revealed and Lewis was strongly reminded of the provocative poses of the models in the girlie magazines. It could almost have been an erotic experience – looking through those pictures; but Lewis remembered the back of the blonde head and the cruelly shattered skull. He thought of his own darling daughter – thirteen now; she was getting a nice little figure . . . God, what a world to bring up children in. He hoped and prayed that she would be all right, and he felt a deep and burning need to find the man who did all that to Sylvia Kaye.

Morse had finished.

'Can you put me in the picture, sir?' asked Lewis.

Morse sat back and thought for a few minutes. 'I suppose I ought to have told you before, Lewis. But I couldn't be sure – well, can't be sure now – about one or two things. Pretty well from the beginning I thought I had a good idea of the general picture. I thought it was like this. Two girls want a lift to Woodstock and we've got some fairly substantial evidence that they *were* picked up – *both* of them.' Lewis nodded. 'Now neither the driver nor the other girl came forward. The question I asked myself was "why?". Why were both these people anxious to keep quiet? There were pretty obvious reasons why *one* of them should keep his mouth shut. But why both? It seemed most improbable to me that the pair of them could be partners in crime. So. What are we left with? One very strong possibility, as I saw it, was that they knew each other. But that didn't seem quite good enough, somehow. Most people don't withhold evidence, certainly don't tell complicated lies, just because they know each other. But what if they have, between them, some guilty reason for wanting to keep things very quiet indeed? And what if such a guilty reason is the fact that they know each other rather *too* well? What if they are – not to put too fine a point on things – having an affair with each other? The situation's not so good for them, is it? With a murder in the background – not so good at all.' Lewis wished he'd get on with it. 'But let's go back a bit. On the face of it our evidence suggested from the word go that the encounter between the two girls and the driver of the car was pure chance: Mrs Jarman's evidence is perfectly clear on that point. Now we have discovered, after a good deal of unnecessary trouble, who the driver of the red car was: Crowther. In his evidence he admits that he is having an affair with another woman and that the venue for these extramarital excursions is Blenheim Park. Furthermore, again on his own evidence, he was going to see his lady-love on the night of Wednesday, 29 September. Now at this point I took a leap in the dark. What if the lady-love was one of the girls he picked up?'

'But . . .' began Lewis.

'Don't interrupt, Lewis. Now, was the lady-love Sylvia Kaye? I don't think so. We know that Mr John Sanders had a date, however vague, with Sylvia on the 29th. It doesn't prove things one way or the other, but Sylvia is the less likely choice of the two. So. We're left with our other passenger – Miss, or Mrs X. It is clear from Mrs Jarman's evidence that Miss X seemed anxious and excited, and I think no one gets too anxious and excited about going to Woodstock unless that person has a date, and an important date at that, and not very much time to spare. Crowther said an hour or so at the most, remember?'

'But . . .' He thought better of it.

'We also learned from what Mrs Jarman said that Sylvia knew the other girl. There was that business of having a giggle about it in the morning. So, we try the place where Sylvia works and we find an extraordinary, quite inexplicable letter written to Miss Jennifer Coleby, who has become my odds-on favourite for the Miss X title. I agree that the evidence of the letter is not conclusive; worth following up though. She's a clever girl, our Jennifer. She has two spanners to throw in the works. First, she seems to have been at a pub this side of Woodstock instead of in Blenheim Park; second – and this really worried me and still does – why does she have to bus to Woodstock, or hitchhike, if she's got a car? Which, as we know, she has. It seemed a fatal objection. But is it? *My* car wouldn't start on Wednesday morning because the battery was flat. You said that *you* had a few punctures recently and you said you could mend them. You said you were not an old woman. Now Jennifer Coleby is not an old woman – but *she's a woman*. What if she discovered that her car wouldn't start? What would she do? Ring up her garage. That was pretty obvious and hence your visit to Barkers, where you drew a blank. I thought I saw the light, though, this morning. I had a bill for my car-battery and you mentioned the tyre and battery people. The real question then is *when* did Jennifer discover her car was out of order? Surely not before she got back from work, at about 5.30 p.m. Now not many garages these days are going to do much at that time; the staff has all gone. But your little tyre and battery men don't work, methinks, to union hours, and they are worth trying. I must assume that Jennifer could get no one to see to her car that night – not because they couldn't do it, but because they *couldn't do it in time*. She may not have discovered the trouble until about 6.15 or 6.30 p.m. But I think she tried to get something done – and failed. Well, what's she to do? Naturally, she can get a bus. She's never had to bus before, but she's seen the Woodstock buses often enough and that's why I believe it was Jennifer who was seen at Fare Stage 5 on the night Sylvia was murdered. She meets an impatient fellow-traveller, Sylvia, and the two of them decide to hitchhike. They walk past the roundabout and a car stops: Crowther's car. It's hardly a coincidence, is it? He's got to get to Woodstock, too, and he's bound to be going there at roughly the same time as Jennifer. Whether he knew it was her – it was getting fairly dark – I just don't know. I suspect he did.' Morse stopped.

'And what happened then, do you think, sir?'

'Crowther has told us what happened for the next few miles.'

'Do you believe him?'

Morse sat thoughtfully and didn't answer immediately. The phone rang. 'No,' said Morse, 'I don't believe him.' Lewis watched the Inspector. He could not hear what was being said on the other end of the line. Morse listened impassively.

'Thank you very much,' he said finally. 'What time would be convenient? All right. Thank you.' He put down the phone, and Lewis looked at him expectantly.

'Well, sir?'

'I told you Lewis. You're a genius.'

'Her car *was* out of order?'

Morse nodded. 'Miss Jennifer Coleby rang the Cowley Tyre and Battery Co. at 6.15 p.m. on the evening of Wednesday, 29 September. She said it was urgent – a very flat front tyre. They couldn't get there until sevenish and she said that was too late.'

'We're making headway, sir.'

'We are, indeed. Now what about our bus ride?'

*

The two men caught the 11.35 4A to Woodstock. It was half empty and they sat in the front seat on the upper deck. Morse was silent and Lewis mulled over the strange developments in the case. The bus made good speed and stopped only four times before reaching Woodstock. At the third of these stops Morse gave his sergeant a dig in the ribs and Lewis looked out to see where they were. The bus had pulled into a shallow lay-by just outside Begbroke, at a large, thatched house with its garden crowded with tables and chairs set under brightly striped umbrellas; he bent his head down to the bottom of the side window to see the name of the public house and read the two words Golden Rose.

'Interesting?' said Morse.

'Very,' replied Lewis. He thought he might as well say something.

They alighted at Woodstock and Morse led the way. 'Ready for a pint, Sergeant?'

They walked into the cocktail bar of the Black Prince. 'Good morning, Mrs McFee. You won't remember me, I suppose?'

'I remember you very well, Inspector.'

'What a memory,' said Morse.

'What can I get for you, gentlemen?' She was clearly not amused.

'Two pints of best bitter, please.'

'Official business?' Her dislike of Morse's manner was not quite enough to stifle her natural curiosity.

'No, no. Just a friendly visit to look at you again.' He's in good spirits this morning, thought Lewis.

'I see from the paper that you're hoping . . .' she fumbled for the words.

'We're making progress, aren't we, Sergeant?'

'Oh yes,' said Lewis. After all, he was the other half of those intensive enquiries.

'Don't they ever give you a few hours off?' asked Morse.

'Oh, they're very good really.' She was softening a little towards him; it was always nice to be reminded how hard she worked. 'As a matter of fact I've got tonight and all of Saturday and Sunday off.'

'Where shall we go?' asked Morse.

The hostess smiled professionally. 'Where do you suggest, Inspector?' Good for you, my girl, thought Lewis.

Morse asked for the menu and studied it in some detail.

'What's the food like here?' asked Morse.

'Why don't you try it?'

Morse appeared to consider the possibility but asked instead if there was a good fish-and-chip shop near by. There wasn't. Several customers had come in and the policemen left by the side entrance and walked into the yard. To their right, a car was sitting up on its haunches, with each of the front wheels off. Underneath the car, suitably protected from the grease and oil, and wielding a formidable wrench, lay the landlord of the Black Prince, and by his side the folding tool-box which had so recently housed a long and heavy tyre-spanner.

Unnoticed by Morse and Lewis as they left the premises, a young man had entered the cocktail bar and ordered a tonic water. Mr John Sanders had apparently made a sufficient recovery from his bouts of shivery fever to join once more in the social life of Woodstock, if not to resume his duties with Messrs Chalkley and Sons.

On the bus journey back Morse was deeply engrossed in a Midland Counties bus timetable and a map of North Oxford. Occasionally he looked at his watch and made a brief entry in a notebook. Lewis felt hungry. It had been a pity about the fish-and-chip shop.

CHAPTER TWENTY-ONE
Friday, 15 October, p.m.

A bulky envelope marked 'Confidential' arrived on Morse's desk at 3.30 that afternoon – 'from the Principal'. He had done a very careful and thorough job – that was quite clear. There were ninety-three typewriters, it appeared, in Lonsdale College. Most of them belonged to the college and had found their various ways into the rooms of the fellows; over twenty were the personal property of members of the college. Ninety-three sheets of paper, each numbered, were neatly arranged beneath a bull-dog clip. Two further sheets, stapled together, provided the key to the typewritten specimens, and, appropriately enough, the Principal's typewriter was given the No. 1 designation. Morse riffled the sheets. It was going to be a bigger job than he'd thought, and he rang the laboratory boys. He learned it would take an hour or so.

Lewis had spent most of the afternoon typing his reports and did not return to Morse's office until 4.15 p.m.

'You hoping to have the weekend off, Lewis?'

'Not if there's something you want me for, sir.'

'I'm afraid we have rather a lot to do. I think it's time we had a little confrontation, don't you?'

'Confrontation?'

'Yes. A gentle little confrontation between a certain Miss Coleby and a certain Mr Crowther. What do you think?'

'Might clear the air a bit.'

'Ye-es. Do you think the old establishment could run to four clean cups of coffee in the morning?'

'You want me to join you?'

'We're a team, Lewis, my boy. I've told you that before.' Morse rang Town and Gown and asked for Mr Palmer.

'Hew shell I see is calling?' It was the prim little Judith.

'Mister Plod,' said Morse.

'Howld on, please, Mr Plod . . . you're threw.'

'I didn't quite catch your name, sir? Palmer here.'

'Morse. Inspector Morse.'

'Oh, hullo, Inspector.' Stupid girl!

'I want to have a word with Miss Coleby. Confidential. I wonder if . . .'

Palmer interrupted him. 'I'm awfully sorry, Inspector. She's not here this afternoon. She wanted to spend a long weekend in London and, well . . . we do occasionally show a little er flexibility, you know. It sometimes helps the er the smooth running . . .'

'London, you say?'

'Yes. She said she was going to spend the weekend with some friends. She caught the lunch-time train.'

'Did she leave an address?'

'I'm sorry. I don't think she did. I could try to er . . .'

'No. Don't bother.'

'Can I take a message?'

'No. I'll get in touch with her when she comes back.' Perhaps he could see Sue again . . . 'When will she be back, by the way?'

'I don't really know. Sunday evening I should think.'

'All right. Well, thank you.'

'Sorry I couldn't be . . .'

'Not your fault.' Morse put down the phone with less than average courtesy.

'One of our birds has flown, Lewis.' He turned his attention to Bernard Crowther and decided to try the college first.

'Porter's Lodge.'

'Can you put me through to Mr Crowther's rooms, please?'

'Just a minute, sir.' Morse drummed the table with the fingers of his left hand. Come on!

'Are you there, sir?'

'Yes. I'm still here.'

'No reply, I'm afraid, sir.'

'Is he in college this afternoon?'

'I saw him coming in this morning, sir. Just a minute.' Three minutes later Morse was wondering if the wretched porter had taken a gentle stroll around the quad.

'Are you there, sir?'

'Yes, I'm still here.'

'He's away somewhere, sir, for the weekend. It's a conference of some sort.'

'Do you know when he's due back?'

'Sorry, sir. Shall I put you through to the college office?'

'No, don't bother. I'll ring him later.'

'Thank you, sir.'

Morse held the phone in his hands for a few seconds and finally put it down with the greatest circumspection. 'I wonder. I wonder . . .' He was lost in thought.

'It seems *both* of our birds have flown, sir.'

'I wonder if the conference is being held in London.'

'You don't think . . .'

'I don't know what to think,' said Morse.

Nor was he sure what to think when half an hour later the findings of the laboratory were phoned through. Lewis watched the Inspector's curious reactions.

'Are you sure . . . ? You're quite sure . . . ? Yes. Well, many thanks. You'll bring them over? Good. Thank you.'

'Well, Lewis, you're in for a surprise.'

'About the note?'

'Yes. About the note – the note someone wrote to the young lady who is now visiting "some friends" in London. They say they know whose typewriter it was.'

'And whose was it?'

'That's what's puzzling me. We've never heard of him before! He's a Mr Peter Newlove.'

'And who's Mr Peter Newlove?'

'It's time we found out.' He rang Lonsdale College for the second time that afternoon and found the same slow-motion porter presiding over the Lodge.

'Mr Newlove, sir? No, I'm afraid he's not in college. Just let me check in the book . . . No, sir. He's away till Monday. Can I take a message? No? All right. Goodbye, sir.'

'Well, that's that,' said Morse. '*All* our birds have flown. And I don't see much point in staying here, do you?' Lewis didn't.

'Let's just tidy up all this mess,' said Morse.

Lewis gathered together the papers on his side of the table – the photographs of Sylvia Kaye and the carefully drawn diagrams of the yard at the Black Prince, annotated in think spidery writing with details of everything found therein. He looked again at the close-ups of the murdered girl lying there, and felt a paternally protective urge to cover the harsh nakedness of her beautiful body.

'I'd like to get the bastard who did this,' he muttered.

'What's that?' Morse took the photographs from him.

'He must be a sex maniac, don't you think, sir? Tearing off her clothes like that and leaving her for anyone and everyone to see. God, I wish I knew who he was!'

'Oh, I don't think there's much difficulty about that,' said Morse.

Lewis looked at him incredulously. 'You mean you *know*?'

Morse nodded slowly, and locked away the file on Sylvia Kaye.

PART THREE

Search for a killer

CHAPTER TWENTY-TWO
Sunday, 17 October

Sue saw David off on the Birmingham train at 7.13 on Sunday evening. She told him what a marvellous weekend it had been – and so it had. On Saturday they had gone to the cinema, had a delicious Chinese meal, and generally luxuriated in being together. Most of Sunday they had spent in Headington at the home of David's parents, pleasant, warm-hearted people, sensible enough to leave the two young love-birds alone for the greater part of the day. They hoped to marry some time next autumn, after David had finished his post-graduate year of research in metallurgy at the University of Warwick. He was hopeful (for he had taken a 'first') of getting a lectureship somewhere, and Sue encouraged him: she would rather be married to a lecturer than to an industrial chemist, or whatever metallurgists became. She thought that was the only thing about David of which she couldn't wholeheartedly approve – his choice of metallurgy. It had something to do with her own schooldays and the distaste she'd always felt amid the smells and silver slivers of the metalwork shop. There was something, too, about the *hands* of people who worked with metal: a sort of ingrained griminess, however patiently they were scrubbed.

The train lingered at Oxford station for several minutes and Sue kissed David fully and freely as he leaned from the window of an empty carriage.

'It's been lovely seeing you again, darling,' said David.

'Super.'

'You enjoyed it, didn't you?'

'Of course I did.' She laughed gaily. 'Why on earth did you ask that?'

David smiled. 'It's just nice to know, that's all.' They kissed again, and Sue walked along with him for a few yards as the train pulled out.

'See you in a fortnight. Don't forget to write.'

'I won't,' said Sue. 'Bye.' She waved until the train had left the platform and she watched it curving its way towards the north, the red light on the rear coach bobbing and winking in the gathering darkness.

She walked slowly back down the platform, along the subway and up to the barrier on the other side. She gave in her platform-ticket and made her way to Carfax. Here she had to wait for half an hour before a number 2 bus came along, and it was eight o'clock before she got off in North Oxford. She crossed the road and with her head down walked along Charlton Road and thought about the last two days. She could never have told David about Wednesday night. There was nothing to tell anyway, was there? Just a minor peccadillo. She supposed most people had their foolish moments – even engaged people – and there were some things that just could not be told. Not that David would have been jealous; he wasn't that sort, at all – mild, equable, balanced David. Perhaps she wouldn't mind if he *were* a bit jealous. But she knew, or thought she knew, that he wasn't; she could spot jealousy a mile off. She thought of Morse. She really had been very naughty at the Sheridan with Doctor Eyres, and Morse had been jealous – rabidly, furiously jealous. She'd secretly enjoyed making him jealous until . . . Well, she wasn't going to think of him any more . . . But she'd never cried over David . . . She wondered if Morse believed her when she said she would be crying herself to sleep on Wednesday night. She hoped he had, for it was true. There she went again, starting with David and finishing with *him*. He'd probably not given her another thought . . . David! He was her man. Married to David she would be happy at last. Marriage. A big step, they all said. But she was twenty-three now . . . She hoped Morse *had* given her another thought . . . Forget him!

But she was not to be allowed to forget him. As she reached the house she saw the Jaguar outside. Her heart pounded against her ribs and a wave of involuntary joy coursed through her blood. She let herself in and went straight to the living-room. There he was, sitting talking to Mary. He stood up as she came in.

'Hullo.'

'Hullo,' she said weakly.

'I really called to see Miss Coleby, but I gather she may not be back yet for a while. So I've been having a delightful little chat with Mary here.'

Mary indeed! Dumpy, freckled little man-eater! Why don't you go, Mary? Mary, why don't you leave us alone – just for a few minutes? Please! She felt viciously jealous. But Mary seemed very taken with the charming Inspector and showed no signs of imminent surrender. Sue, still wearing her summer coat, sat on the arm of a chair, trying to resist the wave of desperation that threatened to engulf her.

She heard herself say: 'She'll catch the eight fifteen from Paddington, I should think. Probably get here about ten.'

That was two hours. Two whole hours. If only Mary would go! He might ask her out for a drink and they could talk. But the wave swept her over, and she left the room and rushed upstairs. Morse got up as she left and thanked Mary for her hospitality. As he opened the front door he turned to Mary. Would she ask Sue to come down for a second? He would like to have a quick word with her. Mary, too, disappeared upstairs and blessedly faded from the scene. Morse stepped out into the concrete drive and Sue appeared, framed in the doorway. She stopped there.

'You wanted a word with me, Inspector?'

'Which room do you sleep in, Sue?' She stepped out and stood next to him. Her arm brushed his as she pointed to the window immediately above the front door, and Morse felt a jagged ache between his temples. He wasn't a tall man and she was almost his own height in the very high wedge-heeled shoes she wore. She dropped her arm and their hands met in an accidental, beautiful way. Leave your hand there, Sue. Leave it there, my darling. He felt the electric thrill of the contact and gently, softly he ran his fingertips along her wrist.

'Why do you want to know that?' Her voice sounded hoarse and breathless.

'I don't know. I suppose if I drive past and see a light on in your window I shall know it's you in there.'

Sue could bear it no longer. She took her hand from his and turned away. 'You came to see Jennifer, then?'

'Yes.'

'I'll tell her, of course – when she comes in.' Morse nodded.

'You think she's got something to do with the Woodstock business, don't you?'

'Something, perhaps.'

They stood in silence for a minute. Sue was wearing a sleeveless dress and she was trying not to shiver.

'Well, I'd better be off.'

'Goodnight, then.'

'Goodnight.' He turned towards the gate and had almost reached it when he turned round. 'Sue?' She stood in the doorway.

'Yes?'

He walked back. 'Sue, would you like to come out with me for a little while?'

'Oh . . .' Sue got no further. She flung her arms around him and cried joyfully on his shoulder, and neither heard the front gate open.

'If you'll excuse me, please?' said a cool, well-spoken voice, and Jennifer Coleby edged past them into the house.

The other wanderers, too, were just returning. Bernard Crowther had returned from London on the same train as Jennifer Coleby; but they had travelled in separate parts of the train, and no one watching them alight at platform number 2 could have formed the slightest suspicion that either was aware of the other's existence.

About this time, too, Peter Newlove was taking his leave of a red-headed, radiant girl in Church Street, Woodstock. They kissed again with eagerness and seeming insatiability.

'I'll be in touch, Gaye.'

'Make sure you do – and thanks again.'

It had been an expensive weekend; very expensive, in fact. But it was, in Peter's view, worth almost every penny.

CHAPTER TWENTY-THREE
Monday, 18 October

On Monday morning, Morse decided that, however embarrassing it would be, he had his job to do. How he dreaded it, though! Here was the big moment, the dénouement of the case (of that he felt quite confident) and yet he felt as if he himself were the guilty party. Lewis collected Jennifer Coleby in his own car; Morse felt he could just about spare her the official trappings. Bernard Crowther said he would make his own way, if that was all right. It was. Morse had tried to think out the likeliest approaches, but his concentration had been lapsing sadly. He decided to let things take their course.

At 10.25 a.m. Crowther arrived, five minutes early, and Morse poured him coffee and asked him a few casual questions about the 'conference'.

'Oh. The usual thing, you know. One long yawn,' said Crowther.

'What was it about exactly?'

'University admissions. Arguing the toss about A-level requirements. We're not very popular with the Schools Council, you know. They think Oxford is the last bastion of academic élitism. Still, I suppose it is really . . .' He had no chance to develop his theme. Lewis came in with Jennifer Coleby, and Crowther got to his feet.

'You two know each other?' asked Morse. There was not a hint of cynicism in his voice. Strangely, or so it seemed to Morse, Jennifer and Crowther shook hands. 'Good mornings' were exchanged, and Morse, a trifle nonplussed, poured two more coffees.

'You *do* know each other?' He sounded rather unsure of himself.

'We live fairly near each other, don't we, Mr Crowther?'

'We do, yes. I've often seen you on the bus. It's Miss Coleby, I think, isn't it? You come round for the SPCC.'

Jennifer nodded.

Morse got up and passed the sugar basin round. He felt he couldn't sit still.

During the next few minutes Lewis was forced to wonder if the Inspector had lost his grip completely. He um'd and ah'd and said 'to be honest with you' and 'we have some reason to suppose' and finally managed to suggest to his pair of prime suspects, almost apologetically, that they might be having an affair with each other.

Jennifer laughed almost aloud and Bernard smiled shyly. It was Bernard who spoke first. 'I'm sure I feel very flattered, Inspector, and I very much wish perhaps that I *was* having some secret affair with Miss Coleby. But I'm afraid the answer's no. What else can I say?'

'Miss Coleby?'

'I think I have spoken to Mr Crowther twice in my life – to ask him for a donation to the SPCC. I sometimes see him on the bus going into town – we get on and off at the same stops. But I think he always goes upstairs and I never do. I hate the smell of cigarettes.'

Morse, who was smoking his third cigarette, felt once more that he was getting the worst of things with Jennifer Coleby. He turned to Crowther.

'I must ask you this, sir. Please think very carefully before you answer, and remember that you are here in connection with a murder, the murder of the girl who was travelling in your car.' Morse saw a look of surprise on Jennifer's face. 'Was Miss Coleby here the other passenger you picked up that night?'

Bernard replied with an immediacy and conviction that sorely troubled Morse. 'No, Inspector, she wasn't. Of that you can be completely assured.'

'And you, Miss Coleby. Do you deny that you were the other passenger in Mr Crowther's car?'

'Yes. I do deny it. Absolutely.'

Morse drained his coffee.

'Do you want us to sign anything, Inspector?' There was a deep cynicism in Jennifer's voice.

Morse shook his head. 'No. Sergeant Lewis has made notes on what you've both said. One more question though, Miss Coleby, if you don't mind. Can you give me the address of the friends you stayed with in London this weekend?'

Jennifer took a plain envelope from her handbag and wrote down an address in Lancaster Gardens. As an afterthought she added the telephone number, and handed the envelope to Morse.

'They're lying – both of 'em,' said Morse when they had gone.

Crowther had to get to the centre of Oxford and had gallantly offered a lift to his fellow-suspect. Morse wondered what they would be talking about. Lewis had said nothing.

'Did you hear me?' Morse was angry.

'Yes, sir.'

'I said they're a pair of prize liars. LIARS.' Lewis remained silent. He thought the Inspector was wrong, terribly wrong. He himself was no stranger to interviewing liars and he had the firm conviction that both Crowther and Coleby were telling the plain truth.

Morse looked hard at his sergeant. 'Come on! Out with it!'

'What do you mean, sir?'

'What do I mean? You know what I mean. You think I'm up the bloody pole, don't you? You think I'm going bonkers. You're willing to believe what everyone else says, but you don't believe *me*. Come on. Tell me! I want to know.'

Lewis was upset. He didn't know what to say, and Morse was losing the last remnants of his self-control, his eyes blazing and his voice growing vicious and deadly. 'Come on. You tell me. You heard what I said. I want to know!'

Lewis looked at him and saw the bitter failure in the Inspector's eyes. He wished he could put things right, but he couldn't. It had been the quality in him that from the start had endeared him to Morse. It was his basic honesty and integrity.

'I think you're wrong, sir.' It took a lot of saying, but he said it, and he deserved better than Morse's cruel rejoinder.

'You think I'm wrong? Well let me tell you something, Lewis. If anyone's wrong here, it's not me – it's *you*. Do you understand that? YOU – not me. If you've not got the nous to see that those two slimy toads are *lying*, lying to save their own necks, you shouldn't be on this case. Do you hear me? *You shouldn't be on this case.*'

Lewis felt a deep hurt; but not for himself. 'Perhaps you ought to have someone else with you, sir. On the case, I mean.'

'You may be right.' Morse was calming down a little and Lewis sensed it.

'There's this man Newlove, sir. Shouldn't we . . .'

'Newlove? Who the hell's he?' Lewis had said the wrong thing, and Morse's latent anger and frustration rose to fever pitch again. 'Newlove? We've never heard of the bloody man before. All right – he's got a typewriter. That's not a sin, is it? He didn't write that letter. CROWTHER DID! And if you don't see that you must be blind as a bloody bat!'

'But don't you think . . .'

'Oh, bugger off, Lewis. You're boring me.'

'Does that mean I'm off the case, sir?'

'I don't know. I don't care. Just bugger off and leave me alone.' Lewis went out and left him alone.

The phone rang a few minutes later. Morse picked the receiver up and closed his mind to everything. 'I'm not here,' he snapped, 'I've gone home.' He slammed down the receiver and sat brooding savagely within himself. He even forgot Sue. The last castle had finally collapsed. Having stood the flood so long, it was now a flattened heap of formless sand. But even as it fell a curious clarification was dawning across his mind. He got up from his leather chair, opened the cabinet, and took out the file on Sylvia Kaye. He opened it at the beginning and was still reading it late into the afternoon, when the shadows crept across the room and he found it difficult to read, and a new and horrifying thought was taking birth in the depths of his tortured mind.

The dramatic news broke at a quarter past seven. Margaret Crowther had committed suicide.

CHAPTER TWENTY-FOUR

Monday, 18 October

Bernard Crowther, after dropping Jennifer Coleby in the High, had been lucky in finding a parking space in Bear Lane. Not even the dons were permitted to park outside the college now. He had lunched in the Senior Common Room and spent the afternoon and early evening working. Both the children were away for a week on a school camping holiday in nearby Wytham Woods. On such ventures it was customary for the parents to visit their children on one evening during the week, but the young Crowthers had told their parents not to bother; and that was that. At least it would be a chance for Bernard and Margaret to have a few decent meals, instead of the inevitable chips and tomato sauce with everything.

Bernard left college at about twenty-past six. The roads were getting free again by now and he had an easy journey home. He let himself in with his Yale key and hung up his coat. Funny smell. Gas?

'Margaret?' He put his brief-case in the front room. 'Margaret?' He walked to the kitchen and found the door locked. 'Margaret!' He rattled the knob of the kitchen door, but it was firmly locked on the other side. He banged on the door. 'Margaret! Margaret! Are you there?' He could smell the gas more strongly now. His mouth went completely dry and there was wild panic in his voice. 'MARGARET!' He rushed back to the front door, through the side-gate, and tried the back door. It was locked. He whimpered like a child. He looked into the kitchen through the large window above the sink. The electric light was on and for a fraction of a second a last ember of hope flared up, and glowed, and then was gone. The surrealistic sight that met his eyes was so strangely improbable that it registered itself blankly as a meaningless picture on the retinas of his eyes – a sight without significance – a waxwork model, bright-eyed and brightly hued, with a fixed, staring smile. What was she doing sitting on the floor like that? Cleaning the oven?

He picked up a house-brick lying by the side of the wall, smashed a pane in the window, and cut his fingers badly as he reached for the catch and opened the window from the inside. The nauseating smell of gas hit him with an almost physical impact, and it was some seconds before, holding his handkerchief to his face, he climbed awkwardly in through the window and turned off the gas. Margaret's head was just inside the oven, resting on a soft red cushion. In a numbed, irrational way he thought he should put the cushion back where it came from; it was from the settee in the lounge. He looked down with shocked, zombie-like eyes at the jagged cuts on his hand and mechanically dabbed them with his handkerchief. He saw the sticky brown paper lining the gaps by the door-jambs and the window, and noticed that Margaret had cut the ends as neatly as she always did when she wrapped the children's birthday presents. The children! Thank God they were away. He saw the scissors on the formica top over the washing machine, and like an automaton he picked them up and put them in the drawer. The smell was infinitely sickly still, and he felt the vomit rising in his gorge. And now the horror of it all was gradually seeping into his mind, like a pool of ink into blotting paper. He knew that she was dead.

He unlocked the kitchen door, picked up the phone in the hall, and in a dazed, uncomprehending voice he asked for the police. A letter addressed to him was lying beside the telephone directory. He picked it up and put it in his breast pocket and returned to the kitchen.

Ten minutes later the police found him there, sitting on the floor beside his wife, his hand on her hair, his eyes bleak and glazed. He had been deaf to the strident ringing of the front door bell.

Morse arrived only a few minutes after the police car and the ambulance. It was Inspector Bell of the Oxford City Police who had called Morse; Crowther had insisted it. The two inspectors had met several times before and stood in the hallway talking together in muted voices. Bernard had been led unresisting from the kitchen by a police doctor and was now sitting in the lounge, his head sunk into his hands. He appeared unaware of what was going on or what was being said, but when Morse came into the lounge he seemed to come to life again.

'Hullo, Inspector.' Morse put his hand on Crowther's shoulder, but could think of nothing to say that might help. Nothing could help. 'She left this, Inspector.' Bernard reached into his breast pocket and pulled out the sealed envelope.

'It's for you, you know, sir; it's addressed to you – not to me,' said Morse quietly.

'I know. But you read it. I can't.' He put his head in his hands again, and sobbed quietly.

Morse looked enquiringly at his fellow inspector. Bell nodded and Morse carefully opened the letter.

Dear Bernard,

When you read this I shall be dead. I know what this will mean to you and the children and it's only this that has kept me from doing it before – but I just can't cope with life any longer. I am finding it so difficult to know what to say – but I want you to know that it's not your fault. I have not been all that a wife should be to you and I have been a miserable failure with the children, and everything has built up and I long for rest and peace away from it all. I just can't go on any longer. I realize how selfish I am and I know that I'm just running away from everything. But I shall go mad if I don't run away. I must run away – I haven't the courage to stand up to things any longer.

On your desk you will find all the accounts. All the bills are paid except Mr Anderson's for pruning the apple trees. We owe him £5 but I couldn't find his address.

I am thinking of the earlier times when we were so happy. Nothing can take them from us. Look after the children. It's my fault – not theirs. I pray that you won't think too badly of me and that you can forgive me.

Margaret.

It wasn't going to be much comfort, but Crowther had got to face it some time.

'Please read it, sir.'

Bernard read it, but he showed no emotion. His despair could plumb no lower depths. 'What about the children?' he said at last.

'Don't worry yourself about that, sir. We'll look after every-thing.' The police doctor's voice was brisk. He was no stranger to such situations, and he knew the procedure from this point on. It wasn't much that he could do – but it was something.

'Look, sir, I want you to take . . .'

'What about the children?' He was a shattered, broken man, and Morse left him to the ministrations of the doctor. He retired with Bell to the front room, and noticed the list of the accounts, insurances, mortgage repayments, and stock-exchange holdings which Margaret had left so neatly ordered under a paper-weight on the desk. But he didn't touch them. They were something between a husband and his wife, a wife who had been alive when he had interviewed Crowther earlier that day.

'You know him, then?' asked Bell.

'I saw him this morning,' said Morse. 'I saw him about the Woodstock murder.'

'Really?' Bell looked surprised.

'He was the man who picked up the girls.'

'You think he was involved?'

'I don't know,' said Morse.

'Has this business got anything to do with it?'

'I don't know.'

The ambulance was still waiting outside and curious eyes were peeping from all the curtains along the road. In the kitchen Morse looked down at Margaret Crowther. He had never seen her before, and he was surprised to realize how attractive she must have been. Fortyish? Hair greying a little, but a good, firm figure and a finely featured face, twisted now and blue.

'No point in keeping her here,' said Bell.

Morse shook his head. 'No point at all.'

'It takes a long time, you know, this North Sea gas.'

The two men talked in a desultory way for several minutes, and Morse prepared to leave. But as he walked out to his car, he was called back by the police doctor.

'Can you come back a minute, Inspector?' Morse re-entered the house.

'He says he must talk to you.'

Crowther sat with his head against the back of the chair. He was breathing heavily and the sweat stood out upon his brow. He was in a state of deep shock, and was already under sedation.

'Inspector,' he opened his eyes wearily. 'Inspector, I've got to talk to you.' He had great difficulty in getting this far, and Morse looked to the doctor, who slowly shook his head.

'Tomorrow, sir,' said Morse. 'I'll see you tomorrow.'

'Inspector, I've got to talk to you.'

'Yes, I know. But not now. We'll talk tomorrow. It'll be all right then.' Morse put his hand to Crowther's forehead and felt the clammy wetness there.

'Inspector!' But the top corner of the walls where Crowther was trying to focus was slowly disintegrating before his eyes; the angles melted and spiralled and faded away.

Morse drove slowly out of Southdown Road and realized just how close Crowther lived to Jennifer Coleby. It was a black night and the moon was hidden away deep behind the lowering clouds. Rectangles of light, shaded by curtains, showed from most of the front-room windows, and in many Morse could see the light-blue phosphorescent glow of television screens. He looked at one house in particular and looked up at one window in it, the window directly above the door. But it was dark, and he drove on.

CHAPTER TWENTY-FIVE
Tuesday, 19 October, a.m.

Morse had slept very badly and woke with a throbbing head. He hated suicides. Why had she done it? Was suicide just the coward's refuge from some black despair? Or was it in its way an act of courage that revealed a perverted sort of valour? Not that, though. So many other lives were intertwined; no burdens were shed – they were merely passed from the shoulders of one to those of another. Morse's mind would give itself no rest but twirled around on some interminable fun-fair ride.

It was past nine o'clock before he was sitting in his leather chair, and his sombre mood draped itself over his sagging shoulders. He summoned Lewis, who knocked apprehensively on the door before going in; but Morse had seemingly lost all recollection of the nasty little episode the day before. He told Lewis the facts of Margaret Crowther's suicide.

'Do you think he's got something important to tell us, sir?'

There was a knock on the door before Lewis could learn the answer to his question, and a young girl brought in the post, said a bright 'Good morning', and was off. Morse fingered through the dozen or so letters and his eye fell on an unopened envelope marked 'strictly private' and addressed to himself. The envelope was exactly similar to the one he had seen the previous evening.

'I don't know whether Crowther's got anything to tell us or not; but it looks as if his late wife has.' He opened the envelope neatly with a letter-knife and read its typewritten contents aloud to Lewis.

Dear Inspector,
    I have never met you, but I have seen from the newspapers that you are in charge of the inquiry into the death of Sylvia Kaye. I should have told you this a long time ago, but I hope it's not too late even now. You see, Inspector, I killed Sylvia Kaye.
    I must try to explain myself. Please forgive me if I get a little muddled, but it all seems very long ago.

I have known for about six months – well, certainly for six months – perhaps I've known for much longer – that my husband has been having an affair with another woman. I had no proof and have none now. But it is so difficult for a man to hide this sort of thing from his wife. We have been married for fifteen years and I know him so well. It was written all over what he said and what he did and how he looked – he must have been terribly unhappy, I think.

On Wednesday, 22nd September, I left the house at 6.30 p.m. to go to my evening class at Headington – but I didn't go immediately. Instead, I waited in my car just off the Banbury Road. I seemed to wait such a long time and I didn't really know what I was going to do. Then at about a quarter to seven Bernard – my husband – drove up to the junction at Charlton Road and turned right towards the northern roundabout. I followed him as best I could – I say that because I'm not a good driver – and anyway it was getting darker all the time. There wasn't much traffic and I could see him clearly two or three cars ahead. At the Woodstock Road roundabout he turned along the A34. He was driving too fast for me, though, and I kept dropping further and further behind. I thought I had lost him – but there were road-works ahead and the traffic had to filter into single line for about a mile. There was a slow, heavy lorry in the front and I soon caught up again – Bernard was only about six or seven cars ahead of me. The lorry turned off towards Bladon at the next roundabout and I managed to keep Bernard in sight and saw him take the first turning on the left in Woodstock itself. I panicked a bit and didn't know what to do – I turned into the next street, and stopped the car and walked back. But it was hopeless. I drove back to Headington and was only twenty minutes late for my evening class.

The next Wednesday, the 29th September, I drove out to Wood-stock again, leaving the house a good ten minutes earlier than usual, parked my car further along the village, and walked back to the street into which Bernard had turned the previous week. I didn't know where to wait and I felt silly and conspicuous, but I found a safe enough little spot on the left of the road – I was terrified that Bernard would see me – if he came that was – and I waited there and watched every car that came round the corner. It was child's play to see the cars turning in – and the occupants as well. He came at quarter-past seven and I felt myself trembling frantically. He was not alone – a young girl with long fair hair, in a white blouse, was sitting next to him in the front seat. I thought they must see me because the car turned – oh, only six or seven yards ahead of me – into the car park of the Black Prince. My legs were shaking and the blood was pounding in my ears, but something made me go through with it. I walked cautiously up to the yard and peered in. There were several cars there already and I couldn't see Bernard's for several minutes. I edged round the back of one car – just to the left of the yard – and then I saw them. The car was on the same side at the far end, with the boot towards the wall – he must have backed in. They were sitting in the front – talking for a while. I felt a cold anger inside me. Bernard and a blowzy blonde – about seventeen she looked! I saw them kissing. Then they got out of the front and into the back. I couldn't see any more – at least I was spared that.

I can't really explain what I felt. As I write now it all seems so flat – and so unimportant somehow. I felt more anger than jealousy – I know that. Burning anger that Bernard had shamed me so. It was about five minutes later when they got out. They said something – but I couldn't hear what it was. There was a lever – a long tyre-lever – I found it on the floor of the yard, and I picked it up. I don't know why. I felt so frightened and so angry. And suddenly the engine of the car was switched on and then the lights and the whole yard was lit up. The car moved off and out of the yard, and after it had gone the darkness seemed even blacker than before. The girl stood where he had left her, and I crept behind the three or four cars between us and came up behind her. I said nothing and I'm sure she didn't hear me. I hit her across the back of the head with an easy strength. It seemed like a dream. I felt nothing – no remorse – no fear – nothing. I left her where she was, against the far wall. It was still very dark. I didn't know when or how she would be found – and I didn't care.

Bernard knew all along that I had murdered Sylvia Kaye – he passed me on my way back to Oxford. He must have seen me because I saw him. He was right behind me for some time and must have seen the number plate. I saw his car as clear as daylight when he overtook me.

I know what you have suspected about Bernard. But you have been wrong. I don't know what he's told you – but I know you have spoken to him. If he has told you lies, it has only been to shield me. But I need no one to shield me any longer. Look after Bernard and don't let him suffer too much because of me. He did what hundreds of men do, and for that I blame myself and no one else. I have neither been a good wife to him nor a good mother to his children. I am just so tired – so desperately tired of everything. For what I have done I am now most bitterly sorry – but I realize that this is no excuse. What else can I say – what else is there to say?
Margaret Crowther.

Morse's voice trailed away and the room was very still. Lewis felt very moved as he heard the letter read aloud, almost as if Margaret Crowther were there. But she would never speak again. He thought of his visit to her and guessed how cruelly she must have suffered these last few months.

'You thought it was something like that, didn't you, sir?'

'No,' said Morse.

'Comes as a bit of a shock, doesn't it? Out of the blue, like. '

'I don't think much of her English style,' said Morse. He handed the letter over to Lewis. 'She uses far too many dashes for my liking.' The comment seemed heartless and irrelevant. Lewis read the letter to himself.

'She's a good, clean typist anyway, sir.'

'Bit odd, don't you think, that she typed her name at the end instead of using her signature?'

Give Morse a letter and his imagination soared to the realms of the bright-eyed seraphim. Lewis groaned inwardly.

'You think she wrote it, don't you, sir?'

Morse reluctantly reined back the wild horses. 'Yes. She wrote it.'

Lewis thought he understood the Inspector's feelings. There would have to be a bit of tidying up, of course, but the case was now substantially over. He'd enjoyed most of his time working with the irascible, volatile Inspector, but now . . . The phone rang and Morse answered. He said 'I see' a dozen times and replaced the receiver.

'Crowther's in the Radcliffe – he's had a mild heart attack. He's not allowed to see anyone for two days at least.'

'Perhaps he couldn't tell us much more,' suggested Lewis.

'Oh yes he could,' said Morse. He leaned back, put his hands on his head like a naughty schoolboy, and stared vacantly at the farthest corner of the wall. Lewis thought it best to keep quiet, but he grew uncomfortably restless as the minutes ticked by.

'Would you like a coffee, sir?' Morse didn't seem to hear him. 'Coffee? Would you like a coffee?' Morse reminded him of a very deaf person with his hearing-aid switched off. Minute after minute slipped by before the blue eyes refocused on the world around him.

'Well, that's cleared up one thing, Lewis. We can cross Mrs Crowther off our list of suspects, can't we?'

CHAPTER TWENTY-SIX

Tuesday, 19 October, p.m.

At midday Peter Newlove was sitting in his rooms. He was expecting no one. Normally Bernard might have dropped in about now for a gin, but the news had swept the college that morning: Margaret had killed herself and Bernard had suffered a heart attack. And the double-barrelled news hit no one harder than Peter. He had known Margaret well and had liked her; and Bernard was his best friend in that academic, dilettante style of friendship which springs up in most collegiate universities. He had rung up the hospital, but there was no chance of visiting Bernard until Thursday at the earliest. He had sent some flowers: Bernard liked flowers and had no wife to send them now . . . He had enquired, too, about the children. They had gone to stay with an aunt in Hendon, though Peter couldn't imagine how such an arrangement could possibly help them very much.

There was a knock on the door. 'It's open.'

He had not met Inspector Morse before and was pleasantly surprised that his offer of a drink was accepted. Morse explained in blunt, unequivocal terms why he had called.

'And it was written on *that* one?' Newlove frowned at the open portable typewriter on the table.

'No doubt about it.'

Newlove looked mildly perplexed, but said nothing.

'Do you know a young lady named Jennifer Coleby, Miss Jennifer Coleby?'

'I don't, I'm afraid.' Newlove's frown grew deeper.

'She works in the High, not far from here. Town and Gown. Assurance place.'

Newlove shook his head. 'I might have seen her, of course. But I don't know her. I've not heard the name before.'

'And you've never written to anyone of that name?'

'No. How could I? As I say, I've never heard of the woman.'

Morse pursed his lips and continued. 'Who else could have used your typewriter, sir?'

'Well, I don't know really. I suppose almost anyone in a way. I don't lock the place up very much unless there are question papers about.'

'You mean you leave your doors open and let anybody just walk in and help himself to your booze or your books – or your typewriter?'

'No, it's not like that. But quite a few of the Fellows do drop in.'

'Who in particular, would you say?'

'Well, there's a new young don here this term, Melhuish, for example. He's been in quite a few times recently.'

'And?'

'And a dozen others.' He sounded a little uneasy.

'Have you ever seen any of these er friends of yours using your typewriter?'

'Well, no. I don't think I have.'

'They'd use their own, wouldn't they?'

'Yes. I suppose they would.'

'Not much "suppose" about it, is there, sir?' said Morse.

'No.'

'You've no idea then?'

'I'm not being very helpful, I know. But I've no idea at all.'

Morse abruptly switched his questioning. 'Did you know Mrs Crowther?'

'Yes.'

'You've heard about her?'

'Yes,' said Newlove quietly.

'And Bernard Crowther?' Newlove nodded. 'I understand he's one of your best friends?' Again Newlove nodded. 'I've been to his room this morning, sir. If you want to put it crudely I've been snooping around. But you see, I often have to snoop around. I take no particular delight in it.'

'I understand,' said Newlove.

'I wonder if you do understand, sir.' There was a clipped impatience in his voice now. 'He often drops in to see you, is that right?'

'Quite often.'

'And do you think he'd come to you if he wanted anything?'

'You mean rather than to somebody else?'

'Yes.'

'He'd come to me.'

'Did you know that his typewriter can't even cope with a comma?'

'No, I didn't,' lied Newlove.

After dropping Morse at Lonsdale College, Lewis had his own duties to perform. For the life of him he couldn't understand the point of this particular errand, but Morse had said it was of vital importance. Something had galvanized the Inspector into new life. But it wasn't the gay, rumbustious Morse of the early days of the case. Something grim had come over him and Lewis found him a little frightening sometimes. He only hoped they got no more letters upon which Morse could practise his misdirected ingenuity.

He pulled the official police car into the small yard of the Summertown Health Centre, situated on the corner of the Banbury Road and Marston Ferry Road. It was a finely built, large, red-brick structure with steps up to a white porch before the front door – one of the many beautiful large houses built by the well-to-do along the Banbury Road in the latter half of the nineteenth century. Lewis was expected and had only a minute or so to wait before being shown into the consulting room of the senior partner.

'That's the lot, Sergeant.' Dr Green handed over a file to Lewis.

'Are you sure it's all here, sir? Inspector Morse was very anxious for me to get everything.'

Doctor Green was silent for a moment. 'The only thing that's not there is . . . is er any record that we had er may have had about any er conversation we er may have had with Miss Kaye about her er private sex life. You understand, I know, Sergeant, that there are er there is the ethical side of er the er confidential nature of the er doctor's relationship with the er patient.'

'You mean she was on the pill, Doctor.' Lewis stepped boldly with his policeman's boots where the angelic Green had so delicately feared to tread.

'Er . . . I er didn't say that, did I, Sergeant? I er said that we er it is er improper to er betray to betray the confidences that we er we er hear in the consulting room.'

'Would you have told us if she *wasn't* on the pill?' asked Lewis innocently.

'Now that's er a very difficult er question. You er we er you er you are putting words into my er mouth a bit aren't you, Sergeant? All I'm saying is er . . .'

Lewis wondered what the senior partner would say to a patient who had malignant cancer. It would be, he was sure, a most protracted er interview. He thanked the good doctor and left as quickly as he could, although he was half-way down the porch steps before he finally shook off the er persistent Green. He'd have to tell his wife about er Doctor Green.

As they had agreed, Lewis picked up Morse outside Lonsdale College at one o'clock. He told the Inspector about the troubled state of Doctor Green's conscience on the problem of professional confidentiality, but Morse was cynically unimpressed.

'We know she was on the pill, remember?' Lewis should have remembered. He had read the reports; in fact Morse had specially asked him to get to know them as well as he could. It hadn't seemed very important at the time. Perhaps, even then, Morse had seen its relevance? But he doubted it, and his doubts, as it happened, were well justified.

As Lewis drove out of the city, Morse asked him to turn off to the motel at the Woodstock roundabout. 'We'll have a pint and a sandwich, eh?'

They sat in the Morris Bar, Morse engrossed in the medical reports on Sylvia Kaye. They covered, at intermittent stages, the whole of her pathetically brief little life, from the mild attack of jaundice at the age of two days to an awkward break of her arm in the August before she had died. Measles, warts on fingers, middle-ear infection, dysmenorrhoea, headaches (myopia?). A fairly uneventful medical history. Most of the notes were reasonably legible, and oddly enough the arch-apostle of indecision, the conscientious Green, had a beautifully clear and rounded hand. His only direct contacts with Sylvia had been over the last two afflictions, the headaches and the broken arm. Morse passed the file over to Lewis, and went to refill the glasses. Some of the details had appeared in the post-mortem report anyway, but his memory wasn't Lewis's strongest asset.

'Have you ever broken your arm?' asked Morse.

'No.'

'They say it's very painful. Something to do with the neurological endings or something. Like when you hurt your foot, Lewis. Very, very painful.'

'You should know, sir.'

'Ah, but if you've got a basically strong constitution like me, you soon recover.' Lewis let it go. 'Did you notice,' continued Morse, 'that Green saw her on the day before she died?'

Lewis opened the file again. He had read the entry, but without noticing the date. He looked again and saw that Morse was right. Sylvia had visited the Summertown Health Centre on Tuesday, 28 September, with a letter from the orthopaedic surgeon at the Radcliffe Infirmary. It read: 'Arm still very stiff and rather painful. Further treatment necessary. Continuation of physiotherapy treatment recommended as before – Tuesday and Thursday a.m.'

Lewis could imagine the consultation. And suddenly a thought flashed into his mind. It was being with Morse that did it. His fanciful suspicions were getting as wild as the Inspector's. 'You don't think, surely, that er . . .' He was getting as bad as Green.

'That what?' said Morse, his face strangely grave.

'That Green was having an affair with Sylvia?'

Morse smiled wanly and drained his glass. 'We could find out, I suppose.'

'But you said this medical stuff was very important.'

'That was an understatement.'

'Have you found what you wanted, sir?'

'Yes. You could say that. Let's say I just wanted a bit of confirmation. I spoke to Green on the telephone yesterday.'

'Did he er did he er,' mimicked Lewis. It was an isolated moment of levity in the last grim days of the case.

Sue had Tuesday afternoon off, and she was glad of it. Working in the casualty department was tiring, especially on her feet. The other girls were out and she made herself some toast and sat in the little kitchen staring with her beautiful, doleful eyes at the white floor-tiles. She'd promised to write to David and she really must get down to it this afternoon. She wondered what to say. She could tell him about work and she could tell him how lovely it had been to see him last weekend and she could tell him how much she looked forward to seeing him again. Yet all seemed empty of delight. She blamed herself bitterly for her own selfishness; but even as she did so, she knew that she was more concerned with her own wishes and her own desires than with anyone else's. With David's – particularly David's. It was futile, it was quite impossible, it was utterly foolish, it was even dangerous to think of him – to think about Morse, that is. But she wanted him so badly. She longed for him to call – she longed just to see him. Anything . . . And as she sat there in the little kitchen staring at the white tiles still, she felt an overwhelming sense of self-reproach and loneliness and misery.

Jennifer was busy on Tuesday afternoon. Palmer had sent her a draft letter and wanted her to look it through. Premiums on virtually everything were to be increased by 10% after Christmas and all the company's clients had to be informed. The dear man, thought Jennifer; he's not so very bright really. The first paragraph of his letter was reminiscent of the tortuous exercises she'd been set in Latin prose. 'Which' followed 'which', which followed yet another 'which'. A coven of whiches, she thought, and smiled at the conceit. She amended the paragraph with a bold confidence; a full stop here, a new paragraph there, a better word here – much clearer. Palmer knew she was by far the brightest girl in the office, and over important drafts he always consulted her. She wouldn't be staying there much longer, though. She had applied for two jobs in the last week. But she wouldn't dream of telling anybody, not even Mr Palmer. Not that it was unpleasant working where she was – far from it. And she earned almost as much as Mary and Sue put together . . . Sue! She thought of Sunday evening when she had returned from London. How glad she had felt to find them like that! She visualized the scene again and a cruel smile played over her lips.

She took the amended drafts to Mr Palmer's office, where Judith was trying to keep pace with the very moderate speed at which her employer was dictating a letter. She handed the draft to him. 'I've made a few suggestions.'

'Oh, thank you very much. I just rushed it off, you know. Put down the first things that came into my head. I realized it was, you know, a bit er a bit rough. Thanks very much. Jolly good.'

Jennifer said no more. She left, and as she walked up the corridor to the typists' room, the same nasty smile was playing about her pretty mouth.

The third of the triad, the undaunted, dumpy, freckled little Mary, worked for Radio Oxon. In the BBC she might have been accorded the distinguished title of 'continuity girl'; but she was in a dead-end job with the local radio station. Like Jennifer she had been thinking of a change, although unlike Jennifer she had few qualifications behind her. Jennifer had some A levels and all her shorthand and typing certificates; she must have been clever at school, thought Mary. Cool, sort of *knowing* all the time . . . It worked well enough, the three of them living together; but she wouldn't mind a move. Sue was all right, she quite liked Sue really, although she'd been a bit moody and broody just recently. Men trouble. Had she fallen for that Inspector chap? She wouldn't blame her, though. At least Sue was human. She wasn't quite so sure about Jennifer.

After lunch on Tuesday one of the assistants came in to chat with her. He had a beard, a light-hearted manner, five young children, and a roving eye for the ladies. Mary did not positively strive to discourage his attentions.

CHAPTER TWENTY-SEVEN

Thursday, Friday; 21, 22 October

Bernard Crowther was, in the words of the ward sister, 'satisfactory', and on Thursday afternoon he was sitting up in bed to receive his first visitor. Strangely, Morse had not seemed anxious to press his claims, and had waived his rights to be at the head of the queue.

Peter Newlove was glad to see his old friend looking so lively. They talked naturally and quietly for a few minutes. Some things just had to be said, but when Peter had said them, he turned to other matters and he knew that Bernard understood. It was almost time to go. But Bernard put his hand on his friend's arm and Peter sat down again beside the bed. An oxygen tube hung over the metal frame behind Bernard's head and a multi-dialled machine stood guard on the other side of the bed.

'I want to tell you something, Peter.'

Peter leaned forward slightly to hear him. Bernard was speaking more labouredly now and taking a deep breath before each group of words. 'We can talk again tomorrow. Don't upset yourself now.'

'Please stay.' Bernard's voice was strained and urgent as he went on. 'I've got to tell you. You know all about that murder at Woodstock?' Peter nodded. 'I picked up the two girls.' He breathed heavily again and a light smile came to his lips. 'Funny really. I was going to meet one of them anyway. But they missed the bus and I picked them up. It ruined everything, of course. They knew each other and – well, it scared me off.' He rested a while, and Peter looked hard at his old friend and tried to keep the look of incredulity out of his eyes.

'To cut a long story short, I finished up with the other one. Think of it, Peter! I finished up with the other one! She was hot stuff, good Lord she was. Peter, can you hear me?' He leaned back, shook his head sadly, and took another deep breath.

'I had her – in the back of the car. She made me feel as randy as an old goat. And then – and then I left her. That's the funny thing about it. I left her. I drove back home. That's all.'

'You left her, you mean, at the Black Prince?'

Bernard nodded. 'Yes. That's where they found her. I'm glad I've told you.'

'Are you going to tell the police?'

'That's what I want to ask you, Peter. You see I . . .' he stopped. 'I don't know whether I should tell you, and you must promise me never to breathe it to a living soul' – he looked anxiously at Peter, but seemed confident of his trust – 'but I'm pretty sure that I saw someone else in the yard that night. I didn't know who it was, of course.' He was becoming progressively more exhausted each time he spoke, and Peter rose to his feet anxiously.

'Don't go.' The uphill climb was nearly done. 'I didn't know – it was so dark. It worried me though. I had a double whisky at a pub near by and I drove home.' The words were coming very slowly. 'I passed her. What a stupid fool I was. She saw me.'

'Who do you mean? Who did you pass, Bernard?'

Bernard's eyes were closed, and he appeared not to hear. 'I checked up. She didn't go to her night class.' He opened his heavy eyes; he was glad he'd told somebody, and glad it was Peter. But Peter looked dazed and puzzled. He stood up and bent over and spoke as quietly but as clearly as he could into Bernard's ear.

'You mean you think it was – it was *Margaret* who killed her?' Bernard nodded.

'And that was why she . . .' Bernard nodded his weary head once more.

'I'll call in again tomorrow. Try to rest.' Peter prepared to go and was already on his way when he heard his name called again.

Bernard's eyes were open and he held up his right hand with a fragile authority. Peter retraced his steps.

'Not now, Bernard. Get some sleep.'

'I want to apologize.'

'Apologize?'

'They've found out about the typewriter, haven't they?'

'Yes. It was mine.'

'I used it, Peter. I ought to have told you.'

'Forget it. What does it matter?'

But it did matter. Bernard knew that; but he was too tired and could think no more. Margaret was dead. That was the overwhelming reality. He was only now beginning to grasp the utter devastation caused by that one terrible reality: *Margaret was dead*.

He lay back and dozed into a wakeful dream. The cast of the scene was assembled and he saw it all again, yet in a detached, impersonal way, as if he were standing quite outside himself.

When he saw them he had known immediately it was her, but he couldn't understand why she was hitchhiking. They exchanged no words and she sat in the back. She must have felt, as he had, how dangerous it had suddenly become; she obviously knew the other girl. It was almost a relief to him when she said she was getting off at Begbroke. He made an excuse – getting cigarettes – and they had whispered anxiously together. It was better to forget it for that night. He was worried. He couldn't afford the risk. But surely he could pick her up later, couldn't he? She had asked it with a growing anger. He'd sensed, as they were driving along, the jealousy she must have felt as the girl in the front had chatted him up. Not that he had given her any encouragement. Not then, anyway. But he felt genuinely worried, and, he told her so. They could meet again next week: he would be writing in the usual way. It was half a minute of agitated whispering – no longer; just inside the door of the Golden Rose. There had been exasperation and a glint of blind fury in her eyes. But he understood how she felt. He wanted her again, too – just as badly as ever.

He got back into the car and drove on to Woodstock. Now that she had the field to herself, the blonde girl seemed even freer from any inhibitions. She leaned back with a relaxed and open sensuality. The top button of her thin, white blouse was unfastened, and the blouse itself seemed like a silken seed-pod ready to burst open, her breasts swelling like two sun-ripened seeds beneath it.

'What do you do?'

'I'm at the University.'

'Lecturer?'

'Yes.' Their eyes met. It had gone on like that until they reached Woodstock. 'Well, where shall I drop you?'

'Oh, anywhere really.'

'You going to see the boy friend?'

'Not for half an hour or so. I've got plenty of time.'

'Where are you meeting him?'

'The Black Prince. Know it?'

'Would you like to come for a drink with me first?' He felt very nervous and excited.

'Why not?'

There was a space in the yard and he backed in, up against the far left-hand wall.

'Perhaps it's not such a good idea to have a drink here,' she said.

'No, perhaps not.'

She lay back again in the seat, her skirt rising up around her thighs. Her legs were stretched out, long, inviting, slightly parted.

'You married?' she asked. He nodded. Her right hand played idly and irregularly with the gear lever, her fingers caressing the knob. The windows were gradually misting over with their breath and he leaned over to the compartment on the near side of the dashboard. His arm brushed her as he did so and he felt a gentle forward pressure from her body. He found the duster and half-heartedly cleaned her side window. He felt the pressure of her right hand against his leg as he moved slightly across her, but she made no effort to remove it. He put his left arm around the back of her seat and she turned towards him. Her lips were full and open and tantalizingly she licked her tongue along them. He could resist her no longer and kissed her with an abrupt and passionate abandon. Her tongue snaked into his mouth and her body turned towards him, her breasts thrusting forward against him. He caressed her legs with his right hand, revelling in sheer animal joy as she swayed slightly and parted them with wider invitation. She broke off the long and frenzied kissing and licked the lobe of his ear and whispered, 'Undo the buttons on my blouse. I'm not wearing a bra.'

'Let's get in the back,' he said hoarsely. His erection was enormous.

It was over all too soon, and he felt guilty of his own reactions. He wanted to get away from her. She seemed quite different now – metamorphosed in a single minute.

'I'd better go.'

'So soon?' She was slowly fastening her blouse but the spell was broken now.

'Yes. I'm afraid so.'

'You enjoyed it, didn't you?'

'Of course. You know I did.'

'You'd like to do it again some time?'

'You know I would.' He was getting more and more anxious to get away. Had he imagined someone out there? A peeping Tom, perhaps?

'You've not told me your name.'

'You've not told me yours.'

'Sylvia. Sylvia Kaye.'

'Look Sylvia.' He tried to sound as loving towards her as he could. 'Don't you think it would be better if we, you know, just thought of this as something beautiful that happened to us. Just the once. Here tonight.'

She turned nasty and sour then. 'You don't want to see me again, do you? You're just like the rest. Bi' of sex and a blow out and you're off.' She spoke differently, too. She sounded like a common slut, a cheap, hard pick-up from a Soho side-street. But she was right, of course – absolutely right. He'd got what he wanted. But hadn't she? Was she a prostitute? He thought of his days in the army and the men who'd caught a dose of the pox. He must get out of here; out of this claustrophobic car and this dark and miserable yard. He put his hand in his pocket and found a £1 note. Except for some loose silver, he had no more money on him.

'A pound no'! One bloody pound no'! Chris' – you must think I'm a cheap bi' of goods. You 'ave a bi' of money on you nex' time mate – or else keep your bloody 'ands off.'

He felt a deep sense of shame and corruption. She got out of the car and he followed her.

'I'll find ou' who you bloody are, mister. I will – you see!'

What had happened then he didn't know. He remembered saying something and he vaguely remembered that she had said something back. He remembered his headlights swathing the yard and he remembered waiting for a gap in the traffic as he reached the main road. He remembered stopping to buy a double whisky and he remembered driving fast down the dual carriageway; and he remembered coming up behind a car and then swerving past it and flying through the night, his mind reeling. And on Thursday afternoon he had read in the *Oxford Mail* of the murder of Sylvia Kaye.

It had been foolish to write that letter, of course, but at least Peter would be out of trouble now. It was always asking for trouble – putting anything down on paper; but it had been a neat little arrangement until then. It was her suggestion anyway, and it seemed necessary. The post in North Oxford was really dreadful – 10.00 a.m. or later now – and no one seemed to mind the girls at the office getting letters. And so often he couldn't be quite sure until the last minute. Sometimes things got into a complex tangle, but more often the arrangement had worked very smoothly. They had worked out a good system between them. Quite clever really. No one even looked at the date anyway. Sometimes he had incorporated a brief message, too – like that last time. That last time . . . Morse must have had his wits about him, but he hadn't been quite clever enough to see the whole picture . . . He couldn't have told Morse the whole truth, of course, but he hadn't deliberately meant to mislead him. A bit, certainly. That height business, for example . . . He'd like to see Morse. Perhaps under other circumstances they could have got to know each other, become friends . . .

He dozed off completely and it was dark when he awoke. The lights were dim. The silent, white figure of a nurse sat behind a small table at the far end of the ward, and he saw that most of the

other patients were lying asleep. The real world rushed back at
him, and Margaret was dead. Why? Why? Was it as she said in
the letter? He wondered how he could ever face life again, and he
thought of the children. What had they been told?

Sharp spasms of agonizing pain leaped across his chest and he
knew suddenly and with certitude that he was going to die. The
nurse was with him, and now the doctor. He was drenched with
sweat. Margaret! Had she killed Sylvia or had he? What did it
matter? The pains were dying away and he felt a strange serenity.

'Doctor,' he whispered.

'Take it gently, Mr Crowther. You'll feel better now.' But
Crowther had suffered a massive coronary thrombosis and his
chances of living on were tilted against him in the balances.

'Doctor. Will you write something for me?'

'Yes. Of course.'

'To Inspector Morse. Write it down.' The doctor took his
notebook out and wrote down the brief message. He looked at
Crowther with worried eyes: the pulse was weakening rapidly.
The machine was working, its black dials turned up to their
maximum readings. Bernard felt the oxygen mask over his face
and saw in a strangely lucid way the minutest details of all around
him. Dying was going to be much easier than he had ever hoped.
Easier than living. He knocked away the mask with surprising
vigour, and spoke his last words.

'Doctor. Tell my children that I loved them.'

His eyes closed and he seemed to fall into a deep sleep. It was
2.35 a.m. He died at 6.30 the same morning before the sun had
risen in the straggly grey of the eastern sky and before the early
morning porters came clattering along the corridors with their
hospital trolleys.

Morse looked down at him. It was 8.30 a.m. and the last mortal
remains of Bernard Crowther had been unobtrusively wheeled
into the hospital mortuary almost two hours ago. Morse had liked
Crowther. Intelligent face; good-looking man really. He thought
that Margaret must have loved him dearly once; probably always
had, deep down. And not only Margaret. There had been someone
else, too, hadn't there, Bernard? Morse looked down at the sheet
of note-paper in his hand, and read it again. 'To Inspector Morse.
I'm so sorry. I've told you so many lies. Please leave *her* alone. She
had nothing to do with it. How could she? I killed Sylvia Kaye.'

The pronouns were puzzling, or so they had seemed to the

doctor as he wrote the brief message. But Morse understood them and he knew that Bernard Crowther had guessed the truth before he died. He looked at the dead man again: the feet were as cold as stone and he would babble no more o' green fields.

Morse turned slowly on his heel and left.

CHAPTER TWENTY-EIGHT
Friday, 22 October, a.m.

Later that same Friday morning Morse sat in his office bringing Lewis up to date with the morning's developments. 'You see, all along the trouble with this case has been not so much that they've told us downright lies but that they've told us such a tricky combination of lies and the truth. But we're nearly at the end of the road, thank God.'

'We're not finished yet, sir?'

'Well, what do you think? It's not a very tidy way of leaving things, is it? It's always nice to have a confession, I know, but what do you do with *two* of 'em?'

'Perhaps we shall never know, sir. I think that they were just trying to cover up for each other, you know – taking the blame for what the other had done.'

'Who do you think did it, Sergeant?'

Lewis had his choice ready. 'I think she did it, sir.'

'Pshaw!' Well, it had been a 50:50 chance, and he'd guessed wrong. Or at least Morse thought he was wrong. But *he* hadn't been on very good form recently, had he? 'Come on,' said Morse. 'Tell me. What makes you pick on poor Mrs Crowther?'

'Well, I think she found out about Crowther going with this other woman and I believe what she said about following him and seeing him at Woodstock. She couldn't have known some of the things she mentioned if she hadn't been there, could she?'

'Go on,' said Morse.

'I mean, for instance, about where the car was parked in the yard. About them getting in the back of the car – *we* didn't know that; but it seems to fit in with the evidence we got when one of Sylvia's hairs was found on the back seat. I just feel she couldn't have made it up. She couldn't have got those things from the newspapers because they were never printed.'

Morse nodded his agreement. 'And I'll tell you something else,

Lewis. She wasn't at her Headington class on that Wednesday night. There's no tick for her on the register anyway. I've looked.'

Lewis was grateful for the corroborative evidence. 'But you don't believe it was her, sir?'

'I know it wasn't,' said Morse simply. 'You see, Lewis, I think that if Margaret Crowther had been in murderous mood that night, it would have been Bernard's skull on the other end of a tyre-lever – not a nonentity like Sylvia's.'

Lewis seemed far from convinced. 'I think you're wrong, sir. I know what you mean, but all women are different. You can't just say a woman would do this and wouldn't do that. Some women would do anything. She must have felt terribly jealous of this other girl taking her husband from her like that.'

'She doesn't say she was jealous, though; she says she felt "burning anger", remember?'

Lewis didn't, but he saw his opening. 'But why are you all of a sudden so anxious to believe what she says, sir? I thought you said you *didn't* believe her.'

Morse nodded his approval. 'That's exactly what I mean. It's all such a mixture of truth and falsehood. Our job is to sift the wheat from the chaff.'

'And how do we do that?'

'Well, we need a bit of psychological insight, for one thing. And I think she was telling the truth when she said she was angry. To me, it's got the right sort of ring about it. I'm pretty sure if she was making it up she'd have said she was jealous, rather than angry. And if she was angry, I think the object of her anger would be her husband, not Sylvia Kaye.'

To Lewis it all seemed thin and wishy-washy. 'I've never cared much for psychology, sir.'

'You're not convinced?'

'Not with that, sir. No.'

'I don't blame you,' said Morse. 'I'm not very convinced myself. But you'll be glad to know that we don't have to depend on my abilities as a psychologist. Just think a minute, Lewis. She said she entered the yard, keeping close in – that is, to her left – and edged her way behind the cars. She saw Crowther at the far end of the yard, also on the left. Agreed?'

'Agreed.'

'But the tyre-lever, if we can believe the evidence, and I can see no possible reason for *not* doing so, was either in, or beside, the tool-box at the farthest right-hand corner of the yard. The weapon with which Mrs Crowther claims she killed Sylvia Kaye was at least twenty yards away from where she stood. She mentions in her statement that she was not only angry but frightened, too. And I can well believe her. Who wouldn't be frightened? Frightened of what was going on, frightened of the dark perhaps; but above all *frightened of being seen*. And yet you ask me to believe that she crossed the yard and picked up a tyre-lever that was almost certainly no more than four or five yards from where Bernard stood with his bottled blonde? Rubbish! She read about the tyre-lever in the papers.'

'Someone could have moved it, sir.'

'Yes. Someone could, certainly. Who do you suggest?'

Lewis felt that his arguing with Morse in this mood was almost as sacrilegious as Moses arguing with the Lord on Sinai. Anyway, he ought to have spotted that business about the spanner from the start. Very bad, really. But something else had bothered him about Margaret's statement. It had seemed so obvious from the start that this was a man's crime, not a woman's. He had himself looked down on Sylvia that first night and he had known perfectly well, without any pathologist's report, that she had been raped. Her clothes were torn and quite obviously someone had not been able to wait to get his hands on her body. It had been no surprise to him, or to Morse surely, that the report had mentioned the semen dribbling down her legs, and the bruising round her breasts. But all that didn't square with Margaret Crowther's evidence. She'd seen them in the back of the car, she said. But had she been right? The hair was found in the back of the car, but that didn't prove very much, did it? It could have got there in a hundred different ways. No. Things didn't add up either way. It beat him. He put his thoughts into words and Morse listened carefully.

'You're right. It's a problem that caused me a great deal of anxiety.'

'But it's not a problem now, sir?'

'Oh no. If that were our only problem we'd have some plain sailing ahead of us.'

'And you don't think we have?'

'I'm afraid we've got some very stormy seas to face.' Morse's face was drawn and grey, and his voice was strained as he continued. 'There's one more thing I should have told you, Lewis. After I left the Radcliffe this morning, I called to see Newlove. He'd been to see Bernard yesterday and was quite willing to talk about him.'

'Anything new, sir?'

'Yes, I suppose you can say there is, in a way. Newlove didn't want to talk about the personal side of things, but he told me that Crowther had spoken to him about the night of the murder. Very much what we already knew or what we've pieced together. Except one thing, Lewis. Crowther said he thought *there was someone else in the yard* that night.'

'Well we knew that, didn't we, sir?'

'Just a minute, Lewis. Let's just picture the scene, if we can. Crowther gets out of the front seat and into the back, right? Sylvia Kaye does the same. Now there was precious little room where the car was, and this was certainly not the place or the occasion for old-world gallantry; and I reckon it's odds-on that she got out the front nearside and into the back nearside and that he did the same on his side. In other words they sat on the same sides in the back of the car as they did in the front – he on the right, she on the left. Now whatever peculiar posture Crowther got himself into, I think that for most of the time he had his back to where his wife was standing – in other words she was almost directly behind him. But Bernard hadn't got eyes in the back of his head, and Margaret, as we've said, was probably scared stiff of being seen. And it tends to lead to one conclusion, as I see it, and one conclusion only: Crowther did not see his wife that night. I'm sure she was there, but I don't think he saw her. But he did see somebody else. In other words *there was yet another person in the yard that night*, another person much nearer to him than Margaret ever got; someone standing very near to the tool-kit, and someone Crowther caught a shadowy glimpse of, as he sat in the back of his car. And I think it may have been that person, Lewis, who murdered Sylvia Kaye.'

'You don't think it was Bernard either, then?'

For the first time Morse seemed oddly hesitant. 'He could have done it, of course.'

'But I just don't see a motive, do you sir?'

'No,' said Morse flatly, 'I don't.' He looked around the room dejectedly.

'Did you get anything else from Mr Newlove, sir?'

'Yes. Crowther told him he'd used his typewriter.'

'Newlove's typewriter, you mean?'

'You sound surprised.'

'You mean Crowther *did* write that letter after all?'

Morse gave him a look of pained disappointment. 'You've never doubted that, surely?'

He opened a drawer in his desk and took out a sealed white envelope which he handed across to Lewis. It was addressed to

Jennifer Coleby. 'I want you to go to see her, Lewis, and give her this, and stay with her while she opens it. Inside there's one sheet of paper and a return envelope addressed to me. Tell her to answer the question I've asked and then to seal up her answer in the return envelope. Is that clear?'

'Wouldn't it be easier to ring her up, sir?'

Morse's eyes suddenly blazed with anger, although when he spoke his words were quiet and controlled. 'As I was saying, Lewis, you will stay with her and when she has written her answer you will make sure that the envelope is sealed tight. You see, I don't want you to see the question I've asked, nor the answer that she gives.' The voice was icy now, and Lewis quickly nodded his understanding. He had never realized quite how frightening the Inspector could be, and he was glad to get away.

CHAPTER TWENTY-NINE
Friday, 22 October, p.m.

After Lewis had gone, Morse sat and thought of Sue. So much had happened since Monday, but Sue had remained uppermost in his thoughts for almost all the time. He had to see her again. He looked at his watch. Midday. He wondered what she was doing, and suddenly spurred himself into action.

'Is that the Radcliffe?'

'Yes.'

'Accident department, please.'

'I'm putting you through, sir.'

'Hallo. Accident department.' It wasn't Sue.

'I want to have a quick word with Miss Widdowson, please.'

'You mean Staff Nurse Widdowson.' He hadn't known that.

'Susan, I think her Christian name is.'

'I'm sorry, sir. We're not allowed to take outside telephone calls except . . .'

'It might be an emergency,' interrupted Morse hopefully.

'Is it an emergency, sir?'

'Not really, no.'

'I'm sorry, sir.'

'Look, this is the police.'

'I'm sorry, sir.' Obviously she had heard that one before.

Slowly Morse was getting angry again. 'Is the Matron there?'

'You want me to put you through to Matron?'

'Yes, I do.'

He had to wait a good two minutes. 'Hullo. Matron here.'

'Matron, I'm speaking from Thames Valley Police HQ. Chief Inspector Morse. I want to speak to Staff Nurse Widdowson. I understand you have your rules about this, and of course I wouldn't in the normal way wish to break them . . .'

'Is it urgent?' *Vox auctoritatis.*

'Well, let's say it's important.'

For the next few minutes Matron coolly and lucidly explained the regulations governing the delivery of personal mail to, and the acceptance of incoming telephone calls by, members of 'my' nursing staff. She spelled out the rules and the reasons for the rules, and Morse fidgeted at his table, the fingers of his left hand drumming the top of his desk in characteristic fashion.

'You see, you have no idea of the volume of official letters and telephone calls that all my departments receive every day. And if we had the additional complication of all personal letters and calls, where would it all end? I have tried and I think I have succeeded . . .'

Morse heard her out. As she had been talking a wildly improbable thought had taken root in his mind. He almost wanted to hear her repeat the tedious catalogue of restraints. 'I'm most grateful to you, Matron. I do want to apologize . . .'

'Oh, not at all. I've enjoyed talking to you. Now, please let me help in any way I can.' She would do anything for him now, he knew that. But the situation had changed. There was just the wildest, slimmest chance now, where before there had been none at all. He rang off as soon as he could, the Matron almost begging for the chance of doing him some favour. But he wanted none: his course was now clear.

Sue was having lunch while Morse was finishing his lengthy call to her immediate superior. She was thinking of him, too. Would she had known him earlier! She knew with a passionate certainty that he could have changed her life. Was it too late even now? Dr Eyres sat next to her, taking every opportunity he decently could of effecting the closest physical contact with the lovely staff nurse; but Sue loathed his proximity and his insinuations and, not worrying about a sweet, she left the table as quickly as she could. Oh Morse! Why didn't I meet you before? She walked back to the outpatients' room at the casualty clinic and sat down on one of the hard benches. Absently she picked up a long-outdated copy of *Punch* and flicked mechanically through the faded pages . . . What was she to do? He hadn't been anywhere near since that wretched night when Jennifer had come home. Jennifer! And she had been fool enough to confide in Jennifer. David? She would have to write to David. He would be so upset; but to live with someone, to sleep with someone, forty, even fifty years – someone you didn't really and truly love . . .

Then she saw him. He stood there, an anxious, vulnerable look in his blue eyes. The tears started in her eyes and she felt an incredible joy. He came and sat beside her. He didn't even try to hold her hand – there was no need of that. They talked, she didn't know what about. It didn't matter.

'I shall have to go,' she said. 'Try to see me soon, won't you?' It was after half-past one.

Morse felt desperately sick at heart. He looked at Sue long and hard, and he knew that he loved her so dearly.

'Sue?'

'Yes?'

'Have you got a photograph of yourself?'

Sue rummaged in her handbag and found something. 'Not all that good, is it, really?'

Morse looked at the photograph. She was right. It didn't really do her justice, but it was his Sue all right. He put it carefully into his wallet, and got up to go. Patients were already waiting: patients with bulky plasters over legs and arms; patients with bandages round their heads and wrists; a road casualty with blood around the mouth, the face an ashen white. It was time to go. He touched her hand lightly and their fingers met in a tender, sweet farewell. Sue watched him go, limping slightly, through the flappy, celluloid doors.

It was almost a quarter to two as Morse walked down from the Radcliffe Infirmary to the broad, tree-lined avenue of St Giles'. He thought of postponing his next task; but it had to be done some time, and he was on the spot now anyway.

Keeping to the right-hand side of St Giles' as he made his way in the general direction of the Martyrs' Memorial, Morse stopped at the first snack-bar he came to, the Wimpy Grill, and walked inside. On his own admission the small, swarthy Italian, turning beefburgers on a hotplate, 'no speake, signor, the English so good,' and promptly summoned his slatternly young waitress into the consultation. Morse left amid a general shaking of heads and a flurry of gesticulation; it wasn't going to be easy. A few yards further down he stopped and entered the 'Bird and Baby' where he ordered a pint of bitter and engaged in earnest, quiet conversation for several minutes with the barman, who also as it happened was the landlord and who always stood lunch-time duty behind his bar. Sorry, no. Oh yes, he'd have noticed; but no. Sorry. It was going to be a long, dispiriting business, but one which only Morse himself could do.

He worked his way methodically along the dozen likely places in the Cornmarket below the ABC Cinema, crossed the road at Carfax, and started up the other side. It was at a little ('snacks served') cake shop nestling alongside the giant pile of Marks and Spencer that he found the person he was searching for. She was a grey-haired, plumpish woman, with a kindly face and a friendly manner. Morse spoke to her for several minutes, and this time too there was much nodding of the head and pointing. But pointing not vaguely outside, up alleys or down side-streets; this time the pointing was towards a little room, beyond the shop, wherein the establishment's snacks were served. To be precise, the pointing was towards one particular small table standing in the far corner of the room, with one chair on each side of it, both now empty, and a cruet, a dirty ashtray, and a bottle of tomato sauce upon its red-and-white striped tablecloth.

It was 3.45 p.m. Morse went over to the table and sat down. He knew that the case was nearly over now, but he could feel no elation. His feet ached, especially the right one, and he was badly in need of something to cheer him up. Again he took out the picture of Sue from his wallet and looked at the face of the girl he loved so hopelessly. The grey-haired waitress came up to him.

'Can I get you anything, sir? I'm sorry I didn't realize you might . . .'

'I'll have a cup of tea, luv,' said Morse. It was better than nothing.

He was not back in his office until 4.45 p.m. A note from Lewis lay on his desk. His sergeant hoped it would be all right going off a bit early. Please to ring him if he was needed. His wife had a touch of 'flu and the kids were a bit of a handful.

Morse screwed up the note and tossed it into the wastepaper basket. Underneath the note lay the letter that Lewis had brought from Jennifer Coleby. Making certain that it was carefully sealed,

Morse placed it unopened into the bottom left-hand drawer of his desk and turned the key in the lock.

He looked up a number in the directory and heard the drumming 'purr purr, purr purr'. He looked at his watch: almost 5.00 p.m. It wouldn't matter of course if he had gone, but he wanted to get things over straight away. 'Purr purr, purr purr.' He was on the point of giving up when the call was answered.

'Hello?' It was Palmer.

'Ah. Glad to catch you, sir. Morse here.'

'Oh.' The little manager sounded none too overjoyed. 'You're lucky. I was just locking up, but I thought I'd better get back and answer it. You never know in this job. Could be important.'

'It is important.'

'Oh.'

Palmer lived in the fashionable Observatory Street at the bottom of the Woodstock Road. Yes. He could meet Morse – of course, he could – if it was important. They arranged a meeting at the Bull and Stirrup in nearby Walton Street at 8.30 p.m. that evening.

It was a mean-looking, ill-lighted, spit-and-sawdust type of pub; a dispiriting sort of place, with gee-gees, darts, and football-pools the overriding claims upon the shabby clientele. Morse wanted to get things over and get out as quickly as he could. It was a struggle for a start, and Palmer was cagey and reluctant; but Morse knew too much for him. Grudgingly, but with apparent honesty, Palmer told his pitiable little tale.

'I suppose you think I should have told you this before?'

'I don't know. I'm not married myself.' Morse sounded utterly indifferent. It was 9.00 p.m. and he took his leave.

He drove up the Woodstock Road at rather more than 30 m.p.h.; but spotting a police car up ahead he slackened off to the statutory speed limit. He swung round the Woodstock roundabout, the starting point of all this sorry mess, and headed for Woodstock. At the village of Yarnton he turned off and parked the Jaguar outside the home of Mrs Mabel Jarman, where he stayed for no more than a couple of minutes.

On his way home he called at police HQ. The corridors were darkened, but he didn't bother to turn on the lights. In his office he unlocked the bottom left-hand drawer and took out the envelope. His hand shook slightly as he reached for his paper-knife and neatly slit open the top. He felt like a cricketer who has made a duck, checking the score-book just in case an odd run made by the other batsman had been fortuitously misattributed to his own name. But Morse had no faith in miracles, and he knew what the note had to say before he opened it. He saw the note; he did not read it. He saw it synoptically, not as the sum of its individual words and letters. Miracles do not happen.

He turned off the light, locked his office door, and walked back along the darkened corridor. The last piece had clicked into place. The jigsaw was complete.

CHAPTER THIRTY
Saturday, 23 October

Since breakfast Sue had been trying to write to David. Once or twice she had written half a page before screwing up the paper and starting a fresh sheet; but mostly the elusive phraseology had failed her after nothing more than a miserably brief sentence. She tried again.

My dear David,
   You've been so kind and so loving to me that I know this letter will come as a terrible shock to you. But I feel I must tell you – it's not fair to keep anything from you. The truth is that I've fallen in love with someone else and I . . .

What else could she say? She couldn't just leave it at that . . . She screwed up the latest draft and added it to the growing collection of tight paper balls upon the table.

A sombre-looking Morse sat in his black leather chair that same morning. Another restless, fitful night. He must have some holiday.

'You look tired, sir,' said Lewis.

Morse nodded. 'Yes, but we've come to the end of the road, now.'

'We have, sir?'

Morse seemed to buoy himself up. He took a deep breath: 'I've taken one or two wrong turnings, as you know, Lewis; but by some fluke I was always heading in the right direction – even on the night of the murder. Do you remember when we stood in that yard? I remember staring up at the stars and thinking how many secrets they must know, looking down on everything. I remember trying even then to see the pattern, not just the bits that form the pattern. There was something very odd, you know Lewis, about that night. It looked like a sex murder right enough. But things are not always what they seem, are they?'

He seemed to be speaking in a dazed, sing-song sort of way, almost as if he were on drugs. 'Now you can *make* things look a bit odd, but I've not met any of these clever killers yet. Or things just *happen* like that, eh? It was odd if Sylvia had been raped where she was found, wasn't it? I know it was very dark in the yard that night, but cars with full headlights were coming in and out all the time. It's surely stretching the imagination a bit to think that anyone would be crazy enough to rape a girl in the full blaze of motorists' headlights.' He seemed to Lewis to be relaxing a little and his eyes had lost their dull stare. 'Well?' That was more like the chief.

'I suppose you're right, sir.'

'But it looked odd. A young, leggy blonde murdered and raped or raped and murdered. Whichever way round it was, it all pointed in the same way. We've got a sex-killer to find. But I wasn't sure. Raping isn't easy they tell me if the young lady isn't too willing, and, as I say, I discounted the likelihood of Sylvia being raped in the yard. She could have screamed and yelled – unless of course she was dead already. But I'm a bit squeamish about that sort of thing, and I thought the chances of us having to deal with a Christie-like necrophiliac were a bit remote. Where does that leave us, then?' Lewis hoped it was a rhetorical question, and so it was. 'Well, let us concentrate our attention separately upon each of the two components – rape and murder. Let us assume two distinct actions – not one. Let us assume that she has intercourse with a man – after all, there was no doubt about the fact of intercourse. Let us assume further that this took place entirely with her consent. Now there was one shred of evidence to support this. Sylvia wasn't a member of Women's Lib, but she wasn't wearing a bra, and it seemed to me, if not unusual, well – a little suggestive. We discovered that Sylvia had several white blouses, but no white bras. Why not? No one as conscious of her figure and her appearance as Sylvia Kaye is going to wear a black bra under a thin, white blouse, is she? I could draw only one conclusion – that Sylvia not infrequently went out without a bra; and if she did wear a bra, it would be a black one, because all the girls believe that black underwear is terribly sexy. Now all this suggested that perhaps she was a young lady of somewhat easy virtue, and I think it's pretty clear she was.'

'She wasn't wearing pants either, sir.'

'No. But the pathologist's report suggests that she had been – there were the marks of elastic round her waist. Yes, I'm pretty sure that she had been wearing pants and that they got stuck in someone's pocket and later got thrown away or burned. Anyway, it's not important. To get back to the separate components of the crime. First, a man had intercourse with Sylvia – pretty certainly without too much opposition. Second, someone murdered her. It could have been the same man, but it's not easy to see the motive. The evidence we got at a very early stage seemed to suggest that this was a completely casual acquaintanceship, a chance pick-up on the road to Woodstock. All right. But since it was established that Bernard Crowther was the man who had stopped at the Woodstock roundabout, certain aspects of the case seemed to get more puzzling rather than less. I could well imagine that Crowther was the sort of man who might now and then be unfaithful to his wife; from what we now know, his relationship with his wife seems to have drifted over the last few years from idyllic bliss to idiotic bickering. But if we were looking for a sex-crazed maniac, I felt fairly sure Crowther wasn't the man we were looking for. He seemed to me an essentially civilized man. You remember when you looked at those photographs of Sylvia, Lewis? You remember you said you'd like to get the bastard who did it? But you had a composite picture of the crime in your mind, I think: you were putting together the rape and the murder and *something else – the obvious interference with Sylvia's scanty clothing*. Now I couldn't fit Crowther into that picture; and if Mrs Crowther's evidence was right in any respect, it was surely right at the point where she described what she saw in the car. You made that point yourself, Lewis. What have we got then? First, he makes love to the girl in the back of the car. Second, he may have had a quarrel with her about something. Let's say she's a mercenary young tart and she agreed to make love with him on the sort of terms a common prostitute would ask. Let's say he couldn't or wouldn't pay her. Let's say they quarrel and he kills her. It's a possibility. But I just couldn't believe that if this had been the sequence of events that we should have found Sylvia in the condition we did – with her blouse torn and ripped away from her. Or at least not if we were right in thinking of Crowther as the guilty party.'

Lewis interrupted him quietly. 'You said that you knew who did that.'

'I think you do, too,' replied Morse. 'As the case progressed there seemed to be only one person who had a mind sufficiently warped and perverted to interfere with the body of a murdered girl. A man who had been waiting to see her anyway; a man we know who perpetually tantalized and tortured himself by thoughts of sex; a man who feasted on a weekly diet of blue films and pornography. You know all about him, Lewis. And I went to see him a week ago. His bedroom is cluttered with the whole paraphernalia of dirty postcards, Danish magazines, hard pornography, and all the rest. He's sick, Lewis, and he knows he's sick, and his mother knows he's sick. But he's not a vicious type of chap. In fact he's not unlikeable in a nasty sort of way. He told me that he'd often had a dream about undressing the body of a dead girl.'

'My God!' said Lewis.

'You shouldn't feel too surprised about it, you know,' said Morse. 'I'm told that Freud mentions that sort of dream as being quite a common form of sexual fantasy among frustrated voyeurs.' Lewis remembered the film. He'd found it a bit erotic himself, hadn't he? But he hadn't wanted to admit it – even to himself.

'He'd met Sylvia several times before. They usually met in the cocktail lounge of the Black Prince, had some booze, and then went back to his house – to his bedroom. He paid for it. He told me so.'

'He had quite a lot of expense one way or another, sir.'

'He did indeed. Anyway, on the night when Sylvia was murdered he'd been waiting since about a quarter to eight. He drank more and more and felt more and more desperate as the time ticked by and Sylvia didn't appear. He went out several times to look for her. But he saw nothing. When he did find her he was sick in mind and body: sick from pent-up sexual frustration and sick from too much drink. He found her quite by chance – so he says – and I believe him.'

'And then . . . you mean he . . . he fiddled about with her?'

Morse nodded. 'Yes. He did.'

'He needs treatment, sir.'

'He's promised me to see a psychiatrist – but I'm not very optimistic about that. I only ever knew one psychiatrist. Funny chap. If ever a man was in need of psychiatric treatment it was him.' Morse smiled ruefully, and Lewis felt his chief was becoming more like his normal self.

'So that's cleared that bit up, sir.'

'Yes. But it didn't help all that much, did it? I was as sure as I could be that Sylvia Kaye was not murdered by Mr John Sanders. She was murdered, so the pathology report says, between 7 and 8 p.m. or thereabouts. Now we know all that stuff about the murderer going back to the scene of the crime, but I just couldn't believe that Sanders had stood for about two and a half to three hours drinking whisky no more than fifty-odd yards away from where his victim lay murdered. He'd have hopped it, that's for sure. What seemed so odd to me was why she wasn't found earlier. But you cleared that up.'

Lewis was glad to know that he had been of value somewhere along the line, and he knew what Morse was referring to, for he had himself interviewed all the drivers of vehicles parked in the yard that night. The driver of the car beside which Sylvia had been found had earlier parked in an awkward position just outside the yard of the Black Prince; but he had been anxious about blocking other cars and he had immediately taken the opportunity, on seeing a car drive out from the yard, of backing his own car into the space left vacant. His light of course could not possibly have picked up Sylvia's body, and when he got out of the driving seat the body was against the wall on the other side of the car.

'Well,' continued Morse, 'by this time, for one reason or another we managed to get on to Crowther. Or rather the Crowthers. Perhaps we shall never know the exact part each of them played that night. But one thing I think we can confidently suggest – that as a result of what happened *Margaret thought that Bernard had murdered Sylvia*. Whether she killed herself just because of what she suspected, I don't know, though it was surely one of the factors that drove her to it. But that's only half the matter. I think, too, that *Bernard thought that Margaret had murdered Sylvia*. If I'm right about this, it seems to me to explain a lot of things. Bernard had two overwhelming reasons for keeping quiet. First, his love affair would almost certainly be brought out into the open, with all the consequences that would entail. But second, and even more important, his evidence might well help us find the murderer who, as Bernard saw things, was probably his own wife, Margaret. Oh dear, Lewis, if only they had spoken to each other about it! You don't suspect someone else of a crime if you've done it yourself. And I think each of them was quite genuine in suspecting the other. So we can say with every confidence that *neither of them did it*. And if Bernard had shown any intelligence he would have known how improbable it was that Margaret was actually involved in the murder. He passed his wife on the way back to Oxford! Now we know from Margaret's evidence that she's a slowish driver and perhaps most cars would pass her anyway. But if he left for Oxford *before* her, it is a physical impossibility for him to have overtaken her. Agreed?'

'Unless he called for a drink or something, sir.'

'I hadn't thought of that,' said Morse slowly. 'But it isn't a vital point. Let's go on. Now the key person in the case from the beginning has been Miss X – the Miss X who was with Sylvia in Bernard Crowther's car. What did we learn about her? The most vital fact we learned was something Mrs Jarman heard; and she's utterly convinced that she *did* hear it – I saw her again last night. She heard Sylvia say, "We'll have a giggle about it in the morning." So. We find the field narrowed very considerably, do we not? We investigate the Town and Gown Assurance Co. and we discover some interesting facts. And the most interesting fact of all is that someone tells Miss Jennifer Coleby to keep her mouth shut.' Lewis opened his own mouth, but got no further. 'I know you think I've been anti that young lady from the beginning, but I am now convinced – more than ever convinced – that the letter we found addressed to Jennifer Coleby was written to her by Bernard Crowther. If you want chapter and verse, it was written on the afternoon of Friday, 1 October in the rooms of Mr Peter Newlove in Lonsdale College on the same Mr Peter Newlove's typewriter. That, Lewis, is a *fact*.'

Again Lewis made an effort to protest, and again Morse waved the protest aside. 'Hear me out, Lewis. Jennifer Coleby lied from the word go. In fact of all the people in this case, it's Jennifer Coleby who had the monopoly of the lies. Lies, lies, and more lies. But why *should* she lie? Why should anyone be so anxious to mislead us to the extent that she did? I felt sure, fairly early on, that the reason was pretty simple really. The young lady who sat in the back of Bernard's car was his mistress, and everything we learned from Margaret confirmed the truth of his own admission that he did in fact have a mistress. Now I needn't go over all the lies we got from Jennifer; but there was some truth amid the tangled web of all the lies. And the one thing she told us that seemed the biggest whopper of the lot was just about the one thing that was true. *She said she'd got a car.*'

Lewis could restrain himself no longer. 'But she had a puncture, sir. We know all about that.'

'Oh, I don't doubt she had a puncture. We know she did. She rang up the Battery and Tyre people. But if they couldn't mend it, someone else could, eh? If you remember, Jennifer didn't ask the tyre man to call some other time; and she didn't have it done at Barkers. But somebody mended her puncture, Lewis. Perhaps she did it herself? She's not a fool, is she? Perhaps she asked the man next door? I don't know. But you can repair a puncture in five minutes without much trouble, and *Jennifer Coleby is a practical girl and she had to have a car that night.'*

'I don't follow that at all,' said the mystified Lewis.

'You will, have no fear.' Morse looked at his watch. 'I want you to go and pick her up, Lewis.'

'You mean Miss Coleby?'

'Who the hell else?'

Morse followed Lewis out, knocked at the office of Chief Superintendent Strange, and went in.

Some half an hour later the door was opened, and Strange stood on the threshold with Morse. Both men looked stern-faced, and Strange nodded his head gravely as the Chief Inspector said a few final words.

'You look tired, you know, Morse. I think you ought to put in for a fortnight's furlough now this is over.'

'Well, not quite over, sir.'

Morse walked slowly back to his office.

When Jennifer Coleby arrived Morse asked her to sit down and then walked over to Lewis. 'I want this to be private, Lewis. You understand, I know.'

Lewis didn't understand and he felt hurt. But he left them together, and walked along to the canteen.

'Look Inspector. I really thought that after your sergeant saw me yesterday that you'd finished . . .'

Morse interrupted her sharply. '*I've* asked you here and *I'll* do the talking. You just sit back and shut up for a few minutes.' There was thinly veiled menace in his voice, and Jennifer Coleby, looking very much on her guard, did as Morse had bidden her.

'Let me tell you what I suspected long ago in this case, Miss Coleby. You can interrupt me if I go wrong, but I want no more of your miserable lies.' She glanced viciously into his hard eyes, but said nothing. 'Let me tell you what I think. I think that two girls were picked up by a man one night and that one of the girls was the man's mistress. I think that this mistress usually travelled by car to see her lover, but on that particular night she couldn't get there by car, and that was why she either had to catch a bus or hitchhike. Unfortunately, and by sheer chance, she was picked up *by the very man she was going to see.* Unfortunately, too, there were two girls, and he had to pick them both up, and *these two girls knew each other*. Now the whole thing suddenly seemed too dangerous – this is what I think, Miss Coleby, you understand – and somehow they decided to forget their date and wait until the next opportunity arose. I think that this girl, the mistress, asked to be dropped off somewhere on the way. She probably made some perfectly natural excuse – she was a good liar – and she asked him to drop her off. But she knew where the other girl was going – no doubt the other girl had told her – and she felt uncontrollably jealous that night. She'd perhaps sensed something as they'd all driven along together. You see, the girl who was sitting in the front was very attractive to men. And perhaps? Who knows? The man, the man she knew so well, had been unfaithful to his wife. He had been unfaithful with her! Why not with some other girl? So I think this is what happened. She got out of the car, but she didn't return home. No. She waited for a bus and one came almost immediately. How she must have cursed her luck. If only she'd not hitched a lift! Anyway, she caught the bus and found her way to the place where she knew she might find them. And she did find them. It was dark there and she couldn't see very much, but she saw enough. And she felt a murderous jealousy welling up inside her, not so much against her lover, but against that cheap slut of a girl, a girl she'd got to know but never liked, a girl she now hated with unspeakable fury. I think perhaps they may have spoken to each other when the man had gone – but I can only guess, and I may be wrong. I think that the girl who had just got out of the car could sense the deadly fury in the other girl's face, and I think she tried to run away. But as she did, a vicious blow crashed across her skull and she lay dead in a heap upon a cobbled yard. I think the dead girl was dragged by the arms into the darkest corner of the yard and I think the girl who murdered her walked out into the night and caught a bus that took her home.'

Morse stopped, and there was utter silence in the room. 'Do you think that's how it happened, Miss Coleby?'

She nodded her head.

'We both know who murdered Sylvia, don't we?' Morse spoke so very softly that she could only just catch his words. Again she nodded.

Morse rang Lewis and told him to come in. 'Take a few notes, Sergeant. Now, Miss Coleby. A few more questions, please. Who mended your puncture for you?'

'The man across the road. Mr Thorogood.'

'How long did it take him?'

'Five, ten minutes. Not long. I helped him.'

'How long have you been the mistress of your employer, Mr Palmer?' Lewis lifted his eyes in amazement.

'Nearly a year.'

'Didn't you think it a bit dangerous – telling someone else?'

'I suppose it was. But it meant we could have a room once a week.'

'Palmer told you this morning that I knew?'

'Yes.' She had answered mildly enough thus far. But the old flash blazed in her eyes once more. 'How did you know?'

'I had to guess. But there had to be some reason. It was accidental, really. I checked the night-school register for Wednesday, 29 September, to see whether Mrs Crowther had been present. She wasn't. But I noticed another name on the list, and she *had* been present, a Mrs Josephine Palmer. Well . . .'

'You've got a suspicious mind, Inspector.'

'And when did this business of the letters start?'

'In the summer. Stupid really. But it worked all right – so they said.'

'Can you give me your solemn word, Miss Coleby, that you will say nothing of this to anyone?'

'Yes, Inspector. I think I owe you that at least.'

Morse got up. 'Well, get someone to take her back to work, Lewis. We've taken up enough of Miss Coleby's time.' A flabbergasted Lewis gaped at them like a fish out of water, and Jennifer looked round and gave him a wan, sad smile.

'You're not being very fair to me are you, sir?' Lewis seemed downcast and annoyed.

'What do you mean?' asked Morse.

'You said the case was nearly over.'

'It is over,' said Morse.

'You know who murdered her?'

'A person has already been arrested and charged with the murder of Sylvia Kaye.'

'When was this?'

'This morning. Here!' Morse took out the letter which Lewis himself had brought from Jennifer Coleby, and passed it over. Lewis took out the sheet of paper and read with blind, blank, uncomprehending disbelief the one line answer that Miss Coleby had written to Morse's question.

'Yes,' said Morse softly. 'It's true.'

Lewis was full of questions, but he received no answers. 'Look, Lewis, I want to be alone. You go home and look after your wife for a change. I'll talk to you on Monday.'

The two men left the office. Lewis got his coat and was soon away. But Morse walked slowly to the cells at the far end of the north wing.

'Want to go in, sir?' said the sergeant on duty.

Morse nodded. 'Leave us alone, will you?'

'Anything you say, sir. Cell number 1.'

Morse took the keys, unbolted the main door to the cells and walked along to cell number 1. He put his hands on the bars and stood staring sadly through.

'Hello, Sue,' he said.

CHAPTER THIRTY-ONE
Monday, 25 October

The day had broken bright and clear, but by mid-morning a melancholy army of heavy grey cloud had massed overhead; and flurries of light rain were already sprinkling the window panes of Morse's office as, for the last time on the case of Sylvia Kaye, the two detectives faced each other across the desk.

'What did we know about Miss X?' asked Morse, and proceeded to answer the question himself. 'We knew roughly what she looked like, we knew roughly what she was wearing, and we knew roughly what age she was. It was a start, but it could never have got us very far. But we also knew that the two girls waiting at the bus stop not only knew each other but that *they would be seeing each other again the following morning*. Now this, without a doubt, was by far the most important single piece of evidence we ever got, and we acted upon it immediately. Naturally we assumed that we could narrow down the field of our enquiries, and quite properly we concentrated our attentions on the office girls who worked with Sylvia Kaye. Of course, it could have been a friend of Sylvia's, someone she would be meeting at lunch-time perhaps, or someone she would be meeting on the bus. It could have been a hundred and one things. But we didn't think so. And we didn't think so because our suspicions were very soon aroused, and with every justification, by the peculiar behaviour of one of the girls who worked in the same office as Sylvia – Miss Jennifer Coleby.

But although we didn't know it at the time, there was someone else Sylvia would be meeting that next morning, and if we'd been a fraction brighter earlier on, Lewis, we might have got on to it more quickly. Sylvia was undergoing physiotherapy treatment at the Radcliffe Infirmary for her broken arm, and she was going for this treatment regularly on Tuesday and Thursday mornings. That is, she would be reporting for physiotherapy to the staff nurse in charge of the Accident Outpatients' Department *on the morning of Thursday, 30 September*. In other words, she would be reporting to Staff Nurse Widdowson.' Lewis got up to close the windows upon which the rain was splattering more heavily now. 'This, of course,' continued Morse, 'meant nothing very much by itself. But we learned that Sylvia didn't have many close girl friends, didn't we? It was interesting. Yes, at the very least it was interesting.' Morse's attention wandered momentarily, and he stared as Lewis had done through the windows to the concrete yard outside, now gleaming under the lowering sky. 'But let's return to Jennifer Coleby. Crowther wrote to her – that's established now beyond any question of doubt. But Crowther didn't write the note *for* Jennifer: she was merely the messenger boy. She's admitted that, and she had no option really. When I wrote to her I didn't ask her to accuse anyone of murder; but I did ask her if the letter was meant for Sue Widdowson, and she confirmed that it was. You'll never know, Lewis, how much I dreaded the truth of all this . . .'

The rain plashed across the yard, and the room was sombre and dark. Electric lights flashed on in several adjoining rooms, but not in Morse's office. 'Just consider a minute, Lewis. *Jennifer had a car.* That was a central fact in the case. And in spite of the temporary trouble she had with a puncture, *she used her car on the night of the 29th.* She said she did, remember? And she did. I didn't believe her at the time, but I was wrong. She met someone that night who saw her car and saw Jennifer Coleby in it. Someone who had nothing whatsoever to do with Sylvia's murder. And that was someone with whom Jennifer was having an affair – her employer, Mr Palmer. So, although the evidence had pointed at almost every stage to Jennifer Coleby, she suddenly acquired for herself a wholly incontrovertible alibi. Up to that point I had felt utterly convinced that the other girl in this affair was Jennifer; but I now had to face the undoubted, unchallengeable fact that whoever it was who sat behind Sylvia Kaye that night in Bernard Crowther's car, it was not, quite definitely *not*, Jennifer Coleby. Who was it, then? Although I was forced to abandon Jennifer as suspect number one – indeed, forced to abandon her as a suspect at all – I stuck stubbornly to my original idea that whoever the girl was, she was Crowther's mistress, and that it was to her that Crowther had sent his message. So let us look at things from Crowther's angle for a few minutes. I think that without a shadow of doubt he must have been a very frightened man. Just put yourself in his shoes, Lewis. He had left Sylvia Kaye alive and well – he knew that – on the Wednesday night. And the next day – what does he discover? He reads in the press that this same girl has been found murdered. But not murdered *anywhere*. Murdered on the very spot where he had last seen her – in the courtyard of the Black Prince. Who *knew* that he'd been there? Just himself and Sylvia – and she could never again say anything to anyone. But Sue Widdowson would have *guessed*, because Sylvia would have told her where she was going. He must have been worried out of his wits, and certainly for an intelligent man he doesn't seem to have been very sensible in what he did. Again and again the thought must have flashed across his mind: would Sue realize how dangerous it would be to say one single word to a living soul? He must have thought she would surely realize this. But still the doubts must have nagged away at his mind. She was the one person who could upset the whole apple-cart – not only bring him under suspicion for Sylvia's murder but throw the whole of his family life into a turmoil he felt he couldn't face. He just had to make sure, or at least he had to do *something*. He daren't see her. So he wrote.' Lewis showed the familiar signs of unease and Morse nodded his understanding. 'I know, Lewis. Why does he write to *Jennifer*?'

'Why did he write at all, sir? Why not just ring?'

'Yes. I'm coming to that. But first let's be absolutely certain about the *fact* of the matter – and the fact is that Crowther *did* write to Jennifer Coleby. For if we fully recognize the significance of that, we can begin to answer the perfectly valid question you raise. Why not ring her? Why not? The answer is fairly straightforward, I think. *Who* was he to ring, and *where*? Let's assume for the minute that he wants to ring up Jennifer – the faithful messenger girl. At work? No. It was too dangerous. All the girls in the office knew Palmer's views on using his company's phones, and they played it fair because he turned a blind eye to personal correspondence coming in. But more than that. It was also far too dangerous, because all incoming telephone calls – except to the private phone in Palmer's office, which his personal secretary handled – came through the switchboard; and as you well know anyone on the switchboard can listen in with complete impunity to whatever's

being said. No. That was out. Well? Why not ring Sue Widdowson
herself? Why not ring his mistress and speak to her direct, either
at her home or at the hospital? Again it's not difficult to see why
he didn't. If he rang Sue up at home, he could never be sure that
the other two weren't there, could he? He could risk Jennifer, but
not Mary. He must have felt pretty certain – and I'm sure he was
right – that listening in, even to a one-sided telephone call, is a
temptingly easy and interesting pastime.'

After politely knocking on Morse's door, the young girl with
the office correspondence entered brightly and placed the Inspector's morning mail into his in-tray.

'Not a very nice day, sir.'

'No,' said Morse.

'It'll probably clear up later.' She gave him a warm and pleasant
smile as she left, and Morse nodded in a kindly way. It was some
vague consolation to know that life was still going on around him.
He stared absently out of the window and noticed that the rain
had slackened. Perhaps she was right. It would probably clear up
later . . .

'But why couldn't he ring her at work, sir?'

'Ah yes. I'm sorry, Lewis. Why couldn't he ring her at work,
you say? I found the answer to that only last Friday. It is virtually
impossible for any outsider, even for the police, to get into direct
contact with any of the nursing staff at the Radcliffe. I tried it
myself, and you might as well ask directory enquiries for a number
if you haven't got the address. There's an old battle-axe of a
matron there . . .'

'Couldn't Crowther have written to her, though? Surely . . .'

'He could, yes. And I don't know why he didn't really, except
. . . You see, Lewis, he'd got into this routine with Sue Widdowson. Let me try to explain how it must have started. As you know,
the post gets worse and worse everywhere. But in North Oxford it
seems it's particularly bad. It seldom arrives before ten in the
morning – far too late for anyone to receive a letter before setting
off for work. And even if it arrived early, say at eight, it would
still not be in time. Why not write to her at the hospital, then? The
answer is that our dear Matron puts her foot down there as well;
she positively forbids all private mail being accepted in the
hospital.'

'But if Crowther had posted a letter to her home address, she
would have got it as soon as she came back from work, wouldn't
she?'

'Yes, you're right. But you put your finger on the central

difficulty, and this is why I should think Jennifer Coleby was brought into the picture in the first place. Bernard Crowther, you see, like most of these University fellows, didn't work any regular hours at Lonsdale College. Something would always be cropping up at odd times – disciplinary matters, unexpected visitors, un-scheduled meetings – and he could never plan his extra-marital escapades with any more than the hopeful anticipation that he might be free at any particular time in the days ahead. But much more important than this, he had to keep a very careful eye on the day-to-day comings and goings of his own family. Margaret might arrange something, the children might get a half-day holiday out of the blue, or be ill or . . . well here, too, there was plenty that could go wrong and mess up the best-laid plans completely. So it seems to me that Crowther often didn't know for certain until the day itself, even perhaps until a few hours beforehand, if and when and where he was going to be free to meet his mistress. But, Lewis, *Lonsdale College is no more than a hundred yards or so* from the premises of the Town and Gown Assurance office in the High.'

'You mean Crowther just walked along and dropped a note in?'

'He did just that.'

'But Jennifer wouldn't be able to contact Sue during the day either, would she? You just said . . .'

'I know what you're going to say. He might just as well have written to Sue's home address. She wouldn't get the message any earlier, because the letter would be lying on the door-mat when she got in. In fact she'd almost certainly get it later. But all this is assuming that Crowther could write *the day before* to arrange a meeting, and as I say I suspect that he very often couldn't. But there's another much more important point, Lewis. You say that Jennifer couldn't contact Sue during the day. *But she could, and she often did.* The two of them met fairly regularly for a snack at lunch-time. They met in a little café next to M and S. I know that, Lewis. I've been there.' Morse intoned the last words in a melancholy, mechanical way, and Lewis looked at him curiously. There was something that Morse had said a few minutes ago. It was almost as if . . .

'Jennifer Coleby must have known all about it then, sir.'

'I don't know about *all*. She knew enough, though. Too much I suppose . . .' He lapsed into silence for a few moments, but when he resumed there was more spring and spirit in his voice. 'I don't know how it started, but at some stage they must have told each other about themselves. They tell me that women, and men, too, for that matter, enjoy talking to someone else about their conquests; and some chance remark probably brought the two of them together, and a bond of conspiracy was soon forged. I think there can be no doubt about that. I suspect it was Crowther, perhaps after a couple of misunderstandings and disappointments over meetings with Sue, who suggested the idea of dropping some harmless-looking note addressed to Jennifer Coleby into the letter-box of Town and Gown. I'm pretty sure he had the sort of mind that enjoyed the idea of cryptic messages, and the practice grew and this became their normal channel of communication. He would stroll past and put a letter or a postcard through the front door of the office. Simple – not even out of his way. It probably only happened at first when an unexpected opportunity arose, but as time went on it became the normal practice, so normal that he even followed it for his last and crucial message to her. And quite apart from being a neat and extremely useful device, it must have seemed a godsend to Crowther not to have to write any actual letters as such to Sue. Like most people in such illicit affairs he must have had a dread of a letter going astray, being opened by the wrong person, or being found somewhere. No one could learn very much this way, could he, even if he did find the letters?'

'When did you first think it was Miss Widdowson, sir?' Lewis asked his question with an unwonted gentleness, for at last he had begun to understand.

Morse stared wearily and sadly at the desk in front of him, the fingers of the left hand drumming nervously on the surface. 'I suppose there were the vaguest hints – oh, I don't know. But I wasn't certain until last Friday. Perhaps the first time I began to suspect the truth was when I checked the evening-class register for Margaret Crowther's attendance record. I happened to notice, purely by accident really, that by some divine mischance Palmer's wife was a member of the same class. And it made me wonder; it made me wonder a lot. I thought it most improbable that Jennifer Coleby was the sort of person to grant a lot of favours without getting some in return; and I pondered on the bond that must exist between her and the other girl. In a roundabout way I considered the possibility of both girls being in similar circum-stances, in the same sort of relationship with other people. With men. And so I did a lot of guessing, and I thought of Crowther with somebody and Jennifer with somebody; and then Palmer fitting in somewhere perhaps? And then . . . Well, and then I thought of Sue Widdowson, and suddenly the pieces began to click together. Could Jennifer be having an affair with Palmer? So often in this sort of situation it's someone you meet at work; and who was there at Town and Gown but Palmer? He was the only man on the premises. I kept wondering what it was that Jennifer was getting out of the bargain. And it suddenly struck me that there was one thing that she would want above all. Do you know what that was, Lewis?'

'I'm afraid I've no experience in that sort of thing, sir.'

'Nor have I,' said Morse.

'Well, I suppose you'd want a place where you could be alone together . . . Oh, I see. You mean . . .'

'Yes, Lewis. Someone could offer Jennifer a room where she could be alone with Palmer. Mary wasn't out all that much. But whenever she was, the coast was clear, because the other member of the trio could also arrange to be conveniently absent at the same time. And that's what she did.'

'Just a minute, sir.' Some worry was nagging away at the back of Lewis's mind. He was thinking back to the night of Wednesday, 29 September . . . Then he had it. 'But the house would have been free, wouldn't it, on that Wednesday night? I thought you said that Mary had gone to the pictures or something.'

'We'll make a detective of you yet, Lewis.' Morse got up from his leather chair, clapped his hand on his sergeant's shoulder, and stood watching the threatening clouds roll slowly westward. It had stopped raining now and the shallow puddles in the yard lay undisturbed. 'That was another of Jennifer's lies, I'm afraid. Mary was at home that night – she told me so. But even if Mary had been out, I don't think it would have made any difference. I'm pretty sure that Jennifer's job was to drive Sue to meet Crowther. That was her part of the bargain. And on Wednesday, 29 September, they both had their dates – as we know.'

'But why didn't they . . .' Lewis appeared reluctant to continue the sentence, and Morse did it for him.

'Why didn't the four of them take the opportunity of using the house whenever Mary was out? Is that what you mean?'

'Yes.'

'Well, it was a pretty safe bet for Palmer, of course. He lives a good way off and very few people would be likely to know him in North Oxford. Anyway it was a reasonable risk. In fact I know he's been there. I had the house watched all last week, and on Wednesday night Palmer's car was parked in the next road. McPherson found it – I'd put him on special duty.' A slightly pained expression crossed Lewis's face, but Morse ignored it. 'He didn't actually see Palmer go in, but he saw him come out, and I saw Palmer myself on Friday night when I had it all out with him.'

'But it was too risky for Crowther?'

'What do you think? He lived only a stone's throw from the place. No, it would be the stupidest thing imaginable for him to do. He'd lived there for years. Virtually everyone knew him, and he walked along the same street almost every night when he went for a drink at the Fletcher's Arms. People would have started talking immediately. No, no. That was not on from the start.'

'So when they both had dates . . .'

'It was Jennifer's job to give Sue a lift, yes.'

'So if Jennifer hadn't suddenly found a puncture in her tyre that night, Sylvia might never have been murdered.'

'No, she wouldn't.' Morse crossed the room and sat down again in his chair. He had almost finished. 'On the night of the murder, Sue Widdowson was impatient and probably a bit annoyed with Jennifer. I don't know. Anyway she felt she couldn't wait while Jennifer was ringing up about the puncture, and finally finding some decent old boy across the way who might take ages. She thought she'd be late and so she decided to catch a bus. She walked over to the Woodstock Road and she stood at Fare Stage 5 and . . . well you know the rest. She found someone else waiting. She found Miss Sylvia Kaye.'

'If only she'd waited.'

Morse nodded. 'If only she'd waited, yes. Jennifer got the puncture mended in no more than five or ten minutes, so she says. She'd arranged to meet Palmer at the Golden Rose that night. You see she always took Sue to Woodstock and it was convenient for her and Palmer to meet at some pub near by – Begbroke, Bladon, or Woodstock itself. And they met that night, we know that. In fact, in spite of all her troubles, Jennifer was there before Palmer. She bought herself a lager and lime and went out to sit in the garden to watch out for him coming.'

'Funny, isn't it, sir. If Sue Widdowson . . .'

'You're full of "ifs", Lewis.'

'Life *is* full of "ifs", sir.'

'Yes, that's true.'

'But you were still guessing, weren't you? I mean, you had no solid evidence to go on.'

'Perhaps not then. But everything was adding up. Sue and Jennifer were about the same height, same sort of colouring, except . . .'

'Except what, sir?'

'It doesn't matter. Forget it. Dress? I saw the coat that Mrs Jarman described; I saw the same sort of slacks; and Sue Widdowson was wearing them. On Friday night I showed Mrs Jarman a photograph of Sue and she recognized her immediately. No wonder the poor woman couldn't pick anybody out at the identity parade. The girl she had seen at the bus stop just wasn't there.'

'People do make mistakes, sir.'

'If only they did, Lewis. If only they did!'

'But it's still not *proof*.'

'No, I suppose it isn't. But I found something else. When I called at the Radcliffe to see Crowther's body, I got his keys from the ward sister – they'd been in his trouser pocket. I asked her if anyone from the nursing staff had been along to see him, and she said that no one had. But she said that Staff Nurse Widdowson had asked her how he was getting along and that she had stood at the top of the ward and looked for a long time at the bed where Crowther lay.'

Morse's voice was growing agitated, but he pulled himself together as quickly as he could. Once more he walked over to the window and saw the sun beginning to filter through the thinning cloud. 'I went to Lonsdale College and I looked through Crowther's room. I found only one drawer locked up in the whole place, one of the drawers in his table desk – the bottom drawer on the left, if you're interested.' He turned round and glared at Lewis, and his voice sounded harsh and fierce. 'I opened the drawer, and I found . . . I found a photograph of Sue.' His voice had suddenly become very quiet and he turned again to look out of the window. 'A copy of the same photograph she gave to me.' But he spoke these last words so softly that Lewis was unable to catch them.

EPILOGUE

It was done.

Lewis drove home for his lunch, hoping that his wife was feeling better. He passed a newspaper placard with bold, large headlines: WOODSTOCK MURDER – WOMAN HELPING POLICE. He didn't stop to buy a copy.

Morse went along once more to the cell block, and spent a few minutes with Sue. 'Anything you want?'

There were tears in her eyes as she shook her head, and he stood by her in the cell, awkward and lost. 'Inspector?'

'Yes.'

'Perhaps you can't believe me, and it doesn't matter anyway. But . . . I loved you.'

Morse said nothing. He felt his eyes prickling and he rubbed his left hand across them, and prayed that she would notice nothing. For a while he could not trust himself to speak, and when he did he looked down at his darling girl and said only, 'Goodbye, Sue.'

He walked outside and locked the door of the cell behind him. He could say no more. He tore himself away and walked along the corridor, and he heard her voice for the last time.

'Inspector?'

He turned. She stood by the bars of the cell, her face streaming with tears of anguish and despair. 'Inspector, you never did tell me your Christian name.'

It was getting dark when Morse finally left his office. He climbed into his Jaguar, drove out of the yard on which the puddles now had almost dried, and turned left into the main stream of the city-bound traffic. As he passed the ring-road roundabout, he saw two people standing on the grass verge thumbing a lift. One was a girl, a pretty girl by the look of her. Perhaps the other was a girl, too. It was difficult to tell. He drove on to his home in Oxford.

The
Wench
is Dead

The
Wench
is Dead

Thou hast committed –
Fornication; but that was in another country,
And besides, the wench is dead

(Christopher Marlowe, *The Jew of Malta*)

For
Harry Judge,
lover of canals, who introduced me to
The Murder of Christine Collins,
a fascinating account of an
early Victorian murder,
by
John Godwin.
To both I am deeply indebted.
(Copies of John Godwin's publication are obtainable
through the Divisional Librarian, Stafford
Borough Library.)

ACKNOWLEDGEMENTS

The author and publishers wish to thank the following who have kindly given permission for use of copyright materials:

Map of the Oxford Canal reproduced by permission of Oxfordshire Museum Services;

Century Hutchinson Limited for extracts from *Adventures in Wonderland* by David Grayson;

Faber and Faber Ltd for extracts from 'Little Gidding' from *Four Quartets* by T. S. Eliot;

David Higham Associates Limited on behalf of Dorothy L. Sayers for extracts from *The Murder of Julia Wallace*, published by Gollancz;

Methuen London Limited for extracts from *A Man's a Man* by Bertolt Brecht;

Oxfordshire Health Authority for extracts from *Handbook for Patients and Visitors*;

Oxford Illustrated Press for extracts from *The Erosion of Oxford* by James Stevens Curl;

E. O. Parrott for extracts;

Routledge, Chapman and Hall for extracts from *Understanding Media* by Marshall McLuhan;

The Society of Authors on behalf of the Bernard Shaw Estate for extracts from *Back to Methuselah*, published by Longman.

Every effort has been made to trace all the copyright holders but if any has been inadvertently overlooked, the author and publishers will be pleased to make the necessary arrangement at the first opportunity.

THE OXFORD CANAL

CHAPTER ONE

Thought depends absolutely on the stomach; but, in
spite of that, those who have the best stomachs are not
the best thinkers

(Voltaire, *in a letter to d'Alembert*)

Intermittently, on the Tuesday, he felt sick. Frequently, on the
Wednesday, he *was* sick. On the Thursday, he felt sick frequently,
but was actually sick only intermittently. With difficulty, early on
the Friday morning – drained, listless, and infinitely weary – he
found the energy to drag himself from his bed to the telephone,
and seek to apologize to his superiors at Kidlington Police HQ for
what was going to be an odds-on non-appearance at the office that
late November day.

When he awoke on the Saturday morning, he was happily
aware that he was feeling considerably better; and, indeed, as he
sat in the kitchen of his bachelor flat in North Oxford, dressed in
pyjamas as gaudily striped as a Lido deckchair, he was debating
whether his stomach could cope with a wafer of Weetabix – when
the phone rang.

'Morse here,' he said.

'Good morning, sir.' (A pleasing voice.) 'If you can hold the line
a minute, the Superintendent would like a word with you.'

Morse held the line. Little option, was there? No option, really;
and he scanned the headlines of *The Times* which had just been
pushed through the letter-box in the small entrance hall – late, as
usual on Saturdays.

'I'm putting you through to the Superintendent,' said the same
pleasing voice – 'just a moment, please!'

Morse said nothing; but he almost prayed (quite something for
a low-church atheist) that Strange would get a move on and come
to the phone and say whatever it was he'd got to say . . . The
prickles of sweat were forming on his forehead, and his left hand
plucked at his pyjama-top pocket for his handkerchief.

'Ah! Morse? Yes? Ah! Sorry to hear you're a bit off-colour, old
boy. Lots of it about, you know. The wife's brother had it – when
was it now? – fortnight or so back? No! I tell a lie – must have been
three weeks, at least. Still, that's neither here nor there, is it?'

In enlarged globules, the prickles of sweat had re-formed on

Morse's forehead, and he wiped his brow once more as he mumbled a few dutifully appreciative noises into the telephone.

'Didn't get you out of bed, I hope?'

'No – no, sir.'

'Good. Good! Thought I'd just have a quick word, that's all. Er . . . Look here, Morse!' (Clearly Strange's thoughts had moved to a conclusion.) 'No need for you to come in today – no need at all! Unless you feel suddenly very much better, that is. We can just about cope here, I should think. The cemeteries are full of indispensable men – eh? Huh!'

'Thank you, sir. Very kind of you to ring – I much appreciate it – but I am officially off duty this weekend in any case—'

'Really? Ah! That's good! That's er . . . *very* good, isn't it? Give you a chance to stay in bed.'

'Perhaps so, sir,' said Morse wearily.

'You say you're *up*, though?'

'Yes, sir!'

'Well you go back to bed, Morse! This'll give you a chance for a jolly good rest – this weekend, I mean – won't it? Just the thing – bit o' rest – when you're feeling a bit off-colour – eh? It's exactly what the quack told the wife's brother – when was it now . . .?'

Afterwards, Morse thought he remembered concluding this telephone conversation in a seemly manner – with appropriate concern expressed for Strange's convalescent brother-in-law; thought he remembered passing a hand once more over a forehead that now felt very wet and very, very cold – and then taking two or three hugely deep breaths – and then starting to rush for the bathroom . . .

It was Mrs Green, the charlady who came in on Tuesday and Saturday mornings, who rang treble-nine immediately and demanded an ambulance. She had found her employer sitting with his back to the wall in the entrance hall: conscious, seemingly sober, and passably presentable, except for the deep-maroon stains down the front of his deckchair pyjamas – stains that in both colour and texture served vividly to remind her of the dregs in the bottom of a coffee percolator. And she knew exactly what *they* meant, because that thoughtlessly cruel doctor had made it quite plain – five years ago now, it had been – that if only she'd called him immediately, Mr Green might still . . .

'Yes, that's right,' she heard herself say – surprisingly, imperiously, in command: 'just on the southern side of the Banbury Road roundabout. Yes. I'll be looking out for you.'

At 10.15 a.m. that same morning, an only semi-reluctant Morse condescended to be helped into the back of the ambulance, where, bedroom-slippered and with an itchy, grey blanket draped around a clean pair of pyjamas, he sat defensively opposite a middle-aged, uniformed woman who appeared to have taken his refusal to lie down on the stretcher-bed as a personal affront, and who now sullenly and silently pushed a white enamel kidney-bowl into his lap as he vomited copiously and noisily once more, while the ambulance climbed Headley Way, turned left into the grounds of the John Radcliffe Hospital complex, and finally stopped outside the Accident, Casualty, and Emergency Department.

As he lay supine (on a hospital trolley now) it occurred to Morse that he might already have died some half a dozen times without anyone recording his departure. But he was always an impatient soul (most particularly in hotels, when awaiting his breakfast); and it might not have been quite so long as he imagined before a white-coated ancillary worker led him in leisurely fashion through a questionnaire that ranged from the names of his next of kin (in Morse's case, now non-existent) to his denominational preferences (equally, alas, now non-existent). Yet once through these initiation rites – once (as it were) he had joined the club and signed the entry forms – Morse found himself the object of considerably increased attention. Dutifully, from somewhere, a young nurse appeared, flipped a watch from her stiffly laundered lapel with her left hand and took his pulse with her right; proceeded to take his blood-pressure, after tightening the black swaddling-bands around his upper-arm with (for Morse) quite needless ferocity; and then committing her findings to a chart (headed MORSE, E.) with such nonchalance as to suggest that only the most dramatic of irregularities could ever give occasion for anxiety. The same nurse finally turned her attention to matters of temperature; and Morse found himself feeling somewhat idiotic as he lay with the thermometer sticking up from his mouth, before its being extracted, its calibrations consulted, its readings apparently unsatisfactory, it being forcefully shaken thrice, as though for a few backhand flicks in a ping-pong match, and then being replaced, with all its earlier awkwardness, just underneath his tongue.

'I'm going to survive?' ventured Morse, as the nurse added her further findings to the data on his chart.

'You've got a temperature,' replied the uncommunicative teenager.

'I thought *everybody* had got a temperature,' muttered Morse.

For the moment, however, the nurse had turned her back on him to consider the latest casualty.

A youth, his legs caked with mud, and most of the rest of him encased in a red-and-black-striped Rugby jersey, had just been wheeled in – a ghastly looking Cyclopean slit across his forehead. Yet, to Morse, he appeared wholly at his ease as the (same) ancillary worker quizzed him comprehensively about his life-history, his religion, his relatives. And when, equally at his ease, the (same) nurse put him through his paces with stethoscope, watch, and thermometer, Morse could do little but envy the familiarity that was effected forthwith between the young lad and the equally young lass. Suddenly – and almost cruelly – Morse realized that she, that same young lass, had seen him – Morse! – exactly for what he was: a man who'd struggled through life to his early fifties, and who was about to face the slightly *infra dignitatem* embarrassments of hernias and haemorrhoids, of urinary infections and – yes! – of duodenal ulcers.

The kidney-bowl had been left within easy reach, and Morse was retching violently, if unproductively, when a young house-man (of Morse's age no more than half) came to stand beside him and to scan the reports of ambulance, administrative staff, and medical personnel.

'You've got a bit of nasty tummy trouble – you realize that?'

Morse shrugged vaguely: 'Nobody's really told me anything yet.'

'But you wouldn't have to be Sherlock Holmes to suspect you've got something pretty radically wrong with your innards, would you?'

Morse was about to reply when the houseman continued. 'And you've only just come in, I think? If you could give us – Mr, er, *Morse*, is it? – if you give us a chance, we'll try to tell you more about things as soon as we can, OK?'

'I'm all right, really,' said the duly chastened Chief Inspector of Police, as he lay back and tried to unloose the knot that had tied itself tight inside his shoulder muscles.

'You're *not* all right, I'm afraid! At best you've got a stomach ulcer that's suddenly decided to burst out bleeding' – Morse experienced a sharp little jerk of alarm somewhere in his diaphragm – 'and at worst you've got what we call a "perforated ulcer"; and if that *is* the case . . .'

'If that *is* the case . . .?' repeated Morse weakly. But the young doctor made no immediate answer, and for the next few minutes prodded, squeezed, and kneaded the paunchy flesh around Morse's abdomen.

'Found anything?' queried Morse, with a thin and forced apology for a grin.

'You could well lose a couple of stone. Your liver's enlarged.'

'But I thought you just said it was the stomach!'

'Oh yes, it is! You've had a stomach haemorrhage.'

'What's – what's that got to do with my liver?'

'Do you drink a lot, Mr Morse?'

'Well, most people have a drink or two most days, don't they?'

'Do you drink a *lot*?' (The same words – a semitone of exasperation lower.)

As noncommitally as his incipient panic would permit, Morse shrugged his shoulders once more: 'I like a glass of beer, yes.'

'How many pints do you drink a week?'

'A week?' squeaked Morse, his face clouding over like that of a child who has just been given a complex problem in mental multiplication.

'A day, then?' suggested the houseman helpfully.

Morse divided by three: 'Two or three, I suppose.'

'Do you drink spirits?'

'Occasionally.'

'What spirits do you drink?'

Morse shrugged his tautened shoulders once again: 'Scotch – sometimes I treat myself to a drop of Scotch.'

'How long would a bottle of Scotch last you?'

'Depends how big it was.'

But Morse immediately saw that his attempt at humour was ill appreciated; and he swiftly multiplied by three: 'Week – ten days – about that.'

'How many cigarettes do you smoke a day?'

'Eight . . . ten?' replied Morse, getting the hang of things now and smoothly dividing by three.

'Do you ever take any exercise – walking, jogging, cycling, squash . . .?'

But before Morse could switch back to his tables, he reached for the kidney-bowl that had been left within reach. And as he vomited, this time productively, the houseman observed with some alarm the coffee-grounds admixed with the tell-tale brightly crimsoned specks of blood – blood that was de-oxygenated daily with plentiful nicotine and liberally lubricated with alcohol.

For some while after these events, Morse's mind was somewhat hazy. Later, however, he could recall a nurse bending over him – the same young nurse as earlier; and he could remember the beautifully manicured fingers on her left hand as she flipped the watch out again into her palm; could almost follow her thoughts as with contracted brow she squinted at the disturbing equation between his half-minute pulse-rate and the thirty-second span upon her watch . . .

At this point Morse knew that the Angel of Death had fluttered its wings above his head; and he felt a sudden frisson of fear, as for the first time in his life he began to think of dying. For in his mind's eye, though just for a second or two, he thought he almost caught sight of the laudatory obituary, the creditable paragraph.

CHAPTER TWO

Do you know why we are more fair and just towards the dead? We are not obliged to them, we can take our time, we can fit in the paying of respects between a cocktail party and an affectionate mistress – in our spare time.

(Albert Camus, *The Fall*)

When Morse awoke the following morning, he was aware of a grey dawn through the window of the small ward, to his left; and of a clock showing 4.50 a.m. on the wall above the archway to his right, through which he could see a slimly attractive nurse, sitting in a pool of light behind a desk, and writing in a large book. Was she writing, Morse wondered, about *him*? If so, there would be remarkably little to say; for apart from one very brief bout of vomiting in the small hours, he had felt, quite genuinely, so very much better; and had required no further attention. The tubing strapped to his right wrist, and stretching up to the saline-drip bottle hooked above his bed, was still dragging uncomfortably against his skin most of the time, as if the needle had been stuck in slightly off-centre; but he'd determined to make no mention of such a minor irritant. The awkward apparatus rendered him immobile, of course – at least until he had mastered the skills of the young man from the adjacent bed who had spent most of the

previous evening wandering freely (as it seemed) all over the
hospital, holding his own drip high above his head like some
Ethiopian athlete brandishing the Olympic torch. Morse had felt
most self-conscious when circumstances utterly beyond his control
had finally induced him to beg for a 'bottle'. Yet – thus far – he
had been spared the undignified palaver of the dreaded 'pan'; and
he trusted that his lack of solid nutriment during the preceding
days would be duly acknowledged with some reciprocal inactivity
by his bowels. And so far so good.

The nurse was talking earnestly to a slightly built, fresh-faced
young houseman, his white coat reaching almost to his ankles, a
stethoscope hooked into his right-hand pocket. And soon the two
of them were walking, quietly, unfussily, into the ward where
Morse lay; then disappearing behind the curtains (drawn across
the previous evening) of the bed diagonally opposite.

When he'd first been wheeled into the ward, Morse had noticed
the man who occupied that bed – a proud-looking man, in his late
seventies, perhaps, with an Indian Army moustache, and a thin
thatch of pure-white hair. At that moment of entry, for a second
or two, the old warrior's watery-pale eyes had settled on Morse's
face, seeming almost to convey some faint message of hope and
comradeship. And indeed the dying old man would certainly have
wished the new patient well, had he been able to articulate his
intent; but the rampaging septicaemia which had sent a bright-
pink suffusion to his waxen cheeks had taken from him all the
power of speech.

It was 5.20 a.m. when the houseman emerged from behind the
curtains; 5.30 a.m. when the swiftly summoned porters had
wheeled the dead man away. And when, exactly half an hour
later, the full lights flickered on in the ward, the curtains round
the bed of the late Colonel Wilfrid Deniston, OBE, MC, were
standing open, in their normal way, to reveal the newly laundered
sheets, with the changed blankets professionally mitred at the
foot. Had Morse known how the late Colonel could not abide a
chord of Wagner he would have been somewhat aggrieved; yet
had he known how the Colonel had committed to memory
virtually the whole poetic corpus of A. E. Housman, he would
have been most gratified.

At 6.45 a.m. Morse was aware of considerable activity in the
immediate environs of the ward, although initially he could see no
physical evidence of it: voices, clinking of crockery, squeaking of
ill-oiled wheels – and finally Violet, a happily countenanced and
considerably overweight West Indian woman, hove into view

pushing a tea-trolley. This was the occasion, clearly, for a pre-dawn beverage, and how Morse welcomed it! For the first time in the past few days he was conscious of a positive appetite for food and drink; and already, and with envy, he had surveyed the jugs of water and bottles of squash that stood on the bedside tables of his fellow-patients, though for some reason not on the table of the man immediately opposite, one Walter Greenaway, above whose bed there hung a rectangular plaque bearing the sad little legend NIL BY MOUTH.

'Tea or coffee, Mr Greenaway?'

'I'll just settle for a large gin and tonic, if that's all right by you.'

'Ice and lemon?'

'No ice, thank you: it spoils the gin.'

Violet moved away massively to the next bed, leaving Mr Greenaway sans ice, sans everything. Yet the perky sixty-odd-year-old appeared far from mortified by his exclusion from the proceedings, and winked happily across at Morse.

'All right, chief?'

'On the mend,' said Morse cautiously.

'Huh! That's exactly what the old Colonel used to say: "On the mend". Poor old boy!'

'I see,' said Morse, with some unease.

After Greenaway's eyes had unclouded from their appropriate respect for the departed Colonel, Morse continued the dialogue.

'No tea for you, then?'

Greenaway shook his head. 'They know best, though, don't they?'

'They do?'

'Wonderful – the doctors here! And the nurses!'

Morse nodded, hoping indeed that it might be so.

'Same trouble as me?' enquired Greenaway confidentially.

'Pardon?'

'Stomach, is it?'

'Ulcer – so they say.'

'Mine's perforated!' Greenaway proclaimed this fact with a certain grim pride and satisfaction, as though a combination of the worst of disorders with the best of physicians was a cause for considerable congratulation. 'They're operating on me at ten o'clock – that's why I'm not allowed a drink, see?'

'Oh!' For a few seconds Morse found himself almost wishing he could put in some counter-claim for a whole gutful of mighty ulcers that were not only perforated but pierced and punctured into the bargain. A more important matter, however, was now demanding his attention, for Violet had effected a U-turn and was (at last!) beside his bed.

She greeted her new charge with a cheerful grin. 'Morning, Mr, er' (consulting the Biro'd letters on the name-tab) 'Mr Morse!'

'Good morning!' replied Morse. 'I'll have some coffee, please – two spoonfuls of sugar.'

'My, my! *Two – sugars!*' Violet's eyes almost soared out of their whitened sockets towards the ceiling; then she turned to share the private joke with the grinning Greenaway. 'Now, look you here!' (reverting to Morse): 'You can't have no coffee nor no tea nor no sugar neither. Oh right?' She wagged a brown forefinger at a point somewhere above the bed; and twisting his neck Morse could see, behind his saline apparatus, a rectangular plaque bearing the sad little legend NIL BY MOUTH.

CHAPTER THREE

Flowers, writing materials, and books are always welcome gifts for patients; but if you wish to bring food or drink, do ask the Sister, and she will tell you what is advisable

(Oxford Health Authority,
Handbook for Patients and Visitors)

Detective Sergeant Lewis came into the ward just after seven o'clock that Sunday evening, clutching a Sainsbury carrier-bag with the air of a slightly guilty man walking through the Customs' shed; and at the sight of his old partner, Morse felt very glad, and just a little lachrymose.

'How come you knew I was here?'

'I'm a detective, sir – remember?'

'They phoned you, I suppose.'

'The Super. He said you sounded awful poorly when he rang yesterday morning. So he sent Dixon round, but you'd just been carried off in the ambulance. So he rang me and said I might like to see if the NHS is still up to scratch – see if you wanted anything.'

'Something like a bottle of Scotch, you mean?'

Lewis ignored the pleasantry: 'I'd've come in last night, but they said you weren't to have any visitors – only close relatives.'

'I'll have you know I'm not quite your "Orphan Annie", Lewis. I've got a great-aunt up in Alnwick somewhere.'

'Bit of a long way for her to come, sir.'

'Especially at ninety-seven . . .'

'Not a bad fellow, Strange, is he?' suggested Lewis, after a slightly awkward little pause.

'Not when you get to know him, I suppose,' admitted Morse.

'Would you say *you've* got to know him?'

Morse shook his head.

'Well?' said Lewis briskly. 'How *are* things? What do they say's the trouble?'

'Trouble? No trouble! It's just a case of mistaken identity.'

Lewis grinned. 'Seriously, though?'

'Seriously? Well they've put me on some great big round white pills that cost a couple of quid a time, so the nurses say. Do you realize you can get a very decent little bottle of claret for that price?'

'What about the food – is that all right?'

'Food? *What* food? Except for the pills they haven't given me a thing.'

'No drink, either?'

'Are you trying to set back my medical progress, Lewis?'

'Is that what – what *that* means?' Lewis jerked his eyes upwards to the fateful warning above the bed.

'That's just precautionary,' said Morse, with unconvincing nonchalance.

Lewis's eyes jerked, downwards this time, towards the carrier-bag.

'Come on, Lewis! What have you got in there?'

Lewis reached inside the bag and brought out a bottle of lemon-and-barley water, and was most pleasantly surprised to witness the undisguised delight on Morse's face.

'It was just that the missus thought – well, you know, you wouldn't be allowed to drink – to drink anything else much.'

'*Very* kind of her! You just tell her that the way things are I'd rather have a bottle of that stuff than a whole crate of whisky.'

'You don't mean that, do you, sir?'

'Doesn't stop you telling her, though, does it?'

'And here's a book,' added Lewis, withdrawing one further item from the bag – a book entitled *Scales of Injustice: A Comparative Study of Crime and its Punishment as Recorded in the County of Shropshire, 1842–1852.*

Morse took the thick volume and surveyed its inordinately

lengthy title, though without any obvious enthusiasm. 'Mm! Looks a fairly interesting work.'

'You don't mean that, do you?'

'No,' said Morse.

'It's a sort of family heirloom and the missus just thought—'

'You tell that wonderful missus of yours that I'm very pleased with it.'

'Perhaps you'll do me a favour and leave it in the hospital library when you come out.'

Morse laughed quietly; and Lewis was strangely gratified by his chief's reactions, and smiled to himself.

He was still smiling when an extraordinarily pretty young nurse, with a freckled face and mahogany-highlighted hair, came to Morse's bedside, waved an admonitory finger at him, and showed her white and beautifully regular teeth in a dumbshow of disapproval as she pointed to the lemon-and-barley bottle which Morse had placed on his locker-top. Morse, in turn, nodded his full appreciation of the situation and showed his own reasonably regular, if rather off-white, teeth as he mouthed a silent 'OK'.

'Who's that?' whispered Lewis, when she had passed upon her way.

'That, Lewis, is the Fair Fiona. Lovely, don't you think? I sometimes wonder how the doctors manage to keep their dirty hands off her.'

'Perhaps they don't.'

'I thought you'd come in here to cheer me up!'

But for the moment good cheer seemed in short supply. The ward sister (whom Lewis had not noticed as he'd entered – merely walking straight through, like everyone else, as he'd thought) had clearly been keeping her dragon's eye on events in general, and in particular on events around the bed where the dehydrated Chief Inspector lay. To which bed, with purposeful stride, she now took the few steps needed from the vantage point behind the main desk. Her left hand immediately grasped the offending bottle on the locker-top, while her eyes fixed unblinkingly upon the luckless Lewis.

'We have our regulations in this hospital – a copy of them is posted just outside the ward. So I shall be glad if you follow those regulations and report to me or whoever's in charge if you intend to visit again. It's absolutely vital that we follow a routine here – try to understand that! Your friend here is quite poorly, and we're all trying our vairy best to see that he gets well again quickly. Now we canna do that if you are going to bring in anything *you* think might do him good, because you'd bring in all the *wrong* things, OK? I'm sure you appreciate what I'm saying.'

She had spoken in a soft Scots accent, this grimly visaged, tight-lipped sister, a silver buckle clasped around her dark-blue uniform; and Lewis, the colour tidally risen under his pale cheeks, looked wretchedly uncomfortable as she turned away – and was gone. Even Morse, for a few moments, appeared strangely cowed and silent.

'Who's that?' asked Lewis (for the second time that evening).

'You have just had an encounter with the embittered soul of our ward sister – devoted to an ideal of humourless efficiency: a sort of Calvinistic Thatcherite.'

'And what she says . . .?'

Morse nodded. 'She is, Lewis, in charge, as I think you probably gathered.'

'Doesn't have to be so *sharp*, does she?'

'*Forget* it, Lewis! She's probably disappointed in her love-life or something. Not surprising with a face—'

'What's her name?'

'They call her "Nessie".'

'Was she born near the Loch?'

'*In* it, Lewis.'

The two men laughed just a little; yet the incident had been unpleasant and Lewis in particular found it difficult to put it behind him. For a further five minutes he quizzed Morse quietly about the other patients; and Morse told him of the dawn departure of the ex-Indian-Army man. For still another five minutes, the two men exchanged words about Police HQ at Kidlington; about the Lewis family; about the less-than-sanguine prospects of Oxford United in the current soccer campaign. But nothing could quite efface the fact that 'that bloody sister' (as Morse referred to her) had cast a darkling shadow over the evening visit; had certainly cast a shadow over Lewis. And Morse himself was suddenly feeling hot and sweaty, and (yes, if he were honest) just a fraction wearied of the conversation.

'I'd better be off then, sir.'

'What else have you got in that bag?'

'Nothing—'

'Lewis! My stomach may be out of order for the minute but there's nothing wrong with my bloody ears!'

Slowly the dark clouds began to lift for Lewis, and when, after prolonged circumspection, he decided that the Customs Officer was momentarily off her guard, he withdrew a small, flattish bottle, wrapped in soft, dark-blue tissue-paper – much the colour of Nessie's uniform.

'But not until it's *official* like!' hissed Lewis, palming the gift surreptitiously into Morse's hand beneath the bedclothes.

'Bell's?' asked Morse.

Lewis nodded.

It was a happy moment.

For the present, however, the attention of all was diverted by another bell that sounded from somewhere, and visitors began to stand and prepare for their departure: a few, perhaps, with symptoms of reluctance; but the majority with signs of only partially concealed relief. As Lewis himself rose to take his leave, he dipped his hand once more into the carrier-bag and produced his final offering: a paperback entitled *The Blue Ticket*, with a provocative picture of an economically clad nymphet on the cover.

'I thought – I thought you might enjoy something a little bit lighter, sir. The missus doesn't know—'

'I hope she's never found you reading this sort of rubbish, Lewis!'

'Haven't read it *yet*, sir.'

'Well, the, er, title's a bit shorter than the other thing . . .'

Lewis nodded, and the two friends shared a happy grin.

'Time to go, I'm afraid!' The Fair Fiona was smiling down at them, especially (it seemed) smiling down at Lewis, for whom every cloud was suddenly lifted from the weather-chart. As for Morse, he was glad to be alone again; and when the ward finally cleared of its last visitor, the hospital system smoothly, inexorably, re-orientated itself once more to the care and treatment of the sick.

It was only after further testings of pulse and blood pressure, after the administration of further medicaments, that Morse had the opportunity (unobserved) of reading the blurb of the second work of literature (well, literature of a sort) which was now in his possession:

Diving into the water, young Steve Mingella had managed to pull the little girl's body on to the hired yacht and to apply to her his clumsy version of the kiss of life. Miraculously, the six-year-old had survived, and for a few days Steve was the toast of the boat clubs along the Florida Keys. After his return to New York he received a letter – and inside the letter a ticket – from the young girl's father, the playboy proprietor of the city's most exclusive, expensive, and exotic night-spot, a club specializing in the wildest sexual fantasies. The book opens as Steve treads diffidently across the thick carpeted entrance of that erotic wonderland, and shows to the topless blonde seated at Reception the ticket he has received – *a ticket coloured deepest blue* . . .

CHAPTER FOUR

My evening visitors, if they cannot see the clock, should find the time in my face

(Emerson, *Journals*)

Half an hour after Lewis's departure, Fiona came again to Morse's bedside and asked him to unfasten his pyjama bottoms, to turn over on his left side, and to expose his right buttock. Which orders having been obeyed (as Morse used to say when he studied the Classics), the unsmiling Nessie was summoned to insert a syringe of colourless liquid into his flank. This insertion (he could see nothing over his right shoulder) seemed to Morse to have been effected with less than professional finesse; and he heard himself grunt 'Christ!' when the plunger was pressed, his body twitching involuntarily as what felt like a bar of iron was implanted into his backside.

'You'll feel a wee bit sleepy,' was the laconic comment of the Loch Ness Monster; and Fiona was left to pour some disinfectant on to a piece of gauze, which she proceeded to rub vigorously across and around the punctured area.

'She'd have landed a top job in Buchenwald, that woman!' said Morse. But from the uncomprehending look on her face, he suddenly realized that Nazi concentration camps were as far back in the young nurse's past as the relief of Mafeking was in his own; and he felt his age. It was forty-four years now since the end of the Second World War – and this young . . . nurse . . . could only be . . . Morse was conscious of feeling very weary, very tired. 'What I mean is . . .' (Morse pulled his pyjama bottoms up with some difficulty) '. . . she's so . . . sharp!' Yes, Lewis had used that word.

'Did you realize that was my very first injection? Sorry if it hurt a bit – I'll get better.'

'I thought it was . . .'

'Yes, I know.' She smiled down at him and Morse's eyelids

drooped heavily over his tired eyes. Nessie had said he'd feel a wee bit . . . weary . . .

His head jerked down against his chest, and Fiona settled him against the pillows, gently looking at him as he lay there, and wondering for the dozenth time in her life why all the men who attracted her had either been happily married long, long since, or else were far, far, far too old.

Morse felt a soft-fingered hand on his right wrist, and opened his eyes to find himself staring up into the face of an extraordinary-looking personage. She was a very small woman, of some seventy-five to eighty summers, wispily white-haired, her face deeply wrinkled and unbeautiful, with an old-fashioned NHS hearing-aid plugged into her left ear, its cord stretching down to a batteried appliance in the pocket of a dirty, loose, grey woollen cardigan. She appeared naïvely unaware that any apology might perhaps be called for in wakening a weary patient. Who was she? Who had let her in? It was 9.45 p.m. by the ward clock and two night nurses were on duty. Go away! Go away, you stupid old crow!

'Mr Horse? Mr Horse, is it?' Her rheumy eyes squinted myopically at the Elastoplast name-tag, and her mouth distended in a dentured smile.

'Morse!' said Morse. 'M–O . . .'

'Do you know, I think they've spelt your name wrong, Mr Horse. I'll try to remember to tell—'

'Morse! M–O–R–S–E!'

'Yes – but it *was* expected, you know. They'd already told me that Wilfrid had only a few days left to live. And we all do get older, don't we? Older every single day.'

Yes, yes, clear off! I'm bloody tired, can't you *see*?

'Fifty-two years, we'd been together.'

Morse, belatedly, realized who she was, and he nodded more sympathetically now: 'Long time!'

'He *liked* being here, you know. He was so grateful to you all—'

'I'm afraid I only came in a couple of days ago—'

'That's exactly why he wanted me to thank *all* of you – all his old friends here.' She spoke in a precise, prim manner, with the diction of a retired Latin mistress.

'He was a fine man . . .' began Morse, a little desperately. 'I wish I'd got to know him. As I say, though, I only got in a day or two ago – stomach trouble – nothing serious . . .'

The hearing-aid began to whistle shrilly, picking up some internal feedback, and the old lady fiddled about ineffectually with the ear-piece and the control switches. 'And that's *why*' (she began now to talk in intermittent italics) 'I've got this little *book* for you. He was *so* proud of it. Not that he *said* so, of course – but he *was*. It took him a very long time and it was a *very* happy day for him when it was printed.'

Morse nodded with gratitude as she handed him a little booklet in bottle-green paper covers. 'It's very kind of you because, as I say, I only came in—'

'Wilfrid would have been *so* pleased.'

Oh dear.

'And you will *promise* to read it, won't you?'

'Oh yes – certainly!'

The old lady fingered her whistling aid once more, smiled with the helplessness of a stranded angel, said 'Goodbye, Mr Horse!' and moved on to convey her undying gratitude to the occupant of the adjacent bed.

Morse looked down vaguely at the slim volume thus presented: it could contain no more than – what? – some twenty-odd pages. He would certainly look at it later, as he'd promised. Tomorrow, perhaps. For the moment, he could think of nothing but closing his weary eyes once more, and he placed *Murder on the Oxford Canal*, by Wilfrid M. Deniston, inside his locker, on top of *Scales of Injustice* and *The Blue Ticket* – the triad of new works he'd so recently acquired. Tomorrow, yes . . .

Almost immediately he fell into a deep slumber, where he dreamed of a long cross-country race over the fields of his boyhood, where there, at the distant finishing-line, sat a topless blonde, a silver buckle clasped around her waist, holding in her left hand a pint of beer with a head of winking froth.

CHAPTER FIVE

This type of writing sometimes enjoys the Lethean faculty of making those who read it forget to ask what it means, or indeed if it means anything very substantive

(Alfred Austin, *The Bridling of Pegasus*)

The endoscopy, performed under a mild anaesthetic at 10 o'clock the following morning (Monday), persuaded the surgeons at the JR2 that in Morse's case the knife was probably not needed; their prognosis, too, was modestly encouraging, provided the patient could settle into a more cautiously sober and restrictive regimen for the months (and years) ahead. Furthermore, as a token of their muted optimism, the patient was that very evening to be allowed one half-bowl of oxtail soup and a portion of vanilla ice-cream – and for Morse any gourmand *à la carte* menu could hardly have been more gloriously welcome.

Lewis reported to Sister Maclean at 7.30 p.m., and was unsmilingly nodded through Customs without having to declare one get-well card (from Morse's secretary), a tube of mint-flavoured toothpaste (from Mrs Lewis), and a clean hand-towel (same provenance). Contentedly, for ten minutes or so, the two men talked of this and that, with Lewis receiving the firm impression that his chief was recovering rapidly.

Fiona the Fair put in a brief appearance towards the end of this visit, shaking out Morse's pillows and placing a jug of cold water on his locker.

'Lovely girl,' ventured Lewis.

'You're married – remember?'

'Done any reading yet?' Lewis nodded towards the locker.

'Why do you ask?'

Lewis grinned: 'It's the missus – she was just wondering . . .'

'I'm half-way through it, tell her. Riveting stuff!'

'You're not serious—'

'Do you know how to spell "riveting"?'

'What – one "t" or two, you mean?'

'And do you know what "stools" are?'

'Things you sit on?'

Morse laughed – a genuine, carefree, pain-free laugh. It was good to have Lewis around; and the vaguely puzzled Lewis was glad to find the invalid in such good spirits.

Suddenly, there beside the bed, re-mitreing the bottom right-hand corner of the blankets, was Sister Maclean herself.

'Who brought the jug of water?' she enquired in her soft but awesome voice.

'It's all right, Sister,' began Morse, 'the doctor said—'

'Nurse Welch!' The ominously quiet words carried easily across the ward, and Lewis stared at the floor in pained embarrassment as Student Nurse Welch walked warily over to Morse's bed, where she was firmly admonished by her superior. Free access to liquids was to be available only w.e.f. the following dawn – *and not before*. Had the student nurse not read the notes before going the rounds with her water-jugs? And if she had, did she not realize that no hospital could function satisfactorily with such sloppiness? If it mightn't seem important on *this* occasion, did the student nurse not realize that it could be absolutely vital on the *next*?

Another sickening little episode; and for Lewis one still leaving a nasty taste when a few minutes later he bade his chief farewell. Morse himself had said nothing at the time, and said nothing now. Never, he told himself, would he have reprimanded any member of his own staff in such cavalier fashion in front of other people: and then, sadly, he recalled that quite frequently he had done precisely that . . . All the same, he would have welcomed the opportunity of a few quiet words with the duly chastened Fiona before she went home.

There was virtually no one around in the ward now: the Ethiopian athlete was doing the hospital rounds once more; and two of the other patients had shuffled their way to the gents. Only a woman of about thirty, a slimly attractive, blonde-headed woman (Walter Greenaway's daughter, Morse guessed – and guessed correctly) still sat beside her father. She had given Morse a quick glance as she'd come in, but now hardly appeared to notice him as she made her way out of the ward, and pressed the 'Down' button in front of the top-floor lifts. It was her father who was monopolizing her thoughts, and she gave no more than a cursory thought to the man whose name appeared to be 'Morse' and whose eyes, as she had noticed, had followed her figure with a lively interest on her exit.

The time was 8.40 p.m.

Feeling minimally guilty that he had not as yet so much as opened the cover of the precious work that Mrs Lewis had vouchsafed to his keeping, Morse reached for the book from his locker, and skimmed through its first paragraph:

> Diversity rather than uniformity has almost invariably been seen to characterize the criminal behaviour-patterns of any technologically developing society. The attempt to resolve any conflicts and/or inconsistencies which may arise in the analysis and interpretation of such patterns (see Appendix 3, pp. 492 ff.) is absolutely vital; and the inevitable re-interpretation of this perpetually variable data is the raw material for several recent studies into the causation of criminal behaviour. Yet conflicting strategic choices within hetero-geneous areas, starkly differentiated creeds, greater knowledge of variable economic performances, as well as physical, physiological, or physiognomical peculiarities – all these facts (as we shall main-tain) can suggest possible avenues never exhaustively explored by any previous student of criminal behaviour in nineteenth-century Britain.

'Christ!' muttered Morse (for the second time that evening). A few years ago he might possibly have considered persevering with such incomprehensible twaddle. But no longer. Stopping momen-tarily only to marvel at the idiocy of the publisher who had allowed such pompous polysyllaby ever to reach the compositor in the first place, he closed the stout work smartly – and resolved to open it never again.

As it happened, he was to break this instant resolution very shortly; but for the moment there was a rather more attractive proposition awaiting him in his locker: the pornographic paper-back which Lewis (praise the Lord!) had smuggled in.

A yellow flash across the glossy cover made its promise to the reader of Scorching Lust and Primitive Sensuality – this claim supported by the picture of a superbly buxom beauty sunning herself on some golden-sanded South Sea island, completely naked except for a string of native beads around her neck. Morse opened the book and skimmed (though a little more slowly than before) a second paragraph that evening. And he was immediately aware of a no-nonsense, clear-cut English style that was going to take the palm every time from the sprawling, spawning, sociolog-ical nonsense he had just encountered:

> She surfaced from the pool and began to unbutton her clinging, sodden blouse. And as she did so, the young men all fell silent, urging her – praying her! – in some unheard but deafening chorus,

to strip herself quickly and completely – their eyes now rivetted to the carmined tips of her slimly sinuous fingers as they slipped inside her blouse, and so slowly, so tantalizingly, flicked open a further button . . .

'Christ!!' It was the third time that Morse had used the same word that evening, and the one that took the prize for blasphemous vehemence. He leaned back against his pillows with a satisfied smile about his lips, clasping to himself the prospect of a couple of hours of delicious titillation on the morrow. He could bend those covers back easily enough; and it would be no great difficulty temporarily to assume the facial expression of a theological student reading some verses from the Minor Prophets. But whatever happened, the chances that Chief Inspector Morse would ever be fully informed about crime and its punishment in nineteenth-century Shropshire had sunk to zero.

For the moment, at any rate.

He replaced *The Blue Ticket* in his locker, on top of *Scales of Injustice* – both books now lying on top of the hitherto neglected *Murder on the Oxford Canal*, that slim volume printed privately under the auspices of The Oxford and County Local History Society.

As Morse nodded off once more, his brain was debating whether there was just the one word mis-spelled in the brief paragraph he had just read. He would look it up in Chambers when he got home. Lewis hadn't seemed to know, either . . .

CHAPTER SIX

I enjoy convalescence. It is the part that makes the illness worth while

(G. B. Shaw, *Back to Methuselah*)

At 2 a.m. the inevitable occurred; but fortunately Morse managed to attract the quick attention of the nurse as she'd flitted like some Nightingale around the darkened wards. The noise of the curtains being drawn around his bed sounded to Morse loud enough to rouse the semi-dead. Yet none of his fellow-patients seemed to stir, and she – the blessed girl! – had been quite marvellous.

'I don't even know which way up the thing should go,' confided Morse.

'Which way *round*, you mean!' Eileen (such was her name) had whispered, as she proceeded without the slightest embarrassment to explain exactly how the well-trained patient would negotiate this particular crisis. Then, leaving him with half a roll of white toilet-paper, and the firm assurance of a second coming within the next ten minutes, she was gone.

It was all over – consummated with a bowl of warm water and a brief squirt of some odiferous air-freshener. Whew! Not half as bad as Morse had feared – thanks to that ethereal girl; and as he smiled up gratefully at her, he thought there might have been a look in her eyes that transgressed the borders of perfunctory nursing. But Morse would always have thought there was, even if there wasn't; for he was the sort of man for whom some area of fantasy was wholly necessary, and his imagination followed the slender Eileen, as elegantly she walked away: about 5' 8" in height – quite tall really; in her mid-twenties; eyes greenish-hazel, in a delicately featured, high-cheekboned face; no ring of any sort on either hand. She looked so good, so wholesome, in her white uniform with its dark-blue trimmings.

Go to sleep, Morse!

At 7.30 a.m., after breakfasting on a single wafer of Weetabix with an inadequate pour-over of semi-skimmed milk (and no sugar), Morse noted with great satisfaction that the NIL BY MOUTH embargo was now in abeyance, and he poured himself a glass of water with the joy of a liberated hostage. There followed for him, that morning, the standard readings of pulse-rate and blood-pressure, a bedside wash in a portable basin, the remaking of his bed, the provision of a fresh jug of water(!), a flirting confab with Fiona, the purchase of *The Times*, a cup of Bovril from the vivacious Violet, and (blessedly) not a single spoke stuck in the hospital machinery from the *éminence grise* installed at the seat of power.

At 10.50 a.m. a white-coated cohort of consultant-cum-under-lings came to stand around his bed, and to consider the progress of its incumbent. The senior man, after briefly looking through Morse's file, eyed the patient with a somewhat jaundiced eye.

'How are you feeling this morning?'

'I think I'll live on for a few more weeks – thanks to you,' said Morse, with somewhat sickening sycophancy.

'You mention here something about your drinking habits,'

continued the consultant, unimpressed as it appeared with such spurious gratitude.

'Yes?'

'You drink a lot.' It was a statement.

'That's a lot, you think?'

The consultant closed the file with a sigh and handed it back to Nessie. 'During my long years in the medical profession, Mr Morse, I have learned that there are two categories of statistics which can invariably be discounted: the sexual prowess of those suffering from diabetes mellitus; and the boozing habits of our country's middle management.'

'I'm not a diabetic.'

'You will be if you keep drinking a bottle of Scotch a week.'

'Well – perhaps not *every* week.'

'You sometimes drink *two* a week, you mean?'

There was a twinkle in the consultant's eye as he waved his posse of acolytes across to the bed of the weakly Greenaway, and sat himself down on Morse's bed.

'Have you had a drop yet?'

'Drop of what?'

'It's a dreadful give-away, you know' (the consultant nodded to the locker) ' – that tissue paper.'

'Oh!'

'Not *tonight* – all right?'

Morse nodded.

'And one further word of advice. Wait till Sister's off duty!'

'She'd skin me alive!' mumbled Morse.

The consultant looked at Morse strangely. 'Well, since you mention it, yes. But that wasn't what I was thinking of, no.'

'Something worse?'

'She's about the most forbidding old biddy in the profession; but just remember she comes from north of the border.'

'I'm not quite sure . . .'

'She'd probably' (the consultant bent down and whispered in Morse's ear) ' – she'd probably draw the curtains and insist on fifty-fifty!'

Morse began to feel more happily settled; and after twenty minutes with *The Times* (Letters read, Crossword completed), one-handedly he folded back the covers of *The Blue Ticket*, and moving comfortably down against his pillows started Chapter One.

*

'Good book?'

'So-so!' Morse had not been aware of Fiona's presence, and he shrugged non-committally, holding the pages rigidly in his left hand.

'What's it called?'

'Er – *The Blue* – *The Blue City*.'

'Detective story, isn't it? I think my mum's read that.'

Morse nodded uneasily. 'Do *you* read a lot?'

'I used to, when I was young and beautiful.'

'This morning?'

'Sit up!'

Morse leaned forward as she softened up his pillows with a few left hooks and right crosses, and went on her way.

'Lovely girl, isn't she?' It wasn't Lewis this time who made the obvious observation, but the stricken Greenaway, now much recovered, and himself reading a book whose title was plain for all to see: *The Age of Steam*.

Morse pushed his own novel as unobtrusively as possible into his locker: it was a little disappointing, anyway.

'*The Blue Ticket* – that's what it is,' said Greenaway.

'Pardon?'

'You got the title wrong – it's *The Blue Ticket*.'

'Did I? Ah yes! I, er, I don't know why I'm bothering to read it, really.'

'Same reason I did, I suppose. Hoping for a bit of sex every few pages.'

Morse grinned defeatedly.

'It's a bit of a let-down,' went on Greenaway in his embarrassingly stentorian voice. 'My daughter sometimes brings me one or two books like that.'

'She was the woman – last night?'

The other nodded. 'In library work ever since she was eighteen – twelve years. In the Bodley these last six.'

Morse listened patiently to a few well-rehearsed statistics about the mileage of book-shelving in the warrens beneath the Bodleian; and was already learning something of the daughter's *curriculum vitae* when the monologue was terminated by cleaners pushing the beds around in a somewhat cavalier fashion, and slopping their mops into dingily watered buckets.

At 1.30 p.m., after what seemed to him a wretchedly insubstantial lunch, Morse was informed that he was scheduled that afternoon to visit various investigative departments; and that for this purpose the saline-drip would be temporarily removed. And

when a hospital porter finally got him comfortably into a wheel-
chair, Morse felt that he had certainly climbed a rung or two up
the convalescence ladder.

It was not until 3.30 p.m. that he returned to the ward, weary,
impatient, and thirsty – in reverse order of severity. Roughly,
though oddly painlessly, a silent Nessie, just before going off
duty, had reaffixed into his right wrist the tube running down
from a newly hung drip; and with the eyes of a now fully alert
Greenaway upon him, Morse decided that Steve Mingella's sexual
fantasies might have to be postponed a while. And when a small,
mean-faced Englishwoman (doubtless Violet's understudy) had
dispensed just about enough viscous liquid from her tureen to
cover the bottom of his soup bowl, Morse's earlier euphoria had
almost evaporated. He wouldn't even be seeing Lewis – the latter
(as he'd told Morse) taking out the missus for some celebration
(reason unspecified). At 7.05 p.m. he managed to sort out his
headphones for *The Archers*; and at 7.20 p.m., he decided to dip
into the late Colonel's *magnum opus*. By 7.30 p.m. he was so
engrossed that it was only after finishing Part One that he noticed
the presence of Christine Greenaway, the beautiful blonde from
the Bodley.

CHAPTER SEVEN

Murder on the Oxford Canal

Copyright © 1978 by Wilfrid M. Deniston, OBE, MC. No part
whatsoever of this publication may be reproduced, by any
process, without the written authority of the copyright owner.

The author wishes to acknowledge the help he has so freely
received from several sources; but particularly from the Bodleian
Library, Oxford; from the *Proceedings of the North Oxford Local
History Society*; and from the *Court Registers* of the City of Oxford
Assizes, 1859 and 1860.

Further details of the trials mentioned in the following pages
may be found in the editions of *Jackson's Oxford Journal* for 20th

and 27th August, 1859; and of the same journal for 15th and 22nd April, 1860.

PART ONE

A Profligate Crew

Those who explore the back-streets and the by-ways of our great cities, or indeed our small cities, will sometimes stumble (almost literally, perhaps) upon sad memorials, hidden in neglected church-yards – churchyards which seem wholly separated from any formal ecclesiastical edifice, and which are come across purely by accident at the far side of red-bricked walls, or pressed upon by tall houses – untended, silent, forgotten. Until recent years, such a churchyard was to be found at the lower end of the pretty little road in North Oxford, now designated Middle Way, which links the line of Summertown shops in South Parade with the expensively elegant houses along Squitchey Lane, to the north. But in the early nineteen-sixties most of those tomb-stones which had stood in irregular ranks in the Summertown Parish Churchyard (for such was its official name) were removed from their original, supra-corporal sites in order to afford a rather less melancholic aspect to those who were about to pay their deposits on the flats being built upon those highly desirable if slightly lugubrious acres. Each there in his narrow cell had once been laid, and each would there remain; yet after 1963 no one, for certain, could have marked that final resting place.

The few headstones which are adequately preserved and which are to be found – even to this day – leaning almost upright against the northern perimeter of the aforesaid enclave, are but one tenth or so of the memorials once erected there, in the second and third quarters of the nineteenth century, by relatives and friends whose earnest wish was to perpetuate the names of those souls, now perhaps known only to God, who passed their terrestrial lives in His faith and fear.

One of these headstones, a moss-greened, limestone slab (standing the furthest away but three from the present thoroughfare) bears an epitaph which may still be traced by the practised eye of the patient epigraphist – though make haste if you are to decipher that disinte-grating lettering!

Beyond this poignant (if unusually lengthy) epitaph there lies a tale of unbridled lust and drunken lechery; a tale of a hapless and a helpless young woman who found herself at the mercy of coarse and most

To the Memory of

JOANNA FRANKS

wife of Charles Franks of London,
who having been primitively and
cruelly assaulted was found most
tragically drowned in the Oxford
Canal on June 22nd 1859,
aged 38 years.

This stone is erected by
some members of the Summertown
Parish Council in commemoration
of the untimely death of this
most unhappy woman.

Lord have mercy upon her soul

Requiescat in Pace Aeterna

brutally uninhibited boatmen, during an horrendous journey made nearly one hundred and twenty years ago – a journey whose details are the subject-matter of our present narrative.

Joanna Franks hailed originally from Derby. Her father, Daniel Carrick, had been accredited as an agent to the Nottinghamshire and Midlands Friendly Society; and for a good deal of his married life he appears to have maintained a position as a reasonably prosperous and well-respected figure in his home community. Later, however – and certainly in the few years prior to the tragic death of his only daughter (there was a younger brother, Daniel) – he encountered a period of hard times.

Joanna's first husband was F. T. Donavan, whose family sprang from County Meath. He is described by one of his contemporaries as "an Irishman of many parts", and being a man of large physique we learn that he was familiarly (and predictably) known by the nickname of 'Hefty' Donavan. He was a conjurer by profession (or by one of them!) and appeared in many theatres and music-halls, both in London and in the provinces. In order to attract some badly needed publicity, he had at some unspecified date assumed the splendidly grandiloquent title of 'Emperor of all the Illusionists'; and the following theatre handbill was printed at his own expense to herald his appearance at the City of Nottingham Music Hall in early September 1856:

'Mr DONAVAN, citizen of the World and of Ireland, most humbly and respectfully informs all members of the upper and the lower nobilities, folk of the landed gentry, and the citizens of the historic district of Nottingham, that in view of his superior and unrivalled excellencies in MAGIC and DECEPTION, he has had conferred upon him, by the supreme conclave of the Assembly of Superior Magicians, this last year, the unchallenged title of EMPEROR of all the Illusionists, and this particularly by virtue of the amazing trick of cutting off a cockerel's head and then restoring the bird to its pristine animation. It was this same DONAVAN, the greatest man in the World, who last week diverted his great audience in Croydon by immersing his whole body, tighty secured and chained, in a tank of the most corrosive acid for eleven minutes and forty-five seconds, as accurately measured by scientific chronometer.'

Three years earlier Donavan had written (and found a publisher for) his only legacy to us, a work entitled *The Comprehensive Manual of the Conjuring Arts.* But the great man's career was beginning to prove progressively unsuccessful, and no stage appearances whatsoever are traceable to 1858. In that year, he died, a childless and embittered man, whilst on holiday with a friend in Ireland, where his grave now rests in a burial-plot overlooking Bertnaghboy Bay. Some time afterwards his widow, Joanna, met and fell deeply in love with one Charles Franks, an ostler from Liverpool.

Like her first, Joanna's second marriage appears to have been a happy one, in spite of the fact that times were still hard and money still scarce. The new Mrs Franks was to find employment, as a dressmaker and designers' model, with a Mrs Russell of 34 Runcorn Terrace, Liverpool. But Franks himself was less successful in his quest for regular employment, and finally decided to try his luck in London. Here his great expectations were soon realized for he was almost immediately engaged as an ostler at the busy George & Dragon Inn on the Edgware Road, where we find him duly lodged in the spring of 1859. In late May of that same year he sent his wife a guinea (all he could afford) and begged her to join him in London as soon as possible.

On the morning of Saturday, June 11th, 1859, Joanna Franks, carrying two small trunks, bade her farewell to Mrs Russell in Runcorn Terrace, and made her way by barge from Liverpool to Preston Brook, the northern terminus of the Trent and Mersey Canal, which had been opened some eighty years earlier. Here she joined one of Pickford & Co.'s express (or 'fly') boats[1] which was departing for Stoke-on-Trent and Fradley Junction, and thence, via the Coventry and Oxford Canals, through to London on the main Thames waterway. The fare of sixteen shillings and eleven pence was considerably cheaper than the fare on the Liverpool–London railway line which had been opened some twenty years earlier.

Joanna was an extremely petite and attractive figure, wearing an Oxford-blue dress, with a white kerchief around her neck, and a figured silk bonnet with a bright pink ribbon. The clothes may not have been new; but they were not inexpensive, and they gave to Joanna a very tidy appearance indeed. A very tempting appearance, too, as we shall soon discover.

The captain of the narrow-boat *Barbara Bray* was a certain Jack 'Rory' Oldfield from Coventry. According to later testimony of fellow boat-people and other acquaintances, he was basically a good-natured sort of fellow, of a blunt, blustery type of address. He was

---

[1] A 'fly' boat travels round the clock, with a double crew, working shifts, with horses exchanged at regular intervals along the canals.

married, though childless, and was aged 42 years. The fellow-
members of his crew were: the 30-year-old Alfred Musson, alias
Alfred Brotherton, a tall, rather gaunt figure, married with two
young chidren; Walter Towns, alias Walter Thorold, the 26-year-old
illiterate son of a farm-labourer, who had left his home town of
Banbury in Oxfordshire some ten years earlier; and a teenaged lad,
Thomas Wootton, about whom no certain facts have come down to
us beyond the probability that his parents came from Ilkeston in
Derbyshire.

The *Barbara Bray* left Preston Brook at 7.30 p.m. on Saturday,
11th June. At Fradley Junction, at the southern end of the Mersey
Canal, she successfully negotiated her passage through the locks; and
at 10 p.m. on Sunday, 19th June, she slipped quietly into the northern
reaches of the Coventry Canal, and settled to a course, almost due
south, that would lead down to Oxford. Progress had been surprisingly good, and there had been little or no forewarning of the tragic
events which lay ahead for the *Barbara Bray*, and for her solitary
paying passenger – the small and slimly attractive person of Joanna
Franks, for whom such a little span of life remained.

CHAPTER EIGHT

Style is the hallmark of a temperament stamped upon
the material at hand
(André Maurois, *The Art of Writing*)

After reading these few pages, Morse found himself making some
mental queries about a few minor items, and harbouring some
vague unease about one or two major ones. Being reluctant to
disfigure the printed text with a series of marginalia, he wrote a
few notes on the back of a daily hospital menu which had been
left (mistakenly) on his locker.

The Colonel's style was somewhat on the pretentious side – a
bit too high-flown for Morse's taste; and yet the writing was a
good deal above the average of its kind – with a pleasing perora-
tion, calculated to ensure in most readers some semi-compulsive
page-turning to Part Two. One of the most noticeable character-
istics of the writing was the influence of Gray's 'Elegy Written in a
Country Churchyard' – a poem doubtless stuck down the author's
throat as a lad in some minor public school, and one leaving him
with a rather lugubrious view of the human lot. One or two *very*

nice touches, though, and Morse was prepared to give a couple of ticks to that epithet 'supra-corporal'. He wished, though, he had beside him that most faithful of all his literary companions, *Chambers English Dictionary*, for although he had frequently met 'ostler' in crossword puzzles, he wasn't sure *exactly* what an ostler did; and 'figured' bonnet wasn't all that obvious, was it?

Thinking of writing – and writing books – old Donavan (Joanna's first) must have been pretty competent. After all, he'd 'found a publisher' for his great work. And until the last few years of his life, this literate Irish conjurer was seemingly pulling in the crowds at all points between Croydon and Burton-on-Trent . . . He must certainly have had *something* about him, this man of many parts. 'Greatest man in the World' might be going over the top a bit, yet a mild degree of megalomania was perhaps forgivable in the publicity material of such a multi-talented performer?

'Bertnaghboy Bay?' – Morse wrote on the menu. His knowledge of geography was minimal. At his junior school, his teachers had given him a few assorted facts about the exports of Argentina, Bolivia, Chile, and the rest; and at the age of eight he had known – and still knew (with the exception of South Dakota) – all the capital cities of the American states. But that was the end of his apprenticeship in that discipline. After winning a scholarship to the local grammar school, the choice of the three 'G's had been thrust upon him: Greek, German, or Geography. Little real choice, though, for he had been thrust willy-nilly into the Greek set, where the paradigms of nouns and verbs precluded any knowledge of the Irish counties. Where *was* – what was the name? – Bertnaghboy Bay?

It was paradoxical, perhaps, that Morse should have suddenly found himself so fascinated by the Oxford Canal. He was aware that many people were besotted with boat-life, and he deemed it wholly proper that parents should seek to hand on to their offspring some love of sailing, or rambling, or keeping pets, or bird-watching, or whatever. But in Morse's extremely limited experience, narrow-boating figured as a grossly over-rated activity. Once, on the invitation of a pleasant enough couple, he had agreed to be piloted from the terminus of the Oxford Canal at Hythe Bridge Street up to the Plough at Wolvercote – a journey of only a couple of miles, which would be accomplished (he was assured) within the hour; but which in fact had been so fraught with manifold misfortunes that the finishing line was finally reached with only five minutes' drinking-time remaining – and that on a hot and thirsty Sunday noon. That particular boat had required a couple of people – one to steer the thing and one to keep hopping out for locks and what the handbook called 'attractive little drawbridges'. Now, Joanna's boat had got four of them on it – five with her; so it must surely have been awfully crowded on that long and tedious journey, pulled slowly along by some unenthusiastic horse. Too long! Morse nodded to himself – he was beginning to get the picture . . . Far quicker by rail, of course! And the fare she'd paid, 16s 11d, seemed on the face of it somewhat on the steep side for a trip as a passenger on a working-boat. In 1859? Surely so! What would the rail-fare have been then? Morse had no idea. But there were ways of finding out; there were people who knew these things . . .

He could still see in his mind's eye the painting on the cabin in which he'd travelled, with its lake, its castle, its sailing boat, and range of mountains – all in the traditional colours of red, yellow, green. But what was it like to *live* in such boats? Boats that in the nineteenth century had been crewed by assortments of men from all over the place: from the Black Country; from the colliery villages around Coventry and Derby and Nottingham; from the terraced cottages in Upper Fisher Row by the terminus in Oxford – carrying their cargoes of coal, salt, china, agricultural produce . . . other things. *What* other things? And why on earth all those 'aliases'? Were the crewmen counted a load of crooks before they ever came to court? Did every one on the canal have two names – a 'bye-name', as it were, as well as one written in the christening-book? Surely any jury was bound to feel a fraction of prejudice against such . . . such . . . even before . . . He was feeling tired, and already his head had jerked up twice after edging by degrees towards his chest.

Charge Nurse Eileen Stanton had come on duty at 9 p.m., and Morse was still sound asleep at 9.45 p.m. when she went quietly to his bedside and gently took the hospital menu from his hand and placed it on his locker. He was probably dreaming, she decided, of some *haute cuisine* from Les Quat' Saisons, but she would have to wake him up very shortly, for his evening pills.

CHAPTER NINE

What a convenient and delightful world is this world of books – if you bring to it not the obligations of the student, or look upon it as an opiate for idleness, but enter it rather wth the enthusiasm of the adventurer

(David Grayson, *Adventures in Contentment*)

The following morning (Wednesday) was busy and blessed. Violet's early offerings of Bran Flakes, semi-burnt cold toast, and semi-warm weak tea, were wonderfully welcome; and when at 10 a.m. Fiona had come to remove the saline-drip (permanently), Morse knew that the gods were smiling. When, further, he walked down the corridor now to the washroom, without encumbrance, and without attendant, he felt like Florestan newly released from confinement in Act 2 of *Fidelio*. And when with full movement of both arms he freely soaped his hands and face, and examined the rather sorry job he'd earlier made of shaving, he felt a wonderfully happy man. Once out of this place (he decided) he would make some suitable, not too startling, donation to the staff in general, and invite, in particular, his favourite nurse (odds pretty even for the moment between the Fair and the Ethereal) to that restaurant in North Oxford where he would show off his (limited) knowledge of modern Greek and order a Mezéthes Tavérnas menu, the one billed as 'an epicurean feast from first dip to final sweet'. Ten quid per person, or a little more; and with wine – and liqueurs, perhaps – and one or two little extras, £30 should cover it, he hoped . . . Not that the creamy-skinned Eileen would be on duty that night. Some domestic commitments, she'd said. 'Domestic?' It worried Morse, just a little. Still, so long as Nessie wasn't going to be prowling around . . . because Morse had decided that, in the interests of his convalescence, he might well twist the little bottle's golden cap that very night.

Back in the ward, the time passed, one could say, satisfactorily. A cup of Bovril at 10.30 a.m. was followd by a further recital from Mr Greenaway of his daughter's quite exceptional qualities – a woman without whom, it appeared, the Bodleian would have considerable difficulty in discharging any of its academic functions. After which, Morse was visited by one of the ten-a-penny dietitians in the place – a plain-looking, serious-souled young madam, who took him *seriatim* through a host of low-calorie vegetables on which he could 'fill up' *ad libitum*: asparagus; bamboo-shoots; beans (broad); beans (French); beans (runner); bean-sprouts; broccoli; Brussels sprouts; cabbage (various); cauliflower; celery; chicory; chives; courgettes; cucumber – and that was only the first three letters in the eternal alphabet of a healthy dietary. Morse was so impressed with the recital of the miraculous opportunities which awaited him that he even forbore to comment on the assertion that both tomato-juice and turnip-juice were wonderfully tasty and nutritious alternatives to alcoholic beverages. Dutifully, he sought to nod at suitable intervals, knowing deep down that he could, should and bloody well *would* shed a couple of stone fairly soon. Indeed, as an earnest of his new-found resolution, he insisted on only one scoop of potatoes, and no thickened gravy whasoever, when Violet brought her lunch-time victuals round.

In the early afternoon, after listening to the repeat of *The Archers*, the most pleasing thought struck him: no work that day at Police HQ; no worries about an evening meal; no anxieties for the morrow, except perhaps those occasioned by his newly awakened consciousness of infirmity – and of death. Not that even *that* worried him too much, as he'd confessed to Lewis: no next of kin, no dependants, no need for looking beyond a purely selfish gratification. And Morse knew exactly what he wanted now, as he sat upright, clean, cool, relaxed against the pillows. Because, strange as it may seem, for the present he wouldn't have given two Madagascan monkeys for a further couple of chapters of *The Blue Ticket*. At that moment, and most strongly, he felt the enthusiasm of the voyager – the voyager along the canal from Coventry to Oxford. Happily, therefore, he turned to *Murder on the Oxford Canal*, Part Two.

CHAPTER TEN

PART TWO

A Proven Crime

Although at the time there were a few conflicting statements about individual circumstances in the subsequent, and fatal, sequence of events, the general pattern as presented here is – and, indeed, always has been – undisputed.

The 38-odd-mile stretch of the Coventry Canal (of more interest today to the industrial archaeologist than to the lover of rural quietude) appears to have been negotiated without any untoward incident, with recorded stops at the Three Tuns Inn at Fazely, and again at the Atherstone Locks, further south. What can be asserted with well-nigh certitude is that the *Barbara Bray* reached Hawkesbury Junction, at the northern end of Oxford Canal, an hour or so before midnight on Monday, 20th June. Today, the distance from Hawkesbury Junction down to Oxford is some 77 miles; and in 1859 the journey was very little longer. We may therefore assume that even with one or two protracted stops along the route, the double crew of the 'fly' boat *Barbara Bray* should have managed the journey within about thirty-six hours. And this appears to have been the case. What now follows is a reconstruction of those crucial hours, based both upon the evidence given at the subsequent trials (for there were two of them) and upon later research, undertaken by the present author and others, into the records of the Oxford Canal Company Registers and the Pickford & Co. Archives. From all the available evidence, one saddening fact stands out, quite stark and incontrovertible: the body of Joanna Franks was found just after 5.30 a.m. on Wednesday, 22nd June, in the Oxford Canal – in the triangular-shaped basin of water known as 'Duke's Cut', a short passage through to the River Thames dug by the fourth Duke of Marlborough in 1796, about two and a half miles north of the (then) canal terminus at Hayfield Wharf in the City of Oxford.

For the moment, however, let us make a jump forward in time. After a Coroner's inquest at the Running Horses Inn (now demolished, but formerly standing on the corner of Upper Fisher Row by Hythe Bridge in Oxford) the four crew members of the *Barbara Bray* were straightly charged with the murder of Joanna Franks, and were duly committed to the nearby Oxford Gaol. In the preliminary trial, held at the Oxford Summer Assizes of August 1859, there were three indictments against these men: the wilful murder of Joanna Franks by throwing her into the canal; rape upon the said woman, with different counts charging different prisoners with being principals in the commission of the offence and the others as aiders and abettors; and the stealing of various articles, the property of her husband. To a man, the crew pleaded not guilty to all charges. (Wootton, the boy, who was originally charged with them, was not named in the final indictments.)

Mr Sergeant Williams, for the prosecution, said he should first proceed on the charge of rape. However, after the completion of his case, the Judge (Mr Justice Traherne) decided that there could be no certain proof of the prisoners having committed the crime, and the Jury was therefore directed to return a verdict of 'Not Guilty' on that charge. Mr Williams then applied to the Court for a postponement of the trial under the indictment for murder, until the next Assizes, on the grounds that a material witness, Joseph Jarnell, formerly a co-prisoner in Oxford Gaol, and previously committed for bigamy, could not be heard before the Court until he had obtained a free pardon from the Secretary of State. Oldfield, the boat's captain, was understood to have made some most important disclosure to Jarnell while the two men shared the same prison-cell. Although this request was strenuously opposed by Oldfield's Counsel, Mr Judge Traherne finally consented to the suggested postponement.

The Judge appointed for the second trial, held in April 1860, was Mr Augustus Benham. There was intense public feeling locally, and the streets leading to the Assize Court in Oxford were lined with hostile crowds. The case had also excited considerable interest among many members of the legal profession. The three prisoners appeared at the bar wearing the leather belts and sleeve waistcoats usually worn at that time by the canal boatmen, and were duly charged with "wilful murder, by casting, pushing, and throwing the said Joanna Franks into the Oxford Canal by which means she was choked, suffocated, and drowned". What exactly, we must ask, had taken place on those last few, fatal miles above the stretch of water known as Duke's Cut on the Oxford Canal? The tragic story soon began to unfold itself.

There are more than adequate grounds for believing that the journey from Preston Brook down to the top of the Oxford Canal at Hawkesbury was comparatively uneventful, although it soon became known that Oldfield had sat with Joanna in the cabin while the boat was negotiated through the Northwich and Harecastle Tunnels. However, from the time the *Barbara Bray* reached the lonely locks of Napton Junction – 30-odd miles down from Hawkesbury, and with Oxford still some 50 miles distant – the story appears to change, and to change (as we shall see) dramatically.

William Stevens, a canal clerk employed by Pickford & Co., confirmed[1] that the *Barbara Bray* reached the Napton Locks at about 11 a.m. on Tuesday, 21st June, and that the boat remained there, in all, for about an hour and a half. "There was a woman passenger on board", and she complained immediately to Stevens about "the conduct of the men with whom she was driven to associate". It would, he agreed, have been proper for him to have logged the complaint (the *Barbara Bray* was, after all, a Pickford & Co. transport);

[1] Many of the facts in the account used here are taken from the *Court Registers* of the Oxford Assizes, 1860, and from the *verbatim* transcript of those parts of the trial reported in *Jackson's Oxford Journal*, April 1860 (passim).

but he had not done so, confining his advice to the suggestion that the woman should report forthwith to the Company offices in Oxford, where it should be possible for her to switch to another boat on the last leg of her journey. Stevens had witnessed some shouted altercations between Joanna and a member of the crew, and remembered hearing Joanna speak the words: "Leave me alone – I'll have nothing to do with you!" Two of the men (Oldfield and Musson, he thought) had used some utterly disgraceful language, although he agreed with Counsel for the defence that the language of almost all boatmen at these times was equally deplorable. What seemed quite obvious to Stevens was that the crew were beginning to get very much the worse for drink, and he gave it as his opinion that they were "making very free with the spirit which was the cargo". Before setting off, the woman had complained yet again about the behaviour of the men, and Stevens had repeated his advice to her to reconsider her position once the boat reached the terminus of the Oxford Canal – where a partial off-loading of the cargo was officially scheduled.

It appears, in fact, that Stevens's advice did not go unheeded. At Banbury, some twelve miles further down the canal, Joanna made a determined effort to seek alternative transport for the remainder of her journey. Matthew Laurenson, wharfinger at Tooley's Yard, remembered most clearly Joanna's "urgent enquiries" about the times of "immediate coaches to London – and coaches from Oxford to Banbury". But nothing was convenient, and again Joanna was advised to wait until she got to Oxford – now only some 20 miles away. Laurenson put the time of this meeting as approximately 6.30–7 p.m. (it is hardly surprisng that times do not always coincide exactly in the court evidence – let us recall that we are almost ten months after the actual murder), and was able to give as his general impression of the unfortunate woman that she was "somewhat flushed and afeared".

As it happened, Joanna was now to have a fellow passenger, at least for a brief period, since Agnes Laurenson, the wharfinger's wife, herself travelled south on the *Barbara Bray* down to King's Sutton Lock (five miles distant); she, too, was called to give evidence at the trial. Recalling that there was "a fellow passenger aboard who looked very agitated", Mrs Laurenson stated that Joanna may have had a drink, but that she seemed completely sober, as far as could be judged – unlike Oldfield and Musson – and that she was clearly most concerned about her personal safety.

The tale now gathers apace towards its tragic conclusion; and it was the landlord of the Crown & Castle at Aynho (just below Banbury) who was able to provide some of the most telling and damning testimony of all. When Mrs Laurenson had left the boat three miles upstream at King's Sutton, it would appear that Joanna could trust herself with the drunken boatmen no longer, according to the landlord, who had encountered her at about 10 p.m. that night. She had arrived, on foot, a little earlier and confessed that she was so frightened of the lecherous drunkards on the *Barbara Bray* that she had determined to walk along the tow-path, even at that late hour, and to take her chances with the considerably lesser evils of foot-pads and cut-purses. She hoped (she'd said) that it would be safely possible for her to rejoin the boat later when its crew might be a few degrees the more sober. Whilst she waited for the boat to come up, the landlord offered her a glass of stout, but Joanna declined. He had kept an eye on her, however, and noticed that as she sat by the edge of the canal she appeared to be secretly sharpening a knife on the side of the lock (Musson was later found to have a cut on his left cheek, and this could have been, and probably was, made with the same knife). As the boat had drawn alongside Aynho wharf, one of the crew (the landlord was unable to say which) had "cursed the eyes of the woman and wished her in hell flames, for he loathed and detested the very sight of her". As she finally re-boarded the boat, the landlord remembered seeing Joanna being offered a drink; and, in fact, he thought she might have taken a glass. But this evidence must be discounted wholly, since Mr Bartholomew Samuels, the Oxford surgeon who conducted an immediate *post-mortem*, found no evidence whatsoever of any alcohol in poor Joanna's body.

George Bloxham, the captain of a northward-bound Pickford boat, testified that he had drawn alongside Oldfield's boat just below Aynho, and that a few exchanges had been made, as normal, between the two crews. Oldfield had referred to his woman passenger in terms which were completely "disgusting", vowing, in the crudest language, what he would do with her that very night "or else he would burke her".[2] Bloxham added that Oldfield was very drunk; and Musson and Towns, too, were "rather well away, the pair of 'em".

James Robson, keeper of the Somerton Deep Lock, said that he and his wife, Anna, were awakened at about midnight by a scream of terror coming from the direction of the lock. At first they had assumed it was the cry of a young child; but when they looked down from the bedroom window of the lock-house, they saw only some men by the side of the boat, and a woman seated on top of the cabin with her legs hanging down over the side. Three things the Robsons were able to recall from that grim night, their evidence proving so

---

[2] Burke was a criminal who had been executed some thirty years earlier for smothering his victims and then selling their bodies for medical dissection.

crucial at the trial. Joanna had called out in a terrified voice "I'll not go down! Don't attempt me!" Then one of the crew had shouted "Mind her legs! Mind her legs!" And after that the passenger had resumed her frightened screams: "What have you done with my shoes – oh! please tell me!" Anna Robson enquired who the woman was, and was told by one of the crew: "A passenger – don't worry!", the crewman adding that she was having words with her husband, who was with her aboard.

Forbidding to Joanna as the tall lock-house must have appeared that midnight, standing sentinel-like above the black waters, it presented her with her one last chance of life – had she sought asylum within its walls.

But she made no such request.

At this point, or shortly after, it appears that the terrified woman took another walk along the tow-path to escape the drunken crew; but she was almost certainly back on board when the boat negotiated Gibraltar Lock. After which – and only some very short time after – she must have been out walking (yet again!) since Robert Bond, a crew-hand from the narrow-boat *Isis*, gave evidence that he passed her on the tow-path. Bond recorded his surprise that such an attractive woman should be out walking on her own so late, and he recalled asking her if all was well. But she had only nodded, hurriedly, and passed on into the night. As he approached Gibraltar Lock, Bond had met Oldfield's boat, and was asked by one of its crew if he had seen a woman walking the tow-path, the man adding, in the crudest terms, what he would do to her once he had her in his clutches once again.

No one, apart from the evil boatmen on the *Barbara Bray*, was ever to see Joanna Franks alive again.

CHAPTER ELEVEN

'Pon my word, Watson, you are coming along wonderfully. You have really done very well indeed. It is true that you have missed everything of importance, but you have hit upon the method
(Sir Arthur Conan Doyle, *A Case of Identity*)

As with Part One, Morse found himself making a few notes (mentally, this time) as he read through the unhappy narrative. For some reason he felt vaguely dissatisfied with himself. Something was nagging at his brain about Part One; but for the present he was unable to put a finger on it. It would come back to him once he'd re-read a few pages. No hurry, was there? None. The theoretical problem which his mind had suddenly seized upon was no more than a bit of harmless, quite inconsequential amusement. And yet the doubts persisted in his brain: could anyone, *anyone*, read this story and not find himself questioning one or two of the points so confidently reported? Or two or three of them? Or three or four?

What was the normal pattern of entertainment for canal boatmen, like Oldfield, on those 'protracted stops' of theirs? Changing horses was obviously one of the key activities on such occasions, but one scarcely calculated to gladden every soul. Dropping in at the local knocking-shop, then? A likely port-of-call for a few of the more strongly sexed among them, most surely. And drink? Did they drink their wages away, these boatmen, in the low-beamed bars that were built along their way? How not? Why not? What else was there to do? And though drink (as the Porter once claimed) might take away the performance, who could gainsay that it frequently provoked the desire? The desire, in this case, to rape a beautiful woman-passenger.

So many questions.

But if sex was at the bottom of things, why were the rape charges dropped at the first trial? Agreed, there was no DNA biological fingerprinting in the 1850s; no genetic code that could be read into some desperate fellow's swift ejaculations. But even in that era, the charge of rape could often be made to stick without too much difficulty; and Confucius's old pleasantry about the comparative immobility of a man with his trousers round his ankles must have sounded just as hollow then as now. Certainly to the ears of Joanna Franks.

The footnote referring to the *Court Registers* had been a surprise, and it would be of interest, certainly to the sociologist, to read something of contemporary attitudes to rape in 1859. Pretty certainly it would be a few leagues less sympathetic than that reflected in Morse's morning copy of *The Times*: 'Legal Precedent in Civil Action – £35,000 damages for Rape Victim'. Where were those *Registers*, though – if they still existed? They might (Morse supposed) have explained the Colonel's bracketed caveat about discrepancies. But *what* discrepancies? There must have been *something* in old Deniston's mind, something that bothered him just that tiny bit. The Greeks had a word for it – *parakrousis* – the striking of a slightly wrong note in an otherwise tuneful harmony.

Was that 'wrong note' struck by Mrs Laurenson, perhaps?

Whatever the situation had been with Joanna, this Laurenson woman (with her husband's full assent, one must assume) had joined the *Barbara Bray* for the journey down to King's Sutton with – as the reader was led to believe – a boat-load of sexually rampant dipsomaniacs. Difficult to swallow? Unless of course the wharfinger, Laurenson, was perfectly happy to get rid of his missus for the night – or for any night. But such a line of reasoning seemed fanciful, and there was a further possibility – a very simple, and really rather a startling one: that the crew of the *Barbara Bray* had *not* been all that belligerently blotto at the time! But no. Every piece of evidence – surely! – pointed in the opposite direction; pointed to the fact that the boatmen's robes of honour (in Fitzgeraldian phrase) were resting, like the Confucian rapist's, only just above their boot-laces.

Boots . . . shoes . . .

What *was* all that about those shoes? Why were they figuring so repeatedly in the story? There would surely have been more intimate items of Joanna's wardrobe to pilfer if the crewmen had been seeking to effect some easier sexual congress. One of them *might*, perhaps, have been a clandestine foot-fetishist . . . ?

Morse, telling himself not to be so stupid, looked again at the last couple of pages of the text. A bit over-written, all that stuff about the sentinel-like old lock-house, looking out over the dark waters. Not bad, though: and at least it made Morse resolve to drive out and see it for himself, once he was well again. Unless the planners and the developers had already pulled it down.

Like they'd pulled down St Ebbe's . . .

Such were some of Morse's thoughts after reading his second instalment. It was quite natural that he should wish to eke out the pleasures afforded by the Colonel's text. Yet it must be admitted that, once again, Morse had almost totally failed to conceive the real problems raised by this narrative. Usually, Morse was a league and a league in front of any competitive intellects; and even now his thought processes were clear and unorthodox. But for the time being, he was far below his best. Too near the picture. He was standing where the coloured paints on the narrow-boat's sides had little chance of imposing any pattern on his eye. What he really needed was to stand that bit further back from the picture; to get a more synoptic view things. 'Synoptic' had always been one of Morse's favourite words. Quickly Morse re-read Part Two. But he seemed to see little more in general terms than he had done earlier, although there were a few extra points of detail which had evaded him on the first reading, and he stored them away, haphazardly, in his brain.

There was that capital 'J', for example, that the Colonel favoured whenever he wished to emphasize the enormity of human iniquity and the infallibility of Jury and Judicature – like the capital 'G' the Christian Churches always used for God.

Then there were those journeys through the two tunnels, when Oldfield had sat with Joanna . . . or when, as Morse translated things, he put his arm around the frightened girl in the eerie darkness, and told her not to be afraid . . .

And those last complex, confusing paragraphs! She had been desperately anxious to get off the boat and away from her tipsy persecutors – so much seemed beyond any reasonable doubt. But, if so, why, according to that selfsame evidence, had she always been so anxious to get back *on* again?

Airy-fairy speculation, all this; but there were at least two things that could be factually checked. 'Nothing was convenient', it had said, and any researcher worth his salt could easily verify *that*. What *was* available, at the time Joanna reached Banbury? He could also soon discover how much any alternative route to London would have cost. What, for example, was the rail-fare to London in 1859? For that matter, what exactly had been the rail-fare between *Liverpool* and London, a fare which appeared to have been beyond the Franks's joint financial resources?

Interesting . . .

As, come to think of it, were those double quotation marks in the text – presumably the actual words, directly transcribed, and reported *verbatim*, and therefore primary source material for the crewmen's trial. Morse looked through the interspersed quotations again, and one in particular caused his mind to linger: "coaches to London – and coaches from Oxford to Banbury". Now, if those were the *exact* words Joanna had used . . . *if* they were . . . Why had she asked for the times of coaches "from Oxford to Banbury"? Surely, she should have been asking about coaches *from Banbury to Oxford*. Unless . . . unless . . .

Again, it all seemed most interesting – at least to Morse. What, finally, was he to make of that drink business? Had Joanna been drinking – or had she not? There was some curious ambivalence in the text; and perhaps this may have been in the Colonel's mind when he referred to 'a few conflicting statements'? But no – that was impossible. Mr Bartholomew Samuels had found no alcohol in Joanna's body, and that was that!

Or, rather, would have been, to most men.

The thought of drink had begun to concentrate Morse's mind powerfully, and with great circumspection and care, he poured a finger of Scotch into his bedside glass, with the same amount of plain water. Wonderful! Pity that no one would ever believe his protestations that Scotch was a necessary stimulant to his brain cells. For after a few minutes his mind was flooding with ideas – exciting ideas! – and furthermore he realized that he could begin to test one or two of his hypotheses that very evening.

That is, if Walter Greenaway's daughter came to visit.

CHAPTER TWELVE

Th' first thing to have in a libry is a shelf. Fr'm time to time this can be decorated with lithrachure. But th' shelf is th' main thing

(Finley Peter Dunne, *Mr Dooley Says*)

As she walked down Broad Street at 7.40 a.m. the following morning (Thursday), Christine Greenaway was thinking (*still* thinking) about the man who had spoken to her the previous evening in Ward 7C on the top floor of the JR2. (It was only on rare occasions that she welcomed her father's pride in his ever-loving daughter.) It wasn't that she'd been obsessively preoccupied with the man ever since; but there had been a semi-waking, overnight awareness of him. All because he'd asked her, so nicely, to look up something for him in the Bodley. So earnest, so grateful, he'd seemed. And that was silly, really, because she'd willingly have helped him anyway. That's why she'd become a librarian in the first place: to be able to locate some of the landmarks in the fields of History and Literature, and to provide where she could the correct map-references for so many curious enquiries. Even as a five-year-old, with her blonde plaits reaching half-way down her bony back, she'd envied the woman in the Summertown Library who similarly located tickets somewhere in the long drawers behind the high counter; envied, even more, the woman who stamped the dates in the front of the borrowed books, and inserted each little ticket into its appropriate, oblong folder. Not that she, Christine Greenaway, performed any longer such menial tasks herself. Almost forgotten now were those inevitable queries of who wrote *The Wind in the Willows*; for she, Christine, was now

the senior of the three august librarians who sat at the northern
end of the Bodleian's Lower Reading Room, where her daily duties
demanded assistance to both senior and junior members of the
University: checking slips, identifying shelf-marks, suggesting
reference-sections, making and taking phone-calls (one, yesterday,
from the University of Uppsala). And over these last years she
had felt a sense of importance and enjoyment in her job – of
functioning happily in the workings of the University.

Of course, there had been some major disappointments in her
life, as there had been, she knew, with most folk. Married at
twenty-two, she had been a divorcee at twenty-three. No other
woman on his part; no other man on hers – although there'd been
(still were) so many opportunites. No. It was simply that her
husband had been so immature and irresponsible – and, above all,
so boring! Once the pair of them had got down to running a home,
keeping a monthly budget, checking bank-statements – well, she'd
known he could never really be the man for her. And as things
now stood, she could no longer stomach the prospect of another
mildly ignorant, semi-aggressively macho figure of a bed-mate.
Free as she was of any financial worries, she could do exactly as
she wished about issues that were important to *her*; and she had
become a modestly active member of several organizations, including Greenpeace, CND, the Ramblers' Association, and the RSPB.
Quite certainly, she would never join one of those match-making
societies with the hope of finding a more interesting specimen
than her former spouse. If ever she *did* look for another husband,
he would have to be someone she could, in some way, come to
respect: to respect for his conversation or his experience or his
intellect or his knowledge or his – well, his anything at all, really,
except a pride in his sexual prowess. So what (she asked herself)
had all this got to do with *him*? Not much to look at, was he?
Balding, and quite certainly carrying considerable excess weight
around the midriff. Though, to be honest with herself, she was
beginning to feel a grudging regard for those men who were just
slightly overweight, perhaps because she herself seemed never
able to put on a few pounds – however much she over-indulged
in full-cream cakes and deep-fried fish and chips.

Forget him! Forget him, Christine!

Such self-admonition prevailed as she walked that morning
down the Broad, past Balliol and Trinity on her left, before crossing
over the road, just before Blackwell's, and proceeding, *sub imperatoribus*, up the semi-circular steps into the gravelled courtyard of
the Sheldonian. Thence, keeping to her right, she walked past the

SILENCE PLEASE notice under the archway, and came out at last into her real home territory – the Quadrangle of the Schools.

For many days, when six years earlier she had first started working at the Bodleian, she had been conscious of the beautiful setting there. Over the months and years, though, she had gradually grown over-familiar with what the postcards on sale in the Proscholium still called 'The Golden Heart of Oxford'; grown familiar, as she'd regularly trodden the gravelled quad, with the Tower of the Five Orders to her left, made her way past the bronze statue of the third Earl of Pembroke, and entered the Bodleian Library through the great single doorway in the West side, beneath the four tiers of blind arches in their gloriously mellowed stone.

Different today though – so very different! She felt once again the sharp irregularities of the gravel-stones beneath the soles of her expensive, high-heeled, leather shoes. And she was happily aware once more of the mediaeval Faculties painted over those familiar doors around the quad. In particular, she looked again at her favourite sign: SCHOLA NATURALIS PHILOSOPHIAE, the gilt capital letters set off, with their maroon border, against a background of the deepest Oxford-blue. And as she climbed the wooden staircase to the Lower Reading Room, Christine Greenaway reminded herself, with a shy smile around her thinly delicious lips, why perhaps it had taken her to long to re-appreciate those neglected delights that were all around her.

She hung her coat in the Librarians' Cloakroom, and started her daily duties. It was always tedious, that first hour (7.45–8.45 a.m.), clearing up the books left on the tables from the previous day, and ensuring that the new day's readers could be justifiably confident that the Bodley's books once more stood ready on their appointed shelves.

She thought back to the brief passages of conversation the previous evening, when he'd nodded over to her (only some six feet away):

'You work at the Bodleian, I hear?'

'Uh – huh!'

'It may be – it is! – a bit of a cheek, not knowing you—'

'—but you'd like me to look something up for you.'

Morse nodded, with a winsome smile.

She'd known he was some sort of policeman – things like that always got round the wards pretty quickly. His eyes had held hers for a few seconds, but she had been conscious neither of their blueness nor of their authority: only their melancholy and their vulnerability. Yet she had sensed that those complicated eyes of his had seemed to look, somehow, deep down inside herself, and *to like what they had seen.*

'Silly twerp, you are!' she told herself. She was behaving like some adolescent schoolgirl, smitten with a sudden passion for a teacher. But the truth remained – that for that moment she was prepared to run a marathon in clogs and calipers for the whitish-haired and gaudily pyjamaed occupant of the bed immediately opposite her father's.

CHAPTER THIRTEEN

Ah, fill the Cup: – what boots it to repeat
  How Time is slipping underneath our Feet:
  Unborn To-morrow, and dead Yesterday,
Why fret about them if To-day be sweet!
(Edward Fitzgerald,
The Rubaiyat of Omar Khayyam)

He'd been rather vague, and it had been somewhat difficult precisely to assess what he wanted: some specific details about any assurance or insurance companies in the mid-nineteenth century – especially, if it were possible, about companies in the Midlands. Off and on, during the morning, it had taken her an hour or more to hunt down the appropriate catalogues; and another hour to locate the pertinent literature. But by lunch-time (praise be!) she had completed her research, experiencing, as she assumed, an elation similar to that of the scholars who daily dug into the treasury of her Great Library to extract their small nuggets of gold. She had found a work of reference which told her exactly what Morse (the man responsible for ruffling her wonted calm) had wanted her to find.

Just after twelve noon, with one of her female colleagues, she walked over to the King's Arms, on the corner of Holywell Street – in which hostelry she was accustomed to enjoy her fifty-five-minute lunch-break, with a single glass of white wine and a salmon-and-cucumber sandwich. It was when Christine got to her feet and offered to get in a second round of drinks, that her colleague eyed her curiously.

'You always said two glasses sent you to sleep.'

'So?'

'So I'll go to sleep as well, all right?'

They were good friends; and doubtless Christine would have given some castrated account of her visit to the JR2 the previous evening, had not another colleague joined them. Whereafter the three were soon engaged in happily animated conversation about interior decorating and the iniquity of current mortgage repayments.

Or two of them were, to be more accurate. And the one who had been the least lively of the trio found herself doing rather less work than usual that same afternoon. After carefully photocopying her finds, she wished the p.m. hours away, for she was impatient to parade the fruits of her research; and she just, simply – well, she just wanted to see the man again. That was all.

At 6.30 p.m. at her home in the village of Bletchington, some few miles out of Oxford, towards Otmoor, she slowly stroked red polish on to her smoothly manicured oval nails, and at 7 p.m. started out for the JR2.

Equally, from his own vantage point, Morse was looking forward to seeing Christine Greenaway once again. The previous evening he'd quickly appreciated her professionalism as she'd listened to his request, as she'd calculated how it might be implemented. In a more personal way he'd noted, too, the candour and intelligence of her eyes – eyes almost as blue as his own – and the quiet determination around her small mouth. Thus it was that at 7.25 p.m. he was sitting in his neatly re-made bed, newly washed, erect against his pillows, his thinning hair so recently re-combed – when his stomach suddenly felt as though it was being put through a mangle; and for two or three minutes the pain refused to relax its grinding, agonizing grip. Morse closed his eyes and squeezed his fists with such force that the sweat stood out on his forehead; and with eyes still shut he prayed to Someone, in spite of his recent conversion from agnosticism to outright atheism.

Two years earlier, at the Oxford Book Association, he had listened to a mournful Muggeridge propounding the disturbing philosophy of The Fearful Symmetry, in which the debits and the credits on the ledgers are balanced inexorably and eternally, and where the man who tries to steal a secret pleasure will pretty soon find himself queuing up to pay the bill – and more often than not with some hefty service-charges added in. What a preposterous belief it was (the sage had asserted) that the hedonist could be a happy man!

Oh dear.

Why had Morse ever considered the pleasure of a little glass? The wages of sin was death, and the night before was seldom worth the morning after (some people said). All mortals, Morse knew, were ever treading that narrow way by Tophet flare to Judgement Day, but he now prayed that the last few steps in his own case might be deferred at least a week or two.

Then, suddenly as it had come, the pain was gone, and Morse opened his eyes once more.

The clock behind Sister's desk (as earlier and darkly rumoured, Nessie was going to be on the night-shift) was showing 7.30 when the visitors began to filter through with their offerings stashed away in Sainsbury or St Michael carriers, and, some few of them, with bunches of blooms for the newly hospitalized.

Life is, alas, so full of disappointments; and it was to be an unexpected visitor who was to monopolize Morse's time that evening. Bearing a wilting collection of white chrysanthemums, a sombre-looking woman of late-middle age proceeded to commandeer the sole chair set at his bedside.

'Mrs Green! How very nice of you to come!'

Morse's heart sank deeply, and took an even deeper plunge when the dutiful charlady mounted a sustained challenge against Morse's present competence to deal, single-handedly, with such crucial matters as towels, toothpaste, talcum-powder, and clean pyjamas (especially the latter). It was wonderfully good of her (who could deny it?) to take such trouble to come to see him (*three* buses, as Morse knew full well); but he found himself consciously *willing* her to get up and *go*.

At five minutes past eight, after half a dozen 'I-really-must-go's, Mrs G. rose to her poorly feet in preparation for her departure, with instructions for the care of the chrysanthemums. At last (at last!), after a mercifully brief account of her latest visit to her 'sheeropodist' in Banbury Road, Mrs G. dragged her long-suffering feet away from Ward 7C.

On several occasions, from her father's bedside, Christine Greenaway had half-turned in the course of her filial obligations; and two or three times her eyes had locked with Morse's: hers with the half-masked smile of understanding; his with all the impotence of some stranded whale.

Just as Mrs Green was on her way, a white-coated consultant, accompanied by the Charge Nurse, decided (inconsiderately) to give ten minutes of his time to Greenaway Senior, and then in some *sotto voce* asides, to confide his prognosis to Greenaway Junior. And for Morse, this hiatus in the evening's ordering was getting just about as infuriating as waiting for breakfast in some 'Fawlty Towers' hotel.

Then Lewis came.

Never had Morse been less glad to see his sergeant; yet he *had* instructed Lewis to pick up his post from the flat, and he now took possession of several envelopes and a couple of cards: Morse's shoes (his other pair) were now ready for collection from Grove Street; his car licence was due to be renewed within the next twenty days; a ridiculously expensive book on *The Transmission of Classical Manuscripts* now awaited him at OUP; a bill from the plumber for the repair of a malfunctioning stop-cock was still unpaid; the Wagner Society asked if he wanted to enter his name in a raffle for Bayreuth *Ring* tickets; and Peter Imbert invited him to talk in the new year at a weekend symposium, in Hendon, on inner-city crime. It was rather like a cross-section of life, his usual correspondence: half of it was fine, and half of it he wanted to forget.

At twenty-three minutes past eight, by the ward clock, Lewis asked if there was anything else he could do.

'Yes, Lewis. Please *go*, will you? I want to have five minutes with—' Morse nodded vaguely over to Greenaway's bed.

'Well, if that's what you want, sir.' He rose slowly to his feet.

'It *is* what I bloody want, Lewis! I've just *told* you, haven't I?'

Lewis took a large bunch of white seedless grapes (£2.50 a pound) from his carrier-bag. 'I thought – we thought, the missus and me – we thought you'd enjoy them, sir.'

He was gone; and Morse knew, within a second of his going, that he would not be forgiving himself easily for such monumental ingratitude. But the damage was done: *nescit vox missa reverti.*

The bell rang two minutes later, and Christine came across to Morse's bed as she left, and handed him six large photocopied sheets.

'I hope this is what you wanted.'

'I'm ever so grateful. It's – it's a pity we didn't have a chance to . . .'

'I understand. I *do* understand,' she said. 'And you will let me know if I can do anything else?'

'Look . . . perhaps if we—'

'Come along now, please!' The Charge Nurse's voice sounded to Morse almost as imperious as Nessie's as she walked quickly around the beds.

'I'm so grateful,' said Morse. 'I really am! As I say it's . . .'

'Yes,' said Christine softly.

'Will you be in tomorrow?' asked Morse quickly.

'No – not tomorrow. We've got some librarians coming from California—'

'Come along now, *please!*'

Mrs Green, Sergeant Lewis, Christine Greenaway – now all of them gone; and already the medicine-trolley had been wheeled into the ward, and the nurses were starting out on yet another circuit of measurements and medicaments.

And Morse felt sick at heart.

It was at 9.20 p.m. that he finally settled back against his piled pillows to glance quickly through the photocopied material Christine had found for him. And soon he was deeply and happily engrossed – his temporary despondency departing on the instant.

CHAPTER FOURTEEN

Being in the land of the living was itself the survivor's privilege, for so many of one's peers – one's brothers and sisters – had already fallen by the wayside, having died at birth, at infancy or childhood

(Roy & Dorothy Porter, *In Sickness and in Health*)

The documents which Morse now handled were just the thing (he had little doubt) for satisfying the original-source-material philosophy which was just then swamping the GCSE and A-level syllabuses. And for Morse, whose School Certificate in History (Credit) had demanded little more than semi-familiarity with the earliest models of seed-drills and similar agricultural adjuncts of the late eighteenth century, the reading of them was fascinating. Particularly poignant, as it appeared to Morse, was the Foreword to the *Insurance Guide and Hand-Book 1860* (bless the girl! – she'd even got the exact year) where the anonymous author stated his own determination to soldier along in 'this vale of tears' for as long as decently possible:

Thus it is that all our efforts are forever required, not to surpass what we may call the biblical 'par' for life – that famous 'three-score years and ten' – but to come reasonably near to attaining it at all. For it is only by continuous vigilance and energy in the work for self preservation that the appointed average can be brought into view; and with good fortune and good sense (and God's grace) be achieved.

It was interesting to find the Almighty in parenthesis, even in 1860, and Morse felt he would like to have known the author. Yet when that same author went on to assert that 'mortality had decreased by two-fifths between 1720 and 1820', Morse began to wonder what on earth such a bafflingly unscientific – indeed, quite nonsensical – statement might mean. What did seem immediately clear, as he read through the small print, was that people during those years were beginning to live rather longer, and that by the middle of the nineteenth century insurance companies were beginning to match this sociological phenomenon with increasingly attractive rates and premiums, in spite of the sombre statistics appended to each year, right up to the 1850s. Like 1853, e.g. – the figures for which Morse now considered. Of the half million or so departed souls reported in the pages of the *Guide*, 55,000 had died of consumption, 25,000 of pneumonia, 24,500 of convulsions, 23,000 of bronchitis, 20,000 of premature death and debility, 19,000 of typhus, 16,000 of scarlatina, 15,000 of diarrhoea, 14,000 of heart disease, 12,000 of whooping cough, 11,000 of dropsy, 9,000 of apoplexy, 8,500 of paralysis, 6,000 of asthma, 5,750 of cancer, 4,000 of teeth troubles, 3,750 of measles, 3,500 of croup, 3,250 of small-pox, 3,000 of (mothers) giving birth; and so on to the smaller numbers succumbing to diseases of brain, kidney, liver, and other perishable parts of the anatomy – and to old age! As he added up such numbers quickly in his head, Morse realized that about two-thirds of the 500,000 were unaccounted for; and he had to assume that even with a few more categories added ('murder' for one!) there must have been vast numbers of people in those days whose deaths were for some reason or other not specifically 'accounted for' at all, albeit being registered in the national statistics. Perhaps a lot of them were just not important enough to get their own particular malady spelled out on any death certificate; perhaps many of the physicians, midwives, nurses, poor-law attendants, or whatever, just didn't know, or didn't want to know, or didn't care.

As he lay back in the pillows and thought of the circumstances besetting the luckless Joanna Franks, who had died neither of consumption nor pneumonia . . . nor . . . he suddenly fell into a sleep so deep that he missed his 10 p.m. Horlicks and his treasured Digestive biscuit; and then he woke up again, somewhat less than refreshed, at 11.45 p.m., with a dry throat and a clear head. The lights in the ward were turned down to half power, and the other patients around him seemed contentedly asleep – apart from the man who'd been admitted late that afternoon and around whom the medical staff had been fussing with a rather ominous concern; the man who now lay staring at the ceiling, doubtless contemplating the imminent collapse of his earthly fortunes.

Nessie was nowhere to be seen: the desk was empty.

He'd just had a nasty little dream. He'd been playing cricket in his early days at Grammar School; and when it came to his turn to bat, he couldn't find his boots . . . and then when he did find them the laces kept snapping; and he was verging on a tearful despair – when he'd awoken. It might have been Mrs Green talking about her chiropody? Or was it Lewis, perhaps, who'd brought the card from the cobblers? Or neither of them? Was it not more likely to have been a young woman in 1859 who'd shouted, with her particular brand of terrified despair, 'What have you done with my shoes?'

He looked around again: the desk was still empty.

Surely he wasn't likely to imperil the well-being of the ward if he turned on his angle-lamp? Especially if focused directly into a small pool of light on his own pillows? No. Reading a book wasn't going to hurt anyone and the sick man had had *his* light on all the time.

Pushing in the button switch, he turned on his own light, with no reaction from anyone; and still no sign of Nessie.

Part Three of *Murder on the Oxford Canal* was close to hand; but Morse was reluctant to finish *that* too quickly. He remembered when he'd first read *Bleak House* (still to his mind the greatest novel in the English language) he'd deliberately decelerated his reading as the final pages grew ever thinner beneath his fingers. Never had he wanted to hang on to a story so much! Not that the Colonel's work was anything to wax all that lyrical about; and yet Morse *did* want to eke it out – or so he told himself. Which left the not displeasing possibility of a few further chapters of *The Blue Ticket* – with Mr Greenaway now fast asleep. The pattern of crime in nineteenth-century Shropshire had already joined the local legion of lost causes.

Morse was soon well into the exploits of a blonde who would have had arrows on her black stockings, pointing northward and reading 'This way for the knickers' – that is, if she'd worn any stockings; or worn any knickers, for that matter. And it was amid much parading of bodies, pawing of bosoms, and patting of buttocks, that Morse now spent an enjoyable little interval of erotic pleasure; indeed, was so engrossed that he did not mark her approach.

'What do you think you're doing?'

'I was just—'

'Lights go out at ten o'clock. You're disturbing everyone on the ward.'

'They're all asleep.'

'Not for much longer, with you around!'

'I'm sorry—'

'What's this you're reading?'

Before he could do anything about it, Nessie had removed the book from his hands, and he had no option but to watch her helplessly. She made no comment, passed no moral judgement, and for a brief second Morse wondered if he had not seen a glint of some semi-amusement in those sharp eyes as they had skimmed a couple of paragraphs.

'Time you were asleep!' she said, in a not unkindly fashion, handing him back the book. Her voice was as crisp as her uniform, and Morse replaced the ill-starred volume in his locker. 'And be careful of your fruit juice!' She moved the half-filled glass one millimetre to the left, turned off the light, and was gone. And Morse gently eased himself down into the warmth and comfort of his bed, like Tennyson's lily sliding slowly into the bosom of the lake . . .

That night he dreamed a dream in Technicolor (he swore it!), although he knew such a claim would be contradicted by the oneirologists. He saw the ochre-skinned, scantily clad siren in her black, arrowed stockings, and he could even recall her lavender-hued underclothing. Almost it was the perfect dream! Almost. For there was a curiously insistent need in Morse's brain which paradoxically demanded a *factual* name and place and time before, in *fantasy*, that sexually unabashed freebooter could be his. And in Morse's muddled computer of a mind, that siren took the name of one Joanna Franks, provocatively walking along towards Duke's Cut, in the month of June in 1859.

When he awoke (was woken, rather) the following morning, he felt wonderfully refreshed, and he resolved that he would take no risks of any third humiliation over *The Blue Ticket*. With breakfast, temperature, wash, shave, blood-pressure, newspaper, tablets, Bovril, all these now behind him – and with not a visitor in sight –

he settled down to discover exactly what had happened to that young woman who had taken control of his nocturnal fantasies.

CHAPTER FIFTEEN

PART THREE

A Protracted Trial

Joanna Franks's body was found at Duke's Cut at about 5.30 a.m. on Wednesday, 22nd June 1859. Philip Tomes, a boatman, said he was passing down-canal towards Oxford when he saw something in the water – something which was soon identified as, in part, a woman's gown; what else, though, he could not for the moment make out in the darkened waters. The object was on the side of the canal opposite the tow-path, and in due course he discovered it to be the body of a female, without either bonnet or shoes. She was floating alongside the bank, head north, feet south, and there was no observable movement about her. She was lying on her face, which seemed quite black. Tomes stopped his boat, and with a boat-hook gently pulled the body to the tow-path side, where he lifted it out of the water, in which latter task he was assisted by John Ward, a Kidlington fisherman, who happened to be passing alongside the canal at that early hour. In fact, it was Ward who had the presence of mind to arrange for the body, which was still warm, to be taken down to the Plough Inn at Wolvercote.

It appears from various strands of inter-weaving evidence, albeit some of it from the guilty parties themselves, that Oldfield and Musson (and, by one account, Towns also) left the *Barbara Bray* at roughly the point where Joanna met her death, and that they were seen standing together on the tow-path side of the canal just below Duke's Cut. A certain man passed by the area at the crucial time, 4 a.m. or just after, and both Oldfield and Musson, with great presence of mind, asked him if he had seen a woman walking beside the canal. The man had replied, as they clearly recalled, with a very definite 'No!', and had made to get further on his way with all speed. Yet the two (or perhaps three) men had asked him the same question again and again, in rather an agitated manner.

(It is clear that this man's testimony could have been vital in substantiating the boatmen's claims. But he was never traced, in spite of wide-scale enquiries in the area. A man roughly answering his description, one Donald Favant, had signed the register at the Nag's Head in Oxford for either the 20th or the 21st June – there was some doubt – but this man never came forward. The strong implication must therefore remain, as it did at the time, that the whole story was the clever concoction of desperate men.)

Jonas Bamsey, wharfinger in the employ of the Oxford Canal Authority at Oxford's Hayfield Wharf, gave evidence at the trial that the *Barbara Bray* had duly effected its partial unloading, but that Oldfield had not reported the loss of any passenger – which quite certainly should have been the duty of the boat's captain under the Authority's Regulations. Instead, according to the scant and inconsistent evidence at this point, the boatmen do appear to have confided in some of their acquaintances in Upper Fisher Row, claiming that their passenger had been out of her mind; that she had committed suicide; and that on at least one occasion they had been called upon to save her from an attempted drowning on the journey down from Preston Brook.

Later that dreadful day, when the crew of the *Barbara Bray* came to negotiate the lock on the Thames at Iffley, two miles downstream from Folly Bridge, Oldfield spoke to the keeper, Albert Lee, and reported to him and his wife (coincidentally also named Joanna) that a passenger on his boat had been drowned; but that she was most sadly deranged, and had been a sore trial to him and his fellow crew-members ever since she had first embarked at Preston Brook. Oldfield was still obviously very drunk. Pressed to explain what he was seeking to say, Oldfield asserted only that "It was a very bad job that had happened". The passenger was "off her head" and had been last seen by the crew of Gibraltar Lock. Yet Oldfield was vehemently unwilling to listen to Lee's suggestion of returning to Oxford to sort out the whole tragedy; and this made Lee more than somewhat suspicious. On the departure of the *Barbara Bray*, therefore, he himself immediately set off for Oxford, where he contacted the Pickford Office; and where the Pickford Office, in turn, contacted the Police Authority.

When the infamous boat finally arrived at Reading (for some reason, over two hours behind schedule) Constable Harrison was on hand, with appropriate support, to take the entire crew into custody, and to testify that all of them, including the youth, were still observably drunk and excessively abusive as he put them in darbies and escorted them to temporary cell-accommodation in the gaol at Reading. One of them, as Harrison vividly recalled, was vile enough to repeat some of his earlier invective against Joanna Franks, and was heard to mutter "Damn and blast that wicked woman!"

Hannah MacNeil, a serving woman at the Plough Inn, Wolvercote, testified that when the sodden body had been brought from the canal, she had been employed, under direction, to take off Joanna's clothes. The left sleeve was torn out of its gathers and the cuff on the same hand was also torn. Tomes and Ward, for their part, were quite firm in their evidence that they themselves had made no rips or tears in Joanna's clothing as they lifted her carefully from the water at Duke's Cut.

Katharine Maddison testified that she was a co-helper with Hannah MacNeill in taking off Joanna's drenched garments. Particularly had she noticed the state of Joanna's calico knickers which had been ripped right across the front. This garment was produced in Court; and many were later to agree that the production of such an intimate item served further to heighten the universal feeling of revulsion against those callous men who were now arraigned with her murder.

Mr Samuels, the Oxford surgeon who examined the body at the inquest, reported signs of bruising below the elbow of the left arm, and further indications of subcutaneous bruising below left and right cheekbones; the same man described the dead woman's face as presenting a state of "discoloration and disfigurement". Mr Samuels agreed that it was perhaps possible for the facial injuries, such as they were, to have been caused by unspecified and accidental incidents in the water, or in the process of taking-up from the water. Yet such a possibility was now seeming, both to Judge and Jury, more and more remote.

The youth Wootton then gave his version of the tragic events, and on one point he expressed himself forcefully: that Towns had got himself "good and half-seas-over" the night before Joanna was found, and that he was sound asleep at the time the murder must have occurred, for he (Wootton) had heard him "snoring loudly". We shall never be in a position to know whether Towns had forced Wootton to give this evidence to the Court – under some threat or other, perhaps. From subsequent developments, however, it seems clear that we may give a substantial degree of credence to Wootton's testimony.

Joseph Jarnell, the co-prisoner pending whose evidence the re-trial had been agreed, related to the Court the damning confessions Oldfield had betrayed whilst the two men shared a prison-cell. In essence such 'confessions' amounted to a rather crude attempt on Oldfield's part to settle the majority of blame for almost everything which had happened on Musson and Towns. But in spite of the man's earnest manner and the consistency of his account, Jarnell's story made little or no impression. Yet his testimony carried interest, if not conviction. Amongst the strongest of the fabrications which Oldfield had sought to put about was that Joanna Franks had in excess of fifty golden sovereigns in one of her two boxes; that Towns had discovered this fact, and that Joanna had found him rummaging through her trunks. She had threatened (so the allegation ran) to report him to the next Pickford Office if he did not mend his ways and make immediate apology and restoration. (Such nonsense was wholly discredited at the time, and may be safely discounted now.)

Together with many other items, the knife which Joanna had been observed sharpening was later found in one of her trunks, the cord of which had been cut, and which still remained untied. The assumption was that at some point the men had opened Joanna's belongings after the murder, and had replaced the knife in one of the trunks. It must certainly be considered a strong possibility that the men intended to steal some of her possessions, for as we have seen a charge of theft was included, in the most strongly worded terms, in the original indictment of the crew at the first trial in August 1859. It seems, however, that Prosecuting Counsel at the second trial were sufficiently confident as to forgo such a charge and to concentrate their accusations on murder, since the lesser charge (difficult, in any case, as it would have been to substantiate) was subsequently excluded. We have seen a similar procedure operating, in the first trial, concerning the charges of rape; and perhaps it is of some strange and macabre interest to note that in the original trial the charges of both rape and theft (as well as murder) were made against each individual member of the crew – including the youth Wootton.

Out of all the evidence given at that memorable second trial at Oxford in April 1860, fairly certainly that of Charles Franks himself evoked the greatest feeling and the widest sympathy. The poor man was weeping aloud as he entered the witness-box, and it seemed as if it were almost beyond his physical powers to raise his eyes in order to bear the sight of the prisoners and to look upon their faces. He had obviously been deeply in love with Joanna, and turning his back on the vile men arraigned before the Court he explained how, in consequence of some information, he had come into Oxfordshire and seen his wife's dead body at the time of the inquest. For although it was dreadfully disfigured (here the poor fellow could not at all restrain his feelings) yet he knew it by a small mark behind his wife's left ear, a mark of which only a parent or an intimate lover could have known. Corroboration of identification (if, in fact, corroboration was needed) was afforded by the shoes, later found in the fore-cabin of the *Barbara Bray*, which matched in the minutest degrees the contours of the dead woman's feet.

At the conclusion of the hearing, and after a lengthy summing-up by Mr Augustus Benham, the Jury, under their duly appointed chairman, begged permission of his Lordship to retire to consider their verdict.

CHAPTER SIXTEEN

At a hotel facing the sea at Brighton, he ate a good breakfast of bacon and eggs, toast and marmalade; then took a stroll round the town before returning to the station and boarding a train for Worthing
(Court Record of evidence given in the trial of Neville George Clevely Heath, on the morning after the murder of Margery Gardner)

Perhaps it was the dream.

Whatever it was, Morse knew that something had at last prodded him into a slightly more intelligent appraisal of the Colonel's story, because he was now beginning to take account of two or three major considerations which had been staring at him all the while.

The first of these was the character of Joanna Franks herself. How had it come about – whatever the fortuitous, involuntary, or deliberate circumstances in which Joanna had met her death – that the crew of the *Barbara Bray* had insisted time and time again that the wretched woman had been nothing but one long, sorry trial to them all ever since she'd first jumped on board at Preston Brook? How *was* it that they were still damning and blasting the poor woman's soul to eternity way, way *after* they had pushed her into the Canal and, for all Morse or anyone else knew, held her head under the black waters until she writhed in agony against their murderous hands no longer? Had a satisfactory explanation been forthcoming for such events? All right, there was still Part Four of the story to come. But so far, the answer was 'no'.

There was, though (as it now occurred to Morse), one possible dimension to the case that the good Colonel had never even hinted at – either through an excessive sense of propriety, or from a lack of imagination – namely that *Joanna Franks had been a seductive tease*:

a woman who over those long hours of that long journey had begun to drive the crew towards varied degrees of insanity with her provocative overtures, and to foster the inevitable jealousies arising therefrom.

Come off it, Morse!

Yes, come off it! There was no evidence to support such a view. None! Yet the thought stayed with him, reluctant to leave. An attractive woman . . . boredom . . . drink . . . a tunnel . . . continued boredom . . . more drink . . . another tunnel . . . darkness . . . desire . . . opportunity . . . still more drink . . . and more Priapic promptings in the loins . . . Yes, all that, perhaps, the Colonel himself may have understood. But what if she, Joanna herself, had been the active catalyst in the matter? What if she had craved for the men just as much as they had craved for her? What (put it simply, Morse!) *what if she'd wanted sex just as badly as they did*? What if she were the precursor of Sue Bridehead in *Jude the Obscure*, driving poor old Phillotson potty, as well as poor old Jude?

'Men's questions!' he heard a voice say. 'Just the sort of thoughts that would occur to an ageing MCP like you!'

There was a second general consideration which, from the point of view of criminal justice, struck Morse as considerably more cogent and a good deal less contentious. In the court-room itself, the odds did seem, surely, to have been stacked pretty heavily against the crew of the *Barbara Bray* – with 'presumption of innocence' playing decidedly second fiddle to 'assumption of guilt'. Even the fair-minded Colonel had let his prejudgements run away with him a little: already he'd decided that any ostensible concern on the part of the boatmen for the missing passenger (believed drowned?) was only shown 'with great presence of mind' in order to establish a semi-convincing alibi for themselves; already he'd decided that these same boatmen, 'still obviously very drunk' (and by implication still knocking it back at top-tipplers' rates) had manoeuvred their 'infamous' craft down the Thames to Reading without having the common decency to mention to anyone the little matter of the murder they'd committed on the way. Did (Morse asked himself) wicked men tend to get more *drunk* – or more *sober* – after committing such callous crimes? Interesting thought . . .

Yes, and there was a third general point – one that seemed to Morse most curious: the charges both of theft and of rape had, for some reason, been dropped against the boatmen. Was this because the prosecution had been wholly confident, and decided to go for the graver charge of murder – with the expectation (fully justified) that they had sufficient evidence to convict 'Rory' Oldfield and Co. on the capital indictment? Or was it, perhaps, because they had too *little* confidence in their ability to secure conviction on the *lesser* charges? Obviously, as Morse seemed vaguely to remember from his schooldays, neither rape nor theft would have been considered too venial an offence in the middle of the last century, but . . . Or was it just possible that these charges were dropped because there was no convincing evidence to support them? And if so, was the indictment for murder entered upon by the prosecution for one simple reason – that it presented the *only* hope of bringing those miserable men to justice? Certainly, as far as multiple rape was concerned, the evidence must have been decidedly dodgy – as the Judge in the first trial had pronounced. But what about theft? The prerequisite of theft was that the aggrieved party possessed something worth the stealing. So what was it that poor Joanna had about her person, or had in either of her two travelling-boxes, that was worth the crime? The evidence, after all, pointed to the fact that she hadn't got a couple of pennies to rub together. Her fare for the canal-trip had been sent up from her husband in London; and even facing the terrible risks of travelling with a drunken, lecherous crew – certainly after Banbury had been reached – she had *not* taken, or not been *able* to take, any alternative means of transport to get to the husband who was awaiting her in the Edgware Road. So? So what had she got, if anything, that was worth stealing?

There were those shoes again, too! Did Joanna deliberately leave off her shoes? Did she enjoy the feel of the mud between her toes along the tow-path – like some bare-foot hippie on a watery walk round Stonehenge in the dawn?

What a strange case it had been! The more he thought about it, the greater the number of questions that kept occurring to Morse's mind. He had a good deal of experience in cases where the forensic and pathological evidence had been vital to the outcome of a court case. But he wasn't particularly impressed with the conclusions that (presumably) must have been drawn from Mr Samuel's comparatively scientific findings. For Morse (wholly, it must be admitted, without medical or scientific qualifications) the state of the dress, and the bruising described, would have been much more consistent with Joanna being held firmly from behind, with the assailant's (?) left hand gripping her left wrist; and his (her?) right hand being held forcibly across her mouth, where thumb and forefinger would almost invariably produce the sort of bruising mentioned in the recorded description.

What of this Jarnell fellow? The prosecution must have been considerably impressed, at the first hearing, with his potential testimony. Why, otherwise, would anyone be willing to postpone a trial for six months – on the word of a gaolbird? Even the Colonel had given the fellow a good write-up! So why was it that when he duly turned up to tell his tale, at the second trial, no one wished to listen to him? Had there been something, some knowledge, somewhere, that had caused the court to discount, or at least discredit, the disclosures his cell-mate, Oldfield, had allegedly made to him? Because whatever accusations could be levelled against Oldfield, the charge of inconsistency was *not* amongst them. On three occasions, after Joanna's death, he had insisted that she was "out of her mind", "sadly deranged", "off her head" . . . And there had, it appeared, been no conflict of evidence between the crewmen that on one occasion at least (did that mean two?) they had been called upon to save Joanna from drowning herself. The one vital point Jarnell disclosed was that Oldfield had not only protested his own innocence of the murder, but had also sought to shift all responsibility on to his fellow crewmen. Not, to be sure, a very praiseworthy piece of behaviour! Yet, *if Oldfield himself were innocent*, where else could he have laid the blame? At the time, in any case, no one had been willing to listen seriously either to what Jarnell or to what Oldfield might have to say. But if they were right? Or if *one* of them were right?

A curious little thought struck Morse at this point, and lodged itself in a corner of his brain – for future reference. And a rather bigger thought struck him simultaneously: that he needed to remember he was only playing a game with himself; only trying to get through a few days' illness with a happy little problem to amuse himself with – like a tricky cryptic crossword from *The Listener*. It was just a little worrying, that was all . . . the way the dice had been loaded all the time against those drunkards who had murdered Joanna Franks.

And the niggling doubt persisted.

If they had . . .

CHAPTER SEVENTEEN

> The detective novelist, as a class, hankers after compli-
> cation and ingenuity, and is disposed to reject the
> obvious and acquit the accused if possible. He is uneasy
> until he has gone further and found some new and
> satisfying explanation of the problem
> (Dorothy L. Sayers, *The Murder of Julia Wallace*)

The thought that the crewmen may not have been guilty of Joanna
Franks's murder proved to be one of those heady notions that
evaporate in the sunrise of reason. For if the crewmen had not
been responsible, who on earth had? Nevertheless, it seemed to
Morse pretty much odds-on that if the case had been heard a
century later, there would have been no certain conviction. Doubtless, at the time, the jury's verdict had looked safe and satisfactory,
especially to the hostile crowds lining the streets and baying for
blood. But *should* the verdict have been reached? True, there was
enough circumstantial suspicion to sentence a saint; yet no really
direct evidence, was there? No witnesses to murder; no indication
of *how* the murder had been committed; no adequately convincing
motive for *why*. Just a time, and a place, and Joanna lying face-
downwards in Duke's Cut all that while ago.

Unless, of course, there were some passages of evidence not
reported – either from the first or the second trial? The Colonel
had clearly been rather more interested in the lax morals of the
boatmen than in any substantiation of the evidence, and he could
just have omitted the testimony of any corroborative witnesses
who might have been called. Perhaps it would be of some interest
– in this harmless game he was playing – to have a quick look
through those *Court Registers*, if they still existed; or through the
relevant copies of *Jackson's Oxford Journal*, which certainly *did* exist,
as Morse knew, filed on microfiche in the Oxford Central Library.
(Doubtless in the Bodley, too!) And, in any case, he hadn't finished
the Colonel's book yet. Why, there might be much still to be
revealed in that last exciting episode.

Which he now began to read.

Almost immediately he was conscious of Fiona standing beside
him – the amply bosomed Fiona, smelling vaguely of the summer
and strongly of disinfectant. Then she sat down on the bed, and

he felt the pneumatic pressure of her against him as she leaned across and looked over his shoulder.

'Intereeeesting?'

Morse nodded. 'It's the book the old girl brought round – you know, the Colonel's wife.'

Fiona stayed where she was, and Morse found himself reading the same short sentence for the third, fourth, fifth time – without the slightest degree of comprehension – as her softness gently pressed against him. Was she conscious, herself, of taking the initiative in such memorable intimacy, however mild?

Then she ruined everything.

'I don't go in much for reading these days. Last book I read was *Jane Eyre* – for GCSE, that was.'

'Did you enjoy it?' (Poor, dear Charlotte had long had a special place in Morse's heart.)

'Pretty boring stuff. We just had to do it, you know, for the exam.'

Oh dear!

Crossing her black-stockinged legs, she took off one of her flat-heeled black shoes, and shook out some invisible irritant on to the ward floor.

'When do people take their shoes off?' asked Morse. 'Normally, I mean?'

'Funny question, isn't it?'

'When they've a stone in them – like you?'

Fiona nodded. 'And when they go to bed.'

'And?'

'Well – when they go paddling at Blackpool.'

'Yes?'

'When they sit watching the telly with their feet on the sofa – if they've got a mum as fussy as mine.'

'Anything else?'

'What do you want to know all this for?'

'If they've got corns or something,' persisted Morse, 'and go to the chiropodist.' ('Kyropodist', in Morse's book.)

'Yes. Or if their feet get sore or tired. Or if they have to take their tights off for some reason—'

'Such as?'

Morse saw the flash of sensuous amusement in her eyes, as she suddenly stood up, pulled his sheets straight, and shook out his pillows. 'Well, if you don't know at your age—'

Oh dear!

Age.

Morse felt as young as he'd ever done; but suddenly, and so clearly, he could see himself as he was seen by this young girl.

Old!

But his mood was soon to be brightened by the totally unexpected re-appearance of Sergeant Lewis, who explained that the purpose of his unofficial visit (it was 2.15 p.m.) was to interview a woman, still in intensive care, in connection with yet another horrendous crash on the A34.

'Feeling OK this morning, sir?'

'I shall feel a jolly sight better once I've had the chance of apologizing to you – for being so bloody ungrateful!'

'Oh yes? When was that, sir? I thought you were always ungrateful to me.'

'I'm just sorry, that's all,' said Morse simply and quietly.

Lewis, whose anger had been simmering and spitting like soup inadvertently left on the stove, had come into the ward with considerable reluctance. Yet when some ten minutes later he walked out, he felt the same degree of delight he invariably experienced when he knew that Morse needed *him* – even if it were only, as in this case, to do a bit of mundane research (Morse had briefly explained the case) and to try to discover if the *Court Registers* of the Oxford Assizes, 1859–60, were still available; and if so to see if any records of the trials were still extant.

After Lewis had gone, Morse felt very much more in tune with the universe. Lewis had forgiven him, readily; and he felt a contentment which he, just as much as Lewis, could ill define and only partly comprehend. And with Lewis looking into the *Court Registers*, there was another researcher in the field: a qualified librarian, who could very quickly sort out *Jackson's Oxford Journals*. Not that she was coming in that evening, alas!

Patience, Morse!

At 3 p.m. he turned once again to the beginning of the fourth and final episode in the late Colonel Deniston's book.

CHAPTER EIGHTEEN

PART FOUR

A Pronounced Sentence

A bailiff was sworn in to attend the Jury, who immediately retired to the Clerk of Indictments' Room. After an absence of three-quarters of an hour, they returned to the Court; and, their names having been read over, every person appeared to wait with breathless anxiety for their verdict. In reply to the usual questions from Mr Benham, the foreman replied that the Jury was all agreed and that they were unanimous in finding each of the three prisoners at the bar GUILTY of the murder of Joanna Franks. It is said that no visible alteration marked the countenances of the crew on the verdict being given, except that Oldfield for the moment became somewhat paler.

The black coif, emblematical of death, was placed on the Judge's head; and after asking the prisoners if they had anything to say, he passed his sentence in the following awesome terms:

Jack Oldfield, Alfred Musson, Walter Towns – after a long and patient hearing of the circumstances in this case, and after due deliberation on the part of the Jury, you have each and all of you been found guilty of the most foul crime of murder – the murder of an unoffending and helpless woman who was under your protection and who, there is now no doubt as to believe, was the object of your lust; and thereafter, to prevent detection of your crime, was the object of your cruelty. Look not for pardon in this world! Apply to the God of Mercy for that pardon which He alone can extend to sinners who are penitent for their misdeeds, and henceforth prepare yourselves for the ignominious death which now awaits you. This case is one of the most painful, the most disgusting, and the most shocking, that has ever come to my knowledge, and it must remain only for me to pass upon you the terrible and just sentence of the Law, that you be taken whence you came, and from thence to the place of execution, and that you, and each of you, be hanged by the neck until you be dead, and that your bodies be afterward buried within the precincts of the prison and be not accorded the privilege of consecrated ground. And may God have mercy on your souls!

After the trial was over, and sentence pronounced, the three men still persisted in maintaining their innocence. Indeed, Oldfield's wife, who visited the prison, was so agitated by her husband's protestations that "she herself was thrown into a sore fit".

It had seemed reasonably clear from various statements including those of Oldfield and Musson that Towns had been somewhat less involved in the happenings on the canal journey than the other two. It was no surprise, therefore, that some members of the legal profession now thought there was a case for the last-minute reconsideration of the sentence imposed upon Towns; so a letter setting forth their agreed view was taken to London by a barrister, and a special interview with the Secretary of State was obtained. As a result of such representations, Towns was reprieved at (almost literally) the eleventh hour. The good news was broken to him as the three men were receiving for the last time the Holy Sacrament from the Prison Chaplain. Towns immediately burst into a flood of tears, and taking each of his former associates by the hand kissed them affectionately, repeating "God bless you, dear friend!" "God bless you, dear friend!" He was later transported to Australia for life, where he was still alive in 1884 when he was seen and interviewed by one Samuel Carter (like Oldfield and Towns, a citizen of Coventry), who took a lively interest in local history and who wrote of his experiences on his return to England the following year.[1]

Oldfield and Musson were duly hanged in public at Oxford. According to the newspaper reports, as many as ten thousand people were estimated to have witnessed the macabre spectacle. It is reported that from an early hour men sat high on walls, climbed trees, and even perched on the roofs of overlooking houses in order to obtain a good view of those terrible events. A notice-board placed by the Governor in front of the gaol-door stated that the execution would not proceed until after eleven o'clock; but although this occasioned much disappointment among the spectators, it did not deter their continued attendance, and not a spare square-foot of space was to found when, at the appointed hour, the execution finally occurred.

First to appear was the Prison Chaplain, solemnly reading the funeral service of the Church of England; next came the two culprits; and following them the Executioner, and the Governor, as well as some other senior officers from the prison. After the operation of pinioning had been completed, the two men walked with firm step to the platform, and ascended the stairs to the drop without requiring assistance. When the ropes had been adjusted round their necks, the Executioners shook hands with each man; and then, as the Chaplain

---

[1] *Travels and Talks in the Antipodes*, Samuel Carter (Farthinghill Press, Nottingham, 1886).

intoned his melancholy service, the fatal bolt was drawn, and in a minute or two, after much convulsion, the wretched malefactors were no more. The dislocation of the cervical vertebrae and the rupture of the jugular vein had been, if not an instantaneous, at least an effective procedure. The gallows appeared to have sated the sadistic fascination of the mob once more, for there are no reports of any civic disorders as the great throng dispersed homewards on that sunlit day. It was later disclosed, though it had not been observable at the time, that Oldfield's last action in life had been to hand over to the Chaplain a postcard, to be delivered to his young wife, in which to the very end he proclaimed his innocence of the crime for which he had now paid the ultimate penalty.

Locally produced broadsheets, giving every sensational detail of trial and execution, were very quickly on sale in the streets of Oxford – and were selling fast. They were even able to give a full account, with precise biblical reference, of the last sermon preached to the men at 6 p.m. on the Sunday before their hangings. The text, clearly chosen with ghoulish insensitivity, could hardly have brought the condemned prisoners much spiritual or physical solace: 'Yet they hearkened not unto me, nor inclined their ear, but hardened their neck: they did worse than their fathers' (*Jeremiah*, ch. 7, v. 26).

The horror felt by the local population at the murder of Joanna Franks did not end with the punishment of the guilty men. Many, both lay and clerical, thought that something more must be done to seek to improve the morals of the boatmen on the waterways. They were aware, of course, that the majority of boatmen were called upon to work on the Sabbath, and had therefore little or no opportunity of attending Divine worship. A letter from the Revd Robert Chantry, Vicar of Summertown Parish, was typical of many in urging a greater degree of concern amongst the boatmen's employers, and suggesting some period of time free from duties on the Sabbath to allow those having the inclination the opportunity of attending a Church service. Strangely enough, such attendance would have been readily possible for the crew-members of the *Barbara Bray* had Oxford been a regular port-of-call, since a special 'Boatmen's Chapel' had been provided by Henry Ward, a wealthy coal-merchant, in 1838 – a floating chapel, moored off Hythe Bridge, at which services were held on Sunday afternoons and Wednesday evenings. For Joanna Franks, as well as for her sorrowing husband and parents, it was a human tragedy that the sermon preached to the murderers on the Sunday prior to their execution was perhaps the first – as well as the last – they ever heard.

But it is all a long time ago now. The floating chapel has long since gone; and no one today can point with any certainty to the shabby plot in the environs of Oxford Gaol where notorious criminals and murderers and others of the conjecturally damned were once buried.

CHAPTER NINETEEN

We read fine things but never feel them to the full until
we have gone the same steps as the author
(John Keats, *letter to John Reynolds*)

Morse was glad that the Colonel had ignored Doctor Johnson's advice to all authors that once they had written something particularly fine they should strike it out. For Part Four was the best-written section, surely, of what was proving to be one of the greatest assets in Morse's most satisfactory (so far) convalescence; and he turned back the pages to relish again a few of those fine phrases. Splendid, certainly, were such things as 'sated the sadistic fascination'; and, better still, that 'ghoulish insensitivity'. But they were *more* than that. They seemed to suggest that the Colonel's sympathies had shifted slightly, did they not? Where earlier the bias against the boatmen had been so pronounced, it appeared that the longer he went on the greater his compassion was growing for that disconsolate crew.

Like Morse's.

It was such a good *story*. So it was no surprise that the Colonel should have disinterred the bare bones of this particular one from the hundreds of other nineteenth-century burial-grounds. All the ingredients were there for its appealing to a wide readership, if once it got its foot wedged in the doorway of publicity. Beauty and the Beasts – that's what it was, quintessentially.

At least as the Colonel had seen it.

For Morse, who had long ago rejected the bland placebos of conventional religion, the facility offered to errant souls to take the Holy Sacrament before being strangled barbarously in a string seemed oddly at variance with the ban on the burial of these same souls within some so-called 'holy ground'. And he was reminded of a passage which had once been part of his mental baggage, the words of which now slowly returned to him. From *Tess of the d'Urbervilles* – where Tess herself seeks to bury her illegitimate infant in the place where 'the nettles grow; and where all

unbaptized infants, notorious drunkards, suicides, and others . . .'
What was the end of it? Wasn't it – yes! – 'others of the
conjecturally damned are laid'. Well, well! A bit of plagiarism on
the Colonel's part. He really should have put quotation marks
around that memorable phrase. Cheating just a little, really. Were
there any other places where he'd cheated? Unwittingly, perhaps?
Just a little?

Worth checking?

That floating chapel interested Morse, too, particularly since he
had read something about it in a recent issue of the *Oxford Times*.
He remembered, vaguely, that although the Oxford Canal Company gave regular monies towards its upkeep the boat on which it
was housed had finally sunk (like the boatmen's hopes) and was
terrestrialized, as it were, later in the century as a permanent
chapel in Hythe Bridge Street; was now, at its latest conversion,
metamorphosed to a double-glazing establishment.

Without looking back, Morse could not for the moment remember which of the other crew-members had been married. But it
was good to learn that Oldfield's wife had stood beside her
husband, for better or for worse. And a pretty bloody 'worse' it
had turned out to be! How interesting it would have been to know
something of *her* story, too. How Morse would like to have been
able to interview her, then and there! The recipient (presumably
she had been) of that terrible card addressed to her, and handed
to the Chaplain at the very foot of the gallows, she must have
found it well-nigh impossible to believe that her husband could
commit so foul a deed. But hers had been only a small role in the
drama: only a couple of walking-on appearances, the first ending
with a dead faint, and the second with a poignant little message
from the grave. Morse nodded rather sadly to himself. These days
there would be a legion of reporters from the *News of the World*,
the *Sunday Mirror*, and the rest, hounding the life of the poor
woman and seeking to prise out of her such vital information as
whether he'd snored, or been tattooed on either upper or nether
limbs, or how frequently they'd indulged in sexual intercourse, or
what had been the usual greeting of the loving husband after
coming back from one of his earlier murderous missions.

We live in a most degenerate age, decided Morse. Yet he knew,
deep down, what nonsense such thinking was. He was no better
himself, really, than one of those scandal-sheet scouts. He'd just
confessed – had he not? – how much he himself wanted to
interview Mrs Oldfield and talk about all the things she must have
known. And what (sobering thought!) what if *she* had invited each

of them in, one after the other, separately – and asked for £20,000 a time?

No chance of any interview or talk now though – not with any of them . . . But, suddenly, it struck Morse that perhaps there was: Samuel Carter's *Travels and Talks in the Antipodes*. That might be a most interesting document, surely? And (it struck Morse with particular pleasure) it would certainly be somewhere on the shelves of the three or four great UK libraries, the foremost of which was always going to be the Bodleian.

Lewis had already been given his research project; and work was now beginning to pile up for his second researcher in the field: what with *Jackson's Oxford Journal*, and now Carter's book . . . Had the Colonel consulted that? Must have done, Morse supposed – which was a little disappointing.

That Friday evening, Morse was visited by both Sergeant Lewis and Christine Greenaway, the latter suddenly changing her mind and forgoing a cocktail reception in Wellington Square. No trouble at all. Just the opposite.

Morse was very happy.

CHAPTER TWENTY

Those hateful persons called Original Researchers
(J. M. Barrie, *My Lady Nicotine*)

As usual when she went into Oxford on a Saturday, Christine Greenaway drove down to the Pear Tree roundabout and caught the Park-and-Ride bus. Alighting in Cornmarket, she walked up to Carfax, turned right into Queen's Street, and along through the busy pedestrian precinct to Bonn Square, where just past the Selfridges building she pushed through the doors of the Westgate Central Library. Among the wrong assumptions made by Chief Inspector Morse the previous evening was the fact that it would be sheer child's play for her to fish out the fiche (as it were) of any newspaper ever published, and that having effected such effortless entry into times past she had the technical skill and the requisite equipment to carry out some immediate research. She hadn't told him that the Bodleian had not, to the best of her knowledge, ever micro-filmed the whole of the nation's press from the nineteenth century, nor that she herself was one of those people against whom all pieces of electrical gadgetry waged a non-stop war. She'd just agreed with him: yes, it would be a fairly easy job; and she'd be glad to help – again. To be truthful, though, she was. Earlier that morning she'd telephoned one of her acquaintances in the Reference Section of the Westgate Central, and learned that she could have immediate access to *Jackson's Oxford Journal* for 1859 and 1860. How long did she want to book things for? One hour? Two? Christine thought one hour would be enough.

10.30–11.30 a.m., then?

Perhaps Morse had been right all along. It *was* going to be easy.

On the second floor of the Central Library, in the Local History and Study Area, she was soon seated on an olive-green vinyl chair in front of a Micro-Film-Reader, an apparatus somewhat resembling the upper half of a British Telecom telephone-kiosk, with a vertical surface, some two feet square, facing her, upon which the photographed sheets of the newspaper appeared, in columns about $2\frac{1}{2}$ inches wide. No lugging around or leafing through heavy bound volumes of unmanageable newspapers. 'Child's play.' The controls marked Focusing Image, Magnification, and Light Control had all been pre-set for her by a helpful young library assistant (male), and Christine had only to turn an uncomplicated winding-handle with her right hand to skip along through the pages, at whatever speed she wished, of *Jackson's Oxford Journal*.

She was relieved, nevertheless, to discover that the *Journal* was a weekly, not a daily publication; and very soon she found the appropriate columns relating to the first trial of August 1859, and was making a series of notes about what she found; and, like Morse, becoming more and more interested. Indeed, by the time she had finished her research into the second trial, of April 1860, she was fascinated. She would have liked to go back and check up a few things, but her eyes were getting tired; and as soon as the print began to jump along like a line of soldiers dressing by the right, she knew that what the splendid machine called the Viewer Operator had better have a rest. She'd found a couple of pieces of information that might please Morse. She hoped so.

She was looking quickly through her scribbled notes, making sure that she could transcribe them later into some more legible form, when she became aware of a conversation taking place only three or four yards behind her at the Enquiries desk.

'Yes, I've tried County Hall – no help, I'm afraid.'

'Your best bet I should think, then, is the City Archivists. They've got an office in—'

'They sent me here!'

'Oh!' The phone rang and the assistant excused himself to answer it.

Christine gathered up her notes, turned off the MFR (as it seemed to be known), and went up to the desk.

'We met yesterday evening—' began Christine.

Sergeant Lewis smiled at her and said, 'Hullo.'

'Seems I'm having more luck than you, Sergeant.'

'Augh! He always gives me the lousy jobs – I don't know why I bother – my day off, too.'

'And mine.'

'Sorry we can't help, sir,' said the assistant (another query dealt with). 'But if they've got no trace at the Archivists . . .'

Lewis nodded. 'Well, thanks, anyway.'

Lewis escorted Christine to the swing doors when the assistant had a final thought: 'You could try St Aldates Police Station. I *have* heard that quite a lot of documents and stuff got housed by the police in the war' ('Which war?' mumbled Lewis, inaudibly) 'and, well, perhaps—'

'Thanks very much!'

'They can't really be *all* that helpful to the public, though – I'm sure you know—'

'Oh yes!'

But the phone had been ringing again, and now the attendant answered it, convinced that he'd sent his latest customer on what would prove a wholly unproductive mission.

When alone in crowded streets, Christine sometimes felt a little apprehensive; but she experienced a pleasing sense of being under protection as she walked back towards Carfax with the burly figure of Sergeant Lewis beside and above her. Great Tom was striking twelve noon.

'I don't suppose you fancy a drink—' began Lewis.

'No – not for me, thank you. I don't drink much, anyway, and it's a bit – bit early, isn't it?'

Lewis grinned: 'That's something I don't hear very often from the Chief!' But he felt relieved. He wasn't much good at making polite conversation; and although she seemed a very nice young lady he preferred to get about his business now.

'You like him, don't you? The "Chief", I mean?'

'He's the best in the business.'

'Is he?' asked Christine, quietly.
'Will you be going in tonight?'
'I suppose so. What about you?'
'If I find anything – which seems at the moment very doubtful.'
'You never know.'

CHAPTER TWENTY-ONE

From the cradle to the coffin, underwear comes first
(Bertolt Brecht, *The Threepenny Opera*)

In the late 1980s the premises of the City Police HQ in St Aldates were being extensively renovated and extended – and the work was still in progress when Sergeant Lewis walked in through the main door that Saturday morning. The Force had always retained its obstinately hierarchical structure, and friendship between the higher and the lower ranks would perhaps always be slightly distanced. Yet Lewis knew Chief Superintendent Bell fairly well from the old days up at Kidlington and was glad to find him in the station.

Yes, of course Bell would help if he could: in fact, the timing of Lewis's visit might be very opportune, because many corners and crannies had only just been cleared out, and the contents of scores of cupboards and dust-covered cases and crates had recently seen the light of day for the first time within living memory. Bell's orders on this had been clear: if any documents seemed even marginally worth the keeping, let them be kept; if not, let them be destroyed. But strangely, up to now, almost everything so newly rediscovered had appeared potentially valuable to *someone*; and the upshot was that a whole room had been set aside in which the preserved relics and mementoes from the earliest days – certainly from the 1850s onwards – had been unsystematically stacked, awaiting appropriate evaluation by academic historians, sociologists, criminologists, local-history societies – and authors. In fact a WPC was in the room now, as Bell thought – doing a bit of elementary cataloguing; and if Lewis wanted to look around . . .

Explaining that this was her lunch-break, WPC Wright, a pleasant enough brunette in her mid-twenties, continued eating her sandwiches and writing her Christmas cards, waving Lewis to any quarter of the room he wished after he had briefly stated his mission.

'It's all yours, Sergeant. Or, at least, I wish it was!'

Lewis could see what she meant. Morse had given him a copy of the Colonel's work (several spares had been left on the ward); but for the moment Lewis could see little or no chance of linking anything that had occurred in 1860 with the chaotic heaps of boxes, files, bags, crates, and piles of discoloured, dog-eared documents that lay around. To be fair, it was clear that a start had been made on sorting things out, for fifty-odd buff-coloured labels, with dates written on them, were attached to the rather neater agglomeration of material that had been separated from the rest, and set out in some semblance of chronological order. But amongst these labels Lewis looked in vain for 1859 or 1860. Was it worth having a quick look through the rest?

It was at 1.45 p.m., after what had proved to be a long look, that Lewis whistled softly.

'You found something?'

'Do you know anything about this?' asked Lewis. He had lifted from one of the tea-chests a chipped and splintered box, about two feet long, by one foot wide, and about nine to ten inches deep; a small box, by any reckoning, and one which could be carried by a person with little difficulty, since a brass plate, some four inches by half an inch, set in the middle of the box's top, held a beautifully moulded semi-circular handle, also of brass. But what had struck Lewis instantly – and with wondrous excitement – were the initials engraved upon the narrow plate: 'J.D.'! Lewis had not read the slim volume with any great care (or any great interest, for that matter); but he remembered clearly the two 'trunks' which Joanna had taken on to the boat and which presumably had been found in the cabin after the crew's arrest. Up to that point, Lewis had just had a vague mental picture of the sort of 'trunks' seen outside Oxford colleges when the undergraduates were arriving. But surely it had said that Joanna was *carrying* them, hadn't it? And by the well-worn look of the handle it looked as if this box had been carried – and carried often. And the name of Joanna's first husband had begun with a 'D'!

The policewoman came over and knelt beside the box. The two smallish hooks, one on each side of the lid, moved easily; and the lock on the front was open, for the lid lifted back to reveal, inside the green-plush lining, a small canvas bag, on which, picked out in faded yellow wool, were the same initials as on the box.

Lewis whistled once more. Louder.

'Can you – can we—?' He could scarcely keep the excitement from his voice, and the policewoman looked at him curiously for a few seconds, before gently shaking out the bag's contents on to the floor: a small, rusted key, a pocket comb, a metal spoon, five dress-buttons, a crochet-hook, a packet of needles, two flat-heeled, flimsy-looking shoes, and a pair of calico knickers.

Lewis shook his head in dumbfounded disbelief. He picked up the shoes in somewhat gingerly fashion as if he suspected they might disintegrate; then, between thumb and forefinger, the calico knickers.

'Think I could borrow these shoes and the er . . .?' he asked.

WPC Wright eyed him once again with amused curiosity.

'It's all right,' added Lewis. 'They're not for me.'

'No?'

'Morse – I work for Morse.'

'I suppose you're going to tell me he's become a knicker-fetishist in his old age.'

'You know him?'

'Wish I did!'

'He's in hospital, I'm afraid—'

'Everybody says he drinks far too much.'

'A bit, perhaps.'

'Do you know him well, would you say?'

'Nobody knows him all *that* well.'

'You'll have to sign for them—'

'Fetch me the book!'

' – and bring them back.'

Lewis grinned. 'They'd be a bit small for me, anyway, wouldn't they? The shoes, I mean.'

CHAPTER TWENTY-TWO

Don't take action because of a name! A name is an
uncertain thing, you can't count on it!
(Bertolt Brecht, *A Man's a Man*)

During that same Saturday which saw Sergeant Lewis and Christine Greenaway giving up their free time on his behalf, Morse
himself was beginning to feel fine again. Exploring new territory,
too, since after lunch-time he was told he was now free to wander
along the corridors at will. Thus it was that at 2.30 p.m. he found
his way to the day room, an area equipped with armchairs, a
colour TV, table-skittles, a book-case, and a great pile of magazines
(the top one, Morse noted, a copy of *Country Life* dating from nine
years the previous August). The room was deserted; and after
making doubly sure the coast was clear, Morse placed one of the
three books he was carrying in the bottom of the large wastepaper
receptacle there: *The Blue Ticket* had brought him little but embarrassment and humiliation, and now, straightway, he felt like
Pilgrim after depositing his sackful of sin.

The surfaces of the TV set seemed universally smooth, with not
the faintest sign of any switch, indentation, or control with which
to set the thing going; so Morse settled down in an armchair and
quietly contemplated the Oxford Canal once more.

The question for the Jury, of course, had not been 'Who committed
the crime?' but only 'Did the prisoners do it?'; whilst for a
policeman like himself the question would always have to be the
first one. So as he sat there he dared to say to himself, honestly,
'All right! If the boatmen didn't do it, *who did*?' Yet if that were
now the Judge's key question, Morse couldn't see the case lasting
a minute longer; for the simple answer was he hadn't the faintest
idea. What he *could* set his mind to, though, was some considered
reflection upon the boatmen's guilt. Or innocence . . .

A quartet of questions, then.

First. Was it true that a jury should have been satisfied, beyond
any reasonable doubt, that the boatmen murdered Joanna Franks?
Answer: no. Not one shred of positive evidence had been produced by the prosecution which could be attested in court by any
corroborative witnesses to murder – and it had been on the count
of murder that the boatmen had been convicted.

Second. Was it true that the prisoners at the bar had been

afforded the time-honoured 'presumption of innocence' – the nominal glory of the British legal system? Answer: it most definitely was not. Prejudgements – wholly pejorative prejudgements – had been rife from the start of the first trial, and the attitude of the law officers no less than the general public had been, throughout, one of unconcealed contempt for, and revulsion against, the crude, barely literate, irreligious crew of the *Barbara Bray*.

Third. Was it true that the boatmen, or some of them, were likely to have been guilty of something? Answer: almost certainly, yes; and (perversely) most probably guilty on the two charges that were dropped – those of rape and theft. At the very least, there was no shortage of evidence to suggest that the men had lusted mightily after their passenger, and it was doubtless a real possibility that all three – all four? – had sought to force their advances on the hapless (albeit sexually provocative?) Joanna.

Fourth. Was there a general sense – even if the evidence *was* unsatisfactory, even if the Jury *were* unduly prejudiced – in which the verdict was a reasonable one, a 'safe' one, as some of the jurisprudence manuals liked to call it? Answer: no, a thousand times no!

Almost, now, Morse felt he could put his finger on the major cause of his unease. It was all those conversations, heard and duly reported, between the principal characters in the story: conversations between the crew and Joanna; between the crew and the other boatmen; between the crew and lock-keepers, wharfingers, and constables – all of it was *wrong* somehow. *Wrong, if they were guilty*. It was as if some inexperienced playwright had been given a murder-plot, and had then proceeded to write page after page of inappropriate, misleading, and occasionally contradictory dialogue. For there were moments when it looked as if it were Joanna Franks who was the avenging Fury, with the crewmen merely the victims of her fatal power.

Then, too, the behaviour of Oldfield and Musson *after* the murder seemed to Morse increasingly a matter of considerable surprise, and it was difficult to understand why Counsel for the Defence had not sought to ram into the minds of Judge and Jury alike the utter *implausibility* of what, allegedly, they did and said. It was not unknown, admittedly, for the odd psychopath to act in a totally irrational and irresponsible manner. But these men were *not* a quartet of psychopaths. And, above all, it seemed quite extraordinary to Morse that, even after (as was claimed) the crew had somehow and for some reason managed to murder Joanna Franks, they were – some twenty-four, thirty-six hours later – still knocking back the booze, still damning and blasting the woman's soul to eternity. Morse had known many murderers, but never one who had subsequently acted in such a fasion – let alone *four*. No! It just didn't add up; didn't add up at all. Not that it mattered, though – not really – after all these years.

Morse flicked open the index of the stout volume recording the misdeeds of Old Salopians, and his eye caught 'Shropshire Union Canal (The)'. He turned idly to the page reference, and there read through the paragraph, and with growing interest. (Well done, Mrs Lewis!) The author was still most horribly enmeshed in his barbed-wire style, still quite incapable of calling a spade anything else but a broad-bladed digging-tool; but the message was clear enough:

> With such an incidence of crime on the canals, it can scarcely be a source of surprise that we find countless instances of evasiveness, on the part of many of the boatmen, in matters such as the registering of names, both those of the boats they crewed and of their own persons. Specifically, with regard to the latter of these deceptions, we discover that many of those working both on the water and on the wharfs had a duality of names, and were frequently considerably better known by their 'bye-names' than by their christened nomenclature. For varied sociological reasons (some of which we have yet to analyse) it can more than tentatively be suggested that boatmen as a generality were likely to be potentially predisposed to the regular commission of crime, and certain it must be held that their profession (if such it may be called) afforded ample opportunities for the realization of such potentiality. Sometimes they sold parts of their cargoes, replacing, for example, quantities of coal with similar quantities of rocks or stone; frequently we come across recorded instances (see esp. SCL, *Canal and Navigable Waters Commission*, 1842, Vol. IX, pp. 61–4, 72–5, 83–6, *et passim*) of crewmen drinking from their cargoes of fine wines and whiskies, and refilling the emptied bottles with water. Toll officials, too, do not always appear blameless in these affairs, and could occasionally be bribed into closing their eyes . . .

Morse's eyes were beginning to close, too, and he laid the book aside. The point had been made: boatmen were a load of crooks who often nicked bits of their cargoes. Hence Walter Towns, aka Walter Thorold, and the rest. All as simple as that – once you knew the answers. Perhaps it would *all* be like that one day, in that Great Computer Library in the Sky, when the problems that had beset countless generations of sages and philosophers would be answered immediately, just by tapping in the questions on some celestial key-board.

The youth with the portable saline-drip walked in, nodded to Morse, picked up a small TV control-panel from somewhere, and began flicking his way around the channels with, for Morse, irritating impermanence. It was time to get back to the ward.

As he was leaving his eyes roamed automatically over the book-case, and he stopped. There, on the lower row, and standing side by side, were the titles *Victorian Banbury* and *OXFORD (Rail Centres Series)*. Having extracted both, he walked back. Perhaps, if you kept your eyes open, you didn't need any Valhallan VDUs at all.

Walter Algernon Greenaway had been trying, with little success, to get going with the *Oxford Times* crossword. He had little or no competence in the skill, but it had always fascinated him; and when the previous day he had watched Morse complete *The Times* crossword in about ten minutes, he felt most envious. Morse had just settled back in his bed when Greenaway (predictably known to his friends, it appeared, as 'Waggie') called across.

'You're pretty good at crosswords—'

'Not bad.'

'You know anything about cricket?'

'Not much. What's the clue?'

'"Bradman's famous duck".'

'How many letters?'

'Six. I saw Bradman at the Oval in 1948. He got a duck then.'

'I shouldn't worry too much about cricket,' said Morse. 'Just think about Walt Disney.'

Greenaway licked the point of his pencil, and thought, unproductively, about Walt Disney.

'Who's the setter this week?' asked Morse.

'Chap called "Quixote".'

Morse smiled. Coincidence, wasn't it. 'What was *his* Christian name?'

'Ah! I have you, sir!' said Waggie, happily entering the letters at 1 across.

CHAPTER TWENTY-THREE

All that mankind has done, thought, gained, or been, it
is all lying in magic preservation in the pages of books
(Thomas Carlyle)

Embarras de richesses – for Morse couldn't have chosen a more
informative couple of books if he'd sauntered all day round the
shelves in the local Summertown Library.

First, from *Victorian Banbury*, he gleaned the information that by
about 1850 the long-distance stage-coach routes via Banbury to
London had been abandoned, almost entirely as a result of the
new railway service from Oxford to the capital. Yet, as a direct
result of this service, coaches between Banbury and Oxford had
actually *increased*, and regular and efficient transportation was
readily available between Banbury and Oxford (only twenty miles
to the south) during the 1850s and 1860s. Furthermore, the author
gave full details of the actual stage-coaches that would have been
available, on the day in question, and about which Joanna Franks
must have made enquiry: quite certainly coach-horses would have
been seen galloping southwards on three separate occasions in the
earlier half of the following day, delivering passengers picked up
at the Swan Inn, Banbury, to the Angel Inn in the High at Oxford.
That for the sum of 2s/1d. Even more interesting for Morse was the
situation pertaining at Oxford itself, where trains to Paddington,
according to his second work of reference, were far more frequent,
and far quicker, than he could have imagined. And presumably
Joanna herself, at Banbury on that fateful day, had been presented
with *exactly* the same information: no less than *ten* trains daily,
leaving at 2.10 a.m., 7.50 a.m., 9 a.m., 10.45 a.m., 11.45 a.m.,
12.55 p.m., 2.45 p.m., 4.00 p.m., 5.50 p.m., and 8.00 p.m. *Embarras
du choix*. Admittedly, the fares seemed somewhat steep, with 1st-,
2nd-, and 3rd-class carriages priced respectively at 16s, 10s, and
6s, for the 60-odd-mile journey. But the historian of Oxford's
railways was fair-minded enough to add the fact that there were
also three coaches a day, at least up until the 1870s, making the
comparatively slow journey to London via the Henley and Reading
turnpikes: *The Blenheim* and *The Prince of Wales*, each departing at
10.30 a.m., with *The Rival* an hour later, the fare being a 'whole
shilling' less than the 3rd-class railway fare. And where did they
finish up in the metropolis? It was quite extraordinary. The
Edgware Road!

So, for a few minutes Morse looked at things from Joanna's

point of view – a Joanna who (as he had no option but to believe) was *in extremis*. Arriving at Banbury, as she had, in the latish evening, she would very soon have seen the picture. No chance of anything immediately, but the ready opportunity of a stay over-night in Banbury, in one of the taverns along the quay-side, perhaps. Not four-star AA accommodation – but adequate – and certainly costing no more than 2s or so. Then one of the coaches to Oxford next morning – the book of words mentioned one at 9.30 a.m., reaching Oxford at about 1 p.m. That would mean no difficulty at all about catching the 2.45 p.m. to Paddington – or one of the three later trains, should any accident befall the horses. Easy! If she *had* eventually made a firm decision to escape her tormentors for good, then the situation was straightforward. 2s overnight, say, 2s/1d coach-fare, 6s 3rd-class rail-fare – that meant that for about 10s she was offered a final chance of saving her life. And without much bother, without much expense, she *could* have done so.

But she hadn't. Why not? Received wisdom maintained that she hadn't got a penny-piece to her name, let alone half a guinea. But had she nothing she could sell, or pawn? Had she no negotiable property with her? What *had* she got in those two boxes of hers? Nothing of any value whatsoever? Why, then, if that were so, could there ever have been the slightest suspicion of *theft*? Morse shook his head slowly. Ye gods! – how he wished he could have a quick look into one of those boxes!

It was tea-time, and Morse was not aware that his wish had already been granted.

CHAPTER TWENTY-FOUR

Magnus Alexander corpore parvus erat
(Even Alexander the Great didn't measure up to the
height-requirement of the Police Force)

(Latin proverb)

Normal shifts for the nursing staff at the JR2 were Early (07.45–15.45), Late (13.00–21.30), and Night (21.00–08.15). Always more of an owl than a lark, Eileen Stanton shared none of the common objections that were levelled against the Night shift: born with a temperament slightly tinged with melancholy, she was perhaps a natural creature of the dark. But this particular week had been unusual. And that day she was on Late.

Married at the age of nineteen and divorced at twenty, she was now, five years later, living out at Wantage with a man, fifteen years her senior, who had celebrated his fortieth birthday the previous evening (hence the re-arrangements). The party had gone splendidly until just after midnight when the celebrant himself had been involved in a pathetic little bout of fisticuffs, over *her!* Now, in films or on TV, after being knocked unconscious with a vicious blow from an iron bar, the hero has only to rub the sore spot for a couple of minutes before resuming his mission. But life itself, as Eileen knew, wasn't like that – the victim was much more likely to end up in the ICU, with permanent brain-damage, to boot. Much more cruel. Like last night (this morning!) when her cohabitee had been clouted in the face, his upper lip splitting dramatically, and one of his front teeth being broken off at the root. Not good for his looks, or his pride, or the party, or Eileen, or anybody. Not good at all.

For the umpteenth time her mind dwelt on that incident as she drove into Oxford, parked her apple-jack-green Metro in the Staff Only park of the JR2, and walked down to the basement cloak room to change her clothes. It would do her good to get back on the ward, she knew that. She'd found it easy enough so far to steer clear of any emotional involvement with her patients, and for the moment all she wanted was to get a few hours of dutiful nursing behind her – to forget the previous night, when she'd drunk a little too freely, and flirted too flagrantly with a man she'd never even met before . . . No hangover – although she suddenly began to wonder if she *did* have a hangover after all: just didn't notice it amid her other mental agitations. Anyway, it was high time she forgot all her own troubles and involved herself with other people's.

She'd noticed Morse (and he her) as he'd walked along to the day room; watched him walk back, half an hour later, and spend the rest of the afternoon reading. Bookish sort of fellow, he seemed. Nice, though – and she would go and have a word with him perhaps once he put his books down. Which he didn't.

She watched him again, at 7.40 p.m., as he sat against the pillows; and more particularly watched the woman who sat beside him, in a dark-blue dress, with glints of gold and auburn in her hair, the regular small-featured face leaning forward slightly as she spoke to him. To Eileen the pair of them seemed so eager to

talk to each other – so different from the conversational drought
which descended on so many hospital visitations. Twice, even as
she watched, the woman, in the middle of some animated little
passage of dialogue, placed the tips of her fingers against the
sleeve of his gaudy pyjamas, fingers that were slim and sinewy,
like those of an executant musician. Eileen knew all about *that* sort
of gesture. And what about him, Morse? He, too, seemed to be
doing his level, unctuous best to impress *her*, with a combination
of that happily manufactured half-smile and eyes that focused
intently upon hers. Oh yes! She could see what each of them was
feeling – nauseating couple of bootlickers! But she knew she
envied them; envied especially the woman – Waggie's clever-clogs
of a daughter! From the few times she'd spoken to Morse, she
knew that his conversation – and perhaps, she thought, his life,
too – was so *interesting*. She'd met just a few other men like that –
men who were full of fascinating knowledge about architecture,
history, literature, music . . . all the things after which over these
last few years she'd found herself yearning. How relieved she
suddenly felt that most probably her swollen-lipped forty-year-old
wouldn't be able to kiss her that evening!

A man (as she now realized) had been standing patiently at the
desk.

'Can I help you?'

Sergeant Lewis nodded and looked down at her. 'Special
instructions. I've got to report to the boss whenever I bring the
Chief Inspector a bag of plastic explosive. You're the boss tonight,
aren't you?'

'Don't be too hard on Sister Maclean!'

Lewis bent forward and spoke softly. 'It's not me – it's him! He
says she's an argumentative, bitchy old . . . old something.'

Eileen smiled. 'She's not very tactful, sometimes.'

'He's, er – looks like he's got a visitor for the moment.'

'Yes.'

'Perhaps I'd better not interrupt, had I? He gets very cross
sometimes.'

'Does he?'

'Especially if . . .'

Eileen nodded, and looked up into Lewis's kindly face, feeling
that menfolk weren't quite so bad as she'd begun to think.

'What's he like – Inspector Morse?' she asked.

*

Christine Greenaway stood up to go, and Morse was suddenly conscious, as she stood so closely beside the bed, how small she was – in spite of the high-heeled shoes she habitually wore. Words came back to his mind, the words he'd read again so recently: '. . . petite and attractive figure, wearing an Oxford-blue dress . . .'

'How tall are you?' asked Morse, as she smoothed her dress down over her thighs.

'How *small* am I, don't you mean?' Her eyes flashed and seemed to mock him. 'In stockinged feet, I'm five feet, half an inch. And don't forget that half-inch: it may not be very important to you, but it is to me. I wear heels all the time – so I come up to about normal, usually. About five three.'

'What size shoes do you take?'

'Threes. You wouldn't be able to get your feet in them.'

'I've got very nice feet,' said Morse seriously.

'I think I ought to be more worried about my father than about your feet,' she whispered quietly, as she touched his arm once more, and as Morse in turn placed his own left hand so briefly, so lightly upon hers. It was a little moment of magic, for both of them.

'And you'll look up that—?'

'I won't forget.'

Then she was gone, and only the smell of some expensive perfume lingered around the bed.

'I just wonder,' said Morse, almost absently, as Lewis took Christine's place in the plastic chair, 'I just wonder what size shoes Joanna Franks took. I'm assuming, of course, they *had* shoe-sizes in those days. Not a modern invention, like women's tights, are they? – shoe sizes? What do you think, Lewis?'

'Would you like me to show you exactly what size she *did* take, sir?'

CHAPTER TWENTY-FIVE

Those who are incapable of committing great crimes do
not readily suspect them in others
(La Rochefoucauld, *Maxims*)

Morse was invariably credited, by his police colleagues, with an
alpha-plus intelligence, of a kind which surfaced rarely on the
tides of human affairs, and which almost always gave him about
six furlongs' start in any criminal investigation. Whatever the truth
of this matter, Morse himself knew that one gift had never been
bestowed on him – that of *reading* quickly. It was to be observed,
therefore, that he seemed to spend a disproportionately long time
that evening – Christine gone, Lewis gone, Horlicks drunk, pills
swallowed, injection injected – in reading through the photocopied
columns from *Jacksons's Oxford Journal.* Christine had not mentioned to him that, dissatisfied with her hand-written notes, she
had returned to the Central Library in the early afternoon and
prevailed upon one of her vague acquaintances there to let her
jump the queue and photocopy the original material directly from
their bulky originals. Not that Morse, even had he known, would
have exhibited any excessive gratitude. One of his weaknesses
was his disposition to accept loyalty without ever really understanding, certainly not appreciating, the sacrifices that might be
involved.

When, as a boy, he had been shepherded around various
archaeological sites, Morse had been unable to share the passion
of some fanatic drooling over a few (disintegrating) Roman bricks.
Even then, it had been the written word, rather than the tangible
artefact, which had pricked his curiosity, and promoted his subsequent delight in the ancient world. It was to be expected,
therefore, that although Lewis's quite extraordinary discovery was
to prove the single most dramatic break-through in the supposed
'case', the sight of a sad-looking pair of shrivelled shoes and an
even sadder-looking pair of crumpled knickers was, for Morse, a
little anti-climactic. At least, for the present. As for Christine's
offerings, though, how wonderfully attractive and suggestive they
were!

From the newspaper records, it was soon clear that the Colonel
had omitted no details of any obvious importance. Yet, as in most
criminal cases, it was the apparently innocuous, incidental, almost
irrelevant, details that could change, in a flash, the interpretation
of accepted facts. And there were quite a few details here (to

Morse, hitherto unknown) which caused him more than a milli-
metric rise of the eyebrows.

First, reading between the somewhat smudged lines of the
photocopied material, it seemed fairly clear that the charge of theft
had probably been dropped at the first trial for the reason that the
evidence (such as it was) had pointed predominantly to the youth,
Wootton, therefore necessitating an individual prosecution – and
that against a minor. If any of the other crewmen were involved,
it was Towns (the man deported to Australia) who figured as the
safest bet; and quite certainly no obvious evidence could be
levelled against the two men eventually hanged for *murder*. What
was it then that the young man's covetous eyes may have sought
to steal from Joanna Franks's baggage? No answer emerged clearly
from the evidence. But there was surely one thing, above all, that
thieves went for, whether in 1859 or 1989: *money*.

Mmm.

Second, there was sufficient contemporary evidence to suggest
that it was Joanna who was probably the sustaining partner in her
second marriage. Whatever it was that had caused her to 'fall
deeply in love with Charles Franks, an ostler from Liverpool', it
was *Joanna* who had besought her new husband to keep up his
spirits during the ill fortune which had beset the early months of
their marriage. An extract from a letter to Charles Franks had
indeed been read out in court, presumably (as Morse saw things)
to substantiate the point that, quite contrary to the boatmen's
claim of *Joanna* being demented, it was *Charles* who seemed the
nearer to a mental breakdown: 'Sorry I am to read, my dear
husband, your sadly wandering letter – do, my dear, strive against
what I fear will await you should you not rest your tortured mind.
The loss of reason is a terrible thing and will blight our hopes. Be
strong and know we shall soon be together and well provided for.'
A poignant and eloquent letter.

Were *both* of them a bit unbalanced?

Mmm.

Third, various depositions from both trials made it clear that
although 'fly' boats worked best with a strict enforcement of a
'two on – two off' arrangement, it was quite usual, in practice, for
the four members of such a crew to permutate their different
duties in order to accommodate individual likings or requirements.
Or *desires*, perhaps? For Morse now read, with considerable
interest, the evidence adduced in court (Where were you, Colonel
Deniston?) that Oldfield, captain of the *Barbara Bay*, had paid
Walter Towns 6d to take over him the arduous business of 'legging'

the boat through the Barton tunnel. Morse nodded to himself: for his imagination had already travelled there.

Mmm.

Fourth, the evidence, taken as a whole, suggested strongly that for the first half of the journey Joanna had joined in quite happily with the boatmen at the various stops: staying in their company, eating at the same table, drinking with them, laughing with them at their jokes. Few jokes, though, on the latter half of the journey, when, as the prosecution had pressed home again and again, Joanna figured only as a helpless, hapless soul – crying out (at times, literally) for help, sympathy, protection, mercy. And one decisive and dramatic fact: as the crew themselves grew progressively inebriated, Joanna was becoming increasingly sober; for the coroner's evidence, as reported at the trial, was incontestable: *no alcohol at all was found in her body.*

Mmm.

Morse proceeded to underline in blue Biro the various, and most curious, altercations which the law-writer of *Jackson's Oxford Journal* had deemed it worthy to record:

'Will you have anything of this?' (Oldfield) 'No, I have no inclination.' (Bloxham) '——'s already had his concerns with her tonight: and I will, or else I shall——her.' (Oldfield) 'D——n and blast the woman! If she has drowned herself, I cannot help it.' (Oldfield) 'She said she'd do it afore, and now she seems to 'a done it proper.' (Musson) 'I hope the b——y w——e is burning in hell!' (Oldfield) 'Blast the woman! What do we know about her? If she had a mind to drown herself, why should we be in all this trouble?' (Towns) 'If he is going to be a witness against us, it is for other things, not for the woman.' (Oldfield)

Mmm.

Randomly quoted, incoherent, unchronological as they were, these extracts from the trials served most strongly to reinforce Morse's earlier conviction that they were not the sort of comments one would expect from murderers. One might expect some measure of shame, remorse, fear – yes! – even, in a few cases, triumph and jubilation in the actual performance of the deed. But not – no! – not the fierce anger and loathing perpetuated by the boatmen through the hours and the days after Joanna had met her death.

Finally, there was a further (significant?) passage of evidence which the Colonel had *not* cited. It was, apparently, Oldfield's claim that, at about 4.a.m. on the fateful morning, the boatmen *had*, in fact, caught up with Joanna – the latter in a state of much mental confusion; both he and Musson had discovered her whereabouts only by the anguished cries in which she called upon the name of her husband: 'Franks! Franks! Franks!' Furthermore, Oldfield claimed, he had actually persuaded her to get back on the boat, although he agreed that she had fairly soon jumped off again (again!) to resume her walking along the tow-path. Then, according to Oldfield, two of them, he and Towns on this occasion, had once more gone ashore, where they met another potential witness (the Donald Favant mentioned in the Colonel's book). But the boatmen had not been believed. In particular this second meeting along the tow-path had come in for withering scorn from the prosecution: at best, the confused recollection of hopelessly drunken minds; at worst, the invention of 'these callous murderers'. Yes! That was exactly the sort of comment which throughout had disquieted Morse's passion for justice. As a policeman, he knew only the rudiments of English law; but he was a fervent believer in the principle that a man should be presumed innocent until he was pronounced guilty: it was a fundamental principle, not only of substantive law, but of natural justice . . .

'You comfy?' asked Eileen, automatically pulling the folds of his sheets tidy.

'I thought you'd gone off duty.'

'Just going.'

'You're spoiling me.'

'You enjoy reading, don't you?'

Morse nodded: 'Sometimes.'

'You like reading best of all?'

'Well, music – music, I suppose, sometimes more.'

'So, if you're reading a book with the record-player going—'

'I can't enjoy them both together.'

'But they're the *best*?'

'Apart from a candle-lit evening-meal with someone like you.'

Eileen coloured, her pale cheeks suddenly as bright as those of the dying Colonel.

Before going to sleep that night, Morse's hand glided into the bedside cabinet and poured out a small measure; and as he sipped the Scotch, at his own pace, the world of a sudden was none too bad a place . . .

When he awoke (was awoken, rather) the following morning (Sunday) he marvelled that the blindingly obvious notion that now occurred to him had taken such an age to materialize. Usually, his cerebral analysis was as swift as the proverbial snap of a lizard's eyelid.

Or so he told himself.

CHAPTER TWENTY-SIX

Now, there is a law written in the darkest of the Books of Life, and it is this: If you look at a thing nine hundred and ninety-nine times, you are perfectly safe; if you look at it for the thousandth time, you are in frightful danger of seeing it for the first time
(G. K. Chesterton, *The Napoleon of Notting Hill*)

Just the same with crossword puzzles, wasn't it? Sit and ponder more and more deeply over some abstruse clue – and get nowhere. Stand away, though – further back! – futher back still! – and the answer will shout at you with a sort of mocking triumph. It was those shoes, of course . . . shoes at which he'd been staring so hard he hadn't really seen them.

Morse waited with keen anticipation until his morning ablutions were complete before re-reading the Colonel's work, lingering over things – as he'd always done as a boy when he'd carved his way meticulously around the egg-white until he was left with only the golden circle of the yolk, into which, finally, to dip the calculated balance of his chips.

What were the actual words of the trial report? Yes, Morse nodded to himself: when Charles Franks had looked at the body, he had recognized it, dreadfully disfigured as it was, by 'a small mark behind his wife's left ear, a mark of which only a parent or an intimate lover could have known'. *Or a scoundrel.* By all the gods, was *ever* identification so tenuously asserted and attested in the English courts? Not only some tiny disfigurement in a place where no one else would have been aware of it, but a tiny disfigurement which existed *on* the head of Joanna Franks only because it existed *in* the head of her new husband! Oh, it must have been there all right! The doctor, the coroner, the inspector of police, those who'd undressed the dead woman, and redressed her for a proper Christian burial – so many witnesses who could, if need ever arose, corroborate the existence of such a blemish on what had once been such a pretty face. But who could, or did, corroborate the fact that the face had been *Joanna's*? The husband? Yes, he'd had his say. But the only others who might have known, the parents – where were they? Apparently, they'd played no part at all in the boatmen's trial at Oxford. Why not? Was the mother too stricken with grief to give any coherent testimony? Was she *alive*, even, at the time of the trial? The father was alive, though, wasn't he? The insurance man . . .

Morse brought his mind back to the central point he was seeking to establish before his own imagined jury (little 'j'). No court would have accepted such unilateral identification without *something* to support it – and there *had* been something (again Morse looked back to the actual words): corroboration was afforded 'by the shoes, later found in the fore-cabin of the *Barbara Bray*, which matched in the minutest degrees the contours of the dead woman's feet'. So, the matter was clear: one, the shoes in the cabin belonged to Joanna Franks; two, the shoes had been worn by the drowned woman; therefore, three, the drowned woman was Joanna Franks – QED. Even Aristotle might have been satisfied with such a syllogism. Incontrovertible! All three statements as true as the Eternal Verities; and if so, the shoes *must* belong to the woman who was drowned. But . . . but what if the first statement was *not* true? What if the shoes had *not* belonged to Joanna? Then the inexorable conclusion must be that whatever was found floating face-downward at Duke's Cut in 1859, *it was not the body of Joanna Franks*.

Just one moment, Morse!! (The voice of the prosecution was deafening against his ear.) All right! The identification as it stood, as it stands, may perchance appear a trifle tenuous? But have you – *you* – any – *any* – reason for discrediting such identification? And the answering voice in Morse's brain – *Morse's* voice – was firm and confident. Indeed! And if it should please my learned friends I shall now proceed to tell you exactly what *did* happen between 3 a.m. and 5 a.m. on the morning of Wednesday, the 21st June, in 1859.

Gentlemen! We who are engaged in seeking to reconstruct the course as well as the causation of crime are often tormented by the same insistent thought: *something* must have happened, and happened *in a specific way*. All theory, all reconstruction, all probability, are as nothing compared with *the simple, physical truth of what actually happened at the time*. If only . . . if only, we say, we could see it all; see it all as it actually happened! Gentlemen, I am about to tell you—

Proceed! said the judge (little 'j').

CHAPTER TWENTY-SEVEN

Imagination, that dost so abstract us
That we are not aware, not even when
A thousand trumpets sound about our ears!

(Dante, *Purgatorio*)

Standing by the door at the left of the fore-cabin, she could see them both. A reporter, perhaps, would have had them dribbling or vomiting; snoring 'stertorously', certainly. But Joanna was to notice, at that point, only the simple fact, the undramatic circumstance: asleep, the pair of them – Oldfield and Musson – only the slight rise and fall of the faded maroon eiderdown that covered them both betraying their fitful breathing. Drunk? Yes, *very* drunk: but Joanna herself had seen to that. Little or no persuasion required – but the *timing* important . . . She smiled grimly to herself, and consulted the little silver time-piece she always kept so carefully about her person: the watch her father had given her on her twenty-second birthday (not her twenty-first) – when some fees had been forthcoming from the London Patent Office. And again, now, her hand closed around the precious watch as if it were a talisman for the success of the imminent enterprise.

Occasionally she spoke quietly – very quietly – to the shifty, silly, spotty-faced youth who stood beside her at the entrance to the cabin: his left hand upon the Z-shaped tiller, painted in alternate bands of red, green, yellow; his right hand (where she had placed it herself!) fondling the bosom of her dress. Twenty-five yards ahead, the horse (rather a good one!) was plodding along a little more slowly now, the wooden bobbins stretched taut along its flanks as it forged forward along the silent tow-path – with only the occasional flap of the waters heard as they slurped against the *Barbara Bray*, heading ever southwards into the night.

Joanna looked briefly behind her now, at the plaited basket-work that protected the narrow-boat's stern. 'Over a bit *more*, Tom!' she whispered, as the boat moved into the elbow-bend at Thrupp, just past the village of Hampton Gay. 'And don't forget

THE WENCH IS DEAD

our little bargain,' she added as she stepped up on to the side, whilst Wootton gently manoeuvred the boat ever closer in towards the right-hand bank.

Wootton would not be celebrating his fifteenth birthday until the February of 1860, but already, in several ways, he was a good deal older than his years. Not in *every* way, though. Never, before Joanna had come on board at Preston Brook, had he felt so besotted with a woman as he was with *her*. Exactly, as he knew, the rest of the crew had been. There was something sexually animated, and *compelling*, about Joanna Franks. Something about the way she flashed her eyes when she spoke; something about the way her tongue lightly licked the corners of her mouth after a plate of mutton chops and peas at some low-roofed tavern alongside the canal; something wickedly and calculatedly controlled about her, as she'd drunk her own full share of liquor – that happily awaited, worry-effacing liquor that all the boatmen (including Wootton) drank so regularly along their journeys. *And Oldfield had taken possession of her* – of that Wootton was quite sure! Taken her in one of the pitch-black transit-tunnels when he, Wootton, had gladly taken Oldfield's 6d, and 'legged' the *Barbara Bray* slowly towards that pin-point of light which had gradually grown ever larger as darkly he'd listened to the strangely exciting noises of the love-making taking place in the bunk below him. Towns, too, had taken Oldfield's 6d in a tunnel further south. And both Towns and Musson – the lanky, lecherous-eyed Musson! – knew only too well what was going on, soon wanting a share of things for themselves. No surprise, then, that nasty incident when Towns had gone for Musson – with a knife!

As agreed, Thomas Wootton provided her with the lantern. The night, though dark, was dry and still; and the flame nodded only spasmodically as she took it, and leaped lightly off the *Barbara Bray* – her bonnet around her head, her shoes on her feet – on to the tow-path bank where, very soon, she had disappeared from the youth who now kept looking straight ahead of him, a smile around his wide, lascivious mouth.

It was not unusual, of course, for women passengers to jump ashore at fairly regular intervals from a narrow-boat: female toiletry demanded a greater measure of decorum than did that for men. But Joanna might be gone a little longer than was usual that night . . . so she'd said.

She stood back in the undergrowth, watching the configuration of the boat melt deeper and deeper into the night. Then, gauging she was out of ear-shot of the crew, she called out the man's name

– without at first receiving a reply: then again; then a third time –
until she heard a rustling movement in the bushes beside her,
against the stone wall of a large mansion house – and a suppressed, tense, 'Shsh!'

The night air was very still, and her voice had carried far too
clearly down the canal, with both the youth at the helm, and the
man with the stoical horse, turning round simultaneously to look
into the dark. But they could see nothing; and *hearing* nothing
further, neither of them was giving the matter much further
thought.

But one of the men supposedly asleep had heard it, too.

Meanwhile Joanna and her accomplice had flitted stealthily
along the row of small, grey-stoned, terraced cottages which lined
the canal at Thrupp, keeping to the shadows; then, gliding
unobserved past the darkened, silent windows of the Boat Inn,
they moved, more freely now, along the short hedge-lined lane
that led to the Oxford–Banbury highway.

For the *Barbara Bray*, the next three miles of the Oxford Canal
would interpose the Roundham, Kidlington Green, and Shuttleworth's locks – the latter just north of the basin of water known as
Duke's Cut. Negotiation of these locks (so carefully calculated!)
would afford appropriate opportunity. No real problem. Much
more difficult had been the arrangements for meeting each other;
and certainly Oldfield, more than once, had looked at Joanna
suspiciously in the last twenty-four hours as she had taken (but of
necessity!) her diurnal and nocturnal promenades. She knew,
though, how to deal with Oldfield, the skipper of the *Barbara
Bray* . . .

'Everything ready?'

He nodded, brusquely. 'Don't talk now!'

They walked across to a covered carrier's wagon which stood, a
piebald horse between its shafts, tethered to a beech tree just
beside the verge. The moon appeared fitfully from behind a slow-
moving cloud; not a soul was in sight.

'Knife?' he asked.

'I sharpened it.'

He nodded with a cruel satisfaction.

She took off her coat and handed it to him, taking, in return,
the one he passed to her – similar to her own, though cheaper in
both cloth and cut, and slightly longer.

'You didn't forget the handkerchief?'

Quickly she re-checked, drawing from the right-hand pocket of her former cloak the small, white square of linen, trimmed with lace, the initials J. F. worked neatly in pink silk in one corner.

Clever touch!

'She's – she's in there?' Joanna half-turned to the back of the wagon, for the first time her voice sounding nervous, though unexpectedly harsh.

He jerked his head, once, his small eyes bright in the heavily bearded face.

'I don't really want to see her.'

'No need!' He had taken the lantern; and when the two of them had climbed up to the front of the wagon, he shone it on a hand-drawn map, his right forefinger pointing to a bridge over the canal, some four-hundred yards north of Shuttleworth's Lock. 'We go down to – here! You wait there, and catch up with them, all right? Then get on board again. Then after that – *after* you get through the lock – you . . .'

'What we agreed!'

'Yes. Jump in! You can stay in the water as long as you like. But be sure no one sees you getting out! The wagon'll be next to the bridge. You get in! And lie still! All right? I'll be there as soon as I've . . .'

Joanna took the knife from her skirt. 'Do you want *me* to do it?'

'No!' He took the knife quickly.

'No?'

'It's just,' he resumed, 'that her face, well – well, it's gone *black*!'

'I thought dead people usually went white,' whispered Joanna.

The man climbed on to the fore-board, and helped her up, before disappearing briefly into the darkness of the covered cart; where, holding the lantern well away from the face, he lifted the dead woman's skirts and with the skill of a surgeon made an incision of about five or six inches down the front of her calico knickers.

The man was handing Joanna two bottles of dark-looking 'Running Horse' ale, when he felt the firm grip of her hand on his shoulder, shaking, shaking, shaking . . .

'Some soup for you, Mr Morse?'

It was Violet.

(Not the soup.)

CHAPTER TWENTY-EIGHT

Mendacity is a system that we live in. Liquor is
one way out and death's the other
(Tennessee Williams, *Cat on a Hot Tin Roof*)

The 'Report' was a regular feature of all the wards in the JR2,
comprising a meeting of hospital and medical staff at the change-
over points between the Early, Late, and Night shifts. In several
of the wards, the weekends offered the chance for some top
consultants and other senior medical personnel to concentrate
their attention on such sidelines as boating and BMWs. But in
many of the semi-surgical wards, like Ward 7C, the Reports went
on very much as at any other times; as they did on what was now
the second Sunday of Morse's stay in hospital.

The 1 p.m. meeting that day was, in fact, well attended: the
Senior Consultant, a junior houseman, Sister Maclean, Charge
Nurse Stanton, and two student nurses. Crowded into Sister's
small office, the group methodically appraised the patients in the
ward, briefly discussing convalescences, relapses, prognoses,
medications, and associated problems.

Morse, it appeared, was no longer much of a problem.

'Morse!' The hint of a smile could be observed on the Consultant's face as he was handed the relevant notes.

'He's making fairly good progress,' Sister asserted, slightly
defensively, like some mother at a Parents' Evening hearing that
her child was perhaps not working as hard as he should be.

'Some of us,' confided the Consultant (handing back the notes)
'would like to persuade these dedicated drinkers that water is a
wonderful thing. I wouldn't try to persuade you, of course, Sister,
but . . .'

For a minute or two Sister Maclean's pale cheeks were flooded
with a bright-pink suffusion, and one of the student nurses could
barely suppress a smile of delight at the Dragon's discomfiture.
But oddly, the other of the two, the Fair Fiona, was suddenly
aware of lineaments and colouring in Sister's face that could have
made it almost beautiful.

'He doesn't seem to drink *that* much, does he?' suggested the
young houseman, his eyes skimming the plentiful notes, several
of which he had composed himself.

The Consultant snorted contemptuously: 'Nonsense!' He flicked
his finger at the offending sheets. 'Bloody liar, isn't he? Drunkards

and diabetics!' – he turned to the houseman – 'I've told you that before, I think?'

It was wholly forgivable that for a few seconds the suspicion of a smile hovered around the lips of Sister Maclean, her cheeks now restored to their wonted pallidity.

'He's not diabetic—' began the houseman.

'Give him a couple of years!'

'He *is* on the mend, though.' The houseman (and rightly!) was determined to claim *some* small credit for the reasonably satisfactory transit of Chief Inspector Morse through the NHS.

'Bloody lucky! Even I was thinking about cutting half his innards away!'

'He must be a fundamentally strong sort of man,' admitted Sister, composure now fully recoverd.

'I suppose so,' conceded the Consultant, 'apart from his stomach, his lungs, his kidneys, his liver – especially his liver. He might last till he's sixty if he does what we tell him – which I doubt.'

'Keep him another few days, you think?'

'No!' decided the Consultant, after a pause. 'No! Send him home! His wife'll probably do just as good a job as we can. Same medication – out-patients' in two weeks – to see *me*. OK?'

Eileen Stanton was about to correct the Consultant on his factual error when a nurse burst into the office. 'I'm sorry, Sister – but there's a cardiac arrest, I think – in one of the Amenity Beds.'

'Did he die?' asked Morse.

Eileen, who had come to sit on his bed, nodded sadly. It was mid-afternoon.

'How old was he?'

'Don't know exactly. Few years younger than you, I should think.' Her face was glum. 'Perhaps if . . .'

'You look as if you could do with a bit of tender loving care yourself,' said Morse, reading her thoughts.

'Yes!' She looked at him and smiled, determined to snap out of her mopishness. 'And *you*, my good sir, are not going to get very much more of our wonderful loving care – after today. We're kicking you out tomorrow – had quite enough of you!'

'I'm going out, you mean?' Morse wasn't sure if it was good news or bad news; but she told him.

'Good news, isn't it?'

'I shall miss you.'

'Yes, I shall . . .' But Morse could see the tears welling up in her eyes.

'Why don't you tell me what's wrong?' He spoke the words softly; and she told him. Told him about her wretched week; and how kind the hospital had been in letting her switch her normal Nights; and how kind, especially, *Sister* had been . . . But the big tears were rolling down her cheeks and she turned away and held one hand to her face, searching with the other for her handkerchief. Morse put his own grubby handkerchief gently into her hand, and for a moment the two sat together in silence.

'I'll tell you one thing,' said Morse at last. 'It must be pretty flattering to have a couple of fellows fighting over you.'

'No! No, it *isn't*!' The tears were forming again in the large, sad eyes.

'No! You're right. But listen! It won't do you any good at all – in fact' (Morse whispered) 'it'll make you feel far worse. But if *I'd* been at that party of yours – when they were fighting over you – I'd have taken on the *pair* of 'em. You'd have had *three* men squabbling over you – not just two.'

She smiled through her tears, and wiped her wet cheeks, already feeling much better. 'They're big men, both of them. One of them takes lessons in some of those martial arts.'

'All right – I'd've lost! Still have fought for you, though, wouldn't I? Remember the words of the poet? 'Better to have fought and lost than . . . something . . . something . . .' (Morse himself had apparently *forgotten* the words of the poet.)

She brought her face to within a few inches of his, and looked straight into his eyes: 'I wouldn't have minded a little bit if you *had* lost, providing you'd let me look after you.'

'You *have* been looking after me,' said Morse, 'and thank you!'

Getting to her feet, she said no more. And Morse, with a little wistfulness, watched her as she walked away, Perhaps he should have told her that she'd meant 'provided', not 'providing'? No! Such things, Morse knew, were no great worry to the majority of his fellow men and women.

But they were to him.

CHAPTER TWENTY-NINE

I think it frets the saints in heaven to see
How many desolate creatures on the earth
Have learnt the simple dues of fellowship
And social comfort, in a hospital
(Elizabeth Barrett Browning, *Aurora Leigh*)

There is a sadness which invariably and mysteriously accompanies the conclusion of any journey, and the end of any sojourn. Whether or not such sadness is a presage of the last journey we all must take; whether or not it is, more simply, a series of last, protracted goodbyes – it is not of any import here to speculate. But for Morse, the news that he was forthwith to be discharged from the JR2 was simultaneously wonderful – and woeful. Music awaited him. Indeed! Soon he would be luxuriating again in Wotan's Farewell from the last act of *Die Walküre*; and turning up Pavarotti *fff* from one of the Puccinis – certainly in mid-morning, when his immediate neighbours were always out and about on their good works for Oxfam. Books, too. He trusted that the Neighbourhood Watch had done its duty in North Oxford, and that his first edition of *A Shropshire Lad* (1896) was still in its place on his shelves, that slim, white volume that stood proudly amongst its fellows, carrying no extra insurance-cover, like a Royal Prince without a personal bodyguard. Yes, it would be good to get home again: to please himself about what he listened to, or read, or ate . . . or drank. Well, within reason. Yet, quite certainly, he would miss the hospital. Miss the nurses, miss the fellow-patients, miss the routine, miss the visitors – miss so much about the institution which, with its few faults and its many virtues, had admitted him in his sickness and was now discharging him in comparative health.

But the departure from Ward 7C was not, for Morse, to be a memorable experience. When the message came – hardly a bugle-call! – to join a group of people who were to be ambulanced up to North Oxford, he had little opportunity of saying farewell to anyone. One of his ward-mates ('Waggie') was performing his first post-operatively independent ablutions in the wash-room; another was very fast asleep; one had just been taken to the X-ray Department; the Ethiopian torch-bearer was sitting in his bed, with Do-Not-Disturb written all over him, reading *The Blue Ticket* (!); and the last was (and had been for hours) closeted behind his curtains, clearly destined little longer for this earthly life; perhaps, indeed, having already said his own farewells to everybody. As for the nurses, most were bustling purposively about their duties (one or two new faces, anyway), and Morse realized that he was just another patient, and one no longer requiring that special care of just one week ago. Eileen he had not expected to see again, now back to her normal Nights, as she'd told him. Nor was Sister herself anywhere to be seen as he was wheeled out of the ward by a cheerful young porter with a crew-cut and ear-rings. The Fair Fiona, though, he did see – sitting patiently in the next bay beside an ancient citizen, holding a sputum-pot in front of his dribbling lips. With her free hand she waved, and mouthed a 'Good luck!'. But Morse was no lip-reader and, uncomprehending, he was pushed on through the exit corridor where he and his attendant waited for the service-lift to arrive at Level 7.

CHAPTER THIRTY

Lente currite, noctis equi!
(Oh gallop slow, you horses of the night!)
(Ovid, *Amores*)

Although Mrs Green had kept Morse's partial central-heating partially on, the flat seemed cold and unwelcoming. It would have been good for *anyone* to be there to welcome him: certainly (and especially) Christine – or Eileen, or Fiona; even, come to think of it, the dreaded Dragon of the Loch herself. But there was no one. Lewis had not been in to clear up the stuff stuck through the letter-box, and Morse picked up two white-enveloped Christmas cards (one from his insurance company, with the facsimiled signature of the managing director); and his two Sunday newspapers. Such newspapers, although there was an occasional permutation of titles, invariably reflected the conflict in Morse's mind between the Cultured and the Coarse – the choice between the front page of the present one, SYNOD IN DISPUTE OVER DISESTAB-LISHMENT, and SEX SLAVE'S SIX-WEEK ORDEAL IN SILK-LINED COFFIN of the other. If Morse chose the latter first (as, in fact, he did) at least he had the excuse that it was undoubtedly the finer headline. And this Sunday, as usual, he first flicked through the pages of full-breasted photographs and features on Hollywood intrigues and soap infidelities. Then he made himself a cup of instant coffee (which he much preferred to 'the real thing') before settling down to read about the most recent fluctuations on the world's stock-markets, and the bleak prospects for the diseased and starving millions of the world's unhappy continents.

At half-past five the phone rang, and Morse knew that if he had one wish only it would be for the caller to be Christine.

The caller was Christine.

Not only had she located the rare (and extraordinarily valuable) book of which Morse had enquired, but she had spent an hour or so that afternoon ('Don't tell anyone!') reading through the relevant pages, and discovering ('Don't be disappointed!') that only one short chapter was given over to the interview, between Samuel Carter and an ageing Walter Towns, concerning the trial of the boatmen.

'That's wonderful!' said Morse. 'Where are you ringing from?'

'From, er, from home.' (Why the hesitation?)

'Perhaps—'

'Look!' she interrupted. 'I've made a photocopy. Would you like me to send it through the post? Or I could—'

'Could you read it quickly over the phone? It's fairly short, you say?'

'I'm not a very good reader.'

'Put the phone down – and I'll ring you back. Then we can talk as long as we like.'

'I'm not as hard up as all *that*, you know.'

'All right – fire away!'

'Page 187, it begins – ready?'

'Ready, miss!'

Of the persons encountered in Perth in these last months of 1884 was a man called Walter Towns. Although he was known as a local celebrity, I found it difficult to guess the quality which had avowedly brought such renown to the rather – nay, wholly! – miserable specimen to whom I soon was introduced. He was a small man, of only some five feet in stature, thin, and of a gaunt mien, with deeply furrowed creases down each of his cheeks from eye to mouth; furthermore, his exceedingly sallow complexion had remained untouched by the rays of a sun that is powerful in this region, and his hollow aspect was further enhanced by the complete absence of teeth in the upper jaw. Yet his eyes spoke a latent (if limited) intelligence; and also a certain dolefulness, as if he were remembering things done long ago and things done ill. In truth, the situation pertaining to this man was fully as melodramatic as my readers could have wished; for he had been reprieved from the gallows with minutes only to spare. It was with the utmost interest and curiosity, therefore, that I questioned him.

A woman had been murdered near Oxford in 1860, on the local canal, and suspicion had centred on the crew of a narrow-boat plying south towards London. The four members of the crew, including both Towns himself and a lad of some fourteen years, had duly been arrested and brought to Court. Whilst the youth had been acquitted, the three others had been convicted, and incarcerated in the gaol in the city of Oxford, awaiting public execution. It was here, two or three minutes following the final visit of the Court Chaplain to the prisoners in their condemned cells, that Towns had received the news of his reprieve. Few humans, certainly, can have experienced a peripeteia [Christine here reverted to the spelling] so dramatic to their fortunes. Yet my conversation with Towns proved a matter of some considerable disappointment. Barely literate as the man was (though wholly understandably so) he was also barely comprehensible. His West Country dialect (as I straightaway placed it) was to such an extent o'erlaid with the excesses of the Australian manner of speech that I could follow some of his statements only with great difficulty. In short, the man I now met seemed ill-equipped to cope with the rigours of life – certainly those demanded of a free man. And Towns *was* a 'free' man, after serving his fifteen years' penal servitude in the Longbay Penitentiary. A broken, witless man; a man old before his time (he was but 47), a veteran convict (or 'crawler') who had experienced the ineffable agonies of a man faced with execution on the morrow.

Concerning the gruesome and macabre events invariably associated with the final hours of such criminals, I could learn but little. Yet a few facts may be of interest to my readers. It is clear, for example, that the prisoners each breakfasted on roasted lamb, with vegetables, although it seems probably from Towns' hazy recollection that such or similar breakfasts had been available during the whole period following the fixing of the date for their execution. More distressing, from Towns' viewpoint, was being denied access to his fellow criminals; and if I understood the unfortunate man aright it was this 'deprivation' which had been the hardest thing for him to bear. Whether he had slept little or not at all during the fateful night, Towns could not well remember; nor whether he had prayed for forgiveness and deliverance. But a miracle had occurred!

Surprisingly, it had not been the hanging itself which had been the focal-point of Towns' tortured thoughts that night. Rather it had been the knowledge of the public interest aroused in the case – the notoriety, the infamy, the horror, the abomination, the grisly spectacle, *the fame*; a fame which might bring those hapless men to walk the last few, fatal yards with a degree of fortitude which even the most pitiless spectators could admire.

Of the crime itself, Towns protested his complete innocence – a protestation not without precedent in criminal archives! But his recollection of the canal journey – and especially of the victim herself, Joanna Franks – was vivid and most poignant. The woman had been, in Towns' eyes, quite wondrously attractive, and it may cause no surprise that she became, almost immediately, the object of the men's craving, and the cause of open jealousies. Indeed, Towns recalled an occasion when two of the crew (the two who were eventually hanged) had come to blows over that provocative and desirable woman. And one of them with a knife! Even the young boy, Harold Wootton, had come under her spell, and the older woman had without much doubt taken advantage of his infatuation. At the same time, from what Towns asserted, and from the manner of his assertion, I am of the view that he himself did not have sexual dealings with the woman.

There is one interesting addendum to be made. In the first indictment (as I have subsequently read) the charge of either rape or theft would possibly have been prosecuted with more success than that of murder. Yet it was to be the charge of murder that was brought in the second trial. In similar instances, we may observe that the minor charge will frequently be suppressed when the major charge appears the more likely to be sustained. Was this, then, the reason why Towns seemed comparatively loquacious about the suggestion of *theft*? I know not. But it was his belief, as recounted to me, that Wootton had rather more interest in theft than in rape. After all, the availability of sexual dealings in 1860 was, as now, hardly a rarity along the English canals.

'Well, that's it! I'll put it in the post tonight, so you should—'
'Can't you call round, and bring it?'
'Life's, well, it's just a bit hectic at the minute,' she replied, after a little, awkward silence.
'All right!' Morse needed no further excuses. Having dipped the thermometer into the water, he'd found the reading a little too cold for any prospect of mixed bathing.
'You see,' said Christine, 'I – I'm living with someone—'
'And he doesn't think you should go spending all your time helping me.'
'I kept talking about you, too,' she said quietly.
Morse said nothing.

'Is your address the same as in the telephone directory? E. Morse?'

'That's me! That is I, if you prefer it.'

'What does the "E" stand for? I never knew what to call you.'

'They just call me "Morse".'

'You won't forget me?' she asked, after a little pause.

'I'll try to, I suppose.'

Morse thought of her for many minutes after he had cradled the phone. Then he recalled the testimony of Samuel Carter, and marvelled that a researcher of Carter's undoubted experience and integrity could make so many factual errors in the course of three or four pages: the date of the murder; Towns's accent; Towns's age; Wootton's Christian name; the dropping of the rape charge . . . Very interesting, though. Why, Morse had even guessed right about that dust-up with the knife! Well, almost right: he'd got the wrong man, but . . .

CHAPTER THIRTY-ONE

The second coastline is turned towards Spain and the west, and off it lies the island of Hibernia, which according to estimates is only half the size of Britain
(Julius Caesar, *de Bello Gallico* –
on the geography of Ireland)

Ten minutes later the phone rang again, and Morse knew in his bones that it was Christine Greenaway.

It was Strange.

'You're out then, Morse – yes? That's good. You've had a bit of a rough ride, they tell me.'

'On the mend now, sir. Kind of you to ring.'

'No *great* rush, you know – about getting back, I mean. We're a bit understaffed at the minute, but give yourself a few days – to get over things. Delicate thing, the stomach, you know. Why don't you try to get away somewhere for a couple of days – new surroundings – four-star hotel? You can afford it, Morse.'

'Thank you, sir. By the way, they've signed me off for a fortnight – at the hospital.'

'Fortnight? A *fort*-night?'

'It's er, a delicate thing, the stomach, sir.'

'Yes, well . . .'

'I'll be back as soon as I can, sir. And perhaps it wouldn't do me any harm to take your advice – about getting away for a little while.'

'Do you a world of good! The wife's brother' (Morse groaned inwardly) 'he's just back from a wonderful holiday. Ireland – Southern Ireland – took the car – Fishguard – Dun Laoghaire – then the west coast – you know, Cork, Kerry, Killarney, Connemara – marvellous, he said. Said you couldn't have spotted a terrorist with a telescope!'

It *had* been kind of Strange to ring; and as he sat in his armchair Morse reached idly for the World Atlas from his 'large-book' shelf, in which Ireland was a lozenge shape of green and yellow on page 10 – a country which Morse had never really contemplated before. Although spelling errors would invariably provoke his wrath, he confessed to himself that he could never have managed 'Dun Laoghaire', even with a score of attempts. And where was Kerry? Ah yes! Over there, west of Tralee – he was on the right bit of the map – and he moved his finger up the coast to Galway Bay. Then he saw it: *Bertnaghboy Bay*! And suddenly the thought of going over to Connemara seemed overwhelmingly attractive. By himself? Yes, it probably had to be by himself; and he didn't mind that, really. He was somewhat of a loner by temperament – because though never wholly happy when alone he was usually slightly more miserable when with other people. It would have been good to have taken Christine, but . . . and for a few minutes Morse's thoughts travelled back to Ward 7C. He would send a card to Eileen and Fiona; and one to 'Waggie' Greenaway, perhaps? Yes, that would be a nice gesture: Waggie had been out in the wash-room when Morse had left, and he'd been a pleasant old—

Suddenly Morse was conscious of the tingling excitement in the nape of his neck, and then in his shoulders. His eyes dilated and sparkled as if some inner current had been activated; and he sat back in the armchair and smiled slowly to himself.

What, he wondered, was the routine in the Irish Republic for *exhumation*?

CHAPTER THIRTY-TWO

Oh what a tangled web we weave
When first we practise to deceive!
(Sir Walter Scott, *Marmion*)

'You *what*?' asked a flabbergasted Lewis, who had called round at
7.30 p.m. ('Not till *The Archers* has finished' had been his strict
instruction.) He himself had made an interesting little discovery –
well, the WPC in St Aldates had made it, really – and he was
hoping that it might amuse Morse in his wholly inconsequential
game of 'Find Joanna Franks'. But to witness Morse galloping
ahead of the Hunt, chasing (as Lewis was fairly certain) after some
imaginary fox of his own, was, if not particularly unusual, just a
little disconcerting.

'You see, Lewis' (Morse was straightway in full swing) 'this is
one of the most beautiful little deceptions we've ever come across.
The *problems* inherent in the case – almost all of them – are resolved
immediately once we take one further step into imaginative
improbability.'

'You've lost me already, sir,' protested Lewis.

'No, I haven't! Just take one more step *yourself*. You think you're
in the *dark*? Right? But the dark is where we *all* are. The dark is
where *I* was, until I took one more step into the dark. And then,
when I'd taken it, I found myself in the *sunshine*.'

'I'm very glad to hear it,' mumbled Lewis.

'It's like this. Once I read that story, I was uneasy about it –
doubtful, uncomfortable. It was the *identification* bit that worried
me – and it would have worried any officer in the Force today, *you*
know that! But, more significantly, if we consider the psychology
of the whole—'

'Sir!' (It was almost unprecedented for Lewis to interrupt the
Chief in such peremptory fashion.) 'Could we – could you – please
forget all this psychological referencing? I just about get my fill of
it all from some of these Social Services people. Could you just tell
me, simply and—'

'I'm boring you – is that what you're saying?'

'*Exactly* what I'm saying, sir.'

Morse nodded to himself happily. 'Let's put it *simply*, then, all
right? I read a story in hospital. I get interested. I think – *think* –
the wrong people got arrested, and some of 'em hanged, for the
murder of that little tart from Liverpool. As I say, I thought the
identification of that lady was a bit questionable; and when I read

the words the boatmen were alleged to have used about her – well, I knew there must be something fundamentally *wrong*. You see—'

'You said you'd get to the point, sir.'

'I thought that Joanna's father – No. Let's start again! Joanna's father gets a job as an insurance rep. Like most people in that position he gets a few of his own family, if they're daft enough, to take out a policy with him. He gets a bit of commission, and he's not selling a phoney product, anyway, is he? I think that both Joanna and her *first* husband, our conjuror friend, were soon enlisted in the ranks of the policy-holders. Then times got tough; and to crown all the misfortunes, Mr Donavan, the greatest man in all the world, goes and dies. And when Joanna's natural grief has abated – or evaporated, rather – she finds she's done very nicely thank you out of the insurance taken on his life. She receives £100, with profits, on what had been a policy taken out only two or three years previously. Now, £100 plus, in 1850 or whenever, was a very considerable sum of money; and Joanna perhaps began, at that point, to appreciate the potential for *malpractice* in the system. She began to see the insurance business not only as a potential *future* benefit, but as an actual, *present* source of profit. So, after Donavan's death, when she met and married Franks, one of the first things she insisted on was his taking out a policy – not on *his* life – but on *hers*. Her father could, and did, effect such a transaction without any trouble, although it was probably soon after this that the Notts and Midlands Friendly Society got a *little* suspicious about Joanna's father, Carrick – Daniel Carrick – and told him his services were no longer—'

'Sir!'

Morse held up his right hand. 'Joanna Franks was *never* murdered, Lewis! She was the master-mind – mistress-mind – behind a deception that was going to rake in some considerable, and desperately needed, profit. It was *another* woman, roughly the same age and the same height, who was found in the Oxford Canal; a woman provided by Joanna's *second* husband, the ostler from the Edgware Road, who had already made his journey – not difficult for *him*! – with horse and carriage from London, to join his wife at Oxford. Or, to be more accurate, Lewis, at some few points *north* of Oxford. You remember in the Colonel's book?' (Morse turned to the passage he had in mind.) 'He – here it is! – "he explained how in consequence of some information he had come into Oxfordshire" – Bloody liar!'

Lewis, now interested despite himself, nodded a vague

concurrence of thought. 'So what you're saying, sir, is that Joanna worked this insurance fiddle and probably made quite a nice little packet for herself and for her father as well?'

'Yes! But not only that. Listen! I may just be wrong, Lewis, but I think that not only was Joanna wrongly identified as the lawful wife of Charles Franks – by Charles Franks – but that Charles Franks was the *only* husband of the woman supposedly murdered on the *Barbara Bray*. In short, the "Charles Franks" who broke down in tears at the second trial was *none other than Donavan*.'

'Phew!'

'A man of many parts: he was an actor, he was a conjuror, he was an impersonator, he was a swindler, he was a cunning schemer, he was a callous murderer, he was a loving husband, he was a tearful witness, he was the first and *only* husband of Joanna Franks: F. T. Donavan! We all thought – you thought – even *I* thought – that there were three principal characters playing their roles in our little drama; and now I'm telling you, Lewis, that in all probability we've only got *two*. Joanna; and her husband – the greatest man in all the world; the man buried out on the west coast of Ireland, where the breakers come rolling in from the Atlantic . . . so they tell me . . .'

CHAPTER THIRTY-THREE

Stet Difficilior Lectio
(Let the more difficult of the readings stand)
(The principle applied commonly by editors faced with
variant readings in ancient manuscripts)

Lewis was silent. How else? He had a precious little piece of evidence in his pocket, but while Morse's mind was still coursing through the upper atmosphere, there was little point in interrupting again for the minute. He put the envelope containing the single photocopied sheet on the coffee-table – and listened further.

'In the account of Joanna's last few days, we've got some evidence that she could have been a bit deranged; and part of the evidence for such a possibility is the fact that at some point she kept calling out her husband's name – "Franks! Franks! Franks!" Agreed? But she *wasn't* calling out that at all – she was calling her *first* husband, Lewis! I was sitting here thinking of "Waggie" Greenaway—'

'And his daughter,' mumbled Lewis, inaudibly.

' – and I thought of "Hefty" Donavan. F. T. Donavan. And I'll put my next month's salary on that "F" standing for "Frank"! Huh! Who's ever heard of a wife calling her husband by his surname?'

'I have, sir.'

'Nonsense! Not these days.'

'But it's *not* these days. It was—'

'She was calling *Frank Donavan* – believe me!'

'But she *could* have been queer in the head, and if so—'

'Nonsense!'

'Well, we shan't ever know for sure, shall we, sir?'

'Nonsense!'

Morse sat back with the self-satisfied, authoritative air of a man who believes that what he has called 'nonsense' three times must, by the laws of the universe, be necessarily untrue. 'If *only* we knew how tall they were – Joanna and . . . and whoever the other woman was. But there is just a chance, isn't there? That cemetery, Lewis—'

'Which do you want first, sir? The good news or the bad news?'

Morse frowned at him. 'That's . . .?' pointing to the envelope.

'That's the good news.'

Morse slowly withdrew and studied the photocopied sheet.

> Twenty five minutes past 7 o'clock.
> Drowned body was in cut
> of wtr licensed to D of M —
> taken to Plough Inn at Wolv—
> probable identity? unknown.
> Prelim findings wd suggest
> death by drowning – no obvious
> injury was seen – 5 3¾ in —
> well nour – c 35 yrs. Bruise
> on mouth (rt side) – body warm
> full clothes, *not* bonnet &
> shoes – face discoloured, black.

'Not the Coroner's Report, sir, but the next best thing. This fellow must have seen her before the *post-mortem*. Interesting, isn't it?'

'*Very* interesting.'

The report was set out on an unruled sheet of paper, dated, and subscribed by what appeared as 'Dr Willis', for the writing was not only fairly typical of the semi-legibility forever associated with the medical profession, but was also beset by a confusion with 'm's, 'w's, 'n's, and 'u's – all these letters appearing to be incised with a series of what looked like semi-circular fish-hooks. Clearly the notes of an orderly-minded local doctor called upon to certify death and to take the necessary action – in this case, almost certainly, to pass the whole business over to some higher authority. Yet there were one or two real nuggets of gold here: the good Willis had made an exact measurement of height, and had written one or two most pertinent (and, apparently, correct) observations. Sad, however, from Morse's point of view, was the unequivocal assertion made here that *the body was still warm*. It must have been this document which had been incorporated into the subsequent *post-mortem* findings, thenceforth duly reiterated both in Court and in the Colonel's history. And it *was* a pity; for if Morse had been correct in believing that another body had been substituted for that of Joanna Franks, that woman must surely have been killed in the early hours of the morning, and could *not* therefore have been drowned some three or four hours later. *Far* too risky. It was odd, certainly, that the dead woman's face had turned black so very quickly; but there was no escaping the plain fact that the first medical man who had examined the corpse had found it still *warm*.

Is that what the report had said, though – 'still warm'? No! No, it hadn't! It just said 'warm' . . . Or *did* it?

Carefully Morse looked again at the report – and sensed the old familiar tingling around his shoulders. *Could* it be? Had everyone else read the report wrongly? In every case the various notes were separated from each other by some form of punctuation – either dashes (eight of them) or full stops (four) or question-marks (only one). All the notes *except one*, that is: the exception being that 'body warm/full clothes . . .' etc. There was neither a dash nor a stop between these two, clearly disparate, items – unless the photocopier had borne unfaithful witness. No! The solution was far simpler. There had been *no* break requiring any punctuation. Morse looked again at line 10 of the report, *on mouth (rt side) – body warm*

and considered three further facts. Throughout, the 's's were written almost as straight vertical lines; of the fifteen or so 'i' dots, no fewer than six had remained un-dotted; and on this showing Willis seemed particularly fond of the word 'was'. So the line should perhaps – should certainly! – read as follows: 'on mouth (rt side) – body was in'. The body 'was in full clothes'! The body was *not* 'warm'; not in Morse's book. There, suddenly, the body was very, very cold.

Lewis, whilst fully accepting the probability of the alternative reading, did not appear to share the excitement which was now visibly affecting Morse; and it was time for the bad news.

'No chance of checking this out in the old Summertown grave-yard, sir.'

'Why not? The gravestones are still there, some of them – it says so, doesn't it? – and I've seen them myself—'

'They were all removed, when they built the flats there.'

'Even those the Colonel mentioned?'

Lewis nodded.

Morse knew full well, of course, that any chance of getting an exhumation order to dig up a corner of the greenery in a retire-ment-home garden was extremely remote. Yet the thought that he might have clinched his theory . . . It was not a matter of supreme moment, though, he knew that; it wasn't even important in putting to rights a past and grievous injustice. It was of no great matter to anyone, except to himself. Ever since he had first come into contact with problems, from his early schooldays onwards – with the meanings of words, with algebra, with detective stories, with cryptic clues – he had always been desperately anxious to know the *answers*, whether those answers were wholly satisfactory or whether they were not. And now, whatever had been the motive leading to that far-off murder, he found himself irked in the extreme to realize that the woman – or *a* woman – he sought had until so very recently been lying in a marked grave in North Oxford. Had she been Joanna Franks, after all? No chance of knowing now – not for certain. But if the meticulous Dr Willis had been correct in his measurements, she *couldn't* have been Joanna, surely?

*

After Lewis had gone, Morse made a phone call.

'What was the average height of women in the nineteenth century?'

'Which end of the nineteenth century, Morse?'

'Let's say the middle.'

'Interesting question!'

'Well?'

'It varied, I suppose.'

'Come *on*!'

'Poor food, lack of protein – all that sort of stuff. Not very big, most of 'em. Certainly no bigger than the Ripper's victims in the 1880s: four feet nine, four feet ten, four feet eleven – that sort of height: well, that's about what *those* dear ladies were. Except one. Stride, wasn't her name? Yes, Liz Stride. They called her "Long Liz" – so much taller than all the other women in the work-houses. You follow that, Morse?'

'How tall was *she* – "Long Liz"?'

'Dunno.'

'Can you find out?'

'What, now?'

'And ring me back?'

'Bloody hell!'

'Thanks.'

Morse was three minutes into the love duet from Act One of *Die Walküre* when the phone rang.

'Morse? Five feet three.'

Morse whistled.

'Pardon?'

'Thanks, Max! By the way, are you at the lab all day tomorrow? Something I want to bring to show you.'

So the 'petite' little figure had measured three quarters of an inch *more* than 'Long Liz' Stride! And her shoes as Lewis had ascertained, were about size 5! Well, well, well! Virtually every fact now being unearthed (though that was probably not *le mot juste*) was bolstering Morse's bold hypothesis. But, infuriatingly, there was, as it seemed, no chance whatever of establishing the truth. Not, at any rate, the truth regarding Joanna Franks.

CHAPTER THIRTY-FOUR

Marauding louts have shot the moping owl:
The tower is silent 'neath the wat'ry moon;
But Lady Porter, lately on the prowl,
Will sell the place for pennies very soon
(E. O. Parrot, *The Spectator*)

The communication from the insurance company had been a third and final demand for his previous month's premium; and the first thing Morse did the following morning was to write out a cheque, with a brief letter of apology. He understood very little about money, but a dozen or so years previously he had deemed it provident (as it transpired, Prudential) to pay a monthly premium of £55 against a lump sum of £12,000, with profits, at sixty – an age looming ever closer. He had never given a thought about what would happen if he pre-deceased his policy. No worry for him: for the present he had no financial worries, no dependants, a good salary, and a mortgage that would finish in two years' time. He knew it, yes! – compared with the vast majority of mankind he was extremely fortunate. Still, he ought perhaps to think of making a will . . .

Coincidentally, he had been talking to Lewis about insurances the day before and (he admitted it to himself) largely making it all up as he went along. But it was *far* from improbable, wasn't it – what he'd guessed? Those insurance fiddles? He looked out the first material that Christine had brought in to him at the JR2, and once again studied the facts and figures of the Nottinghamshire and Midlands Friendly Society for 1859.

Joanna had been born in 1821, so she was thirty-eight in 1859. If she'd taken out a policy a year, two years earlier, that would be – age next birthday thirty-six – an annual premium of £3. 8s. 9d. Under £7, say, for a return of £100. Not bad at all. And if Donavan had already pocketed a similar packet . . .

Morse left his flat in mid-morning (the first excursion since his return) and posted his single letter. He met no one he knew as he turned right along the Banbury Road, and then right again into Squitchey Lane; where, taking the second turning on his left, just past the evangelical chapel (now converted into a little group of residences), he walked down Middle Way. It was a dark, dankish morning, and a scattering of rooks (mistaking, perhaps, the hour)

PLAN OF THE ASSOCIATION.   7

The following Table (I.) exhibits the scale of Premiums for the assurance of £100 on the lives of Members ; also the Net Premiums payable after seven years, allowing a reduction of 72 per cent., to which persons now assuring will then be entitled if the present rate of abatement be maintained.

Age next Birthday.	Annual Premium.	Reduction 72 per cent.	Net Premium.	Age next Birthday.	Annual Premium.	Reduction 72 per cent.	Net Premium.
	£ s. d.	£ s. d.	£ s. d.		£ s. d.	£ s. d.	£ s. d.
21	2 10 0	1 16 0	0 14 0	45	4 9 0	3 4 7	1 5 2
22	2 10 9	1 16 6	0 14 3	46	4 12 0	3 6 0	1 6 0
23	2 11 6	1 17 1	0 14 5	47	4 16 3	3 9 4	1 6 11
24	2 12 6	1 17 10	0 14 8	48	4 19 3	3 11 10	1 7 11
25	2 13 6	1 18 6	0 15 0	49	5 3 6	3 14 6	1 9 0
26	2 14 6	1 19 3	0 15 3	50	5 7 6	3 17 5	1 10 1
27	2 15 6	2 0 0	0 15 6	51	5 11 9	4 0 6	1 11 3
28	2 16 6	2 0 8	0 15 10	52	5 16 0	4 3 6	1 12 6
29	2 17 9	2 1 7	0 16 2	53	6 0 6	4 6 9	1 13 9
30	2 19 3	2 2 8	0 16 7	54	6 5 0	4 10 0	1 15 0
31	3 0 6	2 3 7	0 16 11	55	6 9 6	4 13 3	1 16 3
32	3 2 0	2 4 8	0 17 4	56	6 14 6	4 16 10	1 17 8
33	3 3 6	2 5 9	0 17 9	57	6 19 6	5 0 5	1 19 1
34	3 5 3	2 7 0	0 18 3	58	7 4 6	5 4 0	2 0 6
35	3 7 0	2 8 3	0 18 9	59	7 9 6	5 7 8	2 1 10
36	3 8 9	2 9 6	0 19 3	60	7 15 0	5 11 7	2 3 5
37	3 10 9	2 10 11	0 19 10	61	8 0 9	5 15 9	2 5 0
38	3 12 9	2 12 5	1 0 4	62	8 7 0	6 0 3	2 6 9
39	3 14 9	2 13 10	1 0 11	63	8 13 9	6 5 1	2 8 8
40	3 17 0	2 15 5	1 1 7	64	9 1 0	6 10 4	2 10 8
41	3 19 3	2 17 1	1 2 2	65	9 8 9	6 15 11	2 12 10
42	4 1 6	2 18 8	1 2 10	66	9 17 0	7 1 10	2 15 2
43	4 4 0	3 0 6	1 3 6	67	10 5 0	7 7 7	2 17 5
44	4 6 0	3 2 6	1 4 3				

squawked away in the trees to his right. Past Bishop Kirk Middle School he went on, and straight along past the attractive terraced houses on either side with their mullioned bay-windows – and, on his left, *there it was*: Dudley Court, a block of flats built in cinnamon-coloured brick on the site of the old Summertown Parish Cemetery. A rectangle of lawn, some fifty by twenty-five yards, was set out behind a low containing wall, only about eighteen inches high, over which Morse stepped into the grassy plot planted with yew-trees and red-berried bushes. Immediately to his left, the area was bounded by the rear premises of a social club; and along this wall, beneath the straggly branches of winter jasmine, and covered with damp beech-leaves, he could make out the stumps of four or five old headstones, broken off at their roots like so many jagged teeth just protruding from their gums. Clearly, any deeper excavation to remove these stones in their entirety had been thwarted by the proximity of the wall; but all the rest had been removed, perhaps several years ago now – and duly recorded no doubt in some dusty box of papers on the shelves of the local Diocesan Offices. Well, at least Morse could face one simple fact: no burial evidence would be forthcoming from these fair lawns. None! Yet it would have been good to know where the stone had marked (as the Colonel had called it) the 'supra-corporal' site of Joanna Franks.

Or whoever.

He walked past Dudley Court itself, where a Christmas tree, bedecked with red, green, and yellow bulbs, was already switched on; past the North Oxford Conservative Association premises, in which he had never (and would never) set foot; past the Spiritualist Church, in which he had never (as yet) set foot; past the low-roofed Women's Institute HQ, in which he had once spoken about the virtues of the Neighbourhood Watch Scheme; and finally, turning left, he came into South Parade, just opposite the Post Office – into which he ventured once a year and that to pay the Jaguar's road-tax. But as he walked by the old familiar land-marks, his mind was far away, and the decision firmly taken. If he was to be cheated of finding one of his suspects, he would go and look for the other! He needed a break. He would *have* a break.

There was a travel agency immediately across the street, and the girl who sat at the first desk to the right smiled brightly.

'Can I help you, sir?'

'Yes! I'd like' (Morse sat himself down) 'I'd like to book a holiday, with a car, in Ireland – the Republic, that is.'

Later that day, Morse called at the William Dunn School of Pathology in South Parks Road.

'Have a look at these for me, will you?'

Refraining from all cynical comment, Max looked dubiously across at Morse over his half-lenses.

'Max! All I want to know is—'

'—whether they come from M&S or Littlewoods?'

'The tear, Max – *the tear.*'

'Tear? *What* tear?' Max picked up the knickers with some distaste and examined them (as it seemed to Morse) in cursory fashion. 'No tear here, Morse. Not the faintest sign of any irregular distension of the fibre tissue – calico, by the way, isn't it?'

'I think so.'

'Well, we don't need a microscope to tell us it's a cut: neat, clean, straight-forward *cut*, all right?'

'With a knife?'

'What the hell else do you cut things with?'

'Cheese-slicer? Pair of—?'

'What a wonderful thing, Morse, is the human imagination!'

It was a wonderful thing, too, that Morse had received such an unequivocal answer to one of his questions; the very first such answer, in fact, in their long and reasonably amicable acquaintanceship.

CHAPTER THIRTY-FIVE

Heap not on this mound
Roses that she loved so well;
Why bewilder her with roses
That she cannot see or smell?
(Edna St Vincent Millay, *Epitaph*)

Inspector Mulvaney spotted him parking the car in the 'Visitor' space. When the little station had been converted ten years earlier from a single detached house into Kilkearnan's apology for a crime-prevention HQ, the Garda had deemed it appropriate that the four-man squad should be headed by an inspector. It seemed, perhaps, in retrospect, something of an over-reaction. With its thousand or so inhabitants, Kilkearnan regularly saw its ration of fisticuffs and affray outside one or more of the fourteen public-houses; but as yet the little community had steered clear of any involvement in international smuggling or industrial espionage. Here, even road accidents were a rarity – though this was attributable more to the comparative scarcity of cars than to the sobriety of their drivers. Tourists there were, of course – especially in the summer months; but even they, with their Rovers and BMWs, were more often stopping to photograph the occasional donkey than causing any hazard to the occasional drunkard.

The man parking his Jaguar in the single (apart from his own) parking-space, Mulvaney knew to be the English policeman who had rung through the previous day to ask for help in locating a cemetery (for, as yet, no stated purpose) and who thought it was probably the one overlooking Bertnaghboy Bay – that being the only burial ground marked on the local map. Mulvaney had been able to assure Chief Inspector Morse (such was he) that indeed it would be the cemetery which lay on the side of a hill to the west of the small town: the local dead were always likely to be buried there, as Mulvaney had maintained – there being no alternative accommodation.

From the lower window, Mulvaney watched Morse with some curiosity. It was not every day (or week, or month) that any contact was effected between the British Police and the Garda; and the man who was walking round to the main (only) entrance looked an interesting specimen: mid-fifties, losing his whitish hair, putting on just a little too much weight, and exhibiting perhaps, as was to be hoped, the tell-tale signs of liking his liquor more than a little. Nor was Mulvaney disappointed in the man who was shown into his main (only) office.

'Are you related to Kipling's Mulvaney?' queried Morse.

'No, sor! But that was a good question – and educashin, that's a good thing, too!'

Morse explained his unlikely, ridiculous, selfish mission, and Mulvaney warmed to him immediately. No chance whatsoever, of course, of any exhumation order being granted, but perhaps Morse might be interested in hearing about the business of grave-digging in the Republic? A man could never *dig* a grave on a Monday, and that for perfectly valid reasons, which he had forgotten; and in any case it wasn't Monday, was it? And if a grave *was* dug, even on a Monday, it had always – *always*, sor! – to be in the morning, or at least the previous evening. That was an important thing, too, about all the forks and shovels: placed across the open grave, they had to be, in the form of the holy cross, for reasons which a man of Morse's educashin would need no explanation, to be sure. Last, it was always the custom for the chief mourner to supply a little quantity of Irish whiskey at the graveside for the other members of the saddened family; and for the grave-diggers, too, of course, who had shovelled up the clinging, cloggy soil. 'For sure, 'tis always a t'irsty business, sor, that working of the soil!'

So Morse, the chief mourner, walked out into the main (only) High Street, and purchased three bottles of Irish malt. An understanding had been arrived at, and Morse knew that whatever the problems posed by the Donavan–Franks equation, the left-hand side would be solved (if solved it *could* be) with the full sympathy and (unofficial) co-operation of the Irish Garda.

In his mind's eye, Morse had envisaged a bank of arc-lights, illuminating a well-marked grave, with barricades erected around the immediate area, a posse of constables to keep the public from prying, and press photographers training their telescopic lenses on the site. The time? That would be 5.30 a.m. – the usual exhumation hour. And excitement would be intense.

It was not to be.

Together, Morse and Mulvaney had fairly easily located the final habitation of the greatest man in all the world. In all, there must have been about three or four hundred graves within the walled area of the hill-side cemetery. Half a dozen splendidly sculptured angels and madonnas kept watch here and there over a few former dignitaries, and several large Celtic crosses marked other burial-plots. But the great majority of the dead lay unhonoured here beneath untended, meaner-looking memorials. Donavan's stone was one of the latter, a poor, mossed-and-lichened thing, with white and ochre blotches, and no more than two feet high, leaning back at an angle of about 20 degrees from the vertical. So effaced was the weathered stone that only the general outlines of the lettering could be followed – and that only on either side of a central disintegration:

'That's him,' said Morse triumphantly. It looked as if his name *had* been Frank.

'God rest his soul!' added Mulvaney. 'That's if it's there, of course.'

Morse grinned, and wished he'd known Mulvaney long ago. 'How are you going to explain . . .?'

'We are digging yet another grave, sor. In the daylight – and just as normal.'

It was all quite quick. Mulvaney had bidden the two men appointed to the task to dig a clean rectangle to the east of the single stone; and after getting down only two or three feet, one of the spades struck what sounded like, and was soon revealed to be, a wooden coffin. Once all the dark-looking earth had been removed and piled on each side of the oblong pit, Morse and Mulvaney looked down to a plain coffin-top, with no plate of any sort screwed into it. The wood, one-inch elm-boarding, and grooved round the top, looked badly warped, but in a reasonable state. There seemed no reason to remove the complete coffin; and Morse, betraying once again his inveterate horror of corpses, quietly declined the honour of removing the lid.

It was Mulvaney himself, awkwardly straddling the hole, his shoes caked with mud, who bent down and pulled at the top of the coffin, which gave way easily, the metal screws clearly having disintegrated long ago. As the board slowly lifted, Mulvaney saw, as did Morse, that a whitish mould hung down from the inside of the coffin-lid; and in the coffin itself, covering the body, a shroud or covering of some sort was overspread with the same creeping white fungus.

Round the sides at the bottom of the coffin, plain for all to see, was a bed of brownish, dampish sawdust, looking as fresh as if the body which lay on it had been buried only yesterday. But *what* body?

"Tis wonderfully well preserved, is it not, sor? 'Tis the peat in the soil that's accountin' forrit.'

This from the first grave-digger, who appeared more deeply impressed by the wondrous preservation of the wood than by the absence of any body. *For the coffin contained no body at all.* What it did contain was a roll of carpet, of some greenish dye, about five feet in length, folded round what appeared to have been half a dozen spaded squares of peat. Of Donavan there was no trace whatsoever – not even a torn fragment from the last handbill of the greatest man in all the world.

CHAPTER THIRTY-SIX

A man's learning dies with him; even his virtues fade
out of remembrance; but the dividends on the stocks he
bequeaths may serve to keep his memory green
(Oliver Wendell Holmes, *The Professor at the
Breakfast Table*)

Morse grew somewhat fitter during the days following his return
from Ireland; and very soon, in his own judgement at least, he
had managed to regain that semblance of salubrity and strength
which his GP interpreted as health. Morse asked no more.

He had recently bought himself the old Furtwängler recording
of *The Ring*; and during the hours of Elysian enjoyment which that
performance was giving him, the case of Joanna Franks, and the
dubious circumstances of the Oxford Tow-path Mystery, assumed
a slowly diminishing significance. The whole thing had brought
him some recreative enjoyment, but now it was finished. Ninety-
five per cent certain (as he was) that the wrong people had been
hanged in 1860, there was apparently nothing further he could do
to dispel that worrying little five per cent of doubt.

Christmas was coming up fast, and he was glad not to have
that tiring traipsing round the shops – no stockings, no scent to
buy. He himself received half a dozen cards; two invitations to
Drinks Evenings; and a communication from the JR2:

Xmas Party

*The Nursing Staff of the John Radcliffe Hospital
request the pleasure of your company
on the evening of Friday, 22nd December,
from 8 p.m. until midnight,
at the Nurses' Hostel, Headington Hill, Oxford.
Disco Dancing, Ravishing Refreshments, Fabulous Fun!*

Please Come! Dress informal. RSVP.

The printed card was signed, in blue Biro, 'Ward 7C' – and
followed by a single 'X'.

It was on Friday, 15th December, a week before the scheduled
party, that Morse's eye caught the name in the *Oxford Times'*
'Deaths' column:

DENISTON, Margery – On December 10th, peace-
fully at her home in Woodstock, aged 78 years. She
wished her body to be given to medical research.
Donations gratefully received, in honour of the late
Colonel W. M. Deniston, by the British Legion Club,
Lambourn.

Morse thought back to the only time he'd met the quaint old
girl, so proud as she had been of her husband's work – a work
which had brought Morse such disproportionate interest; a work
which he'd not even had to pay for. He signed a cheque for £20,
and stuck it in a cheap brown envelope. He had both first- and
second-class stamps to hand, but he chose a second-class: it wasn't
a matter of life and death, after all.

He would (he told himself) have attended a funeral service, if
she'd been having one. But he was glad she wasn't: the stern and
daunting sentences from the Burial Service, especially in the A.V.,
were ever assuming a nearer and more personal threat to his peace
of mind; and for the present that was something he could well do
without. He looked up the British Legion's Lambourn address in
the telephone directory, and after doing so turned to 'Deniston,
W. M.'. There it was: 46 Church Walk, Woodstock. Had there
been any family? It hardly appeared so, from the obituary notice.
So? So what happened to things, if there was no one to leave them
to? As with Mrs Deniston, possibly? As with anyone childless or
unmarried . . .

It was difficult parking the Jaguar, and finally Morse took advantage of identifying himself to a sourpuss of a traffic warden who
reluctantly sanctioned a temporary straddling of the double-
yellows twenty or so yards from the grey-stoned terraced house in
Church Walk. He knocked on the front door, and was admitted
forthwith.

Two persons were in the house: a young man in his middle
twenties who (as he explained) had been commissioned by Blackwells to catalogue the few semi-valuable books on the late Denis-
tons' shelves; and a great-nephew of the old Colonel, the only
surviving relative, who (as Morse interpreted matters) was in for a
very pretty little inheritance indeed, if recent prices for Woodstock
property were anything to judge by.

To the latter, Morse immediately and openly explained
what his interest was: he was begging nothing – apart from the

opportunity to discover whether the late Colonel had left behind
any notes or documents relating to *Murder on the Oxford Canal*.
And happily the answer was 'yes' – albeit a very limited 'yes'. In
the study was a pile of manuscript, and typescript, and clipped to
an early page of the manuscript was one short letter – a letter with
no date, no sender's address, and no envelope:

> Our dear Daniel,
>   We do both trust you are keeping well these past months. We
> shall be in Derby in early Sept. when we hope we shall be with you.
> Please say to Mary how the dress she did was very successfull and
> will she go on with the other one if she is feeling recovered.
>   Yours Truely and Afectionatly,
>   Matthew

That was all. Enough, though, for the Colonel to feel that it was
worth preserving. There was only one 'Daniel' in the case, Daniel
Carrick from Derby; and here was that one piece of primary-source
material that linked the Colonel's narrative in a tangible, physical
way to the whole sorry story. Agreed, Daniel Carrick had never
figured all that prominently in Morse's thinking; but he *ought* to
have done. He was surely just as damningly implicated as the
other two in the deception – the twin deception – which had seen
the Notts and Midlands Friendly Society having to fork out, first
for the death of the great uncoffined Donavan, and then for the
death of the enigmatic Joanna, the great undrowned.

Morse turned over the faded, deeply creased letter and saw, on
the back, a few pencilled notes, pretty certainly in the Colonel's
hand: 'No records from Ins. Co. – Mrs C. very poorly at this time?
Not told of J.'s death? 12 Spring St. still occupied 12.4.76!'

There it was then – palpable paper and writing, and just a
fingertip of contact with one of the protagonists in that nineteenth-
century drama. As for the two principal actors, the only evidence
that could have been forthcoming about them was buried away
with their bodies. And where Joanna was buried – or where the
greatest man in all the world – who knew, or who could ever
know?

CHAPTER THIRTY-SEVEN

Modern dancers give a sinister portent about our times.
The dancers don't even look at one another. They are
just a lot of isolated individuals jiggling in a kind of self-
hypnosis

(Agnes de Mille, *the New York Times*)

The party-goers were fully aware that when the caretaker said
midnight he meant 11.55 p.m.; but few had managed to arrive at
the Nurses' Hostel before 9 p.m. In any case, the event was never
destined to be of cosmic significance, and would have little to
show for itself apart from a memory or two, a few ill-developed
photographs, and a great deal of clearing up the following
morning.

As soon as he took his first steps across the noisy, throbbing,
flashing room – it was now 10.30 p.m. – Morse realized that he
had made a tragic error in accepting the invitation. 'Never go
back!' – that was the advice he should have heeded; yet he had
been fool enough to recall the white sheets and the Fair Fiona and
the Ethereal Eileen. Idiot! He sat down on a rickety, slatted chair,
and sipped some warm insipid 'punch' that was handed out in
white plastic cups to each new arrival. Constituted, if taste were
anything to go by, of about 2% gin, 2% dry Martini, 10% orange
juice, and 86% lemonade, it was going to take a considerable time,
by Morse's reckoning, before such Ravishing Refreshments turned
him on; and he had just decided that the best thing about it was
the little cubes of apple floating on the top when Fiona detached
her sickly-looking beau from the dance-floor and came up to him.

'Happy Christmas!' She bent down, and Morse could still feel
the dryness of her lips against his cheek as she introduced the
embarrassed youth, repeated her Christmas greeting, and then
was gone – throwing herself once more into a series of jerky
contortions like some epileptic puppet.

Morse's plastic cup was empty and he walked slowly past a
long line of tables, where beneath the white coverings he glimpsed
sugared mince-pies and skewered sausages.

'We'll be starting on them soon!' said a familiar voice behind
him, and Morse turned to find Eileen, blessedly alone and, like
only a few of the others, wearing her uniform.

'Hullo!' said Morse.

'Hullo!' she said softly.

'It's good to see you!'

She looked at him, and nodded, almost imperceptibly.

A tall man, looking as if he might have been involved in a fight recently, materialized from somewhere.

'This is Gordon,' said Eileen, looking up into the shaded planes of Gordon's skull-like face. And when Morse had shaken hands with the man, he once more found himself alone, wondering where to walk, where to put himself, how to make an inconspicuous exit, to cease upon the five-minutes-to-eleven with no pain.

He was only a few feet from the main door when she was suddenly standing in front of him.

'You're not trying to sneak away, I hope!'

Nessie!

'Hullo, Sister. No! I'm – I mustn't stay too long, of course, but—'

'I'm glad you came. I know you're a wee bit old for this sort of thing . . .' Her lilting Scottish accent seemed to be mocking him gently.

Morse nodded; it was difficult to argue the point, and he looked down to pick out the one remaining apple-cube from his cup.

'Your sergeant did you rairther better – with the drink, I mean.'

Morse looked at her – suddenly – almost as if he had never looked at her before. Her skin in this stroboscopic light looked almost opaline, and the colour of her eyes was emerald. Her auburn hair was swept upward, emphasizing the contours of her face, and her mouth was thinly and delicately lipsticked. For a woman, she was quite tall, certainly as tall as he was; and if only (as Morse thought) she'd worn something other than that miserably dowdy, unflattering dress . . .

'Would you like to dance, Inspector?'

'I – no! It's not one of my, er, things, dancing, I'm afraid.'

'What—?'

But Morse was never to know what she was going to ask him. A young houseman – smiling, flushed, so happily at home here – grabbed her by the hand and was pulling her to the floor.

'Come on, Sheila! *Our* dance, remember?'

Sheila!

'You won't try to sneak away—?' she was saying over her shoulder. But she was on the dance-floor now, where shortly all the other dancers were stopping and moving to the periphery as the pair of them, Sheila and her young partner, put on a dazzling display of dance-steps to the rhythmic clapping of the audience.

Morse felt a stab of jealousy as his eyes followed them, the young man's body pressed close to hers. He had fully intended to stay, as she had asked. But when the music had finished, the newly metamorphosed Nessie, pretending to collapse, had become the centre of enthusiastic admiration, and Morse placed his plastic cup on the table by the exit, and left.

At 9.30 the following morning, after a somewhat fitful sleep, he rang the JR2 and asked for Ward 7C.

'Can I speak to Sister, please?'

'Who shall I say is calling?'

'It's – it's a personal call.'

'We can't take personal calls, I'm afraid. If you'd like to leave your name—'

'Just tell her one of her old patients from the ward—'

'Is it Sister Maclean you wanted?'

'Yes.'

'She's left – she left officially last week. She's off to be Director of Nursing Services—'

'She's left Oxford?'

'She's leaving today. She stayed on for a party last night—'

'I see. I'm sorry to have bothered you. I seem to have got the wrong end of things, don't I?'

'Yes, you do.'

'Where is she going to?'

'Derby – Derby Royal Infirmary.'

CHAPTER THIRTY-EIGHT

> The very designation of the term 'slum' reflects a middle-class attitude to terrace-housing, where grand values are applied to humble situations
> (James Stevens Curl, *The Erosion of Oxford*)

Since fast driving was his only significant vice (apart from egg-and-chips) Lewis was delighted, albeit on one of his 'rest'-days, to be invited to drive the Jaguar. The car was a powerful performer, and the thought of the stretch of the M1 up to the A52 turn-off was, to Lewis, most pleasurable. Nor had Morse made the slightest secret of the fact that the main object of the mission was to find out if a thoroughfare called 'Spring Street' still stood – as it had stood until 1976 – on the northern outskirts of Derby.

'Just humour me, Lewis – that's all I ask!'

Lewis had needed little persuasion. It had been a momentous 'plus' in his life when Morse had intimated to his superiors that it was above all with him, Sergeant Lewis, that his brain functioned most fluently; and now – moving the Jaguar across into the fast lane of the M1 at Weedon – Lewis felt wholly content with the way of life which had so happily presented itself to him those many years since. He knew, of course, that their present mission was a lost cause. But then Oxford was not unfamiliar with such things.

Spring Street proved difficult to locate, in spite of a city-map purchased from a corner-newsagent in the northern suburbs. Morse himself had become progressively tetchier as the pedestrians to whom Lewis wound down his window appeared either totally ignorant or mutually contradictory. Finally, however, the Jaguar homed in on an area, marked off by hoardings, announcing itself as the 'Derby Development Complex', with two enormously tall, yellow cranes tracing and retracing their sweeping arcs above the demolition squads below.

'Could be too late, could we?' ventured Lewis.

'It doesn't *matter* – I've *told* you, Lewis.' Morse wound down his own window and spoke to a brick-dusted, white-helmeted workman.

'Have you flattened Spring Street yet?'

'Won't be long, mate,' the man replied, pointing vaguely towards the next-but-one block of terraced houses.

Morse, somewhat irked by the 'mate' familiarity, wound up his window, without a 'thank you', and pointed, equally vaguely, to Lewis, the latter soon pulling the Jaguar in behind a builder's skip a couple of streets away. A young coloured woman pushing a utility pram assured Morse that, yes, this *was* Spring Street, and the two men got out of the car and looked around them.

Perhaps, in some earlier decades, the area had seen some better times; yet, judging from its present aspect it seemed questionable whether any of the houses in this unlovely place had ever figured in the 'desirable' category of residences. Built, by the look of them, in the early 1800s, many were now semi-derelict, and several boarded-up completely. Clearly a few remained tenanted, for here and there smoke rose up into the grey air from the narrow, yellow chimney-pots; and white-lace curtains still framed the windows yet unbroken. With distaste, Morse eyed the squashed beer-cans and discarded fish-and-chip wrappings that littered the narrow pavement. Then he walked slowly along, before stopping beside a front door painted in what fifty years earlier had been a Cambridge blue, and into which a number-plaque '20' was screwed. The house was in a terraced group of six; and walking further along, Morse came to the door of an abandoned property on which, judging from the outlines, the figures '16' had once been fixed. Here Morse stopped and beckoned to Lewis – the eyes of both now travelling to the two adjacent houses, boarded up against squatters or vandals. The first house must, without question, have once been Number 14 – and the second, Number 12.

The latter, the sorry-looking object of Morse's pilgrimage, stood on the corner, the sign 'Burton Road' still fastened to its side-wall, although no sign of Burton Road itself was any longer visible. Below the sign, a wooden gate, hanging forlornly from one of its rusted hinges, led to a small patch of back-yard, choked with litter and brownish weeds, and cluttered with a kiddy's ancient tricycle and a brand-new trolley from a supermarket. The dull-red bricks of the outer walls were flaking badly, and the single window-frame here had been completely torn away, leaving the inside of the mean little abode open to the elements. Morse poked his face through the empty frame, across the blackened sill, before turning away with a sickened disgust: in one corner of the erstwhile kitchen was what appeared to be a pile of excrement; and beside it, half a loaf of white bread, its slices curled and mildew-green.

'Not a pretty sight, is it?' whispered Lewis, standing at Morse's shoulder.

'She was brought up here,' said Morse quietly. 'She lived here with her mother . . . and her father . . .'

'. . . and her brother,' added Lewis.

Yes! Morse had forgotten the brother, Joanna's younger brother, the boy named after his father – forgotten him altogether.

Reluctantly Morse left the small back-yard, and slowly walked round to the front again, where he stood in the middle of the deserted street and looked at the little terrace-house in which Joanna Carrick-Donavan-Franks had probably spent – what? – the first twenty or so years of her life. The Colonel hadn't mentioned exactly where she was born, but . . . Morse thought back to the dates: born in 1821, and married to the great man in 1842. How reassuring it would have been to find a date marked on one of the houses! But Morse could see no sign of one. If the house had been built by the 1820s, had she spent those twenty years in and around that pokey little kitchen, competing for space with the sink and the copper and the mangle and the cooking-range and her parents . . .? And her younger brother? He, Morse, had his own vivid recollections of a similarly tiny kitchen in a house which (as he had been told) had been demolished to make way for a carpet-store. But he'd never been back. It was always a mistake to go back, because life went on perfectly well without you, thank you very much, and other people got along splendidly with their own jobs – even if they were confined to selling carpets. Yes, almost always a mistake: a mistake, for example, as it had been to go back to the hospital; a mistake as it would have been (as he'd intended) to go along to the Derby Royal and nonchalantly announce to Nessie that he just happened to be passing through the city, just wanted to congratulate her on becoming the Big White Chief . . .

Lewis had been talking whilst these and similar thoughts were crossing and recrossing Morse's mind, and he hadn't heard a word of what was said.

'Pardon, Lewis?'

'I just say that's what we used to do, that's all – over the top of the head, as I say, and put the date against it.'

Morse, unable to construe such manifest gobbledegook, nodded as if with full understanding, and led the way to the car. A large white-painted graffito caught his eye, sprayed along the lower wall of a house in the next terrace: HANDS OFF CHILE – although it was difficult to know who in this benighted locality was being exhorted to such activity – or, rather, inactivity. TRY GEO. LUMLEY'S TEA 1s 2d, seemed a more pertinent notice, painted over the bricked-up first-floor window of the next corner house, the lettering originally worked in a blue paint over a yellow-ochre background, the latter now a faded battleship-grey; a notice (so old was it) that Joanna might well have seen every day as she walked along this street to school, or play – a notice from the past which a demolition gang of hard-topped men would soon obliterate from the local-history records when they swung their giant skittle-balls and sent the side-wall crumbling in a shower of dust.

Just like the Oxford City Council Vandals when . . .

Forget it, Morse!

'Where to now, sir?'

It took a bit of saying, but he said it: 'Straight home, I think. Unless there's something else *you* want to see?'

CHAPTER THIRTY-NINE

And what you thought you came for
Is only a shell, a husk of meaning
From which the purpose breaks only when it is fulfilled
If at all. Either you had no purpose
Or the purpose is beyond the end you figured
And is altered in fulfilment

(T. S. Eliot, *Little Gidding*)

Morse seldom engaged in any conversation in a car, and he was predictably silent as Lewis drove the few miles out towards the motorway. In its wonted manner, too, his brain was meshed into its complex mechanisms, where he was increasingly conscious of that one little irritant. It had always bothered him not to know, not to have heard – even the smallest things.

'What was it you were saying back there?'

'You mean when you weren't listening?'

'Just *tell* me, Lewis!'

'It was just when we were children, that's all. We used to measure how tall we were getting. Mum always used to do it – every birthday – against the kitchen wall. I suppose that's what reminded me, really – looking in that kitchen. Not in the front room – that was the best wallpaper there; and, as I say, she used to put a ruler over the top of our heads, you know, and then put a line and a date . . .'

Again, Morse was not listening.

'Lewis! Turn round and go back!'

Lewis looked across at Morse with some puzzlement.

'I said just turn round,' continued Morse – quietly, for the moment. '*Gentle* as you like – when you get the *chance*, Lewis – no need to imperil the pedestrians or the local pets. But just *turn round*!'

Morse's finger on the kitchen switch produced only an empty 'click', in spite of what looked like a recent bulb in the fixture that hung, shadeless, from the disintegrating plaster-boards. The yellowish, and further yellowing, paper had been peeled away from several sections of the wall in irregular gashes, and in the damp top-corner above the sink it hung away in a great flap.

'Whereabouts did you use to measure things, Lewis?'

'About here, sir.' Lewis stood against the inner door of the kitchen, his back to the wall, where he placed his left palm horizontally across the top of his head, before turning round and assessing the point at which his fingertips had marked the height.

'Five-eleven, that is – unless I've shrunk a bit.'

The wallpaper at this point was grubby with a myriad finger-prints, appearing not to have been renovated for half a century or more; and around the non-functioning light-switch the plaster had been knocked out, exposing some of the bricks in the partition-wall. Morse tore a strip from the yellow paper, to reveal a surprisingly well-preserved, light-blue paper beneath. But marked memorials to Joanna, there were none; and the two men stood silent and still there, as the afternoon seemed to grow perceptibly colder and darker by the minute.

'It was a thought, though, wasn't it?' asked Morse.

'Good thought, sir!'

'Well, one thing's certain! We are *not* going to stand here all afternoon in the gathering gloom and strip all these walls of generations of wallpaper.'

'Wouldn't take all that long, would it?'

'What? All this bloody stuff—'

'We'd know where to look.'

'We would?'

'I mean, it's only a little house; and if we just looked along at some point, say, between four feet and five feet from the floor – downstairs only, I should think—'

'You're a genius – did you know that?'

'And you've got a good torch in the car.'

'No,' admitted Morse. 'I'm afraid—'

'Never mind, sir! We've got about half an hour before it gets too dark.'

It was twenty minutes to four when Lewis emitted a child-like squeak of excitement from the narrow hallway.

'Something here, sir! And I think, I *think*—'

'Careful! *Careful!*' muttered Morse, coming nervously alongside, a triumphant look now blazing in his blue-grey eyes.

Gradually the paper was pulled away as the last streaks of that December day filtered through the filthy skylight above the heads of Morse and Lewis, each of them looking occasionally at the other with wholly disproportionate excitement. For there, inscribed on the original plaster of the wall, below three layers of subsequent papering – and still clearly visible – were two sets of black-pencilled lines: the one to the right marking a series of eight calibrations, from about 3' 6" of the lowest one to about 5' of the top, with a full date shown for each; the one to the left with only two calibrations (though with four dates) – a diagonal of crumbled plaster quite definitely precluding further evidence below.

For several moments Morse stood there in the darkened hallway and gazed upon the wall as if upon some holy relic.

'Get a torch, Lewis! And a tape-measure!'

'Where—?'

'Anywhere. Everybody's got a torch, man.'

'Except you, sir!'

'Tell 'em you're from the Gas Board and there's a leak in Number 12.'

'The house isn't *on* gas.'

'Get *on* with it, Lewis!'

When Lewis returned, Morse was still considering his wall-marks – beaming as happily at the eight lines on the right as a pools-punter surveying a winning-line of score-draws on the Treble Chance; and, taking the torch, he played it joyously over the evidence. The new light (as it were) upon the situation quickly confirmed that any writing below the present extent of their findings was irredeemably lost; it also showed a letter in between the two sets of measurements, slightly towards the right, and therefore probably belonging with the second set.

The letter 'D'!

Daniel!

The lines on the right *must* mark the heights of Daniel Carrick; and, if that were so, then those to the left were those of *Joanna Franks*!

'Are you thinking what I'm thinking, Lewis?'

'I reckon so, sir.'

'Joanna married in 1841 or 1842' – Morse was talking to himself as much as to Lewis – 'and that fits well because the measurements end in 1841, finishing at the same height as she was in 1840. And her younger brother, Daniel, was gradually catching her up – about the same height in 1836, and quite a few inches taller in 1841.'

Lewis found himself agreeing. 'And you'd expect them that way round, sir, wouldn't you? Joanna first; and then her brother, to Joanna's right.'

'Ye-es.' Morse took the white tape-measure and let it roll out to the floor. 'Only five foot, this.'

'Don't think we're going to need a much longer one, sir.'

Lewis was right. As Morse held the 'nought-inches' end of the tape to the top of Joanna's putative measurements, Lewis shone the torch on the other end as he knelt on the dirty red tiles. No. A longer tape-measure was certainly not needed here, for the height measured only 4' 9", and as Lewis knew, the woman who had been pulled out of Duke's Cut had been 5' 3¾" – almost seven inches taller than Joanna had been after leaving Spring Street for her marriage! Was it possible – even wildly possible – that she had grown those seven inches between the ages of twenty-one and thirty-eight? He put his thoughts into words:

'I don't think, sir, that a woman could have – '

'No, Lewis – nor do I! If not impossible, at the very least unprecedented, surely.'

'So you were right, sir . . .'

'Beyond any reasonable doubt? Yes, I think so.'

'Beyond *all* doubt?' asked Lewis quietly.

'There'll always be that one per cent of doubt about most things, I suppose.'

'You'd be happier, though, if—'

Morse nodded: 'If we'd found just that *one* little thing extra, yes. Like a "J" on the wall here or . . . I don't know.'

'There's nothing else to find, then, sir?'

'No, I'm sure there isn't,' said Morse, but only after hesitating for just a little while.

CHAPTER FORTY

The world is round and the place which may seem like
the end may also be only the beginning
(Ivy Baker Priest, *Parade*)

It sounded an anti-climactic question: 'What do we do now,
sir?'

Morse didn't know, and his mind was far away: 'It was done a
long time ago, Lewis, and done ill,' he said slowly.

Which was doubtless a true sentiment, but it hardly answered
the question. And Lewis pressed his point – with the result that
together they sought out the site-foreman, to whom, producing
his warranty-card, Morse dictated his wishes, making the whole
thing sound as if the awesome authority of MI5 and MI6 alike lay
behind his instructions regarding the property situated at Number
12 Spring Street, especially for a series of photographs to be taken
as soon as possible of the pencil-marks on the wall in the entrance
hall. And yes, the site-foreman thought he could see to it all
without too much trouble; in fact, he was a bit of a dab hand with
a camera himself, as he not so modestly admitted. Then, after
Lewis had returned torch and tape-measure to a slightly puzzled-
looking householder, the afternoon events were over.

It was five minutes to six when Lewis finally tried once again to
drive away from the environs of Derby (North) and to make for
the A52 junction with the M1 (South). At 6 p.m., Morse leaned
forward and turned on the car-radio for the news. One way or
another it had been a bad year, beset with disease, hunger, air
crashes, railway accidents, an oil-rig explosion, and sundry earth-
quakes. But no cosmic disaster had been reported since the earlier
one o'clock bulletin, and Morse switched off – suddenly aware of
the time.

'Do you realize it's gone opening time, Lewis?'

'No such thing these days, sir.'

'You know what I mean!'

'Bit early—'

'We've got something to celebrate, Lewis! Pull in at the next
pub, and I'll buy you a pint.'

'You *will*?'

Morse was not renowned for his generosity in treating his
subordinates – or his superiors – and Lewis smiled to himself as

he surveyed the streets, looking for a pub-sign; it was an activity with which he was not unfamiliar. 'I'm driving, sir.'

'Quite right, Lewis. We don't want any trouble with the police.'

As he sat sipping his St Clements and listening to Morse conducting a lengthy conversation with the landlord about the wickedness of the lager-brewers, Lewis felt inexplicably content. It had been a good day; and Morse, after draining his third pint with his wonted rapidity, was apparently ready to depart.

'Gents?' asked Morse.

The landlord pointed the way.

'Is there a public telephone I could use?'

'Just outside the Gents.'

Lewis thought he could hear Morse talking over the phone – something to do with a hospital; but he was never a man to eavesdrop on the private business of others, and he walked outside and stood waiting by the car until Morse re-appeared.

'Lewis – I, er – I'd like you just to call round quickly to the hospital, if you will. The Derby Royal. Not too far out of our way, they tell me.'

'Bit of stomach trouble again, sir?'

'No.'

'I don't think you should have had all that beer, though—'

'Are you going to drive me there or not, Lewis?'

Morse, as Lewis knew, was becoming increasingly reluctant to walk even a hundred yards or so if he could ride the distance, and he now insisted that Lewis park the Jaguar in the AMBULANCES ONLY area just outside the Hospital's main entrance.

'How long will you be, sir?'

'How long? Not sure, Lewis. It's my lucky day, though, isn't it? So I may be a little while.'

It was half an hour later that Morse emerged to find Lewis chatting happily to one of the ambulance-men about the road-holding qualities of the Jaguar family.

'All right, then, sir?'

'Er – well. Er . . . Look, Lewis! I've decided to stay in Derby overnight.'

Lewis's eyebrows rose.

'Yes! I think – I think I'd like to be there when they take those photographs – you know, in, er . . .'

'*I* can't stay, sir! I'm on duty tomorrow morning.'

'I know. I'm not asking you to, am I? I'll get the train back – no problem – Derby, Birmingham, Banbury – easy!'

'You *sure*, sir?'

'*Quite* sure. You don't *mind* do you, Lewis?'

Lewis shook his head. 'Well, I suppose, I'd better—'

'Yes, you get off. And don't drive too fast!'

'Can I take you – to a hotel or something?'

'No need to bother, I'll – I'll find something.'

'You look as though you've already found something, sir.'

'Do I?'

As the Jaguar accelerated along the approach road to the M1 (South) Lewis was still smiling quietly to himself, recalling the happy look on Morse's face as he had turned and walked once more towards the automatic doors.

EPILOGUE

The name of a man is a numbing blow from which he
   never recovers
                        (Marshall McLuhan, *Understanding Media*)

On the morning of Friday, 11th January (he had resumed duties on New Year's Day), Morse caught the early Cathedrals' Express to Paddington. He was programmed to speak on Inner City Crime at 11 a.m. at the Hendon Symposium. Tube to King's Cross, then out on the Northern Line. Easy. Plenty of time. He enjoyed trains, in any case; and when Radio Oxford had announced black ice on the M40, his decision was made for him; it would mean, too, of course, that he could possibly indulge a little more freely with any refreshments that might be available.

He bought *The Times* and the *Oxford Times* at the bookstall, got a seat at the rear of the train, and had solved *The Times* crossword by Didcot. Except for one clue. A quick look in his faithful *Chambers* would have settled the issue immediately; but he hadn't got it, and as ever he was vexed by his inability to put the finishing touch to anything. He quickly wrote in a couple of bogus letters (in case any of his fellow-passengers were waiting to be impressed) and then read the letters and the obituaries. At Reading he turned to the *Oxford Times* crossword. The setter was 'Quixote'; and Morse smiled to himself as he remembered 'Waggie' Greenaway finally solving the same setter's 'Bradman's famous duck (6)' and writing in DONALD at 1 across. Nothing *quite* so amusing here – but a very nice puzzle. Twelve minutes to complete. Not bad!

Morse caught a subliminal glimpse of 'Maidenhead' as the train sped through, and he took a sheaf of papers from his briefcase, first looking through the alphabetical list of those who would be attending the conference. Nobody he knew in the A–D range, but then he scanned the E–F:

> Eagleston
> Ellis
> Emmett
> Erskine
> Farmer
> Favant
> Fielding

Tom Eagleston, yes; and Jack Farmer, yes; and . . .

Morse stopped, and looked again at the middle of the three delegates in the Fs. The name was vaguely familiar, wasn't it? Yet he couldn't remember where . . . Unusual name, though. Morse's eye continued down the list – and then he remembered. Yes! It was the name of the man who had been walking along the Oxford Canal at the time when Joanna Franks was murdered – when Joanna Franks was *supposedly* murdered; the man, perhaps, who had been traced to the Nag's Head where he'd signed the register. A mystery man. Maybe not his real name at all, for the canal had been full of men who used an alias. In fact, as Morse recollected, two of the crew of the *Barbara Bray* itself had done so: Alfred Musson, alias Alfred Brotherton; Walter Towns, alias Walter Thorold. It might well be of some deep psychological significance that criminals sometimes seemed most unwilling to give up their names, even if this involved a greater risk of future identification: Morse had known it quite often. It was as if a man's name were almost an intrinsic part of him; as if he could never shed it *completely*; as if it were as much part of his personality as his skin. Musson had kept his Christian name, hadn't he? So had Towns.

Morse spent the rest of the journey looking idly out of the window, his brain tidying up a few scattered thoughts as the train drew into Paddington: Donald Bradman – Don Bradman, the name by which everyone recognized the greatest batsman ever born; and F. T. Donavan, the greatest man in all the world; and . . .

Ye Gods!!

The blood was running cold through Morse's limbs as he remembered the man who had identified the body of Joanna Franks; the man who had been physically incapable (as it seemed!) of raising his eyes to look into the faces of the prisoners; the man who had held his hands to his own face as he wept and turned his back on the men arraigned before the court. Why did he do these things, Morse? Because *the boatmen might just have recognized him*. For they had seen him, albeit fleetingly, in the dawn, as 'he had made to get further on his way with all speed'. Donald Favant! – or Don Favant, as he would certainly have seen himself.

Morse wrote out those letters D-O-N-F-A-V-A-N-T along the bottom margin of the *Oxford Times*; and then, below them, the name of which they were the staggering anagram: the name of F T DONAVAN – the greatest man in all the world.

The Jewel
That Was Ours

For my wife, Dorothy

Espied the god with gloomy soul
  The prize that in the casket lay,
Who came with silent tread and stole
  The jewel that was ours away.

(*Lilian Cooper*, 1904–1981)

ACKNOWLEDGEMENTS

The author and publishers wish to thank the following who have kindly given permission for use of copyright materials:

Extract from *Oxford* by Jan Morris published by Oxford University Press 1987, reprinted by permission of Oxford University Press;

Extract from the introduction by Lord Jenkins of Hillhead to *The Oxford Story*, published by Heritage Projects (Management) Ltd, reprinted by permission of the Peters Fraser & Dunlop Group Ltd;

Extract from *Lanterns and Lances*, published by Harper & Row and by Hamish Hamilton in the United Kingdom and Commonwealth, copyright © 1961 James Thurber. Copyright © 1989 Rosemary A. Thurber;

Julian Symons for the extract from *Bloody Murder*;

Marilyn Yurdan for the extract from *Oxford: Town & Gown*;

Basil Swift for the extracts from *Collected Haiku*;

Martin Amis for the extract from *Other People*, published by Jonathan Cape;

Max Beerbohm for the extract from *Mainly on the Air*, published by William Heinemann Ltd;

A. P. Watt Ltd on behalf of Crystal Hale and Jocelyn Herbert for the extract from 'Derby Day', *Comic Opera*, by A. P. Herbert;

Extract from *Aspects of Wagner* by Bryan Magee, reprinted by permission of the Peters Fraser & Dunlop Group Ltd;

The Estate of Virginia Woolf for the extract from *Mrs Dalloway*, published by The Hogarth Press.

Every effort has been made to trace all the copyright holders but if any has been inadvertently overlooked, the author and publishers will be pleased to make the necessary arrangement at the first opportunity.

This novel is based in part on an original storyline written by Colin Dexter for Central Television's *Inspector Morse* series.

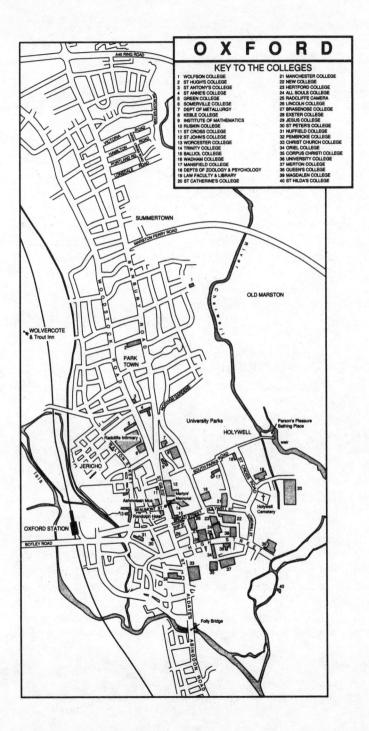

PART ONE

CHAPTER ONE

It is not impossible to become bored in the presence of
a mistress

(Stendhal)

The red-seal *Brut Imperial Moët & Chandon* stood empty on the top
of the bedside table to her left; empty like the champagne glass
next to it, and like the champagne glass on the table at the other
side of the bed. Everything seemed empty. Beside her, supine and
still, hands behind his head, lay a lean, light-boned man in his
early forties, a few years older than herself. His eyes were closed,
and remained closed as she folded back her own side of the floral-
patterned duvet, rose quickly, put her feet into fur-lined slippers,
drew a pink silk dressing-gown around a figure in which breasts,
stomach, thighs, were all a little over-ripe perhaps – and stepped
over to peer through the closed curtains.

Had she consulted her Oxford University Pocket Diary, she
would have noticed that the sun was due to set at 16.50 that early
Wednesday evening in late October. The hour had gone back the
previous weekend, and the nights, as they said, were pulling in
fast. She had always found difficulty with the goings back and
forth of the clock – until she had heard that simple little jingle on
Radio Oxford: Spring Forward/Fall Back. That had pleased her.
But already darkness had fallen outside, well before its time; and
the rain still battered and rattled against the window-panes. The
tarmac below was a glistening black, with a pool of orange light
reflected from the street lamp opposite.

When she was in her junior school, the class had been asked
one afternoon to paint a scene on the Thames, and all the boys
and girls had painted the river blue. Except her. And that was
when the teacher had stopped the lesson (in midstream, as it
were) and asserted that young Sheila was the only one of them
who had the natural eye of an artist. Why? Because the Thames
might well be grey or white or brown or green or yellow –
anything, in fact, except those little rectangles of Oxford blue and

Cambridge blue and cobalt and ultramarine into which all the wetted brushes were dipping. So, would all of them please start again, and try to paint the colours they saw, and forget the postcards, forget the atlases? All of them, that is, except Sheila; for Sheila had painted the water black.

And below her now the street was glistening black . . .

Yes.

Everything seemed black.

Sheila hugged the thin dressing-gown around her and knew that he was awake; watching her; thinking of his wife, probably – or of some other woman. Why didn't she just tell him to get out of her bed and out of her life? Was the truth that she needed him more than he needed her? It had not always been so.

It was so very hard to say, but she said it: 'We were happy together till recently, weren't we?'

'What?' The tongue tapped the teeth sharply at the final 't'.

She turned now to look at him lying there, the moustache linking with the neatly trimmed Vandyke beard in a darkling circle around his mouth – a mouth she sometimes saw as too small, and too prim, and, yes, too bloody *conceited*!

'I must go!' Abruptly he sat up, swung his legs to the floor, and reached for his shirt.

'We can see each other tomorrow?' she asked softly.

'Difficult not to, won't it?' He spoke with the clipped precision of an antique pedagogue, each of the five 't's articulated with pedantic completion. With an occasional lisp, too.

'I meant – afterwards.'

'Afterwards? Impossible! Impothible! Tomorrow evening we must give our full attention to our American clients, must we not? *Motht* important occasion, as you know. Lucky if we all get away before ten, wouldn't you say? And then—'

'And then you must go home, of course.'

'Of course! And you know perfectly well *why* I must go home. Whatever your faults, you're not a fool!'

Sheila nodded bleakly. 'You could come here before we start.'

'No!'

'Wouldn't do much harm to have a drink, would it? Fortify ourselves for—'

'No!'

'I see.'

'And it's healthy for the liver and kindred organs to leave the stuff alone for a while, uh? Couple of days a week? Could you manage that, Sheila?'

He had dressed quickly, his slim fingers now fixing the maroon bow-tie into its usual decadent droop. For her part, she had nothing further to say; nothing she could say. She turned once again towards the window, soon to feel his hand on the back of her shoulders as he planted a perfunctory kiss at the nape of her neck. Then the door downstairs slammed. Miserably she watched the top of the black umbrella as it moved along the road. Then she turned off the bedside lamp, picked up the champagne bottle, and made her way down the stairs.

She needed a drink.

Dr Theodore Kemp strode along swiftly through the heavy rain towards his own house, only a few minutes' walk away. He had already decided that there would be little, if any, furtherance of his affair with the readily devourable divorcée he had just left. She was becoming a liability. He realized it might well have been his fault that she now seemed to require a double gin before starting her daily duties; that she took him so very seriously; that she was demanding more and more of his time; that she was prepared to take ever greater risks about their meetings. Well, *he* wasn't. He would miss the voluptuous lady, naturally; but she *was* getting a little too well-padded in some of the wrong places.

Double chin . . . double gin . . .

He'd been looking for some semblance of love – with none of the problems of commitment; and with Sheila Williams he had thought for a few months that he had found it. But it was not to be: *he*, Theodore Kemp, had decided that! And there *were* other women – and one especially, her tail flicking sinuously in the goldfish bowl.

Passing through the communal door to the flats on Water Eaton Road, whither (following the accident) he and Marion had moved two years earlier, he shook the drenched umbrella out behind him, then wiped his sodden shoes meticulously on the doormat. Had he ruined them, he wondered?

CHAPTER TWO

For the better cure of vice they think it necessary to
study it, and the only efficient study is through practice
(Samuel Butler)

Much later that same evening, with iron grids now being slotted
in from bar-top to ceiling, John Ashenden sat alone in the
University Arms Hotel at Cambridge and considered the morrow.
The weather forecast was decidedly brighter, with no repetition of
the deluge which earlier that day had set the whole of southern
and eastern England awash (including, as we have seen, the city
of Oxford).

'Anything else before we close, sir?'

Ashenden usually drank cask-conditioned beer. But he knew
that the quickest way to view the world in a rosier light was to
drink whisky; and he now ordered another large Glenfiddich,
asking that this further Touch of the Malt be added to the account
of the Historic Cities of England Tour.

It would help all round if the weather were set fairer; certainly
help in mitigating the moans amongst his present group of
Americans:

- too little sunshine
- too much food
- too much litter
- too early reveilles
- too much walking around (especially that!)

Not that they were a particularly complaining lot (except for that
one woman, of course). In fact, by Ashenden's reckoning, they
rated a degree or two above average. Twenty-seven of them.
Almost all from the West Coast, predominantly from California;
mostly in the 65–75 age-bracket; rich, virtually without exception;
and fairly typical of the *abcde* brigade – alcohol, bridge, cigarettes,
detective-fiction, ecology. In the first days of the tour he had
hoped that 'culture' might compete for the 'c' spot, since after
joining the ranks of non-smokers he was becoming sickened at
seeing some of them lighting up between courses at mealtimes.
But it was not to be.

The downpour over Cambridge that day had forced the cancellation of trips to Grantchester and the American War Cemetery at
Madingley; and the change of programme had proved deeply

unpopular – especially with the ladies. Yes, and with Ashenden himself, too. He had duly elected himself their temporary cicerone, pointing neck-achingly to the glories of the late-Gothic fan-vaulting in King's; and then, already weary-footed, shuffling round the Fitzwilliam Museum to seek out a few of the ever-popular Pre-Raphaelite paintings.

'They have a far better collection in the Ashmolean, Mr Ashenden. Or so I've *read*. William Holman Hunt, and – and Mill-*ais*.'

'You'll be able to judge for yourself tomorrow, won't you?' Ashenden had replied lightly, suspecting that the doom-laden lady had forgotten (never known, perhaps) the Christian names of a painter she'd pronounced to rhyme with 'delay'.

It had irked Ashenden that the Cambridge coach company would have to be paid in full for the non-outings that day. It had irked him even more that he had been obliged to forgo the whole of the afternoon in order to enlighten and entertain his ageing charges. He was (he knew it) a reasonably competent courier and guide. Yet in recent years he had found himself unable to cope properly without a few regular breaks from his round-the-clock responsibilities; and it had become his policy to keep his afternoons completely free whenever possible, though he had never fully explained the reasons for this to anyone . . .

In November 1974 he had gone to Cambridge to take the entrance examination in Modern Languages. His A-level results had engendered not unreasonable optimism in his comprehensive school, and he had stayed on for a seventh term to try his luck. His father, as young John knew, would have been the proudest man in the county had his son succeeded in persuading the examiners of his linguistic competence. But the son had not succeeded, and the letter had dropped on to the doormat on Christmas Eve:

From the Senior Tutor, Christ's College, Cambridge

Dear Mr Ashenden,   21.12.74

After giving full and sympathetic consideration to your application, we regret that we are unable to offer you a place at this college. We can understand the disappointment you will feel, but you are no doubt aware how fiercely competition for places

There had been a huge plus from that brief time in Cambridge, though. He had stayed for two nights, in the Second Court at Christ's, in the same set of rooms as a fellow examinee from Trowbridge: a lanky, extraordinarily widely read lad, who apart from seeking a scholarship in Classics was anxious to convert the University (or was it the Universe?) to the self-evident truths of his own brand of neo-Marxism. John had understood very little of it all, really; but he had become aware, suddenly, of a world of scholarship, intelligence, imaginative enthusiasm, sensitivity – above all of sensitivity – that he had never known before in his comprehensive school at Leicester.

On their last afternoon together, Jimmy Bowden, the Trotskyite from Trowbridge, had taken him to see a double-bill from the golden age of the French cinema, and that afternoon he fell in love with a sultry, husky-voiced whore as she crossed her silk-clad legs and sipped her absinthe in some seedy bistro. It was all something to do with 'the synthesis of style and sexuality', as Jimmy had sought to explain, talking into the early hours . . . and then rising at six the following morning to stand outside Marks & Spencer to try to sell the *Socialist Worker*.

A few days after being notified of his own rejection, Ashenden had received a postcard from Jimmy – a black and white photograph of Marx's tomb in Highgate Cemetery:

The idiots have given me a major schol – in spite of that Greek prose of mine! Trust you've had your own good news. I enjoyed meeting you and look forward to our first term together – Jimmy.

He had never replied to Jimmy. And it was only by chance, seven years later, that during one of his Oxford tours he'd met a man who had known Jimmy Bowden . . .

After gaining his pre-ordained First in both parts of the Classical Tripos, Jimmy had been awarded a Junior Research Fellowship at Oxford to study early Etruscan epigraphy; and then, three years later, he had died of Hodgkin's disease. He had been an orphan (as events revealed) and been buried in Oxford's Holywell Cemetery, amongst many dead, but once pre-eminent, dons – only some twenty feet or so, as Ashenden learned, from the grave of Walter Pater. Yet though Jimmy had died, some small part of his legacy lived on – for John Ashenden had for many years subscribed to several specialist film magazines, printed in the UK and on the Continent, for cinema buffs such as he himself had soon become.

Exactly where and when the degeneration had set in (if, indeed, 'degeneration' it were) John Ashenden could not be all that sure.

Born in 1956, John had not grown up amidst the sexually repressive mores of his own father's generation. And once he started to work (immediately after school), started to travel, he had experienced little sense of guilt in satisfying his sexual curiosities by occasional visits to sauna clubs, sex cinemas, or explicit stage shows. But gradually such experiences began to nourish rather than to satisfy his needs; and he was becoming an inveterate voyeur. Quite often, at earlier times, he had been informed by his more experienced colleagues in the travel business (themselves totally immune, it appeared, from any corrupting influences) that the trouble with pornography was its being so *boring*. But *was* it?

From his first introduction, the squalid nature of his incipient vice had been borne upon him – groping his way like a blind man down a darkened aisle of a sleazy cinema, the Cockney voice still sounding in his ears: 'It's the real fing 'ere, sir, innit? No messin' about – nuffin like that – just straight inta fings!' And it disturbed him that he could find himself so excited by such crude scenes of fornication. But he fortified his self-esteem with the fact that almost all the cinemas he attended were fairly full, probably of people just as well adjusted as himself. Very soon, too, he began to understand something of that 'synthesis' that Jimmy had tried to explain to him – the synthesis of style and sexuality. For there *were* people who understood such things, with meetings held in private dwellings, the High Priest intoning the glorious Introit: 'Is everybody known?' That Ashenden had been forced to miss such a meeting of initiates that afternoon in Cambridge had been disappointing. Very disappointing, indeed.

But the next stop was Oxford . . .

CHAPTER THREE

'O come along, Mole, do!' replied the Rat cheerfully, still plodding along.

'*Please* stop, Ratty!' pleaded the poor Mole, in anguish of heart. 'You don't understand! It's my home, my old home! I've just come across the smell of it, and it's close by here, really quite close. And I *must* go to it'
(Kenneth Grahame, *The Wind in the Willows*)

'Arksford? This is *Arksford*?'

Seated on the nearside front seat of the luxury coach, John Ashenden glanced across at the diminutive septuagenarian from California: 'Yes, Mrs Roscoe, this is Oxford.' He spoke rather wearily, yet wholly without resentment. Hitherto little on the Historic Cities of England Tour (London–Cambridge–Oxford–Stratford–Bath–Winchester) had appeared unequivocally satisfactory to the well-read, eager, humourless (insufferable!) Mrs Roscoe; and yet as he looked out of his own side-window Ashenden could sympathize with that lady's disappointment. The eastern stretch of the A40 could hardly afford the most pleasing approach to the old University City; and as the coach slowly moved, one car-length at a time, towards the Headington roundabout, a litter-strewn patch of ill-kempt grass beside a gaudily striped petrol station lent little enchantment to the scene.

The tour party – eighteen women, nine men (three registered husband-and-wife combinations) – sat back in their seats as the coach drove past the sign for 'City Centre' and accelerated for a few miles along the featureless northern section of the Ring Road, heading for the Banbury Road roundabout.

For some reason Mrs Laura Stratton was ill-at-ease. She recrossed her legs and now massaged her left foot with her right hand. As agreed, it would be Eddie who would sign the forms and the Visitors' Book, and then identify the luggage and tip the porter – while she would be lying in a hot herbal bath and resting her weary body, her weary *feet* . . .

'Gee, I feel so *awful*, Ed!'

'*Relax*, honey. Everything's gonna be OK.' But his voice was so quiet that even Laura had difficulty in picking up his words. At sixty-six, four years younger than his wife, Eddie Stratton laid his hand briefly on the nylon-clad left foot, the joints of the toes disfigured by years of cruel arthritis, the toe-nails still painted a brightly defiant crimson.

'I'll be fine, Ed – just once I get in that bairth.' Again Laura switched legs and massaged her other foot again – a foot which like its partner had recently commanded the careful ministrations of the most expensive chiropodist in Pasadena.

'Yeah!' And perhaps someone else on the coach apart from his wife might have noticed Eddie Stratton's faint smile as he nodded his agreement.

The coach had now turned down into the Banbury Road, and Ashenden was soon into his well-rehearsed commentary: '. . . and note on each side of the road the cheerful orange-brick houses, built in the last two decades of the nineteenth-century when the dons in the University – there, look! – see the date? – 1887 . . .'

Immediately behind Ashenden sat a man in his early seventies, a retired civil engineer from Los Angeles, who now looked out of his window at the string of shops and offices in Summertown: banks, building societies, fruiterers, hairdressers, housing agents, newsagents, wine shops – it could almost have been back home, really. But then it *was* back home, decided Howard Brown.

Beside him, Shirley Brown was the second wife who had seen a smile upon a husband's lips – a smile this time of wistful satisfaction; and suddenly she felt a sharp regret.

'Howard?' she whispered. 'Howard! I *am* glad – you know I am – glad we booked the tour. *Really* I am!' She laid her right arm along his long thigh and squeezed it gently. 'And I'm sorry I was such' (*pianissimo*) 'such an ungrateful bitch last night.'

'Forget it, Shirl – forget it!'

But Howard Brown found himself wishing that for a little while at least his wife would perpetuate her sullen ill-humour. In such a mood (not infrequent) she presented him with the leeway he needed for the (not infrequent) infidelities of thought and deed which he could never have entertained had she exhibited a quarter of the affection he had known when they'd agreed to marry. But that was in 1947 – forty-three years ago – before she'd ever dreamed of checking his automobile mileage, or scrutinizing the postmarks on his private mail, or sniffing suspiciously at him after his coming home from the office . . .

'. . . and here' (Ashenden was in full and rather splendid spate) 'we see the Ruskin influence on domestic architecture during that period. You see – there! – on the left, look! – the neo-Gothic, mock-Venetian features . . . And here, on the left again, this is Norham Gardens, with the famous University Parks lying immediately behind. There! You see the iron gates? The Parks are one of the greatest open spaces in Oxford – still, even now, liable to be

closed to the public at the whim of the University authorities –
unless, of course, you get to know how to sneak in without being
noticed by the keepers at the main entrance.'

'And to sneak *out* again, surely, Mr Ashenden?'

For once, one of Mrs Roscoe's inevitable interruptions was both
pertinent and good-humoured, and her fellow passengers laughed
their light-hearted approval.

Howard Brown, however, had been quite unaware of the
exchange. He was craning his neck to look across at the Keeper's
Lodge; and as he did so, like Mole, he sensed and smelled his old
home territory, and inside him something long dormant woke into
sudden life. He felt his eyes welling up with nostalgic tears, before
fiercely blowing his nose and looking obliquely at his wife once
more, gratified to observe that her lips had once again settled into
their accustomed crab-crumpet discontent. She suspected nothing,
he was virtually certain of that.

As the coach drew into St Giles', the sky was an open blue, and
the sunlight gleamed on the cinnamon-coloured stone along the
broad tree-lined avenue. 'Here we are, in St Giles'.' (Ashenden
slipped into over-drive now.) 'You can see the plane trees on
either side of us, ablaze with the beautifully golden tints of autumn
– and, on the left here, St John's College – and Balliol just beyond.
And here in front of us, the famous Martyrs' Memorial, modelled
on the Eleanor Crosses of Edward the First, and designed by
Gilbert Scott to honour the great Protestant martyrs – Cranmer
and Latimer and, er . . .'

'Nicholas Ridley,' supplied Mrs Roscoe, as the coach turned
right at the traffic lights and almost immediately pulled in on the
left of Beaumont Street beneath the tall neo-Gothic façade of The
Randolph Hotel.

'At last!' cried Laura Stratton, with what might have been the
relief of a prisoner learning of a late reprieve.

In retrospect, it would have seemed an odd coincidence (though
not an important one) that the middle-aged man housed in a
nondescript block of flats at the top of the Banbury Road had been
looking out from his second-floor double-glazed windows as the
long luxury coach carrying Ashenden's group had passed by that
late afternoon. Inside, a recently renewed needle glided through
the well-worn grooves of the Furtwängler recording of *Götterdämm-
erung*; but the man's mind was more closely concentrated with an
almost physical hurt on the greasy wrappings discarded by the

previous night's fish-and-chip brigade as they'd walked homeward from the Chicken Barbecue in Summertown.

CHAPTER FOUR

'The cockroach *Blattella germanica*,' it was observed darkly in 1926, 'was at one time recorded as present in the Randolph Hotel kitchen'

(Jan Morris, *Oxford*)

Roy, concierge of the five-star Randolph Hotel, a cheerful florid-faced man of sixty, had been on duty since midday, and had, as always, been fully apprised by the Reception Manager of the scheduled afternoon arrivals – especially, of course, of the biggish bus-load of American tourists at 4.30 p.m. Roy, who had started with the hotel as a page-boy in 1945 – forty-five years since – quite liked the Americans. Not that he'd ever wished to fly over there for a holiday or anything drastic like that; but they *were* a nice lot, usually, the Yanks; friendly, communicative, generous. And although an incorrigibly biased patriot himself, he had recently begun to query the automatic superiority of his own countrymen, particularly that night the previous month when he'd returned on a Euro-Ferry after an abortive 0–0 draw between England and Holland.

It was five minutes before schedule that from his cubby-hole immediately inside the main entrance he saw the patrician coach pull slowly in beside the white canopy, flanked by a pair of elegant lamp-posts, at the front of Oxford's premier hotel. And a few seconds later he was standing at the top of the steps outside, in his yellow-piped blue uniform, beaming semi-beatifically, and ready to greet the new arrivals with an appropriate degree of that 'warmth' attested to on several separate pages of the hotel's Technicolor brochure. As he stood there, the flags – Union Jack, EEC, USA – fluttered lightly above him in the afternoon breeze. He enjoyed his work – always had; in fact seldom referred to it as 'work' at all. Seldom, too, did anything much go wrong in an establishment so happily and so predictably well-ordered as The Randolph. Seldom indeed.

But once in a while?

Yes, once in a while.

*

Phil Aldrich, a small, mournful-visaged dolichocephalic senior citizen (from California, too) moved from his habitual and lonely seat on the back row of the coach and came to sit next to Mrs Roscoe; his hearing was not quite what it had been and he wanted to know what was going on. The Deputy Manager had appeared on the coach itself to welcome them all and to announce that tea – or coffee, if preferred – was immediately available in the St John's Suite on the first floor; that all bedrooms were now ready for occupancy and that every hotel facility from telephone to trouser-press was at his guests' disposal forthwith; that even as he spoke their baggage was being unloaded, counted, checked, and por-tered to the appropriate rooms. It would save a good deal of time, the Deputy Manager concluded, if everyone would fill in now, on the coach, the Guest Registration Cards.

With appreciative nods observable on each side of the gangway, Ashenden duly distributed the Welcome Trusthouse Forte forms, already completed for the sections dealing with Company, Next Destination, Settlement of Account, Arrival, Departure, and Nationality. Only remaining for the tourists to fill in were the four sections headed Home Address, Telephone, Passport Number, and Signature.

Phil expressed an unqualified approval: 'Gee! That's what I'd say was pretty darned efficient, Janet.'

For once Mrs Roscoe was unable to identify any obvious flaw in the procedures, and, instead, appeared to concentrate her thoughts upon the perils of the unpredictable future.

'I do hope the people here realize the great difference between vegetarian and vegan—'

'Janet! This is one of the finest hotels in the UK—'

But Ashenden's voice now cut across their conversation:

'So! If we can all . . . St John's Suite, St John's – that's on the first floor, just up the main staircase – tea or coffee – right away. I know some of you will just want to settle in and have a wash and . . . So if you take your forms to Reception – that's straight ahead of you as you go through the main doors here – and just sign the documentation forms there and get your keys . . . The lift, the guest-lift, is just to your right, in the corridor . . .'

'Get a *move* on!' hissed Laura under her breath.

'. . . I shall be calling round to your rooms later, just to make sure everything's . . .'

Ashenden knew what he was doing. Experience had taught him that the first hour or so in any new hotel was always the most vital, since some small problem, dealt with promptly, could make the difference between a contented life and an anxious existence. Blessedly, Ashenden was seldom, if ever, confronted with such positive complaints as cockroaches, mice, or the disgusting habits of a room's previous occupants. But a range of minor niggles was not unfamiliar, even in the best regulated of establishments: no soap in the bathroom; only two tubs of cream beside the self-service kettle; no instructions on how to operate the knobless TV; no sign – *still* no sign – of the luggage . . .

Eddie Stratton had managed to squeeze into second spot in the queue for keys, and Laura had grabbed their own key, 310, from his hand before he'd finished the documentation.

'I'm straight up, Ed, to draw me a bairth – I can't wait.'

'Yeah, but leave the door, honey – there's only the one key, OK? I'll have a cup of tea in the Saynt Jarn Suite.'

'Sure. I'll leave the door.'

She was gone.

As Laura hobbled away towards the guest-lift, Eddie turned round and looked directly into the eyes of Mrs Shirley Brown. For a few seconds, there seemed to be no communication between the two of them; but then, after glancing briefly towards her husband, Shirley Brown nodded, almost imperceptibly, and her eyes smiled.

CHAPTER FIVE

All saints can do miracles, but few can keep a hotel
(Mark Twain, *Notebook*)

'*At last!*' muttered Laura Stratton for the third (and final) time as she inserted her key and turned it clockwise (and correctly) in the lock.

The room itself did not open immediately off the main corridor on level three; but a small plaque fixed beside double swing-doors (a FIRE EXIT sign above them) had pointed the way to Room 310. Once through these doors Laura had found herself in a further corridor, only four or five feet wide, which ran parallel to the main corridor, along which (after she had turned left) she walked the five yards or so to the bedroom door – on her right. Just beyond this door, the corridor turned at right angles and came to an almost immediate stop in the shape of another double-doored FIRE EXIT – doubtless, as Laura guessed (again correctly), leading down some back stairs to the ground floor. It did not occur to her that a person could stand in this narrow square of space, pressed tightly back behind the wall, and remain completely unobserved from the narrow corridor leading to her room.

If anyone wished to remain thus unobserved . . .

Laura extracted the key and carefully let the door close, or almost close, behind her, with the tongue of the lock holding it slightly ajar. The two large black-leather cases were on the floor immediately inside, and she looked around to find herself in a most pleasantly appointed room. A double bed stood immediately to her right, covered by a pale-green quilt, with a free-standing wardrobe beyond it; facing her were the three lancet windows of the outside wall, with curtains down to the carpeted floor; and in front of these windows, from right to left, a tea-maker, a TV, a low, mirrored dressing-table, and a red-plush chair. Her swift glance around missed little, except for the rather fine reproduction of Vermeer's *View of Delft* above the bed. Laura and her first husband had once seen the original of this in the Mauritshuis in The Hague, when the guide had mentioned that it was Marcel Proust's favourite painting; but strangely enough she had found it disappointing, and in the very few minutes of life remaining to her she was to have no opportunity of revising that rather harsh judgement.

She stepped to the window and looked across at the tetrastyle portico of Ionic columns, with the figure of Apollo, right arm raised and seated (a little precariously, as Laura judged) at the apex of the low-pitched pediment. Between the two central columns, a large Oxford-blue banner was suspended: *Musaeum Ashmoleanum apud Oxonienses*. Oh yes, Laura knew quite a lot about the Ashmolean Museum, and there appeared the flicker of a smile around her excessively lipsticked mouth as she let the curtain fall back and turned to the door on her left, half-open, which led to the champagne-tiled bathroom. Without for the moment entering, she pushed the door a little further open: WC to the right; bath immediately facing her, the shower-curtains half drawn across; and to the left a hand-basin with a series of heated rails beside it, fully laden with fluffy white towels.

Laura had always slept on the left-hand side of any double bed, both as a young girl with her sister and then with both her husbands; and now she sat down, rather heavily, on the side of the bed immediately beside the main door, placed her white leather handbag below the various switches for lights, radio, and TV, on the small table-top next to the bed – and removed her shoes.

Finally removed her shoes.

She fetched the kettle, filled it from the wash-basin in the bathroom, and switched on the current. Then, into the bathroom once more where she put the plug in the bath and turned on the hot tap. Returning to the main room again she picked up a DO NOT DISTURB sign, hung it over the outside door-knob, and returned to the bathroom to pour some pink Foaming Bubbly into the slowly filling bath.

Beryl Reeves had noted the single arrival in Room 310. At 4.40 p.m. she had put in a final burst of corridor hovering and hoovering, and knew even from her very limited experience that before she went off duty at 5.00 there would be several queries from these Americans about the whereabouts of the (non-existent) 'ice-machine' and the (readily available) replenishments of coffee sachets. Beryl was from Manchester; and her honest, if slightly naïve attitude to life – even more so, her *accent* – had already endeared her to many of her charges on Level Three. All in all, she was proving a very good employee: punctual, conscientious, friendly, and (as Morse was later to discover) a most reliable witness.

It had been exactly 4.45 that afternoon (and who could be more accurate than that?) when she had looked in at Room 310; noticed the sign hanging over the door-knob, wondering why the door itself was slightly ajar; peered momentarily into the room itself; but immediately retreated on seeing the steam emanating from the bathroom. Yes, she *thought* she would have probably noticed a white leather handbag if it had been somewhere just inside. No, she had *not* passed beyond the door and looked around the corner beside the Fire Exit. She had seen an American guest going into Room 308 shortly after this – a man; a friendly man, who'd said 'Hi!'. Yes, of course she would recognize him. In fact she could tell them who he was straightaway: a Mr Howard Brown from California.

Just before 6 p.m. the phone rang in the office of Chief Superintendent Strange at the Thames Valley Police HQ at Kidlington. The great man listened fairly patiently, if with less than obvious enthusiasm, to his colleague, Superintendent Bell from St Aldates in Oxford.

'Well, it doesn't sound particularly like Morse's cup of tea, Bell, but if you're really short . . . No, he's trying to get a few days off, he tells me, says he never gets his full ration of furlough. Huh! If you take off the hours he spends in the pubs . . . what? Well, as I say, if you *are* short . . . Yes, all right. You know his home number? . . . Fine! Just tell him you've had a word with me. He's usually happier if Lewis is with him, though . . . What? Lewis is already *there*? Good. Good! And as I say, just tell him that you've had a word with me. There'll be no problems.'

CHAPTER SIX

There are worse occupations in this world than feeling a woman's pulse

(Laurence Sterne, *A Sentimental Journey*)

'You here already, Lewis?'

'Half an hour ago, sir. The Super called me. They're short-staffed at St Aldates—'

'Must be!'

'I've already been upstairs.'

'No problems?'

'I'm – I'm not quite sure, sir.'

'Well – "Lead on, Macduff!"'

'That should be "Lay on Macduff!", sir. So our English teacher—'

'Thank you, Lewis.'

'The lift's just along here—'

'Lift? We're not climbing the Empire State Building!'

'Quite a few stairs, sir,' said Lewis quietly, suspecting (rightly) that his chief was going through one of his temporary get-a-little-fitter phases.

'Look! Don't you worry too much about me, Lewis. If by any chance things become a bit too strenuous in the ascent, I shall stop periodically and pant, all right?'

Lewis nodded, happy as always (almost always) to be working with the curmudgeonly Morse once more.

For a few seconds Morse stood outside Room 310, breathing heavily and looking down at the door-knob. He raised his eyebrows to Lewis.

'No, sir – waste of time worrying. Four or five people been in.'

'Who's in there now?' asked Morse quietly.

'Only the quack – Doc Swain – he's been the house-doctor here for a few years.'

'Presumably the *corpse* as well, Lewis?'

'The corpse as well, sir.'

'Who else has been in?'

'The Manager, Mr Gascoigne, and Mr Stratton – that's the husband, sir. He was the one who found her – very shaken up, I'm afraid, he is. I asked Mr Gascoigne to take him to his office.' Lewis pointed vaguely to one of the lower floors.

'No one else?'

'Me, of course.'

Morse nodded, and almost smiled.

Mrs Laura Stratton lay neatly supine on the nearer side of the double bed. She wore a full-length peach-coloured dressing robe, and (so far as Morse could see) little else. And she was dead. Morse glanced briefly at the face, swallowed once, and turned away.

Dr Swain, a fresh-faced, youngish-looking man (early thirties?) was seated at the low dressing-table, writing. He turned his head and almost immediately answered Morse's unspoken question.

'Heart attack. Massive coronary.'

'Thank you, Dr – *Swain*, I think?'

'And you are?'

'I am Morse. Chief Inspector Morse.'

Swain got to his feet and handed Morse a sheet of paper, headed 'Oxfordshire Health Authority', with an impressively qualified column of medical men printed top right, in which (second from bottom) Morse read 'M. C. Swain, MA, MB, BCh, MRCP, MRCGP'.

'Congratulations!' said Morse.

'Pardon?'

'Sixteen, isn't it? Sixteen letters after your name, and I haven't got a single one after mine.'

'Well, er – that's how things go, isn't it? I'll be off now, if you don't mind. You've got my report. BMA dinner we've got this evening.'

Seldom was it that Morse took such an irrationally instant dislike to one of his fellow men; but there are always exceptions, and one of these was Dr M. C. Swain, MA, MB, BCh, MRCP, MRCGP.

'I'm afraid no one leaves for the moment, Doctor. You know, I think, that we've got slightly more than a death here?'

'I'm told something valuable's been stolen. Yes, I know that.

All I'm telling *you* is that the cause of death was a massive coronary. You can read it in *that!*' Swain flung his forefinger Morse's way, towards the sheet just handed over.

'Do you think that was before – or after – this valuable something went missing?'

'I – I don't know.'

'She died there – where she is now – on the bed?'

'On the floor, actually.'

Morse forced his features to the limits of credulity: 'You mean you *moved* her, Dr Swain?'

'Yes!'

'Have you ever heard of murder in the furtherance of theft?'

'Of course! But this *wasn't* murder. It was a massive—'

'Do you really think it necessary to tell me things three times, sir?'

'I knew nothing about the theft. In fact I only learned about it five minutes ago – from the Manager.'

'That's true, sir,' chipped in Lewis, greatly to Morse's annoyance.

'Yes, well, if the doctor has a dinner to attend, Lewis – a BMA dinner! – who are we to detain him? It's a pity about the *evidence*, of course. But I suppose we shall just have to try our best to find the man – or the woman – responsible for this, er, this massive coronary, brought on doubtless by the shock of finding some thief nicking her valuables. Good evening, Doctor. Make sure you enjoy your dinner!' Morse turned to Lewis: 'Tell Max to get over here straightaway, will you? Tell him it's as urgent as they get.'

'Look, Inspector—' began Swain.

But Morse was doing a reasonably convincing impression of a deaf man who has just turned off his hearing-aid, and now silently held the door of Room 310 open as the disconcerted doctor was ushered out.

It was in the Manager's office, on the first floor of The Randolph, that for the first time Morse himself was acquainted with the broad outlines of the story. Laura Stratton had taken her key up to her room soon after 4.30 p.m.; she had earlier been complaining of feeling awfully weary; had taken a bath – presumably after hanging a DO NOT DISTURB notice outside her door; had been discovered at 5.20 p.m. when her husband, Mr Eddie Stratton, had returned from a stroll around Broad Street with a fellow tourist, Mrs Shirley Brown. He had found the door to 310 shut, and after being unable to get any response from within had hurried down to Reception in some incipient panic before returning upstairs to find . . . That was all really; the rest was elaboration and emotional overlay. Except of course for the handbag. But who is the man, with his wife lying dead on the carpet, who thinks of looking around to see if her handbag has disappeared?

Well, Mr Eddie Stratton, it seemed.

And that for a most important reason.

CHAPTER SEVEN

Almost all modern architecture is farce
(Diogenes Small (1797–1812), *Reflections*)

The Randolph boasted many fine rooms for dinners, dances, conferences, and exhibitions: rooms with such splendid names as Lancaster, Worcester, and the like – and the St John's Suite, a high-ceilinged room on the first floor where the reception had been arranged. In the daylight hours the view from the east window took in the Martyrs' Memorial, just across the street, with Balliol and St John's Colleges behind. And even now, at 6.45 p.m., with the floral, carpet-length curtains drawn across, the room still seemed so light and airy, the twin candelabra throwing a soft light over the maroon and pink and brilliant-white décor. Even Janet Roscoe could find little to criticize in such a grandly appointed room.

Sheila Williams, a large gin and tonic in her left hand, was trying to be pleasantly hospitable: 'Now are we all here? Not *quite* I think? Have we all got drinks?'

News of Laura Stratton's death had been withheld from the rest of the group, with only Sheila herself being officially notified of that sad event. It was a burden for her, certainly; but also a wonderful excuse for fortifying the inner woman, and Sheila seldom needed any such excuse.

'Mrs Roscoe! You haven't got a drink. What can I—?'

'I don't drink, Mrs Williams!' Janet turned her head to a sheepish-looking Phil Aldrich, standing stoically beside her: 'I've already told her *once*, Phil.'

'Janet here is a deacon in our church back home, Mrs Williams—'

But Sheila had already jerked into a tetchy rejoinder: 'Well I *do* drink, Mrs Roscoe! In fact I'm addicted to the stuff. And my

reasons for such addiction may be just as valid as your own
reasons for abstinence. All right?'

With which well-turned sentence she walked back to the table
just beside the main door whereon a dozen or so bottles of gin
(Booth's and Gordon's), Martini (French and Italian), sherry (dry,
medium, sweet) stood in competition with two large jugs of orange
juice. She handed over her half-empty glass to the young girl
dispensing the various riches.

'Gin – large one, please! – no ice – and no more tonic.'

Thus, fully re-equipped for her duties, Sheila looked down once
more at the yellow sheet of A4 which John Ashenden had earlier
prepared, typed up, photocopied, and distributed. It was high time
to get things moving. Of the tourists, only Howard and Shirley
Brown (apart from Eddie Stratton) seemed now to be missing –
no, that was wrong: apart from Eddie and *Laura* Stratton. Of the
two distinguished speakers (*three*, if she herself were included),
Theodore Kemp had not as yet put in an appearance. But the third
of the trio, Cedric Downes, seemed to Sheila to be doing a splendid
job as he stood behind a thinly fluted glass of dry sherry and
asked, with (as she saw it) a cleverly concealed indifference,
whence the tourists hailed and what their pre-retirement professions had been.

It was 7.25 p.m. before Dr Kemp finally entered, in the company
of a subdued-looking Ashenden; and it was almost immediately
apparent to Sheila that both of them had now been informed of
the disturbing events that had been enacted in the late afternoon.
As her eyes had met Kemp's there was, albeit for a moment, a
flash of mutual understanding and (almost?) of comradeship.

'Ladies and gentlemen . . .' Sheila knocked a table noisily and
repeatedly with the bottom of an ash-tray, and the chatter subsided. 'Mr Ashenden has asked me to take you through our
Oxford itinerary – briefly! – so if you will all just look at your
yellow sheets for a minute . . .' She waved her own sheet; and
then, without any significant addition (although with a significant
omission) to the printed word, read vaguely through the dates
and times of the itemized programme:

THE HISTORIC CITIES OF ENGLAND TOUR
27TH OCT–10TH NOV
(Oxford Stage)

Thursday 1st November

4.30 p.m. (approx.)	Arr. The Randolph
4.30–5.30 p.m.	English teas available

6.45 p.m.	Cocktail reception (St John's Suite) introduced by Sheila Williams, MA, B.Litt. (Cantab.), with Cedric Downes, MA (Oxon.)
8.00 p.m.	Dinner (main dining room)
9.30–10.15 p.m.	Talk by Dr Theodore Kemp, MA, D.Phil. (Oxon.) on 'Treasures of the Ashmolean'.

Friday 2nd November

7.30–9.15 a.m.	Breakfast (main dining room)
10.30–11.30 a.m.	Visit to The Oxford Story, Broad Street (100 yards only from the hotel)
12.45 p.m.	Lunch (St John's Suite) – followed by an informal get-together with our lecturers in the coffee-lounge
3.00 p.m.	We divide into groups (details to be announced later)
4.30–5.00 p.m.	English tea (Lancaster Room)
6.30 p.m.	The Tour Highlight! The presentation, by Mrs Laura Stratton, of the Wolvercote Tongue (Ashmolean Museum)
8.00 p.m.	Dinner (N.B. extra charge) in The Randolph. Otherwise group members are offered a last opportunity to dine out, wine out, and find out – wherever they wish – on our final night in this wonderful University City

Saturday 3rd November

| 7.30–8.30 a.m. | Breakfast (Please be punctual!) |
| 9.30 p.m. | Departure from The Randolph for Broughton Castle (Banbury), and thence to Stratford. |

'The only thing that needs much expansion here' (Shelia was talking more confidently now) 'is the three p.m. spot tomorrow afternoon. So let me just fill in a bit there. Dr Kemp, Keeper of Anglo-Saxon and Mediaeval Antiquities at the Ashmolean – the museum just opposite us here – will be taking his group around there tomorrow – as well as talking to us after dinner tonight, as you can see. Then, Mr Cedric Downes' (Sheila duly signified that distinguished gentleman) 'will be taking his own group round several colleges – including the most interesting of the dining halls – and addressing himself particularly to' (Sheila looked at her brief notes) '"Architectural Design and Technique in the Sixteenth and Seventeenth Centuries". That, again, is at three p.m. . . . Well, you've heard almost enough from me now . . .' (Janet Roscoe was nodding) '. . . but I'd just like to mention that there is a *third* group tomorrow.' ('Hear, hear!' said Phil Aldrich happily.) 'You see, *I* shall be taking a group of you – perhaps only two or three of you, I don't mind – on an "Alice Tour". As most of you will know, the Reverend Charles Lutwidge Dodgson – "Lewis Carroll"

– was in real life a "Student" – I shall explain that tomorrow – at Christ Church in the latter half of the nineteenth century; and we shall be looking at many mementoes of him, in the Deanery Garden, the Cathedral, and the Dining Hall; and also looking at a unique collection of old photographs, drawings, and cartoons in the Bodleian Library. Well, that's what's on the menu. I'm sorry we're running just a bit late but . . . Anyway, it's my great pleasure now to introduce you to Cedric here – Mr Cedric Downes – who is going to set the scene for his talk tomorrow, in a rather light-hearted way, he tells me, by giving us a few thoughts on *modern* architecture. Ladies and gentlemen – Cedric Downes.'

'Thank you, Sheila! I sometimes feel that some of our tourists must think that here in Oxford we're all mediaeval, Early English, Gothic, Tudor, Jacobean, Georgian, and so on. But we do have – though I'm no expert in this field – we do have a few fine examples of contemporary design. I don't want to get too serious about things – not tonight! But take St Catherine's, for example – the work of that most famous Danish architect, Arne er Johansen—'

'Jacobsen!' (*Sotto voce* from Kemp.)

'Pardon?'

'You said "Johansen",' murmured Kemp.

'Surely not! I said "Jacobsen", didn't I?'

A chorus of assorted tourists assured Downes that he had most certainly *not* said 'Jacobsen'; and for a second or two Downes turned upon his fellow lecturer a look of what might have been interpreted as naked detestation, were it not for the slightly weary resignation in his eyes. To his audience he essayed a charming smile, and resumed:

'I'm sorry! It's all these Danes, you know! You never actually meet one called "Hamlet", do you? And talking of *Hamlet*, I see you'll all be at Stratford-on-Avon—'

'I thought it was Stratford-uparn-Avon,' chirruped a shrill, thin voice.

But by now Downes was getting into his stride: 'How good it is for us all in Oxford, Mrs, er—'

'Mrs Roscoe, sir. Mrs Janet Roscoe.'

'How good it is for Dr Kemp and Mrs Williams and myself to meet a scholar like you, Mrs Roscoe! I was just going to mention – only in passing, of course – that the Swan Theatre, in my view . . .'

But everyone had seen the door open, and now looked with some puzzlement at the newcomer, a man none of them had seen before.

'Mrs Williams? Is there a Mrs Williams here?'

The said lady, still standing beside the drinks-table, no more than a couple of yards from the door, raised the index-finger of her non-drinking hand to signify her identity.

'Could I have a quiet word with you, madam?' asked Sergeant Lewis.

CHAPTER EIGHT

Madame, appearing to imbibe gin and It in roughly equal measure, yet manages to exude rather more of the gin than of the 'it'
(Hugh Sykes-Davies, *Obiter Dicta*)

Inside the Manager's office, situated at the head of the first flight of stairs, Morse found his attention almost immediately drifting towards the large drinks-cabinet which stood to the left of the high-ceilinged suite of rooms wherein Mr Douglas Gascoigne, a bespectacled, intelligent-looking man in his early forties, sought, and sought successfully, to sustain the high standards of service expected from his multi-starred establishment. Early photographs, cartoons, diplomas, framed letters, and a series of pleasing water-colours, lined the walls of the main office, above the several tables on which VDU screens, print-out machines, telephones, in-and out-trays, fax machines, and file-cases abstracted from surrounding shelves, vied with each other for a few square feet of executively justifiable space. As in the St John's Suite, the curtains were drawn, this time across the window behind Gascoigne as he sat at his desk, concealing the view of the Ashmolean façade upon which, though from a higher elevation, Mrs Laura Stratton had gazed so very briefly some three hours earlier.

'It's just' (Gascoigne was talking) 'that we've never had – well, not in my time – anyone actually *dying* in the hotel.'

'Some thefts, though, I suppose?'

'Yes, a few, Inspector. Cameras left around – that sort of thing. But never anything so valuable . . .'

'Wonder why she didn't leave it in your safe, sir?'

Gascoigne shook his head: 'We always offer to lock away anything like that but—'

'Insured, was it?'

'Mr Stratton' – the Manager lowered his voice and gestured to the closed door on his right – 'thinks probably yes, but he's still in a bit of a daze, I'm afraid. Dr Swain gave him some pills and he's still in there with one of his friends, a Mr Howard Brown.' And indeed Morse thought he could just about hear an occasional murmur of subdued conversation.

Lewis put his head round the door and signified his success in securing the appearance of Mrs Sheila Williams. Gascoigne got to his feet and prepared to leave the two detectives to it.

'As I say, just make use of any of our facilities here for the time being. We may have to keep coming in occasionally, of course, but—'

'Thank you, sir.'

So Gascoigne left his own office, and left the scene to Morse.

And to Sheila Williams

She was – little question of it – a most attractive woman, certainly as Morse saw her: mid-thirties (perhaps older?), with glistening dark-brown eyes that somehow managed to give the simultaneous impression of vulnerability, sensuality, and mild inebriation.

A heady mixture.

'Sit down! Sit down! You look as if you could do with a drink, Mrs Williams.'

'Well, I – it *is* all a bit of a shock, isn't it?'

'Anything suitable in there, Lewis?' Morse pointed to the drinks-cabinet, not without a degree of self-interest.

'Looks like he's just about got the lot, sir.'

'Mrs Williams?'

'G and T – that would be fine.'

'Gin and tonic for the lady, Lewis . . . Ice?'

'Why dilute the stuff, Inspector?'

'There's no ice anyway,' muttered Lewis.

'Look,' began Sheila Williams, 'I'm not myself in charge of this group. I do liaise *with* the group and arrange speakers and so on – but it's John Ashenden who's the tour leader.'

Morse, however, appeared wholly uninterested in the activities of Mr Ashenden: 'Mrs Williams, I'm going to have to ask everyone in the group what they were doing between about four-thirty and five-fifteen this afternoon – that's between the time Mr Stratton last saw his wife and when he got back from his walk with, er, with Mrs Brown . . .'

As Sheila tossed back the last of her G and T, Lewis thought he saw the hint of a smile about her full lips; but Morse had turned to the wall on his left where he was minutely studying a late nineteenth-century Henry Taunt photograph of some brewery drays, and his last few words may well have been spoken without the slightest hint of implication or innuendo.

'I'm sure they'll all co-operate, Inspector, but they don't know yet about . . .'

'No. Perhaps we should wait a while? After dinner? No later than that. I wouldn't want Sergeant Lewis here to be too late in bed— Ah! Another, Mrs Williams?'

'I'm sorry . . . I seem to be—'

'Nothing to be sorry about, is there?'

'Same again then, please, Sergeant. Little less tonic, perhaps?'

Lewis's eyebrows rose a centimetre. 'Anything for you, sir?'

'No thank you, Lewis. Not on duty.'

Lewis's eyebrows rose a further centimetre as he collected Mrs Williams's glass.

The tour was, as Morse and Lewis learned, a pretty expensive, pretty exclusive business really. Most of them had been to England before (not all, though) and most of them were well enough off to be coming back again before *too* long, whatever the strength of the pound sterling. One of them wouldn't be, though . . . Yes, Sheila Williams knew quite a bit about the Wolvercote Tongue, although Dr Kemp was the real authority, of course. It seemed that Laura Stratton's first husband, a real-estate man operating in California and, in later life, quite a collector, had come to find himself in possession of a jewelled artefact which, after learning of its provenance, he had bequeathed – he had died two years since – to the Curators of the Ashmolean Museum in Oxford. Oh yes, she had seen it dozens of times, though only in a series of Technicolor slides, from which she had been able to sketch out a diagram of the whole jewel, buckle *and* tongue; and in fact she herself had executed the final coloured illustration which was at that moment on show at the Ashmolean. Come to think of it, she was glad she *had* done the drawings; whatever happened now, people could know exactly how the Wolvercote Jewel in its entirety *would* have appeared. Doubtless the police would find the tongue, but . . .

'We shall certainly do our best, madam,' Lewis had interposed, the tone of his voice suggesting something less than brimming optimism.

The Tongue itself? Well, again, *Kemp* was really the one to ask. But she could certainly tell them all about the look of it: of triangular shape, some 3 inches long, and 2 inches wide at the base; of a dull dirtyish brown colour (gold!), with (originally) three ruby-stones, one on each corner of the triangle – but now reduced to just the one, and that at the narrower end of things. The great, the unique, value of the tongue was the fact that it fitted (perfectly!) into the gold buckle which had been discovered during an archaeological dig at the village of Wolvercote in the early 1930s; and which, since 1947, had been proudly exhibited in the Ashmolean as evidence (hitherto unsuspected) of the exquisite craftsmanship of the goldsmith's art in the late eighth century AD. Laura Stratton (so Sheila had learned from John Ashenden) had carried the jewel with her, in a black velvet-lined case, and kept it in her handbag – refusing to entrust the precious artefact either to transatlantic postal services, international tour operators, or burglar-and-fire-proof safe-deposit boxes. In the same handbag, it appeared, Laura had also carried a beautiful-looking string of wholly phoney pearls, which she had worn on most evenings with her dinner-dresses. Of any other valuables which might have been stolen with the handbag, Sheila had no idea whatsoever, although she volunteered the information that from her own recent experiences – and in spite of the equally recent strength of the pound sterling – some of the Americans seemed less than fully aware of the denominational value of the English currency they carried on their persons. With almost all of the party (she suspected) several £10, £20, even £50, notes would hardly be strangers in the purses and wallets of some of California's wealthier citizens. So a casual thief might have been pleasantly surprised by the sum of the monies often carried? But Mr Stratton – Eddie Stratton – *he'd* be the man to ask about such things, wouldn't he? Really?

She turned her large, melancholy eyes upon Morse; and for a few seconds Lewis found himself wondering if his chief wasn't temporarily mesmerized. So much so that he decided not to withhold his own contribution:

'You say, Mrs Williams, that the group won't perhaps mind me asking them all where they were between four thirty and five fifteen? Would you mind if you told us where *you* were?'

The effect of such an innocent question was quite unexpectedly melodramatic. Sheila Williams placed the empty glass on the table in front of her, and immediately burst into tears, during which time Morse glowered at his subordinate as if he had simultaneously broken all the rules of diplomacy, etiquette, and Freemasonry.

But Morse himself, as he thought, was equal to the task: he nodded peremptorily to the empty glass, and immediately Lewis found himself pouring yet another generous measure of Gordon's gin, tempered again with but a little slim-line tonic.

Suddenly, and with a defiant glare at the two policemen, Sheila sat up in her chair, sought to regain a precarious state of equipoise, and drank down the proffered mixture in a single draught – much to Morse's secret admiration. She spoke just five words: 'Ask Dr Kemp – he'll explain!'

After she was gone, guided in gentlemanly fashion along the corridor by Sergeant Lewis, Morse quickly opened the drinks-cabinet, poured himself half a tumbler of Glenfiddich, savoured a large and satisfying swallow, thereafter placing the tumbler stra-tegically on a convenient shelf, just below the line of vision of anyone entering. Including Sergeant Lewis.

Strangely, neither Sergeant Lewis nor Inspector Morse himself seemed particularly conscious of the fact that Mrs Sheila Williams had signally failed to answer the only significant question that had been put to her.

Such is the wonderful effect of any woman's tears.

CHAPTER NINE

Often I have wished myself dead, but well under my
blanket, so that neither death nor man could hear me
(George Lichtenberg)

John Ashenden would later remember exactly what he had done during the vital forty-five minutes that Morse had specified . . .

It was a quarter to five when he had walked out of The Randolph, and crossed over by the Martyrs' Memorial into Broad Street. The sun no longer slanted across the pale-yellow stone, the early evening was becoming much cooler, and he was wearing a lightweight rain-coat. He strode fairly quickly past the front of Balliol, the great gates of Trinity, Blackwells Book Shop; and was waiting by the New Bodleian building to cross at the traffic lights into Holywell Street when he saw them standing there outside the Sheldonian, *sub imperatoribus*, her arm through his, neither of them (as it seemed) taking too much notice of anything except their mutual selves. Even more briskly now, Ashenden walked past the King's Arms, the Holywell Music Room, the back of New College – until he came to Longwall Street. Here he turned left; and after two hundred yards or so went through the wooden gate that led into Holywell Cemetery, where under the stones and crosses – so many Celtic crosses! – were laid to rest the last remains of eminent

Oxford men, in these slightly unkempt, but never neglected, acres
of the dead. A curving path through the grass led him to a wooden
seat above which, wired to a yew tree, was a rectangular board
showing the plot of the cemetery, with the memorials of the
particularly eminent marked by numbers:

1 Kenneth Grahame (1859–1932)
2 Maurice Bowra (1898–1971)
3 Kenneth Tynan (1927–1980)
4 H. V. D. Dyson (1896–1975)
5 James Blish (1921–1975)
6 Theodore and Sibley, Drowned (1893)
7 Sir John Stainer (1840–1901)
8 Walter Pater . . .

That was him!

It took Ashenden some twenty minutes or so, treading through
overgrown grasses, and parting ivy from many semi-decipherable
inscriptions, to find the strong, squat cross:

> In te, Domine, speravi
> **WALTER PATER**
> Died July 30 1894

Then, almost immediately, he saw that other stone, the one he
was looking for – an even simpler memorial:

> **JAMES ALFRED BOWDEN**
> 1956–1981
> Requiescat

For several minutes Ashenden stood there silently under the
darkening shadows: it seemed a wonderfully unforbidding piece
of ground in which to find a final resting-place. Yet no one wanted
to die – certainly not John Ashenden, as he remained standing by
the grave, wondering whether Jimmy Bowden, during the pain of
his terminal illness, had ever recanted the dogmatic and confident
atheism he had once propounded in the early hours of one most
memorable day. But Ashenden doubted it. He recalled, too, that
final postcard to which he had never replied . . .

There was no one else in the cemetery; no one there to observe the strange little incident when Ashenden, after looking round about him for a last reassurance, parted the thickly twined rootage of ivy at the rear of Bowden's small cross, took something from the right-hand pocket of his rain-coat, and laid it carefully at the foot of the stone before replacing the ivy and patting it, almost effeminately, back into its pristine state.

He was in no hurry, and on his leisurely way back to the cemetery gate he stopped and read several of the gravestones, including 'Kenneth Grahame, who passed the river on the 6th July 1932, leaving childhood and literature through him the more blest for all time'. Ashenden loved the wording. He looked vaguely for 'Theodore and Sibley, drowned (1893)'; but it was too dark now, and he could find no clue as to who they were and where they had perished.

He regained the main street, and on his way back to The Randolph called in the back bar of the King's Arms to order a pint of cask-conditioned Flowers. For which choice, Inspector Morse would have been quietly proud of him.

Shirley Brown had disengaged her arm as she and Eddie Stratton crossed into Beaumont Street at ten-past five.

'Whatever you say, Ed, I'd still like to know where he was going.'

'Like I say, *forget* it, Shirl!'

'He was trying to get out of sight – quick. You *know* he was.'

'You still reckon he saw us?'

'I still reckon he saw us,' said Shirley Brown, in her Californian drawl.

They were the only two in the guest-lift; and Eddie bade his temporary leave as they reached the third floor.

'See you in a little while, Shirl.'

'Yeah. And tell Laura I hope her feet are rested.'

Eddie Stratton had made no reply as he walked towards Room 310.

CHAPTER TEN

A foolish consistency is the hobgoblin of little minds
(Ralph Waldo Emerson, *Essays*)

Too long had Morse been in the police business for him to believe
that a death and a theft, or (as he was now beginning to think) a
theft and a death, were likely to be a pair of fortuitously contingent
events. Not that he was even remotely hopeful about the *theft*. He
would never mind pitting his brains against a *murderer*; but he'd
always discounted his chances against a reasonably competent
burglar – even, come to think of it, against a reasonably *in*competent burglar. And if, as seemed the consensus of opinion now,
Laura Stratton had left her door ajar for her husband to let himself
in; if she had carelessly left her handbag on the bedside table
immediately inside her partially opened door; if someone had
known of these things – even if someone had *not* known of these
things . . . well, certainly, the odds were pretty strong on the
prompt disappearance of the handbag. Give it fifteen minutes? At
the outside, thought Morse. We all might pray (*some* of us might
pray) 'Lead us not into temptation', yet most people seemed
perfectly happy to stick their cameras, binoculars, radios, squash
rackets, handbags . . . mm . . . yes, stick any of 'em on the back
seats of their cars, and then complain to the police when they
found their rear windows smashed into splinters and—
  Come off it!
  The truth was, of course, that Morse had virtually lost all
interest in the case already, his only enduring memory being the
admiration he'd felt for the alcoholic capacity of a lady named Mrs
Sheila Williams.
  He just managed to hide the tumbler when without even a
sociable knock Max put his head round the door and, seeing
Morse in the Manager's chair, promptly entered and seated
himself.
  'They told me I'd find you here. Not that I needed much
direction. Any pathologist worth his meagre remuneration tends
to develop a fairly keen sense of smell.'
  'Well?'
  'Heart attack. Massive coronary.' (*Swain*'s words.)
  Morse nodded slowly.
  'God knows why you ask me along here to confirm the obvious.
Where's the booze, by the way?'
  Reluctantly, Morse pointed to the drinks-cabinet.

'You're not paying for it, are you?'

'What do you fancy?'

'Nothing for me, Morse. I'm on duty.'

'All right.'

'Is, er, is it drinkable – the Scotch?'

Morse got to his feet, poured a miniature into a plastic cup, and handed it over. For a few minutes the two old enemies sat sipping in friendly silence.

'You *quite* sure, Max . . .?'

'Not so bad, is it, this stuff?'

'. . . about the time of death?'

'Between four thirty and five fifteen.'

'*Really?*' Never before had Morse heard anything remotely approaching such a definitive statement from the lips of the hump-backed police-surgeon. 'How on earth—?'

'Girl at Reception, Morse. Said the poor old dear had gone up to her room at four thirty, on her own two tootsies, too. Then your people told me she was found by her ever-loving husband at five fifteen.' Max took a large swallow of the Glenfiddich. 'We professionals in the Force, Morse, we have to interpret all the available clues, you know.' He drained his cup with deep appreciation.

'Another?'

'Certainly not! I'm on duty . . . And anyway I'm just off to a very nice little dinner.'

A distant temple-bell was tinkling in Morse's mind: 'Not the same nosh-up as whatshisname?'

'The very same, Morse.'

'He's the house-doctor here.'

'Try telling me something I *don't* know.'

'It's just that he looked at Mrs Stratton, that's all.'

'And you didn't have much faith in him.'

'Not much.'

'He's considered quite a competent quack, they tell me.'

'To be honest, I thought he was a bit of a . . .'

'Bit of a *membrum virile*? You're not *always* wrong, you know . . . Er, *small* top-up, perhaps, Morse?'

'You know him?'

'Oh yes. And you're *quite* wrong, in this case. He's not just a— No, let's put it the other way: he's the *biggest* one in Oxford.'

'She still died of a heart attack, though?'

'Oh yes! So don't go looking for any silly bloody nonsense here. And it's not Swain who's telling you, Morse . . . it's *me*.'

When, some ten minutes later, Max had departed for his BMA

dinner, Morse had already performed what in political parlance would be termed a compromising U-turn. And when Lewis came in, with Dr Theodore Kemp immediately in tow, Morse knew that he had erred in his earlier thinking. The coincidence of a theft and a death (in whichever order) might often be shown to be causally connected.

But not in this case.

Lewis would have to interview them all, of course; or most of them. But that would be up to Lewis. For himself, Morse wished for nothing more fervently than to get back to his bachelor flat in North Oxford, and to listen once again to the Second Movement of the Bruckner No. 7.

But he'd better see one or two of them.

CHAPTER ELEVEN

> *History*, n. An account mostly false, of events mostly unimportant, which are brought about by rulers mostly knaves, and soldiers mostly fools
> (Ambrose Bierce, *The Devil's Dictionary*)

Almost immediately Kemp slotted into Morse's preconceptions of the we-are-an-Oxford-man, although he was aware that he could well be guilty of yet another instant inaccuracy. The bearded, clever-looking, ugly-attractive man (late thirties – Sheila's age?) who sat down only after lightly dusting the seat with a hyper-handkerchief, had clearly either been told (by Sheila?) or heard (gossip inevitable) something of what had occurred. Other persons might have been irritated only temporarily by the man's affected lisp. Not so Morse.

'Abtholutely pritheless, Inthpector!'

'Perhaps you could tell us a little more about the Wolvercote Tongue, sir.'

Kemp was well prepared. He opened his black brief-case, took out a pile of pale-blue leaflets, and handed one across the desk to Morse, one to Lewis.

The Wolvercote Jewel

During the last century or so archaeologists and historians have become increasingly conscious of the splendid workmanship of the late Saxon period, and the discovery in 1931 of a gold 'buckle' at Wolvercote had been extremely exciting. Particularly so since this buckle linked up with a corresponding 'tongue', fully documented and authenticated, known to be in the collection of one Cyrus C. Palmer Jnr, a citizen of Pasadena, California. The *cloisonné* enamel of the pear-shaped tongue, set in a solid gold frame, decorated in a distinctive type of delicate filigree, and set (originally) with three large ruby-stones, appeared to match the Ashmolean buckle with exact precision. And if further proof were sought, the tongue's lettering – [AE]LFRED[1] MEC HE[HT GEWYR]CAN – was identical in figuration and engravure to that of the gold buckle – into which (as all experts now concur) the tongue had once fitted.

That the tongue will shortly fit into its buckle once more is due to the philanthropy of Mr Palmer and to the gracious co-operation and interest of his wife, (now) Mrs Laura M. Stratton. The only major problem remaining to be resolved (according to Dr Theodore Kemp of the Ashmolean Museum) is the exact purpose of this most beautifully wrought artefact, henceforth to be known, in its entirety, as 'The Wolvercote Jewel'. Whether it was the clasp of some royal garment, or whether it served some symbolic or ceremonial purpose, is a matter of fascinating speculation. What is certain is that The Wolvercote Jewel – tongue and buckle at last most happily conjoined – will now be numbered amongst the finest treasures of the Ashmolean Museum.

[1] Alfred the Great, Ad 871–901. For a full discussion, see *Pre-Conquest Craftsmanship in Southern Britain*, Theodore S. Kemp, Babington Press, June 1991

'You write this, sir?' asked Morse.

Kemp nodded bitterly: the whole bloody thing now cancelled (Morse learned) – the ceremony that was all fixed up – the presentation – the press – TV. God!

'We learnt the dates of the kings and queens of England at school,' said Morse. 'Trouble is we started at William the First.'

'You ought to have gone back earlier, Inspector – much earlier.'

'Oh, I'm always doing that, sir.' Morse fixed his eyes on the pallid face across the table. 'What were you doing earlier this evening between four thirty and five fifteen, Dr Kemp?'

'What? What wath I doing?' He shook his head like a man most grievously distraught. 'You don't – you can't understand, can you! I wath probably buggering around in . . .' He pointed vaguely over Morse's head in the direction of the Ashmolean. 'I don't know. And I don't care!' He picked up the pile of leaflets and, with a viciousness of which Morse would not have thought the effeminate fingers capable, tore them across the middle, and threw them down on the desk.

Morse let him go.

Kemp was the second witness that evening who had been less than forthcoming in answering the only pertinent question that had been put to him.

'You didn't like him much, did you sir?'

'What's that got to do with anything?'

'Well, somebody must have stolen this Wolvercote thing.'

'Nobody pinched it, Lewis! They pinched the *handbag*.'

'I don't see it. The handbag's worth virtually nothing – but the, you know, it's priceless, he says.'

'Abtholutely pritheless!' mimicked Morse.

Lewis grinned. 'You don't think *he* stole it?'

'I'd rather not *think* at all about that inflated bladder of wind and piss. What I *know* is that he'd be the last person in Oxford to steal it. He's got everything lined up – he's got this literature all ready – he'll get his name in the papers and his face on the telly – he'll write a monograph for some learned journal – the University will give him a D.Litt. or something . . . No, he didn't pinch it. You see you can't *sell* something like that, Lewis. It's only "priceless" in the sense of its being unique, irreplaceable, crucial for historical and archaeological interpretation . . . You couldn't sell the *Mona Lisa*, could you?'

'You knew all about it, did you, sir? This Wolvercote thing?'

'Didn't *you*? People come from far and wide to view the Wolvercote Tongue—'

'"Buckle", isn't it, sir? Isn't it just the *buckle* that's there?'

'I've never heard of the bloody thing,' growled Morse.

'I've never even been *inside* the Ashmolean, sir.'

'Really?'

'The only thing we learned about King Alfred was about him burning the cakes.'

'That's something though, isn't it? It's a fact – *perhaps* it's a fact. But they don't go in for facts in History these days. They go in for empathy, Lewis. Whatever that is.'

'What's the drill then, sir?'

So Morse told him. Get the body moved quietly via the luggage-lift while the tourists were still at dinner; get a couple of DCs over from Kidlington to help with statements from the group, including the speakers, re their whereabouts from 4.30 to 5.15 p.m.; *and* from the occupants of bedrooms adjacent or reasonably proximate to Room 310. Maids? Yes, better see if any of them were turning down counterpanes or restocking tea-bags or just walking around or . . . Morse suddenly felt himself utterly bored with the whole business. 'Find out the *system*, Lewis! Use a bit of initiative! And call round in the morning. I'll be at home – *trying* to get a few days' furlough.'

'We're not going to search the rooms then, sir?'

'Search the rooms? Christ, man! Do you know how many rooms there *are* in The Randolph?'

Morse performed one final task in what, by any criterion, had hitherto been a most perfunctory police inquiry. Briefly he spoke with Mr Eddie Stratton, who earlier had been sympathetically escorted up to the Browns' quarters in Room 308. Here, Morse found himself immediately liking the tall, bronzed Californian, in whose lived-in sort of face it seemed the sun might soon break through from behind the cloud of present adversity. Never particularly competent at expressing his personal feelings, Morse could do little more than mumble a few clichés of condolence, dredged up from some half-remembered funerals. But perhaps it was enough. For Stratton's face revealed little sign of grief; certainly no sign of tears.

The Manager was standing by Reception on the ground floor; and Morse thanked him for his co-operation, explaining that (as invited) he had made some, er, little use of the, er, the facilities available in the Manager's office. And if Sergeant Lewis and his men could continue to have the use of the office until . . .?

The Manager nodded his agreement: 'You know it's really most unfortunate. As I told you, Inspector, we always advise our guests that it's in their own best interests *never* to leave any unattended valuables in their rooms—'

'But she didn't leave them, did she?' suggested Morse mildly. 'She didn't even leave the room. As a matter of fact, sir, she still hasn't left it . . .'

In this last assertion Morse was somewhat behind the times, for Lewis now came down the main staircase to inform both of them that at that very moment the body of the late Laura M. Stratton was being transferred from Room 310, via the luggage-lift, en route for the Chapel of Rest in the Radcliffe Infirmary, just up the Woodstock Road.

'Fancy a drink, Lewis?'

'Not for me, sir. I'm on duty.'

The faithful sergeant allowed himself a wry grin, and even Morse was vaguely smiling. Anyway, it would save him, Lewis, a quid or two – that was for sure. Morse never seemed to think it was *his* round; and Lewis had occasionally calculated that on about three-fifths of his chief's salary he usually bought about three-quarters of the considerable quantities of alcohol consumed (though little by himself) on any given case.

Morse nodded a curt understanding, and walked towards the Chapters Bar.

CHAPTER TWELVE

Water taken in moderation cannot hurt anybody
(Mark Twain)

Pouring a modicum of slim-line tonic into the large gin that her present drinking companion had just purchased for her, Sheila Williams asked the key question: 'Might you have to cancel the rest of the tour, John?'

'Oh, I don't think it need come to that. I mean, they've all *paid* for it, haven't they? Obviously we could refund if, well, if Mr Stratton or—'

'He's fine. I've spoken to him. *You* haven't.'

'I can't do everything, you know.'

'Please don't misunderstand me, John, but wasn't it perhaps a little unfortunate that you were nowhere within hailing distance when one of your charges busts her arteries and gets burgled into the bargain?'

Ashenden took a sip from his half-pint glass of bitter, appearing to acknowledge the truth of what Sheila had just said, though without volunteering any further comment. He'd once read (or heard) – Disraeli, was it? (or Jimmy Bowden?) – that a man ought never to apologize; never to explain.

He did neither now.

'We go ahead with everything, Sheila – except for the presentation bit, of course.'

'Unless they find it.'

'Which they won't.'

'Which they won't,' agreed Sheila.

'In spite of this fellow—'

'*That's him!*' whispered Sheila, laying a beautifully manicured hand across Ashenden's fore-arm. '*That's* Morse!'

Ashendon looked across at the greying man, of middle height and middle age, who beamed briefly at the brunette behind the bar as he ordered a pint of best bitter.

'Drinks too much – *beer*,' volunteered Ashenden, sticking in the last word rapidly as he found Sheila's eyes switch to his with a glare of displeasure. 'Bit overweight – round the middle – that's all I meant.'

'Yes! I know.' Her eyes softened, and Ashenden was aware – had *often* been aware – that he found her attractive, especially (what a cussèd world it all was!) as she was now, when all that seemed required was a pair of strong arms to cart her up to the nearest bed.

But she suddenly ruined every bloody thing!

She had moved nearer to him, and spoke close to his ear – softly and sensuously: 'I shouldn't really tell you this, John, but I find him awfully attractive. Sort of, you know, dishy, and . . . sexy . . .'

Ashenden removed the hand that had found his sleeve once more. 'For Christ's sake, Sheila!'

'Clever, too, John. *Very* clever – so they say.'

'And what's that supposed to mean?' Ashenden's voice sounded needlessly tense.

'I'll tell you,' replied Sheila, the clarity of her articulation beginning to disintegrate: 'He's going to wanna know wha' – wha' you were up to between – between – about – four thirty and five fifteen.'

'What's that got to do with *him*?'

'It's not *me* wants to know, darling. All I say is, that's . . . that's wha' he's goin' to ashk – ask you. That's wha' he's goin' to ask *everybody*.'

Ashenden looked down silently at his drink.

'Where *were* you, John?' (Was the lovely Sheila sober once again already?)

'There's no law against anyone having a look round the colleges, is there?'

'Quite a few people were wondering where you'd got to—'

'I've just told you, for Heaven's sake!'

'But where *exactly* was it you went, John? Tell me! Come on! Tell Mummy all about it!'

Ashenden decided to humour her: 'If you must know I went and had a look round Magdalen—'

But he got no further. A few yards away Morse was walking towards the Bar-Annexe as Sheila greeted him:

'Inspector! Inspector Morse! Come and join us!'

Morse's half-smile, grudging and potentially aloof, suggested he might have preferred his own company. But Sheila was patting the settee beside her, and Morse found himself looking down into the same dark-brown, pleading eyes that had earlier held such a curious fascination for him on the floor above.

'I, er—'

'Meet John Ashenden, Inspector – our leader!'

Morse nodded across, hesitated, then surrendered, now positioning himself and his pint with exaggerated care.

'John was just saying he'd been round Magdalen this afternoon. That's right, isn't it, John?'

'Yep. It's, er, not a college I've ever got to know really. Wonderful though, isn't it? I'd known about the deer-park, but I'd never realized what a beautiful walk it was along the Cherwell there – those hundreds of acres of fields and gardens. As well as the tower, of course. Surely one of the finest towers in Europe, wouldn't you agree, Inspector?'

Morse nodded, seeming that evening to have a particular predisposition to nodding. But his brain was suddenly engaged, as it had never been engaged at any other point since arriving on the scene . . .

He had always claimed that when he had to think he had to drink – a dictum indulgently interpreted by his colleagues as an excellent excuse for the disproportionate amount of time the chief inspector seemed to spend at various bars. Yet Morse himself was quite convinced of its providential truth; and what is more, he knew that the obverse of this statement was similarly true; that when he was drinking he was invariably thinking. And as Ashenden had just spoken, Morse's blue eyes had narrowed slightly and he focused on the leader's face with a sudden hint of interest, and just the slightest tingle of excitement.

*

It was twenty minutes later, after a dinner during which they had spoken little, that Howard and Shirley Brown sat brooding over their iced tomato-juices at a table just inside the main bar.

'Well,' maintained Howard, '*you've* gotten yourself an alibi OK, Shirl. I mean, you and Eddie . . . No prarblem! What about me, though?' He grinned wryly, good-humouredly: 'I'm lying there next door to Laura, right? If I'd wanted to, well—'

'What you thinking of, honey? Murder? Theft? Rape?'

'You don't think I'm capable of rape, Shirl!'

'No, I don't!' she replied, cruelly.

'And you saw Ashenden, you say. That gives *him* an alibi, too.'

'Half an alibi.'

'He saw *you* – you're sure?'

'Sure. But I don't reckon he thought we saw *him*.'

'Down Holywell Street, you say?'

'Uh-huh! I noticed the sign.'

'What's down there?'

'Eddie looked it up on the street map. New College, then Magdalen College – that's without the "e".'

DCs Hodges and Watson were now going systematically through their lists; and, almost simultaneously, Hodges was requesting both Mrs Williams and Mr Ashenden to accompany him to the Manager's office, with Watson asking Howard and Shirley Brown if they would please mind answering a few questions in the deserted ballroom.

On the departure of his two drinking companions – the lady reluctantly, the gentleman with fairly obvious relief – Morse looked again at the Osbert Lancaster paintings on the walls around him and wondered if he really liked these illustrations for *Zuleika Dobson*. Perhaps, though, he ought at last to *read* Beerbohm's book; even discover whether she was called 'Zuleeka' or 'Zuleyeka' . . .

His glass was empty and he returned to the bar, where Michelle, the decidedly bouncy brunette, declined to accept his proffered payment.

'The lady, sir. The one that was with you. She paid.'

'Uh?'

'She just said to get a pint for you when you came up for a refill.'

'She said "when", did she?'

'She probably knows your habits, sir,' said Michelle, with an understanding smile.

Morse went to sit in the virtually deserted Annexe now, and thought for more than a few minutes of Sheila Williams. He'd had a girl-friend called Sheila when he'd been an undergraduate just across St Giles' at St John's – the very college from which A. E. Housman, the greatest Latinist of the twentieth century, had also been kicked out minus a degree. A hundred years ago in Housman's case, and a thousand years in his own. Sheila . . . the source, in Milton's words, of all our woe.

After his fourth pint of beer, Morse walked out to Reception and spoke to the senior concierge.

'I've got a car in the garage.'

'I'll see it's brought round, sir. What's the number?'

'Er . . .' For the moment Morse could not recall the number. 'No! I'll pick it up in the morning if that's all right.'

'You a resident here, sir?'

'No! It's just that I don't want the police to pick me up on the way home.'

'Very sensible, sir. I'll see what I can do. Name? Can I have your name?'

'Morse. Chief Inspector Morse.'

'They wouldn't pick *you* up, would they?'

'No? Funny lot the police, you know.'

'Shall I call a taxi?'

'Taxi? I'm walking. I only live at the top of the Banbury Road, and a taxi'd cost me three quid at this time of night. That's three pints of beer.'

'Only *two* here, sir!' corrected Roy Halford as he watched the chief inspector step carefully – a little *too* carefully? – down the shallow steps and out to Beaumont Street.

CHAPTER THIRTEEN

Solvitur ambulando
(The problem is solved by walking around)
(Latin proverb)

As he walked up the Banbury Road that Thursday night, Morse was aware that by this time Lewis would know considerably more than *he* did about the probable contents of Laura Stratton's handbag, the possible disposition of the loot, and the likely circle of suspects. Yet he was aware, too, that his mind seemed – was! – considerably more lucid than he deserved it to be, and there *were* a few facts to be considered – certainly more facts than Lewis had gleaned in his school-days about Alfred the Great.

Facts: carrying her handbag, a woman had gone up to Room 310 at about 4.35 p.m.; this woman had not been seen alive again – or at least no one so far would *admit* to seeing her alive again; inside 310 a bath had been run and almost certainly taken; a coffee-sachet and a miniature tub of cream had been used; a DO NOT DISTURB sign had been displayed on the outside door-knob at some point, with the door itself probably left open; the woman's husband had returned at about 5.15 p.m., and without reporting to Reception had gone up to the third floor, in the guest-lift, with a fellow tourist (female); thence a hurried scuttle down to Reception via the main staircase where a duplicate key was acquired. On finally gaining access to his room, the husband had discovered his wife's body on the floor, presumably already dead; the hotel's house-doctor had arrived some ten or fifteen minutes later, and the body duly transferred from floor to bed – all this by about 5.40 p.m. At some point before, during, or after these latter events, the husband himself had noticed the disappearance of his wife's handbag; and at about 6 p.m. a call had been received by St Aldates CID with a request for help in what was now looking a matter of considerably more moment than any petty theft.

Yes, those were the facts.

So move on, Morse, to a few non-factual inferences in the problem of the Wolvercote Tongue. Move on, my son – and hypothesize! Come on, now! Who *could* had stolen it?

Well, in the first place, with the door to 310 *locked*, only those who had a key: the Manager, the housekeeper, the room-maids – namely, anyone with, or with access to, a duplicate key to the

aforementioned room. *Not* the husband. In the second place, with
the door to 310 *open*, a much more interesting thieves' gallery was
open to view: most obviously, anyone at all who would happen to
be passing and who had glimpsed, through the open door, a
handbag that had proved too tempting an opportunity. Open to
such temptation (if not necessarily susceptible to it) would have
been the room-maids, the occupants of nearby rooms, any casual
passer-by . . . But just a moment! Room 310 was *off* the main
corridor, and anyone in its immediate vicinity would be there *for a
reason*: a friend, perhaps, with a solicitous enquiry about the lady's
feet; a fellow tourist wanting to borrow something; or learn
something . . . Then there was Ashenden. He'd said he would be
going around at some point to all the rooms to check up on the
sachets, shampoos, soaps, switches. Opportunity? Yes! But hardly
much of a motive, surely? What about the three guest speakers?
Out of the question, wasn't it? They hadn't been called to the
colours at that point – weren't even *in* The Randolph. Forget them!
Well, no – not altogether, perhaps; not until Lewis had checked
their statements.

So that was that, really. That set the 'parameters' (the buzz-
word at HQ recently) for the crime. No other portraits in the
gallery.

Not really.

No.

Or were there?

What about the husband? Morse had always entertained a
healthy suspicion of anyone found first on the scene of a crime;
and Eddie Stratton had been a *double* first: the first to report both
the death of his wife, *and* the theft of the jewel. But any man who
finds his wife dead – dead! – surely he's not going to . . . Nobody
could suspect that.

Except Morse.

And what about – what about the most unlikely, improbable,
unthinkable . . . Unthinkable? Well, *think* about it, Morse! What
about the wife herself: Mrs Laura Stratton? Could she have been
responsible for the disappearance of the jewel? But why? Was it
insured? Surely so! And doubtless for a hefty sum. All right, the
thing was unsellable, unbuyable; the thing was useless – except,
that is, as a link in a cultural continuum in a University Museum.
Or else – yes! – or else as an insurance item which in terms of cash
was worth far more lost than found; and if the Strattons were
getting a bit hard up it might not have been so much *if* it were lost
as *when*. And what – it was always going to hit Morse's brain

sooner or later – what if the thing had never been there to get lost in the first place? Yes, the possibility had to be faced: what if the Wolvercote Tongue had never been inside the handbag at all? (Keep going, Morse!) Never even left America?

Morse already found himself in the Summertown shopping centre; and it was some five minutes later, as he came to his bachelor flat just south of the A40 Ring Road, that the oddest possibility finally struck him: what if the Wolvercote Tongue didn't *exist* at all? But surely there would have been all sorts of descriptive and photographic pieces of evidence, and so on? Surely such an authority as Dr Theodore Kemp could never have been so duped in such a matter? No. And he'd almost certainly flown over to see it, anyway. No. Forget it! So Morse almost forgot it, and let himself into his flat, where he played the first two movements of the Bruckner No. 7 before going to bed.

He woke up at 2.50 a.m., his mouth very dry. He got out of bed and went to the bathroom, where he drank a glass of water; and another glass of water. In truth, water – a liquid which figured little during Morse's waking life – was his constant companion during the early hours of almost every morning.

CHAPTER FOURTEEN

It is only shallow people who do not judge by appearances. The true mystery of the world is the visible, not the invisible

(Oscar Wilde, *The Picture of Dorian Gray*)

The bachelor Morse had only the wraith-like, gin-ridden spectre of a lush divorcée to share his pillow that night, unlike the male speakers scheduled for the following day's Historic Cities of England programme, both of whom, when Morse had made his first visit to the bathroom, were dutifully asleep beside their respective spouses and in their own homes – homes in North Oxford, separated by only about a quarter of a mile.

The traveller who heads north from the centre of Oxford may take, at St Giles' Church, either the fork which leads up the Woodstock Road, or the right-hand fork, the Banbury Road, which leads after a mile or so to Summertown. Here, just past the shopping area, he will come to the new, yellow-bricked premises of Radio Oxford on his left; and then, almost immediately on his right, the first of the four roads – Lonsdale, Portland, Hamilton, Victoria – which stretch between the main Banbury Road and the River Cherwell (pronounced by most of the locals 'Charwell'). At all hours, each of these roads is suitable only for one-way traffic because of the continuous lines of parked cars on either side. The majority of houses here, built in the 1920s and 30s, are without integral garages; and many an amateurishly painted sign, alongside the edges of the pavement or on boards beside front gates, urges with courtesy, warns with threats of trespass, or simply begs with a pathetic 'Please', those motorists who commute to Summertown not to park their wretched vehicles *there*. In vain! For the life-blood along these roads ever flows, as it were, through arteries clogged with atherosclerosis.

But Dr Kemp no longer drives a car . . .

Any person meeting for the first time those two distinguished academics, Theodore Kemp and Cedric Downes, would be fairly sure to come to the following judgements. Kemp would perhaps appear to merit such epithets as artistic, flamboyant, high-brow, selfish, aloof, rakish – the list could go on and on, in much the same direction; and this impression would be formed largely from a certain arrogance in the pale features, an affected upper-class diction, the almost invariable silk shirt and bow-tie, the casual elegance of the light-beige lightweight suits which he favoured in both summer and winter to bedeck his slim and small-boned figure. And what of Downes? Certainly not by any means such a clear-cut impression: rather languid in movement, somewhat overweight, a not-quite-top-echelon-public-school-man, a slightly bored expression round the mouth, the promise of a humorous twinkle in the eyes, a semi-florid colouring, a heavyish suit with trousers sorely in need of a press, longish and lank brown hair, and a careless, unpretentious drawl in a voice which still bore the flat traces of his Midlands origins. Everything about him qualified; everything 'rather', 'quite', 'somewhat'. And finally – most import-antly, maybe – the obvious impression that he was going a bit, more than a bit deaf. For increasingly noticeable was his habit of shepherding any interlocutor to his right-hand side; his frequent cupping of the hand behind his right ear; and occasionally his use of an NHS hearing-aid, recently provided for his rapidly developing otosclerosis.

Which things being so, it might be assumed that Kemp was probably having all the fun that was going in life in general, and in Oxford in particular; whilst the seedier, world-weary Downes was slowly running out of steam, and like as not running out of luck, too. Yet such an assumption would not be wholly correct: in fact it would be some considerable way distant from the truth.

Kemp's life had not blossomed as once it had promised. After fathering (as was rumoured) almost as many illegitimate offspring as almighty Zeus himself, and after successfully disclaiming most of the responsibility for such excessive multiplication of the species, he had married a rather plain, though neatly figured woman, named Marion (with an 'o'), whose parents were rumoured to be fairly wealthy. Then, now two years since, he had managed to crash his BMW in such a way that his not wholly fair but fully pregnant wife had lost both her child and the use of her lower limbs, whilst he himself had received only a broken collar-bone, with a few slivers of glass embedded in his back. But at least Marion had survived: the driver of the other car involved, a thirty-five-year-old married woman, had been instantly killed. Definitive responsibility for the accident could not be fully determined, since the coroner found some of the evidence confusing, and far from competently reported. Yet Kemp *had* been drinking: and the charge he faced, a charge resulting in a fine and a three-year disqualification, had been one of driving whilst under the influence of alcohol, not that of reckless or of dangerous driving. Some of those who knew Kemp well, most of his University colleagues, and all of those who could never abide the man, considered him to have been extremely fortunate. Such disapprobation had probably accounted for the refusal of his college to elevate his status as a post-graduate researcher (or 'graduate researcher', as the pedantic Morse would have preferred) to that of the fellowship which had suddenly fallen vacant. Six weeks after this humiliation, he had been appointed to the post of Keeper of Anglo-Saxon and Mediaeval Antiquities at the Ashmolean. He now lived in a ground-floor flat in Cherwell Lodge, a brick-built block along Water Eaton Road – the latter stretching from the bottom of Victoria Road into the Cutteslowe Estate. The enforced move, made to accommodate his wheel-chaired wife, had taken place at exactly the wrong time in the housing market, and his property was presently worth little more than a quarter of the price likely to be fetched by that of his fellow-lecturer, the one who had temporarily forgotten the name of a Danish architect.

At the age of forty, five years previously, Cedric Downes had married Lucy, an engagingly attractive woman, eleven years his junior, fair-skinned and blonde, fully-figured and fully-sexed – though with a tendency towards a nervousness of manner on occasion – and with an IQ which was rated quite high by those meeting her for the first time, but which usually dipped a little upon more intimate acquaintance. Downes, a mediaeval historian, was a Fellow of Brasenose, and lived in a large detached house at the far end of Lonsdale Road, its beautifully tended back garden stretching down to the banks of the River Cherwell . . .

In the back bedroom of Number 6 Cherwell Lodge, Marion Kemp lay supine. Marion Kemp *had* to lie supine. It would have been beneficial to the two of them, certainly would have guaranteed longer periods of sleep, if after the accident they had abandoned the double bed and settled for twin beds – perhaps even for separate rooms. Surprisingly, however, her husband would hear nothing of such a suggestion, and at first she had felt pleased and, yes!, flattered that he still wished to lie each night beside her fruitless body. And even on that Thursday night some of the hatred which for so long had been slowly coalescing in her soul had perhaps abated minimally . . .

As he had promised, he had been home at 10 p.m., had clearly not been drinking much at all, had brought her a cup of Ovaltine and a Digestive biscuit, and quite definitely had *not* been with that bitchy, boozy, whoreson *Williams* woman.

Unlike Lucy Downes, Marion Kemp did not convey any immediate impression of a lively mind. Yet those who knew her well (a diminishing group) were always aware of a shrewd and observant intelligence. Earlier she had watched Theo carefully as he had spoken to her about what had occurred that evening, and she had been wholly conscious of his own colossal frustration and disappointment. But in truth she could not find herself caring two milk-tokens about the loss of the Wolvercote Tongue; nor indeed find herself unduly distressed about the death of some bejewelled old biddy from the far side of America. Yet she could find no sleep in the small hours of that Friday morning, her mind considering many things: above all the growing suspicion that the man asleep beside her was looking now beyond that bloody Williams woman . . .

And Marion thought she knew exactly where.

Cedric Downes had come home rather later than usual that Thursday evening. He had been one of the last to give the police an account of his movements from 4.30 to 5.15 p.m. ('Is this *really* necessary, officer?') God! He'd had a tutorial at that time! And now, when finally he went through into the bedroom, all was very quiet, with Lucy lying motionless along her own side of the bed. He nestled gently against the contours of her body, hoping that she might sense his need for her, but realizing almost immediately that she was distanced, and would not be conjoined. He turned on to his right-hand side, as now he usually did when seeking sleep. With his left ear becoming so deaf, he would consciously press his right ear deep into the pillow, thereafter hearing virtually nothing of the nightly groans of the central-heating pipes, or the inexplicable creaking of the wood, or the rushing of the wind in the towering pine trees. Briefly his mind dwelt on the evening's events; briefly dwelt on his loathing for Kemp; but within a few minutes he could feel the tug of the warm tide and soon he was floating down to the depths of slumber.

Not so his wife, still breathing quietly and rhythmically, and not so much as twitching a lumbrical muscle.

But very much asleep that night was Sheila Williams, the bedroom window wide open in her dingily stuccoed semi in the lower reaches of Hamilton Road, a house (as it happened) almost exactly equidistant from that of Kemp and that of Downes.

At 4.45 a.m. Morse made his third visit to the bathroom – *and suddenly he remembered.* He went into his living room, looked along his book-shelves, extracted a volume, consulted its index, turned to the pages given, and read through the entry he had sought. His head nodded a few degrees, and his dry mouth widened into a mildly contented smile.

He was asleep when Lewis rang the doorbell at 8.30 a.m.

CHAPTER FIFTEEN

The best-laid schemes o' mice and men
   Gang aft a-gley,
And lea'e us naught but grief and pain
   For promised joy
                    (Robert Burns, *To a Mouse*)

Few English families living in England have much direct contact with the English Breakfast. It is therefore fortunate that such an endangered institution is perpetuated by the efforts of the kitchen staff in guest houses, B & Bs, transport cafés, and other no-starred and variously starred hotels. This breakfast comprises (at its best): a milkily-opaque fried egg; two rashers of non-brittle, rindless bacon; a tomato grilled to a point where the core is no longer a hard white nodule to be operated upon by the knife; a sturdy sausage, deeply and evenly browned; and a slice of fried bread, golden-brown, and only just crisp, with sufficient fat not excessively to dismay any meddlesome dietitian. That is the definitive English Breakfast. And that is what the French, the Germans, the Italians, the Japanese, the Russians, the Turks . . . and the English, also, with their diurnal diet of Corn Flakes and a toasted slice of Mother's Pride – that is what they all enjoy as much as almost anything about a holiday.

The Americans, too, though there are always exceptions.

Janet Roscoe leaned across the table, lowered the volume switch on her abnormally loud voice, and spoke to Sam and Vera Kronquist, the third of the married couples originally registered on the tour.

'I just don't know how he' – her sharp eyes singled out Phil Aldrich, seated at the next table – 'how he can even think of eating – *that*.'

The vehement emphasis accorded to this last word might perhaps have suggested that Janet's co-worshipper in Sacramento's Temperance Hall of Christian Scientists was devouring a plateful of raw maggots or the roasted flesh of sacrificial infants, instead of his slim rasher of streaky bacon. But Sam Kronquist, though content with his croissant, was happily tolerant about the tastes of others:

'We're only on vaycation once a year, you know, Janet. So perhaps we can forgive him?'

Or perhaps not; for Janet made no reply, and in silence completed her own modest breakfast of naturally juiced grapefruit segments, and one slice of unbuttered toast smeared over with diabetic marmalade. She was just finishing her cup of black de-caffeinated coffee when John Ashenden, after his peripatetic trip around the other tables, came to tell the three of them that there would be a short meeting in the St John's Suite at 9.15 a.m. in order to fit the coming day's events into a schedule that would have to be slightly revised . . .

'If you refer,' began Ashenden, 'to your original sheets' (he held up a copy of the yellow sheets distributed the previous day) 'you will see that quite a few amendments, sadly, will have to be made to it. But the tour will quite definitely be going ahead as normal – or as normal as it can do in the circumstances. Eddie – Eddie Stratton – wants this, wants it to go ahead, and he believes that Laura would have wished that, too. So . . . First of all then: our visit to The Oxford Story, scheduled for ten-thirty. This has been put back to ten a.m. Make a note, please: ten a.m. instead of—'

'Don't you mean brought *forward*, Mr Ashenden?'

Yes, probably Ashenden *did* mean exactly what Mrs Roscoe said. And he beamed a smile towards her, in fact welcoming rather than resenting the interruption: '—has been brought for-ward to ten a.m. There's been a cancellation of a Spanish block-booking and it will help the people there if we take the earlier spot. Yes? No problems?'

Thereupon Ashenden duly distributed an extra sheet to each of his rather subdued audience:

The Oxford Story

It was here in Oxford that Lewis Carroll created the immortal 'Alice'; here that King Charles I held his Civil War Parliament; here where Archbishop Cranmer was burned at the stake; here where Penicillin was developed. So take a seat aboard a flying desk – Ride the Spiral! – and travel backwards through time to the earliest days of Oxford University when Friar Roger Bacon (1214–1294) sat in his rooms overlooking Folly Bridge and . . . But let *Oxford* tell its own story, as you sit comfortably in your car and witness whole centuries of fascinating men and glorious events. (Wheel-chair access and toilet facilities for the disabled.)

There being no murmurs of demurral, even from the customary quarter, Ashenden proceeded to extol the virtues of such a visit: to whisk oneself back to the origins of the University in the twelfth century, and thence be spiralled to the present day – seated, foot-happily – with the wonderful bonus, betweenwhiles, of listening to a commentary on the passing pageants by no less a personage than Sir Alec Guinness himself. The visit had in fact figured as an 'extra' in the published brochure, but in view of the, er, the sad, *sad* events . . . Well, the company had agreed that the £2 supplement should now be waived.

'That's a very kindly gesture, sir,' volunteered Phil Aldrich, and several of his fellow tourists audibly concurred.

Sam Kronquist, suffering from incipient prostate trouble, found himself wondering whether that final parenthesis signified a lack of toilet facilities for those persons as yet unwilling to label themselves 'disabled'; but he held his peace.

That meant, Ashenden continued, that there would be something of an uncomfortable gap between about 11.15 and 12.30; and he was very glad to be able to announce that Mrs Williams and Mr Downes and Dr Kemp had agreed to hold an impromptu question-and-answer session on Oxford: Town and Gown. This would be in the Ball Room, beginning at 11.30 a.m.

To the afternoon, then.

Ashenden exhorted his audience once again to consult the original sheet, confirming that, apart from the 6.30 p.m. presentation, the scheduled programme would go ahead as stated. Perhaps it would be sensible, though, to start the afternoon groups at 2.45 p.m., please, at which time Dr Kemp would meet *his* group immediately outside the main entrance to the Ashmolean; Mr Downes *his* group at the Martyrs' Memorial; Mrs Williams *her* group in the foyer of the hotel. Was that all clear? And would they all please try if possible to keep to the group they had first opted for? There was a nice little balance at the moment; not that he would want to *stop* anyone changing, of course . . .

Again the touring party appeared to find the arrangements wholly unexceptionable, and Ashenden came to his last point. Would everyone please change the time given on their sheets for dinner: this was now brought forward ('Right, Mrs Roscoe?') from 8 p.m. to 7.30 p.m. Three of the Trustees of the Ashmolean would be joining them, and he would assume unless he was informed to the contrary that everyone would be coming to this final dinner. It *had* been optional, he knew that; but in view of . . .

In the crowded hotel foyer, ten minutes later, Mrs Roscoe failed to decrease her decibel level as she called across to the Bacon Man from Sacramento: 'They tell me we sit in those cars two at a time, side by side, Phil . . .'

'Yeah! OK, Janet. Yeah, OK.'

CHAPTER SIXTEEN

As you go through, you see the great scientists, scholars, and statesmen; the thinkers, writers, actors, mon-
archs, and martyrs who are part of Oxford's history. By
passing this doorway you have a glimpse of the people
whom Oxford has moulded, and many of whom have,
in their turn, gone on to help mould the world
(Lord Jenkins of Hillhead, *The Oxford Story*)

At 9.50 a.m. Cedric Downes led the way as the tourists trooped down the front steps of The Randolph, turned right, and moved across the road. Here, just by the Martyrs' Memorial, Downes stopped.

'Here we have . . .' He pointed to the heavy iron sign on which the letters MAGDALEN STREET were painted in white, and the group gathered around him. 'Everyone – nearly everyone – knows that this is pronounced "Maudlin" Street, as if it were a sentimental, tearful sort of street. That's what the bus drivers call it. Now out in East Oxford we've got a Magdalen Road, and the same bus drivers call that one "M-a-g-dalen" Road. I only mention this, my friends, to show you that life here in Oxford is never quite so simple as it may appear. Off we go!'

'I didn't know *that*, Phil,' said Janet Roscoe quietly. '*Very* interesting.'

The group progressed to Broad Street, where Downes brought them all to a stop again, this time immediately outside the Master's Lodge at Balliol. 'Here – on your left here – the plaque on the wall – this is where Latimer and Ridley, and later Cranmer, were burned at the stake in 1555 and 1556. Not difficult to remember the date, is it? You can see the actual spot, the cross there – see it? – right in the middle of the road.'

A little silence fell on the group: those with the faculty of a visual imagination watching as the long, grey beards began to sizzle, and then the ankle-length shirts suddenly leap up in a scorching mantle of fire, and others hearing perhaps those agonized shrieks as the faggot-fired flames consumed the living flesh . . . For a few moments it seemed that everyone was strangely affected by Cedric Downes's words. Perhaps it was the way he'd spoken them, with a sad and simple dignity . . .

'Here we are then! No more walking to do at all.' He pointed immediately across the way to the triple-arched entry of the three-storeyed building that housed The Oxford Story.

That same evening Miss Ginger Bonnetti (not 'Ginger', but christened Ginger) wrote a longish letter to her married sister living in Los Angeles, one Mrs Georgie (as christened!) Bonnetti, who had married a man named Angelo Bonnetti. (Morse would have had great joy in learning of this, for he gloried in coincidences; but since Miss Ginger Bonnetti was destined to play no further role in the theft of the Wolvercote Tongue, he never did.)

Hi, sis! We had a great morning in Oxford. There's a kind of tourist attraction here called The Oxford Story and we got into these sort of cars, but they're more like those old-fashioned desks from schooldays really – sitting side by side, remember? Made of some dark sort of wood with slightly sloping tops as if you'd just got to listen to the class teacher or write out the alphabet again if you didn't. Then we went up a sort of spiral gradiant at .000001 mph – no kidding! I wish I could remember all those great names we saw, and I do mean great! And you sit. You sit in these double desks and listen to a commentary from you guess who! Sir Alec Guiness. I mean, the _voice_! So the pen was working away as we went around and I've kept a brochure for you somewhere of all these people, Roger Bacon, Thomas Bodley, Charles First (what a little guy _he_ was), Hobbes and Locke, Wilkins (? — I can't read my own handwriting). Sir Christopher Wren, Boyle (you remember _our_ Physics teacher?), John Wesely (or is it Wessley?), Alice (yeah, the same!), William Ewart Gladstone and no end of those other PMs. And of course Cranmer and the Protestant Martyrs, and I'm starting to remember I've forgotten so many of the others. Does that last bit make sense, Georgie? Anyway it was marvellous, the only trouble was that the poor fellow in front of me had to put up with all this incessant chatter from a really _dreadful_ little woman who's clearly trying to trap another victim. But I've left the big news till now. You remember I told you about the jewel one of the group was going to bring to the Oxford museum here?

Well yesterday this poor woman had a coronary and died and someone stole her handbag with this jewel inside it! Where _is_ safe these days? You tell me that. She'd been a little poorly and her husband said she always knew it was going to be sooner or later but it's a bad time just now, for the tour I mean. Eddie, he's the husband, doesn't want us to be too upset and the tour goes on as sheduled, and well he was her second! He's a pretty nice guy really. But I reckon she was the one with the money and I just hope she was pretty well insured all round. So as you can see we're having plenty happening here!

Love to Angelo,
Ginger

P.S. I forgot to tell you it was just a bit _spooky_ for a start in that Oxford Story.

P.P.S My room looks right out on the Ashmolean - see that X on the enclosed card?

In the Oxford Story Gift Shop, the group had stayed quite some time, examining aprons, busts, chess-sets, Cheshire cats, cufflinks, games, gargoyles, glassware, jewellery, jigsaws, jugs, maps, pictures, postcards, posters, stationery, table-mats, thimbles, videos – everything a tourist could wish for.

'Gee! With *her* feet, how Laura would have loved that ride!' remarked Vera Kronquist. But her husband made no answer. If he were honest he was not wholly displeased that Laura's feet were no longer going to be a major factor in the determination of the tour's itineraries. She was always talking about lying down; and now she *was* lying down. Permanently.

'Very good,' said Phil Aldrich as he and Mrs Roscoe and the Browns emerged through the exit into Ship Street.

'But the figures there – they weren't nearly as good as the ones in Madame Tussaud's, now were they?'

'No, you're quite right, Janet,' said Howard Brown, as he gently guided her towards Cornmarket and back towards The Randolph.

When, five days later, Mrs Georgie Bonnetti received her sister's interesting letter, she was a little disappointed (herself a zealous Nonconformist) that with neither cartridge from the double-barelled rifle had her sister succeeded in hitting the saintly founder of Methodism. (The unbeliever Morse would have been rather more concerned about the other four mis-spellings.)

CHAPTER SEVENTEEN

Clever people seem not to feel the natural pleasure of
bewilderment, and are always answering questions
when the chief relish of a life is to go on asking them
(Frank Moore Colby)

After his *in situ* briefing outside Balliol, Downes left the scene of the barbarous burnings and strolled thoughtfully along to Blackwells. An hour and a quarter (Ashenden had suggested) for The Oxford Story; then back to The Randolph where he and Sheila Williams and Kemp (the man would always remain a surname to Downes) had agreed to hold the question-and-answer session with the Americans. Downes sometimes felt a bit dubious about 'Americans'; yet like almost all his colleagues in Oxford, he often found himself enjoying actual Americans, without those quotation marks. That morning he knew that as always some of their questions would be disturbingly naïve, some penetrating, all of them *honest*. And he approved of such questions, doubtless because he himself could usually score a pretty point or two with answers that were honest: quite different from the top-of-the-head comments of some of the spurious academics he knew.

People like Kemp.

After spending fifty minutes browsing through the second-hand books in Blackwells, Downes returned to The Randolph, and was stepping up the canopied entrance when he heard the voice a few yards behind him.

'Cedric!'

He turned round.

'You must be deaf! I called along the road there three or four times.'

'I *am* deaf – you know that.'

'Now don't start looking for any sympathy from me, Cedric! What the hell! There are far worse things than being deaf.'

Downes smiled agreement and looked (and not without interest) at the attractively dressed divorcée he'd known on and off for the past four years. Her voice (this morning, again) was sometimes a trifle shrill, her manner almost always rather tense; but there were far worse things than . . .

'Time for a drink?' asked Sheila – with hope. It was just after eleven.

They walked together into the foyer and both looked at the noticeboard in front of them:

HISTORIC CITIES TOUR ST JOHN'S SUITE 11.30 a.m.

'Did you hear me?' continued Sheila.

'Pardon?'

'I said we've got almost half an hour before—'

'Just a minute!' Downes was fixing an NHS hearing-aid to his right ear, switching it on, adjusting the volume – and suddenly, so clearly, so wonderfully, the whole of the hotel burst into happily chattering life. 'Back in the land of the living! Well? I know it's a bit early, Sheila, but what would you say about a quick snifter? Plenty of time.'

Sheila smiled radiantly, put her arm through his, and propelled him through to the Chapters Bar: 'I would say "yes", Cedric. In fact I think I would say "yes" to almost anything this morning; and especially to a Scotch.'

For a few delightful seconds Downes felt the softness of her breast against his arm, and perhaps for the first time in their acquaintanceship he realized that he could want this woman. And as he reached for his wallet, he was almost glad to read the notice to the left of the bar: 'All spirits will be served as double measures unless otherwise requested.'

They were sitting on a beige-coloured wall-settee, opposite the bar, dipping occasionally into a glass dish quartered with green olives, black olives, cocktail onions, and gherkins – when Ashenden looked in, looked around, and saw them.

'Ah – thought I might find you here.'

'How is Mr Stratton?' asked Sheila.

'I saw him at breakfast – he seems to be taking things remarkably well, really.'

'No news of . . . of what was stolen?'

Ashenden shook his head. 'Nobody seems to hold out much hope.'

'Poor Theo!' pouted Sheila. 'I must remember to be nice to him this morning.'

'I, er,' Ashenden was looking decidedly uncomfortable: 'Dr Kemp won't be joining us this morning, I'm afraid.'

'And why the hell *not*?' This from a suddenly bristling Sheila.

'Mrs Kemp rang earlier. He's gone to London. Just for the morning, though. His publisher had been trying to see him, and with the presentation off and everything—'

'That was this *evening*!' protested Downes.

'Bloody nerve!' spluttered Sheila. 'You were here, John, when he promised. Typical! Leave Cedric and me to do all the bloody donkey-work!'

'He's getting back as soon as he can: should be here by lunchtime. So if – well, I'm sorry. It's been a bit of a disappointment for the group already and if you . . .'

'One condition, John!' Sheila, now smiling, seemed to relax. And Ashenden understood, and walked to the bar with her empty glass.

The tour leader was pleased with the way the session had gone. Lots of good questions, with both Sheila Williams and Cedric Downes acquitting themselves *magna cum laude*, especially Downes, who had found exactly the right combination of scholarship and scepticism.

*

It was over lunch that Sheila, having availed herself freely of the pre-luncheon sherry (including the rations of a still-absent Kemp), became quite needlessly cruel.

'Were you an undergraduate here – at Arksford, Mr Downes?'

'I was here, yes. At Jesus – one of the less fashionable colleges, Mrs Roscoe. Welsh, you know. Founded in 1571.'

'I thought Jesus was at Cambridge.'

Sheila found the opening irresistible: 'No, no, Mrs Roscoe! Jesus went to Bethlehem Tech.'

It was a harmless enough joke, and certainly Phil Aldrich laughed openly. But not Janet Roscoe.

'Is that what they mean by the English sense of humour, Mrs Williams?'

'Where else would he go to do carpentry?' continued Sheila, finding her further pleasantry even funnier than her first, and laughing stridently.

Downes himself appeared amused no longer by the exchange, and his right hand went up to his ear to adjust an aid which for the past few minutes had been emitting an intermittent whistle. Perhaps he hadn't heard . . .

But Janet was not prepared to let things rest. She had (she knew) been made to look silly; and she now proceeded to make herself look even sillier. 'I don't myself see anything funny in blasphemy, and besides they didn't have colleges in Palestine in those days.'

Phil Aldrich laid a gently restraining hand on Janet's arm as Sheila's shrill amusement scaled new heights: 'Please don't make too much fun of us, Mrs Williams. I know we're not as clever, some of us, as many of you are. That's why we came, you know, to try to learn a little more about your country here and about your ways.'

It was a dignified little speech, and Sheila now felt desperately ashamed. For a few seconds, a look of mild regret gleamed in her slightly bloodshot eyes, and she had begun to apologize when immediately next to them, on a table below the window overlooking the Taylor Institution, the phone rang.

It was 12.35 p.m. when Mrs Celia Freeman, a pleasantly spoken and most competent woman, took the call on the telephone exchange at the rear of the main Reception area. Only approximately 12.35 p.m., though. When later questioned (and questioned most earnestly) on this matter, she had found on her notepad that both the name of the caller ('Dr Kemp') and the name of the person called ('Mr Ashenden') had been jotted down soon after a timed call at 12.31 p.m. And it was at 12.48 p.m., exactly, that John Ashenden phoned back from the St John's Suite to Reception to order a taxi to meet the train from Paddington arriving 15.00, and to pick up a Dr Theodore Kemp at Oxford Station.

CHAPTER EIGHTEEN

In the police-procedural, a fair degree of realism is possible, but it cannot be pushed too far for fear that the book might be as dull as the actual days of a policeman

(Julian Symons, *Bloody Murder*)

It was not until 10 a.m. that same morning that Morse had recovered the Jaguar; 10.15 a.m. when he finally put in an appearance at Kidlington HQ.

'Hope you had a profitable evening, Lewis?'

'Not particularly.'

'Not arrested the thief yet?'

Lewis shook his head. He'd already put in three hours' work, trying to sort out and collate various statements, and he was in no mood to appreciate the sarcasm of a man who had seemingly lost most of the little enthusiasm he'd started with.

'Well?' asked Morse.

'Nothing, really. These Americans – well, they seem a nice lot of people. Some of 'em not all that sure about *exactly* where they were – but you'd expect that, wouldn't you? Settling in, drinking tea, unpacking, having a wash, trying to get the telly going—'

'Studying the Fire Instructions, I hope.'

'Doubt it. But as far as I could see, they all seemed to be telling the truth.'

'Except one.'

'Pardon, sir?'

'Ashenden was lying.'

Lewis looked puzzled: 'How can you say that?'

'He said he had a look round Magdalen.'

'So?'

'He told me all about it – he was virtually reciting phrases from the guide-book.'

'He *is* a guide.'

'Pages 130 – something of Jan Morris's *Oxford*. Word for word – nearly.'

'He'd probably swotted it up for when he was going round with the group.'

'Magdalen's not on the programme.'

'But you can't just say he's lying because – '

'Ashenden's a liar!'

Lewis shook his head: it was hardly worth arguing with Morse in such a mood, but he persisted a little longer. 'It doesn't *matter* though, does it? If Ashenden decided to go and look round Magdalen—'

'He didn't,' said Morse quietly.

'No?'

'I rang the Porters' Lodge there this morning. The College was closed to visitors all day: they're doing some restoration in the cloisters and the scaffolders were there from early morning. No one, Lewis – *no one* – was allowed in Magdalen yesterday except the Fellows, by order of the Bursar, an order the Head Porter assured me was complied with without a single exception – well only a fellow without a capital "f" who brought a stock of superfine toilet paper for the President.'

'Oh!' Lewis looked down and surveyed the sheets on his desk, neatly arranged, carefully considered – and probably wasted. They might just as well be toilet paper, too. Here was Morse making a mockery of all his efforts with just a single phone call. 'So he was telling us lies,' he said, without enthusiasm.

'Some of us spend most of our lives telling lies, Lewis.'

'Do you want me to bring him in?'

'You can't arrest a man for telling lies. Not *those* lies, anyway. He's probably got a fancy bit of skirt along Holywell Street somewhere. Just as well he *was* there, perhaps.'

'Sir?'

'Well, it means he wasn't in The Randolph pinching handbags, doesn't it?'

'He could have pinched it *before* he went out. Mrs Stratton was one of the first up to her room, and Ashenden was there for a good ten minutes or so—'

'What did he do with it?'

'We ought to have searched the rooms, sir.'

Morse nodded vaguely, then shrugged his shoulders.

'We wasting our time?' asked Lewis.

'What? About the handbag? Oh yes! We shall never find that –
you can safely put your bank balance on that.'

'I wouldn't lose all that much if I did,' mumbled the dispirited
Lewis.

'Has Max rung?'

'No. Promised to, though, didn't he?'

'Idle sod!' Morse picked up the phone and dialled the lab. 'If he
still says it was just a heart attack, I think I'll just leave this little
business in your capable hands, Lewis, and get back home.'

'I reckon you'd be happy as a sandboy if he tells you she was
murdered.'

But Morse was through: 'Max? Morse. Done your homework?'

'Massive coronary.'

'Positive?'

Morse heard the exasperated expiration of breath at the other
end of the line; but received no answer.

'Could it have been brought on, Max – you know, by her
finding a fellow fiddling with her powder-compact?'

'Couldn't say.'

'Someone she didn't expect – coming into her room?'

'Couldn't say.'

'No sign of any injury anywhere?'

'No.'

'You looked everywhere?'

'I always look everywhere.'

'Not much help, are you.'

'On the contrary, Morse. I've told you exactly what she died of.
Just like the good Dr Swain.'

But Morse had already put down the phone; and five minutes
later he was driving down to North Oxford.

Lewis himself remained in the office and spent the rest of the
morning rounding off the dull routine of his paper work. At 12.50
p.m., deciding he couldn't emulate the peremptory tone that
Morse usually adopted with commissionaires, he took a number
21 bus down to St Giles', where he alighted at the Martyrs'
Memorial and began to walk across to The Randolph. Sheila
Williams was stepping out briskly, without glancing behind her,
up the left-hand side of St Giles', past the columns of the Taylorian
and the front of Pusey House, before being lost to the mildly
interested gaze of Sergeant Lewis. And as the latter turned into
Beaumont Street, with the canopy of The Randolph immediately
in front of him, he stopped again. A man walked down the steps

of the hotel, looking quickly back over his shoulder before turning left and scurrying along the street towards Worcester College, where he turned left once more at the traffic lights, and passed beneath the traffic sign there announcing 'British Rail'. In normal circumstances, such an innocent-seeming occurrence would hardly have deserved a place in the memory. But these were not normal circumstances, and the man who had just left The Randolph in such haste was *Eddie Stratton*.

Diffidently, Lewis followed.

It was during this hour, between 1 p.m. and 2 p.m., as Morse and Lewis were later to learn, that the scene was irreversibly set for murder.

At 3.20 p.m., to an audience slightly smaller than anticipated, Cedric Downes was pointing to the merits of the stained-glass windows in University College chapel, and especially to the scene in the Garden of Eden, where the apples on the tree of knowledge glowed like giant golden Jaffas. At 3.30 p.m., in the Archive Room of the new Bodleian, Sheila Williams was doing her best to enthuse over a series of Henry Taunt photographs taken in the 1880s – also to an audience slightly smaller than anticipated. But the slides selected by Dr Theodore Kemp, to illustrate the development of jewelled artefacts in pre-Conquest Britain, were destined to remain in their box in the Elias Ashmole Memorial Room that sunny afternoon.

CHAPTER NINETEEN

At Oxford nude bathing was, and sometimes still is, indulged in, which used to cause mutual embarrass- ment when ladies passed by in boats
(Marilyn Yurdan, *Oxford: Town & Gown*)

At 9.30 p.m. the University Parks had long been closed – since before sundown in fact. Yet such a circumstance has seldom deterred determined lovers, and others slightly crazed, from finding passage-ways through or over fences and hedges into this famous precinct – the setting for countless copulations since the Royalist artillery was quartered on its acres during the Civil War.

Two of these latter-day lovers, Michael Woods (aged seventeen) and Karen Jones (two years older), and both from the village of Old Marston to the east of the Parks, had sauntered over the high-arched Rainbow Bridge across the Cherwell, and come to 'Meso-potamia', a pathway between two branches of the river, when young Michael, encouraged by the fact that he was now resting the palm of his right hand upon the right buttock of the slightly forbidding Karen – and without any perceptible opposition on her part – steered the nymphet into the enclosure known as Parson's Pleasure. This famous and infamous bathing place is to be found at a point where the Cherwell adapts itself to a pleasingly circum-scribed swimming area at a bend of the river, with a terrace of unsophisticated, though adequate, cubicles enabling would-be bathers to shed their clothing and to don, or not to don, their swimming costumes there. Green-painted, corrugated-iron fenc-ing surrounds Parson's Pleasure, with the access gate fairly jeal-ously guarded during the summer months, and firmly locked after the waters are deemed too cold even for the doughtiest of its homoerotic habitués. But whether from an unseasonable gale, or whether from recent vandalism, one section of the perimeter fencing lay forlornly on the ground that evening; and very soon the young pair found themselves seated side by side in one of the cubicles. In spite of her seniority in years, Karen was considerably the more cautious of the two in the progress of this current courtship. And justifiably so, for Michael, as vouched for by several of the village girls, was a paid-up member of the Wander-ing Hands Brigade. After several exploratory fingerings along the left femur, a sudden switch of tactics to the front of her blouse had heralded a whole new manual offensive – when at that point she decided to withdraw to previously prepared positions.

'Mike! Let's get out of here, please! I'm getting a bit chilly—'

'I'll soon see to that, love!'

'And it's a bit spooky. I don't like it here, Mike.'

He'd known, really, ever since they'd slipped through the hedge at half-past eight; known when he'd kissed her briefly on the Rainbow Bridge above the swollen and fast-flowing waters, testing the temperature and finding it not warm enough for any further penetration into the underclothing of a girl who seemed dressed that balmy evening as if for some Antarctic expedition. He stood up now, and (as she thought) with a surprisingly gallant, almost endearing gesture, refastened the only button on her blouse he'd thus far managed to disengage.

'Yeah! Gettin' a bi' chilly, innit?' he lied.

The moon as they walked from the cubicle was bright upon the waters, and Karen was wondering whether she might slightly have misjudged this lively, fun-loving youth when her eyes caught sight of something lying lengthways across the top of the weir in front of them.

'Yaaaaahhhhh!'

PART TWO

CHAPTER TWENTY

The moon jellyfish
like a parachute in air
sways under the waves
(Basil Swift, *Collected Haiku*)

It was half-way through the slow movement of Dvořák's American Quartet – with Morse mentally debating whether that wonderful work might just edge out the 'In Paradisum' from the Fauré *Requiem* for the number eight spot in his Desert Island cassettes – when the phone rang. For the second time that evening. Some while earlier, a weary-sounding Lewis had informed Morse that Mr Eddie Stratton had gone off somewhere just after lunchtime – from the railway station – and had still not returned to The Randolph. Naturally such a prolonged absence was a little worrying, especially in view of, well, the circumstances; and in fact an anxious Ashenden had rung Kidlington a few minutes previously, just in case the police knew anything. So Lewis thought he perhaps ought to mention it before going off duty . . . To that earlier call Morse had listened with a grudging, half-engaged attention; but he was listening far more carefully now.

Both Lewis and Max were already on the scene when Morse arrived, the surgeon (incongruously suited in evening dress) immediately putting the Chief Inspector into the picture – in a somewhat flushed and florid manner:

'The dead man lay there, Morse' – pointing to the moonlit water by the weir – ' "something pale and long and white", as the young lady said. Rather good, eh? Somebody'd poked him along here with a punt-pole; and when I arrived his body – his naked, semi-waterlogged body – was nudging against the side of the bank – just here – just in front of the changing cubicles, face down, his head washed clean of blood – much blood, methinks, Morse! – his hair rising and falling—'

'Have you been rehearsing all this stuff, Max?'

'Just drinking, dear boy . . . hair rising and falling in the water like some half-knackered jelly-fish.'

'Very fine!'

'I read that bit about the jelly-fish somewhere. Too good to let it go, eh?'

'He needed a hair-cut, you mean?'

'You've no poetry in your soul.'

'What party was it *tonight*?'

'Oxfordshire Health Authority. Guest Speaker – no less!' Max flicked his bow-tie with the index-finger of his right hand, before pointing the same finger at the figure of a man lying covered with a plastic sheet on the splashed grass beside the water's edge.

'Who is it?' asked Morse quietly.

'Ah, I was hoping you could tell *me* that. You're the detective, Morse. Have a guess!'

'A seventy-year-old Californian whose wife died yesterday – died, according to the best informed medical opinion, of purely natural causes.'

'And what did *he* die of?'

'Suicide – suicide by drowning – about three or four hours ago, just as it was getting dark. Crashed his head against a jagged branch as he was floating by. Anything else you want to know?'

'Back to school, Morse! I'm not sure he's an American or whether he was recently severed from his spouse. But he's certainly not in his seventies! Forties more like – you could put your pension on the forties.'

'I propose keeping my pension, thank you.'

'See for yourself!'

Max drew back the covering from the corpse, and even Lewis gave his second involuntary shudder of the night. As for Morse, he looked for a second or two only, breathed very deeply, lurched a fraction forward for a moment as if he might vomit, then turned away. It was immediately clear, as Max had said, that there had earlier been much blood; soon clear, too, that the body was that of a comparatively young man; the body of the man whom Morse had interviewed (with such distaste) the previous evening; the man who had been cheated of the Wolvercote Jewel – and the man who now had been cheated of life.

Dr Theodore Kemp.

*

Max was putting his bag into the boot of his BMW as Morse walked slowly up to him.

'You got here early, Max?'

'Just round the corner, dear boy. William Dunn School of Pathology. Know it?'

'How did he die?'

'Blood probably coagulated *before* he entered the water.'

'Really? I've never heard you say anything so definite before!'

'I know, Morse. I'm sorry. It's the drink.'

'But you'll know for certain tomorrow?'

'"Tomorrow and tomorrow and tomorrow . . ."'

'It wasn't suicide, then?'

'Oh no, Morse. That was *your* verdict.'

'No chance?'

'I'm only a pathologist.'

'How long in the water?'

'Couldn't possibly say.'

'Roughly?'

'Eight, seven, six, five, four hours . . . "Roughly", you said?'

'Thank you very much.'

Max walked round to the front of his car: 'By the way, I was talking to Dr Swain again this evening. He's reporting you to the Chief Constable.'

'Night, Max.'

'Night, Morse.'

When the surgeon had departed, Morse turned with unwarranted ferocity upon his ill-used sergeant: 'You told *me*, Lewis, that Mr Eddie bloody Stratton had been missing in quite extraordinarily suspicious circumstances since early afternoon, and that a frenetically distraught Ashenden had rung you up—'

'I didn't! I didn't say that!'

'What *did* you tell me, then?'

'Well, I did mention that Stratton had gone AWOL. And I *also* said that Dr Kemp hadn't turned up at the railway station when they'd arranged for a taxi to pick him up and take him—'

'What time was that?'

'Three o'clock, sir.'

'Mm. So if there's some evidence of a whacking great crack on his head . . . and if this had been deliberately inflicted rather than accidentally incurred . . . about seven hours ago, say . . . Three o'clock, you say, Lewis, when Kemp turned up again in Oxford?'

'When he *didn't* turn up in Oxford, sir.'

So many lights: the yellow lights of the arc-lamps that shone down on the river-bank; the white lights from the flashes of the police photographers; the blue lights of the police cars that lingered still around the scene. But little light in Morse's mind. He could hang around, of course, for the following hour or two, pretending to know what it was that he or anybody else should seek to discover. Or go back to HQ, and try to think up a few lines of enquiry for the staff there to pursue – men and women looking progressively more unwashed and unkempt and incompetent as the small hours of the morning gradually wore on.

But there *was* another option. He could drive down to The Randolph, and sort out that lying sod Ashenden! The bar would still be open, wouldn't it? At least for residents. Surely the bar *never* closed in a five-star hotel? Isn't that what you paid for? Yes. And occasionally, as now, it so happened that duty and pleasure would fall together in a sweet coincidence; and from Parson's Pleasure, after dutifully forbidding Lewis to linger more than a couple of hours or so, Morse himself departed.

It was twenty-five minutes after Morse had left the scene that Lewis discovered the first, fat clue: a sheet of yellow A4 paper on which the details of the Historic Cities of England Tour had been originally itemized; and on which the time of the final item that day had been crossed through boldly in blue Biro, with the entry now reading:

7.30 8.00 p.m.   Dinner

CHAPTER TWENTY-ONE

> You did not come,
> And marching Time drew on, and wore me numb
> (Thomas Hardy, *A Broken Appointment*)

The parking plots on either side of St Giles' were now virtually empty and Morse drew the Jaguar in outside St John's. It was two minutes past midnight when he walked through into the Chapters Bar, where a dozen or so late-night (early-morning) drinkers were still happily signing bills. Including Ashenden.

'Inspector! Can I get you a drink?'

After 'a touch of the malt' had been reasonably accurately

translated by Michelle, the white-bloused, blue-skirted barmaid, as a large Glenlivet, Morse joined Ashenden's table: 'Howard and Shirley Brown, Inspector – and Phil here, Phil Aldrich.' Morse shook hands with the three of them; and noted with approval the firm, cool handshake of Howard Brown, whose eyes seemed to Morse equally firm and cool as he smiled a cautious greeting. The reason for such a late session, Ashenden explained, was simple: Eddie Stratton. He had not been seen again since he was observed to leave the hotel just after lunch; observed by Mrs Roscoe (who else?) – and also, as Morse knew, by Lewis himself. No one knew where he'd gone; everyone was worried sick; and by the look of her, Shirley Brown was worried the sickest: what could a man be doing at *this* time of night, for Heaven's sake? Well, perhaps supping Glenlivet, thought Morse, or lying with some lovely girl under newly laundered sheets; and indeed he would have suggested to them that it was surely just a little early to get *too* worried – when the night porter came through and asked Chief Inspector Morse if he was Chief Inspector Morse.

'How the hell did you know I was here, Lewis?'

'You said you were off home.'

'So why—?'

'No answer when I rang.'

'But how—?'

'I'm a detective, sir.'

'What do you want?'

A phone call made just before midnight to St Aldates Police Station had been relayed to the murder scene at Parson's Pleasure: Mrs Marion Kemp, of 6 Cherwell Lodge, had reported that her husband, who had left for London early that morning, had still not arrived back home; that such an occurrence was quite unprecedented, and that she was beginning (had long begun!) to feel a little (a whole lot!) worried about him. She was herself a cripple, constantly in need of the sort of attention her husband had regularly given her in the evenings. She knew something, though not all, of his day's programme: she'd rung The Randolph at 10.45 p.m. and learned from the tour leader that her husband had not turned up at any point during the day to fulfil his commitments – and that in itself was quite out of character. After an evening of agonizing and, now, almost unbearable waiting, she'd decided to ring the police.

Such was the message Lewis passed on, himself saying nothing for the moment of his own extraordinarily exciting find, but agreeing to pick up Morse in about ten minutes' time, after briefly reporting in to St Aldates.

'News? About Eddie?' asked an anxious Phil Aldrich, when the frowning Morse walked back into the bar.

Morse shook his head. 'We get all sorts of news, sir, in the Force: good news, sometimes – but mostly bad, of course. No news of Mr Stratton, though. But I wouldn't worry too much, not about him, anyway . . .' (the last words mumbled to himself). He wondered whether to tell the four of them seated there about the death of Dr Kemp, for they'd have to know very soon anyway. But he decided they probably had enough on their minds for the moment; and swiftly tossing back the Glenlivet, he left them, making his way thoughtfully to the front entrance, and wondering something else: wondering whether any announcement of Kemp's death – Kemp's murder – would have come as too much of a surprise to *one* of the four people who still sat round the table in the Chapters Bar.

There was no time, however, for him to develop such a fascinating, and probably futile thought; for as he stood waiting on the pavement outside the hotel entrance, a taxi drew up, and with the help of the driver a very drunken man staggered stupidly into the foyer. Morse was usually reasonably tolerant about fellow-tipplers, and indeed occasionally rather enjoyed the company of slightly tipsy sirens; but the sight of this fellow pathetically fighting to extricate a wallet from an inner pocket, and then forking out and handing over three £10 notes – such a sight filled even Morse with mild disgust. Yet at least it was all a bit of a relief, wasn't it?

For the man was Eddie Stratton.

Clearly there could be little point in interviewing Stratton then and there; and already a solicitous (if censorious) Shirley Brown on one side, and a business-like (if unsmiling) Howard Brown on the other, were guiding the prodigal son to the guest-lift. No. Stratton could wait. With any luck he'd still be there the following morning.

Unlike the taxi-driver.

Morse caught the man's arm, and held him back as he was walking down the steps.

'You must have brought him quite a way?'

'You wha'?'

'Thirty quid? Must have been – Banbury, was it?'

'Yeah – could a' bin. Nothin' to do with you, mate.'

'I'm not your mate,' said Morse, fishing for his warranty.

'So? Wha's the trouble?'

'Where did you pick him up?'

'North Oxford.'

'Expensive ride!'

'I didn't ask for—'

'You *took* it.'

'Not short of a quid or two though, these Yanks—'

'I quite like the Yanks.'

'Me too, officer.'

'There's a bottle there' (Morse pointed back to Reception). 'Leukaemia fund. Doesn't look as if it's quite full yet.'

'How much?'

'Twenty?'

Shrugging, the taxi-man handed Morse two of the £10 notes.

'Where was it in North Oxford? What was the address?'

'I forget.'

'Shall we make it twenty-five?'

'Down the bottom of Hamilton Road, somewhere – ninety-seven, I think it was.'

'Name?'

'Same name as mine. Huh! Coincidence, eh?'

'I've always liked coincidences.'

'She rang up an' said, you know, take this feller down to The Randolph.'

'Good! Thanks! Good night then, Mr, er . . .'

'Williams. Jack Williams.'

Lewis had pulled in behind the taxi, and was in time to find Morse slowly – reluctantly? – pushing two £10 notes into the slot of a Charity Bottle. He smiled happily. Morse had a *bit* of money – he knew that. But the chief's generosity, certainly in pubs, was seldom in evidence; and it was most reassuring to find that there was an unexpectedly munificent side to the Chief Inspector's soul. So Lewis watched, and said nothing.

CHAPTER TWENTY-TWO

Duty is what one expects from others; it is not what one
does one's self
                    (Oscar Wilde, *A Woman of No Importance*)

It was not difficult for Lewis to find his way to the Kemps' home
in Cherwell Lodge, the ground-floor flat on the extreme right of
the three-storey building, since it was the only window in the
whole street, let alone the block of flats, wherein electric light still
blazed at a quarter to one that morning. By this time, Lewis had
shown Morse the yellow A4 sheet; and Morse had seemed so
delighted with it that he'd turned on the car's internal light in
transit. He folded the sheet along its original creases, and was
putting it inside his breast-pocket as Lewis quietly pulled the car
alongside the pavement outside Number 6.

'We can ring from *there* – be easier really,' suggested Morse,
pointing to the Kemps' property. 'We'll need a WPC – there
should be one at HQ, don't you think?'

Lewis nodded.

'And a doc,' continued Morse. '*Her* doc, if he's not too far sunk
in slumber or wine.'

Again Lewis nodded. 'You're right, sir. The more the merrier,
isn't it, with this sort of thing? It's about the only time I really hate
the job, you know – with accidents and so on . . . having to tell
the relatives, and all that.'

It was Morse's turn to nod. 'Always hard, isn't it, Lewis? I hate
it too, you know that.'

'Well, at least there are the two of us tonight, sir.'

'Pardon?'

'I said, at least with the two of us—'

'No! Only *you*, Lewis. We can't waste precious resources at this
unearthly hour.'

'You mean you're not—'

'Me? I'm just going to walk round to, er, talk to our other
witness.'

'Who's that?'

'That, Lewis, is Mrs Sheila Williams. She could very well have
something vital to tell us. It was Mrs Williams, remember, who
ordered the taxi—'

'But she'll be in *bed*!'

By not the merest flicker of an eyebrow did Morse betray the
slightest interest in the prospect of interviewing an attractively

proportioned and (most probably) scantily clad woman at such an ungodly hour.

'Well, I shall have to wake her up then, Lewis. Our job, as you rightly say, is full of difficult and sometimes distasteful duties.'

Lewis smiled in spite of himself. Why he ever enjoyed working with this strange, often unsympathetic, superficially quite humourless man, well, he never quite knew. He didn't even know if he *did* enjoy it. But his wife did. For whenever her husband was working with Morse, Mrs Lewis could recognize a curious contentment in his eyes, that was not only good for him, but good for her, too. Very good. And in a strange sort of way, she was almost as big an admirer of Morse as that faithful husband of hers – a husband whose happiness had always been her own.

'Perhaps, I'd better run you round there, sir.'

'No, no, Lewis! The walk may do me good.'

'As you say.'

'Er . . . just one more thing, Lewis. About the Jaguar. I left it just outside St John's, I think. If, er . . .' He held up his car-keys between the thumb and forefinger of his right hand, as if saving his nostrils the distress of some malodorous handkerchief. Then he got out of the car.

As Lewis watched him walk away up to Hamilton Road, he wondered, as he'd so often wondered, what exactly Morse was *thinking*; wondered about what was going on in Morse's mind at that very moment: the reading of the clues, those clues to which no one else could see the answers; those glimpses of motive that no one else could ever have suspected; those answers to the sort of questions that no one else had even begun to ask . . .

When Morse opened the ramshackle gate to Number 97, his mind was anticipating a potentially most interesting encounter. If a diabetic patient was in need of so-called 'balance' – namely, the appropriate injection of human insulin for the control of blood-sugar levels – equally so did Morse require the occasional balance of some mildly erotic fancy in order to meet the demands of what until recently he had diagnosed as a reasonably healthy libido. Earlier that very week, in fact, as he'd filled up the Jaguar with Gulf-inflated gasoline, he'd found himself surveying the display of semi-pornographic magazines arranged along the highest shelf above the dailies; and re-acquainted himself with such reasonably familiar titles as *Men Only*, *Escort*, *Knave*, *Video XXXX*, and so many others, each of them enticing the susceptible motorist with its cover of some provocatively posed woman, vast-breasted and voluptuous. And it was just after he'd flicked through one of them that Detective Constable Hodges (blast his eyes!) had come in, walked over to the newspaper stall, and picked up the top copy but one from the *Daily Mirror* pile. Morse had immediately picked up a copy of *The Times*, and proceeded to hold this newspaper like a crusader flaunting his emblazoned shield as he'd stood beside Hodges at the check-out.

'Nice day, sir?'

'Very nice.'

It had seemed to Morse, at that moment, that the dull eyes of Hodges had betrayed not the slightest suspicion of Morse's susceptibility. But even Morse – especially Morse! – was sometimes wholly wrong.

CHAPTER TWENTY-THREE

Yet the first bringer of unwelcome news
Hath but a losing office
(Shakespeare, *King Henry IV*, Part 2)

Lewis watched the silhouette gradually form behind the opaque glass in the upper half of the front door.

'Hullo? Who is it?' The voice sounded sharp, and well educated.

'Police, Mrs Kemp. You rang—'

'All right! All right! You took your time. Let me take mine!'

With much clicking of locks and a final scrabbling of a chain, the door was opened, and Lewis looked down with ill-disguised surprise.

'For Heaven's sake! Didn't they *tell* you I was a cripple?' And before Lewis could reply: 'Where's the policewoman?'

'Er, *what* policewoman, Mrs Kemp?'

'Well, I'm not going to be put to bed by *you* – let's get that straight for a start!'

Lewis might almost have been amused by the exchanges thus far, were it not for the heavy burden of the news he was bearing.

'If I could just come in a minute . . .'

Marion Kemp turned her chair through one hundred and eighty degrees with a couple of flicks of her sinewy wrists, then wheeled

THE JEWEL THAT WAS OURS

herself swiftly and expertly into the front room. 'Close the door behind you, will you? Who *are* you by the way?'

Lewis identified himself, though Marion Kemp appeared but little interested in the proffered warranty.

'Have you found him yet?' The voice which Lewis had earlier thought well under control now wavered slightly, and with her handkerchief she quickly wiped away the light film of sweat that had formed on her upper lip.

'I'm afraid—' began Lewis.

But for the moment Marion simulated a degree of hospitality. 'Do sit down, Sergeant! The settee is quite comfortable – though I have little first-hand experience of it myself, of course. Now, the only reason I rang – the chief reason – was that I need a little help, as you can see.'

'Yes, I do see. I'm, er, sorry . . .'

'No need! My husband managed to crash into another car on the Ring Road down near Botley.'

'Er, I'll just, er . . .' Lewis had seen the phone in the entrance-hall and with Mrs Kemp's permission he now quickly left the room and rang HQ for a WPC. He felt profoundly uneasy, for he'd known the same sort of thing on several previous occasions; surviving relatives rabbiting on, as if so fearful of hearing the dreaded information.

'She'll be along soon, madam,' reported Lewis, seating himself again. 'Very dangerous that stretch by the Botley turn . . .'

'Not for the driver, Sergeant! Not on this occasion. One broken collar-bone, and a cut on the back of his shoulder – and even *that* refused to bleed for more than a couple of minutes.' The bitterness in her voice had become so intense that Lewis couldn't think of anything, even anything inadequate, to say. 'It would have been better if he'd killed me, and had done with the whole thing! I'm sure *he* thinks that. You see, he can't get rid of me – not the way he could get rid of any *normal* wife. He has to keep coming back all the time to look after my needs when . . . when he'd much rather be out having *his* needs looked after. You *do* know what I'm talking about, don't you, Sergeant?'

Lewis knew, yes; but he waited a little, nodding his sympathy to a woman who, for the moment, had said her immediate say.

'What time did your husband leave this morning?' he asked quietly, noting a pair of nervous eyes suddenly flash across at him.

'Seven twenty. A taxi called. My husband was banned for three years after he'd killed me.'

Lewis shook his head helplessly: 'He *didn't* kill you, madam—'

'Yes he did! He killed the woman in the other car – and he killed *me*, too!'

Lewis it was who broke the long silence between them, and took out his notebook: 'You knew *where* he was going?'

'His publishers. He's just finished a book, and now he's doing some chapters for the new *Cambridge History of Early Britain*.'

'And he actually – *went*, did he?'

'Don't be silly! Of course he went. He rang me up from London. The post hadn't come when he left, and he wanted to know if some proofs had arrived.'

'What time did you expect him back?

'I wasn't sure. There'd been some trouble at The Randolph. You know all about that?'

Lewis nodded – ever dreading that inexorable moment when she, too, would have to know all about something else.

'They'd changed the programme – I forget exactly what he said. But he'd have been home by half-past ten. He's never later than that . . .'

The slim, dark-haired, rather plain woman in the wheel-chair was beginning to betray the symptoms of panic. Talk on, Lewis! Write something in that little book of yours. Do anything!

'You've no idea where he might have gone to when he came back from London?'

'No, no, no, Sergeant! How could I? He'd hardly even have the time to see his precious Sheila bloody Williams, would he? That over-sexed, pathetic, alcoholic . . .'

Talk on, Lewis!

'He must have been pretty upset about the Wolvercote Jewel.'

'He'd been waiting long enough to see it.'

'Why didn't he go over to America to see it?'

'I wouldn't let him.'

Lewis looked down at the uncarpeted floor-boards and put his notebook away.

'Oh no! I wasn't going to be left here on my own. Not after what he did to me!'

'Mrs Kemp, I'm afraid I've got—'

But Marion was staring down into some bleak abyss. Her voice, so savagely vindictive just a moment since, was suddenly tremulous and fearful – almost as if she already knew. 'I wasn't very nice to him about it, was I?'

Blessedly the front-door bell rang, and Lewis rose to his feet. 'That'll be the policewoman, Mrs Kemp. I'll – if it's OK – I'll go

and . . . Look, there's something we've got to tell you. I'll just go
and let her in.'

'He's dead. He's dead, Sergeant, isn't he?'

'Yes, Mrs Kemp. He's dead.'

She made no sound but the tips of her taut and bloodless fingers
dug into her temples as if seeking to sever the nerves that carried
the message from ears to brain.

CHAPTER TWENTY-FOUR

There are several good protections against temptations,
but the surest is cowardice
(Mark Twain, *Following the Equator*)

'Sit down, Inspector! Can I get you a drink?'

Sheila Williams, fairly sober and fully respectable, was drinking
a cup of black coffee.

'What – coffee?'

Sheila shrugged: 'Whatever you like. I've got most things – if
you know what I mean.'

'I drink too much as it is.'

'So do I.'

'Look, I know it's late – '

'I'm never in bed before about one – not on my own!' She
laughed cruelly at herself.

'You've had a long day.'

'A long boozy day, yeah.' She took a few sips of the hot coffee.
'There's something in one of Kipling's stories about a fellow who
says he knows his soul's gone rotten because he can't get drunk
any more. You know it?'

Morse nodded. '"Love o' Women".'

'Yeah! One of the greatest stories of the twentieth century.'

'Nineteenth, I think you'll find.'

'Oh, for Christ's sake! Not a literary copper!' She looked down
miserably at the table-top; then looked up again as Morse
elaborated:

'It was Mulvaney, wasn't it? "When the liquor does not take
hold, the soul of a man is rotten in him." Been part of my mental
baggage for many a year.'

'Jesus!' whispered Sheila.

The room in which they sat was pleasantly furnished, with some good quality pieces, and several interesting and unusual reproductions of Dutch seventeenth-century paintings. A few touches of good taste all round, thought Morse; of femininity, too – with a beribboned teddy-bear seated upright on the settee beside his mistress. And it was in this room, quietly and simply, that Morse told her of the death of Theodore Kemp, considering, in his own strange fashion, that it was perhaps not an inappropriate time for her to know.

For a while Sheila Williams sat quite motionless, her large, brown eyes gradually moistening like pavements in a sudden shower.

'But how . . . why . . .?'

'We don't know. We were hoping you might be able to help us. That's why I'm here.'

Sheila gaped at him. 'Me?'

'I'm told you had a – well, a bit of a row with him.'

'Who told you that?' (The voice sharp.)

'One of the group.'

'That Roscoe bitch!'

'Have another guess.'

'Ugh, forget it! We had a row, yes. God, if anyone was going to kill themselves after that, it was me – *me*, Inspector – not him.'

'Look! I'm sorry to have to ask you at a time like this—'

'But you want to know what went on between us – between Theo and me.'

'Yes. Yes, I do, Mrs Williams.'

'Sheila! My name's Sheila. What's yours?'

'Morse. They just call me Morse.'

'All bloody "give" on my part, this, isn't it?'

'What did pass between you and Dr Kemp, Mrs – er, Sheila?'

'Only my *life* – that's what! That's all!'

'Go on.'

'Oh, you wouldn't understand. You're married, I'm sure, with a *lovely* wife and a couple of *lovely* kids—'

'I'm a bachelor.'

'Oh, well. That's all right then, isn't it? All right for *men*.' She drained her coffee and looked, first wildly, then sadly around her.

'G and T?' suggested Morse.

'Why not?'

As Morse poured her drink (and his), he heard her speaking in a dreamy, muted sort of voice, as though dumbfounded by the news she'd heard.

'You know, I was married once, Morse. That's how I got most of this' (gesturing around the room).

'It's nice – the room,' said Morse, conscious that the shabby exterior of the property belied its rather graceful interior, and for a second or two he wondered whether a similar kind of comment might not perhaps be passed on Mrs Williams herself . . .

'Oh, yes. He had impeccable taste. That's why he left me for some other woman – one who didn't booze and do embarrassing things, or get moody, or stupid, or passionate.'

'And Dr Kemp – he'd found another woman, too?' asked Morse, cruelly insistent. Yet her answer surprised him.

'Oh, no! He'd already *found* her; found her long before he found me!'

'Who—'

'His wife – his bloody wife! He was always looking at his watch and saying he'd have to go and—'

She burst into tears and Morse walked diffidently over to the settee, where he temporarily displaced the teddy-bear, put his arm along her shoulder, and held her to him as she sobbed away the storm.

'I don't know whether I'm in shock or just suffering from a hangover.'

'You don't get hangovers at this time of night.'

'Morning!'

'Morning.'

She nuzzled her wet cheek against his face: 'You're nice.'

'You've no idea why Dr Kemp—?'

'Might kill himself? No!'

'I didn't say "kill himself".'

'You mean—?' For a few seconds she recoiled from him, her eyes dilated with horror. 'You can't mean that he was murdered?'

'We can't be sure, not yet. But you must be honest with me, please. Did you know anyone who might have wanted to kill him?'

'Yes! *Me*, Inspector. Kill his wife as well while I was at it!'

Morse sedately disentangled himself from Mrs Williams. 'Look, if there's anything at all you think I ought to know . . .'

'You don't really think I had anything to do with – with whatever's happened?'

'You were seen walking up St Giles' towards North Oxford, just after lunch yesterday. And it wasn't Mrs Roscoe this time, either. It was Sergeant Lewis.'

'I was going—' replied Sheila slowly, 'I *went* – to the "Bird and

Baby". Would *you* like a guess, this time? A guess about what I went for?'

'You were on your own there, in the pub?'

'Ye-es.' She had hesitated sufficiently, though.

'But you saw someone in there?'

'No. But – but I saw someone cycling past; cycling up towards the Banbury Road. It was Cedric – Cedric Downes. And he saw me. I know he did.'

Morse was silent.

'You do *believe* me, don't you?'

'One of the secrets of solving murders is never to believe anybody – not completely – not at the start.'

'You don't *really* see me as a suspect, surely!'

Morse smiled at her: 'I promise to take you off the list as soon as possible.'

'You know, I've never been suspected of murder before. Thank you for being so civilized about it.'

'It'll be just as well if you don't say anything to the group about it. Not till we're a bit further forward.'

'And you're not very far forward at the minute?'

'Not far.'

'Couldn't *we* make a little more progress, Morse?' The fingers of her left hand were toying with the top button of her scarlet blouse, and Morse heard the siren voice beside his ear: 'What would you say to another little drink before you go?'

'I'd say "no", my lovely girl. Because if I'm not reasonably careful, if I do have another drink, in fact if I stay a further minute even *without* another drink – then I shall probably suggest to you that we proceed – don't forget that we don't "progress" in the police force, we always "proceed" – to, er . . .' Morse waved a hand vaguely aloft, drained his glass, rose from the settee, and walked to the door.

'You'd enjoy it!'

'That's what's worrying me.'

'Why not, then?'

Sheila had not moved from the settee, and Morse stood in the doorway looking back at her: 'Don't you know?'

A few minutes later, as he turned right into the Banbury Road, now beginning to think once more with some semblance of rationality, Morse considered whether his witness had been telling him the whole truth. Just as ten minutes earlier, as he had driven back to St Aldates, Lewis had wondered the same about Mrs Kemp; in particular recalling the curious fact that, for a woman

who had so manifestly hated her husband, she had reacted to the
news of his death with such terrible distress.

CHAPTER TWENTY-FIVE

Going by railroad I do not consider as travelling at all; it
is merely being 'sent' to a place, and very little different
from becoming a parcel

(John Ruskin, *Modern Painters*)

At Kidlington HQ Morse and Lewis swapped notes at 7.45 a.m.:
both felt very tired, but neither confessed to it; and one of them
had a headache, about which he likewise made no comment. The
Jaguar had been parked outside his flat that morning, with the
keys found on the door-mat; but just as of his weariness and of his
hangover, Morse made no mention of his gratitude.

At least the morning plan was taking shape. Clearly the biggest
problem was what to do about the tour, scheduled to leave Oxford
at 9.30 a.m. bound for Stratford-upon-Avon. It would certainly be
necessary to make some further enquiries among the tourists,
particularly about their activities during the key period between
the time Kemp had arrived back in Oxford, and the pre-dinner
drinks when everyone except Eddie Stratton, it appeared, was
accounted for. *One* of the tourists, quite definitely, would not be
able to produce his or her copy of the Oxford stage of the
programme, for the yellow sheet found in Parson's Pleasure was
now safely with forensics; might even produce some new evidence. And even if no fingerprints could be found on it, even if
several of the tourists had already discarded or misplaced their
own sheets, there would not be too many Americans, surely, who
regularly wrote down their sevens with a continental bar across
the down-stroke. Then there was Cedric Downes. He would have
to be seen a.s.a.p., and would have to come up with a satisfactory
explanation of exactly why and when he'd left The Randolph.

In addition it was to be hoped that Max could come up with
some fairly definite *cause* of death; and it was even possible (if only
just) that the surgeon might throw caution to the wind for once
and volunteer a tentative approximation of the time it had actually
happened.

An hour later, as he drove the pair of them down to Oxford,
Lewis felt strangely content. He was never happier than when

watching Morse come face to face with a mystery: it was like watching his chief tackle some fiendishly devised crossword (as Lewis had often done), with the virgin grid on the table in front of him, almost immediately coming up with some sort of answer to the majority of the clues – and then with Lewis himself, albeit only occasionally, supplying one blindingly obvious answer to the easiest clue in the puzzle, and the only one that Morse had failed to fathom. Whether or not he'd be of similar help in the present case, Lewis didn't know, of course. Yet he'd already solved a little 'quick' crossword, as it were, of his own, and he now communicated his findings to Morse. The first part of Kemp's day had probably been something like this:

Left home earlyish for his visit by rail to London to see his publishers; been picked up by taxi at about 7.20 a.m., almost certainly to catch the 07.59, arriving Paddington at 09.03; obviously with only some fairly quick business to transact, since he'd appeared confident of meeting his commitments with the tourists at lunchtime at The Randolph, and then again during the afternoon; likely as not, then, he would originally have intended to catch the 11.30 from Paddington, arriving Oxford at 12.30.

'Have you checked with BR?'

'No need.' Lewis reached inside his breast-pocket and handed Morse the Oxford–London London–Oxford Network South-East timetable; but apart from briefly checking the arrival time of the 13.30 from Paddington, Morse seemed less than enthusiastic.

'Did you know, Lewis, that before nine o'clock the third-class rail fare—'

'*Second-class* sir!'

' – is about, what, seven times – eight times! – more expensive than getting a coach from Gloucester Green to Victoria?'

'*Five* times, actually. The coach fare's—'

'We ought to be subsidizing public transport, Lewis!'

'You're the politician, sir – not me.'

'Remember Ken Livingstone? He subsidized the Tube, and everybody used the Tube.'

'Then they kicked him out.'

'You know what Ken Livingstone's an anagram of?'

'Tell me!'

' "Votes Lenin King." '

'They wouldn't be voting him king now, though.'

'I thought you might be interested in that little snippet of knowledge, that's all.'

'Sorry, sir.'

'Why are you driving so slowly?'

'I make it a rule never to drive at more than forty-five in a built-up area.'

Morse made no reply, and two minutes later Lewis drew up in front of The Randolph.

'You've not forgotten Ashenden, have you, sir? I mean, he was the one who took the call from Kemp – and he was the one who wasn't looking round Magdalen.'

'I'd not forgotten Mr Ashenden,' said Morse quietly, opening the passenger door. 'In fact I'll get him to organize a little something for me straightaway. I'm sure that all these tourists – *almost* all these tourists – are as innocent as your missus is—'

'But one of 'em writes these peculiar sevens, right?'

'They're not "peculiar"! If you live on the Continent it's *ours* that look peculiar.'

'How do we find out which one it is?'

Morse permitted himself a gentle grin: 'What date did the tour start?'

CHAPTER TWENTY-SIX

Wilt thou have this Woman to thy wedded wife, to live together after God's ordinance in the holy estate of Matrimony? Wilt thou love her, comfort her, honour, and keep her in sickness and in health; and, forsaking all other, keep thee only unto her, so long as ye both shall live?

(*Book of Common Prayer,
Solemnization of Matrimony*)

At just after 9.30 a.m., Morse sat with Lewis, Ashenden, Sheila Williams, and the (now fully apprised) Manager of The Randolph in a first-floor suite which the latter had readily put at police disposal. Without interruption, quietly, quickly, Morse spoke.

'I've no wish to hold up the tour a minute longer than necessary, Mr Ashenden, but I've got certain duties in this case which will involve your co-operation. Likewise, sir' (to the Manager) 'I shall be grateful if you can help in one or two practical ways – I'll tell you how in a few minutes. Mrs Williams, too – I shall . . . we, Sergeant Lewis and I, shall be grateful for your help as well.'

Morse proceeded to expound his preliminary strategy.

The tour, originally scheduled to leave at 9.30 a.m., could not now leave until well after a buffet lunch, if this latter could be arranged by the kitchen staff (the Manager nodded). A meeting of all the tourists would be summoned straightaway (Ashenden felt a pair of unblinking blue eyes upon him) – summoned to meet *somewhere* in the hotel (the Manager nodded again – the St John's Suite was free), and Morse himself would then address the group and tell them as much or as little as he wanted to tell them, believing, he admitted, that Rumour had probably lost little of her sprinting speed since Virgil's time, and that most of the tourists already had a pretty good idea of what had happened. After that meeting had finished, it would help police enquiries if the tourists could be kept amused for the rest of the morning. And if Mrs Williams – and how very grateful Morse was that she'd agreed to his earlier telephone request to be present! – if Mrs Williams could possibly think of some diversion . . . some talk, some walk. Yes, that would be excellent.

So! There was much to be done fairly quickly, was there not?

Ashenden left immediately, with the manifold brief of herding his flock together; of informing the coach-driver of the postponed departure; of phoning Broughton Castle to cancel the special out-of-season arrangements; of explaining to the Stratford hotel the cancellation of the thirty lunches booked for 1 p.m.; and finally of reassuring the lunchtime guest-speaker from the Royal Shakespeare Company that her fee would still be paid.

The Manager was the next to leave, promising that his secretary could very quickly produce thirty photocopies of the brief questionnaire that Morse had roughed out:

(a) Name ....

(b) Home Address ....
    ....

(c) Whereabouts 3–6.30 p.m., Friday 2nd Nov.
    ....
    ....
    ....

(d) Name of one fellow-tourist able to
    corroborate details given in (c)
    ....

(e) Date of arrival in UK ....

(f) Signature .... Date ....

Sheila Williams, however, appeared less willing to co-operate than her colleagues: 'I willingly agreed to come here, Inspector – you know that. But my only specialism is mediaeval manuscripts, and quite honestly not many of this lot are going to be particularly ecstatic about *them*, are they? I could – well, I *will*, at a pinch – traipse around these inhabited ruins and try to remember whether Queens is apostrophe "s" or "s" apostrophe. But like Dr Johnson I must plead ignorance, Inspector – sheer ignorance.'

Here Lewis chipped in with his first contribution: 'What about shipping them all off on one of these circular tours – you know, on the buses?'

Morse nodded.

'Or,' pursued an encouraged Lewis, '"The Oxford Story" – *brilliant*, that!'

'They went on it yesterday – most of them,' said Sheila.

'I suppose we could just ask them to stay in their rooms and watch the telly,' mused Morse; but immediately withdrew the suggestion. 'No! People will be arriving—'

'They could just walk around Oxford, couldn't they, sir? I mean there's an awful lot to see here.'

'Christ, Lewis! That's what I suggested, at the *start*. Don't you remember?'

'What about Cedric, Inspector?' (This from Sheila.) 'I'm pretty sure he's free this morning, and he's a wonderfully interesting man once he gets going.'

'Could he do the sort of talk Dr Kemp was going to give yesterday?'

'Well, perhaps not that. But he's a bit of a Renaissance Man, if you know what I mean. The only thing he's a bit dodgy on is modern architecture.'

'Good! That's fine, then. If you could ring this polymath pal of yours, Mrs Williams . . . ?'

'He'd take far more notice of *you* if you rang him, Inspector. And . . . he probably won't know yet about—'

'Not unless he was the one who murdered Kemp,' interposed Morse quietly.

Cedric Downes had himself been on the phone for about five minutes, trying frustratedly to contact British Rail about times of trains to London that day; yet he could have had little notion of the irrational and frenetic impatience of the man who was trying to contact *him*; a man who was betweenwhiles cursing the

incompetence of British Telecom and bemoaning the cussedness
of the Universe in general.

'Hullo! Is that British Rail?' (It was, by the sound of it, Mrs
Downes, surely.)

'What?' answered Morse.

'Oh, I'm sorry. It's just that my husband couldn't get through
to BR, and he rang the operator and I thought . . .' Clearly Mrs
Downes had little idea *what* she'd thought. Her manner was rather
endearingly confused, and Morse switched on what he sometimes
saw in himself as a certain charm.

'I do know what you mean. I've been trying to get your
number . . . er . . . Mrs Downes, isn't it?'

'Yes. I'm Mrs Downes. Can I help you?'

'If you will. Chief Inspector Morse here.'

'Oh!'

'Look, I'd much rather be talking to you than . . .'

'Ye-es?' The voice, as before, sounded a little helpless, more
than a little vulnerable. And Morse liked it.

'. . . but is your husband in?'

'Ah! You want Cedric. Just a minute.'

She must, thought Morse, have put her hand over the mouth-
piece, or perhaps Downes himself had been waiting silently (for
some reason?) beside the phone, for there was no audible sum-
mons before a man's voice sounded in his ear.

'Inspector? Cedric Downes here. Can I be of help?'

'Certainly, if you will, sir. We have a bit of a crisis here with the
American Tour. I'm speaking from The Randolph, by the way.
The sad news is—'

'I know.' The voice was flat and unemotional. 'Theo's dead – I
already knew.'

'Do you mind telling me *how* you know?'

'John Ashenden phoned a couple of hours ago.'

'Oh, I see!' On the whole Morse was not unhappy that Ashenden had been ringing around. 'Why I'm calling, sir, is to ask if
you're free to come to The Randolph this morning.'

'This *morning*? Well . . . er . . . er . . . Well, I've got commitments after lunch, but this morning's free, I think.'

'If you *could* get down here, sir, I'd be very grateful. We've got
our hands a bit full with things.'

'Of course.'

'If you could—'

'Walk 'em round Oxford again?'

'A different route, perhaps?'

'Or I might be able to get the Oxford University Museum to open up a bit early – you know, Inspector, the dodo and Darwin and the dinosaurs.'

'Wonderful idea!'

'Glad to help, really. It's awful, *terrible* – isn't it? – about Theo.'

'You'll contact the Museum, sir?'

'Straightaway. I know someone there who's still trying to classify a few of the South American crabs that Darwin left to the Museum. Fascinating things, crabs, you know.'

'Oh yes!' said Morse. 'I'm most grateful to you, sir.'

'Anyway, I'll call at The Randolph, so I'll see you soon.'

'Er, just before you ring off, sir?'

'Yes?'

'It's only fair to tell you that we shall be asking everyone here a few questions about what they were doing yesterday afternoon.'

'As is your duty, Inspector.'

'Including *you*, sir.'

'Me?'

'I shall be asking you why you were cycling up St Giles' towards North Oxford after lunch yesterday. So if you can have your answer ready? It's only a formality, of course.'

'Would that all questions were so easy to answer!'

'Where were you going, sir?'

'I was going home to get a new hearing-aid. I almost always carry a spare, but I didn't yesterday. At lunchtime the aid started going off and I suddenly realized that I wasn't going to get through the afternoon—'

'Your hearing's not all *that* bad, is it, sir? You don't seem to have much of a problem hearing me now.'

'Ah, but I'm very fortunate! My dear wife, Lucy, bought me a special phone-attachment – bought it for my last birthday, bless her heart.'

Something had stirred in the back of Morse's brain, and he sought to keep the conversation going.

'It sounds as if you're very fond of your wife, sir?'

'I love my wife more than anything else in the world. Can that be so surprising to you?'

'And you'd do anything to keep her?' It seemed a brusque and strange reply, but Downes seemed in no way disconcerted.

'Yes! Certainly.'

'Including murdering Kemp?'

From the other end of the line there was no manic laughter; no silly protestation; no threat of lawyers to be consulted. Just the simple, gentle confession: 'Oh yes! Including that, Inspector.'

For the moment, Morse was completely wrong-footed, and he would have discontinued the exchange without further ado. But Downes himself was not quite finished.

'It was Sheila, I know that, who saw me yesterday afternoon. And I don't blame her in the slightest for telling you. If you *have* got a murder on your hands, it's the duty of all of us to report anything, however insignificant or innocent it may appear. So I may as well tell you straightaway. As I biked up St Giles' yesterday afternoon I passed one of the group walking up to North Oxford. Would you like to know who *that* was, Inspector?'

CHAPTER TWENTY-SEVEN

It is a matter of regret that many low, mean suspicions
turn out to be well founded
            (Edgar Watson Howe, *Ventures in Common Sense*)

As Lewis saw things, Morse's talk to the tourists was not one of his chief's most impressive performances. He had informed his silent audience of the death – just 'death' – of Dr Kemp; explained that in order to establish the, er, totality of events, it would be necessary for everyone to complete a little questionnaire (duly distributed), sign and date it, and hand it in to Sergeant Lewis; that the departure of the coach would have to be postponed until late afternoon, perhaps, with lunch by courtesy of The Randolph; that Mr Cedric Downes had volunteered to fix something up for that morning, from about 10.45 to 12.15; that (in Morse's opinion) activity was a splendid antidote to adversity, and that it was his hope that *all* the group would avail themselves of Mr Downes's kind offer; that if they could all think back to the previous day's events and try to recall anything, however seemingly insignificant, that might have appeared unusual, surprising, out-of-character – well, that was often just the sort of thing that got criminal cases solved. And here, sad to relate, was more than one case – not only the theft of a jewel, but also two deaths: of the person who was to present that jewel to the Ashmolean, and of the person who was to take official receipt of such benefaction.

When he had finished Morse had the strong feeling that what

he had just implied was surely true: there *must* be some connection between the disturbing events which had developed so rapidly around the Wolvercote Tongue. Surely, too, it must be from within the group of American tourists, plus their tutors and their guide, that the guilty party was to be sought. And fifteen minutes later, with all the completed questionnaires returned, there was good reason to suppose that Morse could be right, since three of those concerned, Eddie Stratton, Howard Brown, and John Ashenden, appeared temporarily unable to provide corroboration of their individual whereabouts and activities during the key period of the previous afternoon – the afternoon when the original groups, three of them, had been re-formed slightly (following Kemp's telephone call), and when anyone wishing to absent himself for some purpose would have been presented with a wonderful opportunity so to do. And keeping check on who was doing what, and when, and where, could well have proved as complicated as calling the roll after Dunkirk.

For Morse, the information gleaned from the questionnaires was eminently pleasing; and when, at 10.50 a.m., Cedric Downes led the way out of The Randolph towards South Parks Road and the University Museum, with every single member of the group present (except Mr Eddie Stratton), he looked tolerably pleased with himself. Especially of interest was the fact that one of the two men clearly experiencing difficulty with section (c) on the examination paper, Howard Brown (Morse wondered why his wife hadn't been willing to cover for him), had filled in section (e) with the correct day of arrival, 27 October; or, to be more precise about the matter, '27 October'.

Nor would Morse be forgetting the only man who had not been present at the meeting – the man who still lay with a wicked headache and a barely touched breakfast-tray beside him in Room 201, to which room Shirley Brown had shepherdessed him when, after his unexplained absence, he had reeled into The Randolph the previous night.

But it was with Ashenden that Morse's attention was immediately engaged. Ashenden! – the man whom Cedric Downes now claimed to have passed on his bicycle; the man who had lied about his visit to Magdalen; the man who, like Howard Brown (and possibly Eddie Stratton?), was as yet unable to produce a single witness to his whereabouts the previous afternoon.

Three of them. How easy it had been almost immediately to uncover three possible suspects for the murder of Theodore Kemp! Too easy, perhaps?

CHAPTER TWENTY-EIGHT

Myself when young did eagerly frequent
Doctor and Saint, and heard great Argument
 About it and about: but evermore
Came out by the same Door as in I went
    (Edward FitzGerald, *The Rubaiyat*)

'How are you, Morse?'

'Optimistic.'

'Oh!' Max appeared disappointed by the reply as he peered down again at the grisly work on which he was engaged.

The contrast between the two men would have struck any observer that morning. The stout, hump-backed surgeon – circumspect, but perky and confident; Morse – looking distinctly weary, his jowls semi-shaven by an electric razor that had seemingly passed peak efficiency, and yet somehow, somewhere underneath, a man on the side of the angels.

'There's some deep bruising here,' began Max, pointing to Kemp's left temple, 'but the main blow' – he jerked the head towards him before caressing the crushed skull with a gentle reverence – 'was *here*.'

Characteristically Morse sought to swallow back the bitter-tasting fluid that had risen in his gorge; and the surgeon, with understanding, pulled the rubber sheet over the head again.

'Bit messy, isn't it? Bled a lot, too. Whoever killed him had a bucket of blood to wipe away.'

'He *was* murdered, then?'

'What? Ah! Slipped up a bit there, didn't I?'

'But he was, wasn't he?'

'Your job, that side of things.'

'Which blow killed him?'

'Paper-thin skull like that? Either! Little knock on the right place . . .'

'Probably the blow on the back of the head, Max.'

'Oh yes – certainly could have been that.'

'Or . . .?'

'Yes – *could* have been the crack on the temple.'

'Someone could have hit him and then he fell over and hit himself on the fender or the door-jamb or the bedpost—'

'Or the kerb, if he was out in the street.'

'But you don't believe he was, do you?'

'Not my province, belief.'

'Could he have suffered either of the injuries in the water?'

'"Till that her garments, heavy with their drink, Pull'd the poor wretch from her melodious lay To muddy doom."'

'"Death", Max – not "doom". And he hadn't got any garments, had he?'

'Good point, Morse. And I've got something else to show you.' Max now exposed Kemp's torso and heaved the corpse a few inches off the table. Along the back of the right shoulder was a scratch, some five or six inches long: a light, fairly superficial scratch, it appeared, yet one made quite recently, perhaps.

'What caused that, Max?'

'Dunno, dear boy.'

'Try!'

'An instrument of some sort.'

'Not a blunt instrument, though.'

'I would suggest a sharp instrument, Morse.'

'Amazing!'

'*Fairly* sharp, I should have said.'

'Caused as he was floating along like Ophelia?'

'Oh, I couldn't possibly say.'

'Could it have been done before he was murdered – when he was wearing a shirt, say?'

'Ah! A not unintelligent question!'

Together the two men looked again at the light wound, stretching down diagonally from the back of the neck towards the armpit.

'*Could* it have been, Max?'

'I think not.'

'Then he was possibly naked when he was murdered?'

'Oh, I wouldn't go *that* far. Anyway he might have hit a willow twig in the river.'

'What other possibilities are there?'

'The evidence extends only as far as the lower scapula, does it not? He could have been wearing an off-the-shoulder toga.'

Morse now closed his eyes and turned away from the body: 'A toga pinned together with the Wolvercote Tongue, no doubt.'

'Oh no! I can assure you of one thing: that was not upon his person.'

'You don't mean – you didn't . . .?'

Max nodded. 'And he didn't swallow it, either.'

'And he didn't drown.'

'No. None of the usual muck one finds in the lungs when a man's fighting for his breath. Could he swim, by the way?'

'Don't know. I haven't seen his wife yet.'

The pathologist suddenly dropped his habitual banter, and looked Morse in the eye. 'I know you've got a lot on your plate, old boy. But I'd see her soon, if I were you.'

'You're right,' said Morse quietly. 'Just tell me, *please*, whether you think he was naked when he was murdered – that's all I ask.'

'I've told you. I don't know.'

'Not many reasons why people are naked, are there?'

'Oh, I dunno. Having a bath; standing on the weighing-scales; sun-bathing in Spain – so they tell me.'

'Having sex,' added Morse slowly. 'Not so much a willow's twig, perhaps, as a woman's talon.'

'Less likely, I'd say.'

'But you're sometimes wrong.'

'Not so often as you, Morse.'

'We'll see.'

Max grinned. 'Glad it was *you* who mentioned sex, though. I was beginning to suspect you'd misplaced your marbles.'

'No, no! No chance of that, Max. Not yet, anyway.'

And as Morse left the pathology block, a quiet little smile of confidence could be seen around the Chief Inspector's lips.

CHAPTER TWENTY-NINE

There are an awful lot of drunks about these days. It wouldn't really surprise me if you turned out to be one yourself

(Martin Amis, *Other People*)

Apart from his former wife, Mr Edward Stratton was the only one of the original group who had not listened to Morse that morning. Although his head was throbbing almost intolerably, he'd felt sober enough to ring for breakfast in his room, and had done his best to contemplate the 'Full English' he'd so foolishly ordered for 7 a.m. His brain drew a veil over the sickening consequences.

Edward Stratton had always been interested in machinery, or 'working parts' as he'd always liked to think of things. As a boy in high school he'd progressed from World War I aircraft-kits to model railways, his mind and his hands responding most happily to the assemblage of pistons, valves, wheels, with their appropriate adjustments and lubrications. Not marrying, he had set up a small business in specialized agricultural machinery – which had gone bust in 1975. After a long period of depression, and a short period of training, he had taken on a new career – one which also demanded dexterity with the hands: that of a mortician. Was there ever an odder switch of professions? But Stratton had soon grown proficient in the gruesome, sometimes disgusting, demands of his new job; and in the process of preparing an aged philanthropist for his silk-lined resting-place, he had met the man's disconsolate widow, Laura. And married her a year later. Or, perhaps, it may have been that *she* had married him. Convenience, that's what it had been for her – little more. Maybe for him, too? He'd assumed that she had money; everyone assumed that she had money. But he'd never known for certain and still didn't know now.

It was the Wolvercote Tongue which monopolized Stratton's thoughts as he sat on his unmade bed, head between his hands, that Saturday mid-morning. The thing was insured, he knew that – well insured. How otherwise? Yet insured in exactly what circumstances, under exactly what provisions, Stratton was wholly ignorant. *Why* had Shirley Brown had to mention the point on her brief visit to him earlier that morning, and sowed those slowly germinating seeds of doubt? Would it make a difference if it could be maintained that Laura had died *before* the Tongue was stolen? Would the money then go to the Ashmolean? But there could never be any proof on the matter, and if she had died *after* it was stolen, then surely the money would have to be credited to her estate, would it not? Stratton shook his aching head. He could get no real grip on the situation, and the more he pondered, the more confused his thinking became. But if he could get the police to believe it was *after* . . . because that would mean it was still in her possession when she died . . . wouldn't it . . .?

Augh!

Stratton rose from the bed and walked to the bathroom. He was dipping his heavy aching head into a basin of cold water when he heard the sharp knock on the door, and was soon admitting Chief Inspector Morse and Sergeant Lewis into his bedroom.

The former had immediately recognized the symptoms of a Caesar-sized hangover and offered practical aid in the form of two tablets of Alka Seltzer which he appeared to carry regularly on his person.

And almost immediately Stratton had been talking freely . . .

They must have thought him a bit insensitive – running off like that, the day after . . . But he'd seen the advert in the *Oxford Mail*, and the prospect of an Open Day at Didcot had proved irresistible. He'd walked round the engine sheds, he said, where he'd looked long and lovingly at the old locomotives, and where he'd seen schoolboys and middle-aged men carefully recording numbers and wheel-arrangements in their notebooks. ('All of them apparently sane, Inspector!') And then he'd had the thrill of actually *seeing* ('a life-time's ambition') the Flying Scotsman! He'd stayed there ('in Didcart') much longer than he'd intended; and when finally he tore himself away from the Cornish Riviera and the Torbay Express he'd walked back to Didcot Parkway Station at about five o'clock, and caught the next train back to Oxford, where he'd, er, where he'd had a quick drink in the station buffet. Then he'd been walking back to The Randolph when he suddenly felt he just couldn't face his excessively sympathetic countrymen, and he'd called in a pub and drunk a couple of pints of lager.

'The pubs were open, were they, Mr Stratton?' asked Lewis.

But it was Morse who answered: 'If you wish, Lewis, I will give you the names and addresses of the three of them there that open all day. Please continue, Mr Stratton.'

Well, at about half-seven he'd gone into a restaurant in St Giles', Browns; had a nice steak, with a bottle of red wine; left at about half-nine – and was strolling down to The Randolph when he'd met Mrs Sheila Williams, just outside the Taylorian, as she was making for the taxi-rank. They had stood talking for quite some time, each of them perhaps slightly the worse for wear, and then she had invited him up to her North Oxford home for a night-cap.

And that was it.

The strong-bodied American, with his rugged features, had spoken with a quiet simplicity; and as he'd watched him and heard him, Morse thought he could well have enjoyed a pint with the fellow. Yet in Morse's view it was always a good idea to ask a few inconsequential questions. So he did.

'You say you had a drink at Oxford Station?'

'Yep.'

'Which platform would that have been on?'

'Search me! But the same side the train came in, I'd swear to it.'

'And they have booze there, do they?'

'Sure do! I had a can – coupla cans. Expensive it was, too.'

Lewis's eyebrows lifted under a frown, and he looked across at his chief: 'I'm afraid that's not right, sir. Mr Stratton couldn't have got any beer or lager at Oxford Station – not yesterday. There was a great big notice outside: "No Refreshments" or something like that, due to modernization.'

'"Owing to" modernization, Lewis.'

'I've never known the difference.'

'No need. Just say "because of" and you'll always be right.'

'As I was saying, sir, the buffet was shut.'

'Interesting point!' remarked Morse, suddenly turning again to a now distinctly uncomfortable-looking Stratton. 'So if you didn't stay on the station between about five-thirty and six-thirty, where exactly *were* you, sir?'

Stratton sighed deeply, and seemed to be pondering his position awhile. Then he sighed again, before opening the palms of his hands in a gesture of resignation. 'Your Sergeant's right, Inspector. I asked if I could get a drink – anything. But, like he says, they were refurbishing all the places there. I *did* stay, though. I stayed about half an hour – longer, perhaps. I'd gotten myself a *Herald Tribune* and I sat reading it on one of the red seats there.'

'Bit chilly, wasn't it?'

Stratton remained silent.

'Was there someone outside you didn't want to meet?' suggested Morse.

'I didn't – I didn't want to go out of the station for a while. It, er, it might have been a little awkward for me – meeting someone who might . . . might be waiting for a bus, or a taxi.'

'You saw someone from the group on the train, is that what you're saying? Someone sitting in a compartment in front of you when you got on the train at Didcot?'

Stratton nodded.'*He'd* not got on at Didcot, though. He must have come from Reading, I suppose—'

'Or Paddington,' added Morse quietly.

'Yes, or Paddington.'

Morse looked across at Lewis. Paddington was beginning to loom slightly larger than a man's hand on the horizon; Paddington was where the murdered Kemp had stood and phoned The Randolph the previous day. So was it too much to believe that it was *Kemp* that Stratton had seen – about five o'clock, hadn't he said?

'You'll have to tell me, you know that,' said Morse gently.

'It was Phil Aldrich,' replied Stratton quietly, his eyes searching those of the two policemen with a look of puzzlement – and perhaps of betrayal, too.

Phew!

'Let me ask you one more question, please, sir. Do you stand to profit much from your wife's death?'

'I do hope so,' replied Stratton, almost fiercely. 'You see, I'm pretty hard-up these days, and to be honest with you I'm certainly not going to say "no" to any insurance money that might be pushed my way.'

'You're an honest man, Mr Stratton!'

'Not always, Inspector!'

Morse smiled to himself, and was walking over to the door when Stratton spoke again: 'Can I ask you a favour?'

'Go ahead!'

'Can you leave me another coupla those Alka Seltzer things?'

CHAPTER THIRTY

Precision of communication is important, more important than ever, in our era of hair-trigger balances, when a false, or misunderstood word may create as much disaster as a sudden thoughtless act

(James Thurber, *Lanterns and Lances*)

Morse thought it must be the splendid grandfather clock he'd seen somewhere that he heard chiming the three-quarters (10.45 a.m.) as he and Lewis sat beside each other in a deep settee in the Lancaster Room. Drinking coffee.

'We're getting plenty of suspects, sir.'

'Mm. We're getting pretty high on content but very low on analysis, wouldn't you say? I'll be all right though once the bar opens.'

'It *is* open – opened half-past ten.'

'Why are we drinking *this* stuff, then?'

'Stimulates the brain, coffee.'

But Morse was consulting the Paddington–Oxford timetable which Lewis had picked up for him from Reception, and was nodding to himself as he noted that the 13.30 arrived at Oxford 14.57, just as Kemp had claimed. Now if Kemp had been held up, for some reason, for even longer than he'd expected . . . for considerably longer than he'd expected . . . Yes, interesting! The train Stratton must have caught – *said* he'd caught – must have been the 16.20 from Paddington, arriving at Didcot 17.10, and Oxford 17.29. For several seconds Morse stared across Beaumont Street at the great Ionic pillars of the Ashmolean . . . What time *had* Kemp left Paddington? For left Paddington he certainly had, at some point, after ringing through to The Randolph to explain his delayed departure.

But what if . . .?

'You know, sir, I was just wondering about that telephone call. What if—?'

Morse grinned at his sergeant. 'Great minds, Lewis – yours and mine!'

'You really think there's a possibility it *wasn't* Kemp who rang?'

'Yes, I do. And it would give us a whole new time perspective, wouldn't it? You know, with the best will in the world, Max will never give us too much help if he thinks he *can't*. Quite right, too. He's a scientist. But if *we* can narrow the time down – or rather, widen it out, Lewis . . .'

For a while he appeared deep in thought. Then, pushing his half-finished coffee away from him, he stood up and gave Lewis his orders: 'Go and find Ashenden for me. I shall be in the bar.'

'There we are, then!' said John Ashenden.

It was twenty minutes later, and Morse had decided (insisted) that his temporary HQ in the Lancaster Room should be moved to more permanent quarters in the Chapters Bar Annexe. He had questioned Ashenden in detail for several minutes about the crucial phone call with Kemp, and asked him to write down in dialogue-form the exchanges as far as he could recall them. Ashenden himself now sat back in his armchair, crossed his lanky legs, and watched with slightly narrowed eyes as Morse took the sheet from him and proceeded to read the reconstructed conversation:

K. I've been held up at Paddington, John.

A. Oh no! What's you're trouble?

K. Just missed the train, but I'll catch the half-past one and be with you for quarter-past three, at the very latest. Sorry to let you down like this, and miss the drinks and the lunch and the first bit of p.m. Apologies apologies apologies, John!

A. Not the end of the world, though – not quite! (sotto voce.) I'll do my best to sort things out, of course, and let your group know. Trouble is I changed the time to quarter-to three.

K. I'm a bloody nuisance, I know.

A. It could be worse. Shall I arrange a taxi for you from the station?

K. Is it worth it?

A. Save ten minutes.

K. All right. I get in at just before three o'clock.

A. I'll ring Luxicars just in case there's not a taxi there.

K. Thanks.

A. Make sure you don't miss the next one!

K. No danger. Er, before I ring off can I have a quick word with Cedric please — if he's there?

A. He's here. I'll get him. Hold on!

'You write fairly well,' said Morse, after reading through the sheet for a second time, and still refraining from pointing out the single grammatical monstrosity. 'You ought to try your hand at some fiction one of these days.'

'*Fact*, Inspector – it's not fiction. Just ask that nosy Roscoe woman if you don't believe me! She was sitting near the phone and she misses *nothing*.'

Morse smiled, if a little wanly, and conceded the trick to his opponent. Yet he sensed that those next few minutes, after Ashenden had finished speaking with Kemp, might well have been the crucial ones in that concatenation of events which had finally led to murder; and he questioned Ashenden further.

'So you called over to Mr Downes?'

'I *went* over to Mr Downes.'

'But he didn't want to talk to Dr Kemp?'

'I don't know about that. He was having trouble with his hearing-aid. It kept whistling every now and then.'

'Couldn't he have heard without it?'

'I don't know. Perhaps not. The line *was* a bit faint, I remember.'

Morse looked across at Lewis, whose eyebrows had risen a self-congratulatory millimetre.

'Perhaps you only *thought* it was Dr Kemp, sir?' continued Morse.

But Ashenden shook his head firmly. 'No! I'm ninety-nine per cent certain it was him.'

'And Sheila – Mrs Williams – she spoke to him then?'

'Yes. But you put it most accurately, Inspector. She spoke to *him*. And when she did, he put the phone down. So he didn't actually speak to *her* – that's what she told me anyway.'

Oh!

'We've still only got *his* word for it,' said Lewis, after Ashenden had gone. 'Like we said, sir, if it *wasn't* Kemp, we'd have a different time-scale altogether, wouldn't we? A whole lot of alibis that wouldn't wash at all.'

Morse nodded thoughtfully. 'Yes, I agree. If Kemp was already dead at twelve-thirty . . .'

'There was somebody else who heard him, sir.'

'Was there?'

'The woman on the switchboard who put the call through.'

'She wouldn't have known the voice, Lewis! She gets thousands of calls every day—'

'She'd be a very busy girl if she got a *hundred*, sir.'

Morse conceded another trick. 'Fetch her in!'

Celia Freeman was of far greater help than either Morse or Lewis could have wished. Especially Morse. For just as he had begun to survey the picture from a wholly different angle, just as he thought he espied a gap in the clouds that hitherto had masked the shafts of sunlight – the switchboard-operator dashed any hope of such a break-through with the simple statement that she'd known Theodore Kemp very well indeed. For five years she had worked at the Ashmolean before moving across the street to The Randolph; and for the latter part of that time she had actually *worked* for Dr Kemp, amongst others. In fact, it had been Dr Kemp who had written a reference for her when she'd changed jobs.

'Oh yes, Inspector! It was Dr Kemp who rang – please believe that! He said, "Celia? That you?", or some such thing.'

'Mr Ashenden said that the line was a bit faint and crackly.'

'Did he? You *do* surprise me. It may be a little faint on one or two of the extensions, but I've never heard anyone say it was crackly. Not since we've had the new system.'

'He never said it *was* "crackly",' said Lewis after she had gone.

'Do you think I don't know that?' snapped Morse.

'I really think we ought to be following up one or two of those other leads, sir. I mean, for a start there's . . .'

But Morse was no longer listening. One of the most extraordinary things about the man's mind was that any check, any setback, to some sweet hypothesis, far from dismaying him, seemed immediately to prompt some second hypothesis that soon appeared even sweeter than the first.

'. . . this man Brown, isn't there?'

'Brown?'

'The continental-seven man.'

'Oh yes, we shall have to see Brown, and hear whatever cock-and-bull story he's cooked up for us.'

'Shall I go and get him, sir?'

'Not for the minute. He's on the walkabout with Mr Downes.'

'Perhaps he's not,' said Lewis quietly.

Morse shrugged his shoulders, as if Brown's present whereabouts were a matter of indifference. 'At least *Mr Downes* is on the walkabout, though? So maybe we should take the opportunity . . . What's Downes's address again, Lewis?'

CHAPTER THIRTY-ONE

There is much virtue in a window. It is to a human being as a frame is to a painting, as a proscenium to a play

(Max Beerbohm, *Mainly on the Air*)

It was just before mid-day when Lewis braked sedately outside the Downes's residence at the furthest end of Lonsdale Road.

'Worth a few pennies, sir?' suggested Lewis as they crunched their way to the front door.

'Thou shalt not covet thy neighbour's house, Lewis. Just ring the bell!'

Lucy Downes was in, and soon stood at the door: an attractive, slim, fair-haired woman in her early thirties, dressed in a summerish cotton suit of pale green, with a light-beige mackintosh over her left arm. Her eyes held Morse's for a few seconds – eyes that seemed rather timid, yet potentially mischievous, too – until her mouth managed a nervous little 'Hullo'.

'Good morning, madam!' Lewis showed his ID card. 'Is Mr Downes in, please? Mr Cedric Downes?'

Lucy looked momentarily startled: 'Oh! Good Lord! He's not here, I'm afraid, no! He's been showing some Americans round Oxford this morning – and he's got a lecture this afternoon, so . . . Er, *sorry*! Can I help? I'm his wife.'

'Perhaps you can, Mrs Downes,' interposed Morse. 'We spoke earlier on the phone, if you remember? May we, er, come in for a little while?'

Lucy glanced at her watch. 'Yes! Yes, of course! It's just' – she held the door open for them – 'I'm just off to – whoops!'

Morse had knocked his shin against a large suitcase standing just inside the door, and for a moment he squeezed his eyes tight, the whiles giving quiet voice to a blasphemous imprecation.

'Sorry! I should have – that wretched case! It's bitten *me* twice this morning already. Sorry!'

She had a pleasing voice, and Morse guessed that her gushy manner was merely a cover for her nervousness.

Yet nervousness of what?

'I'm just on my way,' continued Lucy. 'London. Got to change some curtains. A friend recommended a reasonably priced shop near King's Cross. But you really can't trust any of the stores these days, can you? I quite specifically ordered French pleats, and then – oh, sorry! Please sit down!'

Morse looked around him in the front living-room, slightly puzzled to find the carpet, the decoration, the furniture, all that little bit on the shabby side, with only the curtains looking bright and new, and (in Morse's opinion) classy and tasteful. Clearly, in any projected refurbishment of the Downes's household, Lucy was starting with the curtains.

'I'd offer you both coffee but the taxi'll be here any time now. Cedric usually takes me to the station—' she giggled slightly, 'I've never learned to drive, I'm afraid.'

'It's purely routine, madam,' began Morse, sitting down and sinking far too far into an antiquated, unsprung settee. 'We just have to check up everything about yesterday.'

'Of course! It's awful, isn't it, about Theo? I just couldn't believe it was true for a start—'

'When exactly *was* that?' Morse asked his question in a level tone, his eyes, unblinking, never leaving hers.

She breathed in deeply, stared intently at the intricate pattern on the carpet, then looked up again. 'Cedric rang up from The Randolph just before he came home. He said – he said he shouldn't know himself really, but one of the people there, the tour leader, told him and told him not to say anything, and Cedric'

– she breathed deeply again – 'told me, and told *me* not to say anything.'

'Bloody Ashenden!' muttered Morse silently.

'His poor wife! How on earth—?'

'How many other people did you tell?'

'Me? I didn't tell anyone. I haven't been out of the house.'

Morse glanced at the phone on the table beside the settee, but let the matter rest. 'Dr Kemp tried to talk to your husband yesterday lunch-time.'

'I know. Cedric told me. He came back here.'

'What time was that?'

'One-ish? Quarter-past one – half-past?'

'He came back for his spare hearing-aid?'

Lucy was nodding. 'Not only that, though. He picked up some notes as well. I forget what they were for. Well, I don't really *forget*. I never knew in the first place!' She smiled nervously, and (for Lewis) bewitchingly, and (for Morse) heart-eatingly. 'Anyway he just grabbed some papers – and he was off again.'

'With his spare hearing-aid, too?'

She looked up at Morse with her elfin grin. 'Presumably.'

'I thought the NHS only issued one aid at a time.'

'That's right. But Cedric's got a spare – two spares in fact. Private ones. But he always votes Labour. Well, he *says* he does.'

'He's not all that deaf, is he, Mrs Downes?'

'He pretends he's not. But no, you're right, he's not *that* bad. It's just that when he talks to people he gets a bit frightened. Not frightened about not knowing the answers but frightened about not hearing the questions in the first place.'

'That's very nicely put, Mrs Downes.'

'Thank you! But that's what *he* says. I'm only copying him.'

'What time did he get home last night?'

'Elevenish? Just after? But he'll be able to tell you better than me.'

The door bell rang; and in any case the three of them had already heard the steps on the gravel.

'Shall I tell him to wait a few minutes, Inspector? He's a bit early.'

Morse rose to his feet. 'No. I think that's all. I – unless Sergeant Lewis here has any questions?'

'What are French pleats?'

She laughed, her teeth showing white and regular. 'Like that!' She pointed up to the curtains on the front window. 'It's the way they're gathered in at the top, Sergeant.'

'Oh! Only the missus keeps on to me about getting some new curtains—'

'I'm sure, Lewis, that Mrs Downes will be able to arrange a private consultation with Mrs Lewis at some convenient point. But some other time, perhaps? She does have a train to catch – her taxi driver is waiting impatiently on the threshold . . .'

'Sorry, sir!'

Lucy smiled again, especially at Sergeant Lewis, as he carried her heavy suitcase out to the taxi.

'You know when you're coming back, Mrs Downes?' Lewis asked.

'Seven o'clock. Just before – or is it just after?'

'Would you like me to ask your husband to meet you? We shall be seeing him.'

'Thank you. But he *is* coming to meet me.'

She climbed aboard, and the two policemen stood and watched as the taxi drove off into Lonsdale Road.

'Lovely woman, that!'

For the moment Morse made no reply, staring back at the house with a slightly puzzled air. 'Thou shalt not covet thy neighbour's wife, Lewis! Exodus, chapter something.'

'I didn't mean anything like that. You've got a one-track mind, sir!'

'You are perfectly correct, Lewis: one track only. My mind wants to know what the theft of the Wolvercote Tongue has got to do with the murder of Theodore Kemp. And I would be very surprised if that "lovely woman" of yours doesn't know a little more than she's prepared to admit – even to you!'

CHAPTER THIRTY-TWO

Man has such a predilection for systems and abstract deductions that he is ready to distort the truth intentionally, he is ready to deny the evidence of his senses in order to justify his logic

(Dostoevsky, *Notes from Underground*)

Of a sudden, on the way back down the Banbury Road, Morse decided to view Parson's Pleasure by daylight. So Lewis drove down to the bottom of South Parks Road, where he was ushered through into the University Parks by a policeman on duty at the

entrance to the single-track road which led down to the bathing
area. Here the whole of the site was lightly cordoned off, and one
of the Park Attendants was talking to (the newly promoted)
Sergeant Dixon as Morse and Lewis moved alongside. The Park
had closed at 4.30 p.m. the previous day, the detectives learned,
yet it was not unknown for nimble adolescents and desperate
adults to gain access to the Parks from half a dozen possible places.
And the number of expended condoms discovered in and around
the bathing-area suggested that not only ingress and egress, but
congress too, was not unusual there, with the cover of the night,
and the cover of the cubicles, combining to promote this latter
activity – even when frost was forecast. But the cubicle in which
the yellow sheet had been found could reveal no further secrets,
and all hope had early been abandoned of learning anything from
the scores of footprints which had criss-crossed the grassy area
since the murder. Two divers had gone down into the river during
the morning, but had found no item of relevance; and perhaps
would not have recognized its relevance had they found it.
Certainly no clothes, Sergeant Dixon asserted.

Morse walked over to the water's edge, the river-level high
against the banks, and there he dipped his fingers in: not quite so
cold as he would have thought. Dixon's mention of clothes had
pulled his mind back to the discovery of Kemp's body, and he
asked Lewis much the same question he had asked Max, receiving
much the same answers.

'But I don't think he'd have been swimming here, sir.'

'Not unknown, Lewis, for people to bathe naked in this stretch.'

'Too chilly for me.'

'What about sex?'

'You don't have to take all your clothes off to do that.'

'No? Well, I'll take your word for it. I'm not an expert in that
area myself.' He stood pondering the waters once more. 'Do you
ever have any rows with your wife?'

'"Not unknown", as *you* would say, sir.'

'Then you patch things up?'

'Usually.'

'When you've patched things up, do you feel even closer
together than before?'

Lewis was feeling puzzled now, and a little embarrassed at the
course of the conversation: 'Probably a good thing now and then
– clears the air, sort of.'

Morse nodded. 'We know of two people who had a row
recently, don't we?'

'Dr Kemp and Mrs Williams? Yes! But she's got a whacking great alibi, sir.'

'A much better alibi than Stratton, certainly.'

'I could try to check on Stratton: Didcot – the pub he mentioned – Browns Restaurant.'

Morse looked dubious: 'If only we knew *when* Kemp was murdered! *Nobody's* got an alibi until we know that.'

'You think Mrs Williams might have killed him?'

'She might have *killed* him all right. But I don't think she could have dumped him. I'd guess it was a man who did that.'

'He wasn't very heavy, Kemp, though. Not much fat on him.'

'Too heavy for a woman.'

'Even a jealous woman, sir?'

'Yes, I know what you mean. I keep wondering if Kemp had found some other floozie – and Sheila Williams found out about it.'

'"Hell hath no fury . . ."'

'If you must quote, quote accurately, Lewis! "Heaven has no rage, like love to hatred turned Nor Hell a fury like a woman scorned."'

'Sorry! I never did know much about Shakespeare.'

'Congreve, Lewis.'

'He seems to have been a bit of a ladies' man—'

'And if he couldn't make love to his wife because she was paralysed from the waist down . . .'

'I got the feeling she wasn't too worried about that, perhaps. It was Mrs Williams she had it in for.'

'She might have forgiven him if it had been anyone else, you mean?'

'I think – I think you ought to go to see her, sir.'

'All *right*,' snapped Morse. 'Give me a chance! We've got these Americans to see, remember? Aldrich and Brown – find out where *they* were yesterday afternoon. Where they *say* they were.'

Morse turned to look at the waters once more before he left, then sat silently in the passenger-seat of the police car as Lewis had a final word with Sergeant Dixon. In the side panel of the door he found a street map of Oxford, together with a copy of *Railway Magazine*; and opening out the map he traced the line of the River Cherwell, moving his right index-finger slowly north-wards from the site marked Bathing Pool, up along the edge of the University Parks, then past Norham Gardens and Park Town, out under the Marston Ferry Road; and then, veering north-westerly, up past the bottom of Lonsdale Road . . . Portland Road . . .

Hamilton Road . . . Yes. A lot of flood water had come down from the upper reaches of the Cherwell; and a body placed in the river, say, at Lonsdale Road . . .

And suddenly Morse knew where the body had been launched into the river and into eternity; knew, too, that if Lucy Downes could so quickly arouse the rather sluggish libido of a Lewis, then it was hardly difficult to guess her effect upon the lively carnality of a Kemp.

Lewis had climbed into the driving seat, and seen Morse's finger seemingly stuck on the map, at the bottom of Lonsdale Road.

'He couldn't have done it, sir – not Downes. He was with the Americans all the time – certainly till after we found the body. If anybody's got an alibi, he has.'

'Perhaps it was your friend Lucy Downes.'

'You can't think that, surely?'

'I'm not thinking at all – not for the minute,' replied Morse loftily. 'I am deducing – deducing the possibilities. When I've done that, I shall begin to *think*.'

'Oh!'

'And get a move on. We can't keep the Americans here all day. We're going to have to let 'em get on their way. Most of 'em!'

So Lewis drove back from Parson's Pleasure, back on to the Banbury Road, down St Giles', and then right at the lights into Beaumont Street. And all the time Chief Inspector Morse sat, less tetchy now, staring at the street map of Oxford.

No doubt, as Lewis saw things, 'deducing'.

CHAPTER THIRTY-THREE

If you are afraid of loneliness, don't marry

(Chekhov)

Sheila Williams was feeling miserable. When Morse, himself looking far from serene, had come into The Randolph and demanded to see Messrs Aldrich and Brown immediately, he had resolutely avoided her eyes, appearing to have no wish to rekindle the brief moments of intimacy which had occurred in the morning's early hours. And the tourists, most of them, were getting restless – understandably so. Only Phil Aldrich had seemed as placid as ever, even after being interrupted in the middle of his lunch, and thereafter being seated in the Lancaster Room, writing busily on the hotel notepaper; and being interrupted just the once, and then only briefly, by Janet Roscoe – the latter intent, it appeared, on fomenting further dissatisfaction whenever possible.

Like now, for instance.

'I really do *think*, Sheila—'

'I do *envy* you so, Mrs Roscoe. I haven't had a genuine thought in *years*! Oh, Cedric! Cedric?'

He had been trying to steal silently away from the post-lunch chatter, but was stopped in his tracks at the foot of the great staircase as Sheila, glass in her left hand, laid the crimson-nailed fingers of her right hand along his lapel.

'Cedric! How that bloody woman has lived this long without getting murdered . . .'

Cedric grinned his sad, lopsided grin, removed the somewhat disturbing hand, and looked at her – her upper and lower lips of almost equal thickness, moist and parted, and temptingly squashable. She was a woman he had known for several years now; one with whom he had never slept; one who half repelled, and ever half attracted him.

'Look! I've got to be off. I've got a tutorial shortly, and I ought to sober up a bit betweentimes.'

'Why do that, darling?'

'Sheila! You're a lovely girl, but you – you let yourself down when you drink too much.'

'Oh, for Christ's sake! Not you as well.'

'Yes! *Me as well!* And I've got to go. I'm meeting Lucy off the train later on anyway, and if you want to know the truth' – he looked about him with rolling eyes – 'I'm completely pissed off with the whole of this bloody set-up. I've done my best, though. First I stood in for—' Suddenly he stopped. 'Sorry, Sheila! I shouldn't have said that. Forgive me!' He kissed her lightly on the cheek, then turned and walked out of the hotel.

As Sheila watched him go, she knew that in spite of the hurtful words he had just spoken she would always have a soft spot for the man. But she knew, too, what a lousy judge of men she'd always been. Her husband! God! A quietly cultivated, top-of-the-head English don, incurably in the grip of the Oxford Disease – that tragic malady which deludes its victims into believing they can never be wrong in any matter of knowledge or opinion. What a disaster that had all been! Then a series of feckless, selfish, vain

admirers . . . then Theo. Poor Theo! But at least he was – had been
– an interesting and vital and daring sort of man.

Sheila walked slowly over to the window and watched Cedric
as he wheeled his bicycle across Beaumont Street towards St
Giles'. He never drove his car if he was having any drink with his
lunch. Not like some people she'd known. Not like Theo, for
instance . . . He'd been over the limit, they'd said, when he'd
crashed his BMW, and there could have been no sympathy
whatsoever for him from the relatives of the woman killed in the
other car. *Or* from his wife, of course – his bloody wife! And yet
there was the suggestion that he'd been just a little unlucky,
perhaps? Certainly many people had mumbled all that stuff about
'there but for the grace of God . . .' And there *was* a lot of luck in
life: some people would go to jail for badger-baiting; but if they'd
baited just the foxes they'd like as not be having sherry the next
day with the Master of the Foxhounds. Yes, Theo *may* have been
a fraction unlucky about that accident.

Even unluckier now.

And Cedric? Was he right – about what he'd just said? Already
that morning she had drunk more than the weekly average for
women she'd noticed displayed on a chart in the Summertown
Health Centre waiting-room. But when she was drinking, she was
(or so she told herself) perfectly conscious of all her thoughts and
actions. It was only when she was reasonably sober, when, say,
she woke up in the morning, head throbbing, tongue parched,
that she suspected in retrospect that she hadn't been quite so
rationally conscious of those selfsame thoughts and actions . . .

God! What a mess her life was in!

She looked miserably back across the coffee-lounge, where
several of the group were mumbling none too happily. Six o'clock.
Morse had changed their departure-time to six o'clock, unless
something dramatic occurred in the mean time.

She walked through into the Lancaster Room again, where Phil
Aldrich was still scribbling away on the hotel's notepaper; and for
the moment (as Sheila stood in the doorway) looking up with his
wonted patience and nodding mildly as Janet propounded her
latest views on the injustice of the tour's latest delay. But even as
Sheila stood there, his mood had changed. None too quietly, he
asked the woman if she would mind leaving him alone, just for a
while, since he had something more important to do for the
minute than listen to her gripes and belly-aching.

Who would have believed it?

Sheila had heard most of the exchange; and, with the volume

of Janet's voice, so probably had several of the others too. It had been a devastating rebuke from the quiet little fellow from California; and as Sheila watched the hurt face of the formidable little woman from the same State (wasn't it the same Church, too?), she almost felt a tinge of sympathy for Mrs Janet Roscoe.

Almost.

Lewis, too, had been watching as Aldrich wrote out his statement; and wondering how a man could write so fluently. Huh! When Aldrich handed it to him there were only three crossings out in the whole thing.

CHAPTER THIRTY-FOUR

Thou hast committed –
Fornication; but that was in another country,
And besides, the wench is dead
(Christopher Marlowe, *The Jew of Malta*)

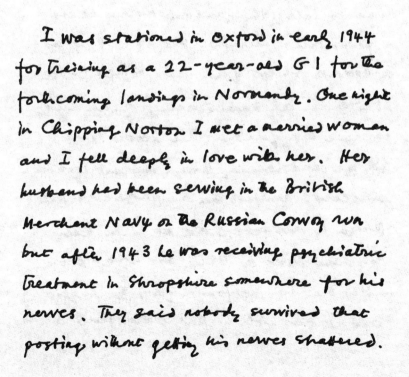

I was stationed in Oxford in early 1944 for training as a 22-year-old GI for the forthcoming landings in Normandy. One night in Chipping Norton I met a married woman and I fell deeply in love with her. Her husband had been serving in the British Merchant Navy on the Russian Convoy run but after 1943 he was receiving psychiatric treatment in Shropshire somewhere for his nerves. They said nobody survived that posting without getting his nerves shattered.

Well while he was in hospital his wife
had gotten herself pregnant and she had
a baby daughter 2nd Jan. 1945. From
what I half learnt the father must have
been a forgiving sort of man because he
treated the daughter (my daughter) as if
she were his own little girl. But there was
some trouble with her in her early teens
and perhaps she'd guessed something of the
truth. The fact is she ran away from her
home in late 1962 and her mother heard
a few months later that she was living as
a common street girl near King's Cross
Station. I only knew something of all this
because the girl's mother kept in touch
with me occasionally through innocent looking
postcards and just the one phone call put
through to our ~~telephone~~ me when her
husband died in 1986. She moved soon
after that to Thetford in your E. Anglia
and I was able to phone her there a

few times. But I could tell there was no real
wish on her part to renew any old ties
of love and friendship and if I am going
to be honest no real wish on my part
either. I valued my independence too much
to get into any deep down involvement and
particularly with a woman who goddamit
I probably wouldn't have recognized anyway!
But I felt so different about my daughter
and tried to learn where she'd gotten to.
She attended the funeral so I guess there
must have been some contact there. Well
then her mother died last Feb. with some
awful cancer and her daughter had been
beside her when she died and probably
learnt then about the secret which must
have burdened her poor mother's life for
so many years. I guess I ought to be
more honest about this because my
daughter wrote me after her mother's funeral
and said she'd guessed what had happened
anyway. I'd never had other children of

my own and somehow she seemed very
prescious just then, but I never expected
to see her. She'd not given any address
but the stamp had a WC1 postmark. So
when this tour was advertised and I saw
three days would be spent in London I
just decided to go, that's all. It would be
good to see old England again and even if
I didn't find her I could tell myself I'd
just tried that little bit. So when we were
there in London I asked around at several
centers for rehabilitating women and I struck
lucky. At one place there were about a dozen
young women having a lunch together. I don't
recall the name of the place but there was
royal blue woodwork there and grey walls
and all the pipes were bright red. It was
a biggish house in a terrace, yellowish brick
and white window frames about five or ten
minutes walk from King's Cross. The only
other thing I remember is that there was litter
everywhere in that street there. The warden

was a wonderful guy and he mentioned my
daughter's name to these girls and one of
them knew her! There were a lot of street
walkers and petty criminals, he called
them his pros and cons, but one of them had
seen my daughter Pippa a week earlier in
a cafeteria somewhere near. So I left
her £10 and asked her to please tell the
warden if she saw her again so that he
could call me with any news. Yesterday
was the last possible day ~~we could have~~
on the tour that was near enough London
to get up there easily, only about an hour
away. Then I had a phone call yesterday
from my daughter herself! I'd given
the warden details of our itinerary,
and the call got put straight through to
my own room here just before we went
for lunch. So we arranged to meet in the
Brunel Bar in the Great Western Hotel
at Paddington at a quarter after two
and I just decided to go without telling

anyone in the group. I got to Paddington just after 2 o'clock right on skedule and I walked straight over to the hotel bar and gotten me a big whiskey because gee was I nervous. You see, I'd never seen my own daughter before. I waited and waited and waited — until about 3 o'clock and then when the bar closed until about 4 o'clock in the lounge there. But she didn't come though I was willing and praying for any women round forty-five or so who came in to be her. So I caught the 4.20 train back to Oxford which stopped at Reading and then Didcot. I didn't see Eddie get on the train at Didcot but I now know he saw me. I only know because he told me this morning, he'd not meant to say anything but his conscience was worrying him so he told me what he'd told you. I just hope the police can come nearer solving the murder if we all tell the truth even if there are a few skeletons in the cuboard. I only ask for my secret to stay a secret. But just one more thing. I asked ~~Janet~~ Mrs Janet Roscoe to sign that she saw me yesterday afternoon at one of the sessions. Please don't blame her because I just told her I'd gotten a bad headache. She is a much nicer lady than the others may think and I admire her such a lot.

Philip Aldrich

CHAPTER THIRTY-FIVE

Just a song at twilight
When the lights are low
And the flick'ring shadows
Softly come and go . . .
(*From the English Song Book*)

For all the swiftness of his thought, Morse was quite a slow reader. And as Lewis (who had already read through the statement) watched his chief going through the same pages, he felt more than a little encouraged. It was like finding a Senior Wrangler from Cambridge unable to add seventy-seven and seventeen together without demanding pencil and paper.

'Well? asked Morse at long last. 'What did you make of that?'

'One odd thing, sir. It's an alibi for Aldrich all right, but not really one for Stratton, is it?'

'It isn't?'

'Surely not. Aldrich didn't actually *see* Stratton – on the train, did he?'

'You mean Stratton might *not* have been on the train? Ye-es . . . But if so, how did he know *Aldrich* was on the train?'

Lewis shook his head: 'I'm thinking about it, sir.'

'But you're right, Lewis,' added Morse slowly, as he sat back and stared at the ceiling for a few seconds. 'And I'll tell you something else: he writes well!'

'Clever man, sir!'

'More literate than his daughter, I should think. Only those couple or so of spelling mistakes, wasn't it?'

'Only the two I spotted,' replied Lewis, his features as impassive as those of a professional poker-player, as Morse, with a half-grin of acknowledgement, started shuffling inconsequentially through the completed questionnaires.

'Bit sad,' ventured Lewis, 'about Mr Aldrich's daughter.'

'Mm?'

'Wonder why she didn't turn up at Paddington.'

'Probably met a well-oiled sheik outside The Dorchester.'

'She'd *agreed* to meet him, though.'

'So he says.'

'Don't you believe him?' Lewis's eyes looked up in puzzlement. 'He can't have made up all that stuff about the army . . . or the train—'

'Not those bits, no.'

'But you don't believe the bits in the middle?'

'As you said, he's a clever man. I think he went up to London, yes, but I'm not at all sure what he *did* there. All a bit vague, don't you think? Just as I'm not quite sure what *Kemp* was doing, after he left his publishers. But if they *met* each other, Lewis . . . ? Interesting, don't you think?'

Lewis shook his head. It was almost invariably the same: half-way through any case Morse would be off on some improbable and complicated line of thought which would be just as readily abandoned as soon as a few more facts emerged. And, blessedly, it was *facts* that Morse now seemed to be concentrating on as, forgetting Aldrich for the moment, he browsed once again through the questionnaires.

'See here, Lewis!' He passed over three of the sheets and pointed to the answers to question (e):

P. Aldrich	10–27–90
E. Stratton	27th Oct 1990
H. Brown	October 27

'Not conclusive though, is it, sir?'

But Morse appeared to have boarded a completely different train of thought: 'I was just wondering about their dates of birth . . .'

'Soon find out. I got Ashenden to collect in all their passports this morning.'

'You did?'

Lewis felt gratified to note the surprise and appreciation in Morse's eyes and voice, and very soon he was back with the passports.

'All here, are they?'

'Except Ashenden's. You're not, er, forgetting Ashenden, are you, sir?'

'Oh no! I'm not forgetting Ashenden,' replied Morse quietly, as taking out his Parker pen he wrote three d.o.b.s on a table napkin:

Aldrich:	8.4.1922
Stratton:	29.9.1922
Brown:	3.8.1918

'Two of 'em sixty-eight now, and one seventy-two . . .'

'You wouldn't *think* Brown was the oldest, though, would you, sir? He trots around like a two-year-old.'

'A two-year-old *what*?'

Lewis sighed, but said nothing.

'He stayed in his room when his wife went off for a jaunt round Oxford, remember? And I still think one of the oddest things in this case is why Stratton didn't see his wife safely up to her room. It's not natural, Lewis. It's not how things *happen*.'

'What are you suggesting?' asked Lewis, vaguely.

'Brown said he stayed in his room when his wife and Stratton decided to look round Oxford. Said he was tired. Huh! As you said, he's as sprightly as a two-year-old.'

'A two-year-old *what*, sir?'

But Morse appeared to have missed the question.

In the Annexe, as if on cue, a tune could be heard quite clearly. First a few exploratory notes, presumably on the Steinway Grand that Morse had earlier admired in the Lancaster Room; then the whole melody as the pianist hired for the afternoon tea-room session fingered his way through the nostalgic chords of 'Love's Old Sweet Song'.

The two men listened in silence, before Morse resumed:

'You know, I'm beginning to wonder exactly who was having an affair with who.'

Lewis's eyebrows shot up yet again.

'All right! "Whom", if you prefer it. Stratton and Shirley Brown go out together and everybody says "tut-tut". Agreed? And we all focus our attention on the potential scandal – completely ignoring a far more suggestive state of affairs. Brown and Laura Stratton are there right next to each other in Rooms 308 and 310. It's shenanigans between the sheets, Lewis! It's a *crime passionnel*! Stratton comes back in and catches Brown in the missionary position – and all this Wolvercote Tongue business is just a secondary blind.'

But Lewis would have nothing to do with such futile speculation: 'She was tired, sir. She'd be far more interested in a bath than . . .'

'. . . than in a bonk?'

'Well, people that age—'

'What? I've heard that sex can be very good for the over sixty-fives.'

'Only ten years for you to go, then.'

Morse grinned, though with little conviction. 'I'm sure of it, though. It's Love's Old Sweet Song – that *must* come into things somewhere. A woman dies. An art-work goes missing. An art-expert gets murdered. You following me, Lewis? There's a link – there's got to be a *link*. But for the present I can't—' He broke off, and looked at the three dates again. 'You realize, don't you, that those three would have been – what? – twenty-two, twenty-two, and twenty-six in 1944?' His eyes gleamed with what might have been taken for some inner illumination. 'What about all of them being stationed in or near Oxford?'

'What difference would that make, sir?'

Morse seemed not to know.

Picking up Aldrich's statement, Lewis rose to his feet. 'Shall I go and get Howard Brown?'

But again Morse's mind seemed to be tuned to another wavelength. 'Why did you say he' – indicating the statement – 'he was a clever man?'

'Well, for a start, there's only the three crossings out, aren't there? And he just – well, he just sort of sat down and wrote it straight off.'

'Ye-es,' said Morse, but to himself, for Lewis had already left the Annexe to summon Brown.

He looked around at the two other tables occupied in the Bar-

Annexe. At the first, a middle-aged woman with an enormous bosom was digging a fork into a plate of salad with the precision of an accountant jabbing at his calculator, before transferring the accumulated forkful up to her rapidly masticating jaws; and Morse knew that if he had married *her*, it would all have been over within the week. But there was another woman, at the second table: a woman only half the age of her executively suited escort; a woman who was having a fairly difficult time by the look of things, earnestly rehearsing a whole chapter of body language with her ringless hands. Perhaps, thought Morse, the illicit little office affair was drawing to its close. Then her sad eyes met Morse's in a sort of distant, anonymous camaraderie: she smiled across, almost fully. And Morse did the same, feeling for a few small moments an intense and splendid happiness.

CHAPTER THIRTY-SIX

Their meetings made December June
(Tennyson)

Faced with the evidence of the tell-tale 7, Howard Brown capitulated immediately. Yes, Morse was right in one respect: Aldrich, Stratton, and himself had been stationed in or around Oxford in 1944, and he (Brown) had in fact known Stratton vaguely in those far-off days. They'd been delighted therefore to renew acquaintanceship at the beginning of the tour; and thereafter had spent many an hour together, talking about old comrades they'd known – those who'd come through, and those who hadn't . . . and reminiscing about some of the 'local talent' the GIs had been only too happy to discover, in Oxford itself and in some of the surrounding towns and villages. Brown had fallen miserably in love (so he said) with a girl named Betty Fowler, whom he'd met one Friday evening at a hop held in the Oxford Town Hall, and already on their second meeting they had vowed a mutual, eternal love.

Then when the war ended in the summer of 1945, after being demobbed from Germany, he'd gone straight back to the US, with no possible hope of any real communication between them except for one or two impermanent and unreliable addresses. So, slowly, the memories of their idyllic times together had faded. He'd met up with a marvellous girl in Münster, anyway; then a fully

consenting Hausfrau from Hamburg . . . and so it had gone on.
He'd gradually come to terms with the fairly obvious fact (as most
of his comrades already had) that wartime associations were
almost inevitably doomed to dissolution.

Back home in California, he'd met Shirley; and married her.
OK, there mightn't perhaps be all that much left over now from
the early joys of their marriage; yet, in an odd sort of way, the
longer they'd abjured the divorce courts, the stronger had grown
the ties that bound them together: home, children, friends, memories, insurance policies; and above all, perhaps, the sheer length
– the ever-increasing length – of the time they'd spent together as
man and wife. Forty-three whole years of it now.

Before marrying Shirley, he'd written an honourable and honest
letter to Betty Fowler, but he'd received no reply. Whatever the
actual reasons for this, in his own mind he'd singled out the fact
that she must have got married. She was an extraordinarily
attractive girl, with a pale complexion, a freckled face, and ginger
hair; a girl for whom most of the other GIs would willingly have
given a monthly pay-packet. Or an annual one.

Then, only six months since, he had received a letter ('Private
and Strictly Confidential'). Although sent to his 1947 address in
Los Angeles, it had finally, almost flukily, caught up with him –
and thereby opened a floodgate of memories upon which the
years had added their sentimental compound-interest. She had
(Betty confessed) received his letter all that while ago; still had it,
in fact. But by that time she had married a car-worker from
Cowley, was four months pregnant, and was eventually to become
the mother of four lovely children – three girls and one boy. Her
husband had retired in 1988 and then, so sadly, died only seven
months later. She was all right, herself. No worries – certainly no
financial worries. And eight (eight!) grandchildren, though she
had not herself been tempted to enter the local 'Glamorous
Grandmother' contest. So, the only reason for her writing was to
say that if he ever *did* get the chance to come over to the UK again,
well, she'd like . . . well, it would be nice . . .

From America, how earnestly he'd longed to reach her on the
telephone! But she had given him neither an address nor a
telephone number; and the complexities of finding either had
posed rather too much of a problem on a transatlantic line. Yet
here he was now – so near to her! And with his wife gone out for
long enough with one of her admirers . . . So, he'd watched her
go from the hotel, and then contacted Directory Enquiries from
the phone-booth in the foyer. Miraculously, within a couple of

minutes, he'd found himself speaking to a woman he'd kissed goodbye in the early May of 1944 – over forty-six years ago! Could she meet him? Would she *like* to meet him? The answer was yes, yes, yes. And so they *had* met (it had been *so* easy, as it happened, for him to sneak away the previous afternoon) nervously and excitedly outside the main entrance to the University Parks at 2.30 p.m.

'And *she* turned up, did she?' asked Morse.

'Yes.' Brown appeared a fraction puzzled by the question. 'Oh, yes! I'd walked up St Giles' about two o'clock, and then down Keble Road to the Parks. And, well, there she was – waiting for me.'

'Then you went to Parson's Pleasure and sat in one of the cubicles.'

'But you won't get me wrong, will you, Inspector? I want to set the record straight. We just had a quiet little kiss and cuddle together and – well, that was that, really.'

'My only wish,' said Morse, looking now with somewhat irrational distaste at the remarkably well-preserved Lothario from Los Angeles, 'is to set, as you say, the record straight. So thank you for your honesty!'

Brown stood up and prepared to leave. He looked, little doubt of it, considerably relieved, but clearly there was something on his mind, for he stood hesitantly beside the table, his eyes scouting around for some object upon which to focus.

'There *is* one thing, Inspector.'

'And that is?'

'When I was walking up to Keble Road yesterday I saw someone standing at the bus-stop outside St Giles' Church, waiting to get up to Summertown. Well, I suppose it was Summertown.'

'And who was that, sir?'

'It was Mr Ashenden.'

'I just don't believe all this,' said Morse after Brown had gone.

'You mean you wonder who *Ashenden* saw, sir?'

'Exactly.'

'He sounded as if he was telling the truth.'

'They all do! But *somebody* isn't telling the truth, Lewis. Somebody stole the Wolvercote Tongue, and somebody murdered Kemp! If only I could find the connection!'

'Perhaps there isn't a connection,' said Lewis.

But he might just as well have been talking to himself.

CHAPTER THIRTY-SEVEN

Sic, ne perdiderit, non cessat perdere lusor
(To recoup his losses, the gambler keeps on backing the losers)
(Ovid, *Ars Amatoria*)

Ashenden, buttonholed as he was once again in the coffee-lounge by the diminutive dynamo from Sacramento, appeared only too glad to be given the opportunity of escaping, albeit to an interview with Chief Inspector Morse.

'Do you always get one like that?' sympathized Lewis.

'Well, she'd probably take the prize,' conceded Ashenden with a weary grin. 'But Janet's not such a bad old stick sometimes – not when you get to know her.'

'Makes you wonder how anyone ever married her, though.'

Ashenden nodded as he walked through into the Bar-Annexe: 'Poor chap!'

With this next hand (Ashenden), Morse took no finesses at all. Just played off his aces and sat back. Question: Why had Ashenden lied about his visit to Magdalen? Answer: It wasn't a lie really. He *had* gone up to Magdalen College, asked at the Porters' Lodge, discovered the grounds were closed; then just carried on walking over the bridge, around the Plain, and back again down the High. Silly to lie, really. But it was only to avoid any tedious and wholly inconsequential explanation. Question: What about the previous afternoon, at about 2 p.m.? (Morse admitted his willingness to listen to a little more 'tedious and wholly inconsequential explanation'.)

'No secret, Inspector. In fact I'd told a couple of the group – Mr and Mrs Kronquist, I think it was – that I was going up to Summertown.'

'Why bother? Why explain? You're a free agent, aren't you, sir?'

Ashenden pondered the question awhile. 'I did realize, yesterday, that you perhaps weren't completely satisfied with the account of my whereabouts when, er—'

'The Wolvercote Tongue was stolen,' supplied Morse.

'Yes. That's why it seemed no bad idea for somebody to know where I was yesterday afternoon.'

'And where was that?'

Ashenden, looking decidedly uncomfortable, drew a deep breath: 'I spent the afternoon in the betting-shop in Summertown.'

Lewis looked up: 'Not a crime, that, is it?'

Morse seemed to appreciate the interjection: 'Surely Sergeant

Lewis is right, sir? Certainly it's not a criminal offence to line a bookie's pockets.'

Ashenden suddenly seemed more relaxed: 'I had a tip. I met this fellow from Newmarket when we were at the University Arms in Cambridge. He said be sure to back this horse – over the sticks at Fontwell Park.'

'Go on.'

'Well, that's it, really. I picked another horse, in the race before – I'd got to the bookie's at about half-past two, I suppose. I put three pounds to win on a horse in the two-fifty, and then five pounds to win on the 'dead cert' this fellow had told me about in the three-fifteen or three-twenty – something like that.'

'How much did you win?'

Ashenden shook his head sadly: 'I don't think you can be a racing man, Inspector.'

'Would they have records at the bookie's to show you'd been there, sir?'

It was Lewis who had asked the question, and Ashenden turned in his chair to face him: 'Are you suggesting I *wasn't* there?'

'No, sir. Certainly not. But it was the key sort of *time*, wasn't it? Three o'clock time? Just the time when Dr Kemp was getting back to Oxford.'

'Yes,' replied Ashenden slowly. 'I take the point.'

'Would anyone recognize you,' continued Lewis, 'if you went there again?'

'I don't know. There were quite a few there during the afternoon – eight, ten – more, perhaps, for some of the time, some of the races. But whether anyone would recognize me . . .'

'They'd have your betting-slips, surely?' suggested Morse.

'Oh yes – they'd keep those – if the horses had won.'

'Bit of bad luck you didn't pick a winner, then. You could have collected your winnings and proved your alibi both at the same time.'

'Life's full of disappointments, Inspector, as I'm sure—' Suddenly he stopped; and his eyes lit up as he withdrew a black-leather wallet from the breast-pocket of his sports jacket. 'With a bit of luck . . . Yes! Thank goodness! I thought I might have torn them up.'

'They tell me betting-shops are littered with torn-up betting-slips,' said Morse, as he looked down at the two pink slips that Ashenden had handed to him.

'You might just as well tear those up as well, Inspector, I'm afraid.'

'Oh, no, sir. We mustn't destroy any evidence, must we, Lewis?'

Ashenden shrugged, and seemed for a moment somewhat less at ease. 'Anything else?'

'I think not,' said Morse. 'But it's a mug's game, betting, you know. A dirty game, too.'

'Perhaps you should go into a betting-shop yourself one day. It's quite a civilized business these days—'

But Morse interrupted the man, and his eyes were ice. 'Look, lad! Once you've lost as much money as me on the horses – *then* you come and give me a sermon on gambling, all right?' He flicked his right hand in dismissal. 'And tell your coach-driver he can leave at *five* o'clock. That should please everybody. It's only thirty-seven or thirty-eight miles to Stratford – and Lewis here once managed it in half an hour.'

CHAPTER THIRTY-EIGHT

The west yet glimmers with some streaks of day:
Now spurs the lated traveller apace
To gain the timely inn

(Shakespeare, *Macbeth*)

On the coach, as it headed north up the Woodstock Road, and thence out on to the A34, the members of the touring party were mostly silent, their thoughts monopolized perhaps by the strange and tragic events they had left behind them in Oxford. What tales they would be able to tell once they got back home again! John Ashenden, seated alone in the front nearside seat, debated with himself about reaching for the microphone and saying a few words about Somerville College, the Radcliffe Infirmary, the tower of the Winds, the large, late nineteenth-century redbrick residences, St Edward's School . . . But he decided against it: the mood was not upon him – nor upon anyone else in the coach, as far as he could gather.

Opposite him, in the seat immediately behind the driver, sat a sour-faced Mrs Roscoe, her nicely shaped little nose stuck deep into the text of *A Midsummer Night's Dream*. Immediately behind him sat Howard and Shirley Brown, silent and sombre, each thinking thoughts that were quite impossible for any observer to ascertain – even for the two of them themselves fully to comprehend. And behind the Browns, the enigmatic Kronquists, now the only other married couple registered on the tour, reluctant, it seemed, to engage in even the most perfunctory of conversations: she now reading *Lark Rise to Candleford*; he, the *Good Beer Guide* (just published) for 1991. At the back, as if distanced to the utmost from the woman who *ab initio* had publicly sought to claim him as escort, friend, and guide, sat Phil Aldrich, slowly reading the evening's edition of the *Oxford Mail*. Nor had the sudden coolness between himself and Mrs J. Roscoe escaped most of the other tourists; indeed, this development was proving one of the few topics of conversation as the coach accelerated along the dual carriageway towards Woodstock.

Only two of the party that had arrived at The Randolph, some fifty hours earlier, were no longer in their original seats – the seats immediately behind Mrs Roscoe. One of these missing persons was still lying (lying still, rather) in the police mortuary in St Aldates; the other person with Morse's full permission, had that afternoon departed by train for London, not stopping on this occasion (as he had claimed to have stopped earlier) at Didcot Parkway, but travelling straight through – past Reading, Maiden-head, Slough – to Paddington, whence he had taken a taxi to the Tour Company HQ in Belgravia in order to discuss the last wishes and the last rites of his erstwhile legal spouse, Mrs Laura Mary Stratton.

As the coach pulled powerfully up the hill away from Wood-stock, Ashenden once again looked slightly anxiously at his watch. He had rung through to the Swan Hotel in Stratford to set a revised time of arrival at 6.15 p.m.; but by the look of things it was going to be, in Wellington's words, 'a damn close-run thing'. Yet he made no attempt to harass the driver into any illegitimate speed. They'd arrive a little late? So what! Twenty-six plates of 'Mousse Arbroath Smokies' were already laid out, they'd said – with just the single carrot juice for just the single vegan girl.

Was Inspector Morse (Ashenden pondered) quite the man most people seemed to think he was? A man with a mind that might have left even the mythical Mycroft just floundering a fraction? Ashenden doubted it, his doubt redoubling as the coach drew further away from Oxford along the A34.

Everything would be all right.

CHAPTER THIRTY-NINE

I feel like I done when Slippery Sun
Romped 'ome a winner at 30 to 1
(A. P. Herbert, *Derby Day*)

From the street-window of the coffee-lounge, Morse and Lewis
had watched them go.

'Think we shall be seeing any of them again, sir?'

'No,' said Morse flatly.

'Does that mean you've got some idea—?'

'Ideas, plural, Lewis! We've seldom had so many clues, have
we? But I can't help feeling we've missed all the really vital ones—'
Morse broke off and resumed the drift of his earlier thought. 'It's
this wretched *love* business – and I still think that Kemp was killed
because he had one too many fancy women.'

'I know I keep on about Mrs Kemp, sir, but don't you think we
ought—'

Morse ignored the interruption. '*Why* was he naked? I thought
for a start it was because moving the dead body might have been
a very messy business. Max said there'd have been buckets of
blood, and if someone's going to get it all over a suit, or a dress
. . . It's a possibility, Lewis. Or he may have been stripped to
delay any identification, I suppose. The longer delayed it is—'

'—the more difficult it gets for us to disprove an alibi.'

Morse nodded. 'But I don't think it was either of those reasons.'

'You think he was making love to a lady?'

'Well, a *woman*, Lewis. And since we know that woman wasn't
likely to have been his wife because she'd . . . well, because of the
car crash, we've got to decide who it could have been. Just think a
minute! We get the husband, or whoever the jealous party was,
bounding into the boudoir and catching 'em copulating. Who was
she, though? I can't for the life of me see how it could have been
Sheila Williams he was with . . . No, we've got to look down the
race-card for some attractive, available, acquiescent filly – and the
likeliest filly is surely—'

Suddenly Morse stopped, his mind once more six furlongs
ahead of the field. He had bought a copy of *The Times* before he
had come to The Randolph that morning, but hitherto had not
even glanced at the headlines. Now he looked again at the two
betting-slips that lay on the table in front of him; then turned to
the back of the Business section for the Sport, his eye running
down the results of the previous day's racing at Fontwell Park.

Ashenden's stake in the 2.50 race, £3 win on Golden Surprise, had contributed further, it appeared, to the luxurious life-style of the bookmaking fraternity. But as Lewis now saw them, Morse's eyes seemed to grow significantly in circumference as they fell upon the result of the 3.15:

1   THETFORD QUEEN (J. Francis) 30–1

'Bloody 'ell!' whispered Morse.

'Sir?'

'Ashenden backed a horse yesterday – a horse he said someone in Cambridge had tipped – he put a fiver on it – and it won! Thetford Queen. There! – it's on the betting-slip.'

'Whew! That means he's got a hundred and fifty pounds coming to him.'

'No. He didn't pay any tax on it, so he'd only get one hundred and forty back – including his stake.'

'I didn't realize you knew quite so much about the gee-gees, sir?'

But again Morse ignored the comment: 'He says he was there, Lewis – in the betting-shop. He's put his money on the hot tip, and the thing wins, and . . . he doesn't pick up his winnings!'

Lewis considered what Morse was saying, and shook his head in puzzlement. Surely Ashenden *would* have gone up to the Pay-Out desk immediately, if he'd been there – especially since that was the only time he was going to be in the betting-shop. And if for some strange reason he'd been misinformed, been told that the horse had lost, then it was difficult to see why he'd kept the slips so carefully in his wallet. Why not tear them up like everyone else and contribute to the litter found on every bookie's floor?

Morse interrupted Lewis's thoughts: 'Shall I tell you exactly what our leader was doing in the betting-shop? Establishing his alibi! If you've backed a couple of horses, and if you'll be gone the next day, you stay there like everybody else and listen to the commentaries. But if you pick a couple of complete no-hopers, rank outsiders, well, there's no need to stay, is there? Look at the odds on Golden Surprise! 50–1! So Ashenden spent eight quid of his money *in order to buy himself an alibi.*'

'Bit of bad luck the horse won, if you see what I mean, sir.'

'Where did he *go*, though?'

'Well he can't be that "jealous husband" you're looking for.'

'No, but he went somewhere he didn't want anyone to know about. I just wonder whether it might have been somewhere like—'

The Manager walked swiftly through: 'Can you come to the phone, Inspector? Very urgent, they say.'

It was Max.

'Morse? Get over here smartish! Bloody Hell! Christ!'

'Tell me, Max,' said Morse softly.

'Mrs Kemp, that's what! Tried to cross the nighted ferry; might've made it but for a district-nurse calling unexpectedly.'

'She's not dead?'

'Not yet.'

'Likely to be?'

'Oh, I couldn't say.'

'*For God's sake, Max!*'

'Not even for His.'

Morse had never seen Mrs Marion Kemp, but from the marriage photograph that hung in the living room he realized that she must once have been quite a vivacious woman: dark, curly hair; slim, firm figure; and curiously impudent, puckish eyes. She had already been removed to the Intensive Care Unit at the JR2, but in the bedroom there seemed quite sufficient evidence that she had planned a deliberate departure. A brown glass bottle of sleeping pills stood capless and empty on the bedside table, and beside it, lying on the top of a Georgette Heyer novel, was a short, soberly legible (though unsigned) note:

If found still alive, please let me die.
If found dead, please contact
Dr M. Davies at the Summertown
Health Centre — the only man who
ever tried to understand my
suffering.

CHAPTER FORTY

He
That kills himself to avoid misery, fears it,
And, at the best, shows but a bastard valour
(Philip Massinger, *The Maid of Honour*)

Morse and Max stood for a few moments silently just outside the front door of the Kemp residence. Nothing, as both men knew, could be quite as sombre and sickening as a suicide (or, as here, an attempted suicide), for it spoke not only of unbearable suffering but also of a certain misguided fortitude. Morse had looked quickly round the flat but had found nothing much to engage his interest.

'Let's try to keep her alive, if we can, Max,' he said quietly.

'Out of my hands, now.'

'Fancy a glass of Brakspear? Only just along the road here.'

'No time, dear boy! Presumably you consider the Henley branch of the Brakspear family to be greater benefactors than that St Albans fellow?'

'Wha—?' For a few seconds even Morse was lost a little; but then he grinned acknowledgement: 'You're a cultured sod.'

'You know, Morse,' panted Max as he eased his overweight frame into his car, 'I've always thought of myself more as a Renaissance man, actually.'

He was gone, and Morse looked around the area somewhat fecklessly. A maintenance man, with a garden fork and wheelbarrow, was tending the herbaceous border that stretched along the frontage of the flats and, in reponse to Morse's question, he said he was one of a small team that looked after the three blocks of flats that stood on the eastern side of Water Eaton Road. And yes, he'd been working there for several days. Had he seen anyone coming in, during the afternoon of the previous day? After three o'clock, say? But the man, looking to Morse far too young to have graduated with any glory from a landscape-gardening apprenticeship, shook his head dubiously.

'Difficult, innit? I mean, I was out the back most o' the time. There *were* some people comin' in, I remember, but they'd probably bin shoppin' and that, 'adn't they?'

'You saw this man?' Morse held up the photograph of Theodore Kemp which he had just removed from the living room. Clearly it had been taken several years earlier, but it showed, even then, the supercilious cast of a face which had looked into the camera with head held well back, and lips that seemed to smile with a curious arrogance above the Vandyke beard.

'Yea! I seen 'im before – but I dunno about yesterday. As I said, I was out the back most o' the time – doin' the bits by the river.'

The river . . .

Morse thanked the man, and walked along to the ramp at the side of the flats, and down to the concreted area where five garages directly in front of him shielded the immediate view. Then, turning to his right, he came to a stretch of well-trimmed lawn that sloped down to the river, the far bank of which was policed by a row of severely pollarded willow trees. Here the water was green-scummed and semi-stagnant. But a bridge ('Residents Only') led him across to the main channel of the Cherwell, where the water was still flowing fairly swiftly after the week's earlier rains, and where pieces of debris were intermittently knocking into the sides of the banks, and then turning and twisting, first one way then the other, like dodgem cars at the funfair. For several minutes Morse looked down at the turbid, turgid river; and his thoughts were as restless as the waters below him. Then, of a sudden, he nodded to himself firmly – and the look around his mouth was almost as arrogant as that of the late Theodore Kemp, who at some time, at some point, had recently been manoeuvred into these selfsame murky, swollen waters.

Lewis was waiting for him as he reached the road again.

'What now, sir?'

'What we need is a little liquid refreshment, and there's a little pub' – Morse got into the passenger seat – 'just along the road here.'

'Might as well walk, sir. It's only fifty yards.'

Morse said nothing, but sat where he was and picked up the *Railway Gazette* from the door-pocket and pretended to read it; then *did* read it – for a few seconds.

Lewis had backed the car a few feet down the ramp and was about to turn towards the Cherwell Arms when he heard his master's voice – a single hissed and incredulous blasphemy:

'Chrissst!'

'More clues, sir?'

'Look! Look at this!'

Lewis took the magazine and read through the brief article to which Morse was pointing:

GOLDEN OLDIES

Members of the GWR Preservation Society will learn with
particular interest that w.e.f. 21st October the world-famous
Torbay Express will be making a nostalgic return visit to a few
stretches of its old track, and will first be housed for three
weeks in Railway Shed 4 at Plymouth.

His eyes looked across at Morse's: 'And he said he'd seen the
Torbay Express at Didcot, didn't he? It's in his statement, surely.'

Morse stared in front of him, his eyes a-glitter: 'He's a liar,
Stratton is; he's a bloody liar!'

'Is – is that a 1990 magazine?' asked Lewis diffidently.

Morse turned to the colourful cover, then placed the magazine
back casually into the door-pocket.

'Well, sir?'

'September 1988,' said Morse, very quietly indeed.

'What's it all mean?' asked Lewis, as he sat at the table, with a
pint of Brakspear for Morse and half of the same for himself. He
had never understood why Morse almost always expected *him* to
buy the beer. It was as though Morse believed that he, Lewis, was
on some perpetual expense-account.

'You mean about Mrs Kemp?'

'I mean about everything. I just don't know what's happening.'

'You think *I* do?'

'I thought you might have an idea.'

'Perhaps I have.' He drained his pint with extraordinary rapidity. 'Is it your round or mine?'

Lewis walked over to the bar with the single glass – almost
happily.

Whilst he was gone, Morse turned to the back of *The Times* and
had filled in the whole of the bottom right-hand quarter of the
crossword when Lewis returned two minutes later.

'Do you always do crosswords that way round, sir?'

'Uh? Oh, yes! I always try solving problems by starting at the
end – never the beginning.'

'I shall have to try that sometimes.'

'I didn't know you did crosswords, Lewis?'

'Yes! Me and the missus, we usually try to do the *Daily Mirror*
Quick Crossword of an evening.'

'Oh!' said Morse, though without much wonderment in his

voice. 'Well, let me tell you something. If I'm doing a crossword, and I think I'm getting stuck—'

'Not that you *do*, sir.'

'No. Not that I do – not very often. But if by some freak mischance I *do* get a bit stuck, you know what I do?'

'Tell me!'

'I *stop* thinking about the problem. Then, when I come back to it? No problem at all!'

'Have *we* got a problem, sir?'

'Oh yes! That's why we need the break – the drinking break.' Morse took an almighty swig from his replenished pint, leaving only an inch of beer in the glass. 'Our problem is to find the connection between the theft of the jewel and the murder of Kemp. Once we find that . . . So the best thing to do is to think of something completely different. Tell me about something, Lewis – something that's got nothing to do with Mrs Kemp.'

'I was just thinking about those betting-slips, sir. They've got the time on them – the time the bet was placed.'

'I said something *different*, Lewis! Anything. Tell me anything! Tell me the name of your first girl-friend! *Anything!*'

'I can't, sir. Not for the minute. I just think I let Mrs Kemp down . . . in a way.'

'What the hell are you talking about? It's *me* who let her down! How many times did you tell me I ought to see her?'

'Why do you think she tried . . . ?'

'How the hell do I know!'

'Just asked, that's all.'

'All right. What do *you* think?'

'I suppose she just felt life wasn't worth living without him – without her husband.'

'You didn't feel that, though, when you met her, did you? From what you told me you seemed to feel the opposite: life might have been worth living if he *wasn't* there.'

Yes, Lewis knew that Morse was right. He'd felt the anger and the bitterness of the woman – far more than any sense of anguish or loss. He knew, too, that his lack of sleep was beginning to catch up with him.

'You talk about giving your mind a rest, sir, but I shall have to give my body a bit of a rest soon. I'm knackered – absolutely knackered!'

'Go home, then! What's stopping you? I can always get Dixon—'

'I don't want to go home, sir. We've got the decorators in and I

keep getting nagged about getting new carpets and new curtains
and—'

Morse jumped up from the table, his face radiant: 'You've done
it, Lewis! You've done it again!'

Lewis too rose from his seat, a tired, bewildered expression
across his honest features.

What had he just said?

CHAPTER FORTY-ONE

Light thickens and the crow makes wing to the
rooky wood

(Shakespeare, *Macbeth*)

It was a quarter past six when Sheila Williams saw the police car
draw up outside, and she answered the front door immediately.

'Come in, Inspector!' The colourless liquid in the glass she
carried might just have been water, perhaps; but whatever it was
she seemed unwontedly sober.

'No. I – we've got a lot to do. Look! I'm very sorry to have to
tell you this – but Mrs Kemp tried to kill herself this afternoon.'

Sheila's right hand jumped to her mouth with a convulsive jerk:
'Oh, no!' she whispered.

'She took enough pills to kill a healthy elephant, Sheila, but
fortunately a nurse found her – in time, we think. If only just.'

'Where—?'

'She's in the JR2. She's having the best care she could get
anywhere.'

Sheila took a deep breath. 'Oh dear!' she managed to say in a
broken voice as the tears began to trickle. Then, somewhat to
Morse's embarrassment, she suddenly buried her head on his
shoulder and clung tightly to him.

'Did she love him?' asked Morse gently.

'She *possessed* him!'

'But did she *love* him?'

Sheila Williams straightened herself and pulled away from him,
searching her pockets for a handkerchief. Her voice was almost
fierce as she answered: 'No! *I* was the only one who really loved
him.'

'Do you know anyone else who loved him? Was there someone
else? A *third* woman in his life?'

Sheila shook her head in deep anguish.

'You quite sure about it, Sheila? It's so very important that you're honest with me,' urged Morse.

'He said not. He swore it!'

'And you believed him?'

She nodded, and wiped her eyes. And Morse nodded, too, and looked very sad.

'All right. Thank you.' He turned to go, but she called him back, the tears springing once more.

'Inspector – please!'

Morse turned, and laid his right hand lightly on her shoulder. 'No need to tell me, really. I *know* there was another woman in his life.'

Her 'yes' was barely audible.

'And I think you knew who it was.'

She nodded again.

'It was only recently though, wasn't it, Sheila? Only recently that he'd started seeing Mrs Downes?'

Lewis, standing at the front gate, had managed to catch most of the exchanges; had watched Mrs Williams as she'd finally turned away from Morse in tearful distress. And now, as they got back into the car, both men sat in silence as they watched the light switched on in the front bedroom – and then the curtains being drawn across.

'Curtains!' said Morse, his voice sounding tired yet triumphant. 'As you said, Lewis – curtains.'

The Downes's house was in darkness, and the sound of the front-door bell seemed somehow to re-echo along empty passageways, around empty rooms. Morse looked at his watch: just after half-past six – and Downes would be meeting his wife at seven o'clock.

A wooden gate at the side of the house led to a neatly tended garden at the back, the lawn sloping down to the river, with a path of paving stones laid along the middle, ending on the edge of the waters at what looked like a small landing-stage, perhaps once used to moor a small boat or punt, but apparently (as Lewis shone his torch across it) not in recent use.

'You think . . . ?' Lewis pointed down to the fast-flowing Cherwell.

'Launched from here? Yes, I do. Launched from here into eternity.'

'But *when*, sir? He wasn't back in Oxford—'

'All in good time, Lewis! For the moment, be a good boy-scout and shine your little torch over those back windows?'

As in the front, the windows here were fully curtained, all of them looking decidedly posh and new; all of them with some approximation to those French pleats whose acquaintance Lewis had so recently made – and, if truth were told, Morse too.

'You see, Lewis,' began Morse, as the two strolled back to the front of the property, 'Kemp had grown tired of Sheila Williams and was starting out on a new conquest – the delectable Lucy Downes. Unfortunately for Kemp, however, Cedric Downes discovered the guilty pair *in flagrante delicto*, which as you will remember, Lewis, is the Latin for having your pants down. He's got to have a woman, has Kemp. His motto's *amo amas amat* it again. And he's at it again when Downes hits him with whatever's to hand; kills him; wonders where he's going to dump the corpse; can't dress him – far too difficult dressing a corpse—'

"Specially for a woman, sir.'

'What?'

'Don't you think it might have been a jealous *woman*? Not a jealous *man*?'

'No, no, Lewis! Not Sheila Williams.'

'She left the group, though – she went to the pub—'

'She hadn't got the *time*! Whoever killed Kemp had time: time to cart him off to the river, and dump him there – *gently*, Lewis – without even a splash to startle the cygnets . . .'

'But it *couldn't* have been like that. The times are all wrong.'

'Speak on, Lewis! Like the murderer, we've got plenty of time.'

'We're waiting *here*, you mean?'

'Oh, yes! I'm very much looking forward to meeting Mr and Mrs Downes again.'

'And you think, in that suitcase of hers . . .?'

But as the two detectives stood beside the car, the radio crackled into life.

'Lewis here!'

'Bad news, Sarge. Mrs Kemp died at the JR2 – fifty minutes ago. We've only just heard.'

Morse stood where he was, listening, and staring up at the sky as if viewing the unsuspected behaviour of some distant galaxy. His shoulders were sagging, and his face looked sad, and very weary.

'You look all in, sir.'

'Me? Don't talk so daft!' Morse looked quickly at his watch.

'He's meeting her in seven minutes! Put your foot down!'
'I thought you said we were waiting here?'
'Get *on* with it Lewis – and turn the bloody siren on!'

CHAPTER FORTY-TWO

No one came
On the bare platform
(Edward Thomas, *Adlestrop*)

The police car drove into the Bus and Taxi area in front of the
railway station. Across on Platform 2, the train from Paddington
was just pulling in; and passengers were already beginning to
stream across the new pedestrian bridge as Morse and Lewis first
ascended, then descended the steps, darting challenging looks
around them as they dodged their way through the bustling
contra-flow.

The train still stood at the platform; and a group of Post Office
workers were lobbing a stack of bulging mail-bags into the guard's
van. And there – yes, there right in front of them! – passing from
one window to another, peering into each of the carriages, his face
drawn and anxious, was Cedric Downes. Morse placed a restraining hand on Lewis's arm, and the two of them stood watching the
man while two or three heavily luggaged travellers finally made
their way along the platform. Soon Downes had reached the last
carriage in front of the diesel locomotive, staring quickly through
the windows of the compartment as the few doors still remaining
open were banged shut and a whistle blew, and with a slight chug
and then with a mighty heave the long, north-bound train began
slowly to move forward, gradually picking up a little speed, before
moving out and away along the curving stretch of line that led to
Banbury.

Downes looked down at his wristwatch, and at last turned
away, walking back along the bare platform towards the footbridge
– where he was confronted by the bulk of the broad-shouldered
Lewis.

'Good evening, sir. We *have* met before.'

Downes seemed slightly surprised – but hardly more than that:
'It's about Theo, I suppose? Theo Kemp?'

'Er – yes.' Lewis hardly managed to climb up to any plateau of
assertiveness.

'Well, I've nothing more to tell you, I'm afraid. Nothing I can add to the statement I've already—'

'Meeting your wife, Mr Downes?' interrupted Morse.

'Pardon? Just a minute, Inspector! I . . . just a minute, please.' Downes fitted a hearing-aid taken from his pocket into his right ear, the aid promptly emitting a series of shrill whistles as he fiddled rather fecklessly with the controls.

'I was asking whether you were meeting—' bawled Morse – to no avail, as it appeared.

'If you'll just bear with me a few minutes, gentlemen, I'll just nip along to the car, if I may. I always keep a spare aid in the glove compartment.' The beseeching grin around the slightly lop-sided mouth gave his face an almost schoolboyish look.

Morse gestured vaguely: 'Of course. We'll walk along with you, sir.'

In front of the railway station, a second police car (summoned by a confident Morse as Lewis had driven him from North Oxford) was now waiting, and the Chief Inspector nodded a perfunctory greeting to the two detective constables who sat side by side in the front seats as they watched, and awaited, developments; watched the three men walk over to the twenty-minute waiting-area set aside for those meeting passengers from British Rail journeys – an area where parking cost nothing at all; watched them as they passed through that area and walked into the main car-park, with the bold notice affording innocent trespassers the clearest warning:

> PARKING FOR BRITISH RAIL
> PASSENGERS ONLY
> FOR OTHER USERS WITHOUT
> PARKING-TOKENS, £10 PER DAY

'Mind telling me, sir, why you didn't just wait in the twenty-minute car-park? Parking where you have done seems a rather unnecessary expense, doesn't it? Doesn't it . . .?'

'Pardon, Inspector? If you give me just a second . . . a second or two . . . just . . .'

Downes took a bunch of car-keys from his pocket, opened the door of a British racing green MG Metro, got into the driver's seat, and leaned over left to open the glove compartment.

Both Morse and Lewis stood, rather warily, beside the car as Downes began to fiddle (once more) with a hearing-aid – one which looked to them suspiciously like the model that had earlier given rise to such piercing oscillation.

'There we are then!' said Downes, as he got out of the car and faced them, his face beaming with an almost childlike pleasure. 'Back in the land of the living! I think you were trying to say something, Inspector?'

'No. I wasn't *trying* to say anything, Mr Downes. I *was* saying something. I was saying how odd it seemed to me that you didn't park your car in the twenty-minute car-park.'

'Ah! Well, I did in a way. I seem to have collected an awful lot of those parking-tokens over the last few months. You see, I often have to go to London and sometimes I don't get back until pretty late. And late at night the barrier here where you slip in your parking-token is often open, and you can just drive straight through.'

'But why *waste* one of your precious tokens?' persisted Morse.

'Ah! I see what you're getting at. I'm a very law-abiding citizen, Inspector. I came here a bit early this evening, and I didn't want to risk any of those clamps or fines or anything. There's an Antiques Fair this week just along Park End Street, and I'd got my eye on a little set of drawers, yew-wood veneer. Lucy's birthday's coming up, November the seventh . . .'

'And then you called in the Royal Oxford, no doubt?'

'I did *not*! I no longer drink and drive. Never!'

'Some people do, sir,' said Morse. 'It's the most common cause of road accidents, you know.'

There was a silence between the three men who now stood slightly awkwardly alongside the MG Metro. Downes, as it appeared, had read the situation adequately, and was expecting to accompany the policemen – well, somewhere! – and he opened the driver's door of the Metro once more. But Morse, leaning slightly towards him, opened his right palm, like a North African Berber begging for alms.

'We'd like you to come with us, sir. If you just hand over your car-keys to me, Sergeant Lewis here will see that your car is picked up later and returned to your home address.'

'Surely this isn't necessary, is it? I know where the police station is, for Christ's sake!' Suddenly, within the last few words, Downes had lost whatever composure he had hitherto sought to sustain.

'The keys, please!' insisted Morse quietly.

'Look! I just don't know what all this bloody nonsense is about. Will you please *tell* me.'

'Certainly! You can *hear* me all right now?'

Downes almost snarled his reluctant 'Yes'; and listened, mouth agape with incredulity, as Morse beckoned over to the two detective constables from the second police car.

'Cedric Downes, I arrest you on suspicion of the murder of Dr Theodore Kemp. It is my duty to advise you that anything you now say may be noted by my sergeant here and possibly used in evidence in any future criminal prosecution.'

But as one of the detective constables clicked a pair of handcuffs round his wrists, Cedric Downes was apparently in no state at all to mouth as much as a monosyllable, let alone give utterance to any incriminating statement. For many seconds he just stood where he was, as still as a man who has gazed into the eyes of the Medusa.

CHAPTER FORTY-THREE

As usual he was offering explanations for what other
people had not even noticed as problems
(Bryan Magee, *Aspects of Wagner*)

After Downes had been driven away, Morse and Lewis walked back to their own car, where Morse gave urgent instructions to the forensic lab to send a couple of their whizz-kids over to the railway station – immediately! – and to Kidlington HQ to see that a breakdown van would be available in about an hour's time to ferry away a certain Metro.

'You're absolutely sure about Downes, aren't you,' said Lewis. But it was a statement, not a question.

'Oh, yes!'

'What now, sir?'

'We'll wait for forensics. Then we'll go and see how Downes is making out – do him good to kick his heels in a cell for half an hour. He was lucky, you know, Lewis. Bloody lucky, one way or another.'

'Hadn't you better start at the beginning, sir? We've got a few minutes' wait, like as not.'

So Morse told him.

The key thing in the case was the phone call made by Kemp. And, yes, it *was* made by Kemp, although some doubt could quite properly have been harboured on the matter: Ashenden knew the man, and knew his voice; and in spite of what was probably a poorish extension-line, confirmation that the call *was* from Kemp had come from the telephone operator, someone else who knew him – knew him very well, in fact. No, the call was not made by anyone *pretending* to be Kemp. But Kemp had not made the call, as he'd claimed, from Paddington! He'd made it from *Oxford*. He was anxious about making absolutely sure that another person was present in The Randolph at the lunch session with the American tourists; and he learned quite unequivocally that this person *was* there, although he didn't actually speak to him. Furthermore, Kemp's absence that afternoon would mean that this other person – yes, Downes – would be all the more committed to *staying* with the tourists for the scheduled 'informal get-together'. This arrangement, cleverly yet quite simply managed, would give him a couple of hours to get on with what he desperately wanted to get on with: to climb into bed with Downes's beautiful and doubtlessly over-sexed wife, Lucy, and get his bottom on the top sheet before his time ran out. The pair of them had probably not been having an affair for long – only perhaps after Kemp's long infatuation with the semi-permanently sozzled Sheila had begun to wear off. But where can they meet? It has to be at Downes's place: Kemp hasn't got a room in college, and it can't be at Kemp's place because his wife is a house-bound invalid. So, that morning presented a wonderful opportunity – and just a little compensation perhaps for the huge disappointment Kemp must undoubtedly have experienced over the theft of the Wolvercote Tongue. The jewel was almost in his grasp; almost about to be displayed and photographed and written up in all the right journals: a jewel he himself had traced, and one he'd worked so hard to get donated to the Ashmolean. No wonder his interest in swopping pleasantries with ageing Americans had sunk to zero; no wonder the prospect of the lubricious Lucy Downes proved so irresistible. Now the deception practised by Kemp was a very clever one. If he was going to be late on parade – 3 p.m., he'd promised – every pressure would be on the other two group leaders, Sheila Williams and Cedric Downes, to keep the tourists adequately amused by each of them shouldering an extra responsibility. It would not, incidentally, have occurred to Kemp that a consequence of such last-minute re-arrangements was that several members of the group took the opportunity thus afforded to perform a strange assortment of extra-mural activities – from viewing steam locomotives to tracing lost offspring. Red herrings, all.

But then things started to go wrong. Downes is not very deaf at all yet; but sometimes, with certain kinds of background noise, and when people are asking questions, well, there can be difficulty. A deaf person, as Lucy Downes told us, is not so much worried about not knowing the answer to any question put to him; he's worried, embarrassingly so, *about not hearing the question.* And at lunch-time – there are witnesses – Downes's hearing-aid began to play up and he discovered he wasn't carrying his spare aid with him. He decided to go home and pick it up, and in fact he was *seen* going up St Giles' on his bicycle towards North Oxford. It's hardly difficult to guess the sequence of events immediately after he'd quietly inserted his key in the Yale lock. He may have had a sixth sense about the presence of some stranger in the house; more likely he saw some physical evidence – a coat, a hat – belonging to a person he knew. He picked up a walking-stick – or something – from the hall-stand, and leapt up the stairs to find his wife and Kemp *in medio coitu*, both of them completely naked. In a fury of hatred and jealousy he thrashed his stick about Kemp's head while Kemp himself tried to extricate himself from the twisted sheets, to get out of the bed, and to defend himself – but he didn't make it. He staggered back and fell, and got his head crashed – a *second* time, as we know – against the corner-post of the double bed or a sharp edge of the fireplace. He had a thin skull – a medical fact – and there was a sudden, dreadful silence; and a great deal of blood. The despairing, faithless, gaping, horrified wife looked down at her lover, and knew that he was dead. Now, sometimes it is extremely difficult to kill a man. Sometimes it is quite extraordinarily easy, as it was then . . .

And Downes himself? The emotions of hatred and jealousy are immediately superseded by the more primitive instinct of survival, and he begins to realize that all may yet be well if he can keep his head. For he is suddenly, miraculously, aware that he has got a wonderful – no! – a *perfect* alibi; an alibi which has been given to him *by the very person he has just killed.* O lovely irony! Kemp had told Ashenden, and Ashenden had then told everyone else, that he (Kemp) would not be back from London until 3 p.m. And that meant that Downes could not *possibly* have killed Kemp before that time, and Downes was going to make absolutely certain – as he did – that he was never out of sight or out of touch with his group – except for the odd, brief visit to the loo – at any time that afternoon or early evening.

It is hardly difficult to guess what happened at the Downes's residence immediately after the death of Kemp. Downes himself could not stay for more than a few minutes. He instructed his panic-stricken, guilt-ridden wife to pack up Kemp's clothes in a suitcase, and to clean up the bloody mess that must have been left on the carpet, and probably on the sheets. The body was left – *had* to be left – in the bedroom. Downes himself would have to deal with that. But later. For the present he seeks to compose himself as he cycles back down to The Randolph.

That evening, at about seven o'clock, he returns to his house in Lonsdale Road, the very far end of Lonsdale Road, where the lawn slopes down directly to the bank of the River Cherwell. He manoeuvres Kemp's body down the stairs and carries it across the lawn, probably in a wheelbarrow. It was a dark night, and doubtless he covered the corpse with a ground-sheet or something. Then slowly, carefully, without even the suspicion of a splash perhaps, he slid Kemp into the swift-flowing waters of a river swollen by the recent heavy rains. Two hours later, the body has drifted far downstream, finally getting wedged at the top of the weir in Parson's Pleasure – the place where the careless Howard Brown had earlier left his yellow programme – and his continental seven . . .

It was at this point in Morse's recapitulation that the forensic brigade arrived; and soon afterwards a royal-blue BMW carrying no lesser a personage than Chief Superintendent Bell from the City Police.

'You know, Morse,' began Bell, 'you seem to breed about as many problems as a pregnant rabbit.'

'You could look at it the other way, I suppose,' replied the radiant Morse. 'Without me and Lewis half of these fellows in forensics would be out on the dole, sir.'

About an hour before these last events were taking place, the American tourists had registered into the two-star Swan Hotel in Stratford-upon-(definitely 'upon')Avon. As throughout the tour, Ashenden had observed the opportunist self-seekers at the front of the queue (as ever) for the room-keys; and in the rear (as ever) the quieter, seemingly contented souls who perhaps knew that being first or last to their rooms would make little difference to the quality of their living. And at the very back, the small, patient figure of Phil Aldrich, seeking (of this, Ashenden could have little doubt) to avoid the embarrassment of refusing to sign Janet Roscoe's latest petition.

The evening meal had been re-scheduled for 8.30 p.m.; and

with time to spare, after throwing his own large hold-all on to the counterpane of his single bed, Ashenden joined a few of the other tourists in the Residents' Lounge, where he took some sheets of the hotel's own note-paper, and began to write a letter. When he had finished, he found a red, first-class stamp in his wallet, fixed it to the envelope, and walked out into Bridge Street to find a pillar-box. The letter was addressed to Chief Inspector Morse, St Aldates Central Police Station, Oxford, and in the top left-hand corner was written the one word: URGENT.

CHAPTER FORTY-FOUR

'When my noble and learned brother gives his Judgment, they're to be let go free,' said Krook, winking at us again. 'And then,' he added, whispering and grinning, 'if that ever was to happen – which it won't – the birds that have never been caged would kill 'em.'

(Dickens, *Bleak House*)

Unwontedly, Lewis was philosophizing as he and Morse sat in the canteen at St Aldate's: 'Amazing, really: you get all these statements and alibis and secret little meetings, and then really, in the end, it's just – well, it's just the same old story, isn't it? Chap goes home and finds the missus in bed with one of the neighbours.'

'Remember, though, this is only *half* the case. And we've got to get some evidence. No, that's wrong. We've *got* some evidence – or we shall have, very soon.'

'Perhaps we shouldn't wait too much longer, sir?'

'It'll be here. Patience, Lewis! Eat your cheese sandwich!'

'I couldn't help feeling just a bit sorry for him, though.'

'Sorry? Why do you say that?'

'Well, you know, it might have been a bit sort of – *accidental*, don't you reckon?'

'I do *not*,' replied Morse, with the fullest conviction.

Downes sat at the table in Interview Room 2 on the ground floor, spell-bound and motionless, as if a witch had drawn a circle round him thrice. Seated opposite, Sergeant Dixon was finding the silence and the stillness increasingly embarrassing.

'Like a cuppa tea?'

'No! Er, yes! Yes please.'

'Milk and sugar?'

But Downes appeared not to hear the supplementary questions, and Dixon nodded to the constable who stood at the door, the latter now making for the canteen on a less than wholly specific mission.

At the Swan Hotel in Stratford, Mrs Roscoe had just completed her evening meal, a concoction of beans so splendidly bleak as to delight the most dedicated vegan. She immediately wrote a brief congratulatory note, insisting that the waiter convey it forthwith to the chef de cuisine himself.

At this same time (it was now 9 p.m.) Eddie Stratton was sitting on the only chair in a small third-floor room of a hotel just north of Russell Square. The facilities here were minimal – a cracked wash-basin, one minuscule bar of soap, and one off-white towel. Yet the bed looked clean-sheeted and felt comfortable; and there was a lavatory just along the corridor (the lady had said), a bathroom one floor down, and a Residents' TV Lounge beside Reception. On the bedside table was a Gideon Bible, and beside it an entry form which, if and when completed and dispatched, would entitle the fortunate applicant to inclusion in a free draw for a ticket to one of the following summer's golfing championships. Stratton availed himself of neither opportunity.

Earlier he had visited the American Consulate, where an attractive and sympathetic fellow countrywoman from North Carolina had advised him on all the sad yet necessary procedures consequent upon the death of an American national in Britain, and acquainted him with the costs of the transatlantic conveyancing of corpses. And now, as he sat staring fixedly at the floral configuration on the faded green carpet, he felt a little sad as he thought of Laura, his wife for only the last couple of years. They had been as contented together as could have been expected, he supposed, from a union which had been largely one of convenience and accommodation; and he would always remember, with a sort of perverse affection, her rather loud voice, her over-daubed war-paint – and, of course, the painful state of those poor feet of hers . . . He nodded slowly to himself, then looked up and across at the lace-curtained window, like a bird perhaps suddenly spotting the open door of its cage. And an observer in that small room would have noticed the suspicion of a smile around his loose and slightly purplish lips.

It was just after 9 p.m. that a PC arrived from the railway station carrying a small brown envelope, which Morse accepted with delight, smiling radiantly at Lewis but saying nothing as he slit open the top and looked briefly inside. Then, with smile unfading, he handed the envelope to Lewis.

'Wish me luck! I'll let you know when to come in.'

CHAPTER FORTY-FIVE

Perchance my too much questioning offends
(Dante, *Purgatorio*)

At least Morse spared Cedric Downes the charade of a cordial re-greeting; he even forbore to express the hope that conditions were satisfactory and that the prisoner was being well treated. In point of fact, the prisoner looked lost and defeated. Earlier he had been officially advised that it was his legal right to have his solicitor present; but surprisingly Downes had taken no advantage of the offer. A cup of tea (sweetened) stood untouched at his right elbow. He raised his eyes, morosely, as Morse took Dixon's seat opposite him and pulled another chair alongside for a very blonde young WPC, who amongst other accomplishments was the only person in St Aldates HQ with a Pitman shorthand qualification for 130 w.p.m. Not that she was destined to get any practice at such a mega-speed, since Downes, at least for the first half of the interview, was to enunciate his words with the slow deliberation of a stupefied zombie. Morse waited patiently. That was always the best way, in the long run. And when Downes finally spoke, it was to ask about his wife.

'Did someone meet the train, Inspector? The next train?'

'Please don't worry about her, sir. She'll be looked after.'

Downes shook his head in stupefaction. 'This is madness – absolute madness! There's been some dreadful misunderstanding somewhere – don't you understand that? I – I can't think straight. I don't know what to say! I just pray I'm going to wake up any second.'

'Tell me about Dr Kemp,' said Morse.

'Tell you what? Everyone knows about Kemp. He was the biggest philanderer in Oxford.'

'You say "everyone"?'

'Yes! Including his wife. *She* knows.'

'*Knew*. She died this afternoon.'

'Oh God!' Downes closed his eyes and squeezed them tightly shut. Then he opened them and looked across at Morse. 'I think I know what you're going to ask me now, Inspector.'

Morse tilted his head to the left: 'You do?'

'You're going to ask me whether Lucy – whether my wife was . . . is aware of it, too.'

Morse tilted his head to the right, but made no reply.

'Well, the answer's "yes". Once or twice he'd – well he'd tried to make some sort of advances to her. At receptions, parties – that sort of thing.'

'Your wife *told* you about this?'

'She was a bit flattered, I suppose.'

'Was she?'

'And amused. More amused than flattered, I think.'

'And you? You, Mr Downes? Were *you* amused?'

'I could have killed the bloody swine!' So suddenly, so dramatically, the manner had changed – the voice now a harsh snarl, the eyes ablaze with hatred.

'It's not all that easy actually to kill a man,' said Morse.

'It isn't?' Downes's eyes appeared perplexed.

'What exactly *did* you hit him with? When you went home for – for whatever it was?'

'I – pardon? – you don't—'

'Just in your own words, sir, if you will. Simply what happened, that's all. The WPC here will take down what you say and then she'll read it back to you, and you'll be able to change anything you may have got wrong. No problem!'

'Wha—?' Downes shook his head in anguished desperation. 'When am I going to wake up?'

'Let's just start from when you put your key – Yale lock, isn't it? – into the front door, and then when you went in . . .'

'Yes, and I got my other hearing-aid, and some notes—'

'Whereabouts do you keep the spare hearing-aid?'

'In the bedroom.'

Morse nodded encouragement. 'Twin beds, I suppose—'

'Double bed, actually – and I keep my spare aid in a drawer of the tallboy' – he looked directly into Morse's eyes again – 'next to the handkerchiefs and the cufflinks and the arm-bands. You do want me to be *precise* about what I tell you?'

'And your wife was in the double bed there – yes, we do want you to be precise, sir.'

'Wha—? What makes you think my wife was in bed? This was at *lunch-time*.'

'Where was she?'

'In the living room? I don't know! I forget. Why don't you ask *her*?' He suddenly sprang to his feet. 'Look! I've got to talk to her! Now! You've no right to hold me here. I know you've got your job to do – I understand that. Some people get held on suspicion – I *know*. But I must speak to Lucy!'

His voice had become almost a screech of anger and frustration. And Morse was glad of it. So often the loss of self-control was the welcome prelude to a confession – a confession that was usually, in turn, a vast relief to the pent-up pressures of a tortured mind. And already Downes seemed calmer again as he resumed his seat, and Morse resumed his questioning.

'You understood, didn't you, the real point of Dr Kemp's phone call? No one else did – but *you* knew.' In contrast to the crescendo of fury from Downes, Morse's voice was very quiet indeed, and beside him WPC Wright was not absolutely sure that she'd transcribed his words with total accuracy.

As for Downes, he was leaning across the table. 'Could you please speak up a bit, Inspector? I didn't hear what you said, I'm afraid.'

It is likely, however, that he heard the loud knock on the door which heralded the entry of a rather harassed-looking Lewis.

'Sorry to interrupt, sir, but—'

'Not *now*, man! Can't you see—?'

'It's very urgent, sir,' said Lewis, in a voice of hushed authority.

WPC Wright had heard what Sergeant Lewis said all right; and she glanced across at Downes. Had *he* heard? Something in his face suggested to her that he might well have done, perhaps.

But it was difficult to tell.

CHAPTER FORTY-SIX

I do love to note and to observe
(Jonson, *Volpone*)

'I just don't believe it!' declared Morse.

It had been Lewis himself who a few minutes earlier had taken the call from the Met.

'Trying to cross over the road by King's Cross Station – about five thirty hit by a car. From Oxford she is. A Mrs Downes: Mrs Lucy Claire Downes according to her plastics. Lonsdale Road.'

'She – is she dead?' Lewis had asked.

'ICU at St Pancras Hospital. That's all we know.'

'Was she carrying a case?'

'No more details – not yet, Sarge. Seems she just stepped off the pavement to get in front of a row of people and . . .'

Morse sat down and rested his forehead on his right hand. 'Bloody 'ell!'

'Circle Line from King's Cross to Paddington, sir – about twenty minutes, say? She must have been going for the six o'clock train, and she was probably in a dickens of a rush when . . .' Lewis had taken the news badly.

'Yes? Dickens of a rush when she *what*?'

'When she stepped off the pavement—'

'An intelligent woman deliberately stepping out into the London traffic – in the rush hour? Do you really believe that? Or do you think she might have been pushed? Do you hear me, Lewis? *Pushed.*'

'How can you *say* that?'

For a few moments Morse sat where he was. Then he rose to his feet, slowly – his eyes glowing savagely. 'He did it, Lewis. *He did it!*'

'But he was in *Oxford*!'

'No he wasn't! He wasn't waiting on the Oxford platform at all. *He'd just got off the train.* And then he saw *us.* So he turned round the second he did, and made it look as though he was waiting for the woman he'd just tried to kill – when they were walking along together . . . He loved her, you see – probably never loved anyone in the world except his Lucy. And when he saw her copulating with Kemp . . . He just couldn't get it out of his mind, not for one second. He thought he was never going to be able to get it out of his mind.' Morse shook his head. 'And I'm an idiot, Lewis. That key! The key they found under the floor-mat in the car, or wherever. I'd guessed that Downes wanted to go back to his car to hide *something*, so I played along with all that hearing-aid rubbish. And when they brought the key, I knew exactly what it was – a left-luggage locker-key. But tell me this, Lewis! How the hell did *he* get hold of that key if he hadn't met his wife?'

'That's what it is, sir? Left-luggage key? You're sure of it?'

Morse nodded. 'And I'll tell you which station, unless you want to tell *me*.'

'King's Cross.'

'Could be Paddington, I suppose.'

'The *bastard*!' muttered Lewis, with an unwonted show of emotion.

Morse smiled: 'You like her, don't you?'

'Lovely woman!'

'That's what Kemp thought.'

'Perhaps . . .?' started Lewis.

'Oh, no! We shall waste no sympathy on Kemp. Look! I want you to get someone to drive you up to the hospital to see her. All right? You can get a bit of kip in the car. Then go to King's Cross and see if there's anything in locker sixty-seven. If there is, bring it back. And if you can get anything in the way of a statement – fine. If not, well, just try to see what she's got to say.'

'If she's . . . shall I say we've got *him* here?'

'Perhaps not . . . I dunno, though. Play it by ear!'

'OK, sir.' Lewis stood up and walked over to the door, where he halted. 'Have you ever thought it might have been *Mrs* Downes who killed Dr Kemp? What if when her husband came home he found Kemp already dead, and then he did all this stuff, you know, to cover up for *her*?'

'Oh, yes, Lewis. I've thought of every possibility in this case. Including Lucy Downes.'

'You don't think—?'

'I think you will be *completely* safe in London. I don't think you'll be in the slightest danger of being knifed as you practise your bedside-manner sitting by a semi-conscious young woman in an intensive care unit.'

Lewis grinned weakly, and felt in his pocket to make sure that the brown envelope containing a small red key, number 67, was still there.

Janet Roscoe had finished re-reading *A Midsummer Night's Dream*, and felt just a little less certain now about her long-held view (she had earlier been an actress) that Mr Shakespeare was sometimes way below his best when it came to the writing of comedy. And she had just turned on the TV, hoping for a late news-programme, when she heard the light knock on her bedroom door. It was Shirley Brown. She had been stung by *something*, and could Janet help? But of course she *knew* Janet could help. Invited in, Shirley watched the little woman delving into her capacious handbag (a gentle little joke with the rest of the group) from whose depths had already emerged, in addition to the usual accessories, a scout-knife, an apostle spoon, and a miniature iron. And something else now: two tubes of ointment. A little bit of each (Janet maintained) could do no possible harm, unsure as Shirley was whether the offending insect had been wasp, bee, gnat, flea, or mosquito.

For five minutes after the medication, the two women sat on the bed and talked. Had Janet noticed how quiet Mr Ashenden had seemed all day? Not his usual self at all, one way or another. Janet had noticed that, yes: and he *was* the courier, wasn't he? Got *paid* for it. And Janet added something more. She thought she *knew* what might have been on his mind, because he'd been writing a letter in the Lounge. And when he'd put the envelope down to put a stamp on it – 'Face upwards, Shurley!' – why, she couldn't *help* noticing who it was addressed to, now could she?

Suddenly, and perhaps for the first time, Shirley Brown felt a twinge of affection for the lonely little woman who seemed far more aware of what was going on than any of them.

'You seem to notice everything, Janet,' she said, in a not unkindly way.

'I notice most things,' replied Mrs Roscoe, with a quiet little smile of self-congratulation.

CHAPTER FORTY-SEVEN

> Some circumstantial evidence is very strong – as when you find a trout in the milk
> (Henry Thoreau, *unpublished manuscript*)

'Are you going to save us an awful lot of time and trouble, sir, or are you determined to burden the taxpayer further?'

Downes licked his dry lips. 'I don't know what this is all about – except that I'm going mad.'

'Oh, no! You're very sane—' began Morse. But Downes, at least for the moment, had taken the initiative.

'And if you're worried about the taxpayer, shouldn't you perhaps be attending to the urgent little matter your sergeant told you about?'

'You *heard* that?' asked Morse sharply.

'He speaks more clearly than you do.'

'Even when he whispers?' For a few seconds a bemused-looking Morse appeared slightly more concerned with the criticism of his diction than with the prosecution of his case, and it was Downes who continued:

'You were commenting on the degree of my sanity, Inspector.'

WPC Wright glanced at Morse, seated to her left. She had never worked with him before, but the man's name was something of a legend in the Oxfordshire Constabulary, and she was experiencing a sense of some disappointment. Morse was talking again now, though – getting into his swing again, it seemed, and she took down his words in her swift and deftly stroked outlines.

'Yes. *Very* sane. Sane enough to cover up a murder! Sane enough to arrange for your wife to cart off the incriminating evidence to King's Cross Station and stick it in a left-luggage locker—'

'I can't be *hearing* you right—'

'No! Not again, sir – please! It's getting threadbare, you know, that particular excuse. You used it when Kemp rang up – *rang up from your own house*. You used it again when you'd just got off the train from Paddington tonight, when you pretended you were waiting for Mrs Downes—'

In her shorthand book, WPC Wright had ample time to write the word that Downes now shrieked; write it in long-hand, and in capitals. In fact she would have had plenty of time to shade in the circles in the last two letters.

She wrote 'STOP!'

And Morse stopped, as instructed – for about thirty seconds. No rush. Then he repeated his accusation.

'You got your wife to take Kemp's clothes to London—'

'Got my wife – got *Lucy*? What? What do you *mean*?'

'It's all right, sir.' Morse's tone now (thought WPC Wright) was rather more impressive. Quiet, cultured, confident – gentle almost, and understanding. 'We've got the key your wife gave you after she'd deposited the clothes and the blood-stained sheets—'

'I've been here all day – here in Oxford!' The voice had veered from exasperation to incredulity. 'I've got a marvellous alibi – did you know that? I had a tutorial this afternoon from—'

But Morse had taken over completely, and he held up his right hand with a confident, magisterial authority. 'I promise you, sir, that we shall interview everyone you saw this afternoon. You have nothing – nothing! – to fear if you're telling me the truth. But listen to me, Mr Downes! Just for a little while *listen* to me! When my sergeant came in to see me – when you yourself heard him – he'd just learned that on my instructions the locker had been opened in London. And that inside the locker was a case, the case your wife took with her to London today; a case which she told me – told me and Sergeant Lewis – contained some curtains. Curtains! We both *saw* her take it, in a taxi. And shall I tell you again what it *really* contained?'

Downes thumped the table with both fists with such ferocity that WPC Wright transferred her shorthand-book to her black-stockinged knee, and failed completely to register the next three words that Downes had thundered.

'No! No! No!'

But Morse appeared wholly unperturbed. 'Please tell me, Mr Downes, how the key came to be in your possession? Under the mat in the driver's seat, was it? Or in the glove compartment? Can you explain that? Are you going to tell me that it was someone who came back on the train from London who gave you the key?'

'Wha—?'

'Couldn't have been your wife, could it?'

'What's Lucy got to do with—'

'The key!' roared Morse. 'What about the key?'

'Key? You mean . . .?' Downes's cheeks were very white, and slowly he started to get up from his chair.

'Sit down!' thundered Morse with immense authority; and simply, silently Downes did as he was bidden.

'Do you remember the number of the key, sir?'

'Of course.'

'Please tell me,' said Morse quietly.

'Number sixty-seven.'

'That's correct. That's correct, Mr Downes.' Morse briefly placed his right hand on WPC Wright's arm, and gave her a scarce-perceptible nod of encouragement. It would be vital, as he knew, for the next few exchanges to be transcribed with unimpeachable certitude. But as Downes spoke, with a helpless little shrug of his shoulders, the newly sharpened pencil of WPC Wright remained poised above the page.

'That's the key to my locker at the North Oxford Golf Club, Inspector.'

Suddenly, Interview Room 2 was still and silent as the grave.

CHAPTER FORTY-EIGHT

Darkness is more productive of sublime ideas than light
(Edmund Burke, *On the Sublime and Beautiful*)

The traffic along Western Avenue had been quiet, and it was only an hour and a quarter after leaving Oxford that Lewis was speaking to the night sister on the third floor of the hospital, a neat, competent-looking brunette who appeared rather more concerned about the unprecedented police interest in matters than in the medical condition of her most recent road-casualty, now lying behind a curtained bed in Harley Ward. A casualty not all *that* badly injured, anyway: broken left humerus, broken left clavicle, some nasty bruising and laceration round the left shoulder – but no broken legs or ribs, and fairly certainly no head injuries, either. Yes, said Sister, Mrs Downes had been remarkably lucky, really; and, yes, Sergeant Lewis could see her for a short while. He would find her under sedation – a bit dopey and drowsy, and still in a state of some disorientation and shock. Quite lucid, though. '*And*,' added Sister, 'you'd better have something ready to tell her if she asks you when her husband's coming. We've put her off as best we can.'

Lewis stood by the bed and looked down at her. Her eyes were open, and guardedly she smiled an instant recognition. She spoke softly, lisping slightly, and Lewis immediately noticed (what he had not been told) that two teeth in the upper left of her jaw had been broken off.

'We met this morning, didn't we?'

'Yes, Mrs Downes.'

'Cedric knows I'm all right, doesn't he?'

'Everything's in hand. Don't worry about anything like that.'

'He'll be here soon, though?'

'I've told you,' said Lewis gently, 'we're looking after everything. No need for you to worry at all.'

'But I want to *see* him!'

'It's just that the hospital don't want you to have any visitors –

not just for the time being. The doctors, you know, they've got to patch you up a bit.'

'I want to thee Thedric,' she moaned quietly, her lips quivering and her eyes now brimming with tears as the good Lewis laid a hand on the pristine-white plaster encasing her upper arm.

'Soon. In good time. As I say—'

'Why can *you* see me if he can't?'

'It's just routine – you know – accidents. We have to make reports on—'

'But I've seen the police already.'

'And you told them—?'

'I told them it was my fault – it wasn't the driver's fault.' Her eyes looked pleadingly up at Lewis.

'Would you just repeat what you said. Please, Mrs Downes.'

'There was nothing *to* say. It was my fault, what else do you want me to say?'

'Just *how*, you know . . .'

'I was walking along there. I was in a hurry to catch the Tube – it was the rush hour – I didn't want to miss the train – Cedric . . . you see, Cedric was waiting—'

'At Oxford, you mean? He was waiting at Oxford?'

'Of course. I was just trying to get past some people in front of me and I stepped off the pavement and the driver – he didn't have a chance. It was *my* fault, don't you believe me? He braked and . . . It was the *case* really. If it hadn't been for the case, I think perhaps . . .'

'The car hit the case, you mean? Hit the case first?'

Lucy nodded. 'It sort of, well – cushioned things, and I hit a litter-bin on the kerb and . . .' She lifted her right hand and pointed vaguely across to the left-hand side of her body.

'So you still had the case with you, then? When the car hit you?'

For the first time the hitherto lucid Lucy looked a little bemused, as if she was unable to follow Lewis's last question. 'I don't quite follow . . . I'm sorry.'

'I just wanted to know if you were carrying the case, that's all.'

'Of course I was.'

'Do you – do you know where it is now, Mrs Downes?'

'Isn't it still under the bed, Sergeant?'

Morse took the call just after 11 p.m.

'You'll never guess what's happened, sir!'

'Don't put your bank balance on it, Lewis!'

'She's going to be all right, they think, sir. The Met got it wrong about the ICU.'

Morse said nothing.

'You are – well, pleased about *that*, aren't you?'

'I take no delight in death, Lewis, and if one thing worries me above all else it is accidents – the random concourse of atoms in the void, as Epicurus used to say.'

'You feeling tired, sir?'

'Yes.'

'You *knew* it was an accident all the time?'

'No. Not all the time.'

'You're losing me – as usual.'

'What is this news of yours, Lewis, that I shall never guess?'

'The case, sir! The case we both saw Mrs Downes take up to London.'

'We both saw her put in the *taxi*, if we are to be accurate.'

'But she did bring it to London! And you won't guess what was in it.'

'Curtains, Lewis? Any good? Curtains with French pleats? By the way, remind me one day to explain this business of French pleats to you. Mrs Lewis would be glad if you took a bit more interest in household furnishings and interior decoration.'

'What do you want me to do about this left-luggage key, sir?'

'What are you talking about? What makes you think that's a left-luggage key?'

After Lewis had rung off, Morse sat at his desk and smoked three Dunhill International cigarettes one after the other. He'd been shaken, certainly, when Cedric Downes had invited him to go along to the North Oxford Golf Club and knock up the caretaker if necessary. And Lewis's phone call had surely hammered the last coffin-nail into the Cedric–Lucy theory. Yet Morse's mind was never more fertile than when faced with some apparently insuperable obstacle, and even now he found it difficult to abandon his earlier, sweet hypothesis about the murder of Theodore Kemp. He gazed out through the curtainless window on to the well-lit, virtually deserted parking-area: only his own red Jaguar and two white police cars. He could – should! – get off now and go to bed. He would be home in ten minutes. Less, perhaps, at this hour . . . Yes, it was extremely useful to have a car, whatever people said about traffic and pollution and expense . . . yes . . .

Morse was conscious that his mind was drifting off into an

interesting avenue of thought, but also that he was drifting off to sleep, as well. It was the cars that had started some new idea . . . For the minute, though, it was gone. Yet there were other new ideas that jostled together in his brain for some more prominent recognition. First, the conviction that there was – must be! – a link, perhaps a blindingly obvious link, between the theft of the Wolvercote Jewel and the murder of Theodore Kemp. Second, the growing belief that *two* people must have been involved in things, quite certainly in the murder. Third, the worrying suspicion that amongst the evidence already accumulated, the statements taken, the people interviewed, the personal relationships observed, the *obiter dicta*, the geography of North Oxford – that amongst all these things *somewhere* there was a fact that he had seen or heard but never fully recognized or understood. Fourth, the strange reluctance he felt about abandoning Downes as Suspect Number One. And as Morse opened his passenger door, he stood for a while looking up at the Pole Star, and asking himself the question he had been asking for the past two hours: was there *any* way in which Downes could still have been the murderer after all?

Many of Morse's ideas were either so strange or so wildly improbable that most of them were always doomed to early disappointment. Yet, as it happened, he was registering well above par that evening, for three of the four ideas he had formulated were finally to prove wholly correct.

Lewis had fallen fast asleep on the back seat of the police car and remained so for the whole of the journey back to Oxford. In his younger days, he had been a middle-weight army boxing champion, and now he dreamed that he was in the ring again, with a right-cross from a swarthy, swift-footed opponent smashing into the left-hand side of his jaw. He had tried to feel inside his mouth to see if any teeth were broken or missing, but the great bulk of his boxing-glove precluded any such investigation.

When the car finally pulled up in St Aldates, the young driver opened the rear door and shook Sergeant Lewis awake, failing to notice that the first action of his passenger was to run the forefinger of his left hand slowly along his upper teeth.

PART THREE

CHAPTER FORTY-NINE

Where water, warm or cool, is
Good for gout – at Aquae Sulis
(Graffito in the Pump Room, Bath, c.1760)

'Bairth? This is *Bairth*?'

Seated on the nearside front seat of the luxury coach, John Ashenden glanced across at the diminutive septuagenarian from California. 'Yes, Mrs Roscoe, this is Bath.'

With less than conspicuous enthusiasm, he leaned forward for his microphone, turned it on, and began. Not quite so confidently as in Stratford; or in Oxford, of course, where he had memorized whole sentences from the Jan Morris guide.

'Bath, ladies and gentlemen, is the site of a Roman spa, *Aquae Sulis*, probably built in the first and second centuries AD. A good deal of the extensive baths has been excavated and the city presents the tourist of today with perhaps the most splendidly restored of all Roman remains in Europe.'

On either side of the central aisle, heads nodded at the buildings and streets around them as a now livelier Ashenden continued, himself (like the site, it appeared) splendidly restored from whatever malaise had affected him over the previous two days, a malaise which had been noted and commented upon by several others of the group besides Mrs Shirley Brown – the latter sitting comfortably now in her usual seat, the effects of the sting having cleared up fairly quickly under the twin application of Mrs Roscoe's unguents.

'Looks a swell place, Shirl,' ventured Howard Brown.

'Yeah. Just wish Laura was with us – and Eddie. It all seems so sad.'

'Too right! Bus seems sorta empty somehow.'

As scheduled, the tourists had lunched at Cirencester, after leaving Stratford earlier that Sunday morning. The weather was still holding, if only just: another golden day in late autumn. And perhaps in the minds of many, the memories of their tragic stay in Oxford were slowly softening at the edges.

One of the slightly younger widows, Mrs Nancy Wiseman, a librarian from Oklahoma City, was seated at the back of the coach beside Phil Aldrich. She had observed with a quiet pleasure how the strident Roscoe woman had markedly cooled towards her former partner after his refusal (and that of most of the others) to sign her petulant letter of complaint concerning Sheila Williams. Although Phil had been slightly reserved in his manner towards her (Nancy), she knew that that was his way and she was enjoying the company of that wiry, small-boned, gently spoken citizen from Sacramento who almost invariably found himself at the back of every queue that ever formed itself. Yes, the tour was definitely looking up a little, and only the previous evening she had written a card to her daughter to say that in spite of a death and a theft and a murder she was 'beginning to make one or two very nice friends on the trip'.

In truth, however, Phil himself was finding Nancy Wiseman a little too effusive for his liking and – perversely, as it seemed – would have preferred sitting next to Janet Roscoe, up there at the front of the coach, as he listened to (and indeed almost wholly managed to hear) the end of Ashenden's introduction to Bath:

'In the eighteenth century the city was transformed into a resort for English high society – being particularly associated, of course, with the name of Beau Nash, the great dandy and gamester who lived here during the 1740s and 50s. Among its many literary connections, Bath can number such great figures as Henry Fielding, Fanny Burney, Jane Austen, William Wordsworth, Walter Scott, Charles Dickens – and most famous of all, perhaps, Geoffrey Chaucer and "The Wife of Bath's Tale".'

It was a good note on which to end.

Opposite him, he noticed that Janet Roscoe had delved once more into the deep handbag, this time producing a very slim volume, whose title it was impossible for him not to see, and which he could have guessed in any case: CHAUCER, *Tale of the Wyf of Bathe*.

He smiled across at her, and as she opened her book at the Prologue, she smiled quite sweetly back at him.

It seemed a good omen for the stay in Bath.

Only seemed.

CHAPTER FIFTY

During late visits to Stinsford in old age he would often
visit the unmarked grave of Louisa Harding
(Florence Emily Hardy,
The Early Life of Thomas Hardy)

According to the hospital bulletin on the Monday afternoon, the
condition of Lucy Downes was now officially listed as 'comfortable', one notch above the 'satisfactory' of the Sunday, and two
above the earlier 'stable'. Three visits from her husband had
helped perhaps (the first in the small hours of the Sunday
morning, two hours after his release from custody), but some
slight complications had arisen with continued internal bleeding,
and she had become deeply and embarrassingly conscious of how
she must appear to everyone whenever she smiled. So she forbore
to do so altogether, even to Cedric, and as she lay in her bed that
day, her arm now beginning to give her some considerable pain,
she would willingly (she knew) have cracked two of her ribs rather
than chipped a couple of her teeth.

Vanity, all is vanity, saith the preacher. And 'satisfactory' was
arguably too favourable a judgement on her circumstances. But that
was the word Morse repeated to the first question Lewis put to him
about Lucy's progress at 8.30 a.m. on the Tuesday. It may have
been that Morse had smiled a little at the question. But it may not.

Activity in the two days following Cedric Downes's release had
hardly afforded a model of investigative collaboration, with Morse
sleeping through until the late afternoon of the Sunday, then
idling away most of the Monday in his office, moodily perusing
the documents in the case; and with Lewis doing the converse,
making what he felt had been a fairly significant contribution to
the case on the Sunday afternoon, and then spending the whole
of the Monday abed, where he had lain dead to the wideawake
world, and where, even when Mrs Lewis had gently rocked his
shoulder at 6.30 p.m. and quietly breathed the prospect of egg
and chips into his ear, he had turned his head over into the pillow
and blissfully resumed his slumbers. But now he felt fully
refreshed.

By the look of him, however, his chief had not perhaps shared
a similarly successful period of recuperation, for he sounded tetchy
as he picked up the brief note Lewis had left him.

'You say Stratton *was* quite definitely out at Didcot when Kemp
was being killed?'

'No doubt about it, sir. I went over there yesterday—'

'You were in bed yesterday.'

'Sunday, I mean. They remembered him.'

'Who's "they"?'

'One of 'em took a photo of him on the footplate of "The Cornishman". He'd already got it developed and was going to post it to America. Stratton gave him a fiver. He's going to get a copy and send it here.'

'And it *was* Stratton?'

'It was Stratton.'

'Oh!'

'Where does all this leave us, sir? I just don't know where we are.'

'And you think *I* do?' mumbled the ill-shaven Morse. 'Here! Read this – came this morning.'

Lewis took the envelope handed him, postmarked Stratford-upon-Avon, and withdrew the two hand-written sheets.

> Swan Hotel,
> Stratford,
> Saturday, 3rd Nov
>
> Dear Inspector,
> My conscience has troubled me since I left Oxford. When you asked about the phone call I tried to remember everything and I don't know what else I could have told you. I want to repeat that the line was faint but it was definitely Dr Kemp on the phone and that what I wrote was as near as anyone could get to what he said. But I lied about the afternoon and I was worried when you wanted to keep the betting slips because you probably know that one of the horses won and I would have won quite a lot of money if I'd stayed in the betting shop. I wanted

people to think I'd gone to Summertown and I could prove it if necessary. So I went to Ladbrokes and picked two rank outsiders and put some money on them and left. The only reason I did this was because I didn't want anyone to know where I really went which was to a flat in Park Town where I am ashamed to say I watched some sex videos with three other people. I think one of them would be willing to back up my story and if it's necessary I will give you a name if you can promise it can all be done with no charges brought. I am worried as well about the way you asked me where I went after we'd arrived in Oxford because I didn't tell you the truth then either, I went to Holywell cemetery and went to the grave of a friend of mine. He wrote to me before he died and I didn't write back and I just wanted to make up for it in some way if I could. His name was James Bowden.
I am sorry to have caused trouble.

John Ashenden

P.S. I forgot to say that I left a small memento at his grave.

P.P.S. I shall be glad if you can pick up my winnings and give the money to Oxfam.

'Well?'

'I suppose you want me to tell you how many spelling mistakes he's made.'

'That would be something.'

'Looks all right to me. There's an apostrophe missing, though.'

Morse's face brightened. 'Well done! Excellent! There *is* the one spelling mistake, but you're *definitely* improving . . . That's a clue, by the way . . . No? Never mind!'

'At least we're getting some of the loose ends tied up.'

'You mean we cross Ashenden off the suspect-list?'

'Don't know, sir. But we can cross Stratton off, I reckon. He was in Didcot most of the afternoon. That's for sure.'

'So he couldn't have killed Kemp?'

'I don't see how.'

'Nor do I,' said Morse.

'Back to square one!'

'You know where we went wrong, don't you? It was that phone call that sent me up the cul-de-sac. You see, we can't get away from the fact that if Kemp *was* in London, he could easily have caught an earlier train. That still puzzles me! He rang at twelve thirty-five and there was a train at twelve forty-five. Ten minutes to walk across from the phone to the platform!'

'You know, we haven't really checked that, have we? I mean the train could have been cancelled . . . or something.'

Morse said, 'I've checked. It's almost the only profitable thing I did yesterday.' He lit a cigarette and sat staring gloomily out of the window.

Lewis found himself looking at the back page of the *Oxford Times* which lay on the desk. Morse had not started the crossword yet ('Ichabod' this week), but just to the right of it Lewis noticed a brief item on a fatal accident at the Marston Ferry Road traffic lights: a young student who had been taking a crash course in EFL. *Crash* course! Huh!

'Don't tell me you've done one across, Lewis?'

'No. Just reading about this accident at the Marston Ferry lights. Bad junction, you know, that is. I think there ought to be a "filter right" as you go into the Banbury Road.'

'Fair point!'

Lewis read on aloud. '"Georgette le . . . something . . . daughter of M. Georges le . . . something of Bordeaux . . ."' But now his eyes had spotted the date. 'Funny! This accident was a week last Saturday, sir, at half-past five. That's exactly one week earlier than Mrs Downes.'

'Life's full of coincidences, I keep telling you that.'

'It's just that when you get two things happening like that, people say there's going to be three, don't they? That's what the wife always says.'

'Look, if a third accident'll please you, volunteer for the ambulance crew this morning. It's a fiver to a cracked piss-pot that some irresponsible sod—' Suddenly Morse stopped, the old tingle of high excitement thrilling strangely across his shoulders.

'Christ! What a fool you've been!' he murmured softly to himself.

'Sir?'

Morse rattled out his words: 'What's the name of Kemp's publisher? The one you rang to make sure he'd been there.'

'"Babington's". The fellow there said it was named after Macaulay' (Lewis smiled with distant memories) 'Thomas Babington Macaulay, sir – you know, the one who wrote the *Lays of Ancient Rome*. That's the one poem I—'

'Get on to the American Consulate! Quick, for Christ's sake! Find out where Stratton is – they'll know, I should think. *We've got to stop him leaving the country.*'

Morse's blue eyes gleamed triumphantly. 'I think I know, Lewis! I think I *know.*'

But Eddie Stratton had left the country the previous evening on a Pan Am jumbo bound for New York – together with his late wife Laura, the latter lying cold and stiff in a coffin in a special compartment just above the undercarriage.

CHAPTER FIFTY-ONE

> At day's end you came,
> and like the evening sun,
> left an afterglow
> (Basil Swift, *Collected Haiku*)

Lewis was enjoying that Tuesday, the day on which Morse had suddenly spurted into a frenetic flurry of activity. Six extra personnel: Sergeant Dixon, three detective PCs, and two WPCs for the telephones. The administrative arrangement and supervision required for such teamwork was exactly the sort of skill in which Lewis excelled, and the hours passed quickly with the progressive gleaning of intelligence, the gradual build up of hard fact to bolster tentative theory – and always that almost insolent gratification that shone in Morse's eyes, for the latter appeared to have known (or so it seemed to Lewis) most of the details before the calls and corroboration had been made.

It was just after a quick, non-alcoholic lunch that Morse had sought to explain to Lewis the nature of his earlier error.

'I once did a crossword in which all of the clues were susceptible of two quite different solutions. A sort of *double entendre* crossword, it was. Get on the wrong wavelength with one across, and everything fits except one single interlocking letter. Brilliant puzzle! – set by Ximenes in the *Observer*. That's what *I* did – got off on the wrong foot. And I did it again in this case, with Downes. You know what one across was? That bloody phone call! I'd assumed it was important, Lewis, and I was *right*. But right for the wrong reasons. When I first learned that the line was bad, I thought it possible – likely, even – that the caller *wasn't Kemp at all*. Then, because he said he'd missed the train – although there was still ten minutes to go – I thought he wasn't at Paddington at all: I thought Kemp was probably in Oxford. And it all fitted, didn't it? Except for that one single letter . . .

'But all the time, that poor line we kept hearing about *was* of crucial significance, but for a totally different reason! It was Kemp all right who made the call. But he wasn't at *Paddington*: he was still at his publisher's in London – Babington Press, Fine Arts Publications, South Kensington – and doubtless he referred to it, like anyone would, as Babington's. Oh, yes! That's where he was, and he did *exactly* what he said he'd do. He caught the next train and arrived in Oxford, dead on schedule.'

In the circumstances 'dead on schedule' hardly seemed to Lewis the happiest of phrases, but he knew that Morse was right about the call from Babington's. It had been he himself, Lewis, who had finally got on to the man there who was in the process of completing the proofs for the forthcoming seminal opus entitled *Pre-Conquest Craftsmanship in Southern Britain*, by Theodore S. Kemp, MA, D.Phil.; the man who had been closeted with Kemp that fateful morning, and who had confirmed that Kemp had not left the offices until about 12.30 p.m.

Sergeant Dixon (stripes newly stitched) was also enjoying himself, although initially he had serious doubts about whether he – or anyone else, for that matter – could successfully handle his assignment in the ridiculously short period of the three or four hours which Morse had asserted as 'ample'.

But he had done it.

He had not realized quite how many customers were attracted by the car hire firms of Oxford, especially American customers; and checking the lists had taken longer than he'd imagined. In this particular respect Morse (suggesting the likelihood of the Botley Road area) had got things quite wrong, for it was at the Hertz 'Rent-a-Car' offices at the top of the Woodstock Road where Dixon had finally spotted the name he was looking for with all the excitement of a young angler just hooking a heavyweight pike.

Tom Pritchard, the manager, went through the key points of the car-hire catechism to be faced by every client:

– Full name and home address?
– How many days' hire?
– Make of car preferred?
– Which dates?
– One driver only?
– Method of payment? (credit card preferred)
– Valid driving licence? (US licence OK)
– Telephone number of one referee?

After that, the manager went through the procedure adopted: a telephone call to the reference number cited; verification of credit card; verification of driving licence; verification of home address (the last three usually completed within ten minutes or so on the International Information Computer); preparation, presentation, and signing of the contract (including appropriate insurance clauses); then, paperwork now completed, the car brought round to the outer forecourt, with an assistant to give the client a quick run-over of the controls, and to hand over the keys. *Bon voyage*, cheerio, and Bob's your uncle.

By good fortune it had been the manager himself who had effected this particular transaction, and who remembered the occasion reasonably clearly. Well, it was only five days ago, wasn't it? The reference call to the hotel, The Randolph – that's what he'd remembered clearest of all, really: he'd looked up the telephone number and then been put through, on the extension given to him by his client, to the Deputy Manageress, who had promptly and effusively vouched for the *bona fides* of Rent-a-Car's prospective customer. Naturally, the manager had more details to offer: the car hired had been a red Cavalier, Registration H 106 XMT; it had been hired at 1.45 p.m. and returned at some time after the offices had closed at 6.30 p.m., with the keys pushed through the special letter-box, as requested. Mileage on the speedometer had been clocked as only 30.7. Probably, thought the manager, the car hadn't left Oxford at all?

Yet for all his own pleasure at tracing this evidence, Dixon could see little in his report which might have accounted for the look of extrordinary triumph he had seen on Morse's face when he reported in at 2.45 p.m.

Sergeant (with a 'g') Lewis's own, self-imposed task would, he suspected, be a fairly tricky undertaking. But even here the gods appeared to be smiling broadly on Morse's enterprise. The distinguished personage known as the Coroner's Serjeant (with a 'j') had been willing to sacrifice what he could of his time if the interests of Justice (capital 'J') were really being served. Yet it had still taken the pair of them more than two hours to assemble and photocopy the material that Morse had so confidently predicted would be found.

And was found.

But by far the most difficult and tiresome task had been that of the telephone girls, who had made scores and scores of transatlantic calls that Tuesday morning, afternoon, and early evening: calls made to one address that led to calls to another address; calls to one friend that led to another friend or colleague; from one police department to another; one State to other States; calls for one set of records that referred to another set of records that led . . . *ad* apparently *infinitum*.

'Couldn't it have waited?' Chief Superintendent Strange had asked, calling in briefly in mid-afternoon. 'Waited till tomorrow?'

But Morse was a man who could never abide the incomplete, could never abide the not-knowing-immediately. One clue unfinished in a *Listener* puzzle, and he would strain the capacity of every last brain-cell to bursting point until he had solved it. And equally so, as now, in a murder case. Tomorrow was too far distanced for his mind to wait for the last piece of evidence – a mind so ceaselessly tossing, as it had been ever since Lewis – wonderful Lewis! – had mentioned that seemingly irrelevant item in the *Oxford Times*.

Those names!

And it was Morse himself who had initiated the arrest of Mr Edward Stratton as he stepped off his plane in New York; Morse himself who had spoken with the aforementioned Stratton for forty-six minutes, seven seconds – as measured by the recently installed meter in the recently constituted Telephone Room at St Aldates. But not even the penny-pinching Strange could have complained overmuch about the price that had been paid for the extraordinary information Morse had gleaned.

It was Morse himself, too, who at 8.30 p.m. had called a halt to everything. He had not returned any fulsome gratitude to his staff for all the work they had put in during the day; but he always found it difficult to express his deeper feelings. However, he *had* returned all but three of the tourists' passports to the safe-keeping of the Manager at The Randolph – the latter just a fraction irked that it now appeared to be his own responsibility to return these passports to whatever location the departed tourists happened to find themselves in.

At 9 p.m. Morse, hitherto that day most remarkably under-beered, made his way up through Cornmarket to the Chapter Bar of The Randolph. There were many times in Morse's life when he needed a drink in order to think. On occasion though (such as now), he needed a drink because he needed a *drink*. What's more, having left the Jaguar down in the police car-park, he was *going* to drink.

And compulsively, happily, thirstily – he drank.

One and a half hours later, as he still sat on a high stool at the bar, he looked down and saw the fingers of a beautifully manicured hand against his left arm, and felt the ghost of a touch of the softest breast against his shoulder.

'Can I buy you a drink, Inspector?' The voice was slightly husky, slightly slurred, and more than slightly disturbing.

Morse had no need to look around. He said, 'Let me buy *you* one, Sheila.'

'No! I insist.' She took his arm, gently squeezing it against herself, then pressed her lips – so full, so dry! – against a cheek that had been hurriedly ill shaven some fourteen hours earlier.

For the moment, Morse said nothing. The day that would soon be drawing to its close had been one of the most wonderful he had experienced: the theft, the murder, the link *between* the theft and the murder – yes, all now known. Well, almost known. And he'd solved it all himself. He'd needed help – yes! Help in crossing the

't's and barring the '7's and dotting the 'j's. Of course he had. Yet
it had been his own vision, his own analysis, his own solution.
   His.
   'What are you doing here?' he asked.
   'Annual Dance. Lit. and Phil. Society. Bloody boring!'
   'You with a partner?'
   'You don't come to these dos without a partner.'
   'So?'
   'So he kept trying to get a bit too intimate during the Veleta.'
   'Veleta? God! That's what I used to dance . . .'
   'We're none of us getting much younger.'
   'And you didn't want – you didn't want that?'
   'I wanted a drink. That's why I'm here.'
   'And you told him . . .'
   '. . . to bugger off.'
   Morse looked at her now – perhaps properly for the first time.
She wore a black dress reaching to just above her knees, sus-
pended from her shoulders by straps no thicker than shoelaces;
black stockings, encasing surprisingly slim legs, and very high
heeled red shoes that elevated her an inch or so above Morse as
he stood up and offered her his stool. He smiled at her, with what
seemed warmth and understanding in his eyes.
   'You look happy,' she said.
   But Morse knew, deep down, that he wasn't really happy at all.
For the last hour his progressively alcoholized brain had reminded
him of the consequences of justice (small 'j'): of bringing a criminal
before the courts, ensuring that he was convicted for his sins (or
was it his crimes?), and then getting him locked up for the rest of
his life, perhaps, in a prison where he would never again go to the
WC without someone observing such an embarrassingly private
function, someone smelling him, someone humiliating him. (And,
yes, it was a *him*.) Humiliating him in that little paddock of privacy
just outside the back of the house where he would try so hard to
keep all that remained of his dignity and self-esteem.
   'I'm not happy,' said Morse.
   'Why not?'
   'G and T, is it?'
   'How did you guess?'
   'I'm a genius.'
   'I'm quite good at some things myself.'
   'Yes?'
   'Do you want me to make you happy for tonight?' Her voice

was suddenly more sober, more sharply etched – and yet more gentle, too.

Morse looked at her: looked at the piled-up hair above her wistful face; looked down at the full and observably bra-less bosom; looked down at the taut stretch of black stocking between the knee and the thigh of her crossed right leg. He was ready for her, and she seemed to sense it.

'I've got a wonderfully comfortable bed,' she whispered into his left ear.

'So have I!' said Morse, oddly defensive.

'But we wouldn't argue *too* much about that sort of thing, would we?' Sheila smiled and reached for her drink. 'Aren't you having another one?'

Morse shook his head: '"It provokes the desire, but it takes away the performance."'

'Do you know, I've never met anyone before who's quoted that thing correctly.'

Perhaps she shouldn't have said it, for suddenly its implications stirred Morse to an irrational jealousy. But soon, as she linked her arm possessively through his, collected her coat from Cloaks, then steered him across towards the taxi-rank in St Giles', he knew that his lust for her had returned; and would remain.

'I ought to make it quite clear to you, ma'am,' he murmured in the taxi, 'that any knickers you may be wearing may well be taken down and used in evidence.'

For the first time in many days, Sheila Williams felt inordinately happy. And was to remain so – if truth is to be told – until the early dawn of the following day when Morse left her to walk slowly to his bachelor flat – only a short distance away up the Banbury Road – bareheaded in the beating rain which an hour since had obliquely streaked the windows of Sheila Williams's front bedroom.

CHAPTER FIFTY-TWO

Rigid, the skeleton of habit alone upholds the human
frame

(Virginia Woolf, *Mrs Dalloway*)

Morse and Lewis arrived at The Chesterton Hotel in Bath at 10.35
a.m. the following morning. Morse had insisted on travelling by
what he called the 'scenic' route – via Cirencester – but, alas, the
countryside was not appearing at its best: the golden days were
gone, and the close-cropped fields where the sheep ever nibbled
looked dank and uninviting under a sky cover of grey cloud. Little
conversation had passed between the two detectives until, an hour
out of Oxford, Morse (looking, as Lewis saw him, still rather tired)
had crossed those final 't's.

'All a bit unusual, though, isn't it, sir?'

'You think so?'

'I do. About as unusual as a . . .' But Lewis found himself
unable to dredge up the appropriate simile.

'"Unusual as a fat postman",' supplied Morse.

'Really? Our postman looks as if he tips the scales at about
twenty stone.'

Morse inhaled deeply upon yet another cigarette, half closed
his eyes, shook his head, and relapsed into the silence that was
customary for him on any journey.

Behind, in a marked police car, Sergeant Dixon sat beside his
driver, a moderately excited PC Watson.

'Drives pretty quick, don't he?' ventured the latter.

'About the only thing he does do quick, I reckon,' said Dixon.

It seemed to Watson a cruel, unfair remark. And Dixon himself
knew it was unfair, for a little while regretting having said it.

It had been forty-five minutes earlier when Dr Barbara Moule had
parked her Fiesta at The Chesterton Hotel, finding John Ashenden
waiting for her a little anxiously. The first part of her illustrated
lecture was scheduled for 10–11 a.m., followed by a coffee break,
and then further slides and questions from 11.30 to noon. Ashenden himself had carried the heavy projector to the Beau Nash
Room at the rear of the hotel, where most of the tourists were now
foregathering. The room was of a narrow, oblong shape, with the
plastic chairs set out two on each side of the central gap in which,
at the front, the projector was placed. Looking around, Ashenden

noted yet again the readily observable fact that (doubtless like animals) tourists from very early on staked out their territories: find them sitting at one particular table for dinner, and almost invariably you would find them sitting at the very same table for breakfast next morning; allocate them to particular seats in a coach on the first part of a journey, and as if by some proprietorial right the passengers would thereafter usually veer towards those self-same seats. And the Beau Nash Room might just as well have been their luxury coach: twenty-three of them only for the minute, with Eddie Stratton now being held in custody by the New York Police, distanced by only a few yards, as it happened, from the mortal remains of his former wife; and with Sam and Vera Kronquist, one of the three married couples originally listed on the tour, still in their room on the second floor of the hotel – Sam watching a mid-morning cartoon on ITV, and Vera, fully dressed, lying back lazily against the pillows of their double bed, reading the previous February's issue of *Country Life*.

'You won't forget, Birdy' (Birdy?) 'that you're supposed to be having a headache, will you?'

His wife, not deigning to look up from the page, smiled to herself slightly. 'Nobody ain't coming in here, Sam – not if we leave that notice there on the door-narb.'

On the front row of the Beau Nash Room, only one of the chairs was occupied – Number 1, if the chairs had been numbered, from left to right, 1, 2, 3, 4 – the seat Janet Roscoe had invariably occupied on every single leg of the coach trip. Behind her the two seats were empty, a troublous reminder of where Eddie and Laura had sat side by side when the coach had first set off from Heathrow Airport . . . and had first arrived at the eastern outskirts of Oxford.

At the back of the room, solitary now, and perfectly prepared to be wholly bored for the next hour (or was it two?) sat Mr Aldrich. His interest in Roman remains was minimal, and in any case his ears (incipient otosclerosis, his personal physician had diagnosed) seemed to be filling up with thicker and thicker wads of cotton-wool each day. He would have liked to exchange a few words with Cedric Downes at Oxford – surely a man suffering from the same kind of trouble? But the opportunity had not arisen, and Aldrich had taken no initiative in effecting any introduction.

Odd, really: Aldrich, with his increasing hearing problems, sitting right at the back of the class; and Mrs Roscoe, whose hearing was so extraordinarily acute, ever seated at the front . . .

So be it!

Three rows in front of Aldrich, on his left-hand side as he looked at the backs of their heads, sat Howard and Shirley Brown.

'Hope these slides are better than your sister's lot on Ottawa.'

'Hardly be wurse,' agreed Shirley, as Ashenden launched into a well-rehearsed eulogy of Dr Moule's incomparable pre-eminence in the field of Romano-British archaeology in Somerset – before walking to the entrance door at the rear, and turning off the lights.

At 10.50 a.m., Aldrich looked across at the two men who had entered quietly by the same door. Surprisingly, he was hearing Dr Moule quite loud and clear, for she had a firm and resonant voice. What's more, he thought, she was good; he *wanted* to hear what she was saying. And everybody thought she was good. Indeed, only three or four minutes into her talk, Shirley Brown had leaned across and whispered into Howard's ear: 'Better than Ottawa!'

Dr Moule had been momentarily conscious, albeit with her back turned, of some silent addition to the audience, though giving this no further thought. But after she had finished the first part of her lecture, after slightly nodding her head to the generous applause; after the lights had gone up again; after Ashenden had said (as every chairman since Creation had said) how much everyone had enjoyed the talk and how grateful everyone was that not only had the distinguished speaker fascinated each and every one of them but also had agreed to answer any questions which he was absolutely sure everyone in the room was aching to put to such a distinguished expert in the field . . . it was only then that Dr Moule was able to survey the two intruders. Sitting together on the back row: the one nearer the exit a burly-looking fellow, with a rather heavy, though kindly mien; and beside him a slimmer, clearly more authoritative man, with thinning hair and pale complexion. It was this second man who now asked the first, the last, question. And it was to this man that almost everyone now turned as the rather quiet, rather cultured, rather interesting, wholly English voice began to speak:

'I was a Classic in my youth, madam, and although I have always been deeply interested in the works of the Roman poets and the Roman historians, I have never been able to summon up much enthusiasm for Roman architecture. In fact the contemplation of a Roman brick seems to leave me cold – quite cold. So I would dearly like to know why it is that you find yourself so enthusiastic . . .'

The question was balm and benison to Barbara's ears. But then the questioner had risen to his feet.

'. . . yes, it would be extremely interesting for all of us to learn your answer. But not – not for the moment, please!'

The man now walked down the central aisle and halted beside the projector, where he turned and spoke. Was it to her? Was it to her audience?

'I'm sorry to interrupt. But the people here know who I am – who we are. And I shall have to ask you, I'm afraid, to leave the next half hour to Lewis and to me.'

Dr Barbara Moule almost smiled. She'd picked up the literary allusion immediately, and enjoyed those few seconds during which the man's intensely blue eyes had held her own.

It was Ashenden who went upstairs to knock on the door of Room 46.

'But didn't Sam here explain? I have a headache.'

'I know. But it's the police, Mrs Kronquist.'

'It is?'

'And they want everybody to be there.'

'Oh my Gard!'

CHAPTER FIFTY-THREE

And summed up so well that it came to far more
Than the Witnesses ever had said
(Lewis Carroll, *The Barrister's Dream*)

The beautiful if bemused Dr Moule, invited to stay if she so wished, took a seat in the front row. The man spoke, she thought, more like a don than a detective.

'Let me outline the case, or rather the two cases, to you all. First, a jewel was stolen from Mrs Laura Stratton's room in The Randolph. At the same time – whether just before or just after the theft – Mrs Stratton died. What is medically certain is that she died of coronary thrombosis: there is no question of any foul play, except of course if the heart attack was brought on by the shock of finding someone in her room stealing the jewel she had come all the way from America to hand over to the Ashmolean Museum, or more specifically to Dr Theodore Kemp on behalf of the Museum. I tried to find out – I may be forgiven – who would benefit from the theft of the jewel, and I learned from Mr Brown here' (heads swivelling) 'that Mrs Stratton was always slightly mysterious – ambivalent, even – about her own financial affairs. So I naturally had to bear in mind the possibility that the jewel had not been stolen at all by any outside party, but "caused to disappear", let us say, by the Strattons themselves. It had been the property of Mrs Stratton's first husband, and it was he who had expressed the wish, as stated in his will, that it be returned to England to find a permanent place in the Ashmolean Museum with its counterpart, the Wolvercote Buckle. As a piece of treasure of considerable historical importance, the Wolvercote Tongue was of course beyond price. In itself, however, as an artefact set with precious stones, it was, let us say, "priceable", and it was insured by Mrs Stratton for half a million dollars. I am not yet wholly sure about the specific terms of the policy taken out, but it appears that in the eventuality of the jewel being stolen, either before or after her death, the insurance money is payable to her husband – and is not to be syphoned off into some trust fund or other. At any rate, that is what Eddie Stratton believed – believes, rather – for I learned most of these facts yesterday from Stratton himself, who is now back in America.' Morse paused a moment and looked slowly around his audience. 'I don't need, perhaps, to underline to you the temptation that faced Mr Stratton, himself a virtually penniless man, and a man who knew – for such seems to be the case – that his wife had run through almost all of the considerable money she had inherited from her first husband.'

Several faces looked pained and incredulous, but Janet Roscoe was the only person who did not restrain her disquietude:

'But that could nart *be*, Inspector! Eddie was out walking—'

Morse held up his right hand, and spoke to her not ungently:

'Please hear me out, Mrs Roscoe . . . It was easy to pin-point the period of time within which the theft must have occurred, and not too difficult – was it? – to find out where the great majority of you had been during the crucial forty-five minutes. Not *all* of you felt willing to be completely honest with me, but I don't wish to labour that point now. As I saw things – still see things – the thief had to be one of you here, one of the touring party, including your courier' (heads swivelling again) 'or one of the staff at The Randolph. But the latter possibility could be, and was, fairly quickly discounted. So you will be able to see where things are heading, ladies and gentlemen . . .

'The immediate effects of the theft were considerably lessened both by the death of Laura Stratton and on the very next day by the murder of Dr Kemp, the man to whom the Tongue was due to be handed over that day at an official little ceremony at the Ashmolean. Now one of the jobs of the police force, and especially the CID, is to try to establish a *pattern* in crime, if this is possible, and in this instance both Sergeant Lewis and myself found it difficult not to believe there was some *link* between the two events. They may of course have been quite coincidental; but already there *was* a link, was there not? Dr Kemp himself! – the man who had one day been deprived of a jewel which he himself had traced to an American collector, a jewel for which he had been negotiating, a jewel that had been found in the waters below the bridge at Wolvercote in 1873, a jewel which once united with its mate would doubtless be the subject of some considerable historical interest, and bring some short-term celebrity, possibly some long-term preferment, to himself – to Kemp. Indeed a photograph of the re-united Buckle and Tongue was going to be used on the cover of his forthcoming book. And then, on the very next day, Kemp is murdered. Interesting, is it not? Did, I asked myself, did the *same* person commit both the theft and the murder? It seemed to me more and more likely. So perhaps I needed just the one criminal, not two; but I needed a reason as well. So my thinking went a little further in that direction – the correct direction. If the criminal was the same in each case, was not the *motive* likely to have been the same? In both crimes, the person who had suffered by far the most had been the same man, Kemp. In the first, he had been robbed of something on which he had set his heart; in the second he was robbed of his life. Why? – that is what I asked myself. Or rather that is *not*, in the first instance, what I asked myself, because I was driven to the view – incorrectly – that there could be no link between the two crimes.

'So let us come to Kemp himself. It is a commonplace in murder investigations that more may often be learned about the murderer from the *victim* than from any other source. Now what did we know of the victim, Dr Kemp? He was a Keeper of Antiquities at the Ashmolean, a man somewhat flamboyant in dress and manner, not only a ladies' man but one of the most dedicated womanizers in the University; a man who patently, almost on first sight, appeared self-centred and self-seeking. Yet life had not gone all his way: far from it. The University had recognized Kemp for what he was: his promotion was slow; a full fellowship was withheld; no family; a very modest two-bedroomed flat in North Oxford; and, above all, a great personal tragedy. Two years ago he was involved in a dreadful crash on the western Ring Road in which his wife, who was sitting beside him in the passenger seat, received such serious injuries to the lower half of the body that for the rest of her life – a life which ended tragically last week – she was confined to a wheel-chair. But that was only the half of it. The driver of the other car was killed instantaneously – a Mrs Mayo from California who was in England doing some research project on the novels of Anthony Trollope. The settlements of the dead woman's Accidental Death Benefit, and of the policy covering the "passenger-liability" responsibility of the surviving driver – a driver by the way almost completely unscathed – were finally settled. But the legal tangle surrounding "culpability" was never really unravelled: no eye-witnesses, contradictory evidence on possible mechanical faults, discrepancies about the time recorded for the breathalyser test – these factors resulted in Kemp getting away comparatively lightly, being banned from driving for three years only, with what must have seemed to many the derisory fine of only four hundred pounds. What had really confused everyone was the fact that Kemp always carried a hip-flask of brandy in the car's glove compartment, and that he had given his wife – trapped by the legs beside him – several sips from this flask before the ambulance arrived; and had even drunk from it himself! Everyone who subsequently learned of this action condemned it as utterly stupid and irresponsible, but perhaps such criticism may be tempered by the fact that the man was in a deep state of shock. At least that was what he said in his own defence.

'But let me revert to the crimes committed last week. The crucial happening, whichever way we look at things, was the telephone call made by Kemp. I formed several theories about that call – all wrong, and I will say nothing about them. Kemp had reported to the group that he would be arriving in Oxford at 3 p.m. – and the simple truth is that he *did* arrive in Oxford at 3 p.m. And somebody knew about that telephone call, *and met Kemp at the railway station*, doubtless informing the taxi-driver who had been hired that he was no longer required.'

Janet Roscoe half opened her mouth as if she were contemplating breaking the ensuing silence. But it was Morse who did so, as he continued:

'A taxi, you see, would have been easily traceable, so a different plan was adopted. Someone went to a car-rental firm in North Oxford in the early afternoon and hired a Vauxhall Cavalier. There was only one real difficulty: after vehicle-licence, credit-worthiness, and so on, were formally checked, the firm required some reference to establish the *bona fides* of the client. But this difficulty was quickly and neatly overcome: the man who hired the car – a *man*, yes! – gave the telephone number of The Randolph, and as the firm's representative was dialling the number he casually mentioned that the Deputy Manageress of The Randolph could be immediately contacted on a certain extension. The call was put through, confirmation obtained, and the car handed over. You will appreciate of course that an *accomplice* was essential at this juncture, but not just someone prepared to perform a casual favour. No! Rather someone who was prepared to be an accomplice to *murder*. Now, I believe it to be true that before this tour – with one exception – none of you had known each other. That exception was Mr Stratton and Mr Brown, who had met in the armed forces. But at the time the car was being hired, Mr Stratton was on his way to Didcot Railway Centre – of that fact there can be no doubt whatsoever. And Mr Howard Brown' (Morse hesitated) 'has given a full and fairly satisfactory account of his own whereabouts that afternoon, an account which has since been substantially corroborated.' Lewis's eyebrows shot up involuntarily, but he trusted that no one had noticed.

'There were one or two other absentees that afternoon, weren't there? Mr Ashenden for one.' The courier was staring hard at the patch of carpet between his feet. 'But he was up in Summertown for the whole of that afternoon with friends – as we've now checked.' (Lewis managed to keep his eyebrows still.) 'And then, of course, there's Mr Aldrich.' Heads were swivelling completely round this time – to the back row where sat Phil Aldrich, nodding his head in gentle agreement, a wry smile on his long, lugubrious face. 'But Mr Aldrich can't possibly have been our guilty party either, can he? He went up to London that day, and in fact was travelling on the same train as Stratton when the two of them arrived back in Oxford. Mr Aldrich himself claims, and I am fully prepared to believe him, that he did not see Mr Stratton on the train. *But Mr Stratton saw Mr Aldrich*; and so in an odd sort of way, even if we had no proof of Stratton being in Didcot, the pair of them quite unwittingly perhaps had given each other an utterly unshakeable alibi. And in addition we now *know* that Stratton was in Didcot most of that afternoon. You see, ladies and gentlemen, whatever happens in life, no person can ever be in two places at the same time, for the laws of the Universe forbid it. And the person perfecting his plans in Oxford, the person who had taken possession of the red Cavalier, that person had plenty to do, and precious little time in which to do it – to do it *in Oxford*. There is, perhaps, a brief additional point to be made. It occurred to me that if Stratton and Brown had known each other, so might their wives, perhaps. But one of these wives was already dead; and it was a *man*,' said Morse slowly, 'and not a woman, who hired the car that afternoon.

'Are we running out of suspects, then? Almost, I agree. Your tour started with only three married couples, did it not? And already we have eliminated two of these: the Strattons and the Browns.' In the tense silence which followed this remark, all eyes now turned upon the couple who had been fetched from their bedroom; the couple who had decided that any further diet of delightful architecture would have amounted to a sort of cultural force-feeding. But the pivoting glances which now fell full upon Sam and Vera Kronquist almost immediately reverted to Chief Inspector Morse as the latter rounded off his background summary.

'But Mr Kronquist, as several of you already know, was assisting Mrs Sheila Williams during most of the afternoon in question with the temperamental kaleidoscope allocated to her for her illustrated talk on "Alice". Now Mr Kronquist may be a very clever man, but *he* is not permitted, either, to suspend the physical laws of the Universe. And you do see, don't you, that Mrs Williams, too, must now be crossed off our list of suspects? And finally we shall cross the name of Cedric Downes off that same list, and for exactly the same reason. If anyone from the group here met Kemp at 3 p.m., it wasn't Downes, because nine or ten of you here will willingly testify to the incontrovertible fact that he was talking to you from that time onwards. Did I say running out of likely suspects? And yet, ladies and gentlemen, someone *did* meet Kemp at the railway station that afternoon.

'One of *you* did!'

CHAPTER FIFTY-FOUR

Either what woman having ten pieces of silver, if she lose one piece, doth not light a candle, and sweep the house, and seek diligently till she find it?

(*St Luke*, ch. 15, v. 8)

Throughout the morning on which Morse was addressing his audience in Bath, and stripping away the deceptions and the half-truths which hitherto had veiled the naked truth of the case, there was much activity at the Trout Inn, a fine riverside hostelry set

between the weir and the Godstow Lock in the village of Wolvercote, only a couple of miles out on the western side of North
Oxford. During the summer months hordes of visitors regularly
congregate there to eat and drink at their leisure on the paved
terrace between the mellow sandstone walls of the inn itself and
the river's edge, where many sit on the low stone parapet and
look below them through the clear, greenish water at the mottled
dark-brown and silvery backs of the carp that rise to the surface to
snap up the crisps and the crusts thrown down to them.

But that Wednesday morning, the few customers who had
called for an early drink were much more interested in other
underwater creatures: four of them, with sleek black skins and
disproportionately large webbed feet, circling up and down, and
round and round, and sweeping the depths diligently below the
weir, streams of bubbles intermittently rising to the surface from
the cylinders strapped to their backs. Each of the four was an
experienced police frogman, and each of them knew exactly what
he was looking for – knew indeed the exact dimensions of the
object and the positioning of the three great ruby eyes once set
into it. Thus far they had found nothing, and above the bed of the
river their searchings were stirring up a cloudy precipitate of mud
as the white waters gushed across the weir. Yet hopes were
reasonably high. The frogmen had been briefed – and with such a
degree of certitude! – as to the exact point on the hump-backed
bridge whence the Tongue had been thrown. So they were able to
plot their operation with some precision as first they swam slowly
abreast across the river, then turning and recrossing the current,
ever feeling, ever searching, as they worked their way slowly
downstream into the more placid reaches of the water.

But nothing.

After its discovery in 1873, the Tongue had found its way into
the hands of a treasure-hunter, who had kept quiet about it and
sold it to a London dealer, who in turn had sold it to an American
collector, who had lent it to an exhibition in Philadelphia in 1922 –
which latter appearance had provided the clues, sixty-five years
later, for a detective-story-like investigation on the part of Theodore Kemp of the Ashmolean Museum – a man who now lay dead
in the mortuary at the Radcliffe Infirmary. But the man who had
agreed to tell Chief Inspector Morse precisely where he had stood,
and with what impetus thrown the Tongue back into the river at
Wolvercote – this man was seated, very much alive, in the vastly
confusing complex of Kennedy Airport. Beside him sat a man of
such immense proportions that Eddie Stratton wondered how he

could ever fit into the seat that had been booked for him on the flight to Heathrow, scheduled to leave in forty minutes' time. He wondered, too, whether the man would be willing to unlock the handcuff that chafed away at his right wrist. For he, Stratton, was comtemplating no high-jinks or high-jacks in mid-Atlantic flight.

CHAPTER FIFTY-FIVE

In great affairs we ought to apply ourselves less to creating chances than to profiting from those that offer
(La Rochefoucauld, *Maxims*)

It was way past coffee-break time in The Chesterton Hotel, but no one seemed to notice.

'Kemp was met at the railway station,' continued Morse. 'He was there told something – I'm guessing – which persuaded him to accompany the driver to his own flat in Water Eaton Road. Perhaps he was told that his wife was suddenly taken very ill; was dead, even. Perhaps some less dramatic disclosure sufficed. There, at Kemp's home – again I'm guessing – a quarrel took place in which Kemp was struck over the head and sent stumbling in his own living room, where his right temple crashed against the kerb of the fire-place – and where he died. I'm amazed how difficult it is occasionally for a murderer to despatch his victim: in the Thames Valley we once had a case where no fewer than twenty-three vicious stab-wounds were insufficient to complete the sorry business. But at the same time it is occasionally so terribly easy to rob a fellow human being of his life: a slight nudge, let us say, from a car-bumper, and a cyclist is knocked down and hits his head against the road – and in a second or two a life has gone. In this case, Kemp had a thin skull, and his murder was no problem. But the body? Oh yes, the body was a problem all right!

'Now, if the murder took place at about three forty-five p.m., as I believe it did, why do we find Kemp's wife, Marion, doing nothing about it? For we can be absolutely sure she was there, the whole time. Maybe the reason for this was that she was vindictively happy *not* to do anything, and it is the opinion of my sergeant here that she probably hated her husband almost as intensely as the murderer himself did. But Marion Kemp could not, in my view, have killed her husband, and quite certainly she could hardly have moved the body a single centimetre from where it lay. On the other hand, Kemp was a slimly built, lightly boned man, and it *would* have been possible for most people here, let us say – anyone reasonably mobile, reasonably fit – to have moved that body at least some small distance. *Even for a woman*, if she were sturdily or athletically built.'

The innuendo in this remark proved too much for the petite figure in the front row, who during the last few words was showing signs of unmistakable distress.

'Inspector! Chief Inspector, rather! For you even to *suggest* that I, for one, could have shifted a bardy, why, that is utterly absurd! And if you think that I am going to sit here—'

Morse smiled wanly at the lady as she sat in the front row, a lady turning the scales at not much more, surely, than about five stone.

'I should never accuse *you* of that, Mrs Roscoe. Please believe me!'

Mollified, it seemed, Janet sat back primly and slimly in her seat, as John Ashenden, seated immediately opposite (beside Dr Moule), looked across at her with a troublous, darkling gaze. And Morse continued:

'In the concreted yard at the back of the flats at Water Eaton Road stood a lightweight, rubber-wheeled, aluminium wheelbarrow which one of the maintenance men had been using earlier that day. It was into this barrow, under cover of the night, at about seven p.m., that the body was put, covered with plastic sacks, themselves in turn covered with a fair sprinkling of autumn leaves, before being wheeled across the low wooden bridge there, across a well-worn path through the field, and across to the swiftly flowing current of the River Cherwell, where unceremoniously the body was tipped into the water. And as I say' (Morse looked slowly around his audience) 'it was one of your own group who performed this grisly task – a *man* – a man who would have felt little squeamishness about first stripping the dead man of his clothes – for there had been much blood, much messy, sticky blood which almost inevitably would have transferred itself to the clothes of the man disposing of the body; a man who for the last ten years of his working life had been inured to such gruesome matters, as a moderately competent "mortician" in America.'

There was a sudden communal intake of breath from the audience, and clearly no need for Morse to spell things out further. But he did:

'Yes! *Mr Eddie Stratton.*'

'*No*, sir!'

The voice from the back of the room caused every head to crane round, although the mild tones of Phil Aldrich were known so well by now to everyone.

'You have my testimony, sir, and you have Eddie's too that we—'

'Mr Aldrich! I do accept your point, and I shall explain. Let us return to Stratton briefly. He had become a small-time mortician, specializing in the beautification – please allow the word! – of corpses that had died an ugly or disfiguring death. And a bachelor. Until two and a bit years ago, that is, when he met and married the widow of a middle-bracket philanthropist. The marriage was mostly an accommodation of interests; a convenience. Eddie did the shopping, tended the garden, mended the taps and the fuses, and serviced the family car. Laura – Laura Stratton as she now was – was reasonably content with the new arrangements: she was less anxious about burglars, she was chauffeured to her twice-weekly consultations with the latest chiropodist, she forgot most of her worries about the upkeep of the household, and she still found herself able to indulge the twin passions of her life, smoking cigarettes and playing contract bridge – simultaneously, wherever possible.

'But there had been disappointed expectations, on both sides, when the estate of the late philanthropist had finally, well almost finally, been settled, with the lawyers still growing fat on the pickings. *Objets d'art* there were aplenty, but most of them were held in trust for some collection or gallery. And so the prospects of a happily monied marriage of convenience were ever diminishing, until an idea occurred to the pair of them – certainly to Laura Stratton. The Wolvercote Tongue was insured for half a million dollars, and one of the safest ways of transferring it over to England had got to be on the person of the traveller: few people would entrust such an item to letter-post or parcel-post or courier-service; and even if they did, the insurance-risk premium would be prohibitive. So the Strattons took it themselves – *and then made sure it was stolen*. That was their plan. The reason the plan went so sadly askew was the not wholly unexpected but extremely untimely death of Laura Stratton herself, though whether this was occasioned by her own complicity, excitement, remorse – whatever! – we shall never really know. The plan – a simple one – was for the Tongue to be stolen immediately after Laura had installed herself in her room at The Randolph. She would be sure to make such a song and dance about her aching feet that she would get right to the head of the queue for the room-key – well, apart from Mrs Roscoe, naturally!'

For the first time during Morse's analysis, his audience was seen reluctantly to smile as it acknowledged the primacy of the perpetually belly-aching little lady from California.

'Once she had the key, and whilst her husband signed the formalities, she was to go up to her room, put the handbag containing the Tongue – and money, pearls, and so on – on a ledge as near as possible to a door which was going to be left deliberately ajar. Meanwhile Eddie Stratton was to enthuse about a quick stroll around the centre of Oxford before it got too dark, and an invitation to accompany him was accepted by Mrs Brown, a woman with whom he'd become friendly on the tour, and who probably felt a little flattered to be asked. All he had to do then was to make it known that he had promised to leave Laura alone so that she could have a rest in peace, to make an excuse about paying a brief visit to the Gents, to go up to his room – probably via the guest-lift – to stick his hand inside the room and grab the handbag, to take out the jewel before dumping the handbag, and then . . .'

Morse stopped, but only briefly. 'Not a *terribly* convincing hypothesis, are you thinking? I tend to agree with you. Everyone would be trying to use the lift at that point – probably queuing for it. And it would be impossible to use the main staircase, because as you'll recall it is immediately next to Reception there. And where does he ditch the emptied handbag? For it was never found. However quickly he may have acted, the actual taking of the handbag must have taken more *time* than seems to have been available – since Eddie Stratton and Shirley Brown were seen walking out of The Randolph almost immediately, if the evidence of at least two of you here is to be believed, the evidence of Mr Brown and Mrs Roscoe. So! So I suggest that something a little more sophisticated may have taken place. Let me tell you what I think. The plan, whatever it was, must have been discussed well in advance of the tour's arrival in Oxford, but a few last-minute recapitulations and reassurances would have been almost inevitable. Perhaps you've noticed that it's often difficult, on a bus or a train, to assess how loudly you are talking? Yes? Too loudly? And where were the Strattons sitting?' Morse pointed dramatically (as he hoped) to the two empty seats just behind Janet Roscoe. 'If they *did* discuss things on the coach, who were the likeliest people to eavesdrop? I'm told, for example, that you, Mrs Roscoe, have quite exceptionally acute hearing for a woman of—'

This time the little lady stood up, if thereby adding only some

seven or eight inches in stature to her seated posture. 'Such
innuendo, Chief Inspector, is wholly without foundation, and I
wish you to know that one of my friends back home is the fiercest
libel lawyer—'

But, again, and with the same patient smile, Morse bade the
excitable lady to hold her peace, and bide her time.

'You were not the only one in earshot, Mrs Roscoe. In the seats
immediately across the gangway from the Strattons sat Mr and
Mrs Brown . . . and in front of them, in the courier's seat . . .'
Eyes, including Morse's, now turned as if by some magnetic
attraction towards John Ashenden, who sat, his eyes unblinking,
in the front row of the seats.

'You see,' resumed Morse, 'Stratton never went up at all to his
room in The Randolph – not at that point. But someone did,
someone *here* did – someone who had overheard enough of the
original plan; someone who had sensed a wonderfully providential
opportunity for himself, or for herself, and who had capitalized
upon that opportunity. How? By volunteering to steal the Wolvercote Tongue, in order that the Strattons could immediately claim –
claim without any suspicion attaching to them – the tempting
prize of the insurance money!

'Let me put the situation to you simply. The person who had
eavesdropped on the proposed intrigue *performed Stratton's job for
him*; stole the jewel; slid thereafter into the background; and
disposed at leisure of the superfluous pearls and the petty cash.
And *that*, ladies and gentlemen, is no wild hypothesis on my part;
it is the truth. Stratton was presented with an offer he could hardly
refuse. At the time, though, he was not aware – could never have
been aware – of the extraordinary service he would have to render
as the *quid pro quo* of the agreement. But he was to learn about it
soon enough. In fact, he was to learn of it the very next day, and
he duly performed his own half of the bargain with a strangely
honourable integrity. As it happens' – Morse consulted his watch
ostentatiously – 'he is very shortly due to take off from Kennedy
Airport to fly back to Heathrow, and he has already made a
substantial confession about his part in the strange circumstances
surrounding the Wolvercote Tongue and Dr Theodore Kemp. But
– please believe me! – it was not *he* who actually stole the one . . .
or murdered the other. Yet I am looking forward to meeting Mr
Stratton again, because thus far he has refused point-blank to tell
me who the murderer was . . .'

*

At the Trout Inn, the frogmen were now seated before a blazing log-fire in the bar. The landlady, an attractive, buxom woman in her mid-forties, had brought them each a hugely piled plate of chilli-con-carne, with a pint of appropriately chilly lager to wash it all down. None of the four had met Morse yet, and didn't know how strongly he would have disapproved of their beverage. But they knew they were working for him, and each of them was hoping that if the jewel were found it would be *he* who would have found it. Some acknowledgement, some gratitude from the man – that was an end devoutly to be wished.

But still nothing. Nothing, that is, except a child's tricycle, an antique dart-board, and what looked like part of a fixture from a household vacuum-cleaner.

Frequently, when Eddie Stratton had flown in the past, his heart had missed a beat or two whenever he heard the 'ding-dong' tones on the aircraft intercom. Indeed, he had sometimes felt that the use of such a system, except in times of dire emergency, should be prohibited by international law. No one Eddie had ever met wished to be acquainted with the pilot and his potential problems. So why not keep an eye on the steering, and forgo any announcements to interested passengers that there was now, say, a splendid view of the Atlantic Ocean down below? *No* announcements, *no* news – that's what passengers wanted. But now, ten minutes before take-off, Stratton felt most curiously relaxed about the possibility of an aerial disaster. Would such an eventuality be a welcome release? No, not really. He would speak to Morse again, yes. But Morse would never learn – at least not from *him* – the name of the person who had murdered Theodore Kemp.

CHAPTER FIFTY-SIX

And as the smart ship grew
In stature, grace, and hue,
In shadowy silent distance grew the Iceberg too
(Thomas Hardy, *The Convergence of the Twain*)

Sergeant Lewis had been gratified by the brief mention of himself in despatches, and he was in any case revising (upwards) his earlier judgement on Morse's rhetorical skills. All right, he (Lewis) now knew the whole picture, but it was good to have the details rehearsed again in front of a different audience. He had never been near the top of the class in any of the subjects he had been taught at school, yet he'd often thought he wouldn't have been all that far below the high-fliers if only some of the teachers had been willing to go over a point a second time; or even a third time. For once Lewis *did* get hold of a thing firmly – suggestion, idea, hypothesis, theory – he could frequently see its significance, its implications, almost as well as anyone; even Morse. It was just that the initial stages were always a bit of a problem; whereas for Morse – well, *he* seemed to jump to a few answers here and there before he'd even read the question-paper. That was one of the big things he admired most about the man, that ability to leap ahead of the field almost from the starting-stalls – albeit occasionally finding himself on completely the wrong race-course. But it wasn't the *biggest* thing. The biggest thing was that Morse appeared to believe that Lewis was not only usually up with him in the race, galloping happily abreast, but that Lewis could sometimes spot something in the stretches ahead that Morse himself had missed, as the pair of them raced on towards the winning-post. It was ridiculous, of course. But Lewis ever found himself trusting that such a false impression might long be perpetuated.

The man's diction is slightly pedantic, thought Dr Moule, but he actually speaks in *sentences* – unusual even for a preacher, let alone a policeman. And – Heaven be praised! – he doesn't stand there with his hands jingling the coins in his pockets. He reminded her of her Latin master, on whom she'd had an extra-special crush, and she wondered whether she wouldn't have had the same for this man. He looked overweight around the midriff, though nowhere else, and she thought perhaps that he drank too much. He looked weary, as if he had been up most of the night conducting his investigations. He looked the sort of man she would like to be going with, and she wondered whether he'd ever been unfaithful to his wife . . . But surely no wife would allow her husband abroad in such an off-white apology for a laundered shirt? Dr Moule smiled quietly, and trusted she was looking her attractive best; and tried to stop herself hoping he had holes in his socks.

*

As the TWA Tristar turned slowly at the head of the runway, Lieutenant Al Morrow tried to pull out a final inch or two from the safety-belt that clamped his enormous girth to the seat. At the same time he unfastened the handcuffs which united him to his fellow-passenger. Morrow had a good deal of experience of the criminal classes, but this particular villain was hardly one of the potentially-dangerous-on-no-account-to-be-accosted variety. OK. He'd accompany him to the loo. But for the rest, the fellow would be fine, imprisoned in his window-seat between the fuselage on the one side and the mighty mountain of flesh that was Morrow on the other. The lieutenant opened his reading matter, *The Finer Arts of Fly-Fishing*, and, as the great jet raced and roared its engines, glanced quickly once again at the man who sat beside him: the features immobile, yet in no way relaxed; the eyes staring, yet perhaps not seeing at all; the forehead unfurrowed, yet tense, it seemed, as though his mind was dwelling on unhappy memories.

'You want sump'n to read, pal?'

Stratton shook his head.

It was as the lieutenant had suspected . . .

. . . It had been extraordinary how the two things had synchronized so perfectly at Oxford: a bit like the iceberg growing as the SS *Titanic* drew ever closer.

It was Laura's fault, of course! The woman could never keep her voice down – a voice that was usually double the decibels needed in normal conversation; and in whispered, conspiratorial communication, just about as loud as normal speech. And particularly on any form of public transport the dotty but endearing old biddy could never seem to gauge the further limits of her penetrating tones. Constantly, had she been fitted with a volume-control attachment somewhere about her person, Stratton would have turned it down. Frequently, as it was, he had enquired of his fairly recently acquired bride whether she was anxious for *the whole world* to know her business! Well, perhaps that was a bit of an exaggeration. Yet someone *had* overheard their plan; or heard enough of their plan to make a firm four out of two and two. And the glory of the thing had been that this someone had been just as anxious – more anxious! – to spirit away the Wolvercote Tongue as Laura was. As *he* was.

It had been the night at the University Arms in Cambridge that

Plan B had been agreed. Such a *simple* plan, that 'plan' seemed far too grand an appellation: audibly (not a difficult task!) Laura would complain about her feet on the journey to Oxford; quite naturally (for her regular seat was on the row second to the front) she would be first in the queue at Reception in The Randolph – even Mrs Roscoe probably conceding her customary prerogative; she would leave her handbag immediately inside the allocated, unlocked bedroom; she would take a bath; she would leave the thief the childishly simple assignment of putting a hand inside the door. His own role? Principally to keep as far away from his room as possible. The police (no way in which they could not be involved) would be primarily interested in who was going to profit from any insurance, and he, Stratton himself, would have to vie with Caesar's wife in immunity from any suspicion. As it happened, he'd already prepared the ground for that by making something of a fuss of Shirley Brown; not at all difficult, because he *wanted* to make a fuss of Shirley Brown; and that lady had been flattered to follow his suggestion for a twilit stroll round Radcliffe Square – a stroll on which they'd seen their courier, Ashenden, and in turn been seen by the all-seeing Roscoe, a woman whom no one could abide, yet one whom everyone believed. Clever little touch, that! The problem that had worried Stratton about the earlier (now discarded) Plan A was where on earth he was going to dispose of the handbag. But need he have worried? Would it really have mattered if the bag had been found fairly soon in the nearest litter-bin? No, it wouldn't! The only thing that had to be disposed of was the jewel itself – not only because the insurance money must not be put in jeopardy, but also because someone else desired *Kemp* to be deprived of it. Desired it desperately.

Then Laura had to put her foot in it! Put her goddamned, aching, corny, foot right in it.

She'd gone and died.

Not that he (Stratton) had been involved in any way in that first death. No! But as far as the second death was concerned? Ah! That was a different matter. And whatever happened he would never tell the whole truth about that to anyone – not voluntarily – not even to that smart-alec copper, Chief Inspector Morse himself.

Yet he respected the man; couldn't help it, remembering the initial broadside on the transatlantic telephone, when Morse had immediately breached the outer fortifications.

'No, Inspector. There's nothing I can tell you about Kemp's death. Nothing.'

'I was more interested in the jewel, sir.'

'Ah! "The jewel that was ours", as Laura used to think of it.'
'Come off it!'
'Pardon, Inspector?'
'I said "Bullshit!"'

CHAPTER FIFTY-SEVEN

What's in a name? that which we call a rose
By any other name would smell as sweet
(Shakespeare, *Romeo and Juliet*)

Although it had been a rather chilly morning, several of the people
seated in the Beau Nash Room wished that the central heating
could be turned down a few degrees. Howard Brown wiped his
high forehead with a large handkerchief, and John Ashenden
brushed the sleeve of his sports jacket across his upper lip where
he felt the sweat-prickles forming. Morse himself drew a forefinger
half a circuit round the neck of his slightly over-tight collar, and
continued:

'I know who stole the Wolvercote Tongue. I know where it is,
and I am quite sure that it will soon be recovered. I also know
which one of you – which one of you here – killed Dr Kemp.' The
hush was now so intense that Lewis found himself wondering
whether his involuntary swallow had been audible, as for thirty
seconds or so Morse stood silent and still, only his eyes moving
left and right, and left and right again across the central aisle. No
one in the audience moved either. No one dared even to cough.

'I'd hoped that the guilty person would have come forward by
now. I say that because you may have read of several cases in
England recently where the police have been criticized – in some
cases rightly so – for depending for a prosecution on the uncorrob-
orated confessions of accused persons, confessions which, certainly in one or two cases, might have been extorted in less than
safe and satisfactory circumstances. How much better it would
have been, then, if Kemp's murderer came forward – *comes
forward* – in the presence of his friends and fellow tourists . . .'
Morse again looked around the room; but if there were any one
person upon whom those blue eyes focused, it was not apparent
to the others seated there.

'No?'

'No?' queried Morse again.

'So be it! There is little more to tell you. The biggest single clue in this case I passed over almost without reading it, until my sergeant jogged my memory. It was contained in a police report of the road accident in which Kemp crippled his wife – and also killed the driver of the other car, a Mrs P. J. Mayo, a thirty-five-year-old woman from California: Mrs Philippa J. Mayo, whose husband had earlier been killed in a gunnery accident on the USS *South Dakota*. That would have been bad enough for Philippa Mayo's parents-in-law, would it not? But at least the man had been serving his country; at least he'd died for some *cause* – whether that cause was justified or not. What of Philippa's own parents, though, when *she* is killed? Their daughter. Their only daughter. Their only child. A child killed needlessly, pointlessly, tragically, and wholly *reprehensibly* – by a man who must have appeared to those parents, from the reports they received, as a drunken, selfish, wicked swine who deserved to be as dead as their daughter . . . Above all, I suspect, the parents were appalled by what seemed to them the quite extraordinary leniency of the magistrates at the criminal hearing, and they came over to England, father and mother, to lay the ghost that had haunted them night and day for the past two years. But why only then, you may ask? I learn that the wife had been suffering from cervical cancer for the previous three years; had just endured her second massive session of chemotherapy; had decided that she could never face a third; had only at the outside six more months to live. So the pair came over to view the killer of their daughter, and if they deemed him worthy of death, they vowed that he would die. They met him the once only on the night before he died: a cocky philanderer, as they saw him; a cruel, conceited specimen; and now a man who, like Philippa Mayo's mother, had so very little time to live. The link between the two crimes, and the motivation for them, was clear to me at last, and the link and the motivation merged into a single whole: the implacable hatred of a man and his wife for the person who had killed their daughter.

'For Theodore Kemp.

'I keep mentioning "man *and* wife" because I finally persuaded myself that no one single person on his own could have carried through the murder of Kemp. It could have been *any* two people, though, and we had to try to find out as much about all of you as we could. When you signed in at The Randolph, you all filled in a form which asked overseas visitors to complete full details of nationality, passport number, place passport issued, permanent home address, and so on. But, as you know, I also had to ask Mr

Ashenden to collect your passports, and from these, my sergeant here' (the blood rose slowly in Lewis's cheeks) 'checked all the details you have given and found that two of you lived in the same block of retirement flats. But these two were not registered as man and wife; rather they had decided to play the waiting game, to take advantage of anything that might crop up, to "optimize the opportunity", as I believe you say in America. And that opportunity materialized – in the person of Eddie Stratton.

'Stratton had been out at Didcot on the afternoon Kemp died, and what is more he could prove his presence there conclusively – with photographic evidence. And I – we – were led to believe that his quite innocent statements about his train journey back to Oxford were equally true. *But they weren't.* Cleverly, unwittingly, as it seemed, he gave a wholly unimpeachable alibi to a man he saw in the carriage ahead of him – a man to whom he owed a very great deal. But he did *not* see that man, ladies and gentlemen! Because that man was *not* on the Didcot–Oxford train that afternoon. He was in Oxford . . . murdering Dr Kemp.'

The last few words sank into the noiselessness of the stifling room. And then Morse suddenly smiled a little, and spoke quietly:

'Can you hear me all right at the back, Mr Aldrich?'

'Pardon, sir?'

'Don't you think it would be far better if you . . .' Morse held out the palm of his right hand and seemed to usher some invisible spirit towards the front row of the seats.

Aldrich, looking much perplexed, rose from his seat and walked forward hesitantly down the central aisle; and, turning towards him, Janet Roscoe smiled expectantly and pointed her hand to the empty seat beside her. But Aldrich ignored the gesture, and slipped instead into one of the empty seats immediately behind her.

'As I say,' resumed Morse, 'the person Stratton claimed to have seen was never on the train at all. That person told me he'd been to London to see his daughter; but he'd only ever had the one daughter . . . and she was *dead.'*

Morse's audience was hanging on his every word, yet few seemed able to grasp the extraordinary implications of what he was saying.

'Names, you know' (Morse's tone was suddenly lighter) 'are very important things. Some people don't like their own names . . . but others are extremely anxious to perpetuate them – both Christian names and surnames. Let's say, for example, that Mr and Mrs Brown here – Howard and Shirley, isn't it – wanted to christen their house, they might think of sticking half of their two names together. What about "W-a-r-d" from his name and "l-e-y" from hers? Make a reasonable house-name, wouldn't it? "Wardley"?'

'Gee, that's exactly—' began Shirley; but Howard laid a hand on her arm, and the embarrassed lady held her peace.

'Not much good trying to perpetuate a surname, though – not if your daughter gets married. She *can* keep her maiden name, of course. Can't she? *Can't* she . . . ? But it's easier with Christian names, especially sometimes. A father whose name is "George", say, can call his daughter "Georgie", "Georgina", "Georgette".' (Lewis glanced up at Morse.) 'And the woman who was killed in the road accident was called Mrs Philippa J. Mayo, remember? Her father couldn't give her his own name exactly, but he could give her the female equivalent of "Philip". And Philippa Mayo was the daughter of the only man here who has that name.'

'*Wasn't she, Mr Aldrich?*' asked Morse in a terrifying whisper.

CHAPTER FIFTY-EIGHT

> . . . that fair field
> Of Enna, where Proserpin gathring flowrs
> Her self a fairer Flowre by gloomie Dis
> Was gathered, which cost Ceres all that pain
> To seek her through the world . . .
> (John Milton, *Paradise Lost, Book IV*)

'You're *serious* about all this, sir?' Phil Aldrich cocked his head to one side and his sad features seemed incredulous, and pained.

'Oh, yes,' said Morse, with a quiet simplicity – perhaps also with some pain. 'You've no daughter in London – or anywhere else now, I'm afraid. You've lost your alibi, too – the very clever alibi provided by Eddie Stratton as the first of his services for you . . . before he performed his *second* service, later that same day, by disposing of Kemp's body in the River Cherwell.'

Momentarily, it seemed, Aldrich was on the point of protesting, but Morse shook his head wearily:

'No point – no point at all in your saying anything to the contrary, Mr Aldrich. We've been in touch with the police department in Sacramento, with your neighbours, with the local institution there, including the High School your daughter attended.

We've got your passport, and we've checked your home address, and it's perfectly correct. You carried through all your details accurately on to the THF Guest Registration Card at The Randolph, and doubtless here too, in Bath. But *your wife*? She was a little "economical with the truth", wasn't she? Your wife – *your accomplice*, Mr Aldrich – she made just a few little changes here and there to her details, didn't she? It was all right for it to be seen that you both lived in the same district, the same street, even – *but not in the same apartment*. Yet you do, don't you, live in the same apartment as your wife? You've been married together, happily married together, for almost forty-two years, if my information is correct. And apart from your daughter, there has only ever been one woman in life you have loved with passion and tenderness – the woman you married. She was a gifted actress, I learned. She was well known on the West Coast of America in many productions in the fifties and sixties – mostly in musicals in the earlier years, and then in a series of Arthur Miller plays. And being an actress, a successful actress, it was sensible for her to keep her stage name – which was in fact her maiden name. But she gave her Christian name to her daughter, just as you did. Philippa J. Aldrich – Philippa *Janet* Aldrich – that was her name.' Morse nodded sadly to himself, and to the two people who sat so near to one another now.

Then a most poignant and exceedingly moving thing occurred. Only a few minutes since, Phil Aldrich had rejected (as it seemed) the blandishments of a diminutive, loud-mouthed, insufferable termagant. But now he accepted her invitation. He rose, and moved forward, just the one row, to sit beside the woman in the front, and to take her small hand gently into his – the tears now spilling down his cheeks. And as he did so, the woman turned towards him with eyes that were pale and desolate, yet eyes which still lit up with the glow of deep and happy love as she looked unashamedly, unrepentantly, into her husband's face; the eyes of a mother who had grieved so long and so desperately for her only daughter, a mother whose grief could never be comforted, and who had journeyed to England to avenge what she saw as an insufferable wrong – the loss of the jewel that was hers.

CHAPTER FIFTY-NINE

Je ne regrette rien

(French song)

After the arrests, after the statements from the two Aldriches and from a repentant Stratton, after a second search of the Kemps' residence, the case – at least from Morse's point of view – was finished.

The major statement (the statement to which Morse awarded the literary prize) was made by Mrs Janet Roscoe, who properly insisted on vetting the transcription of her lengthy evidence typed out by WPC Wright. Except at one point, this agreed with the parallel statement made by Mr Phil Aldrich, with each, in turn, substantially corroborated by Mr Edward Stratton's testimony about his own collusion with the Aldriches. The one colossal discrepancy arose from the two wholly contradictory accounts of Kemp's death. Neither Mr or Mrs Aldrich was willing to give any detail whatsoever about what, as Morse imagined, must have been a savagely bitter altercation between Kemp and themselves before the fateful (though maybe not immediately fatal?) blow struck with the stick that originally had rested across Marion Kemp's knees as she sat in her wheel-chair, her eyes (in Janet's splendid phrase) 'glowing with a sort of glorious revenge'. So much was agreed. Kemp had stumbled blindly against a chair and then fallen heavily, the back of his head striking the corner of the fireplace with 'a noise reminiscent of a large egg trodden under foot – deliberately'. So much was agreed. Then there was all that blood. Such a surprising amount of it! And the carpet where most of it had dripped; and his clothes 'sticky and messy with the stuff'. So much was agreed. But which of the two it was who had lashed out ferociously at Kemp with that stick ('Please return to the Radcliffe Infirmary' branded upon it) – ah! that was proving so difficult to decide. It had been *Phil*, of course – Janet confessed: 'He must have gone quite berserk, Inspector!' But no! It had been *Janet* all the time, as Phil had so sadly admitted to Morse: a frenetic Janet who had been the happy instrument of eternal Justice. But when Morse had told Janet of the wild discrepancy, she'd merely smiled. And when Morse had told Phil of the same ridiculous discrepancy, he too had merely smiled – and lovingly.

There had been one or two minor surprises in the statements, but for the most part things had happened almost exactly as Morse had supposed. What finally, it appeared, had transmuted an intolerable grief into an implacable hatred, and a lust for some sort of retribution, was the fact that in all the reports the parents had received of the coroner's proceedings and the magistrate's hearing, *Philippa's name had never once occurred*. A curious catalyst, perhaps, and yet what a devastating one! But the name of Dr Theodore Kemp had been mentioned many, many times; and when they had read of the Historic Cities of England Tour, *they had seen that name again*. Their plans were made (for what they were) and they duly took their places on the tour – almost enjoying the distanced yet sometimes friendly roles they had assumed. And it was on the coach that Janet had learned of the deceit that the Strattons were plotting . . . And after Janet had taken Laura Stratton's handbag, and put it immediately into her own far more capacious one, she had gone to her own room, on the same floor, and happily discovered that the Wolvercote Tongue fitted almost perfectly into the small case she'd brought with her containing her portable iron . . .

Then it was the telephone call . . .

Janet had heard everything, *clearly*! And a plan was immediately formulated. Eddie Stratton was despatched somewhere – any-where! – so long as he could establish a firm alibi *for himself*; and Phil set off to a nearby car-hire firm, whilst she, Janet, remained seated by the extension-phone in her bedroom to deal with the necessary reference for the car firm. The confusion caused by Kemp's delay that day was a godsend; and Phil, after picking up Janet from Gloucester Green, had met Kemp at the railway station (his train two minutes early) informing him that his wife had been taken ill, that his duties were fully taken care of, and that he (Aldrich) was there to drive him directly up to his North Oxford home . . .

After the deed was done, Janet had found herself waiting anxiously for the return of Eddie Stratton; and as soon as she – and no one else! – had spotted him, she steered him away from The Randolph, handed him the Wolvercote Tongue, and acquainted him with the *second* of his duties in the criminal conspiracy in which he was now a wholly committed accessory: the disposal of the body.

Marion Kemp (this from Stratton's evidence now) had admitted him at Water Eaton Road, where he had divested the corpse of its clothes – how else shift the body without staining his own? And . . . well, the rest was now known. It had not been an unduly gruesome task to a man for whom such post-mortem grotesqueries had been little more than a perfunctory performance. He had wrapped the carpet round the clothes of the murdered man, depositing the bundle behind the boiler in the airing-cupboard. And what of Marion Kemp? Throughout she had sat, Stratton claimed, in the hall-way. In silence.

'And greatly disturbed,' opined Morse.

'Oh no, Inspector!' Stratton had replied.

After leaving Water Eaton Road, Stratton had walked via First Turn and Goose Green to the Trout Inn at Wolvercote where he had thrown the Tongue into the river – and then caught a Nipper bus back to St Giles', where he'd met Mrs Williams.

Sheila's evidence tallied with Stratton's account. She had invited Stratton back to her house in North Oxford, and he had accepted. Anxious as he was to drink himself silly, and with a co-operative partner to boot, Stratton had consumed considerable quantities of Glenfiddich – and had finally staggered into a summoned taxi at around midnight . . .

Such was the picture of the case that had finally emerged; such the picture that Morse painted on the Friday morning of that same week when Chief Superintendent Strange had come into his office, seating himself gruntingly into the nearest chair.

'None of your bullshit, Morse! Just the broad brush, my boy! I'm off to lunch with the CC in half an hour.'

'Give him my very best wishes, sir.'

'Get *on* with it!'

Strange sat back (and looked at his watch) when Morse had finished. 'She must have been an amazing woman.'

'She was, sir. I think Janet Roscoe is possibly the—'

'I'm not talking about *her*! I'm talking about the Kemp woman – Marion, wasn't it? Didn't the Aldrich pair take a huge gamble though? You know, assuming she would play along with 'em, and so on?'

'Oh, yes. But they were gambling all along – with the very highest stakes, sir.'

'And you just think, Morse! Staying in that house – with that bloody corpse – in her bedroom – in the hall – wherever – I don't know. *I* couldn't do it. Could *you*? It'd send me crackers.'

'She could never forgive him—'

'It'd still send me crackers.'

'She *did* commit suicide, sir,' said Morse slowly, beginning only now, perhaps, to see into the abyss of Marion's despair.

'So she did, Morse! So she did!'

Strange looked at his watch again and tilted his heavily jowled head: 'What put you on to 'em? The Aldriches?'

'I should have got there earlier, I suppose. Especially after that first statement Aldrich made, about his fictional trip to London. He wrote it straight out – only three crossings-out in three pages. And if only I'd looked at what he'd crossed out instead of what he'd left in! He was writing under pressure and, if my memory serves me, he crossed out things like "*we* could have done something" and "*our* telephone number". He was worried about giving himself away, because he was writing like a married man . . . He *was* a married man . . . And there was another clue, too. He even mentioned his daughter's name in that statement: "Pippa" – which as you know, sir, is a diminutive of "Philippa".'

Strange rose to his feet and pulled on his heavy winter coat. 'Some nice bits of thinking, Morse!'

'Thank you, sir!'

'I'm not talking about *you*! It's this Roscoe woman. Very able little lady! Did you know that a lot of 'em have been *little* – these big people: Alexander, Augustus, Attila, Nelson, Napoleon . . .'

'They tell me Bruckner was a very small man, sir.'

'Who?'

The two men smiled briefly at each other as Strange reached the door.

'Just a couple of points, Morse. How did Janet Roscoe get rid of that handbag?'

'She says she walked round the corner into Cornmarket, and went into Salisbury's, and stuck it in the middle of the leather handbags on sale there.'

'What about the murder weapon? You say you've not recovered that?'

'Not yet. You see, she walked along to the Radcliffe Infirmary, so she says, and saw a notice there about an Amnesty – for anything you'd had from the place which you should have returned: "Amnesty – No Questions Asked", it said. She just handed it in.'

'Why haven't you got it, then?'

'Sergeant Lewis went along, sir. But there were seventy-one walking sticks in the Physio department there.'

'Oh!'

'Do you want any forensic tests on them?'

'Waste of money.'

'That's what Sergeant Lewis said.'

'Good man, Lewis!'

'Excellent man!'

'Not so clever as this Roscoe woman, though.'

'Few cleverer.'

'She'd be useful in the Force.'

'No chance, sir. She had a thorough medical yesterday. They don't even give her a fortnight.'

'Any doctor who tells you when you're going to die is a bloody fool!'

'Not this one,' said Morse quietly – and sadly.

'Think you'll get that jewel back?'

'Hope so, sir. But *they* won't, will they?'

'Say that again?'

'The jewel that was theirs, sir. They won't ever get *her* back, will they?'

Was Morse imagining things? For a second or two he thought that Strange's eyes might well have glistened with a film of tears. But there was no way of telling this for certain, for Strange had suddenly looked down fixedly at the threadbare carpet beside the door, before departing for his lunch with the Chief Constable.

CHAPTER SIXTY

Accipe fraterno multum manantia fletu,
    Atque in perpetuum, frater, ave atque vale
                                        (Catullus, *Poem CI*)

A week after his meeting with Strange, Morse took the bus down from North Oxford to Cornmarket. He had managed two complete days' furlough, had re-read *Bleak House*, listened again (twice) to *Parsifal*, and (though he would never have admitted it) begun to feel slightly bored.

Not today, though!

When he had said farewell to Sheila Williams the previous week, he had suggested a second rendezvous. He was (he assured her) a reasonably civilized sort of fellow, and it would be pleasant for both of them to meet again fairly soon, and perhaps have lunch together: the Greek Taverna, perhaps, up in Summertown? So a time and a place were carefully agreed: 12 a.m. (twelve *noon*) in the foyer (the *foyer*) of The Randolph.

Where else?

As usual (for appointments), he was ten minutes early, and stood for a while in the foyer talking to Roy, the bespectacled Head Concierge, and congratulating this splendid man on his recent award of the BEM. A quarter of an hour later, he walked down the hotel steps and for several minutes stood immobile on the pavement there, some of his thoughts centred on the Ashmolean Museum opposite and on its former Keeper of Anglo-Saxon and Mediaeval Antiquities; but most of his thoughts, if truth be told, on Mrs Sheila Williams. At 12.20 p.m., when he found himself looking at his wristwatch about three times per minute, he returned to the foyer, and stood there rather fecklessly for a further few minutes. At 12.25 p.m., he asked the concierge if there'd been any messages. No! At 12.30 p.m., he abandoned all hope and decided to drown his disappointment in the Chapters Bar.

As he came to the door, he looked inside – and stopped. There, seated at the bar, a large empty glass held high in her left hand, her right arm resting on the shoulder of a youngish (bearded!) man, sat Sheila Williams, her black-stockinged legs crossed provocatively, her body disturbingly close to her companion's.

'If you insist!' Morse heard her say, as she pushed her glass across the bar. 'Gin – large one, please! – no ice – just *half* a glass of tonic – slim-line.'

Morse held back, feeling a great surge of irrational and impotent jealousy. About which he could do nothing. Absolutely nothing. Like a stricken deer he walked back to the foyer, where he wrote a brief note ('Unavoidable, urgent police business'), and asked the concierge to take it through to the bar in about five minutes or so, and hand it to a Mrs Williams – a Mrs *Sheila* Williams.

Roy had nodded. He'd been there in the hotel for forty-five years, now. That's why he'd been honoured by the Queen. He understood most things. He thought he understood this.

Morse walked quickly along the Broad, past the King's Arms, the Holywell Music Room, the back of New College, turned left at Longwall Street, and after two hundred yards or so went through the wooden gate that led into Holywell Cemetery. He found the grave far more quickly than Ashenden had done; and behind the squat cross the envelope that Ashenden had left there, with the four lines written out neatly on a white card therein. After replacing the envelope, Morse left the cemetery and walked slowly back along Holywell Street to the King's Arms, ordering there (as Ashenden had done before him) a pint of Flowers bitter. He found himself ever thinking of Sheila, and at one point had been on the verge of rushing up to The Randolph to see if she were still there in the Chapters Bar.

But he hadn't.

And gradually thoughts of Mrs Williams were receding; and instead, he found his mind lingering on the sad quatrain he'd found beside the small stone cross in the Holywell cemetery:

> *Life divided us from each other,*
> *Depriving friend of friend,*
> *Accept this leave-taking – with my tears –*
> *For it is all I have to bring.*

At the Trout Inn, the frogmen had given it four days, then called off the search for the Wolvercote Tongue. Sensibly so, as Eddie Stratton (now facing charges of perjury and perverting the course of justice) could have told them from the beginning. It had been a sort of back-up insurance, really – prising out that single remaining ruby, and hiding it privily beneath the white-silk lining of Laura's coffin. In New York his plans had been thwarted, but the jewel would still be there, would it not? Whenever, wherever they finally buried her. Was *anyone* ever likely to suspect such duplicity, such ghoulish duplicity? Surely not. Surely not, reflected Stratton. Yet he found himself remembering the man who had been in charge of things.

Yes, just the one man, perhaps . . .